MW01279786

Bloodlines

K . R. Gangi

Copyright © 2020

All rights reserved. No part of this publication may be reproduced, distributed, or transmitted in any form or by any means, or stored in a database or retrieval system, without the prior written permission of K.R. Gangi, except as permitted under the U.S. Copyright Act of 1976.

This is a work of fiction. Any resemblance of characters to actual persons, living or dead, is purely coincidental. The author holds exclusive rights to this work. Unauthorized duplication is prohibited.

Cover Design: Tricia Reeks
Editing and Formatting: C&D Editing

kylegangi3@gmail.com

Dedication

For Melissa, who kept me focused, listened to my ramblings, and made me feel like an author.
This book would never have been finished if it weren't for you.

Part One

A Vision of Fire

You never get used to the cold. Regardless of how many years you spend making your bed in a field of long grass, or on a thin blanket covering sharp rocks on the side of a mountain, the bite of the bitter wind will always chill you to the bone. You get used to crickets chirping, wolves howling, or even the distant sound of swords clashing together in battle, yet the cold of night is always there to greet you at the end of the day, to grip you tightly within its cold embrace.

A part of Alric wished the cold was the only thing he would have to endure when it came to night, but he wasn't prone to wishful thinking, not anymore.

It wasn't the first time he had woken to find himself soaked in a cold sweat with the vague trace of a nightmare on his mind, and he certainly knew it wouldn't be the last. The ground might not have been able to bring him sleep, but the fire could at least keep him warm.

Alric sat on a rotting log facing the fire, his back toward a small cliff as he chipped away splinters of a stick with the wood-handled knife he carried everywhere. What might seem petty and useless to some, the wood knife was one of those friends that Alric could always rely on, and new friends were hard to come by these days.

Whenever he woke in the night, haunted by the memories that he spent his life running from, his carving knife would always bring him comfort. It didn't ask questions, didn't try to help or judge; it gave him focus on what was there in front of him rather than the echoes of a past life he'd left behind.

As long as he had something to occupy his mind, he had nothing to worry about.

Alric looked around to his brothers, who slept in a wide circle surrounding the fire. Morning was a few hours away, so there really was no point in trying to sleep now, not that he could even if he tried.

He looked at the peaceful faces of the remaining friends he had and felt a hint of envy, jealous of the look of peace that sleep seemed to bring them. He hadn't felt that peaceful with a night's sleep in a very long time.

He heard footsteps behind him but knew it was no threat. If the brotherhood was attacked this deep in Navaleth, it would either be by natives or a group of bandits. Alric knew all too well it couldn't be natives, and if it was Lazar's bandits, they would send someone with lighter feet.

"Getting sloppy, old man," he mumbled while he continued to carve away at the small stick.

"Sloppy, maybe," Benny said, joining Alric at the fire, "but *old man*? I'll take that as a compliment, considering our profession."

"We've outlasted more than most, I suppose. Can't argue with that."

Benny arched his back in a long stretch. "Remember when sleeping on the ground was easy?"

"I remember a time when you could sneak up on a man without waking the entire camp."

"As I remember, we agreed that this was to be *my* watch." Benny paused a moment, letting the words settle on Alric. "I also remember you being able to carve faster than that. Is the mighty wolf getting old and slow, as well?" he said with a smirk.

Alric hesitated for a moment, knowing how this conversation was going to go. "If I were as slow as you are loud, we'd be out of business. It's new," Alric said, holding the carving to the light of the fire. "And don't call me wolf."

"New, you say?"

"New, I said."

"Well, where's the other masterpiece of yours?"

Alric pointed his friendly knife toward the fire. "Right there, with the others."

Benny sighed and rested his elbows on his knees. "I hate that you do that. What was it?"

"And I love how you hate that. A fang."

"A fang? Hmm …" Benny squinted into the fire. "Could mean—"

"It doesn't mean anything." Alric didn't mean to sound so abrupt, but he knew what Benny was doing.

A cramp of guilt tightened his stomach, but he continued to carve.

There was a momentary pause between the two men.

"Out with it," Alric urged. Benny's silence usually meant he was

2

choosing his words carefully.

Benny shifted his eyes. The man had a talent with words. He knew what to say and how to say it, a skill that Alric would never understand nor possess.

"Well, you're awake, covered in sweat, and carving more firewood. Just wondering if you'd like to talk about it."

"There's nothing to talk about," Alric replied shortly.

"Really? How about you save our time and your lies. Tell me what you saw."

Alric hated when Benny pried, even if he meant well. Someone had once told Alric that the less you talk about something, the sooner you'd forget it.

If only it were true.

He chiseled away, sharpening the end of the stick to a point, his force intensifying with each passing second. "Same thing as always," Alric said finally. "Fire and death."

"I see." Benny chewed the side of his lip. "And the arrow?"

Alric held up the wooden stick and looked it over. He was never sure how or why the wood turned out the way it did, only that it felt natural while he was doing it. This time, he held a small wooden arrow, one a child might be caught playing with.

"Looks to be that way," Alric answered.

"But *why* is it that way?"

It was Alric's turn to sigh. "I never know why, Benny." Alric twirled the arrow between his fingers in the firelight. "It just happens."

"All right. Do you plan on keeping this one?"

"You know I don't."

"Why not keep it?" Benny asked with a shrug. "You could think of it as a souvenir?"

Alric felt a sting of annoyance. He looked at his hands, scars covering them from the tips of his fingers all the way up his forearms. Suddenly, he felt vulnerable, naked without his leather gloves. "Got enough of those, if you ask me."

"Alric ..." There was a hint of sadness in Benny's voice now. "You know what I meant."

Alric stopped what he was doing and straightened before facing Benny. He knew his friend meant well, even when he poked at the things that made him mad. Then he looked into the fire before nodding his understanding.

"I'm just curious as to what they mean," Benny continued calmly. "That's all."

3

"Who says they have to mean anything?" Alric asked, his grip on the knife getting tighter.

"Well then, what's the point?"

Alric struggled for words. The truth was that he didn't know what determined what he carved, only that the act of doing it helped him relax. It was peaceful, calming. His mind could completely focus on something small and simple. When you carved, you could make mistakes without catastrophic consequences; each mistake having minimal repercussions. It didn't matter what he carved, only that it helped him when he did it.

He didn't have to explain to Benny why he did it, but he knew he didn't have to hide anything, either. Benny had always been there for him. No matter what darkness Alric was lost in, Benny was a light that helped him get through.

But that didn't mean Alric was good with words. That was Benny's role.

"It … just helps." Alric fumbled with his hands. "Does there need to be another explanation?"

Benny smiled, though it didn't take the concern from his eyes. "That's good. I'm glad it helps. But, wouldn't it be better if you thought about what the carvings could mean? Couldn't *that* help, too?"

Alric opened his arms to the camp, no longer able to hide his annoyance. "Wasn't the point of *this* so I wouldn't think about it *at all*?"

"Al, if that were the case, you wouldn't be awake right now. You think I don't notice when you mumble and holler in your sleep?" It was Benny's turn to gesture toward the brotherhood. "You think *they* haven't?"

"That's different." Alric's face burned with anger now. "I'm handling it."

"I know you're handling it now, but what happens when it becomes too much to bear? How many days has it been since you've slept? How much longer can you go before another episode?"

"I won't let it come to that," Alric stated firmly.

"And how are you going to hold yourself accountable?"

"I'll figure it out when it happens."

"*When* it happens?"

Alric balled his fists in restraint. "You know what I meant. *If* it happens. Don't twist my words."

"I twist nothing. What's said is said. I only point it out. I know you think that you can stop it, but just try to listen—"

"Benny, we're done talking about this." Alric said, anger clear in his voice.

"Just let me help you remember."

"No. We're not doing that."

"Al, I just want—"

"Enough!" Alric growled, locking eyes with Benny.

Noticing the warning in his voice, Benny nodded in defeat and stared back toward the fire.

Alric knew that Benny just wanted answers, and maybe it was selfish not to allow Benny the chance to access those answers. But, how does one explain something they don't fully understand themselves?

Alric held the wooden arrow up in the firelight. After chipping away a tiny sliver near the tip, he deemed it finished and tossed it into the fire. Then he watched as the embers produced a small flame that swirled around the wood, watched it do what fire did best—consume everything in its path.

He glanced around at his brothers lying before him. He would be surprised if they were still asleep. If they wanted to pretend, though, he wouldn't judge. Besides, there was still a few hours until sunrise, and the cave they were looking for shouldn't be too far now. It wouldn't be long until their job was complete and their pockets heavy with gold.

Knowing he would never ease his guilt, he decided to give Benny the benefit of the doubt. He got up and walked to the edge of the cliff, crossing his arms as he looked at distant world beneath him. He could see the small torches of Robins-Port below; close enough to see, but still about a day's ride out.

"All right then," he said aloud, "we'll try it your way."

Benny gave no objections before placing himself at Alric's side, overlooking the dark and peaceful mountainside of trees below them.

"I'm not making any promises, though," he told Benny.

"I only ask that you try. If it doesn't work, we'll burn it with the rest."

"Hm," Alric grumbled. He felt a soft hand on his back while Benny cleared his throat. "I guess."

"Now, what do you remember?"

Alric didn't want to, but he concentrated hard on the brief flashes he could recall of his dream. Always it was the same—flashes of blurred images fading in and out of his mind. However, there was always a detail of something he could never forget, something that haunted his reality for many years now.

"Fire."

"Okay, fire. Now think hard. Was the fire around you? Were you in the fire?"

There was a moment where he could feel Benny's ability working, those ghostly memories fading in from the dark of Alric's mind—blood, trees, houses, bodies. He tried to focus through the images flashing before his eyes, but a searing pain in his head held him back, shifting memory after memory.

Benny might as well spin him around in circles then ask him to paint him a picture of what he saw. Yet, as the seconds passed, the memories began to focus in Alric's mind.

Stars, dead bodies, houses ... on fire.

"No. It's in front of me," he spit between gritted teeth, trying to get out the familiar, bitter taste in his mouth.

"So, you're watching something burn. Now think, Al; where are you? Look around you and think of your arrow. Does anything stick out?"

"I'm going to try to ignore your pun."

"Just focus," Benny said, a slight chuckle in his voice.

Alric looked about in his mind, and an image began to unfold before him. He was crouched in a thicket, burning houses blazing brightly down the street in front of him. Next to him sat a heaping pile of butchered bodies—hands, heads, arms, legs. A dark blood trail led from the pile of bodies to a corpse that lay in front of a burning house. A small corpse. A child with an arrow sticking out of a young boy's chest.

Benny's voice echoed around him, but with each passing word, it sounded more distant.

"I see it, too," Benny's voice echoed. "Go to it."

He walked to the body and realized it was a young boy, a large stain of blood circling around the arrow protruding from his chest. Alric knelt next to the boy.

"Go on, Al," Benny whispered. "Remember, this isn't real. He isn't real."

Alric slowly reached out toward the body. Just as he was inches away from the arrow, though, a cold hand gripped his forearm and the boy's eyes flicked open to reveal two pale eyes looking into him.

Alric tried to pull away, but the grip was too strong. Too strong for a boy this age. Much too strong for a dead one, at that.

The dead boy bore a glare at Alric as he began lifting his head off the ground, slowly inching it closer and closer to Alric's face, the sound of bones popping in his neck.

All was silent in the dream world, all but the sound of the boy's voice. It wasn't one of a child, or a man, pleading for help, but a woman's voice that Alric recognized all too well.

"*Help*," it pleaded to him. "*Help me! I can't get out! Please, help me!*"

Alric tried pulling away, but the grip was too firm.

His surroundings morphed and changed shape around him. He was no longer in a street watching houses burn, but in a burning house himself.

What was silence before erupted into loud cracks of splintering wood and the roar of consuming flames. They grew around him as the air was sucked from his lungs.

Alric looked back to the dead boy and watched in horror as he smiled at him. Not an innocent smile that a father would get from his son, but a malicious smile with bloodstained teeth you would expect from a hungry predator.

"*Please, help me!*" he heard a woman scream. "*I can't get out!*"

The boy vanished before his eyes.

Instead of kneeling on the ground, Alric was lying on his stomach with flames dancing around him. In the next room, someone sat in a chair before him. Alric could see their hands bound with rope behind them, long hair falling behind the chair. A woman's hair.

"*Please, hurry! Help me!*" she screamed as the flames burned closer and closer, spreading slowly like a deadly snake prepping to strike.

He crawled as fast as he could to the next room, but not fast enough. As soon as he was close enough, he went for the knot in the ropes. He went to untie her hands when he noticed she was soaked in a black liquid.

Oil.

Before he knew it, flames climbed up the woman's legs. He tried slapping the flames in order to stifle them, to no avail.

Not seconds later, the women in the chair was completely engulfed in fire, screeching with pain.

"*Help! It hurts. Oh, gods, it hurts!*"

Alric would never forget this moment. The moment where everything was taken from him.

"*Please, help me!*"

He would never forget the smell of burning flesh, the sound it made as it bubbled and boiled.

"*Please, Alric! It hurts!*"

And most of all, the sight of everything he loved burning away before his eyes. The feeling of complete hopelessness. The sound of utter failure.

"Alric!"

He was on his hands and knees as sweat dripped off the bridge of his nose. Benny knelt before him with a look of worry on his face. Were those tears in his eyes?

The rushing sound of footsteps came from behind him, and before he knew it, there was a wooden cup held in front of him.

"Drink this," a familiar voice told him.

Alric was still struggled to breathe, the feel of smoke still clenching his lungs. He coughed frantically and eventually vomited into the grass before him.

"You need to drink this *now*," the voice urged.

The smell was awful, and it tasted even worse, but at least it watered his dry mouth.

Cold air cut through his throat as he gasped for air. His head felt like a blacksmith had taken a hammer to it. He tried to stand, but his legs felt like water. Gentle hands caught under his arms to help steady him.

"He'll be asleep soon," he heard someone say to his right. "Let's get him to his blanket."

"No," Alric tried to say as he was dragged away from the fire, but his tongue was numb in his mouth. He didn't want to go back to sleep, not when he knew what waited there.

The world around him began to swirl, and he felt sickness building in his throat again.

"What'd you give him?" someone asked to his left.

"A tonic that clears the mind. It'll make him sleep, but he won't dream."

Well, that doesn't sound too bad.

Alric was laid down on a soft blanket and flipped onto his back. His entire body felt numb as he tried to stand, only to feel the two people before him pressing him back down.

He raised his hands in front of his face and played with his fingers. They moved before him, but he wasn't sure how. They seemed to have a mind of

8

their own. He laughed at the nonsense of it.

"You've drugged him," one of the men accused.

"Desperate times calls for desperate measures," the other replied. "It'll wear off in a few hours, but he'll sleep until his body is ready. How long has he been awake now?"

"A few days, at least."

"Well, we better get comfortable."

Alric watched as a black blur closed around his vision. Three figures towered above him, their faces distant and cloudy. Their voices echoed around the walls that pressed in, but the words were beyond his understanding.

As two of the figures left, one remained, peering down at Alric. It leaned close to him and whispered into his ear, "Sleep now."

Alric closed his eyes.

Lessons and Patience

The morning darkness rang with echoes of battle. Trevor angled the sword above his head as his opponent was parried away. He glanced, an opening, and went for it, but as he swung, he knew he was too slow.

He felt a pressure behind his knees and was instantly airborne. He saw the sword driving down at him as he fell, leaving him slim chance for defense.

The thud against his chest sucked the air from his lungs before he crashed onto his back.

As he saw the blade rise once more, he knew he had only a split-second or he would be finished.

He rolled to the side just in time as his opponents' blade pierced the ground. Using his momentum, Trevor then circled around and swung his blade wide. Pain shot through his arm as it was deflected, leaving his chest wide open. Instinctively, he jumped back, just out of reach of his enemy's blade.

Not giving his enemy a chance to think, he fixed his stance and pressed forward, sticking to the offensive tactic. Trevor pressed hard, swinging with all the strength he possessed as he drove his opponent back, to no avail. No matter how hard he pressed, or how fast he swung, not one attack met its mark.

He jabbed forward with the point of his sword, knowing well his enemy would easily parry, but he also knew his side would be left vulnerable and open. So, switching his grip, he spun in a quick circle and leveled the sword waist high.

But he wasn't quick enough.

Before he could fully spin, he felt a heavy blow to his back and was knocked away and to the ground. He quickly turned around and rushed his opponent. Slashing left, right, low, high. No matter what angle or what move he used, his blade was deflected.

His arms felt heavy and his strength was fading fast, each breath becoming more laborious.

He saw his opponent swing the blade high, a desperate move hoping to reach a quick end of battle. Easily enough, though, Trevor ducked low, angling his sword up, ready to drive the point into his foe's chest.

He should have known it wouldn't be that easy.

As soon as he ducked below the incoming blow, a large knee crashed against his face, sending him stumbling onto his back.

And just like that, he was finished.

Accepting defeat, he turned and dug the point of his blade into the ground, using it to steady himself. Heavy breath fogged the morning air just as the sun began to crest the surrounding hills. Large beads of sweat trickled down his face as he stared across the yard at his foe.

Uncle Dodge might have stood tall, but Trevor knew he was feeling a burn in his lungs, as well. They were at the end of the morning's lesson after free-sparring for hours.

Dodge stared down at him through the twilight, and Trevor knew he was sizing up his performance.

He wanted nothing more than to let his heavy arms drag him to the ground, but he straightened his back and stood before his mentor.

"What's the problem?" Dodge asked.

Trevor took a deep breath before speaking. "The sword, it's—"

"Are you about to tell me," his uncle interrupted, "that a fight is won only by the weapons you use? Does a man blame his fists when he loses a brawl?"

Trevor hated it when his uncle twisted his words, but he understood it was only to prove a point, to identify an issue and fix it.

"Weapons don't win fights," he responded confidently, staring into his uncle's eyes.

"And what does?" Dodge asked with a raised brow.

"Your knowledge and ability," he answered as if reciting a book read thousands of times. It had been almost two years since the morning of his first lesson, and it was also one of the most important. The one his uncle would never let him forget.

"Explain," Dodge encouraged as he made his way across the yard toward Trevor.

"A weapon is only as deadly as the one yielding it."

Dodge gave a small smile of approval as he handed his wooden practice sword to Trevor, who hesitated before taking it. When he did, it felt as light as a feather.

"So, what's the problem?" his uncle teased, a slight smile curling his lip.

Trevor tossed both practice swords to the ground and pushed his uncle away. "What in all hells did you do to my sword?"

Dodge took a few steps back, laughing, his dark hair bouncing around his rough face as he raised his burly hands in surrender. "Had Tom crack it open and lace the center with a small line of copper, is all."

"*A small line of copper?*" Trevor laughed back. "No wonder my arms feel like lead."

"Don't go using that excuse now. It may have made you slower, which I expected, but your performance was just as sloppy. You're distracted."

Trevor felt a surge of joy twist in his stomach. It was true; he had been distracted about Sarah's return to Robins-Port ever since her last letter. It had been two years since they had last seen each other, since she had made her promise.

"Remember, the only way you'll keep your head in a fight—"

"Is by *keeping* your head in the fight," Trevor finished, another lesson that had been drilled into his brain.

Dodge nodded, picking up the two swords from off the ground.

Trevor felt uneasiness in the air as his uncle scanned the yard. It was another look that he was all too familiar with.

"It's a bit early to brood, don't you think?" Trevor teased.

Dodge exhaled deeply and looked Trevor in the eye. "I was just thinking … It's been a long time since you last saw her."

"That it has. What're you implying?"

"I'm just saying …" Dodge searched the yard for an answer.

"Go ahead," Trevor encouraged. "No harm done."

Dodge shifted on his feet. "All right. No harm done. It's been two years, and I know what her coming back means to you. It's a long time, Trevor, and change always follows close behind time."

"Yeah, it does. But things are the same with us. The plan remains the same."

Dodge looked at Trevor hard before he slapped him playfully on the shoulder. Then he gave a sad smile and looked him in the eyes. "In any case, I'm proud of you. Do you know when she'll be here?"

"Should be a few days now."

"Don't forget you're helping out Tom today."

"I haven't forgotten."

Tom was Robins-Port's local, and only, blacksmith. It always surprised Trevor that there was only one, considering all main trade routes in Navaleth led to Robins-Port. At least, that's what Dodge had told him. Trevor himself never had the opportunity for travel. He had been stuck in the same town his entire life.

Trevor had lived with his uncle Dodge for as long as he could remember. Whenever Trevor would try to get Dodge to talk about his parents, he would always shut down. The only thing he would tell him was that his mother had died giving birth to him, and that his father had died in the last war. Trevor didn't like his uncle's mood after those discussions, so Trevor stayed away from the topic. The way Trevor saw it, Dodge was the only family he had.

It wasn't always easy, living in a town where most residents liked to remind him every day of being an orphan. It had its good days, though. There was Dodge, Tom, Sarah, and the old man near the southern end that Trevor rather enjoyed talking with. There were also the days where nobody seemed to notice him at all. Trevor tallied those up as good days.

On the days the townspeople *did* acknowledge his existence, it was always in a fashion of scolding or whispers under their breaths as he passed by. When they felt to put forth energy enough to scold him verbally, they usually resorted to menacing grimaces when he caught their eyes. It was a town that hated who and what he was, all because his parents had died before he had gotten a chance to meet them. How was that his fault?

Life wasn't fair for Trevor in Robins-Port, where he had been stuck his entire life.

Trevor might have never left Robins-Port, but Sarah Michaelson never stopped leaving it. Trevor grew up with Sarah being his only friend. She never saw him as the monster everyone claimed he was.

As kids, they had never left each other's side. They had run through the town streets, playing tag or sneaking off to the edge of the trees and pretending to fight monsters. Other times, they would just sit and talk, Sarah telling Trevor stories that she heard from her parents. Her favorites were those of Asher, the god-like knight who traveled the world to slay monsters, spending his life protecting innocents.

Growing up with Sarah had made life bearable for Trevor, and whenever they were together, the outside world didn't matter. The scolding, the muttering under

13

the townspeople's breaths, none of that mattered to Sarah; therefore, it didn't matter to Trevor.

The older they got, however, the more frequently Sarah began to leave with her family for business. When it had started, Sarah wouldn't be gone for more than a couple days. Then, as they grew older, the trips had become longer. Sometimes, she would be gone for weeks, or even months. The older she grew, the longer Sarah seemed to be gone. All the while, Trevor remained stuck in Robins-Port, doing the same thing, day after day.

It wasn't until she had been gone for six consecutive months that Trevor realized just how much he cared for Sarah, how much he wanted her in his life. When she was away, the days were longer, nights were quieter.

It was an early morning when he had been shaken awake in his bedroom, only to open his eyes to see Sarah leaning over him. It had been at that moment when he had realized just how beautiful she truly was, and how he wanted to wake up every morning with her by his side.

Another month passed before Sarah had to leave again, for longer this time. Lately, it seemed she was gone more often than she stayed. She had told Trevor that her father had business in a city to the west and that they planned on staying there for a while. How long exactly, she didn't know.

There was a broken wall on the edge of town where hardly anyone ever went, and it was at this spot where Trevor and Sarah would spend most of their free time. They would get lost in conversation for hours, staying there well past sunset. It was on one of those nights when Trevor had truly fell in love with Sarah.

It had been the evening before she had to leave, the sun illuminated an orange glow across the sky, and there was a slight bite to the air, which gave them more reason to sit closer to one another.

He had half-expected Sarah to storm off and never speak to him again after he had confessed his love for her. However, he'd been relieved to hear that her feelings were the same. That was the night everything changed for Trevor.

Now it had been two years since Sarah and Trevor had sat on that broken wall. Since then, Trevor had been waiting for this day.

"Listen," Dodge said, breaking Trevor's daydream, "blacksmithing isn't easy work, but it'll teach you something. It's good for you. And be patient with the man—we both know how he can be."

Dodge didn't have to remind Trevor of Tom the blacksmith. Truth was that Trevor really liked him. Sure, he was vulgar and had a habit of telling people off, but he had always been kind to him. He never once treated him any differently from everyone else simply because he was an orphan.

Growing up, Tom would spend long nights with Dodge at the table, reminiscing about times they'd shared over a dark bottle of liquor. There were even times when Tom had too much to drink, and it was up to Trevor to make sure he got home, for which the drunken blacksmith was always thankful for. He always treated Trevor with a certain amount of respect, and so Trevor gave him respect in return.

"Aye, he's a good man," Trevor replied.

"Good lad."

Dodge's eyes wandered through the air. He squinted against the early sunlight and gave a satisfying look. "For a cold morning, it sure is gonna be a hot day."

Trevor nodded his agreement. Winter was right around the corner. Soon, he would be sparring in the snow.

Winter for Robins-Port, being a smaller town residing in a valley surrounded by hills and mountains, was the slow season for the trading town.

He knew that, within the hour, wagons would be pushed down the street, shutters and windows would open, and the final caravans would be setting out on their supply runs. It was the time of the season when all farmers and shops finished up their work before setting off to another location, escaping the snow that would soon make it near impossible to travel through and leaving the permanent residents, like Trevor and Dodge, behind for the season.

"That being said," Dodge said as he and Trevor made their way to the large wash barrels next to the house, "I want you to pay attention at the smithy. Don't think because you've a history with him that he's gonna take it easy on ya. Just think of it like our practices."

"He's going to cheat me?" Trevor teased.

Dodge gave a soft smile. "No. Well, maybe." Dodge crossed his arms. "What I mean is that it's going to get harder before it gets better."

"Fair enough," Trevor agreed.

"Another thing." Dodge squared with Trevor in front of the barrels. "You're not a child anymore, but that doesn't excuse you from what's expected, and I expect you focused tomorrow morning, regardless of what happens tonight. Understood?"

"Aye, I understand."

Dodge nodded. "Well then, good luck to ya."

"Mind if I take a few eggs down to Eli? Haven't seen him in a bit."

Eli was Trevor's fourth and final friend in Robins-Port. He was an elderly man who gave up his home long ago to live a life of repentance. Trevor didn't know what he lived to rectify, but he cherished the old man's friendship too much to bring up what were probably painful memories.

Dodge grumbled, leaning over the water barrel. "Suppose I could spare a few eggs."

Trevor knew Dodge didn't like sparing the food he had, but he had never once refused to help someone in need.

His uncle rinsed his face in the cold water before patting it with a nearby rag. "Best hurry up, though; Tom likes to get there early," he said before disappearing through the back door that led into their house.

Trevor turned and looked toward the morning sky. An orange glow filled the town and the warm light shone down on him.

"It's going to be a good day," he said to himself. He couldn't help smiling.

The Role of Deceit

Footsteps echoed down the long, torchlit hallway. There was a skip of confidence in his step as he walked, chin high and back straight. He might already have been late for the meeting with his colleagues in the council chamber, but he would not give in to haste. Call it a guilty pleasure, but Francis Balorian enjoyed making people wait for him.

A woman rounded a corner toward him, a familiar elegance in her walk that Francis admired deeply. If he failed to recognize the confidence in her stride, there would be no mistaking her with another while she wore the emerald blouse she was so fond of.

"A bit early for such beauty, is it not, Sabrina?" Francis jested.

"I'm always willing to sacrifice a bit of sleep, Father"—Sabrina smiled— "especially if it's in good company."

"There's no need for that, dear. Please, call me Francis."

Sabrina gave a quick wink as she passed by. "My mistake, Francis."

He stole a glance behind him as she passed, absorbing the melodic sway of her tight hips before he took another turn down a narrow hallway. He would like nothing more than to show Sabrina Helmkat good company, but there were more important things to do at the moment. Duty called, and it was better not to test his master's patience, especially this close to their goal.

Sabrina might have been the most beautiful woman in the castle, possibly the country, for all Francis knew, but she would still be here when it was all done. Well, hopefully.

Sacrifices must be made, after all.

This was Francis's favorite time to travel around the castle. There was something about the quiet of the morning that gave the castle a certain beauty.

It wasn't long until he reached the spiral staircase that descended to the council chamber, where he was greeted with the unique Navalethian history at the bottom of the stairs: paintings, statues, relics on wood shelves, tapestries suspended by gold rope hanging from the ceiling, all bearing the Navalethian sigil—a sword and book set before a large castle—all of them with a story of the greatness of the empire in which Francis currently served.

A history fabricated to serve an old purpose.

Two, large, oak doors stood opposite the base of the stairs. Beyond those doors, Francis's colleagues awaited him. The torches lining the walls illuminated statues of historic former council members. A painting, dedicated to each member, hung next to each statue, another story to help falsify the empire.

Francis took a moment to embrace the history around him. On the left side, stood three, brute-looking men dressed in armor. They held swords upright in front of their bodies to represent Navaleth's strength in battle and war. On the opposite side of the hall, stood three figures decorated in loose robes. Instead of weapons, together, they held thick, stone books that signified wisdom and patience. It was important for all council members to remember that, before making decisions for their kingdom, one must rely on both wisdom and strength in order to succeed.

He couldn't help shaking his head in disappointment as he reached for the heavy oak doors. If Francis had learned anything during the endless nights of his studies, it was that the winners told the history.

For years, he had known the true deeds of the false empire he served. The traitorous lies morphed into a historic fiction that blind Navalethians continued to praise.

The truth was that he was tired. After years of careful planning, of hiding in plain sight, all his tools were now set in place. He simply had to push them into motion.

"Soon," he whispered to himself.

The doors groaned as they swung open, drawing all eyes to him. Three powerful men stared at Francis as he entered the chamber. Two of them shot out of their seats, standing out of respect and tradition, as the third remained seated and paid no heed. Being well acquainted with Vallis for some time now, Francis expected no less from the man.

The council table was massive; a thick rectangle with a gold embroidered mural on its surface. A sword and book, the symbol of Navaleth, was carved into the stone. At the top of the mural stood four, large figures that represented the gods Elinroth and Mariella, with their son and daughter, Volran and Arabella. Below the sigil were small people: guards, peasants, and even royalty. It showed guards helping farmers, royal figures with their arms spread wide in order to thank the hard work of the countrymen.

Francis knew these details well, mostly because, every time he looked upon it, he felt the sudden urge to grind the stone down to rubble. The lies that polluted the castle infuriated him.

More arrogance, Francis thought. *More lies built to control and manipulate.*

His chair sat opposite General Gorman, commander of the garrison stationed at Mendora, which protected the western boundary of Navaleth. The wear of travel was evident on him; dark bags hung from his bloodshot eyes and crusted mud clotted small bits of his black hair.

On Gorman's left sat General Destro, commander of the Walled City of Brackenheart in the north. He had the look of a man who had soldiered his entire life, with a temper as thick as his arms. Like General Gorman, Destro, too, showed signs of travel on his crimson armor.

The third general was Vallis, newly appointed general of the garrison of Servitol, the capital city of Navaleth, the very castle in which they sat now. His baggy tunic matched his short brown hair, looking and smelling as if they had only recently been pressed clean. Considering Vallis was constantly in the kingdom, Francis rarely saw him in his armor, unlike the former colleagues who never took theirs off.

A tall chair lined with a velvet red sat empty at the head of the table where the king would sit. It had been years since the king was able to attend a council meeting, though, and Francis had a feeling that wouldn't change anytime soon. That being the case, it fell unto Francis to speak directly for the king, to convey his plans to the three generals so his orders could be carried to all borders of Navaleth.

"Thank you all for coming," Francis broke the silence, taking his seat at the stone table. "I hope you've had easy travel. I know the nights this time of year get a bit frosty, but the king appreciates your time and effort."

Three pairs of eyes glanced from the velvet chair back to Francis, letting the silence speak for them. A pin hitting the floor could have shattered the quiet in the room.

"I see. Well, to business then." Francis straightened his back while folding his hands on the table. "What news from the west?"

General Gorman crossed his arms and leaned back in his chair, his ragged voice echoing strongly in the room. "Seems quiet now, but the bandits are sure to come back. They always do," Gorman said, his eyes searching his companions around the table. "They seem to have moved farther into Duke Scyllis's territory. Everyone's on edge. People are swelling the streets, seeking shelter and food. Fires have taken their homes and fields, leaving them with nothing but the small coin they had reserved and the clothes on their backs. We've managed food for now, but they'll starve come winter, if they don't freeze to death first."

"Likewise," Destro agreed, clearly irritated at the report. "Same in the north. Bandits have been coming in during the night, burning the stock of our farmers, leaving their fields ash and their bowls empty. I sent a few teams out to track 'em down but found nothing. Sneaky little bastards."

Even the streets of the capital were starting to clutter with the unfortunate. It had started as a minor problem, with a few bandit attacks on a few unlucky farmers. As the years passed, however, larger raids became more frequent, leaving many farmers without homes or trade, left only to beg in the streets of their towns.

"So, start building," Vallis offered with open hands. "Give them shelter and let them fend for themselves during winter. Simple."

Francis could see the annoyance on Destro's face before he managed to speak.

"Have you ever carved through a mountain, *General* Vallis?" he asked without looking at the man.

Vallis pressed a sarcastic finger to his lip. "Nope, can't say I've ever had the chance to."

"Course not. You've been here, in the capital, where you can have men build a small shack within the hour. Carving through a mountain isn't like chopping wood, *boy*."

If Vallis was offended by the insult, he didn't let it show.

Destro continued his rant. "It takes weeks of planning, and that's if you've got hard enough men for it. Of course, it would seem simple for someone who has the luxury of a warm bed while his men and women starve on the cold streets of his home, but the real world isn't as black and white as you may see it."

Hating when his colleagues bickered like children, Francis shot Vallis a warning look that said enough. In response, Vallis gave a nonchalant shrug.

"Fair enough." Vallis reached behind his back and set a small dagger on the table. Eyes lit up with tension as they all stared at him. After seeing everyone's shock, Vallis gave a wry smile and pulled out an apple from beneath his robe. "What?" He shrugged. "It's only a snack."

Francis awkwardly cleared his throat, leaning toward Vallis. "You know there are no weapons permitted in the council chamber."

"Weapons?" He gestured toward the small knife. "Please, I theorize I'll have a harder time cutting this apple, let alone a man."

"Too bad. The law's the law," Gorman warned casually.

"More like a tradition. If you wanted a slice, you'd only have to ask, General." Vallis smiled wickedly. "All you have to do is say please."

"This is your last warning, boy," Destro growled. "Get—"

In a flash, Vallis snatched the knife off the table and pointed it at Destro's chest. "Call me *boy* again, and I might just have to test my theory."

Destro shot out of his chair and squared himself to Vallis. "You dare threaten me? I'll shove that apple down your privileged fucking throat. *Boy.*"

"*Enough!*" Francis's voice boomed off the walls, and all eyes fell to him. "Not five minutes, and you're already at each other's throats. I expect as much from the dukes, but *not* from generals. This is the king's council, and I'm sure he wouldn't tolerate his leadership acting like simpletons at a brothel fighting over a whore. We have the king's business to attend to, and attend to it, we will. What will it be, gentlemen? Shall we take our time or make this quick?"

Gorman remained leaning in his chair, two fingers pressed to the bridge of his nose while he shook his head. After moments of silence, Destro finally took his seat, rage all but steaming off his body. Vallis leaned back in his chair, carved off a piece of his apple, and held it out to Destro with a wink.

"You," Francis said, pointing a firm finger at Vallis, "just eat your apple and shut up."

"Now, there's something we can agree on," he mumbled before tossing the piece into his mouth.

"General Destro, what do you need to help this endeavor?" Francis continued, ignoring Vallis's comment.

Francis could see traces of rage lingering in the man's eye, but he said, "If we're to carve out some more rooms, then I'll need some fresh tools. Lots of them."

"Vallis, write up a work order and have two loads of tools shipped north. The strongest tools we have."

Vallis nodded quietly to himself.

Francis looked to Gorman, who stared at the Vallis's knife. Even after all these years, they still didn't trust one another. That would be a problem for Francis, but a problem he would attend to later.

"General Gorman, what do you need in the west?"

"Can you spare any men?" he asked.

"Unfortunately, the capital has no men to spare, but you are welcome to anything else."

Gorman thought for a moment. "I'll need some tools, as well. Wood, mostly."

Francis looked back to Vallis. "Write out a second order to Duke Gundell for five shipments of oak to be sent west to Mendora. Then another to Duke Scyllis for whatever shipments of grain and wheat he can spare."

"I'm sure he won't like that," Vallis said.

"I don't care what he likes. He controls most of the country's agriculture, so he'll do what's expected of him. It's time we get these farmers off the streets and back to work. Send riders bright and early tomorrow. We'll also need to clear out the barracks and offices for these two gentlemen tonight."

"Don't bother with the office, Father," Gorman said. "I'll be staying with my men."

"Please, call me Francis. And I admire your quality for leadership.

"General Destro, will you and your men be sleeping in the barracks, as well?"

Destro nodded slowly. "We'd appreciate that."

Vallis leaned forward in his chair and slipped the dagger behind his back. Apple core in hand, he stood and gave a theatrical bow to his colleagues. "It seems my work here is done. If you'll excuse me, gentlemen, I've got to play the role of an errand boy." He took a large bite of the apple core and exited the chamber, the giant oak doors slamming behind him.

Francis could feel the tension ease immediately following the departure of Vallis.

Destro gave a long sigh as he pushed back his chair and stretched his legs. "That man sure knows the right way to piss someone off."

Gorman nodded in agreement. "Can't give him all the credit. His fuse is about as short as yours."

Destro chuckled quietly and shook his head. "That may be. Still, I can't believe he's in charge of soldiers. I've recruits more seasoned than him."

"As unexpected and unfortunate the death of General Orlington was," Francis intervened, "we are lucky to have someone like Vallis in charge of the city's garrison. The position just needs to grow on him."

"Is he aware of the notion that leadership is to think about others?" Gorman rebuked.

Destro slowly shook his head, his eyes focused on nothing as he mumbled to himself, "Orlington. Now, that was a great leader."

"That he was," agreed Gorman. "I squired for him as a boy. That man knocked me sideways harder than my father ever had."

Destro chuckled. "He once made me clean the shitters for a month."

"That sounds … quite awful," Francis admitted.

Destro shrugged. "Yeah, well, I never drank before a raid again."

"He never was fond of that 'liquid courage,' was he?" Gorman asked with a smile.

"Not at all." Destro shook his head. "Hard-headed man, that's for sure. Always said courage came from the heart, not the bottle."

"Although, there was that one night …" Gorman said.

"Right." Destro smiled, an awkward look for a brute of a man. "That was a good night."

Frances observed as the two generals reminisced. Being a man of the faith, he never got to achieve great deeds with a sword. His only accomplishments were those of texts and planning. Always planning.

All three men could agree on one thing, though, that General Orlington had indeed been a hard-headed man. Too hard to see the truth before his very eyes. That was his problem. His death was indeed unfortunate, but necessary.

"Is there anything else you require from the crown to assist in your endeavors before we call this meeting to an end?" Francis butted in.

"You sure you can't find a better commander for the capital?" Destro suggested.

Francis felt the bite but chose to ignore the sting. "I assure you, gentlemen, that he will grow on you, as he has on me. If you don't trust his decisions, please trust mine. We must all make do with what we have."

"Aye." Gorman nodded. "That'll be all from me, Father Balorian."

"Same." Destro cleared his throat. "Apologies, Father. The road has not been kind this last week. My patience wears thin tonight."

Francis shied away Destro's apology with a wave of his hand. "There is no need to apologize. And please, call me Francis. I may be the head herald, but I am still a man.

"Rest assured, gentlemen, that the king will hear of your needs and will accommodate you on all the resources we have. If there is anything else you need, do not hesitate to ask. We will meet tomorrow midday when we will discuss the plans of our monarch and the future of our country. Gods be with you, gentlemen."

"Gods be with you," they echoed.

Francis turned his back on the two reminiscing soldiers and left the chamber. Although a bit brief, the morning meeting was still a relative success. He couldn't help feeling a weight lift off his shoulders as he ascended the spiral staircase and made his way to his quarters.

Once inside his room, he locked the door behind him then made way to his desk. He lit a small candle and sunk into his chair.

Scattered papers littered his floor while dozens of books lay open on his desk. Regardless of how strategic and precise his planning had to be, he lacked the appearance of organization.

Hardly a few moments passed before there was a soft knock at his door. He stood and opened it to his expected guest, ushering him to enter. Francis then took his seat as the man stood before him.

"I said to make a scene, not to make yourself look weak," Francis told him.

General Vallis walked over and dropped two work orders onto Francis's desk. "I got carried away. It won't happen again. I just need your seal on these, then I'll send them off."

"Things have changed," he said to Vallis, whose eyes knitted together with curiosity. "There's no need for those."

"Have they now? Can we finally start having fun?"

"Everything's in motion. Soon, the brotherhood will return with the final piece." Francis reached into a drawer and pulled out a piece of parchment. He handed it to Vallis, who accepted it with excitement. "Let them know that they can begin."

"I'm sick of waiting," Vallis complained. "All this fucking *waiting*."

"We have waited long, yes, but remember that *he* has waited longer." Francis let that sink in just a bit. "We are nearing the end, Vallis. You will be well rewarded for your dues; that I promise. From your act earlier, I suspect you've already spoken with Destro?"

"I have, and he understands what's at stake. He's agreed to play his part. No need to worry there."

Francis nodded his approval, hands steepled under his chin. "It's Gorman I'm worried about. He reminds me of Orlington. He might not fully understand our purpose. We need him with us if this is going to work, and he doesn't seem to be your biggest fan."

"Which is why I left it up to Destro. He's charming our friend as we speak. They're old friends, fought in the same war or something, under the command of our late General Orlington, no less. He's confident that he can make him understand."

Francis nodded, picking up the work orders that Vallis had brought him. He held them above his small candle until they caught fire, his eyes staring distantly as the flames consumed the paper. "Nothing bonds two people more than dealing death to a common enemy. I'm confident, as well. Good thinking."

Vallis stared silently at the burning paper, nodding in the confidence of his mentor.

"I don't want him hurt," Francis continued. "We have our king's orders. He has to be capable. However, if he refuses, we will have to resort to … other solutions."

Vallis smiled wickedly. "I'd like to see that."

"And you just might have to. That will be all, Vallis. Do enjoy the day."

"Good morning, Francis. And congratulations on our victory." Vallis unlocked the deadbolts then quietly shut the door behind him, leaving Francis to his thoughts.

Francis let the flames turn to ash on his desk then reached into the collar of his tunic, revealing a small key dangling from a thin chain. He fitted the small key into a small lock on a drawer.

He lifted the lid on the heavy box, mesmerized by the beauty before him. He could feel the power in the tablets as he dragged his fingers across its rough scripture.

"Soon," he promised them.

Eggs and Farewells

The sun was at its peak by the time Trevor found Eli just outside the village. The hermit never stayed long, preferring comfort among the trees rather than the constant clatter in villages. That was something that Trevor and Eli had in common. The only difference between them being that Eli had the opportunity to choose where to live, and Trevor didn't.

It wasn't long ago when Trevor first met Eli. During one of his morning spars with Dodge, Trevor had glimpsed an orange glow in a small patch of woods just beyond the village, a beacon in twilight. When he had asked Dodge what it was, his uncle had been quick to brush it off.

"Traveler or hunter, maybe," he'd said plainly.

Trevor didn't pay much attention to it that morning, but when he came outside the next day and saw the same mysterious glow off in the distance, he couldn't help feeling pulled to that light, like a moth to a lantern.

That morning after practice, Trevor had told Dodge that he was going for a run. He felt guilty lying, but he figured there were worse things to lie about. He hadn't even been sure what he would find—maybe a hunter or traveler like Dodge said. Nevertheless, he couldn't help the urge to know.

Just a few yards past the tree line outside of Robins-Port, Trevor had found the remains of a small camp, the coals of a small fire still burning hot. The grass next to it lay flat, clearly a place where someone had slept.

Trevor had been busy eyeing the camp when he noticed the silhouette of a person standing in the shadow of a tree. His face was hidden beneath a hood as he leaned on a white walking stick. Trevor's heart had frozen for a moment. Either the man had been standing there the entire time, or he was quiet enough to sneak up in front of Trevor without being noticed. Either way, it didn't look good.

The stranger had pulled his hood back to reveal, not the sinister look of a murderous bandit, but the wrinkled face of an old man.

Trevor would never forget the first words the stranger had spoken to him.

"Do you like eggs?" he'd asked Trevor. "I have some spare if you'll join me?"

It was then that the man had introduced himself as Eli, a weary traveler seeking shelter outside of town.

Trevor had been quick to leave, but Eli had begged him to stay.

"I swear, my cooking isn't *that* terrible, and I would really enjoy some company."

With the seed of an awkward first encounter, Trevor and Eli's relationship sprouted into much more. With the absence of Sarah, Trevor had already felt the loneliness of not having a friend to talk to. He had Dodge and Tom, of course, but it wasn't the same. Nothing was ever the same when it came to Sarah, but Eli had become the closest thing.

Eli told stories of the world that Trevor had never seen, of life outside Robins-Port. He told him of the ocean's blue waves, the steep mountains in the north, about the great plains where the wind could knock a man over if he weren't careful, about a world which, in that moment, Trevor realized he had been deprived of his entire life.

Trevor became fascinated by Eli's stories and, as the months went by, found himself visiting the old man every chance he got. Like Sarah, Eli lived a life of travel.

Of course, Trevor told Dodge about Eli.

At first, Dodge had simply grumbled and urged Trevor to stay clear. "When a man gives up a home, his family, and all the benefits of our life, he becomes a man with nothing to live for. There's nothing more dangerous than a man with nothing to lose."

Dodge might never have agreed with Trevor befriending Eli, but he also never forbade him from seeing him. Over the passing months and years, Trevor made a habit of seeing his old friend.

As Trevor entered the woods now, much like the first day he had found his old friend, he saw Eli huddled next to a fire.

"Ah," Eli said with a smile, "Trevor, my boy. It's good to see you. And what's that you carry?"

"Welcome back, Eli," Trevor replied with a wide smile, holding a small box filled with eggs. "Thought you might want some breakfast."

Eli steadied himself off a log, using the old walking stick as a crutch. "Oh, my favorite! You spoil me, young man." He reached into a nearby bag and pulled out a small skillet. "I hope there is enough for both of us?"

"I knew you wouldn't have it any other way," Trevor teased.

"It seems you haven't forgotten about me then, lad." Eli set the pan on a few burning sticks from the fire. "It doesn't get better than this."

Trevor joined him near the log. It was moments like these that he loved the most. The ground was damp with droplets of morning dew, the air warm with the smell of fresh firewood, and he had pleasant company with whom he could pass the time.

"So, did you find what you were looking for?" Trevor asked the hermit.

"If you speak of my salvation, no, I have not, and I don't believe I will for quite some time. But I am farther on the path than the last time we spoke, and that is what matters. Always moving forward, Trevor." Eli smiled softly toward the fire. "Small steps, but closer, nonetheless"

"How so?"

Eli pressed his brows together, a look he favored when in thought. "It shames me to say it, but it felt recently that I had lost my way. When I had arrived at Robins-Port, I was stuck, not knowing which direction to go. But"—Eli lifted a finger into the air—"in recent events, I believe I found a path."

"What did you find?" Trevor asked, always curious of Eli's travels. "Where did you go this time?"

"I'm not sure you will understand, my boy."

"I can try, at least," Trevor answered eagerly.

"All right then." Eli gave a shrug. "I found a wolf."

Trevor wasn't sure if the old man was joking. It took a few passing moments to realize he wasn't.

"You found … a wolf?"

"A wolf," Eli answered.

Trevor searched his friend up and down. "Were you attacked? Are you hurt?"

Eli waved away the question. "Oh dear, no. Not at all. It is a special wolf, not one you are no doubt imagining. This is a rare breed."

Trevor slowly waved his hands in the air, trying to paint the picture Eli was terribly describing. "Are you trying to be vague? What's so special about this rare wolf?"

"It was on the run. Hiding from the world, more or less."

"Wait—are you telling me that you were *tracking* a wolf?"

Eli pressed his lips together and nodded. "In a sense, I suppose I have been."

"How long did it take you?"

"What's that?"

"How long did it take you to find the wolf?" Trevor pressed.

"Ah. Time is so relative, wouldn't you say? What's a few years compared to a lifetime anyway? Maybe *tracking* is the wrong word. *Waiting* is more accurate." Eli looked to the side, staring off into the woods as if talking to someone else. "Sometimes, we don't know what we are looking for until we find it."

"So, what you are saying is that you've been waiting for a wolf to find." Trevor cracked the eggs and let them sizzle in the pan. Eli might have been twice—perhaps even three times—Trevor's age, but his cooking was actually quite terrible.

After a long moment, Eli looked back at Trevor. "Well, I did not know I was until I found it."

"And now that you've found it, you believe you found your path again?"

Eli lifted another finger and smiled with his teeth. "Precisely."

Another silence passed as Trevor waited for the hermit to explain.

Eli rustled through his knapsack and revealed two, small ceramic plates and a pair of forks. When he noticed Trevor's gaze, he raised his eyebrows in question.

"I guess you're right," Trevor said, shrugging. "I just don't understand."

"I do not expect you to, my boy. I hardly understand it myself. Maybe there will be a day when you do. We can only hope. But," Eli indicated a change in subject with his fork, "my woes and adventures can wait. What has been going on in Robins-Port? How is that brooding uncle of yours?"

"How would you know that he broods?" Trevor asked.

Eli thought for a moment. "I suppose he just sounds like a man who favors brooding. How is he, regardless?"

Before Trevor knew it, he was lost in conversation with Eli while they ate their breakfast. He loved talking with the old man about all the places he'd been, what he'd seen, who he talked to, what sorts of dangers he escaped. The way Eli told his stories made it feel as if Trevor were actually there with him, and by the time the food was cleared from their plates, Trevor realized just how much he had missed the old man.

Soon the topics drifted toward Trevor. They talked about his practices with Dodge, about starting to work in the smithy with Tom, and about Sarah's long overdue return. Eli knew the history with Trevor and Sarah.

Then the subject turned back to Eli and what he referred to as his path. It always amazed Trevor just how much the old man had given up for his quest. There were vague details about wealth and power in his stories prior to his recent ideology, about passion and love. However, there were brief moments, very brief moments, when Eli teared with the memory about his life before.

"Don't you get tired?" Trevor asked, trying to respect Eli's secrets.

"Oh"—he sighed a deep breath—"my bones creak and ache more and more with each passing day. I would be lying if I said I even remember my age. I stopped counting long ago."

"Well"—Trevor struggled, trying to find the right words—"how do you know you haven't repented enough?"

It was obvious to Trevor that Eli was uncomfortable with the question. The hermit dug the end of his walking stick into the dirt, carving lines into the ground.

"No, I am not done yet. That is another thing I feel in these old bones of mine. But I know my next move, at least."

Trevor didn't care for the tone of the conversation anymore. He didn't mean to upset Eli or bring up foul memories, so he circled back to something he had been meaning to ask. "Well, I should be heading off. I should have met with Tom nearly an hour ago. I hope he lets me out early to see Sarah."

Eli laughed softly. "He would be a fool to try to stop you."

"Speaking of …" Trevor stood and brushed the dirt from his legs. "Would you like to meet her? It'd mean a lot to me if you would."

"I would love to meet her," Eli said as he struggled to his feet, as well. "Unfortunately, I must be going."

It wasn't the answer Trevor had expected, nor liked in the least bit. "Oh. Already?"

Eli cleared his throat and leaned on his walking stick, a sad look in his eyes as he looked at Trevor. "Admittedly, I have only come back to say goodbye, my boy."

Trevor kicked dirt about, avoided meeting Eli's eyes. A quick lump bulged in his throat, and his eyes began to sting, tears building. "You're leaving for good, aren't you?"

"As I have said, I was lost when I first came here. I had nearly given up at my task. But you"—he pointed with a shaky, thin finger—"you have given me something I was growing unfamiliar with. You gave me hope. So, I continued to search and have found my path again. I have you to thank for that, Trevor, and I can never express just how thankful I am.

"But do not be sad, my boy," Eli encouraged as he approached Trevor. "This may be goodbye, but it is not the end. The world we live in may be vast, but our paths are sure to cross again."

Trevor quickly wiped a tear from his face. He didn't feel shame in crying in front of Eli. As time passed and they'd grown to know one another, shame was a stranger to Trevor around the old hermit.

"If you say so," Trevor replied under his breath. He felt like a pouting child.

Eli put a reassuring hand on Trevor's shoulder. "I know so. I only fear that you will be an entirely different person when we next speak. I do hope it to be for the better. Goodbye, my boy. May you find peace as I search for mine."

Eli turned about, stuffed the dirty pan in his torn knapsack, flipped up his hood, and began walking away. Away from Robins-Port, away from Trevor.

It didn't feel right. It felt too fast. There were so many questions that Trevor still had, so many stories he had yet to hear.

"Eli," he blurted before he even knew what he was saying.

The hermit turned around and gave Trevor a curious look. It reminded him of the day they had first met.

How could I have ever feared this man?

"I don't know what you're looking for," Trevor stumbled with his rushing thoughts, "or where you'll find it, but I hope you do. If anyone deserves forgiveness, it's you."

Trevor saw the smile creep in the shadow beneath Eli's hood.

"I hope you are right, my boy," he said. "Farewell. And do give my regards to that brooding uncle of yours. Tell him he has raised one hell of a man."

Lessons and Mysteries

Quiver crouched under a limp branch as he made his way through the dense green forest, a bow slung over his back and a blade at his waist. The air was sticky and filled with the smell of the trees. Soft dirt welcomed his bare feet, muffling his presence to the life of the forest. Angled gleams of light pierced through gaps between branches, Quiver's only indication of how late it was in the day.

As nervous as the night made him, Quiver was adept at masking his nerves. As chief, he needed to set an example for those he led. If he expected his pack to be fearless, he should be fearless himself. However, it wasn't just the coming darkness that tickled Quiver's gut; it was the state of their mission. They had been at the trail for nearly three weeks now and had failed to find any sign of life, let alone their clansmen.

Food was running short in the village, and it was time for a hunt. Nero, the hunter's chieftain, thought it a perfect time to give the new hunters some firsthand training. Before leaving, Nero declared that, upon their return, in three days hence, there would be a deer slung over every shoulder, and not one by his killing. He would prove the young were trained and ready to provide for the village.

Quiver had grown worried as the fifth day passed, and Nero had yet to return. However, Nero had never let the village down before, so he kept faith in his nephew. But, as a week then passed with still no sign of Nero, Quiver took his worries to Elder Roku. With the shortage of supplies and with no word of Nero or his pack, Quiver pleaded a mission to track down the pack and aid them in their quest for food.

The elder agreed.

Out of the tribe, Quiver held the highest respect, mostly due to his family line. Unfortunately, that status didn't sit well with Elder Roku and, over time, he had become suspicious that Quiver was moving for power within the clan. Because of that, Elder Roku never held back any display of dominance, trying to keep Quiver in line and remind him of who was in charge.

"I give you will to leave, truly, Quiver, but I ask you to take three younglings with you. If you were to find Nero, it may be that he needs aide. If you do not find him, you will still have enough help to carry back food for the village."

There was more meaning behind Roku's words. Deep down, Quiver knew Elder Roku wanted him to fail, to be shamed in front of the entire village, all in fear that Quiver wished to take status as the elder of the village.

It might have been disguised as extra help, but Quiver knew bringing the younglings would only slow him down, making his task even more difficult.

Though Quiver had distanced himself from many of the traditions that his clansmen still practiced, he knew better than to defy Elder Roku. And so, he gathered three of the younglings in training, told them they were to be tested on tracking Nero's party, as well as hunting all the game they could find. He told them to stuff enough rations in their packs to last them a week's time.

On the morning that the pack was due to set off, Quiver made sure to stop at Thread's tent. He could only imagine the wrath that he would face upon his return if he did not say goodbye.

He entered the tent to find her waiting for him, standing with her arms crossed and a smile on her face.

"Off to play the hero again," she'd said.

Quiver had chuckled. "Just doing what anyone else would."

"Except nobody else volunteered. None but you."

Quiver took a step closer to Thread, the sweet smell of flowers radiating off her. "What would you have me do then?"

Thread shrugged. "Convince Elder Roku to send someone else?"

"After I just convinced him to send me?" Quiver shook his head. "Not likely. Besides, that's not my way, Thread. You know that."

"I'm not sure you even know your own way, Chief Quiver. I just wish you'd put your trust in the rest of us."

"The ones who have my trust are the ones I would rather not involve in tasks such as this."

"And what type of task is this?" There was a hint of anger in her voice that kept Quiver on the balls of his feet.

"Nero has been gone for too long. Someone needs to set out and look for him."

"So, send a search party," Thread retorted.

"We also need food before our people starve," Quiver added.

Thread shot back without hesitation, "So send some hunters. None of this you need to involve yourself in."

Quiver shook his head sadly, knowing that what he was saying was breaking Thread's heart. He wanted to tell her what he knew she wanted to hear, but he just couldn't. "I need to do this, Thread."

She looked away from him then. "And what if these people you trust so much to stay would see you disappointed and follow you? Do you think they'll trust your wishes and stay back, or betray you to come with?"

Quiver curled his lips in a smile. "Are you speaking of yourself or the imaginary line of volunteers standing outside the tent?"

Thread averted his eyes, ignoring his question. "Do you trust them to do as you wish?"

Quiver hooked a finger underneath her chin and dragged her attention back to him, the radiance of her brown eyes melting his heart. "I trust you'll decide."

Thread, Quiver's oldest friend, and much more than that, wrapped her arms around him and nestled her head against his chest. "Just promise me something, then."

"Anything," Quiver responded, wrapping his arms around her back.

"Promise me that you'll be all right," she had whispered.

After Quiver's brief goodbye with Thread, he had led his pack of younglings toward the end of the village, on the trail that led into the forest. When he had turned a bend, he'd found a man leaning against a tree, waiting for him. He had a pack slung over his shoulder and was taking a bite out of an apple.

"What do you think you're doing, Rasca?" Quiver had asked the man who was chewing loudly at his fruit.

His friend, one of very few, raised an eyebrow at him. "Leave you alone with the young out there for a week? I wouldn't wish that upon anyone, let alone three younglings who have barely any experience with shooting a bow. Besides, I don't think I could bear Thread's mood while you're out and about, trying to save everybody … again."

Quiver grunted to Rasca, grateful for his friend's aide but refusing to show it.

Quiver had then explained the plan to his friend until the three younglings presented themselves. After a brief introduction, Quiver and his pack had then set out to find Nero.

That was three weeks ago.

As Quiver ducked below a large branch hanging in his path, he came into a small opening. The younglings were on their knees, picking up loose leaves and studying the dirt.

Rasca stood next to Quiver. "More tracks?"

"Guess so," Quiver answered. "It doesn't make any sense, though."

"Besides the fact that Nero was all the way out here?"

"If they'd failed to find game, why not search elsewhere? Why not change course?"

"I think you're missing the strangest part."

Quiver looked to his friend. "Hmm?"

Rasca crossed his arms and gestured his head toward the path behind them. "Where is the life of the forest? The only time we hear anything is at night, and even then, nothing but insects."

Rasca had a point. They'd hardly seen any sign of wildlife during the entire quest. The most they had seen were squirrels, which filled their bellies for the night, keeping them away from using the rations in their packs. Other than that, the forest seemed dead. And the farther out they got, the worse it was, as if all life avoided where their path had taken them.

One of the younglings, Oppo, waved Rasca and Quiver over.

The group slowly dispersed as they approached, opening a wider circle to reveal the ground.

"What did you find?" Quiver asked. It was a quiet moment as the younglings looked to one another for an answer. "Well?"

"We are not sure, Chief Quiver," spoke a youngling. In the dawning sunlight, sweat gleamed as it dripped down the side of his face. His hair was cut short, just barely lifting off a bald scalp with the ink of matching birds on both sides.

"You either know, Sparrow, or you do not."

"I do not know, Chief Quiver." Sparrow bowed his head in shame.

"And that's fine," Quiver reassured. "As long as you do not pretend you do."

Quiver crouched low to the ground. He looked about and studied the pattern within the dirt. According to the tracks, Nero's pack followed farther into the opening then changed course completely. Where obvious tracks should have been, scuttled dirt and fallen leaves littered the ground.

Quiver looked around the opening, taking in the quietness of the jungle and measuring all the shadowed light. Then he stood and walked about the small clearing. Reaching the edge, he crouched and studied the long grass before him.

Just as he was about to turn, a small glint of reflection from the sun caught his eye. He brushed a handful of dried amber leaves near his foot and picked up what was hidden. A hatchet, with a dark coating dried at its edge. Quiver picked at it.

Still a little tough. Not two days dry. Could be blood, but nothing I've ever seen before.

He tucked the hatchet behind his leather belt and hid it beneath his loose shirt.

The pack was waiting quietly for Quiver's guidance as he returned to them.

"You are looking too small," he stated. "Look bigger.

"Oppo, what can you tell me?"

Oppo studied the tracks and mimicked Quiver's interest in the surroundings. "These are not their tracks, Chief," he said, rubbing dirt between two fingers.

"Yes and no," Quiver answered. "Sparrow?"

"I do not know, Chief."

"You best find an answer, or find a way to carry our packs the rest of the way. What do you think, Masco?"

Masco, the youngest of the pack, looked around the clearing in which they stood. After making a small patrol around the open area, peering into the distance, studying the dirt, and finally looking back at the scuffled tracks before them, he looked to Rasca and Quiver.

"Something happened," he stated firmly.

"Something is always happening. Be specific."

"They were attacked."

Quiver watched as Oppo and Sparrow flexed their jaws while Rasca moved away to inspect the area where Quiver had uncovered the hatchet.

"That is right, Masco."

Within the many years of training younglings, Masco had impressed Quiver the most. He was the youngest of the younglings in the village, his mother falling ill to fever and his father dying during the war with the south.

His mind was sharper than most. He had a tendency to see the things that most didn't.

He'll make a strong chieftain someday.

Quiver walked to where Rasca knelt near a bush. "Gather."

The pack hustled to him and waited quietly.

Quiver lifted the low branch and revealed the sight of the endless forest. "Sparrow, what do you see?"

Sparrow took his place in front of the group and peered into the vast openness.

"See before you speak. Be patient. Do not see what is there, see what is not."

After a long moment of silence, Sparrow faced the pack. "Trails."

"Good. Very good, Sparrow." Quiver pointed a finger toward the open green. He narrowed his gesture toward a large patch of bushes near two large trees where the grass parted slightly wider than its surrounding area. Any inexperienced hunter would have missed it, but Quiver was far from inexperienced when it came to tracking. There was only one other person he knew who matched his skill, and he hoped never to see that man again.

"Oppo, which way does the path lead?"

Rasca sat by, peering into the jungle as Quiver questioned the younglings.

"Into the jungle, Chief—"

"Wrong," Masco mumbled.

Quiver rolled his shoulders back and loomed over Masco. "How can you tell?"

Most younglings would cower beneath the shadow of Quiver, but Masco wasn't like most. Quiver could see in the youngling's eyes that he knew he had spoken out of turn, that there would be discipline for his outburst, but he wouldn't stop now.

In a strange way, it reminded Quiver of himself at that age. Quiver had always questioned his father the same way, pushing the limits of his father's patience as Quiver grew up under his training.

But I also learned to be patient.

Masco pointed behind Rasca, toward a bundle of sticks sprouting from the ground. The sticks stood knee high and were angled to a point with a clear sign of being broken. The only indication of travel from the angle of the break showed something not moving into the jungle, but from it, moving toward the clearing.

"There are more trails, too." Masco pointed to several areas surrounding them. "There, there, and there."

37

What others were blind to, Masco saw clearly.

"You're right." Quiver leaned closer to Masco's face. "From this point, you will carry Oppo's bag. You see much, young Masco, but you fail to see where your place is. You will never again speak out of turn. Do you understand?"

Masco did not shy away from Quiver's glare, but he did acknowledge his punishment by putting both arms behind his back and nodding toward his chieftain.

Quiver backed away from Masco. "Since you are so eager to lead, you will teach the others of your findings. Show them what you see, how you see it, and what we can learn from it. When you are done, I will ask each a question. Each question answered wrong will result in ten laps around the village when we return, so hope they understand. Now, I must speak to Chief Rasca. Go."

Masco gave no indication that Quiver's punishment upset him. Without hesitation, he hustled deeper into the jungle and gestured for the others to follow.

Rasca squared with Quiver. "You are hard on the youngling," he said.

"I must be. We all learn to walk before we run, do we not?"

"You think he will become chieftain?"

Quiver thought the question over before nodding slightly. "Only if he learns to follow. My father always said that you cannot lead if you have never followed."

Rasca scoffed. "Sounds like something your father would say."

Rasca looked toward the pack. They knelt near the path as Masco gestured around the area, teaching them what he saw. "You might be right, though. So," changing the topic, he asked, "what do you think?"

Quiver took a moment and pinched the sleep from his eyes. "I think that whatever Nero and his pack followed led them here for an ambush."

"We've seen plenty of ambushes; nothing as clean as this."

Quiver revealed the hatchet from under his belt and handed it to Rasca.

Rasca nodded his agreement. "So, they brought them into a clearing and attacked from all sides. It's smart, coordinated. But it's also forbidden to bring war upon another clan. Who would break a faithful law?"

"Who said anything about a clan?"

There was a moment of silence that followed Quiver's words.

Rasca raised an eyebrow. He picked at the blood on the hatchet. "What is this? This is no blood; it's too dark."

"Nero's too smart to follow straight into an ambush. If he were tracking a clan, it would have gone differently." Quiver nodded to the hatchet. "Someone spotted whatever it was and got a swing in before it took them."

"Still doesn't add up. Nero would back from a fight for the sake of the younglings. The only evidence we have of any encounter is this," Rasca said, lifting the hatchet. He turned around, gesturing to the wide opening. "We both know how messy a fight can be. Where is that mess?"

"Chief!"

Quiver turned to see Masco pointing toward the sky. He followed Masco's finger toward the top of a large oak tree.

For a moment, Quiver forgot to breathe. "What the …?"

Rasca walked toward the giant tree, head tilted toward the dying sun. "Well, I guess you're right about it not being another clan."

See before you speak, he thought, a lesson he often taught to others.

Giant gashes cut through the thick bark across the circle of trees; trees splattered and stained with dark blood. The splinters cut deep into the oak, three lines per gash, as if a wolf with claws the size of a man's torso had discovered how to climb a tree. No animal Quiver had seen could have done this, and no weapon of any tribesman could cut so deeply and precisely to match the pattern before them.

Quiver followed a trail of cuts from tree to tree. Whatever it was, it was strong enough to cut oak. The only thing that made sense was that the beasts hid in the trees until Nero's pack entered the opening.

What could possibly be so big to fit those marks and remain quiet enough to set an ambush on Nero and his pack? It was too strong for any man, and too precise for any beast.

"I guess that would explain the missing bodies," Quiver heard Rasca mumble. "I don't know, Quiver. This makes me uneasy."

Quiver couldn't help agreeing.

He broke his mesmerized attention away from the trees and called the pack to his side. They knelt before him, hands on their knees, waiting for direction. However, Quiver wasn't quite sure what that direction would be. It was possible Nero and his pack were still alive, but Quiver held little faith.

Quiver was fearful, but he refused to show it to the pack. "We're heading back to the village to gather the others. We—"

"We're leaving?" Masco interrupted.

It took all of Quiver's patience not to strike the youngling there and then.

"We're leaving," he confirmed. The sun was setting, and being this far out with the possible danger that hid in the shadows, Quiver wasn't willing to risk the lives of his pack.

Rasca joined at his side.

"But Chief Nero and his pack are still out there," Masco complained.

"There is no evidence of their survival," Sparrow whispered, voice holding fear.

"And there is no evidence of their death, either!" Masco urged. "We cannot leave them out here when they may need our help."

"Whatever Nero was hunting led his pack to this very spot. It chose this spot because it knew not only could it attack from all sides but from above, as well. It's smart. If anyone survived the ambush, they would have made it back to the village by now, yet we saw nothing but tracks leading to nowhere. He had a pack of eight, and we have four. What do you think the odds are with us?"

"Odds?" Oppo questioned, a look of confusion at Quiver's choice of words.

Quiver rubbed his face. *A southern phrase they don't understand. You have to watch yourself, old man.*

"What do you think the chances are for us?" Quiver corrected himself.

"But we have you, Chief Quiver," Oppo pleaded.

The statement took Quiver by surprise as he fumbled for his next words, but it was Rasca who added his say.

"When it comes to battle, it's better to think before you strike. Chief Quiver understands what this means for Nero, but the best thing we can do is warn the village. We must think of all clansmen, not just those who are in these woods right now."

A loud, inhuman shriek echoed through the jungle. It was then that Quiver realized just how low the sun had actually set. Gray shadows replaced what were recently gleams of sunlight. Full darkness was mere moments away.

"What was that?" Sparrow gasped, his eyes wide with fear.

Quiver's arms prickled at the sound. "Nothing I've heard before."

"We need to go," Rasca added. "Now."

Another shriek echoed out, accompanied by another, then another.

Whatever it was, there were more than Quiver would like to count. It sounded distant, but too close for Quiver's liking.

He saw the pale fear on each youngling's face as the night shadowed their bodies.

"Stay in a file and stick to the trail. Keep the pace, and do not lose sight of the one in front of you. We run through the night. Rasca, you take lead, I'll hold the rear."

Rasca replied with a quick nod before disappearing down the trail. Sparrow and Oppo followed, leaving Masco the last one standing before Quiver.

"We are weeks from the village. We'll never make it," he said bluntly.

"If we run, we just might." Quiver tightened the straps at his shoulders. Before setting off, he knelt down and took Masco by the shoulders. "Remember, Masco, there is more than ourselves when it comes to a pack. The pack is the self, not the person. Every chief knows this."

Masco stood in silence, mulling over Quiver's words. After a few moments pause, he nodded, clear determination in his eyes.

Quiver stood up and faced the darkening jungle. "Now, Masco, we run."

The Plague of Robins-Port

Robins-Port was a sparsely populated town near the end of the season. Most people finished their work and took off to spend winter somewhere that offered more than dusty streets and hills of farmland: the luscious forests of Greenworth, the mountainous city of Alvest, or even the bustling streets of the capital city, Servitol.

The streets were small and covered with loose dirt, causing dust clouds to spiral up as wagons and caravans passed. An old rumor of Robins-Port was that, if you spent too much time in the town, you'd start coughing up mud. But in all the years that Trevor had lived there, which was his entire life, he had yet to confirm that myth.

At first glance, Robins-Port would pass as a town of poverty, its residents struggling for a meal every day, but that was simply because of how Robins-Port operated. The town was a means to profit, and those who profited did so very far away. Money didn't pass through Robins-Port, only trade. People didn't need big houses or wealthy shops, only places to reside and for business to get done.

Robins-Port's location was responsible for its profit; It was surrounded by mountains and hills for protection, near dead center of the major cities in Navaleth, and connected with plenty of roads to keep trade moving to anywhere around the country. The three main roads connected to the main cities of Navaleth: Servitol, Brackenheart, and Mendora. No matter what trade route a caravan occupied, if it valued safety, eventually, it would pass through Robins-Port.

Trade tended to slow down quite a bit with the turn of the season, which was undoubtedly Trevor's favorite time of the year. The fewer people who lived in Robins-Port, the happier he was. The less people there were, the fewer people could whisper under their breaths as he passed by, spitting insults when they thought him too far to hear. No more hateful glares, no looks of pity or shame.

Soon, Trevor would be able to walk the streets without the anxious grip in his chest. Until then, there was work to be done. Tom, the blacksmith, made sure of that.

"You pound on that anvil any longer, and you'll lose the shape," Tom hollered at him from across the smithy. "You've gotta dump it while it's still hot. No, put the hammer back first. I'll not have you losing my tools. Quickly now!"

Trevor didn't know how the old man could manage as the only blacksmith with the high demand on tools and weapons. It only took a few minutes of skittering around the smithy for Trevor to be soaked with sweat and gasping for fresh air. There were more than a few moments when he left his station to stand by the door to catch his breath.

Tom was all but unaffected; whether he was pounding the anvil or feeding the forge, he did so with ease. The man was built like an ox, a genius when it came to metals.

Trevor carefully dunked the hot metal into the barrel, mindful not to drop it like the others. Steam hissed and surrounded his face. The constant heat was unbearable, the one thing he already hated about blacksmithing. Trevor wouldn't have wasted time washing himself after the morning's sparring if he knew he would be in a constant sweat anyway.

Tom joined Trevor at the barrel as soon as the steam began to clear. "Aye, that's enough now. Pull her out and let's see what you've got."

Trevor's heart fluttered with excitement. Tom had promised he could keep the first piece of metal that he worked on and had even let him choose what to make. Trevor had decided on a small dagger. However, when he pulled his hours of labor from the steam barrel, his heart dropped.

To say the blade was bent would be an understatement. The metal dulled and warped at different angles. Ripples plagued the blade, resembling what you might see after tossing a rock into a lake. Not to mention the point of the blade resembled a spoon more than a knife.

Tom let out a roar of laughter and gave Trevor a rough slap on his back. Then he left Trevor gazing at his wasted work to grab a small box from a shelf above a table littered with tools.

Tom brought the box over to Trevor. "My mentor told me the same thing when I was but an apprentice: *pick something to build, and you can keep your first one.* And, like you, I chose a weapon. Not a shoe for a horse, or a chain for a fence, but something that would make me feel *strong*."

Tom opened the small box. Inside was a small, warped dagger that resembled Trevor's. Like his, it was bent and deformed. He looked long and hard to compare it to his own before Tom returned the box to the shelf.

"So, you knew I would fail?" he accused the blacksmith.

Tom turned and eyed Trevor. "Fail? You think you've failed this morning? Tell me, when good ol' Dodge handed you that first practice sword, did you know how to use it?"

Trevor knew his answer wasn't needed.

"Of course not," Tom continued. "You just went off what you saw, or heard about, and figured that was all the skill it took. You already knew how to swing, but Dodge showed you how to dance with it." Tom put a reassuring hand on Trevor's shoulder. "Blacksmithing is like swordplay. It takes time and patience, knowledge and skill. There's no failing here, only discovering where you need to improve."

Trevor knew what that meant all too well. "It's going to get harder before it gets easier," Trevor mumbled.

Tom's eyes brightened with approval. "Right you are. Like your lessons with Dodge in your backyard, inside the smithy is where we will learn from our mistakes. Now, don't feel too bad. I've seen much worse than that." He pointed at the dagger in Trevor's hand. "Yours isn't as bad as you might think. In fact, it'll still probably do the trick. Just don't let anybody see it."

"By the gods, what is that abomination?" a voice asked from the doorway.

Both of them turned their gaze toward the entrance. A girl—no, a woman—stood in the doorway, eyes beaming on Trevor's dagger. Her long, blonde hair fell past her shoulders and down her clean, light blue dress that had an intricate white pattern.

"Sarah Michaelson," Tom praised. "Now that's a face I thought I'd never see again."

Sarah stepped farther into the room, never taking her eyes off Trevor. "Thomas Hurling, did you finally take on some help? Or … at least try?" She gestured toward the dagger Trevor still held.

"Hey, Trevor." She smiled.

"Hi," Trevor responded, still stunned by her sudden appearance. "You're very … uh …" Trevor put his arm out and leaned against the water barrel, trying to seem casual in order to save face. His hand slipped, splattering water around the smithy and nearly causing him to fall in himself. Water soaked his arm and splashed around the floor. "Yeah. Hey there, Sarah."

Tom simply responded with tight lips and a shake of his head, thankfully seeing that he didn't need to add to Trevor's current embarrassment.

Sarah giggled to herself, a sound that caused Trevor's heart to flutter. "Yeah. *Hey there, Trev*," she mocked in a voice he could only guess was to mimic his own.

"So," Tom said, interrupting the sudden silence in the smithy, "I'm guessing you came for the boy?"

"Only if you can spare him. Also, my father needs a few things, if you can manage." Sarah handed Tom a small piece of parchment.

His eyes skittered across the parchment as he chewed his lower lip. "This is quite the list, Sarah," he said finally. "How long have I got?"

For the first time during the encounter, Sarah shied away from Trevor's gaze. Was it shame he saw there?

"Will two days be a sufficient amount of time?" she asked.

"Two days?" both Tom and Trevor said in unison.

Tom looked about the room and studied his tools as Sarah gave Trevor an apologetic smile. After a few moments of nobody saying anything, Trevor felt another rough slap on his back.

"Well, looks like today's lesson is done. I've got some real work to do. And truth be told, you'd just get in the way."

Sarah gave Trevor a smile as he met her eyes. "Coming?"

"Hold up," he heard Tom say just as he was about to leave. Trevor turned and faced the blacksmith. "Remember what we talked about today. It's not easy being a blacksmith; you just get used to the challenge. Now, come back in three days and be prepared to learn."

"Thanks, Tom," Trevor said. Trevor took off his apron and tossed it onto a nearby table.

The air cleared as he stepped into the sunlight, a cold breeze cooling his body as he began walking down the dirt-covered streets with Sarah at his side. For a moment, none of it looked dirty, the wood on the houses didn't look rotten, the people passed by without looks of judgement. Everything seemed different when Sarah was there.

***

An orange glow lit the skyline as the sun slowly sank behind the mountains. At the edge of Robins-Port, on top of a rubble pile from a broken wall, two friends searched for the right words to say to one another.

"Tastes a bit like …" Sarah began, smacking her tongue around the inside of her mouth.

Trevor, holding back as long as he possibly could, dramatically spit off the wall. "Like an old foot," he finished for her. "Where did you say this shop was?"

Sarah grimaced, also spitting to her side. "A small town that my father's bank has taken interest in. Somewhere in the west."

"And do these people know what chocolate is *supposed* to taste like?"

"Evidently, no." Sarah tossed the remaining chocolate over her shoulder, "By the gods, that's awful."

"You sure this isn't boot polish?" Trevor asked.

"I was thinking more of some type of fertilizer."

"Is that your high-born way of saying it tastes like shit?"

"Hey"—she slapped his arm playfully—"I'm not a high born."

"I bet you have people who do your laundry now," Trevor accused playfully.

"Only sometimes."

"They spoon feed you, as well?"

"Only when it's soup."

"What about when it's not?"

"That usually means they're too busy with laundry."

The glowing sunset was filled with laughter as they spit out the bitter tastes in their mouths.

Trevor sat quietly, fixated on Sarah. He would ask for nothing more if he could hear that laugh every day and wake up to her smile for the rest of his life.

Gods, I've missed her.

"Beautiful, isn't it?" she asked, casting her eyes at the open sunset before them.

"Breathtaking," he answered, never taking his eyes from her.

Sarah turned and looked at him, a blush rising in her cheeks. Her smile was genuine, yet Trevor could see a hidden sadness in her eyes. She looked away abruptly, kicking her dangling legs out before her.

"What about you?" she asked. "You've seemed to grow into yourself quite a bit while I've been away. Your arms are nearly bigger than my body. Been working at Tom's long?"

"Don't pretend you didn't see my dagger."

"Is that what it was? Thought it was a ladle or something," she said, playfully nudging him.

"And that's not saying much." Trevor held up Sarah's arm. "I'm surprised you're not taken away with the wind. Maybe they should feed Your Highness something more than just soup."

"Please." Sarah snorted, pulling back her arm from Trevor. "I'm far from a princess."

"Could've fooled me."

She still refused to look his way, but Trevor could see a small smile matching the blush in her pale cheeks.

He missed their talks. She was the one person he didn't have to watch what he said, didn't have to tread carefully with his words.

"So, tell me more about this … Everett?"

"Eli," Trevor corrected. "And there's not much else. He moves from place to place pretty frequently. Says he's searching for redemption for something he's done."

"Redemption for what?" Sarah asked.

"I don't know. I've never asked specifically. I can tell he's still hurt from it, so I try not to pry too much."

"Wow. What sort of thing could lead someone to give up his entire life searching for forgiveness?"

"Something about … a fallout maybe? I know it has something to do with his family. '*Changed his world*,' he would always say."

"That's some fallout. I wish I could've met him. I would have loved to hear of his travels. When did you last see him?"

"This morning." Trevor looked to the woods where he had talked with his old friend just this morning, the memory of Eli leaving stinging like a knife to his chest.

"Well, how long is he usually gone for?" Sarah began asking. "Maybe the next—"

"There won't be a next time, Sarah. He said he won't be returning to Robins-Port again." Trevor tried to hide the hurt in his voice, but Sarah knew him too well

47

for that.

"Oh, Trevor, I'm so sorry," she said sincerely.

It took a moment for Trevor to gather his emotions. "I don't know. I mean, I'm going to miss him, but if he's finally found his path, I have to be happy for him. And I am. I'm happy for him. You would have liked him, though. You two have much in common."

"If I've learned anything, it's that the world is smaller than we know. Perhaps one day I will meet him." Although Sarah indicated hope, Trevor couldn't help hearing it as sadness.

For a moment, all was quiet between them. He and Sarah looked to the view before them. The gentle wind swayed the grass back and forth, and the mountains cast a shadow across the field, slowly taking the light and heat of the day.

Trevor looked to Sarah. "I've missed you, Sarah. I really have." He reached for Sarah's hand, but she pulled away abruptly. He could feel his face flush with confusion as he began apologizing, his words sputtering out awkwardly, his body trembling with worry. "I'm … sorry. I didn't mean to. I just, eh—"

"I have to tell you something, Trevor," she said, staring blankly out toward the open world that remained a mystery to him. "And you're not going to like it."

"What do—"

"I've missed you, too, but we've only come back for business." She shifted uncomfortably. "Business for me, mostly."

"That's—"

"Please, Trevor, let me finish." Avoiding his confused stare, she kept her eyes focused on the landscape before them. After what seemed like ages of waiting, she let out a long breath and closed her eyes. "A friend of my father's, who works at the capital with him, has a son my age. His father plans to retire soon, leaving his trade fully to his son. However, they want to find a wife for him first. As you know, my father has been training me with his trade for a while now."

Trevor wasn't exactly sure what any of this had to do with him or Sarah, so he replied with a blank stare. However, his confusion was quickly replaced with worry when he noticed tears building in her eyes.

"My father saw an opportunity," she continued.

"Good for your father, but what—"

"We're to meet them tomorrow."

"Sarah," he said, still confused as to what she was getting at, "what are you trying to say?"

"We're to be married, Trevor," she said with a flare of anger in her eyes.

Trevor's body went numb as he felt the happiness drain from his body, leaving him nearly breathless. Looking past Sarah, his mouth gaped open as he tried to process her last words. One minute he was enjoying the sunset while talking to the only link to a real life he had left, and in the next, he felt he couldn't breathe.

"Please try to understand." Sarah was crying now. "I had ... I *have* no choice in this. I need you to be happy for me. He's a good match. We both come from successful families, so we already know what to expect for the business side.

"My father says he's a nice man, charming, overall. They say that, with our combined business, we can change the world as we know it. Start a new type of commerce. And he ... I ... it's just ..." She searched the air for her next excuse until she gave up.

Trevor, stuck in his dumbfound, sat speechless.

"Please, say something," she pleaded. "Say anything."

There was a pounding in his head, and his ears burned hot. He wasn't even sure he was breathing. He searched for something, anything to say, but couldn't find a single word.

A snide voice broke the silence. "Well, boys, look what we've got here."

Trevor didn't fully understand the phrase "*When it rains, it pours*" until that moment. If he thought he had just hit rock bottom, Warren Robinson would happily hand him a shovel to prove he could dig deeper.

"Has the orphan made a new friend?" Warren asked nobody in particular as he came into view.

"Back off, Warren," Sarah spat as she stood to face him and his posse.

If Warren took offense from Sarah's remark, he didn't show it.

Trevor didn't bother to even glance his way; just sat, transfixed on the land before him, still trying to process the news Sarah had thrown him.

"Wow," Warren gasped. "You remind me of someone I used to know. Couldn't be Sarah Michaelson, though. She didn't look so ... *ripe* the last time I saw her."

The sound of Sarah's name coming from Warren's venomous mouth grabbed more than just Trevor's attention. Before he knew it, he was on his feet, facing Warren's wicked smile, not entirely sure what he was doing but feeling the urge to do something, his anger building toward rage.

Behind Warren stood Plump, a well-rounded boy whose family owned the local bakery in town, famous for its pies and sweets. Jacob was his real name, but ever since Warren started calling him Plump, he didn't respond to anything else. The boy seemed to take the insult as a compliment, adding more weight to his pathetic figure.

The other two were Alec and Alex, twin brothers of a family who delegated the routes for Robins-Port's caravans. They were the spitting image of each other—same size, same shirt, haircut, and boots. They were also known to finish each other's sentences, which Trevor found extremely irritating.

"Maybe," Warren continued as he took a slow step toward Sarah, arms spread with invitation, "you'd like to ditch this pathetic sap and come back to my place? My father is busy with work, and mum is out shopping for a couple of hours. You look like the type of girl who needs a real man to satisfy her."

Trevor fixed his blazing eyes on Warren as the bully's goons laughed. He wasn't sure if it was his future with Sarah being ripped away, or the constant years of Warren's daily torment, but he didn't care. All he felt was the rage boiling in his chest, and he wanted nothing more than to release it on Warren's smug face.

"Put him in his place, Warren," Plump encouraged from behind, strutting out his belly as if it represented his strength.

"Yeah," one of the twins added. "Teach him—"

"—a lesson," the other finished.

Warren returned Trevor's gaze with a smile as he took a long step toward him. Their eyes locked on each other, like vicious wolves waiting for the first strike. Before one of them could make a next move, however, Sarah stepped between them.

"Oh, Mum and Dad are too busy for you again? Sorry, I'll pass," she said calmly to Warren. "Besides, after what you'd refer to as your *few minutes of glory*, what would we do with the remaining time? In fact, Trevor is more a man than you could ever be. Considering he falls so low on the scale in that empty skull of yours, where does that put you? You're no better than the shit our farmers scrape off their boots, Warren Robinson."

Warren's gaze might not have strayed, but Trevor could see in his eyes that Sarah's insult had hit home.

Plump and the twins stood still behind their fearless leader, eyes wide with shock.

"My apologies." Warren bowed dramatically, now meeting Sarah's eyes. "I simply mistook you for a whore. A cheap one at that, considering the company you keep. I'm sure it's a common mistake. Do forgive me, m'lady?"

Laughter erupted from the goon squad, and Trevor could see Warren take pride in his remark, which only pissed him off the more.

Remember what Dodge told you! Breathe deep, exhale deeper. Breathe deep, exhale deeper.

However, Sarah wasn't fazed. "Oh, what's the matter, Warren? Can't handle a minor jest? I thought you were such a *man* not a few minutes ago? Apologies. I'm sure it's a common mistake around here. Do forgive me, *sir*." Sarah moved back, now slowly backing into Trevor, pushing him away from Warren. "Now, excuse us, we've much better things to do than entertain children. Let's go, Trevor."

He felt a tug on his arm, but Trevor refused to budge. Still burning with rage, he squared off with Warren. That was when Sarah edged her way into his vision, locking eyes and taking his focus.

"Please, Trevor, let's go."

Breathe deep, exhale deeper. Breathe deep, exhale deeper.

Trevor felt calm spread from his chest to his limbs.

A small nod to Sarah told her that he was back with her, ready to leave with Warren and his goons defeated at their own game.

They turned to leave when Trevor suddenly lost his balance, feeling weightless for a split moment. He began falling backward, and before he fully realized what was happening, he was pinned to the ground with Warren sitting on his chest. He tried to struggle, to reach for Warren's throat, but his arms were interlocked by Warren's knees. He failed to roll onto his side, for Warren was prepared for that, as well, using his weight to counterbalance Trevor's movement. Trevor was helpless, a mouse trapped by a cat.

A wicked smile crept across Warren's face. There was a familiar sign of malice in his eyes that Trevor recognized all too well—the look of hunger that he had seen the day before he woke up in the infirmary after a run-in with Warren and his posse, which, at the moment, felt like only yesterday.

51

Warren looked up to his friends and joined in on their laughter. He laughed loud enough to catch the attention of nearby villagers, who stopped what they were doing in order to watch the show.

"Get off him!" Trevor heard Sarah scream.

He stared defiantly up at Warren. In return, Warren laid his arm across Trevor's throat and began choking him. Then he leaned so close that Trevor could feel the hot breath on his face as Warren whispered, "How many times must we repeat history in order for you to learn your place? I thought you might have learned the last time when I put you in the hospital. Never mind that; just be sure to remember this moment, *orphan*. Remember how easy it could be to kill you. Who would even notice you'd be gone? Nobody but your uncle and that whore, and even they would quickly forget.

"Don't mistake their pity for love, Trevor. They could never love you. Not truly. They only feel sorry for you." Warren looked up to where Sarah stood, talking to her as much as Trevor. "Especially that one. Why do you think she always leaves?"

Warren's words were as heavy as the arm against Trevor's throat.

Trevor peered toward the streets where the villagers stood, staring at the scene. They showed no emotion for what was happening. No look of concern or entertainment. They just stood there, watching.

"You see?" Warren's smile grew. "They feel nothing for you. To them, you're just a stray dog that needs discipline. A wounded pup better suited to be put down."

Trevor looked to Sarah with a burn in his eyes. She, too, simply stood there and watched as Warren made a mockery of him in front of the town.

It wasn't the pain on his throat, or shortness of breath that released the warm flow of tears down Trevor's face, nor was it the fact that Sarah decided to leave him forever. It was the fact that Warren was right.

It was then that he felt the cold steel of his warped dagger from the smithy. The metal pressed against his fingertips, the temptation near overwhelming.

Tom's words echoed in his head, "*It'll still probably do the trick.*"

Trevor wanted so badly to find out, but how would that end for him? Murdering the only son of the founding family out of sheer anger? And what would Sarah think of him, coming back home to a killer, regardless of the short time that she had left with him?

He relaxed his body, giving in to his beating, just like he always did.

Warren gave a triumphant smile as he crawled off Trevor. "Always remember, you loveless git; *you're* the sheep, *I'm* the fucking wolf." Warren made his point clear by kicking dirt toward Trevor as he and his posse made their exit.

Trevor made no effort to move. He stayed on his back and looked at the sky, tears streaming down the sides of his face. The day's light would soon be gone, and Trevor could finally end another day in the shit-hole he called his life.

He wiped the tears from his face as a shadow fell over him. He wasn't sure exactly when Warren and his friends had left, but Sarah looked down on him now.

He slapped Sarah's hand away as she reached down to help him stand. He didn't want her pity anymore.

Ignoring the stares of the villagers and the gloating few of Warren's posse, he brushed off his britches and headed toward home.

He was partially down the street when he heard Sarah's footsteps catch up to his. He didn't bother looking her way. How could he face her after that?

And what would be the point?

"Gods," Sarah said, "that boy needs—"

"Marriage?" Trevor shouted as he abruptly turned on her.

Sarah jumped at the sudden boom of Trevor's voice, putting her hands in front of her as if to defend herself from an attack.

"You're getting fucking *married?*"

Sarah began looking around to see if anyone was looking, which just pissed him off even more. All this time, Dodge had been teaching him how to control himself, to hold back the rage he had for the world, but he was sick of holding back from a world that offered him nothing in return. He wanted to let loose, to give in to the anger he'd felt for so long. So that's what he did.

"I'm sorry. Am I causing a scene? Am I embarrassing you?" His hands swelled into solid fists at his sides. He wasn't quite sure what he wanted to do with them, but it felt good, nonetheless.

Sarah took a slow step backward as she noticed them. "I wish—"

"*Don't!*" Trevor roared. "Don't you say a fucking word. *He's a nice match. My father says* … Who the fuck are you trying to convince here"—he walked toward Sarah—"me or yourself? But hey, at least people will know who he is. Better to marry a famous stranger, if a stranger at all. Better than an orphan who nobody gives a shit about, right?"

"I know you're upset but, Trevor, we were just kids," Sarah said defensively.

Trevor saw tears building in her eyes again, but he was too mad to care.

"*Kids*? That was two fucking years ago! *You* made *me* promise, Sarah. *You* asked me to wait, said that, when you came back, you'd tell your father you'd be with me. So that's what I did. I waited for two years. *Two fucking years!* And then you come back and tell me you're getting married?" Trevor's chest squeezed tight with each breath, but he tried his best to ignore it.

He shook his head and pointed at Sarah, his dirt covered finger inches away from her nose. "And you want me to be happy for you? Fuck you, Sarah! I wish you'd never come back at all."

It felt good letting it all out, all the built-up anger from the disappointment he called life. What was the point anymore? He had nothing to show for. Everyone hated him, and whoever didn't would soon be leaving him. So, Trevor finally accepted who he was: the plague of Robins-Port.

Sarah stared at the ground in silence as the tears slid down her pale face, and Trevor stormed away down the street before she had a chance to speak. He had heard all he needed to hear.

He left her standing in the middle of Robins-Port's main street as the sun set, sucking all the light from the day, as well as from his heart.

Nightshade

He rubbed at the crust sealing his eyes, the brisk air giving them a cold bite as they fluttered open. The world was a blur, a mist of confusion fogging his vision and memory as he lay on his back, watching the lights of the stars focus distantly as they cast their light down upon him.

What happened?

His muscles were both swollen and stiff, tightening as he climbed to his feet, stretching his arms to his sides as he searched for balance. Once his vision settled, he saw the figure of a man sitting on a log facing a fire, his back toward him.

Alric took a step forward when he felt his face prickle with heat. His head swam once again, and before he knew he was even falling, he'd crashed down onto a knee and began vomiting all over the ground beneath him. He retched until he could no more, his stomach squeezing tight, purging every drop of the black bile projecting from his mouth.

He lay there a moment, his hands and knees covered in the sour smell of his puke, a pool of dark liquid spreading around him. His breaths came short, his arms growing heavier by the minute, as he struggled to hold himself up.

Just before he gave in to the swarming black surrounding his vision, he felt a hand scoop under his arm, dragging him to his feet.

Seroes wrapped Alric's arm around his shoulders, keeping Alric at balance as Seroes sat him on the log in front of the fire.

His head began to clear as a chilled breeze nipped at his skin, bringing the sweet aroma of leaves to his nose. The world was engulfed in the sound of nature— the chirping of crickets, birds singing to one another, and the crackle of the warm fire.

When was the last time I just stopped to enjoy how beautiful nature can be?

When was the last time he even glanced toward the stars and traced remnants of stories about the heroic deeds of gods and men? He used to love doing that, but Alric used to love a lot of things.

Seroes stepped around the fire opposite of Alric. "What's the last thing you remember?"

Alric struggled to answer. The last time he felt like this was after three days of heavy drinking, but he hadn't an ounce of liquor in years.

Then, why is it so hard to think straight?

"I ..." he struggled to explain. "I don't know. I remember setting up camp. We planned to wait before searching for the cave. I must have shut my eyes for a bit or something. Did I sleep through my watch?"

"I guess it was worse than we thought." Benny stepped out of the shadows, the glow of the fire light illuminating his typical look of concern. "Alric, that was nearly three days, before your recent ... *episode*. You've been asleep for three days."

Alric chuckled at the jest.

When the other two didn't smile, he looked around the camp. The sun looked to have recently set, and the others were gone. He, Benny, and Seroes were the only ones in camp.

He leaned forward and pressed the bridge between his eyes. "I don't understand."

"That's normal," Seroes said in his deep crackle of a voice, "considering I dumped an entire vial of nightshade down your throat."

"Nightshade?" Alric asked, puzzled. "Well, that would explain the confusion."

Benny wrinkled his nose at the hint of sour now on the breeze. "And the vomit."

"So, where's everyone else?" Alric asked as Benny sat on a log across from him.

Benny poked at the fire with a dark stick. "Didn't take them long to wake after what happened. Figured they might as well do something while they're awake, so they went in search of the cave. Sure as shit, Evan comes back not a few hours later to tell us they found it. Said it would take a few days to fully search it, so they should be back—"

"Well, isn't this a sight to see," they heard as four, rough-looking men came into the firelight. "Looks like the old man's finally awake. Finally get some beauty sleep there, big guy?"

"Evan, I wish you'd show a bit of sympathy sometimes," Seroes complained.

Evan struck a large spear into the dirt before placing himself on the log next to Benny. "If I possessed sympathy, I'd be out of a job, my friend. Most likely dead."

Alric looked at the men standing around the fire. Garth and Merrick stood with their bows slung over their shoulders, both avoiding Alric's eyes. Baron stood large with his twin hatchets hanging from his belt and two short swords on his back, arms crossed with steady eyes on Alric's.

"How're you feeling?" the old assassin asked him, his voice as soft as a whisper but loud enough for everyone to hear.

"Better than ever." It wasn't necessarily a lie. Now that he had woken up a bit more, he had a strange lift in energy. Maybe it was one of the effects of the nightshade potion. "What'd you find?"

"Same as usual," Garth said. "A few traps here and there, crumbling statues. Not much different from the others."

"On the contrary, you missed one hell of a show with Baron," Evan added with a wide smile. He got up and put a reassuring hand on Baron's shoulder, which was roughly shrugged off. "Our little Flash here nearly took a turn for the worst in there. I don't think I've ever heard the man scream like that before. In fact, not sure I've heard *any* man scream like that before."

"What happened?" Benny asked with a look of interest.

All eyes fell upon Baron as they waited. Garth and Merrick were trying to hide smiles, unlike Evan who could learn a lesson or two in doing just that. Baron, however, just stared off into the fire with his arms still crossed, brows crunched together, and a curl at his lips.

"Looks like I'll have the honors, then," Evan said when he realized Baron wasn't about to share. "So, there we were, trucking through this old, dangerous cave. A walk through hell it was. Danger lurked in every shadow, a trap lay at every step. Then, just as we made our way to a chamber, right when we thought we were safe … a giant spider leapt from the shadows and attacked Baron!"

Benny's jaw dropped, his eyes wide with concern. "A giant … spider?"

"Biggest I've ever seen!" Evan confirmed, followed by a familiar smile Evan tended to share with his punchlines. "You should have seen it, Benny. About as big as a silver coin! The most dangerous and ferocious of all arachnids."

"Oh, fuck off." Baron shook his head. "It was hardly little," he grumbled as he flipped up his hood like a pouting child.

"No, no, no," Evan continued to tease. "You were right to be afraid. It could have crawled into your pocket for a nice sneak attack later."

"The smaller they are, the more poisonous they get," Baron added bitterly.

"I heard that some spiders actually crawl into your mouth while sleeping," Merrick chimed in casually. "They crawl into your throat and lay eggs. You're coughing up a nest by the time you wake up."

His twin brother, Garth, grimaced. "Shame, that. I mean, we do sleep in the woods quite often. And who knows? Maybe one of those little bastards is still on ya somewhere, just waiting for that moment."

Baron shook his body and began patting at his arms. "You evil, little …"

The camp erupted in laughter. Even Benny slapped his knee in amusement.

"Anyway," Garth spoke through the laughter while handing Alric a small bag. "Found this. Same as the others."

Alric reached in and pulled out a large stone. It looked just as old and solid as the rest they'd recovered in the past. He rubbed off the layer of collected dust from the face of the stone and traced the ancient language with his fingers.

How has it come to this? The brotherhood, infamous strength and cunning, hired to search the land of Navaleth for ancient tomes at the request of a priest?

Oh well, who am I to judge? At least the job pays.

"Good work," he said while setting the bag at his feet. Although the job was well done, he couldn't help but feel ashamed by not being there with his brothers. "Let's discuss what happens from here then."

The remaining laughter faded from the camp as all eyes fell to Alric. "Now that we've got all of Balorian's tablets—"

"*Father* Balorian," Seroes corrected.

"Right. Now that we've found the last of *Father Balorian's* tablets, we're near the end of our job. It's about time for that talk that I know we've all been anticipating."

Silence dawned on the group of men as the fire cackled between them. Garth and Merrick, the greatest archers Alric had ever seen—*well, besides one particular native*—looked to one another, speaking without speaking. Evan picked at his fingernail, while Seroes and Baron looked back and forth between Benny and Alric.

Merrick cleared his throat. "A soft bed sounds like a nice change."

Alric nodded. "I'm guessing you wouldn't mind that either, would you, Evan?"

Evan gave a subtle smile, gazing into the fire before them. "Took a bit longer than expected, though I'm not complaining. Would be nice to settle at home for the season."

"Agreed," Seroes added. "We've been at this job for nearly a year, and I'm not sure we'll need much work if Father Balorian pays up what he promised. Home sounds nice, at least until other opportunities stir up."

That left Benny, but Alric already knew what his oldest friend was thinking. Where some saw taking a break to relax as a good thing, he knew Benny saw it differently for Alric. The entire point of the brotherhood was to stay busy, and with how things went last night, he knew Benny was worried about him.

Then again, when isn't Benny worried about him?

Benny gave a soft nod before taking his leave, walking away from the fire and toward the cliff edge.

"Right, then. Seems we've come to an agreement." Alric stood and gave a long stretch. "I'm guessing you'll want to leave soon?"

"We'll leave as soon as you're fit to travel," Seroes stated

"Oh, but thanks to you and your handiness, I've just had the best sleep in years. The sun's just set. If we leave tonight, we should be at Robins-Port for a cozy bed in just a few hours. It's a shit town, but a bed's a bed, at the end of the day."

Alric didn't mean to push Seroes's advice aside so easily. He knew the old man knew his stuff when it came to healing. But the truth was that Alric was feeling fresh and better than ever. He'd rested long enough. Now he wanted to get up and get moving, which always fared better for Alric than idle time.

"So, gentlemen, shall we?"

They all showed their agreement by setting to their packs.

Alric left the fire and joined Benny near the cliff. He could tell his friend wasn't happy, that Benny didn't agree with everything that had just happened. Alric struggled for words to say, so he figured he would try to skip the argument he knew was coming.

"We're setting off soon."

"This is a mistake," Benny said without looking at him.

So much for skipping the argument.

"What happened to you three days ago happens when we slow down," Benny said to Alric.

Alric bit back the angry retort he wanted to throw at his friend. "No, that's what happens when I let you in my head."

Benny turned and faced Alric. "Don't you dare blame me for that." There was anger in his tone, but his eyes showed only concern. "I can help guide you, but where you choose to go is on you. And where you went only guarantees one thing."

"Let me guess, *I'm not ready.*"

If Benny was offended by Alric's mockery, he didn't show it. "I think it's clear to us both that you're not. You didn't sleep for *days* before I tried helping you, and what you saw in your dreams … well, I guess I can't blame you for avoiding them. But it's all the same—you need a distraction. We need to stay busy."

The memory of his dream, of bodies lying in the street, houses aflame, the boy struck with an arrow … The memory of living in that nightmare made his skin prickle. He hated it when Benny used his tricks on him, making him live in his mind when all he wanted to do was avoid it.

"Regardless," Alric said finally, "I let us do it your way. All I ask is for you to try mine. I know you're worried—I am, too—but we're overdue for a break. And honestly, I feel much better already."

Benny gave him a long, hard look. Finally, Alric could see the tension settle in his shoulders. Then they both set their eyes to the landscape below the mountain.

Alric could argue the point further, but he knew that, sometimes, it was best not to say anything at all.

After a long moment of silence, Benny gave a sigh. "Fine," he said in defeat. "Have it your way, then. But if it gets that bad again—"

"I know." Alric didn't let him say it. "But the nightshade helped, although my throat is a bit sore."

Benny suddenly gave a soft laugh.

"What?" Alric asked.

Benny shrugged. "I'd be surprised if it wasn't."

"What do you mean?"

"It was like you were trying to tell all of Navaleth where we are."

It took a moment for Alric to fully realize what Benny was implying. "I snored?" he asked with genuine surprise.

"I'm not sure if that passed for snoring. More like a gargling … howl."

"Now I know you're lying."

"I'm pretty sure that some wolves even howled back to you." Benny chuckled to himself. "A bit ironic, don't you think?"

Alric tried to rub the soreness away from his throat. "I'm no wolf anymore. But I won't argue with you. You'll see, everything is going to be better."

"I hope so." The laughter drained from Benny as he gave Alric the same worried look from before. "I really hope so."

Both of them enjoyed the silence as they watched the world below.

Alric hadn't felt this good in months. It was like seeing a different side of the world for the first time. There was no worry about what was coming next or what they had to do or what they had to look for. It was just them and the life around them. He very much enjoyed it.

The side effects of nightshade had nearly fully worn off, and Alric was able to think back to the night of the episode. He remembered Seroes pouring the vial down his throat. The dizziness from the effects of the potion. Most of all, he remembered …

"Who else was there?" he asked Benny.

"What's that?" Benny questioned, started by Alric breaking the silence.

"The night when … well, that night. You and Seroes walked me to my bed. Who else saw?"

"Nobody. It was just us three."

Alric remembered the moment he lay on his back, looking up at the three blurry figures. "Strange, I thought I remembered seeing another person there."

Benny squinted. "Nope. Just me and Seroes. To be honest, Al, I'm surprised you remember anything at all. You were quite out of it." Benny slapped Alric on the back. "Well, better get ready if we're moving out. Looks like we'll be sleeping on some soft beds tonight."

"Yeah," Alric agreed. "Looks like it."

Two Worlds

Sarah sat quietly at the kitchen table, the emotions of the day racing through her mind. She drowned in an ocean of sorrow, the weight of her guilt dragging her deeper and deeper as she sunk to its depths. She hadn't meant to hurt Trevor—she wanted to be with him just as much as he wanted to be with her—but that wasn't the way things worked anymore. Things were expected of her now, things beyond her control.

Ever since she had learned of her betrothal, the only real pain she'd felt was knowing that she would have to break Trevor's heart. She would imagine scenarios in her mind for months, how the conversation could go and the ways she would respond, but she could never have prepared herself for the way Trevor had responded. Never, not once, had she seen anger like that in his eyes.

Naturally, Warren only had to make things worse.

The cramp in her stomach grew tighter at the memory of Trevor pinned on the ground by the bully. She should have helped, should have just shoved Warren off to the side, but she had just stared, like all the others.

Why had I just stared? One minute I was ready to claw his eyes out. The next ...

Florance, Sarah's mother, set a large bowl of hot soup on the table in front of her.

"Something the matter, dear?" she asked.

"No," Sarah lied.

Her mother sat in the chair next to her and folded her hands on the table. "Oh, silly me, of course there isn't." Florance shook her head, the crook of her smile calling Sarah's bluff. "You know, dear, you really are a terrible liar. Let's not forget that I was once your age; I know young drama when I see it. Now, what's the matter?"

A few seconds of silence passed before Sarah finally met her mother's eyes. Out of all the people Sarah knew, her mother always remained her closest friend. She'd been able to tell her everything that happened in the past, but she couldn't help feeling too ashamed to talk about this.

"It's Trevor," she said finally, shoving her food away. "I saw him today."

"I thought you might." Florance sighed. "I'm guessing you told him the news?"

"Yeah."

"I'm guessing it didn't go well."

Sarah shook her head. "Nope."

Florance leaned back in her chair, arms crossed in front of her chest. "Well, go on, what did you say?"

***

"She says she has no choice, that I should be happy for her. Can you believe that?" Lost in his anger, Trevor slammed his fist on the hard table.

Ever since he had let loose his temper, he'd failed to regain control of himself. Not that he couldn't, but because he liked to let go. He liked the feeling of not having to hide anymore.

"She wants me to be *happy* about this!"

He took deep breaths, trying to calm his nerves, but nothing his uncle had taught him could suppress the rage he felt. He wasn't sure what upset him more: that Sarah wanted him to be happy or the fact that, once she left the day after tomorrow, he would never see her again. After she left, it would mean it was to be with another man. The image alone made him sick to his stomach.

Without saying anything, Dodge walked to a cabinet in the kitchen and pulled out a dusty bottle filled with dark liquid. He set two small glasses on the table in front of Trevor and splashed the bottles contents to their rims.

"I know this isn't what you want to hear," he began, "but you've no right to judge her, especially if she said she doesn't have a choice. What would you do?"

"I'd say no. I have a right to decide my own life. What gives anyone the right to decide hers?"

"He's her father, Trevor. If Harold feels this is the best thing for his daughter's future, who are we to say otherwise?"

Trevor felt a sting in his chest at the mention of the word. "Fathers are overrated," he said through gritted teeth.

When Dodge looked away bashfully, Trevor immediately regretted his hasty words.

"Fathers come in many forms," Dodge said quietly. "And a true father knows what's best for his child."

"I didn't ..." Trevor stuttered, feeling ashamed for a moment. "You know I didn't mean nothin' by it."

An awkward silence passed as Dodge picked up Trevor's glass and offered it to him.

Trevor held it to his nose and breathed in its strong aroma. The burn of his nostrils caught him by surprise as he pulled away from the drink.

"Just toss it back quickly. It'll help," Dodge promised as he emptied his own drink. He swallowed deeply before setting his glass on the table.

Trevor looked at his own glass and followed his uncle's example.

An explosion of heat burst in Trevor's throat as he swallowed. He coughed heavily as he felt the warmth spread to his stomach.

Dodge gave him a rough slap on the back as he struggled to catch a breath.

"So, what'd you say?" Dodge asked.

After the heat of the liquor passed, Trevor looked Dodge in the eye. "At first, nothing. I didn't know what to say. What was I *supposed* to say? Before I could really understand what was happening, Warren decided to say hello."

Trevor could see the red instantly rising to his uncle's face with the news of Warren. "What'd that little prick do now?"

Trevor looked away as the embarrassment from the memory of his encounter with Warren returned. As the memory came back, so did the anger he felt moments ago.

"Nothing."

"Like hell," Dodge growled. "What. Did. He. Do?"

"What he always does," Trevor snapped. "Pinned me down, made it clear to everyone watching that I was still a—"

"Still a what?" Dodge interrupted, angrily leaning forward in his chair.

Trevor couldn't help it. His anger got the best of him, and his uncle trying to avoid what Trevor was didn't help his mood. "An orphan," he said venomously. "That I was nothing but a broken orphan that nobody cares a shit about."

A distant scream broke the heavy silence.

Still a few days till End Harvest, and they're already celebrating?

Trevor ignored his celebrating neighbors.

"No matter how many times I tell myself it doesn't matter, even for the brief moments I forget who I am, it will always come back to haunt me. And that's because it's true. I always have been, and always will be, an orphan. Whether it's Warren and his spoiled, shit-dick friends putting me in my place on the street, or a slight mumble of a passerby, I will always be reminded of what I am, because the world is cruel and will never let me forget."

Trevor waited patiently for his uncles retort, to tell him how much the word didn't matter, to tell him that, regardless of his parents' absences, he still had a family under the very roof he currently sat under. He waited for his uncle to tell him, once again, that family came in different forms. Instead, Dodge filled their glasses once again and offered Trevor another round.

"Did you fight back?" Dodge finally asked, calmer than Trevor expected.

"No," Trevor said as he drank the liquid without a moment's hesitation. It went down a lot smoother than the first time but still felt like liquid fire. "But I wanted to." He remembered the way his dagger had felt against the tips of his fingers, the opportunity to put Warren in his place forever. "I should have."

"Should have what? Beat the governor's only son to a bloody pulp in front of the entire town? No, I don't believe that's what you should have done."

Trevor thought about his uncle's words. Regardless of how upset he was about the things he said, he was more upset because he knew his uncle was right.

"What did Sarah do?" Dodge asked.

***

"I did *nothing*, Mother!" Sarah confessed through snot and tears. "I just sat there, like everyone else, and watched, too scared to do anything."

Sarah wiped away her angry tears as she thought about Warren and his ability to get away with anything simply because he came from the founding family of Robins-Port. She hated the fact that everyone was too scared to confront Warren about his bullying. She wished she could go back in time and do something—do anything.

"You can't blame yourself for what happened to Trevor, dear. That's not fair to you. Warren is a bully, and sooner or later, that young man will be taught a painful lesson. They always learn a lesson before the end."

But I should have done something. Anything but stand there and watch, be a part of the crowd.

Sarah leaned against her mother's shoulder and wiped her tears on a handkerchief. She knew her mother was right. However, she couldn't stop thinking about the blank stare on Trevor's face as Warren said all those nasty things to him.

He didn't even try to defend himself.

Oh, Trevor, why didn't you fight back?

"What should I do?" Sarah asked. "Trevor hates me now. I can't leave things like this."

"Trevor is just upset, dear, he doesn't hate you," she encouraged with a supportive rub over Sarah's back.

"No"—Sarah shook her head—"you weren't there. You didn't see the pain in his eyes. I've seen Trevor upset before. I know what it looks like. Not once has he ever lost control. Not even when Warren and his degenerate friends sent him to the infirmary. This was ... different."

"Sarah ..." Florance cupped her daughter's shaky hands. "This is going to be hard, but I need you to listen. Trevor lives a tough life being ... what he is. However unfortunate that is, he found someone to share his pain with. You two grew up inseparable, creating a bond that nobody could break. And only a few hours ago, you broke his heart. Soon after that, he was publicly humiliated."

Florance never saw Trevor as the town orphan—she respected him like any other one of Sarah's friends—but that didn't mean she was unable to see how it affected his life. It was a part of her mother that Sarah deeply admired—being able to see both sides of the same world. She always taught her to "judge people by what they do, not by who they are." Sarah tried her best to live up to her mother's wisdom.

"He didn't even ask me how *I* felt about it," Sarah complained.

Florance nodded with a small smile. "Which is why you should tell him."

"How am I supposed to do that? We leave the day after tomorrow, how am I supposed to change his mind before then?"

"You aren't here to change his mind, only to tell him how you feel. Eventually, he will begin to understand. What we do now affects what happens later, sweetie. Even seconds can change minutes, days changing months, and months changing years."

"Father wouldn't like it if I snuck off again. Not with tomorrow's plans."

Florance gave Sarah a reassuring wink. "You just leave your father to me."

A woman's scream cut through the silence.

Florance sighed. "I forgot how celebratory this town gets near End Harvest. Your father is probably out enjoying himself as we speak."

Sarah pushed her soup back and forth. Although she felt hunger cramping her stomach, she couldn't bear the thought of eating.

"Do you think he'll understand?" she asked.

"Who, dear?"

"Trevor," Sarah answered. "Do you think he'll understand eventually?"

***

"Understand? The hell am I supposed to understand? She's leaving the day after tomorrow to get married, and we'll never see each other again. Is there something I'm missing?"

It didn't take long for the liquor to find its way to Trevor's head. He replaced his glass with the bottle entirely and waved it around to illustrate the importance of his claims.

"Again, you're telling me," Dodge, who did the same with his glass, said through slurred words, "that the entire time you've known the girl, she's been lying to you?"

"She made me *promise*. Did I ever tell you that?" he asked, ignoring Dodge's question entirely, one drunk trying to lecture another. "She had me promise her."

"More than a few times, but I'm sure you're about to remind me."

Trevor waved the remark away with the half-empty bottle, spilling a few drops on Dodge.

"*She* made *me* promise," he explained slowly while pointing the bottle at nobody. "And while *I* was waiting, as promised, you know what she was doing?"

Dodge coughed to clear his throat. "Again, I'm sure you're about to tell me, whether I know or not."

"She was off getting her laundry done for her."

"Gods, you're an awful drunk." His uncle chuckled, pushing his dark locks behind his shoulders.

"And enjoying exotic foods like … chocolate."

"Look, Trevor, the girl never …" Dodge was taken aback, head shaking, confused as to where the conversation had suddenly gone. "Wait—what?"

"And soup," Trevor mumbled quietly, licking the remains of the liquor from his lips.

Dodge sat there quietly, staring at his nephew as confusion glossed over his eyes. "Did you just say soup?"

"Gods," Trevor continued, staring deeply into the dark bottle of brandy in his hand, "some awful chocolate, but probably delicious soup."

Dodge raised an eyebrow. "Chocolate? What about soup? I make you soup twice every week."

Trevor lifted a confident finger at Dodge. "But you don't feed it to me, do you?"

Dodge was silent for a few moments, squinting hard at Trevor, mouth agape, at a loss for words. Eventually, he threw his arms up. "What the fuck are we talking about? You want me to *feed* you?"

"What? No. No, no, no, no. Don't be ridiculous, Uncle. You're being ridiculous."

"Then what the fuck—"

"I'm saying ..." Trevor searched for the right words to make his point clear. His mind swarmed with thousands of thoughts he couldn't organize, thousands of emotions he didn't know how to express. It was impossible to focus on one alone, and the liquor wasn't helping. There was only one explanation that made sense, as heartbreaking as it was. "I'm saying that we live in two separate worlds." Trevor set down the bottle, leaning forward on the table. "She travels the country for a living, and I've never even left Robins-Port," he explained, poking around the table as if discussing points on a map. "Which I was fine with because, no matter how long she was gone, she always came back. I always knew she was coming back. But now she never will." Tears streamed down Trevor's face.

Dodge grabbed the bottle out of Trevor's hand and sealed the top with a cork. "Look at me," he told Trevor.

Trevor could hardly hear anything besides the pounding in his head.

Another scream came from outside, from a man this time.

"Trevor, look at me." his uncle urged.

Trevor did what he was told, wiping the wetness from his face.

"I want you to imagine that you are Sarah." His uncle looked deep into his eyes. "You're a young, beautiful woman who gets to explore the world and, no offense to the lass, gets whatever she wants. You're lost in the moments of your young life until your father returns from a business trip, only to tell you that you are going to be marrying someone you've never met. You have no idea who this man is, what he looks like, or even what his name is but, very soon, you're told that you'll sleep in the same bed, spend the rest of your life with him, and even bear his children."

Trevor felt his anger coming back once again at the thought of Sarah spending the rest of her life with someone else. "What's your point?"

"The point is, my young and very drunk nephew"—Dodge leaned closer, his dark brown eyes sad with the lesson—"don't you think she's a little scared, too?"

Trevor thought hard about the words being said, his boiling anger quickly simmering to a heavy guilt. He thought back when Sarah was trying to explain herself and realized that it wasn't panic on her face, but fear.

"She was looking for comfort," he realized. "I should have been there for her."

"And you can be. She hasn't left yet, you know."

Trevor leapt to his feet, his chair crashing to the floor behind him. "I have to see her. I'll see her tonight. I have to tell her."

"Whoa, whoa, whoa." His uncle slowly stood. "The last thing the Michaelsons need right now is a drunk Trevor kicking down the front door to confess his love and beg for their daughter's forgiveness."

"Then, when should I?" he asked.

***

"Tomorrow," Sarah confirmed. "I'll see him in the morning, and we won't stop talking until he hears me out."

"And I'm sure he will." Florance patted Sarah's arm. "Now, eat your soup. It's getting cold."

Someone from outside screamed again. It sounded a lot closer, and the laughter could almost pass as crying.

Florance walked toward the door. "I swear, these people have no respect—"

The door burst open and quickly slammed shut as Sarah's father pressed his back against it. His face was pale and dripping with sweat.

"Florance, grab Sarah and get into our bedroom *now*." His words were on the verge of yelling.

"Harold, what's going on?" Florance gasped, pointing at his arm. "Is that … blood?" She rushed to his side. "Honey, are you hurt?"

There was a loud *bang* on the door as it shuddered heavily, as if someone was trying to kick it down.

"Open this fucking door!" a voice screamed from outside.

"Florance, I need you to grab Sarah and get to our room *now*!" her father urged again.

Before she knew it, Sarah was suddenly being dragged out of her chair and pulled into her parents' bedroom. She glimpsed a smile from her father before the bedroom door was slammed shut, her mother sliding the deadbolt to its locked position.

Her mother let go of her arm and ran to her bed. Sprawled on her knees, she reached underneath and pulled out a small box. Sarah remembered finding it when she was younger, but her mother made it very clear that she was never to open it.

What does she need that for?

"Mom?" she whimpered quietly. "What's happening?"

The angry beating on the front door seemed to vibrate off the walls around them.

"What about Father?" she mumbled to her mother, who didn't seem to notice.

Florance took out a small key from around her neck and unlocked the container. After quickly snatching something from inside, she walked over to Sarah and pressed it in her hand. A letter.

"Move to the wall, dear. Off the rug, quickly now!" her mother urged with a few small shoves. Then Florance grabbed the carpet that she'd been standing on and folded it over to reveal a trap door.

There was a loud crash outside the room, the sound of breaking wood and broken dishes, followed by a scream from her father.

Sarah's hands shook uncontrollably as Florance grabbed her by the shoulders.

"Listen to me," she said.

Sarah could hardly hear her mother, focused on the shouting voices coming from outside the room, noticing her father was not among them.

"Anybody else?" asked the first.

"Not in here," answered a second

"Got another door, sir. There in the back," said a third.

Sarah's entire body jolted as her mother shook her shoulders. "Sarah, pay attention."

Heavy footsteps approached the bedroom door. The handle jerked roughly. Someone was trying to get in.

"Locked. Break it down," a muffled voice ordered.

Florance dragged Sarah toward the trapped door, immediately followed by a loud pounding on the door.

"I need you to listen carefully, Sarah." Her mother lifted the heavy latch, revealing a dark hole. "This tunnel will lead you to the other side of town. Walk a few miles west, turn north and you'll find the main road."

There was another heavy shake on the door as she took the silver.

Florance reached into a pocket and pulled out three shiny coins. "Follow the road to the next town and find transportation to the capital. When you get there, hand that letter to the king. You are under no circumstances to give that letter to anyone else. Do you understand? Trust no one."

Sarah nervously nodded, not sure if it was the right answer.

Her mother wiped the tears from Sarah's face and hugged her tightly. "I love you, Sarah," she whispered in her ear. "Never forget that."

"Please, mother," Sarah pleaded. "Please come with me."

The door cracked as splinters shattered to the floor around them. It wouldn't hold much longer.

"I have to stay and cover the door. Now go!"

Sarah was all but pushed into the hole.

She felt cramped in the cold air as she looked up at her mother. Tears crashed from her face as they took a final look at each other.

"No matter what happens," her mother said quietly, "know that I've always been proud to call you my daughter."

The lid slammed shut before Sarah could even say goodbye.

For a moment, she simply sat there, listening to the quiet rustling happening above her. Then there was a muffled crash above her. She held her breath as she heard heavy footsteps walking across the room.

"Who else is in here?" a rough voice asked.

"Nobody," she heard her mother say defiantly.

"Really now? Hands behind your back, you're comin—fuck!"

There was a scuffle sound as the floorboards creaked above Sarah.

"Don't even *think* about touching me!" she heard her mother scream, a sound that Sarah had never heard before.

Sarah heard another set of heavy footsteps enter the room.

"Watch out, sir; she's got a knife!"

"So do you," the new voice said matter-of-factly. "The fuck are you trying to tie her up for? Put her with the others."

"She's quite pretty, sir. Just wanted to have a bit of fun." The words struck Sarah cold.

"We are not here to *have fun*. You have your orders, soldier. *No survivors.*

Now cut her throat and add her to the fire. She'll burn nicely, just like the others."

Sarah's fear peaked as she heard the scraping sound of steel. Then she heard her mother scream, "No, please, *no!*" There was a moment of silence, followed by the sound of someone choking. The sound of spilt water washed across the floor, ending with the collapse of something heavy that shook the floorboards above Sarah.

"Drag them outside and search the place," a man ordered.

Sarah was frozen with fear.

A set of footsteps walked out of the room above her. A heavier set walked closer, nearly standing directly above where she lay hidden beneath the floorboards. Instead of the latch being ripped open, though, she heard the sound of something being dragged across the floor above her. She traced the sound with a frightful stare as it led its way toward the front of the house.

With no other direction to go, Sarah slowly fumbled her way through the darkness and started making her way down the long, dark tunnel to where she hoped was safety.

The Relentless Chase

They spent the next four nights running.

On the morning of the first day, the pack had thought they were free, that they were out of reach of the things that chased them. They had built a small fire, filled their bellies, and had given in to their exhaustion. They'd found an open spot underneath a large oak tree. The branches stretched above their heads, the thick leaves blocking out the sun and cooling the area with shade. As soon as the younglings' heads hit the dirt, snores had followed suit.

Quiver was proud of his pack. At first, he dreaded the idea of leading a pack of untested younglings in the search of his cousin Nero, but he couldn't deny the sense of pride warming his heart as he saw what they had managed to achieve. Not only had they helped discover what had happened with Nero, but they had kept up their pace throughout the previous night, running from whatever it was that chased them.

There was a lot of pride that came with being a chief, but it was moments like these that made his heart swell with happiness to be a part of his people. A pack was always at its strongest when they worked together, and their weakest if they couldn't cooperate together.

Quiver had expected the younglings to have given up during their escape, but not once had any of them given in to their exhaustion until it was time to rest. Not one of them had complained.

As the younglings fell asleep, Quiver decided to take first watch, letting Rasca rest with the others. He sat with his back against the trunk of a tree, watching the shadows stretch as the sun set, when the howls began again.

This time, much closer.

We ran all night and part of the day. How could they possibly be this close?

Quiver didn't know what was chasing them, but he knew they were strong enough to take out Nero's pack with minor resistance, and that was enough to try his hardest to avoid confrontation, leaving only one option.

We have to keep running.

And so they ran through the next night.

Running two days straight was taxing, but, yet again, Quiver was proud to see they'd managed to survive without incident.

Throughout the entirety of the night, the howls rang in the distance behind them. They ran until the sun started to pierce through the gaps between the thick branches of the forest, only to realize that the howls had seized.

That's when a theory came to Quiver.

"We've only heard them when the sun's been down, which means we have the advantage of the daylight," he told the others as they knelt before them, sweat dripping from their pale faces. "Eat some jerky as we walk, but we push for a few more hours. Get more distance between us and ... whatever they are."

Quiver knew how hard he was pushing the pack, but what else could they do? If they had gained on them the first night, running slower the following would only make things worse. They had to take advantage of what little time they had, which wasn't much more than the hours of sunlight.

They had walked a few more hours, pushing through the morning until they settled for a spot in the shade of a large oak tree. The pack didn't bother with a fire, as they didn't need to keep warm—the sun provided enough heat. And they would have to survive off their rations rather than spend time hunting, as none of them wanted to waste time cooking when they could be resting.

Before he completely succumbed to exhaustion, Quiver walked about to each of the pack and checked their supplies. They had just a few waterskins left and barely enough food to last much longer. Their supplies were running short, and they were still quite a ways from the village. At least a few more days. Things were looking grim.

Quiver stood before his pack, each of them on the brink of collapse. "Get some rest," he told them. "I'll take first watch, and then we'll switch after a few hours."

The others didn't argue. They were fully asleep moments after lying down.

After a few hours of scanning the woods, Quiver felt a soft tap on his shoulder as Rasca came to take over his watch.

Quiver fell asleep the moment he closed his eyes.

A dream came in a flash, too quick for his liking. He always liked the nights he dreamt. To him, it was a reassurance of the rest he got.

He dreamt he stood with Thread at the edge of a cliff overlooking the world. Thread took Quiver's hand in hers, gave it a soft squeeze as she smiled at him, and he smiled back. She nodded over her shoulder, and Quiver followed with his eyes.

Behind him, a long wooden bridge stretched across a vast open chasm. He knew nothing of the bridge, but something deep down told him it was *old.* Perhaps the oldest thing he had ever seen. At the end of the bridge was an open landscape leading to the base of a mountain. At the foot of the mountain was a line of trees.

Quiver spotted a blur of movement among them, something pacing before the wood line. When the figure in the distance stopped, he realized he was staring at a giant wolf. Not any wolf, though; *the* wolf.

"You must show him the way," Thread said in a voice that seemed to travel through a tunnel.

She gave him that smile again and, in that moment, Quiver's heart leapt with fear.

Thread's teeth were glistening with red blood, her milky face rotting as blood flowed like a river through the gash in her neck.

Again, Quiver couldn't explain how, but through the horror, he knew the wound couldn't have come from a blade of any sort—the skin was *torn* rather than sliced. He knew it wasn't from a person, but from an animal. A beast.

Even though she represented the very definition of death, Thread still gripped his hand tightly and smiled pleasantly at Quiver, as if the open wound in her neck did not matter. "No more running from who you are. It's time to wake up." Thread walked closer to Quiver, gripping his shoulders tightly. She leaned closer to his face, her fogged eyes locking on to his. "Wake up, Quiver," she said. "Wake up. Wake. UP!"

Quiver jumped as his body shook involuntarily. He looked around, unsure of where he was or what was happening, when his frightened self found Rasca.

"You were mumbling in your sleep," Rasca informed him, looking at him curiously. "Thought it might be a good one, since Thread's name was tossed around here and there. But then you started thrashing about."

Quiver wiped a thick line of sweat from his forehead. "Just a strange dream," he declared. He only then realized that it was early evening, the sun only beginning to descend. "We should get going." With the day of rest they managed, it was time to push through another night.

The following night was worse yet, and only a dark omen of what was yet to come. Long branches scratched at their bodies as they squeezed between trees, bushes with thorns gripped at the sides of their arms as they passed. The sticky sweat poured off Quiver, and more than a few times he picked himself up from a clumsy trip, along with a few others, as well. They were getting passed the point of exhaustion now, using the reserves of their energy to keep going.

Quiver was proud that they had managed to race through the jungle, moonlight and shadows the only guide, but he knew it wouldn't last much longer.

As he turned a sharp bend on the makeshift trail, an enormous boulder stood in his path, a small body slumped against it.

The body can only go so far for so long before it demands rest.

"What happened?" Quiver asked Masco, gesturing to Sparrow's unconscious body slumped against the boulder.

"Turned the corner ..." he said between deep breaths. "Lying on the trail ... must have ... collapsed."

There was a rustle through the bushes as Rasca and Oppo emerged in the darkness. They looked from Sparrow to Masco then gave Quiver a tiny shake of their heads.

"What do we do?" Oppo asked, hunched over his knees, struggling to breathe.

The shrieking howls of their pursuers, too close for comfort, regardless of how hard the pack had pushed these last couple nights, answered for them.

Wasting no time, Quiver hefted Sparrow into his arms. "If we stop, we die."

Not needing any more encouragement, the pack continued on. The sun would rise soon, and then they would be able to put more distance between them and the things that followed. Not that it seemed to matter. The pack ran slower with each passing night, and the distance they had gain in daylight was nearly lost the next evening. It was becoming difficult to judge how far they'd come and how much farther they needed to go. All the while, the relentless chase continued.

We'll never make it at this pace, and I can't push them much faster.

By sunrise, Quiver's arms felt like iron. Regardless of the bumpy path, Sparrow refused to budge awake through the rest of the night. If by midday, he stayed in the same shape, Quiver would have to carry him through the entire night.

Quiver sat Sparrow's limp body against a large tree in the shade and looked him over. He lifted the youngling's upper lip to check his gums.

Pale, he observed. *Nearly the color of his skin. This is not good. He needs water and food. We all do.*

"How is he?" Rasca asked, leaning against a tree, catching his breath.

In Quiver's experience, there was a time to coat the truth and to say it plainly. This was a time for the latter. "Not good. He needs water and rest." Quiver looked about the camp to see Oppo and Masco huddled in the shade. Dark circles weighted their eyes, and their skin was nearly as pale as Sparrow's, sweat glistening, red lines from the trees scratched across their arms and face. Masco began observing his raw, blistered feet, poking it with his finger and bringing it abruptly back with a hiss, as if a viper had snapped at him. "We all do."

"What do you suggest?" Rasca asked.

Being chief was never easy, especially in a situation where people's lives were at risk. It'd been a long time since Quiver's decision could ultimately risk the lives of others, and it wasn't a feeling he missed, but loathed entirely.

Their options were limited. They could rest now and run through the next night in hopes that the beasts would either lose interest or lose their tracks. *Or ...*

That's when Quiver decided what to do. It would be hard, but his father always had said, "Hard times call for hard solutions."

He wasn't sure how they made it this far, nor how much farther they could go. Quiver wasn't even sure how much farther *he* could run, especially if he had to carry Sparrow the rest of the way. The youngling might wake, but for how long would he make it through the next night? If Sparrow collapsed again, how long would Quiver have to carry him then? And what happened if another fainted?

No, being chief was never easy. There were times you had to make a choice between two dark options. A moment when you had to choose the lesser of two evils.

This is one of those moments, he thought. *And a choice has to be made.*

They would never make it back to the village at this rate, and what if they did? They would lead the beasts right to their families.

We'd lead them right to Thread.

"We have to fight," Quiver said plainly.

At first, he didn't think anyone had heard him, until he looked about to see all their eyes wide with worry, even Rasca.

"Fight?" Oppo gasped. "We don't even know what we would be fighting, or how many there are."

"True"—Quiver knelt before Oppo and Masco—"but there are less howls than the night before, which means there is less to fight."

"If there is less, then maybe they are giving up?"

"That may be," Quiver agreed, "but we'll never make it far enough for them to give up fully. No matter how much we rest today, they will be upon us by nightfall. We can either fight with the energy we gather, or we fight when they catch us on the run. Either way, by tomorrow, they'll catch up."

"But"—Oppo's eyes were distant—"if Nero and his pack couldn't fight them off, that would mean—"

Quiver put a hand on Oppo's shoulder. He could see tears welling up in his eyes and could see the fear taking hold. It was the fear nobody could escape. No matter what you survive in life, even the greatest warrior still feared death.

"Nero and his pack may have been great warriors, but they were ambushed, taken by surprise. We will not do the same. We will be ready. We will have the element of surprise, not them."

Quiver took Oppo by both shoulders. "I understand your fear, Oppo. Fear is good. It kept you going through these past nights, did it not?"

Oppo nodded softly, wiping the tears from his eyes.

"We should all use our fear for that reason—to stay alive—but we must not let it fully consume us. Right now, we must be brave, and we cannot be brave without fear." Quiver lifted his head slightly, displaying his broad chin, hoping it made him look stronger than he felt. "Will you be brave with me, Oppo?"

Quiver saw a shift within the youngling, who hardened his face and nodded his answer.

Quiver looked to Masco who stood at a distance beneath a tree. He stood tall and defiant, refusing to show weakness to the pack. After a moment of staring, he nodded.

"Good." Quiver smiled and stood. "This is good."

"We'll need weapons," Rasca added, joining the others. "We can carve spears. Maybe make an axe or two out of rocks and sticks. Won't be able to cut down a tree with it, but it'll crush a skull all the same."

"With your dagger, my bow, and the hatchet we found, that's all we'll need," Quiver said. "We'll make some weapons and get into our positions. Rest there; I'll wake everyone when the sun starts to set."

They all nodded.

There was a groan from Sparrow, immediately followed by coughing. His eyes fluttered open, and he dazed around from one person to the other.

"What's going on?" he muttered to nobody in particular.

"I'll fill him in," Rasca said, handing a waterskin to Sparrow.

Quiver nodded then looked about the clearing. "Oppo, find me some large sticks and rocks, as many as you can find."

The youngling answered by running off into the woods.

"Masco, to me."

A moment later, Masco was on a knee before him.

Quiver matched his height and looked upon his dirt-covered face. "Do you remember what I told you?" he asked quietly.

Masco nodded. "There is only the pack."

"There is only the pack." Quiver nodded back. "Good."

"Chief?" Masco asked just as Quiver was making to stand. "Do you think we'll win?"

The question took Quiver by surprise and, for a moment, he didn't know how to answer.

There is a time to coat the truth, and there is a time to say it plainly.

"I don't know," he answered honestly. "But if this is the night we die, let's be sure to show them hell before we do."

A smile crept across Masco's face. "Aye, Chief. Let's give them hell."

A Night in Hell

"Tell me why I shouldn't," Trevor said as he waved the near empty bottle at Dodge. "Give me one reason why I shouldn't walk down there right now?"

Dodge remained seated at the table, leaning lazily back in his chair. "Besides the fact that you're piss drunk and it's the middle of the night?"

"I said to give me a reason, not state the obvious."

"Stating the obvious is reason enough."

"Why do you do that?" Trevor burrowed his brow. "Why you gotta … twist my words? All the time, you turn my words against me."

"Maybe if you thought before you spoke, I wouldn't—"

"Stop that." Trevor jumped to his feet, nearly tripping over nothing as he wobbled for a brief moment while letting his drunken mind gather itself. "Just … stop. You're not talking me out of this." Trevor made his way toward the door.

"Gods." Dodge rose to his feet. "Would you at least leave the bottle, ya drunken fool?"

Trevor was about to come back with a quip, but as he reached for the door, a loud crash exploded in front of him and launched him onto his back. Splinters of wood flew past his face as the door exploded inward, landing on top of Trevor, as a man with a very large, very malicious hammer walked in.

A smile formed on the man's face when he noticed Trevor pinned beneath the door beneath him. Then the man lifted his hammer to bring it down on Trevor's face when a blur knocked him backward. He hit the wall with a heavy crash as Dodge grabbed the handle of the man's hammer. The stranger roared defiantly before headbutting Dodge in his nose.

As Dodge stumbled back, the stranger came at him, swinging his hammer from the side toward Dodge's face. Trevor wasn't sure how Dodge could have possibly seen the blow coming, but he managed to duck out of the way and step into the man's guard. Twisting sideways, he brought a heavy fist underneath his attacker's chin. When the man began stumbling away,

Dodge then reached out and grabbed his wrist, holding it out before him.

Dodge brought his heavy fist back then punched with all his might at his victim's elbow. The man's elbow shattered, the sound of snapping bones, followed by the clatter of the man's hammer dropping to the floor, as the man roared in agony.

Another man appeared in the doorway, his long hair tied in a tight knot behind his head. He roared as he charged in with a face that screamed murder. Unlike the original attacker, this one carried a mean-looking sword, one already coated with blood.

Trevor tried to wobble and wedge himself out from beneath the door, but with the newcomer's weight above him, he remained pinned.

Noticing the second attacker, Dodge shoved away his original assailant, sending him flying against the new one with the sword. The second attacker simply stepped to the side, letting his friend pass by without interrupting his charge toward Dodge.

Trevor did the only thing he could manage. He shimmied underneath the door, trying to throw the attacker's balance off. It wasn't much, but it was enough to have him stumble for a brief second.

In the moment it took the man to catch his balance, Dodge managed to pick up the hammer and rush forward, bringing it down with a heavy swing onto the swordsman's face.

Crunch!

The sound of the man's face breaking turned Trevor's stomach.

The man dropped his sword and stood dumbfounded, wobbling on his feet like a drunkard as he struggled to keep to his feet, his face a mess of gore as blood streamed down his flattened nose.

Crunch!

The second blow sent him to his knees, his jaw hanging limp to its side, teeth and bone protruding from the skin of his cheek.

The man was dead, Trevor knew that, but it was as if his body refused to accept it. His chest heaved heavily, his deep breaths wheezing through the gurgling sound of him choking on his own blood.

With a third and final swing, Dodge split the man's skull as he brought the hammer against the side of his head, his limp body leaving a bloody trail as it slid two feet away from them.

With his companion dead, the first attacker dragged himself across the floor toward the broken door. He looked at Trevor as he slid by, only a foot away, the look of pure terror on his face.

Dodge's heavy footsteps stepped in close, sending vibrations of rage through the floor close to Trevor.

As Dodge grabbed the man by the ankle and pulled him back, the man screamed in terror. Dodge then put a heavy hand over his mouth, dropped the hammer to the side, only to replace it with the sword from the second attacker.

The man tried his best to struggle, but between a broken arm and the full weight of Dodge straddling his body, there was no hope of escape.

Without hesitation, Dodge set the blade against the man's neck and ripped away, sending a mist of blood in the air.

Trevor, still pinned beneath the heavy door that had trapped him throughout the entire fight, stared as the blood spreading across the floorboards. He watched as the dark pool slowly crawled closer to him. Still, he couldn't find the strength to move.

Before he fully understood what had happened, Dodge threw back the door to free Trevor and lifted him to his feet. "We need to get moving."

Dodge raced off to his bedroom. When he returned, he had a large sword strapped to his back and another one in his other hand. He held the second blade out to Trevor. "Put it on," he said, unfolding a leather belt attached to a scabbard in which the sword was placed in.

Trevor looked from the blade to his uncle, only now noticing the dark droplets of blood that speckled his face, the red mess that painted his hands. Trevor next looked away to the two men on the floor. The sight of them lying there, their corpses a ruined mess of gore, at knowing they were dead, it set Trevor into panic.

They were going to kill me. I saw it in his eyes. That could have been me right there!

"Trevor!" Dodge came over and roughly slapped the satchel into Trevor's hands. "I need you to focus. Look at me, Trevor."

Trevor looked away from the two corpses lying in his kitchen, away from the dark pool of blood soaking the floor. He focused on the words that came out of his uncle's mouth.

"Are you with me?" Dodge searched Trevor's eyes for an answer.

After a few moments, Trevor crossed his arms and nodded.

"Good. Now put this on."

Trevor reached for the belt and found that his hands were too shaky to grab it.

"Here." Dodge undid the strap himself. "Lift your arms; I'll tie it on. Go on; lift them. There you go." Dodge wrapped the belt around Trevor's waist. When it was tight, he situated it so that Trevor's sword hung at his right hip. "Good. See? Fits just right."

"They're dead." Trevor looked back at the two men. "You killed them."

Dodge slowly nodded. "Yes," he answered in a sad voice. "Yes, Trevor, I killed them. Because they were going to kill us." Dodge grabbed Trevor gently under the chin and pulled his gaze away from the gore. "And we're going to kill any more of them we come across. Do you understand?"

Again, it felt that Trevor had to concentrate hard on the words before fully understanding them. As the moments passed, he felt a calm begin to settle inside him, chilling his nerves and steadying his hands. He set a hand softly on the hilt of the sword that hung at his side and nodded.

"Good," Dodge said with a satisfied smile. "Now, go grab your pack. Stuff a blanket and some supplies in there. I'll grab the food. Go. Quickly!"

Finally discovering the strength in his legs, Trevor rushed off to his bedroom. He grabbed the leather bag from under his bed and stuffed inside his small wool blanket, a few pairs of clean socks, a wool sweater, a linen shirt, and a pair of ragged pants.

Once back in the kitchen, he saw that Dodge was peering out the broken doorway, his own leather sack strapped over his free shoulder, large sword over the other.

"Looks clear. Stick close behind me. Don't make a sound and, if it comes to it, don't draw steel unless I say so. All right, let's go."

Trevor did as his uncle said as they rushed out the door, staying close at his heels, not making a sound, but he couldn't help looking at the carnage about him.

A few scattered bodies lay dead in the street, black pools of blood surrounding them. Trevor could see a glow of light, the trail of black smoke rising in the night that told him houses were on fire.

A lot of them, by the looks of it.

Dodge slowed his pace as they were crossing the street, also taking sight of the state the town was in. "It's ... being attacked," he said almost to himself. "Robins-Port is being attacked."

Dodge's house was at the western edge of town, his closest neighbors nothing but a few shops and the woods. If there was someone attacking Robins-Port, Trevor knew they would focus more on the eastern edge, where all the farmers, taverns, and shops were located. Dodge's house could easily be mistaken as a barn, if anything. Maybe that was why there were only two attackers and only a few innocent bystanders killed near here.

Realization stopped Trevor cold.

He looked worriedly at his uncle and whispered, "Sarah."

Understanding dawned on Dodge and, with a deep breath, he pushed his way past Trevor, leading them toward the eastern edge of Robins-Port, to where the glow of light shone brightest.

When they got there, the heat was unbearable. They crouched in the shadow behind a house to catch their breaths, using the smoke and shade to stay invisible.

Trevor's impatience was beginning to overtake him. The longer they took to find Sarah, the more likely something would happen to her.

"Take a look and check the area while I fix this." Dodge fumbled with the strap of his pack.

Trevor cautiously peered around the corner of the house that they were hiding behind and froze with fear.

Bodies were laid out in front of houses, all of them lying in a pool of dark blood. Women, children, men, all of them shared the same fate—facedown in the dirt, awkwardly sprawled out in front of their homes. Dead.

Bodies swung from ropes tied from the awnings of homes, their necks awkwardly angled, blood covering their bodies, swollen tongues and eyes dangling from faces. All faces Trevor knew.

In the center of the street, not two houses away from them, was a large pile of dismembered people. He could see separated arms and legs, and even heads staring back at him with empty eyes. In a strange way, it didn't look real. Things like that only existed in nightmares or stories about the native wars, and since there were no natives in Navaleth anymore, Trevor really wished he would wake up from the nightmare that he was clearly in.

"What do you see?" Dodge whispered.

Trevor wasn't sure how to answer that question. How do you explain something like this? How do you describe such horror and butchery?

"They're dead," was all he managed to whisper.

"Shit," Dodge hissed. "Who?"

Trevor tried to count the families lying in the street, including the purple faced ones that hung. He gave up when he realized he would have to count the pile of mutilated carcasses.

"All of them."

That was when Trevor heard a noise from across the street, the sound of men yelling.

Four men stood in front of a large house. Trevor recognized it was the Robinson's, Warren's house. The men were dressed in chainmail. One held a torch, while the other three held swords.

"Open up or be burnt down!" he heard one scream.

Dodge peeked around Trevor's shoulder. "Fuck," he mumbled. "What are those guards doing? Wait—" Dodge squinted his eyes. "Those aren't the guard's uniforms. This doesn't look good, Trevor. They might—"

"No!" he snapped, not wanting to hear what his uncle was about to say. "We have to find Sarah."

Maybe it was the liquor getting to him, but regardless of how many bodies littered the streets, he wouldn't accept that Sarah was among them. Not unless he saw it for himself. And if there was a chance of her survival, Trevor would skip every other family that was in need of help in order to take it, especially the Robinsons. He felt cruel in that moment, but finding Sarah was everything.

Dodge grumbled again then silently led the way as they crept behind the next house, staying low and invisible in the shadows.

Trevor followed close to his heels as they crossed the silent yards, making their way to the giant orange glow that lit the sky.

Trevor thought back to what it was like working in the forgery during the first couple hours. He remembered the pressure the heat had on his body, making him slow and causing him to sweat profusely. He would take that feeling over this any day.

The eastern side of Robins-Port was a living nightmare. Wood crackled loudly as houses were consumed by fire. More bodies lined the street. Everything was either on fire or already dead, and the closer Trevor got to Sarah's house, the worse the carnage grew. With each step that Trevor took, another piece of his hope was left behind.

Trevor made to move when he felt a firm grip on his shoulder. He turned to see Dodge with a finger to his lips, gesturing to stay silent. He then slowly pointed toward the opposite side of the street where three more men were standing. Trevor couldn't hear what they were saying, but one of the men seemed to be yelling at the others.

"Seven men couldn't have done all this," Dodge whispered. "Wait here."

Dodge dropped to his belly and slowly inched his way toward the street. He made it to a crate hidden in the shadows, still keeping low to the ground as he remained hidden behind it. Trevor wasn't sure what he was doing, but his instincts told him to do as he was told, so that's what he did. He always did what he was told.

The deeper he got into town, the more scared he became to learn Sarah's fate. Did he really want to know? What would he do if he saw that it was her body lying lifeless with the rest? Then he thought about the last words he'd said to her.

"Fuck you, Sarah! I wish you'd never come back at all."

Were those really going to be the last words he'd ever say to her? Would that be the last thing she'd remember by him before she died?

"They've got the entire town surrounded to find stragglers."

Trevor hadn't even noticed that Dodge had returned, too busy lost in his dark thoughts.

"They're about to press to the western side. I'm sorry, Trevor, but everything beyond this point is doomed."

Trevor felt a weight in his knees and sank against the wall. Part of him knew it was true. But the truth was that he didn't know for sure, and if he walked away now and found out later that he could have been there to help her, he would never be able to live with himself.

"I'm not leaving until I see her body," he said flatly.

Dodge must have been anticipating these words, because he was already pulling Trevor to his feet. "It's just a few houses down. Same plan—stick close behind me. We'll have to make this quick if we want to get out alive."

Crouching low to the ground, the two of them snuck through the smoke, away from the thugs in the streets. The smoke and heat was getting thicker, squeezing his lungs tight with each passing breath.

Trevor rubbed his arms roughly as his skin prickled to the heat, but he never slowed his pace. If there was a small chance of saving Sarah, he would take it, even if he had to run into a burning house.

They finally reached far enough down the street where they could see their destination. Trevor leaned against the wall while Dodge peered around the corner.

"What do you see?" he asked.

"Bodies," Dodge mumbled in reply.

Trevor pulled Dodge away and looked himself. There were bodies in front of Sarah's house, but only two. Trevor recognized Harold Michaelson's tunic and Florance's dress. He didn't much care for Harold, not that the man deserved the fate he got, but Florance had always been kind to him. It hurt deeply to see them lying facedown in their own blood.

"She could still be in there," he whispered to Dodge.

"Doubtful. These guys are professionals; they would have searched the place."

"Then what do you suggest!" Trevor snapped with irritation.

Dodge took a deep breath then spoke calmly and quietly. "Sarah isn't amongst the ..."—he paused, catching himself—"with her family. Yes, there's a chance that she's still alive. However, if we don't move quickly, there'll be no chance for us. We can't find her if we're dead, Trevor."

As dark as the words were, Dodge was right. If the thugs had gotten to Sarah, she would be next to her family.

Trevor looked at his uncle, his body tensing the longer they stayed there.

Where could she have gone?

As long as nobody could find her, Trevor figured that was how she could be the safest.

He nodded in defeat to his uncle, and then they stuck to the shadows and made their way back to the western end of Robins-Port, leaving the dead and burnt behind.

The men that they had seen talking in the street were gone now.

As Trevor crept along, he risked a quick glance at Warren's house. Like the rest, the front door had been broken into pieces and bodies were lying in front of the house.

Was Warren among them? Would I even care if I saw his face there?

As they made their way back, Trevor nearly ran into Dodge as he abruptly stopped. He then turned and signaled to Trevor with a finger to his lips. They slowed their pace and pressed up against the neighbor's house. That was when he heard the voices.

Trevor peeked slowly around his uncle's burly shoulder. He saw three men, dressed heavily in armor, and armed to their teeth, pounding violently at the front door of a house.

"We've a warrant," one lazily ordered. "King demands we search the residence. Open up, or we'll break it down."

Small movement drew Trevor's attention toward the street. Someone was slowly making their way toward the house, hunched low with something in their arms, creeping through the shadows. When they came closer, Trevor realized what they were carrying—a battle axe. He was a big, burly man and surprisingly quiet for his size.

It wasn't until he was a few paces away from them when he recognized Tom, the blacksmith.

Before Trevor could relay the information to Dodge, Tom raised his axe above his head and jumped toward the group of men.

"Die, you fuckers!" he roared as he brought his axe down with great force.

There was a soft crunch as it made contact with the back of one of the thug's head. Black blood sprayed all over Tom as the lifeless body dropped to the floor. By the time the two other men had a chance to turn and draw their steel, Tom's axe was already free of the man's skull and swinging wide, whistling through the air toward one of the men's waists.

Dodge drew his sword, springing around the corner. Although the men had time to jump away from Tom's widely swung axe, they weren't anticipating a sword from behind.

Trevor could hear the steel scraping through the thug's armor as the sword point punctured out the other side. He watched slowly as crimson blood dripped from the point of the blade.

Dodge kicked his victim to the ground as he pulled free his blade, immediately taking the defensive stance that Trevor was all too familiar with, anticipating an attack from their final remaining foe. However, the third thug was already engaged with Tom.

Tom cut through the air as he swung high and low, twirling the blade in circles and coming down for an attack. The axe was enormous, yet Tom made it look as light as a feather.

The thug stumbled back, desperately trying to regain his footing as he faltered against Tom's heavy blows. The thug then tried to block with his blade, but even Trevor knew it was hopeless.

There was a loud *clang* as the thug's sword was sent soaring through the air, a severed hand still gripping the pommel. The man dropped to his knees with a loud scream, which was short-lived before his face was split like firewood from Tom's finishing blow. Teeth and bone flew as the blade was ripped free, gushing blood flowing like a waterfall through the gruesome split in what used to be a man's face. With a finality, Tom kicked at the corpse and sent it to the ground with the two others.

Trevor remained in the shadows. He felt awkward with what he had seen. Even with all his practice in fighting, nothing could have prepared him for what real combat looked like. He felt dizzy.

"Come out now, Trevor," Dodge called.

Slowly, Trevor joined the two men at the front of the house. He looked at the bodies lying at their feet, taking a moment to finalize what had just happened. His vision blurred as his face burned with a cold-hotness, which quickly led to him vomiting all over the nearest corpse, the smell of fruity liquor mixed with death.

"Who are these fucking murderers, Dodge?" Tom asked between deep breathes.

Trevor hardly recognized the man. When he had last seen him this morning, he was covered in dirt and grime. Now it looked as if he'd bathed in blood.

"Don't know. Looks as if they started on the eastern end." Dodge stole a glance at Trevor. "We didn't find any survivors."

"Fucking hell." Tom rested his axe on the ground and looked to the east side of Robins-Port. He took a deep breath and violently nodded. "If someone is sacking Robins-Port, we have to tell the king. Where the fuck are the guards?"

Trevor walked away from the scene and vomited again, leaving the two men to theorize just what was going on. When he looked up, his heart sank, nearly sending him back on his ass.

Not twenty paces away, a group of men were sprinting in their direction, their swords held out.

"There!" Trevor yelled.

Dodge and Tom followed Trevor's finger pointing at the fast, closing in enemies.

"Tom, next to me!" Dodge roared as he took his place in front of Trevor. "Don't let them flank you! Trevor, stay a few paces behind us. Don't hesitate, and remember what you've learned!"

Trevor awkwardly pulled his sword free of its scabbard. Sparring with his uncle with wooden swords was one thing. You could make mistakes, the smallest slight leaving you with a bruise or a sore back.

Now the smallest mistake could cost me my life.

His vision shook with fear as the men drew closer. He counted five—no, six men sprinting toward them.

Time slowed. He could feel the throb of his heartbeat through his entire body. The weight in his knees begged him to fall to the ground and curl up in a ball. To turn and flee.

The man leading the charge drew his sword back and came at Dodge. Trevor watched as Dodge gracefully parried the attack wide, leaving the man open and vulnerable. Trevor knew what would come next.

Dodge ducked low, causing the man to roll over his back as his uncle lifted his body, tossing the man into the air like a ragdoll. The man crashed to the ground before Trevor, losing the grip of his sword as it fell out of his reach. Without waiting, Trevor switched his grip and held his sword high. The man's eyes widened with horror as Trevor did exactly what Dodge had told him not to do—he hesitated.

And the thug noticed.

With a heavy kick to the side of Trevor's knee, he lost control of his own sword and crashed to the ground. He fell stomach first, using his now free hands to brace himself. With an arm wrapped around his stomach, he looked up toward his attacker, only to see the bottom of his boot as it crashed into his face.

His neck snapped back in blinding pain.

Rolling onto his back as blood began flowing from his sure to be broken nose, the stars circled above him, his head drowning in dizziness while trying to remember just how he got to be on his back.

The silhouette of a man looked down at him. His face seemed distant but clear enough for Trevor to see the malice burning in the man's eyes. The man reached toward him, his hands stretching from the clouds to wrap tightly around Trevor's throat. Trevor pried at the man's grip, but it was too strong.

His attacker lay on top of him, his weight pushing down on Trevor's neck, squeezing the life out of him, snarling above Trevor like a rabid dog set on its prey.

A fire spread in Trevor's chest. He looked around, desperately for help, for anything that would set him free.

Dodge and Tom were still fighting with the other men, both of them hopping back and forth from their attackers. Tom managed to duck low beneath a wide swing from one of the armed men, only to bring his axe upward underneath toward the man's chin. The man saw it coming, but wasn't quick enough to get fully out of the way of Tom's counterattack, leaving a deep gash in his exposed chest while attempting to lean out of the way.

Dodge was managing to keep himself from being surrounded, using his speed to quickly dodge an attack and step around one of the men. Putting both attackers close to each other, Dodge was limiting their abilities with the cramped space. Trevor watched as this happened, his vision blurring while his solo adversary choked the life out of him.

To his right, Trevor could see the pommel of his own sword, only a couple feet from him. He reached out to it as a dark fog began to tunnel his vision, the image of the sword seeming to crawl farther and farther away, creating a chasm between Trevor and the real world.

His fingers were mere inches away, but it was inches he couldn't gain. He wouldn't be able to reach it, and even if he did, he wasn't sure he'd manage the strength now to use it.

He looked back up at his murderer, upon the face of death. Stories always told that death was a wraith with a scythe, a stranger in the fog with the face of a skeleton, a bony finger held out in invitation to guide you to the afterlife. In Trevor's position, death was but a man, with a crooked nose, saliva stringing from his angled teeth as he snarled behind a vicious smile.

Trevor's tunnel vision was closing in fast now. He dropped his hands to his sides, the fire all but gone now from his chest, when he felt a tingle at his numbed fingertips.

He tapped his right hand, feeling the hardened steel at the side of his leg, and it was in that moment when hope surged life back into his body.

"... *isn't as bad as you might think. It'll still probably do the trick.*"

Trevor gripped the warped dagger he'd made earlier that morning with what strength he had left. He pulled it from the knot at the side of his leg and used the remaining strength he had left to swing it toward his attacker.

"Ugh," the man groaned.

Trevor felt the tension on his neck weaken, the grasp of death loosening as the man began to lean away, eyes looking down at the dagger that Trevor had stabbed into his ribs.

The thug tried to stand, but his knees wobbled heavily before giving out, causing him to fall back on his ass. Delicately, he probed the hilt of the dagger sticking out of his ribs.

Trevor coughed, the fire in his throat burning with each heave of air. He kicked away from the man and managed to get another pace of distance between the two of them when he saw his attacker beginning to pull the dagger from himself.

"You *fucker!*" he roared, a line of blood trailing behind the darkened blade as he pulled the dagger free. He then pressed a hand against the wound as blood seeped through the lines between his fingers. He began to stand, was nearly to his feet, when Trevor realized he wasn't safe yet. "You'll pay for that." He was now on his feet and closing the distance between he and Trevor.

Trevor didn't waste any more time. Dodge had warned him about hesitating, and Trevor had learned the hard way what could happen from it. And so, he lunged to his right, retrieving his sword from the ground with a firm grip, before pulling it back and jutting out the pointy end toward his would-be killer.

Clumsy with the loss of blood, the thug tripped over his own feet just as Trevor's blade was level with his face.

"*Gah—*"

The blade pierced through the man's throat, catching his fall and nearly skewing him down to the pommel. His eyes widened in confusion, the whites of his eyes brightening up the dark world that Trevor now lived in.

Blood flowed down the sword, flowing in a steady stream and wrapping warmly around Trevor's hands, his forearms warm and sticky with the man's lifeblood.

His mouth twitched, moved awkwardly as if trying to speak, but the only sound was a wet gurgle as blood misted onto Trevor's face.

Without fully understanding what was happening, he couldn't find himself able to pull away from the man's eyes. Those placid eyes, wandering back and forth, studying Trevor's face as if the answer to all of life's questions were written on it.

The sound of battle was deaf to him. From his peripheral, Trevor knew Dodge and Tom were still engaged with their enemy, but it was just blurred movement from the corner of his eye.

He watched as the eyes before searched and searched. Trevor watched as those eyes paled, staring distantly, as his victim gurgled a dying breath and the body lay slack on the end of Trevor's sword.

"*Trevor*," a voice called to him, a whisper beyond the edge of his clouded mind.

I just ... killed a man, Trevor thought, reality slowly setting in. *A man just died, and I'm the reason for it.*

Trevor shifted his weight to his left, letting the body awkwardly roll off him like a straw-filled ragdoll.

"*Trevor*," the voice said again, louder. The sound of banging—no, clashing— echoed in the distance, and then finally the sound of the surrounding battle drummed in his ears.

"Trevor! A little help here!" Tom screamed.

Trevor's victim wasn't the only lifeless body on the ground. Three others lay sprawled about, pools of blood surrounding them near where Dodge and Tom fought off the remaining thugs. Trevor watched as the blacksmith fended off two thugs with swords. The blacksmith was impressively fast with his axe, but it was no match for two people. He saw one of the blades split through Tom's tunic, ripping open the flesh on his side. Tom let out a loud roar of pain and stumbled onto his back.

He's going to die. If someone doesn't help him, he's going to die, too.

Trevor jumped to his feet and began tugging at the blade stuck in victim's neck. He tugged as hard as he could, but the blood on his hands made the pommel slick; his hands kept slipping with his grip. He heard another cry from Tom, knew that his old friend, one of his only friends, was in some serious trouble if he couldn't get this fucking blade out of this fucking man's neck so he could fucking help.

Frustrated and panicked, Trevor stepped on the lifeless body and pulled with all his might.

There was a sucking sound as the blade tore free, causing Trevor to fall onto his back, his sword again slipping out of his hands and away from his reach. For as many hours as he had put into sparring with Dodge, he sure did spend a lot of time on his back during a real fight.

As he struggled to stand again, a large body landed on his legs, a large gash in the man's neck. It seemed that Tom was able to take care of one of his attackers.

But, as Trevor looked up and saw that Tom was actually on his back, his second assailant standing over him with his sword coming in fast toward Tom's face, Trevor realized that death had also come for the blacksmith.

"*No!*" Trevor screamed.

The thug's head snapped back with a wet *thud*, an arrow sticking out of the man's face.

The sword fell from his hands as he staggered lazily away from them, eyes crossed and hands pawing at the shaft protruding from his forehead, as if trying to swat away an annoying fly. Trevor mentally compared the look to the drunkards that he'd seen wandering home from a late night at the tavern.

A few moments later, the man sank to his knees and fell onto his side. He didn't move after that.

Trevor wasted no time thinking about what had happened. He used the rest of his strength to shove the dead man off his legs, looked about him for his sword, but only to see it between Dodge and the thug he was fighting with.

He jumped to his feet, about to join, when he saw a quick flash of white.

Trevor watched as the thug's head twirled in the air, blood spraying like a fountain from his severed neck, the severed head tumbling in the air before falling at Dodge's feet.

A figure stood before Dodge, two small axes in both hands, hunched low, as if readying for an attack. A hood from his dark tunic cast a shadow over his face, but Trevor could tell it was a man within the shadow of the hood. Besides the axes in his hands, two short swords latched crossing each other on his back. It was as if he'd appeared out of a shadow itself.

Beyond the fact that he'd helped Dodge slay the thug attacking him, Dodge didn't let his guard down. His blade was waist high and pointing at the stranger.

"Garth?" the stranger yelled in a deep voice, confirming Trevor's suspicion.

Staying as still as the dead around him, the figure kept his eyes fixed on Dodge and the sword in his hands.

"His arm is fine," Trevor heard a voice call from behind him and spun around to see Tom on the ground, a figure kneeling next to him. He had a bow in one hand with a quiver of arrows on his back. "Can't say the same for his side, though. Too deep, but Seroes should be able to help. I'll need help carrying him.

"Ain't nobody fucking carrying me," Tom growled. "I can walk just fine." Tom swatted away the mysterious archer's helping hand as he struggled to his feet.

"Listen," Trevor heard the hooded stranger say, "we've killed a few of them surrounding the town. That's your way out."

The hooded man tucked his axes into small loops at each side of his belt.

Dodge looked from the headless body at his feet then back to the man before him. Seeing that the man was possibly more help than threat, at least for the moment, he sheathed his sword onto his back and nodded.

The hooded man nodded back. "I'll take the rear."

"No," Dodge replied quickly. "I'll take the rear. Both of you up front where I can see you."

Trevor cringed with fear. He half-expected the hooded man to draw steel once more and attack Dodge on the spot. Instead, he looked quietly at the archer, who then returned his look with a soft nod.

"Fair enough," the archer confirmed. "Try to keep up."

"Don't you worry about me," Tom argued as he got to his feet, a hand pressed against his side to cover his wound.

Without waiting, the man walked off toward the one called Garth, leaning in close and whispering under his breath.

Dodge walked to Trevor and grabbed him by his arms, checking him up and down with a worried look.

"I'm fine" Trevor said, gesturing to his blood-covered self. "It's not mine. None of it is mine …" He looked about the small battlefield, blood and gore surrounding them, to the lifeless body of the man he'd just killed.

"Watch carefully," Dodge whispered to him, breaking his concentration of the littered dead around them. "We're not out of this yet. Tom?"

"I'm fine, Dodge," the blacksmith called back, limping off toward where the two strangers walked away from them. "Let's just get out of here before we join the rest of the town, eh?"

Trevor said nothing as he followed Tom. He didn't need to look back to know what was there. He was sure he would remember that sight for the rest of his days.

They were making their way to the edge of the town, the open forest lying before them, when he remembered.

"Did you find any others?" he called up front to the two strangers, not sure if he was ready for the answer they were going to give.

His heart fluttered with hope as the archer called back over his shoulder, "Just one."

Lost in the Dark

The tunnel was as dark and quiet as the dead. The air felt close, wrapping tightly against her chest as she crawled on her hands and knees, reaching out into the pure dark, hands digging deeply into the cold, powdered dirt. Each breath added another thick layer of mud that caked her mouth.

Sarah felt as if she were on the verge of suffocation, breathing just enough air to carry on, but each next breath becoming more laborious than the first.

There was pain everywhere. Each breath was a wheeze, her knees aching with the many scrapes from sharp rocks, her chafing knuckles stung with each grip of dirt she pushed behind her, and she was moving forward blindly. However, though Sarah feared what lay before her, it couldn't possibly be worse than what was behind her.

The memory of her father, and the look of terror on his face just before she and her mother had locked themselves in the bedroom. The sound of his screams after the strange men broke in. Sarah's final glance at her mother before the hatch closed over the hole she had been shoved into, tears dripping from her eyes with that sad smile. A smile that said it would be the last time Sarah would ever see her mother. And then, lastly, the sound of her mother's cry after the men had made their way into the bedroom.

There was a stab of pain in her fingertip as a loose rock wedged itself under her nail. She yanked her arm away and jammed her elbow into the wall, causing her to jump at the pain and jerk up to bang her head against the top of the tunnel, loose dirt now trickling through her hair and down her neck. The overwhelming feeling of being trapped in the tunnel now struck her still.

Breaths came shorter as she began to panic. She moved her body left and right, crashing back and forth into the crowded dirt walls, flailing and crying like a wild animal trying to escape from their cage. But there was no escape for Sarah, not through the dirt walls, and definitely not with the path behind her.

She calmed herself, sunk her head to her chest, and took steady breaths to calm her nerves. She knew she couldn't turn back, and slamming herself into the walls would only cause her more panic, so that left only one option.

I have to keep crawling. The only way out is forward, so that's where I'll go.

The farther that she crawled through the tunnel, the tighter the walls became. She could feel them scraping at her shoulders as she squeezed by, the ceiling snagging at her hair. Fear swept over her again like a heavy blanket. Nobody knew where she was, nobody would hear her scream. She would be stuck underground to wither away from the world all alone.

Suddenly, the walls felt closer than ever.

She began to tremble as she struggled to sit up right, the dirt refusing to let her. She bounced back and forth against the walls, demanding more room, to no avail. She let out a scream, long and loud, but even her shrill voice refused to budge an inch.

Defeated, Sarah buried her face to her chest, accepting that she would die alone in this forsaken tunnel after all.

That's when she heard a noise.

With a sob stuck in her throat, she sat quietly and waited, peering through the darkness toward the way she had come—as much as the tunnel allowed, at least. She could have sworn she heard a distant sound coming from behind her, something sliding through gravel, but the darkness was pure and she couldn't see anything.

Putting her panic aside, she decided to move along.

It only took a few feet of moving to hear the sound again, except it was louder this time, maybe even closer. She stopped again, unable to turn her neck fully around. A cold shiver crept up her spine as the silence drew on.

"Is there anyone there?" she asked, feeling ridiculous calling out, but it wasn't like any hurt could come of it. It was a *hidden* tunnel, ultimately. Nobody knew it existed. No one except her and …

"Mother?" she called. "Mother, is that you?"

When no answer came, she sighed and shook her head, feeling stupid thinking that someone was in there with her.

You're only fooling yourself, Sarah. It's just the dark playing tricks on you. You're all alone down—

"Don't worry, little piggy." The malevolent voice sent a chill all the way up Sarah's spine. Part whisper, part growl, all spoken through the dark from the way she had come. "I won't hurt ya." The voice was deep, ragged, filled with uneasy familiarity.

For a moment, she was frozen solid, too scared to move even a finger.

"Don't wait up for me now," the voice pleaded, coming from much closer than before. A laugh echoed down the tunnel, soft and egregious. "I do like a chase."

Sarah began moving as fast as she could, now barely noticing the rough scrapes against her arms and knees as she desperately tried to distance herself from the threat at her heels.

The walls began to distance and, before she realized it, Sarah had enough space to bear crawl. Even the air felt like it opened up for her. It was as if she had crawled into a large underground room. While there was much more space, there was still no light to help guide her.

Waving her arms out in front of her, she wandered aimlessly through the dark until the rough dirt brushed against her fingertips. She pressed her back against it, trying to get an idea of where she had entered from, but she had been turned about in the dark.

Sliding against the wall, she discovered the small room she was in resembled the shape of a circle. If that were true, then she had finally made it to the end, but without an exit.

With no chance of seeing an alternate route in the pitch dark, she was trapped. She was lost in the dark.

She quickly glanced around the room in desperate search of the entrance she'd crawled through, but she couldn't even see her hand in front of her face. With her heart about to burst through her chest, she scooted across the floor until her back pressed up against the cold, dirt wall. She closed her eyes and breathed low and steady.

Several long minutes dragged by, fear buzzing in her ears as she waited. She silently said a prayer, begging the gods to somehow disperse her pursuer, hoping that there was a turn in the tunnel she had missed that they'd gone down. Her prayers were answered, of course, just not the way she had hoped.

The soft sounds of gravel sliding came from her left. She'd known the man in the dark had followed her into the same room; she just hadn't realized how close he was until the loose gravel he'd been brushing aside sprinkled across her bare foot.

"Little piggy," he called to her. She could smell the alcohol on his breath.

"Little piggy, where did you go?"

She focused on the sound of footsteps moving deeper into the chamber, holding her breath, lest she give away her position. Then an idea struck her. This was her chance. If there was only one entrance, then the man had just come through it, not just a few feet away from her. She could crawl back to her house. With luck, the man would get turned around and lose himself in the tunnel, or find another path leading away from her.

I can make it out!

Sarah began reaching out with her hand, keeping it pressed tightly against the wall. Sure enough, she felt an angle in the dirt, the entrance to the tunnel. Just as she began silently making her way slowly toward the hole, she felt warm breath on the back of her neck, the man all but whispering into her ear.

"Nowhere to run now, little piggy."

Sarah instinctively threw her head back, smashing it against the man's face as he fell away with a groan. She kicked away viciously, trying to hurry down the tunnel that she hoped led back to her house when she felt hands grabbing at her legs. The man's grasp tightened around her ankle with purchase, and she was dragged back, her scream for help piercing the quiet tunnel.

She kicked with her free leg into the darkness and was satisfied when she felt a soft crunch under her foot. The grip on her other ankle recessed, and she began crawling as fast as she could toward freedom.

Somewhere in the scuffle, she managed to lose her sense of direction. She felt the open air above her and realized she could stand. With her hands pressed out before her, she rushed aimlessly into the darkness until she came upon the dirt wall, a curve in its structure. She quickly ran along it with an outstretched arm, all the while her attacker mumbling curses in the darkness, calling her vile names and poisoning the air with his threats.

"My nose," he cried. "You broke my fuckin' nose. Bitch! I'll fucking get you for that. Mark my words, missy; *I'll find you*."

Trying her best to ignore the man's vile promise, she kept at the wall until she discovered an open space, leading her to the entrance of a tunnel. It might not have been the one to her house, but it was better than where she was now.

She managed to get half her body in before she felt another tight grip around her ankle again. Sarah began kicking, reaching out for something, anything that she could grab, but it was hopeless. Another hand grabbed her second ankle. She cried out as she was forced onto her back, the man dragging her closer, climbing

K.R. Gangi

on top of her and using his weight to hold her down.

"Keep squirming, bitch," he grunted, pinning Sarah's arms above her head with a strong hold. "Scream if it makes you feel better; ain't nobody that can hear you. It's just me and you, little piggy, and I much like it when they put up a fight."

Sarah desperately tried to claw at her captor, to kick, even bite at the man's face as she felt a rough hand tearing at her dress, pulling it above her waist, leaving her bare legs exposed. The man shifted his hips awkwardly, forcing Sarah's legs open.

"Please, no!" she begged, tears streaming down her face, her voice crackling with fear. "Please, no. I don't want—"

Her cries were cut short as a cramping pain shot through her, sending splintering tremors through her stomach and up into her chest. The insides of her thighs cramped as the man violently thrust again, and again, and again.

"Just a bit farther," he moaned, spit flecking her face. "Almost done. Don't give up on me now. Keep fighting me."

She wasn't sure how long it lasted, only that time stood still in that moment. The only things that existed were the sounds of the man's moaning echoing in the darkness, the feeling of his tight hands grabbing violently at her wrists. She was numb, barely aware of the pain anymore, barely aware of the tears pouring from her eyes.

Then she saw stars. They shone brightly down at her, a pale light materializing out of the darkness. Between those lights was the shape of a figure, floating in the sky as it looked down upon her. Slowly, the figure reached toward her, and she felt relief knowing that it was death coming to save her.

The Presence of *Bak'am*

The songs of life in the forest sang through the night. Owls calling to one another, crickets chirping up a storm, and even the occasional monkey could be heard off in the distance. It was the most Quiver had heard in the jungle since he and his pack had started their quest to find Nero. And with each passing note the wildlife sang, Quiver felt a bit more at ease.

Out of all the sounds the night had to offer him, Quiver just hoped that one particular sound wouldn't join them; and so far, he'd yet to hear the howler's call. Yet, he was ready for it.

Plan for the worst and hope for the best.

He crouched on a wide branch, a throbbing ache in his back and a spear heavy in his grasp. His pack around him held the same in their separate positions, armed and patiently waiting.

They had a nice spot for the ambush, much like the one set against Nero and his pack. Irony always did like to bite with sharp teeth.

Below him was a wide, circular clearing, nothing but a large boulder in its center and tall grass surrounding it. Rasca hid in a tree across from Quiver, tucked beneath low hanging branches of leaves to keep him out of sight, the branches casting a darker shadow around him and the heavy spear clutched in his hands. Sparrow and Oppo sat in the largest tree in the opening to Quiver's left, both huddled together with makeshift bows, a sling of arrows on their back, and another nocked and ready to be drawn.

To his right sat Masco in his tree, calmer than Quiver had expected. His posture was steady, so steady it took Quiver a moment to search the tree in order to spot him. He scanned the forest around him, another bow in his hands and a few spears next to him, searching for the monsters that hunted them.

Quiver had hoped to get more weapons for their attack, but with the amount of time they had before the sun set, along with the energy they had left in their bodies, they had settled with only a few spears and half a dozen arrows. It was enough to inflict damage, especially with the element of surprise, but their attacks would have to be precise and accurate. Besides that, Rasca had Nero's axe while Quiver had his dagger and bow, the two very things that had led Quiver out of the worst scuffles that he'd ever been in.

They used the dagger and axe to carve the spears, using the cloth of their sacks for fastening the two new bows for the younglings. It wasn't a tough decision to use the last of their supplies to fasten the weapons, since they wouldn't have much need for their sacks if they were dead.

They had done their best to stay ahead of the beasts tracking them the last few days, yet any progress made the day before had been lost near the end of the following night. Not once had they seen the howlers, only the chilling sound of their calls echoing in the dark.

There had been times when Quiver could have sworn one was right on his heels, only a trip away from becoming the beast's next meal, but as he'd peered over his shoulder, he saw nothing but the dark jungle. It was as if the beasts knew how to stay just out of sight before deciding their move.

This led Quiver to believe the beasts relied on their scent, rather than sight, in tracking them. The theory gave his pack an advantage, or at least Quiver had hoped. If not, they wouldn't live to regret it. Everything was riding on Quiver's guesswork, another weight added to the pile on the shoulders of any chief.

Sometimes all you can do is guess and hope it worked out. Nothing is certain.

Quiver's and Rasca's experiences with battle only made it easier for the younglings to trust them for a solid plan, and although the plan might have been simple, Quiver knew that even the simplest of plans could go bad really quick. He was adamant on the younglings understanding this. Once he could see the acknowledgement in their eyes, Quiver explained what was to happen.

The pack would strip down and pile their clothes into a hole in the center of the ambush site. With the remainder of their water, they created mud and smudged it all over their bodies. If Quiver's theory was right, once the mud dried, it would hide the scent of their bodies and leave their clothes for the beasts to follow. Of course, the younglings were more than discouraged to waste the remainder of their water supply, but Quiver explained that there wouldn't be much use for water if they didn't live beyond tonight anyway. The pack was quick to agree.

They would hide in the trees while the howlers were led to the clearing, hopefully drawn close to the pile of clothes while they all waited with their weapons. Once the they managed to make it to the center of the clearing, they were vulnerable to the attack. The pack would wait for Quiver's mark, and then they would all attack from the shadows simultaneously, each picking the closest target and bringing it down as fast as they could.

"The idea is to thin their ranks as fast as we can," he'd told them before the sun had set. "The less of them there are, the more advantage we gain. If we gain superiority in numbers, we gain a better chance at surviving."

Once the attack had begun, and all spears were spent, Rasca and Quiver would jump down and face the remaining beasts with their blades while the younglings continued to attack with their bows from the trees.

Rasca wasn't too fond with that part of the plan. "You'll need to fear me more than the beasts if one of your arrows finds me as a mark," he'd warned the younglings before setting them to their tasks.

There was a familiar feeling that tickled Quiver's gut, that rush through his core, knowing that blood was about to be spilt. It was what his clan referred to as *Bak'am* or, as the southerners would say, *bloodlust.*

Bak'am was the warrior spirit that gave strength to those preparing to fight for their lives. If you were gifted with *Bak'am*, you were given the chance to prove yourself to him. If *Bak'am* found you worthy of his gift in life, then he'd spoil your afterlife with the Forever Calm; a world in which you lived among those you fought against, fought for, and even died from. In the Forever Calm, you meet your enemies once again. Only, instead of a battlefield, it was a grand hall, approaching as friends instead of enemies. Instead of a life of pain and struggle, you were cherished with all the gifts the spirits offered—food, drink, women, and resolve. Most of all, peace.

However, the power of *Bak'am* was vast, almost uncontrollable. Quiver had seen clansmen fight on their knees until their last breath, letting the spirit fuel them until their death. Yet, Quiver had also seen many break under the pressure of *Bak'am*, fleeing from a battle, betraying the gift the spirit bestowed onto them, betraying the spirit itself.

Quiver was no stranger to *Bak'am*, yet he thought—even hoped—that he'd never feel its presence again. He'd spent his life proving to the spirit he was worthy, countless battles with his enemies' lifeblood dripping from his blade, the endless times he'd washed that blood in a stream somewhere in the south. The more he fought, the more he realized that the spirit's craving for blood was insatiable, though Quiver's thirst had been quenched long ago.

Even though Quiver had long ago abandoned the ways of a warrior, that didn't mean he wouldn't fight. He'd always fight to protect those he could. If he fought and won now, he'd not only save his pack, but those at his village, as well, once he warned them of the beasts. And if he fought now and didn't win, he'd be sure to take as many enemies as he could to the afterlife with him.

Hidden in the trees, Quiver's pack waited, stripped naked, caked in dry mud, with hastily made weapons in their hands. They waited to see the monsters that haunted them each night, waited to put an end to the terror at their heels, whether in life or death.

But the terror never came.

It had been nearly an hour now since the sun had set. Quiver expected that, any moment now, the howlers would show themselves, yet nothing came. Birds whistled, crickets chirped, frogs croaked through the fog hanging in the air, bursts of moonlight glaring through the misty branches, but no monsters stepped into the clearing.

With the lack of threat to keep his attention, Quiver lost himself within the beauty of the world around him. He had come to terms with the fact that others in the world had a right to live their life in a way of their choosing, but Quiver never could understand how the southerners would rather live cramped together in their stone towers when the natural world had so much beauty to give. Why would someone want to live that way, away from the beauty of nature?

After what felt like another hour passed, the presence of *Bak'am* that Quiver had felt began to fade. The night made it difficult for him to ignore just how tired his body felt, how exhausted he really was. His ankles strained with a burn that followed all the way up his calves and worked into his shoulders. His head pounded from lack of sleep and water. If he was completely honest, he was beginning to struggle with staying awake. He could only imagine the rest of his pack was doing the same.

Quiver looked across the clearing and could see Sparrow gently nudging Oppo periodically whenever his head bobbed. The youngling would tense for a split moment, look about as if the threat was in his face, and then bob off once again.

Quiver turned to his right, hoping to see Masco awake and ready, and that's when worry struck him cold. Masco's muddied face was staring at Quiver. A glare of moonlight cut through the branches just enough to show the whites of his wide eyes, shining like two full moons in the shadow of the night.

Just as Quiver was going to signal to the youngling, he realized that Masco wasn't looking at him, but *past* him.

It was at that moment when Quiver felt a brush against his shoulder, rough fur rubbing against his naked arm. A large blur radiated warmth and the rank of death, slowly scaling the side of his tree, making its way toward the ground floor. One wrong move, even the slightest sound of his breathing, and that would be it for Quiver.

The same went for Masco's tree. Just feet above him, a creature that easily could have been mistaken for a bear, moved slowly down the tree next to him. However, bears were easy to hear when they climbed. Not only did these beasts appear bigger than your average bear, but you could at least hear a bear climbing a tree, especially in the dead of night. Not this creature, however. Not even the slightest sound betrayed the silence.

Quiver gestured with his eyes to Masco about his danger. He looked above his head to the monster, back down to Masco, and then back again, hoping the youngling caught on to his warning. Quiver wasn't sure if the others were seeing this, or if they found themselves in the same trouble.

By the looks of what Quiver assumed to be the howlers, he now felt a spark of regret for setting the ambush. Suddenly, the thought of running until he collapsed in the jungle didn't seem so bad, as long as he didn't have to face the howlers.

The way the beasts moved down the tree was effortless, their weight showing no signs of restraint. It was no wonder Quiver had never noticed them—their fur was made of shadow. The only distinction Quiver could make between the night and the beasts were the eyes—bloodred orbs that floated in the dark.

If they are this quiet during a hunt, then why the howling at night? Why keep the pack running when the monsters could simply sneak up on them and take them by surprise? Realization hit Quiver like the end of a hammer. *They weren't chasing us; they were* following *us. Following us back to the village. If even one of those monsters make it back ...*

Masco's howler turned his head and looked directly at Quiver; its red eyes like crimson flames peering deep into his soul. He watched as the howler bounced its head slightly up and down.

Quiver's heart stopped in his chest. Fear froze him to his core. He refused to breathe even a breath out of fear the howler would notice him.

Still, the beast kept its red eyes focused on him, continuing to bounce its head up and down in the dark.

Pressure built in Quiver's chest. At any moment now, he expected the monster to leap from the tree at him, to clench its massive jaws down on his head and send him to the Forever Calm.

But it didn't.

It's trying to sniff us out, but it doesn't see me. Stay calm, old man, stick to the plan. The plan is working.

The howler sniffed around a bit more before finally setting eyes of the ground below it.

It's sniffed out the gear.

The life of the jungle disappeared the moment the howlers reached the floor. No birds sang, no crickets chirped. It was so quiet that Quiver feared breathing too loudly. Slowly, very slowly, he glanced down toward the opening.

He could make out two of them pressed low to the ground, slowly working their way toward the center, near the pack's clothing. Whether or not they thought it was them, Quiver couldn't tell. The sight sent shivers up Quiver's arms.

He was right about one thing. If they had never known the beasts were hunting them, they would have never noticed them until it was too late.

He felt a wave of sympathy for Nero and his men for the horror that had happened upon them.

Rasca had a spear already held above his head, ready to be thrown at Quiver's signal. Masco held his bow stretched, an arrow at his cheek. Rasca and Masco both looked ready to fight, regardless of the sudden horror that revealed themselves as the howlers. However, the same could not be said about Sparrow and Oppo.

Sparrow held his bow high, aimed toward his targets, but Oppo fumbled with an arrow, his shaky hands losing grip as he tried to nock it to the string.

Slow down. Just breathe and focus on what you're doing. One step at—

Quiver's heart melted as he saw the arrow slip through Oppo's fingers. He could only watch, as if in slow motion, as the arrow spun over itself toward the ground.

Quiver expected to hear the arrow as it hit the ground, but the howlers were too focused on the pack's gear to notice. A slight moment of relief washed over Quiver as the arrow landed silently on the ground, but that relief was quickly vanquished by pure dread.

The snout of a howler peeked from behind Sparrow and Oppo's tree, just above where the arrow fell. It sniffed the air and pushed around the fallen arrow with its muzzle.

Panic overwhelmed the younglings as they watched the howler beneath their tree. Oppo began fumbling for another arrow, more hastily now.

Quiver nearly sent a prayer to the spirits, but he knew it would be useless. The spirits had either been dead for quite some time now or they had given up hope for his people long ago.

If the spirits do not care on normal circumstances, why would they care when things turn sour?

Another arrow fumbled from Oppo's shaky grip and fell from the tree, bouncing off the giant head of the howler beneath them.

Its shoulders bunched up, and it gave a low growl that seemed to reverberate through everything, which caught the attention of another howler nearby.

The first beast looked up into the tree. Quiver could now see its fangs glistening in the moonlight as the beast spread its jaws and gave a low whine.

Both howlers now patted at the base of the tree. They looked about for a moment, cocking their heads back and forth like confused mutts. Then the second one followed the gaze from the first, both now looking up into the branches where the younglings hid.

Don't move, Quiver thought, hoping his plea could somehow magically be heard by his pack. *Don't move, don't even breathe. They don't see you yet. Just sit still—*

Oppo peered over his branch, looking down at the eyes of the monsters.

A deep growl rumbled in the night as a howler tilted its head up toward the younglings. Then, starting with one massive paw, the howlers began to climb.

Oppo, completely overwhelmed in fear, dropped his bow and looked for an exit. Sparrow kept his calm, though, trying to encourage Oppo to do the same by taking his shoulders in his hands, looking at his friend in the eyes, whispering encouraging words. None of it helped. Oppo's panicked whispers turned into frantic shouting, catching the eyes of the other monsters.

A howler took a massive leap and landed on the large boulder in the center of the clearing. It gave a loud shriek.

The others followed suit, tilting their heads as their haunting howls echoed through the night.

With no time to waste, Quiver stood to give the signal when a final, horrific event caught his attention.

He watched as the youngling fell.

For a moment, time fell still as arms stretched out in hope of grabbing a nearby branch. The youngling let out a small scream as he fell toward the strong jaws of the awaiting howlers.

"No ..." Quiver whispered loud enough so only he could hear.

The body hit the ground with a hollow *thud*, cutting short the youngling's frightful scream.

The beasts wasted no time. They jumped toward their fallen prey with snapping jaws and demonic barks.

Oppo screeched in utter terror, a prayer to the spirits to spare him the pain that awaited him. The spirits didn't answer. His cry was quickly replaced with the sound of tearing flesh and the popping of snapped bone.

The beasts tore him apart, whipping their heads back and forth. Quiver's stomach turned at the savagery before him.

"Now!" he yelled.

Thrusting with all his might, he launched the heavy spear toward the massacre below. An abrupt whine told him that his aim had been true.

Masco was quick with his bow, sending an arrow whistling through the air before Quiver got his hands on his second spear. Rasca roared a loud battle cry as he let loose his own spear, hoping to drive some of the attention away from the fallen youngling.

As Quiver took aim, he could make out a howler below, its massive body hunched with two spears angled out at its flanks, yet the monster barely seemed distracted from its meal.

Quiver drew back another spear just as the howler turned its massive head toward him. Its eyes being the easiest target to identify, Quiver hurled his spear with all the strength he had left toward the monster's face.

The beast rumbled loudly as he crashed to the floor, its body lying still.

The familiar feeling that came with killing washed over Quiver, a craving he felt in his gut, a thirst he thought quenched long ago. The presence of *Bak'am* was with him once more, and regardless of his current lack of faith, he didn't aim to disappoint the spirit.

He grabbed his last remaining spear, picked up his nearby dagger, and ran toward the edge of the large branch. With his last two strides, he leapt off from the tree, his spear angled high above his head as he rushed toward the ground.

At first, everything was silent, the weightlessness of being airborne tickling his stomach. Then, the sound of rushing air was all he could hear and feel. He was falling toward the pack of howlers as they ripped and tore at the fallen youngling's body, shaking their heads violently, bits of flesh flinging in all directions.

He drove his spear down as he landed on one of the beast's back. The wooden shaft vibrated as it scraped past bone and drove deeper into flesh, popping through tough skin and into muscle. The howler let out a loud roar of pain as Quiver then struck out with the dagger. He let out his own roar as he swung wide, again and again, as the blade found its mark in the beast's side, dark lines of blood flying through the air each time he pulled the blade free. The beast stood on its hind legs, roaring in rage.

Quiver tried grasping its fur, but the blood-soaked tuff slipped through his fingers. He fell back and tumbled off the howler.

He knew he was in trouble the moment he hit the ground. The howler turned its vicious snout and snarled at Quiver, blood still dripping from its mouth. It only took a moment for Quiver to realize he no longer had the dagger in his hand.

In his moment of realization, the monster pounced, knocking Quiver onto his back.

Quiver tried to kick at the howler, but the weight was unbearable. Its great body pressed on top of Quiver, the massive jaws snapping toward his face, the smell of death rank on its breath, chunks of meat still fresh in its mouth.

The howler struck at Quiver with its claws, tearing deep into Quiver's sides. Quiver's arms grew weaker by the second as he tried his hardest to fend off the beast.

The howler snapped its snout at Quiver's face, each time getting closer and closer as Quiver managed to turn just out of reach.

There was a flash in the moonlight as the monster screeched in pain, rearing on its hind legs. Quiver took advantage of the moment and rolled himself away.

A firm hand grasped under his arm and helped him to his feet. Next to him stood Masco, blood covering his bare chest and Quiver's dagger bloodied in his hand.

The howler before them was now flailing around frantically, scraping its face in the dirt, pawing at its snout. After shaking its head violently back and forth, the howler then fixed its eyes on Masco and Quiver.

Not eyes—eye. One eye stared angrily back at them, and with a shrieking howl, it charged again.

When the monster was near enough, it drew back its arm and began to swing high. It was a slow attack, making it easy for Quiver and Masco to dodge out of reach, which they did in unison. When they turned about, the howler whined as it tucked an arm tight to the side. The sound reminded Quiver of a wounded wolf that he had found when he'd been a youngling. By the looks of it, Masco had managed to get a stab under its armpit before dodging out of the way.

Then a blur rushed from the side. Masco launched into Quiver, the crash sending him onto his back as another howler stood with a massive paw on Masco's motionless body, a triumphant demon in the night.

"*No!*" Quiver rushed to his feet and dashed at the howler.

The monster raised another paw, razor claws readying to tear at Masco's body.

When he was just a few feet away, Quiver rolled, keeping up with his momentum as he reached out to grab the dagger off the ground. When he turned over to his feet, he launched himself toward the howler. The blade stabbed deep into the howler's chest.

Quiver used the remainder of his strength to tear the blade down to the beast's stomach, releasing a flood of warm blood down his arms and a loud cry from the monster. But it wasn't enough to bring the beast down.

With a roar of pain, the howler now focused its attack on Quiver.

The sound of rushing wind whistled in the night as the howler snapped its head to the side. Even with Nero's axe buried in the side of its head, the beast still managed to stay on his feet.

Rasca jumped out of Quiver's peripheral with a heavy kick toward the monster's snout. It stumbled with the blows, its muzzle crashing into the dirt.

Rasca reached in and ripped free the hatchet that he had buried into the howler's face. "Here," he yelled to Quiver as he tossed something toward him.

My bow!

Quiver caught his bow out of mid-air, pulled free the arrow locked in the groove at the side of the shaft, and nocked an arrow.

Rasca was swinging with a final blow, aiming for the neck of the monster still standing over Masco's body, when the beast backhanded him with a muscled arm. Rasca folded over the blow as he was launched away, smacking against the trunk of a tree with a loud *thud*.

The beast roared in rage, again drawing back the massive paw as it stood on the back of its legs.

Quiver pinched his arrow, drew back, and then released in the matter of a second, burying the arrowhead into the flesh of its massive paw.

The beast stumbled back away from Masco, whimpering as it cowered away, but Quiver wasn't done. Freeing his second arrow from its lock, he nocked, drew, and released just as smoothly as the first.

A lesson his father had told him long ago resonated in his head as the string of his bow left his fingers. "*Do not aim at what is there,*" he had told Quiver. "*Aim for what* will *be there.*"

The beast roared, and that was Quiver's target. Just as the howler opened its mouth, the arrow flew home and lodged itself in the back of its throat, choking off its cry.

The beast flailed about, striking out at anything around him, before crashing to the ground where it sat motionless.

Quiver reached through the gap of his bow and rested it over his shoulder. Knowing that not even a powerful beast such as this could survive such an attack, he walked over and climbed atop its massive body.

The moonlight revealed cuts and scratches bloodied across the entirety of the body, blood streaming from the wounds the beast was suffering. Quiver gripped the spear lodged in the howler's body, ripping it free with a wet, sucking sound.

Rasca, who Quiver thought was unconscious, limped next to Quiver, one hand covering his belly and the other tightly fitted around a dagger. Together, they faced the remaining one-eyed howler.

It was just standing by as we fought the other one, watching as the battle unravel. Was it ... learning how we fight?

These beasts aren't just strong, but they're smart. Smarter than we thought.

The howler looked from Masco's body, now lying in a pool of his own blood, back to the two chiefs standing strong before it with weapons in their hands. After looking about and seeing the bodies of its own pack, the beast gave one last howl before it turned and disappeared into the night.

After waiting a few moments to make sure the howler wouldn't circle back,

Quiver went to Masco's body. The scratch on his back was cut deep. Quiver had seen many wounds as deep as this, none of which the victim lived to tell the tale of how it had happened.

Rasca walked to where the one-eyed howler turned to flee into the woods and picked up Nero's axe off the ground. He studied it in the dark.

"He's breathing," Quiver said, getting Rasca's attention.

Rasca held the axe at his side as he knelt next to Quiver. "We'll need to bandage him up," he said. "I'll find some leaves for you both."

"Both?" Quiver asked.

"Yes, he's not the only one wounded." Rasca gestured to Quiver's side.

Quiver looked down to see dark blood covering his chest, a large scratch of three claws crossing his front. "I'm fine for now. We'll see to him first."

"Check the others, too, and see if they need help." Rasca ignored Quiver's order. "I won't have time to run back in search of more supplies."

Quiver walked to where the battle had begun—the base of Sparrow and Oppo's tree. Sprawled before him laid the dismembered body of one of the younglings in a heaping mess of gore. Bones, organs, strips of meat littered the ground in a dark pool of red.

In the short amount of time the monsters had feasted, there was hardly anything left. The only indication that the victim was even human was the partial clump of skull and a severed hand still clutching a bow. A chunk of skull that bore the tattoo of a bird.

Sparrow ... It was Sparrow who had fallen.

Quiver knelt before the mess. "May you find peace," he whispered.

At that moment, like most moments when Quiver had after battles, he wondered why he bothered to pray to the spirits. These were the spirits that gave birth to the world, yet they encouraged you to soak it with the blood of others.

How is it we worship a deity that punishes you for saving your own life but rewards you for taking others? It was moments like this that reminded Quiver just how distant he had become with his own culture.

"Oppo," he called up the tree; no point in being quiet now. "Where are you, Oppo? It's safe now."

Leaving the mess behind, Quiver limped back to Masco, his sides suddenly burning. As the battle fury began to wear off, pain throbbed through Quiver like a heartbeat. He ached everywhere.

Quiver nodded toward Rasca. "Are you wounded?"

Rasca replied by holding up his hand in the moonlight, showing two empty spaces where fingers should have been. "Could have been worse." He nodded over his shoulder, toward the mess that had once been Sparrow.

Quiver looked around the small battlefield toward the large bodies of the howlers'. Even with the ambush, even with peppering them with spears and arrows, they had managed to keep up a fight. No beast, not even a bear, could muster enough strength to keep up a fight that long with that much damage done.

These were not animals, but fiends of an old world. Creatures of the dark from the old stories, of the old war.

The snap of a twig caused both chiefs to twirl on their heels, ready to defend themselves against another attack, only to see Oppo standing in the darkness.

"Are they …? Is he …?" He crossed his arms, rubbing at his sides as if he were cold. Not a drop of blood was on him. "Is he … dead?"

"No," Rasca said flatly. "Not yet, at least."

Quiver locked eyes with Oppo. He couldn't help feeling a sadness as he looked at the youngling, but he knew he shouldn't judge. You either thrived off of *Bak'am,* or you cowered. There was no middle ground.

"I tried to … He wouldn't listen. I just wanted … He—"

"It doesn't matter," Rasca interrupted Oppo. "What's done is done. What matters now is that we make sure that none of us join Sparrow in the Forever Calm. Let's tend to our wounds and hope we never see those beasts again."

Quiver couldn't have found better words to fit the situation.

He knelt low to Masco once more. "Find us medicine, Rasca. We will tend to our wounds and be on our way after."

Without a reply, Rasca ran off into the woods. If he could find some healing herbs, there was a chance that they could save Masco's life. If not, they'd carry his body back to the village. He hoped it wouldn't be the latter.

Oppo knelt beside Quiver, a hand on Masco's back and a tear dripping from his eyes. "I'm sorry," he whispered in a shaky voice. "I'm so sorry …"

Written in Blood

Alric crouched, hidden in a bush, and watched as the bright flames engulfed the line of houses across the street. The dry wood splintered and cracked as it was fully consumed, bringing back horrid memories of a life stolen from him.

Although the flames would ultimately remind him of what he'd lost, there was something else that felt familiar to him as he watched the houses burn. Something more recent.

During his lifetime of warfare, he had been involved in many different raids. He had snuck over walls with nothing but a dagger, pushed through waist-high sewage to infiltrate a city. Hell, there was even a time when he had walked through the front gates, entering a city as an ally and leaving it as a traitor. Out of all those raids, there was always a common goal: gain entry, kill enough people, then gain control of the city.

This makes no sense, though. What's the point of controlling a village if you burn down all the homes and kill all the people? You can't control a place that doesn't possess anything to control.

Robins-Port held great tactical opportunities for someone in control. It was the arrowhead of all trade within Navaleth. *Why not take advantage of that? If you had enough audacity to take the village, you should have enough men to hold it. Not to mention you'll need housing for barracks, shops for provisions, and people to provide services that troops needed. Why burn it all away?*

People died during raids, of course, and usually with only a few civilian casualties. At least, that's how it was supposed to be. Even then, people were killed with a sense of decency. They were never butchered into pieces and stacked into piles, or hung from rafters and lit on fire.

No military unit in the king's army would be as barbaric as that. So, that left bandits. But what bandit group would dare attack the arrowhead of Navaleth? Lazar and his band were notorious for ransacking farms, but he'd never heard of them ending in a massacre like this.

It occurred to Alric then that this wasn't just a raid, but a message. A message written in blood to strike fear into those who received it.

Three corpses laid in front of a burning house closest to Alric. One of them, a smaller body, had an arrow shaft sticking out toward the sky.

Alric made a move to investigate when he heard the sound of a snapped twig from behind him. Naturally, Alric drew his blade and turned to defend himself, only to find the tip of his dagger inches away from Benny's throat.

"You're getting sloppy, old man," he said while he sheathed his sword and turned back to the carnage.

"I've been told that." Benny took a knee and joined Alric at the scene. "Garth and Baron went to scout the town for survivors. Evan and Seroes are checking the outskirts for stragglers. Should be back soon. Merrick's watching the boy."

Alric replied with a small nod, never taking his eyes away from the fire. "Is he talking yet?"

"No." Benny sighed. "Still a bit confused. Fuck, we're all confused. None of this adds up."

"I was just thinking the same thing. Hopefully, the others find something, or that the kid knows something he can eventually tell us. In any case, we should be moving off soon. It doesn't look like there'll be any more survivors."

"I'll head back and get the others ready."

"Hold on." Alric glanced both ways down the street before revealing himself from the brush, making his way toward the three victims before him. One was a man, not much older than Alric, by the looks of it. The others were a woman around the same age and a lad that couldn't be much older than ten. A family, then. A family soaked in blood.

He lifted the tunic of the father to reveal a single stab wound just beneath his ribs. Unlike the other victims that Alric had come across, it seemed this man had the privilege of a quick and relatively clean death.

Alric studied the wound. *Well, only one way to find out.* He jammed two fingers into the open slit, a trick he learned as a soldier to see how precise an attack was. After checking the boy, he checked the mother's wound, as well. The results were the same—a stab wound that passed through the ribs to penetrate the heart.

Professionally done. This does make matters worse.

He looked at the boy. The pale, lifeless eyes stared at the stars with dried flakes of blood on his chin. Again, Alric felt a wave of déjà vu. Not the nostalgia of a memory relating to his past, but a moment when he had been in this spot, assessing this exact situation before.

He reached for the arrow then hesitated. An overwhelming fear tugged at his stomach as he looked at the boy, a wave of fear he couldn't comprehend. It had been quite some time since Alric had been squeamish over a dead body, even if that body belonged to a child. So, why was he so fearful now?

Get a hold of yourself, Al. He's dead, and there's nothing anyone can do about that.

Pushing past the spontaneous surge of fear, he gripped the shaft and tugged the arrow free of the boy's body. Alric then waited a moment, readying himself in case the child reached for him. After a few slow passing seconds, he tucked the arrow at his side under his belt and returned to the brush where Benny waited.

"Anything new?" Benny asked, indicating the arrow.

"More than I like." Alric shook his head, his eyes focusing on the child's body that he left across the street. "Let's head back."

***

Upon arriving to Robins-Port, the brotherhood had been about half a mile from the village, trekking through the outskirts in the woods, when they'd heard the shouting. A boy sprinting through the woods in front of them had tripped on a large tree root and stumbled into them. It took only a moment to see that he was scared for his life.

"Help me," he'd pleaded, sweat-soaked hair plastered to the side of his face. "Please, help me!"

The bandits had been spotted soon after, the flash of steel in the moonlight. So, Alric had given two soft whistles, signaling for Garth and Merrick to move to their positions. The bandits, who were only a pair, had spotted Alric and the others and had begun to rush them. Unfortunately for them, who hadn't known that they were in the sights of two of the most trustworthy archers Alric had ever come to know.

Alric had held his arms level with his waist, and when the bandits had come closer, he could tell that they weren't typical guards, but men set on violence. When he declared them as a threat, Alric let his arms slowly drop to his sides, giving Merrick and Garth the signal.

Two arrows had whistled through the air, and the bodies dropped to the ground, an arrow sticking out from the side of each of their heads.

After the encounter with the bandits, they had set up a small camp close by, sending out two groups to see what was happening in Robins-Port.

Alric and Benny crouched low now, hidden in the shadows close to where their camp was hidden.

Benny picked up a twig and snapped it, the sound cracking the silence in the dark.

A whisper called out to them in the night, "What flavor?"

"Bitter-sweet," Benny replied.

"Welcome back," the voice called back.

As they entered, Alric saw the corpses of the two thugs lying against an oak tree. Their arms were crossed, indicating they'd already been thoroughly searched. The brotherhood was nothing, if not thorough, especially when seeking answers.

Glancing around, he found the surviving boy sitting against a large boulder. He was in the same position Alric had left him—arms cradling his legs and eyes wide with fear. Alric walked over and knelt next to him.

"Listen. We're going to be making off soon. If you come along, we can take you someplace safe. It doesn't look good for Robins-Port, so I suggest you come along."

Either the boy decided to ignore Alric or he simply didn't understand.

Well, never was good with kids. Never got the chance to be ...

Alric left the boy to join Merrick and Benny. There was nothing he could do for the boy now, but he hoped that, soon enough, the boy could provide them with some answers.

"We should leave as soon as they get back," Alric stated.

They nodded in agreement.

"Let's get our packs set, and then we'll get the others' ready. We need to be miles from here before we stop."

The sound of a snapping twig drew their attention.

"What's the flavor?" Alric asked the darkness in the direction of the sound, his hand firmly tight on the hilt of his dagger.

"Sweet, with a touch of rosemary, if you ask me," Evan replied quietly, sounding as if he was out of breath.

As soon as Alric saw them, he knew something was wrong.

Evan walked in with a hanged head. Seroes had a small body cradled in his arms, trailing behind closely behind him. He walked past the group and set a limp young girl against a tree next to the boy. She was unconscious and covered in blood.

"What happened?" Benny asked Seroes as he approached the girl.

"Strange thing," Seroes responded, rubbing the sweat from his bald head. "We were scouting the perimeter when this old man steps out of nowhere. Said we had to hurry or it would be too late before running off into the woods and disappearing. Thinking it was probably an ambush, we followed slowly. By the time we realized he was gone, we heard some muffled screams. We were led to a trapdoor hidden under some brush. Found the girl inside a make-shift tunnel at the edge of town. Strange luck, that. Wouldn't have heard her if we'd been ten feet farther away."

"Strange indeed," Benny said with a finger pressed to his chin. "And what of this old man? Can you describe him?"

Seroes shrugged. "Not much to describe. He hid his face under a hood. Something like a walking stick with him, too, not that he seemed to need it. Didn't exactly seem threatening; doubt he's with whoever is sacking Robins-Port. Another survivor, perhaps?"

"We must really be getting old," Evan said. "We couldn't even catch an old fart with a cane."

"The girl," Alric said, taking a knee by her side, "she's covered in blood, but I don't make out any wounds. Is she hurt?"

Evan took a hesitant breath, absent of his typical witty demeanor. "Yes and no."

"What happened?" Merrick asked as Seroes joined them by the girl.

The two men looked to one another, as if not sure what they should say, and then back to the group. Alric could tell it was bad news.

"Out with it," Alric snapped with impatience. There was no time for this; they had to leave. Soon.

"Like I said," Seroes began, "we heard a scream. When we lifted the door, we saw the girl inside with a man. We killed him."

"What do you mean, *with a man?*' What does that mean?" Merrick encouraged, his voice getting dangerously loud.

There was a pause, which was cut short by Seroes. "She was … attacked. Violated."

"You don't mean—"

"The fucker was raping her," Evan spit out. "He raped her, so we cut his throat and left him for the worms."

Silence fell over the group as the words weighed in the air.

First raiders, then murderers, now rapists? What the bloody hell is going on in Robins-Port?

Alric studied the bloodied girl. *Not more than fifteen summers old.* He looked at her bare legs, crusted with dried blood. Her dress was torn to ribbons in some areas, and he could see dark purple rings wrapped around her wrists and throat. A rage boiled in Alric's stomach.

"When we dragged her out of the hole, she was in shock," Evan continued. "We couldn't even get a name out of her. Passed out soon after that."

Alric turned toward the surviving boy. "Do you know her?"

At first, he didn't think the boy would respond, but a moment later, the boy turned his head and stared at the girl. Alric could see realization in his eyes as he nodded.

"What's her name?"

"Sarah," the boy said softly. "Her name is Sarah."

Alric looked at Sarah, so young and beautiful, but now robbed of her very soul.

People talked about fates worse than death. Alric knew this was one of them. *Once she wakes up, she'll never be the same again.*

Another twig snapped in the dark.

"What's the flavor?" Alric asked the dark.

"Sweet and tangy, with a few hints of bitter."

A few? Three more survivors.

Their code was simple. Bitter represented a threat, whereas sweet represented friendly. If both were called out, they nullified each other, which usually meant it was only the brotherhood returning. If the answer was sweet, followed by a numerical code, it meant that they had brought someone back with them.

Alric watched as Baron and Garth entered the camp. Trailing behind them were three strangers, one of them limping heavily with a hand pressed to his side, his hand covered in blood.

"We've got a wounded man," Baron announced quietly.

Not a minute later, Seroes had his pack in hand and was inspecting the wounds of a short, burly man holding a giant axe.

Baron shot Alric a glance as he walked by, nodding over his shoulder toward the men behind him. Alric, taking the hint, walked over and looked at the other survivors.

One was a tall, brawny man with a large sword strapped to his back. The shadow of his muscles flexed in the moonlight, and it was obvious he was tense.

Wouldn't you be a bit tense if you stepped out your doorstep to find your entire village butchered like animals and put to the flame?

Alric couldn't blame the man. He knew all too well how drastic your life could change in a matter of moments. These people would know it, too, soon enough.

Next to him was a boy who looked to be around the same age as the first one they'd found, but clearly in better shape. A sword hung at his side, and recently used, by the looks of it.

They'd found three people who knew how to fight. This could be a good thing, or a very bad thing, depending on how well their conversation went.

"What's your name?" Alric asked, approaching the tallest of the trio.

The man shifted his stance into one that Alric recognized all too well. He'd been taught many times about how to look calm but stay ready for a fight, and that's what this man was doing. This was no stranger to combat.

"I'm Dodge. This is my nephew, Trevor. The short one's Tom."

"Oh, fuck off, will ya?" the man named Tom growled at Seroes, who was trying to place a bandage on his wound. "I ain't no babe. Hand it here, and I'll do it."

"My name's Alric," he announced. "Dodge, I can already see you don't trust us, and that's fine. But we're heading out as soon as your man is patched up. You're welcome to come with, if you want. Might be safer for us all. Are any of you two wounded?"

Dodge rolled back his shoulders, giving him an extra three inches in height. "No offense, Alric, but when my man over there is ready, we're going to put ourselves far away from this town, and not in the same direction as you."

"Right." Alric nodded. *Dammit, Al, stop making it look like you're prying. Just do what Benny always does. Stay calm, and they will be calm.* "Where would you be going?" Alric regretted the question immediately after it left his mouth.

"And why would I tell you that? Better yet"—Dodge took a small step toward Alric, angling his body so he could easily grab the sword off his back—"why the fuck do you wanna know?"

This is why you leave the talking to Benny.

Before he knew it, Garth was in front of Dodge with matching hostility. "In case you didn't notice, we just saved your asses back there. So how about you show a little fucking respect?"

Dodge was reaching for his sword, followed by the young one standing beside him, when Benny placed himself between Garth and the brute.

"Hold on, now," Benny urged with a cautious hand on Garth. "If they want to leave, then they can leave. We helped them, not kidnapped them." Benny turned to Dodge, stepping in front of Garth and showing his palms for peace. "Apologies, sir. We haven't fully introduced ourselves. My name is Benjamin, but feel free to call me Benny."

Alric felt his impatience building up again. *Every second we waste here, adds to the possibility of being discovered.* However, Benny seemed to keep enough peace between Garth and Dodge for now, and the faster they could all get on the same page, the faster they could leave.

Benny cleared his throat. "The hot head you met here is Garth, and you've also met Baron."

Baron nodded beneath his hood.

"This here is Alric. Please excuse his uneasy questions. I can assure you his intentions are pure. Merrick, the man you see behind me, is one of our scouts, Garth's brother. The bald guy patching up your friend there goes by Seroes, our medic."

Seroes sighed. "I really wish you'd find a better way of introducing me to strangers."

"And ain't nobody patching me up, *Benny*," Tom said defensively.

"And the one there," Benny continued, pointing toward Evan who stood with his arms crossed at a distance, "is Evan. I apologize in advance on his behalf, he's got a quick tongue on him.

"We are the brotherhood." Benny gestured to the group around them. "And we are here to help you."

Alric could see Dodge studying everyone as Benny introduced them, but it was at the mention of their name when he noticed something change in Dodge's stance.

Dodge took his hand away from his sword. "I thought the brotherhood didn't have a leader?" he asked Benny.

Benny returned a small smile and nodded. "We don't. I can see you've heard of us. And if that is true, you know that we mean you no harm. We only seek to help."

"I guess we can agree on that last bit," Dodge said. "But just because we've met doesn't mean I trust you. The name of a group of strangers can only go so far, even if it is the brotherhood."

"And we expect nothing else from you right now." Within a few moments of Benny's silver tongue, everyone seemed to be at ease with each other.

Alric didn't know how he did it, but Benny could charm people as well as he could fight.

Trevor stepped out from behind Dodge and looked at Alric, speaking for the first time since they'd gotten there. "Where's the other one?"

"What?" Alric responded, not quite sure how to answer.

"Your man said you had a survivor here," Dodge finished for him.

Benny stepped aside and gestured to the remaining survivors.

"No," Trevor gasped. He shoved himself through the crowd before him and rushed to the side of the girl named Sarah. He knelt there, reaching out with his hands but not quite touching her. "Is she …?"

"She just fainted," Benny reassured Trevor. "She'll wake, but only when her body is ready."

"Fainted?" Trevor mumbled to himself. "But she's covered in blood. How can she be alive? What—"

"Trevor," the second boy mumbled from the side. "Is that Trevor?"

When Trevor looked to the other boy, there was a moment's silence. Then, without warning, his hands were shaking, and he reached for his sword.

"No." He pulled the blade free, rage distorting his face as he walked toward the other surviving boy. "*No!* No fucking way! In what world do you deserve to live and she deserves to die?" He raised his sword high, drawing back with murderous intent.

In that moment, everybody moved. Dodge shoved past Benny and Alric, reaching out toward Trevor, but Alric knew he would never make it in time.

The boy that Trevor screamed at held his hands before his face, hoping his bare hands would stop the edge of Trevor's blade.

Seroes and Tom were only looking toward the commotion, a wide stare in their eyes. Merrick and Garth made quick to their bows, reaching for an arrow to nock, just in case.

Out of all the people, it was Evan who stopped Trevor from striking down the cowering boy. He reached out and grabbed Trevor's wrist tightly, bringing the blade down at the boy's side and turning him around.

"Look," Evan said, pulling Trevor close to his face and pointing at Sarah on the ground. "Look closely at her chest. Do you see?"

Trevor panted with wild eyes, struggling to gain back his sword, but Evan kept a firm grip on the pommel.

"I said *look at her*," Evan urged. "She's still breathing, which means she's alive."

Dodge was there now, a hand on Trevor's shoulder and mumbling in his ear. What he was saying was out of earshot for Alric, but whatever was being said seemed to set the boy at ease.

They all looked at Sarah for that moment. Even in the dark, they could see the rise and fall of her chest as she breathed.

"She's just fainted, like we said," Evan stated. "This boy had nothing to do with that."

Seeing the calm in Trevor's eyes, Evan released the pommel of the sword.

Instead of turning to the boy and striking him through, Trevor sheathed it at his side and knelt down next to Sarah, as if his outburst didn't matter.

"You know them?" Alric asked Dodge, who now walked back to Alric and Benny, leaving Trevor kneeling next to Sarah.

He replied with a soft nod. "Yeah."

"Benny, prepare a litter for the girl." Alric looked to the rest of the brotherhood. "We're leaving now."

As everyone began preparing for their departure, Alric took a hesitant step closer to Dodge and spoke softly so only he could hear. "Who's she to Trevor?"

It took a moment for Dodge to speak, but when he finally did, it was in a calm, quiet voice. "They're old friends ... More than friends, you could say."

"And the boy?"

Dodge shook his head, looking off into the distance, toward the weeping survivor they'd first found. "Farthest thing from a friend. What happened?"

"She was found in a tunnel on the western side of town." Alric wanted to choose his words carefully. Then again, how do you explain such a thing? "She's been ... violated," he said, hoping Seroes's choice of words would imply enough.

Dodge scowled at Alric. "Violated?"

Alric nodded in shame. "Raped."

He saw a twinkle of anger in the man's eye. "Those motherfuckers."

As much as Alric wanted to let the information sink, time wasn't exactly on their side.

"Listen. It's clear you can fight, but there's a better chance of surviving this if you stick with us. Tag along for now, and when the girl's better, you can leave. Fair enough?"

There was a moment's silence in which Alric hoped that Dodge could see past his anger toward reason.

"Fair enough," Dodge answered. "But don't you tell Trevor about Sarah," he added.

"Right." Alric nodded. "Another thing, if Trevor and the boy—"

"Warren."

"Right, Warren. If they have bad blood between them, I think it's best they keep their distance."

"That'd be a good idea." Dodge nodded. "Is Warren hurt?"

"No, he stumbled on our path just in time to be saved. He's just … scared. Hasn't said much since we found him."

Dodge only grunted.

"Then it's settled," Alric continued. "We're heading north a few miles. When we set camp, we'll continue this discussion there."

"Sure," Dodge agreed. "You any idea what's going on?"

Alric looked behind him and saw that the girl was lying atop a makeshift litter, the others had their packs strapped and ready to move out.

He rested his hand against the arrow at his side, the one he had pulled off the corpse of the boy earlier. "I have an idea."

But I hope I'm wrong.

Passion

It wasn't the first time that Francis had been shaken awake in the middle of the night, and he was sure that it wouldn't be the last. He longed for a night of solid sleep, yet he was denied that wish once again.

He wiped the crust from his eyes and looked around his room, hoping that the knock at the door was just part of the dream that fluttered away from his memory. His hopes were crushed as the moonlight revealed the face of Vallis looking down at him.

Francis jumped at the sight.

"We have a problem," Vallis said worriedly, face pale and etched with worry in the moonlight.

Francis crawled out of bed, wrapped himself in a thick robe, and rubbed the sleep from his eyes. "What sort of problem?"

Lack of sleep always made it hard for Francis to control his emotions. Vallis knew this better than anyone, since he'd been the usual culprit that denied Francis his rest.

"It seems that our good friend, General Gorman, doesn't exactly trust us," Vallis said plainly.

Francis gave a quick glance at the door, searching the dark for the golden deadbolt near the top, but it was too dark to find.

"I locked it behind me," Vallis assured him after realizing what Francis had been doing. "I still don't understand how it works, but I trust it all the same."

"It's magic," Francis declared with a shrug. "There aren't many left in the world that do understand how it works; we just know it does."

Francis took a seat behind his cluttered desk, lit a candle, and then gestured to the chair across from him.

Just when I think all is well, another problem jumps from the shadows like a mouse to a crumb.

"What do you mean *he doesn't trust us*?" Francis crossed his arms. "I'm not looking for trust, Vallis; I'm looking for understanding. If he understands, he will obey. If he obeys, then we don't have a problem."

"Well ..." Vallis began, fumbling over his words, "you see, he—"

"You told me he wouldn't be a problem, that everything was under control. I thought you and I had an *understanding*, Vallis. Were you lying to me, or have you simply failed?"

Francis shifted uncomfortably. "Yes. No, I mean ... Well—"

"Why don't you just start from the beginning?" Francis cut in impatiently. "We have a rough few days ahead of us, and I'd be content to catch a few more hours of sleep tonight."

"It's about the 'caravans' I dispatched to Robins-Port yesterday." Vallis shifted on his feet as he told his story. "I was in the courtyard, training my men, when I spotted two riders on horseback leaving Servitol. When I talked to the stablemaster, he said the two men simply demanded their horses. They were dressed in garb, but he thought they were soldiers.

"So, I asked some questions and looked around, which eventually led me to find two empty bunks in Gorman's barracks."

Francis could see the red rising in Vallis's neck and cheeks.

"His men felt no shame in telling me that their general sent out two of his best riders to go to Robins-Port and make sure there were no problems with the work orders I dispatched. Apparently, General Gorman feels as if I weren't able to carry out such a simple task."

Francis clenched a fist. "When did they leave?" he snapped.

"Midday yesterday," Vallis answered.

"Midday?" Francis felt his own anger boiling in his chest. "They left at midday, and I'm just now hearing about this?"

Vallis's look of rage was instantly replaced with worry. "I'm sorry. I didn't think to bother you about it before I knew what was actually happening. How was I supposed—"

"Silence!" Francis slammed a fist hard against his desk.

Vallis jumped at the sudden anger then took a cautious step away from Francis.

Usually, Francis was good at holding his anger in check, but timing was everything now, and Francis had no more time to spare.

"Where is Destro?" he growled at Vallis, who was wise enough to avoid his glare.

"In the barracks with his men, I think."

"Do not *think*, Vallis. *Obey*. I am the one who thinks; you are the one who gets it done. Get him. Now!"

Vallis left the room in a hurry without saying a word.

Francis took advantage of the moment's privacy to get fully dressed.

So much for those last few hours of sleep.

By the time Vallis returned with Destro, dressed in a dirty tunic, Francis's office was fully lit with the surrounding candles and he sat in his chair.

"Sit," Francis gestured to the chair across from his desk, in which Destro sluggishly took a seat in. "Tell me, General Destro, what is your mission?"

He looked at Vallis, nodding toward the door. Vallis then slid the golden deadbolt and latched it into its hinge.

This is not a conversation for others to hear.

After rubbing the sleep from his bloodshot eyes, Destro gave a groggy and confused look. "To ensure the safety of—"

"Do you really think that I had you woken in the middle of the night to discuss your loyalty to a false empire?" Call it lack of sleep or the idea of having to put up with people like this for as long as he could remember, but Francis let every ounce of venom fuel his words. "Do I look to be in the mood to play the pretender? No, so I'll ask you again. *Your. Mission.*"

Destro curled his lips back in a snarl. "To gain the favor of General Gorman in our cause."

"And? Have you gained his favor? Does he understand our perspective and wish to join forces?"

"It's too soon to tell. I believe that, with a little more time, I could—"

"Time?" Francis interjected. "You want to speak to me about *time*? No! The answer is no, General. You have not gained his favor, he does not understand our perspective, and he's made it perfectly clear that he suspects something.

"As of midday, General Gorman sent two of his men to Robins-Port to watch over the work orders I've delegated to Vallis. You know, the work orders that I burnt away this last night?"

"Fuck," Destro mumbled, wiping at his face.

"Yes, General Destro, fuck, fuck, *fuck*!" Francis slammed another fist on his oak desk.

Francis had half-expected, hoped even, to see fear in the man's eyes. However, there was only an emotionless stare.

The man has been killing people his entire life. Did you really expect him to budge seeing your temper tantrum? Calm yourself, Francis.

He took a moment to breathe, hoping to calm himself before he did something he'd regret. *No reason to lose yourself like this. Just think of a solution.*

"I'm sure you are well aware of what would happen if Gorman's men report back from Robins-Port when our timing isn't lined up?"

Destro nodded his understanding.

"So, what do we do then?"

For a moment, General Destro just sat and stared at Francis. Finally, he took a deep breath and leaned back in his chair. "Who did he send?"

Francis looked to Vallis, who cleared his throat and approached them.

"I don't have names. They just said they were his best riders."

"Well, I know Gorman's men," Destro said. "If he sent his best riders, it would be Harvey and William, and I saw them an hour before turning in."

"So," Francis said slowly, trying to piece together what Destro was implying, "regardless, he sent men. Does it really matter who—"

"If it wasn't his fastest riders, it means that we can catch them."

Francis wasn't fond of being interrupted, and he'd be lying if he said it didn't irritate him. He remembered an old scroll he'd found in the library about his mentor, written centuries ago. Someone had interrupted him and, in turn, they'd been skewered alive on a pike in front of the entire commanding army. However, times have changed since those dark days.

For now, at least.

"As I've said, they left midday," Vallis reassured his comrade. "They'll be there within the hour."

Destro didn't seem too concerned. "When did you tell Gorman you sent dispatch papers for the caravans?"

"Yesterday morning," Vallis answered curiously, "but I don't see how that matters."

Destro cracked a smile. "That's because you don't understand Gorman. He may be stubborn at times, but he knows what he's doing. If he wanted his men to arrive before our courier, he'd have sent Harvey and William before you sent the papers at all. Whoever he did send will be taking their time. Might be that he didn't mistrust you at all, only wanted to see it done properly. Gorman's good like that."

"Perhaps." Francis steepled two fingers under his chin. "Still, you see the problem at hand, considering the events we've set in motion? If they find out about Robins-Port, things could get complicated."

Destro nodded softly. "Sure. But if he meant for the riders to take their time, they'd probably stop for rest; water their horses, fill their bellies, such and such."

"Which means we can catch them," Francis declared with relief.

"Exactly." Destro nodded. "I could send a few riders to track them down."

"I admire your confidence, General, but what you are asking is to send Navalethian soldiers to track down and kill a pair of Navalethian soldiers."

"We could declare Gorman's soldiers as traitors?" Vallis suggested.

"*Traitors*?" Destro chuckled, a low rumble Francis rarely heard from the man. "In Gorman's crew? Not likely anyone would believe that. He's earned too much respect from his crew to have any traitors. Even if he didn't suspect something before, he sure as hell would the moment you declare his men traitors."

"Then, what do you suggest, General?" Francis asked, sure he already knew the answer.

If Destro tried to hide his bewildered look, it was one of the few skills he didn't possess. "Exactly what I just said. We send a couple of my men, track them, kill them."

Vallis leaned closer to Destro's face. "Are you fucking daft?" he said quietly. "Did you not just hear what—"

In one moment, Destro was sitting calmly in the chair across from Francis, leaning back casually as he promoted his plan. In the next, he was nose-to-nose with Vallis, towering over him like a mountain shadowing a valley.

"Are you doubting my men? *You*? Doubting *my* men? Let me tell you something, *boy*; while you've been sitting here, scheming your way up the chain of command, Gorman and I stood side by side, staring death in the face more times than I can count, and each time, we've welcomed it with open arms." Destro demonstrated by spreading his arms out to his sides.

Destro's voice escalated as he continued, "Side by side, we've cut through our enemies. I've seen Gorman plow through scores of men and not bear a scratch. There hasn't been a single charge we didn't lead, or a single battle that we weren't willing to die for." Destro leaned closer to Vallis, his teeth bared like a wild animal, a predator setting on its prey. "While you've been sitting here, behind these walls, reading your books about warfare, *we were fucking living it!*"

Destro began moving toward Vallis, pushing the man closer and closer to the wall as he continued his raging rant. "You have no idea what bond can come from that. You have no idea what it truly means to be a brother to someone, to know you'd willingly give your own life to save theirs. So, if there is one thing I can guarantee, *boy*, it's that you haven't earned the right to doubt what real soldiers can and will do when they believe in something.

"You've grown up a schemer, and you do it well. But Gorman and I grew up in warfare, and there's none better than us when it comes to a mission."

Vallis was pressed against Francis's bookshelf, cowering before Destro's menacing glare.

Destro had always been quick to temper, but never once had Francis seen a flare of anger this pure.

In that moment, Francis took pity on any who had found themselves on the wrong edge of Destro's blade. However, there was something else beyond the anger that Francis couldn't help but admire—passion.

Francis knew that there was nothing more dangerous than passion. He would have to handle this situation a little more delicately. He already had a problem to fix, and he didn't want to add Destro to that particular list.

"General," Francis started while still searching for the right words, "I ... It seems this night is not kind to any of us. You know your work is well appreciated, not only to us but to your king. Your *true* king. However, I'm not sure this helps."

Francis wasn't sure if the man had even heard him. He stood with clenched fists, staring at Vallis as if he were staring down an enemy.

"The point is," Destro finally said, eyes still burning at Vallis, "when you build a bond with someone, it can't be broken. Not that type of bond, not ever. My men aren't loyal to me because of the title I bear, but because of what I've done to earn it. They trust my judgment more than their own. Not once have I lied to my men, and not once will I ever. There is no need to declare them traitors."

Francis searched Destro's eyes. "And do you trust him?"

For the first time since the outburst, Destro looked at Francis. "Gorman? With my life."

Francis pondered his options, only to soon realize that he didn't have any alternatives. *If we don't work with each other now, then these last ten years would all be for nothing.*

"I trust you, General. *We* trust you," he added, nodding toward Vallis, who stood silently in the corner of the room as if expecting Destro to attack at any moment. "See that it is done."

Destro said nothing. Instead, he took one last glance at Vallis before making his way toward the door. He slid aside the golden deadbolt and rested his hand on the door handle, standing tall and facing the both of them, passion burning in his eyes.

"I'm on your side, Father Balorian, but don't think I'm stupid. Don't think I don't see how convenient General Orlington's death was for Vallis here. The truth is that I honestly never liked the Orlington." Destro paused and looked to Vallis, then back at Francis before stating his last heavy words. "That's the only reason why you are both still breathing."

Francis sat frozen in his chair. Although he was clearly being threatened, he couldn't help admiring Destro's audacity.

"It's like I said," Destro continued. "A bond between brothers never breaks. Gorman and I *have* served together, and for a long time. He's saved my life more times than you can imagine, and I him. We've done things that you wouldn't be able to stomach, problems we've had to work through together. He's my best friend in this entire world.

"Remember, Father, that I am on your side. But also remember that, if anything *unexpected* happens to General Gorman, like what happened with Orlington, no power of any kind will be able to stop me from finding you. No demon, no army, no god would be able to protect you from me. If something happens to my friend, I'll fucking kill the both of you."

Silence passed for a moment, and Francis couldn't help smiling.

Passion. Both beautiful and deadly.

Not waiting for a reply, Destro left Francis and Vallis, his final words floating in the air.

As the silence buzzed in his ears, Francis realized that Destro could be as powerful an enemy as he was an ally.

I'll have to remember that.

Memories of the Past

The world was different from the moment she opened her eyes. The breeze against her face, the lighting casting through the trees, the beautiful melody of nature that blew with the wind. She'd seen it her entire life, but as she noticed these things now, it all felt numb.

She first woke in a daze. She was being carried on a thin blanket by four shadowed figures. She lay still, trying to remember where she was. However, thinking hurt her head, so she decided to focus on what she could sense— large branches of trees passed above her, the sound of heavy breathing by the people surrounding her, and the throbbing ache between her thighs.

She didn't know where she was, who was carrying her, or why she was being carried in the first place.

And she didn't care.

Nothing felt real to her. It was like realizing you were dreaming. You wanted to enjoy it, but you also knew that it was a fabricated world, much like the one Sarah had just woken up to. The world around her felt unreal and mysterious.

"*What happened?*" she tried to say, but the only sound that came out of her mouth was a dry croak. The effort alone was too much to bear.

A surge of pain shot from her thighs up into her chest, her head in a sea of confusion, the peripherals of her vision closing in on her while a pitched tone zinged in her head.

It was easier to close her eyes, so she did, and soon, she was back to sleep.

The rest of the night was spent in a blurred haze, and Sarah was no longer sure what was a dream or reality. One moment, she was staring up at the stars, watching the trails of their white lights pass by. She could tell she was in the woods—sticks snapped underneath her, owls cooed, and bugs whistled to life around her.

She watched, content in the look of the distant stars above her. Then her vision swam and shifted before her, and instead of being in the woods, she was standing in the middle of a wide, dark, ominous cavern.

Vines and vegetation broke through cracks in the walls around her, stretching across the floor and ceiling. The cold, damp air made her skin feel clammy, and there was a distinct smell of wet that hung in the air. At the opposite side of the cavern, facing directly before her, was a statue of a throne of fractured stone. In it sat a tall, hooded figure, its shoulders massive and wide. She suddenly felt a moment of judgment as the figure stared down upon her, a giant overlooking an ant. Her gut told her that she should be afraid of it, that she should turn and flee, there and then. She made to do so when something else caught her eye.

The cavern wall behind the stone figure morphed and changed before her eyes, vibrant colors materializing from nothing, framing itself against the wall opposite her. When she realized what she was looking at, she moved past the statue, her hair standing on end the entire time. Eventually, she stood in front of a painting.

A mural of chaos, depicting a village consumed in fire and death.

There was blood everywhere. Bodies decorated the streets in mangled piles. Figures dressed in black armor were busy cutting down and murdering men, women, and children.

Sarah scanned the painting, the weight in her gut sinking farther into a vast chasm of sorrow, when she was struck cold of her discovery.

The detailed depiction of the massacre was one thing, but the figure, someone dressed in a dark hood with their arms spread wide, welcoming the slaughter, stopped her cold.

They held a large sword in one hand, blood of the villagers still dripping from its sharp point. Although the figure's face was hard to see clearly, Sarah had the overwhelming suspicion that it took pleasure in the massacre, that it was smiling beneath the hood.

The longer she looked at the mural, the more alive it felt. She now heard the distant screams of slaughtered victims, felt the heat of the fire against her face, even smelled the burning bodies that poisoned the air.

The hooded figure let its arms drop to its sides and began to walk toward Sarah. Bigger and bigger the figure became, swelling as it moved closer and closer, malevolence radiating from its aura.

The sound of footsteps on gravel became louder as the figure swelled to the size of half the painting, leaving the village farther behind as it became the sole remaining thing.

Sarah stood, frozen in fear at seeing the hooded figure before her, large enough now in the painting where she could be looking in a mirror. The cavern around her was silent now, her breathing nearly too loud to bear. She stared into the black of the figure's face, the crushing sense of sorrow digging into her very soul.

A hand reached out of the painting in a flash, squeezing around her throat tightly.

She pushed against the cavern walls as the figure in the painting began pulling her forward. She resisted as much as she could, now setting a firm foot against the wall as she tried her best to pull away.

She watched as two red eyes materialized in the shadow of the figure's hood; white, jagged teeth spreading into a malicious smile. That wasn't the worst part, though. No, the worst part for Sarah was the distant laugh she could hear coming from the figure before her.

She squeezed her eyes tightly, gripping at the cold hand strangling her while simultaneously using her foot as leverage to pry herself away. Just when she felt the last of her strength drain away, the hand around her neck disappeared as she launched herself backward, tumbling over herself and landing on her back.

Staring down at her was a woman with long, blonde hair. Her face was flawless in every detail, from the point of her chin to the angle of her cheeks. Sarah was about to scream when the woman spoke to her.

"Lead the haunted wolf to the beginning of time, where you will read the first scripture at the edge of the world. Seek counsel from the sonless father, and accept the creation of the ultimate gift from the fatherless son. At the world's rebirth, a decision will be made." Her voice was as gentle as her features, but Sarah could sense a feeling of power from the woman.

Sarah had no idea what the words meant, so she perked up the courage to ask, "What decision will be made?"

The woman above her gave a sad smile. "To forsake the creators, or forsake the world."

Sarah tried to speak, but her mouth refused to move.

The figure above her began to glow, a blinding light expanding from her chest as a warmth blanketed Sarah.

Then everything went black.

***

Sarah opened her eyes to realize she was propped up against a tree, early morning light nearly blinding her as she rubbed her face. She still felt weak as she glanced about in bewilderment, taking in her surroundings, trying to understand what was happening.

I feel so ... heavy.

There were several people before her, huddled around a small fire; some, she recognized, though most, she didn't. She could see Tom the blacksmith tossing a small log into the pit as the strangers were skinning a squirrel. The more she looked at Tom, the more she realized he didn't look like he usually did.

Normally, he was covered in black dirt and grime that caked his body after working in the smithy, but there was something else there. He looked pale, tired, and there was a white bandage wrapped around his waist with a large red spot at the side of his leg.

She glanced around the campsite, trying to remember how she had gotten there, when she found another pair of eyes locking with hers.

Across the tall grass, leaning against another tree, sat Warren Robinson with his knees bent to his chest.

What a strange feeling. While she hated Warren, she couldn't sum up any feelings toward seeing him at that moment. She remembered him and his bullying goon squad picking on her and Trevor, and she knew that she should feel outraged at the sight of him, but that wasn't the case. She felt nothing.

"You're awake."

She looked away from Warren and snapped toward the sudden voice. She couldn't believe she hadn't noticed him before since he was so close to her.

Trevor's face was stained with black dirt and splattered mud.

No, not mud. Mud doesn't have a red glimmer to it.

She should have been glad to see him. She should have wrapped her arms around his neck and squeezed him and never let go, but she felt too exhausted to do much of anything besides look around. Besides, he was probably still mad at her.

"What do you mean?" she asked, forcing her voice through her dry throat.

"You've been asleep since they found you." Trevor nodded toward the men around the fire. "I was really—"

"Is that ... blood?" Feeling strength return to her body, she reached out a hand and cupped Trevor's cheek.

135

He looked taken aback, and then he furrowed his eyebrows at her. He scraped the side of his face with his nails, peeling a small part of the crust away from his face and rubbed it between two fingers.

"Yeah," he mumbled almost to himself. "It might be."

Behind the numb of her body, Sarah felt a panic build in her stomach and gasped. "My gods, Trevor, why are you covered in blood? Are you okay?" She looked back toward Warren across the opening. "Did *he* do that?"

Trevor looked at her in answer, tears building in his eyes.

Only then did she really look at Trevor. The dark bags under his eyes, the dirt and blood covering his entire body, and the sword hanging from a belt at his side. Not only were his hands shaking, but his entire body was trembling.

"Sarah," he said quietly, "do you remember what happened yesterday?"

She thought to herself for a moment then pressed an awkward finger to her lips when she realized what Trevor was getting at. "You're referring to our fight?"

A tear ran down the side of his face, and he wiped it away quickly, shaking his head as he sniffled. "No. I'm not talking about our fight. That doesn't matter anymore."

They both heard footsteps approaching and both turned to see Dodge looking down at Sarah. She wasn't sure what was more puzzling—the sword strapped over his back or the two strangers at his sides. Like Trevor, Sarah could see dried blood on Dodge's clothes.

One of the strangers wore a dark tunic with gloves, a sword dangling from a strap at his side. His dark, shoulder-length hair was plastered to the side of his face with sweat, and his brown eyes looked empty.

The second stranger stood with his hands folded in front of himself, also wearing leather gloves. Unlike the other man, this one was smiling, as if happy to see Sarah.

Why is everyone looking at me as if I've grown an extra head? And why the bloody hell is everyone wearing a sword?

Dodge knelt and spoke quietly. "Sarah, this here is Alric and Benny. They're … *friends* of mine," he assured hesitantly, as if he didn't believe it himself. "They have some questions for you. You think you're up for that?"

Sarah nodded, puzzled at the question. "Why wouldn't I be?"

There was a silence as Dodge looked into her eyes.

Although Dodge had always been a large man, Sarah had always known him as a gentle giant. But she didn't see that man before her now. This man was stern, yet he looked drained, tired, and unexpectedly guilty of something.

"We are just curious as to how all this has come about," said the man called Benny. "Could you help us with that?"

"What do you mean? Help with what?"

A look of sadness glazed over Dodge's eyes. He glanced at Trevor and shook his head before looking away.

Trevor sniffled and wiped more tears from his face as he stood with the others. "She doesn't remember," Trevor told them all.

There was a long pause as they all stared at her.

She didn't like it. She tried to stand but found her legs too stiff to do it on her own.

Trevor rushed forward to grab her arm and help Sarah to her feet.

It took her a moment for the world to stop spinning, which was strange. Once her vision was clear, she looked at Trevor. "Remember what? What are you going on about?"

He just stood there, mouth gaping as he searched for the right words.

It was the man named Benny who finished for him. "The attack, my dear. Do you remember the attack?"

Sarah thought for a moment, looking beyond the men and toward Warren sitting against a tree across the camp. "Oh! You mean Warren? Just his usual shit. I don't see what that—"

"Sarah, he's not talking about Warren and Trevor," Dodge said, putting a gentle hand on her shoulder. "He's talking about the attack on Robins-Port … Do you remember anything about that?"

"There was an attack at Robins-Port?" Fear sparked like a flame in Sarah's gut.

If there was an attack at home, then my family might be hurt. We have to—

Gods, I really wish they'd stop staring at me like that!

"The looks are getting really annoying really fast, gentlemen."

The stranger, Benny, gave Alric a stern look. Alric returned it with a shake of his head.

"We have to," Benny said flatly.

"Look at her," Alric argued. "She's still in shock, probably still suffering from the loss of blood, and you want her to get thrown right back into it again?"

Dodge was now on his feet, facing the others. "What are you two talking about?"

Both ignored Dodge's question, staring at each other, as if having a discussion without saying words. Alric then looked from Dodge to Sarah, then to Trevor, then back to Benny. "We can figure it out some other way. Do the other one."

"I already did," Benny answered. "He can't move on past his family."

Alric raised a gesturing hand to Sarah. "And you think she'll be any better? No, I'm sure we can figure it out another way."

"I'm sure we can, but nothing is more reliable than what someone remembers," Benny backfired. "We can theorize all we want, or we can return to Servitol with something more solid that theories."

"And you plan on telling them how you got this *solid* information of yours?"

"I won't need to. Sarah will be able to help us with that. Her, Trevor, Dodge, Tom, and Warren. One interview with them will be enough, but it's up to us to figure out this dark puzzle."

Sarah didn't know who these people were, what in the hells they were talking about, why Alric was protecting her, or even what the hell he was protecting her from.

Alric looked back down at her. "No," he settled without taking his eyes from her. "She can't handle it."

Benny let out a long breath. "Unfortunately, old friend, that's not up for you to decide."

"So that leaves it up to you?"

"We can't leave this decision up to anyone. We *must* know what happened. We have to be strong here."

"Will somebody start making some fucking sense?" Tom asked as the rest of the group joined them. "What do you mean to do?"

"I mean," Benny said slowly, not taking his eyes off Alric, "that I know a way to help her remember."

Tom shrugged. "Would that even be a good idea? Seems your man here doesn't agree with you."

"Right," Dodge added cautiously. "What's the catch? If he's opposed to it, why shouldn't we be?"

Everyone looked to Alric, who in return stared furiously back at Benny.

Dodge's question hung in the air, nobody wanting to answer.

"Your call," Alric said flatly as he walked away and toward the fire.

Benny looked at the ground.

For someone who just won an argument, he sure does look defeated.

After a moment, he walked to Sarah and stood before her. "Sarah," Benny said, holding out his hands. "I know you're confused, but we need to know what happened. It could save lives, Sarah. Prevent anything like this ever happening again. I just need you to trust me."

"What is this?" Trevor asked worriedly. "What are you doing? Get away from her!"

"I'm going to help her remember," Benny answered from over his shoulder without breaking eye contact with Sarah. "I need everyone here to trust me."

"And how exactly is this going to help her remember?" Tom asked.

"It's …" For a moment, Benny looked unsure as he removed his gloves, rubbing at his pale hands. "Well, it's an old trick. Something I can't explain; better off just showing."

"There's a term for that," a man from the back said from the fire. "Hocus-pocus, I believe it's called?"

Benny rolled his eyes. "You're not helping, Evan."

The man named Evan shrugged. "Just figured you should be honest with them, at least."

"Why?" Sarah asked, fear suddenly wrapping around her throat. "I don't understand." She looked to Dodge, who seemed to share the same thought but remained silent. Eventually, he crossed his arms and nodded to her.

"Sarah," Benny brought her attention back to him, "I may be able to help you. I just need you to take my hand. I'll guide you through the rest after that."

Her fingers trembled when she lifted it, hesitating before squeezing Benny's callused hand. The only reassurance Sarah felt was approval from Dodge, knowing that he'd never endanger her.

"Close your eyes, dear," Benny told her, and she did. "Now, think back to the last thing you remember. Imagine it. Draw it in your mind."

"I was … sitting with—"

"With your mind, dear," Benny reminded her. "You don't need to use your words; just your mind."

Sarah pictured the broken wall that she and Trevor had sat on the day before. She thought about the chocolate they shared and the stories they told each other after catching up from not seeing each other in so long.

"Great," she heard an echo in her head. "You're doing great. What happened next?"

One moment, she was thinking of the encounter, and the next, she was seeing it. She stood to the side as she and Trevor sat before her on the broken wall in Robins-Port. Sarah had just told him the news of her betrothal; she could tell by the hurt look on Trevor's face.

It was strange. She wasn't just remembering the moment, but actually reliving it from the outside, an observer overlooking the scene.

Her vision flashed, and then she was standing in the street, standing among a crowd, as Warren straddled Trevor on the ground. She saw herself screaming, yelling at Warren to get off, but not actually moving in to help.

Beyond her muffled screams, she could hear Warren's antagonizing voice. "Don't mistake their pity for love, Trevor. They could never love you."

"*Don't listen to him!*" Sarah screamed, but her voice was a wasted effort in this dreamworld. "*He's lying. Don't listen to him, Trevor!*" But nobody heard her. Her voice echoed off into the distance as she, and the rest of the town, simply stood by and watched.

The memory blurred, and then she saw herself standing with Trevor in the middle of the street. His face was red with anger while she cried. He pointed an accusing finger at her chest.

"Fuck you, Sarah! I wish you'd never come back at all." He stormed off toward home.

For a split moment, she wanted to run after him. Turn him about and plant an enormous kiss on his soft lips like she'd wanted to during that first moment of seeing him at Tom's smithy.

"*Do something, you idiot!*" she yelled at the Sarah in front of her. "*Run after him!*"

She didn't move a muscle. She just stood there, watching as her closest friend left her in the dust before turning about and making her way home.

The world shook, and then she was no longer in the street, but in her parents' bedroom. There was a loud bang on the door, and she could hear her father screaming. She watched as her mother grabbed the other Sarah by her shoulders.

"When you get there, hand that letter to the king. You are under no circumstances to give that letter to anyone else."

Mother? When was this? I don't remember this ...

New memories unfolded in Sarah's mind faster than she could keep up. She watched as she was shoved into a dark hole, her mother sobbing goodbye, the shuddering *thud* on the floorboards above her when her mother's scream was cut short. All of it unfolded before her, like watching a play but also being part of the show. She remembered hearing the voices above her head.

"She's quite pretty, sir. Just wanted to have a bit of fun."

"We are not here to have fun. You have your orders, soldier. No survivors. Now cut her throat and add her to the fire. She'll burn nicely, just like the others."

She remembered crawling in the darkness, feeling as if the walls were closing in on her. The feeling of being lost and forgotten forever. She carried a crumpled note in her hand, her mother's voice echoing in her head. *"Follow the road to the next town and find transportation to the capital. When you get there, hand that letter to the king."*

A large hand wrapped around her foot, and she was dragged away, deeper into the darkness.

"Here, little piggy," she heard a voice call.

She wasn't only watching now but reliving the memory. She felt a great pressure on her chest, her arms being pinned above her head, the sour smell of liquor as her throat clenched shut.

"I much like it when they put up a fight."

There was a barrier there, pressing against her mind as she fought against it. She felt it rebelling, forcing her forward into her own memories, trying to move her forward as she fought with everything she had to move back.

"No," the distant voice said. *"I don't understand. How is she ...?"*

The mental barrier she fought against shattered in her mind, the walls of her memories falling away like grains of sand through endless time. They shifted into fog, evaporating in transparent colors, as another image morphed before her.

She now stood before an army of men, a long line of soldiers who stood chest high in a trench. A valley spread out before her, the warm sunlight gleaming down on the forest green grass. Upon the horizon, there was a dark blur growing on top of a large hill.

She looked to the two men closest to her. One's hair was shaved close to his scalp where the other's black hair was tied in a ponytail. Both looked vaguely familiar.

"Well, can't say it lives up to the songs," the shaved headed one yelled to the

other. *"They never do mention how you want to shit yourself scared."*

"Tell me again why we do this," the other replied. Then they laughed, gripping tightly in an embrace before turning toward the hill where an approaching army was running at them.

The soldiers in the trench drew their weapons, waving them high in the air as they roared a battle cry that shook the earth.

She looked out toward the rushing army, but the valley was now vacant. The soldiers around her disappeared. She was alone.

All was still, as silent as the grave, besides the faint voice in the air.

"Sarah, come back to me," the distant voice called to her. *"You must come back to us* now."

She looked about in search of the voice. She spun around, watching as the world around her slowly began to mist away.

Suddenly, she was standing on a large mountain overlooking a valley of rolling hills and a large village off in the distance. Pillars of black smoke swirled through the sky as she realized the village was on fire.

"Sarah!" a familiar voice cried to her, more distant than before.

The echoing sounds from the village below traveled through the air. She could hear people screaming, begging for their lives. The sounds of metal clashing, monsters roaring, men crying, houses burning rang through the air. Beneath it all was the most terrible sound she could make out. Behind all the screams, beyond the burning and fighting, was laughter.

"Come back, Sarah!" She heard a voice surrounding her, this one different than the first. *"What are you doing to her? She's not breathing!"*

The sounds grew louder and louder as she searched for the voice. Then, suddenly, all sound ceased entirely, leaving the dreamlike world as quiet as the dead.

When she turned around, she shrunk back in horror.

A person stood before her, towering above her. They wore a dark robe that hid the face beneath a shadow. They held a crimson blade at their side, blood dripping from its point.

She felt cold all of a sudden, a frigid chill creeping up her legs, past her thighs, onto her waist, over her breasts, and wrapping tightly around her throat. Suddenly, she couldn't move.

The figure breathed out, breath misting the air in a small cloud, emanating the smell of rot and decay.

"*You will fail*," said the deep, rumbling voice, like gravel sliding down a mountainside. "*You cannot stop me. I am eternal.*"

The valley behind the figure began to shift, morphing from a green scenery to a picture of carnage. The orange glow of the setting sun cast a glare onto a battlefield. No, not a battlefield.

A slaughter.

Nothing else could describe it. Bodies littered their way to the limits of the horizon, blood trailing from one carcass to the next. Countless crows circled above in the sky, cawing out to their brethren about the fine meal they'd discovered. Sarah saw heads skewered on pikes, bodies of children butchered into pieces, piles of dismembered cadavers set on fire.

She couldn't see the figure's face beneath the hood, but she could sense it was smiling at her. It lifted an arm and pointed at her.

The cold grasp around her body began to take shape and bend, hovering her off the ground. Then the force began to press at her, bending her backward like a leaf in the wind. Excruciating pain tensed through every muscle in her body as she began to stretch and bend unnaturally back, muscles tearing and bones popping out of place.

The last thing Sarah heard was the deep, grumbling laughter coming from her murderer.

Pieces to a Dark Puzzle

For a few passing moments, Trevor did nothing. An overwhelming dread dawned on him as he looked at Sarah's unconscious body that lay slack against the trunk of a tree.

The rest of them remained in a circle, while Trevor, Dodge, and Tom hovered over Sarah, unsure of what just happened or what else to do.

Dodge reached slowly toward her, cupping her cheek in his hand. "She's warm, and she's breathing." He stood up and turned to face the others, Benny specifically, who was being helped to his feet by Alric. The man was pale and dripping sweat, struggling to catch his breath, like he'd just run for miles.

"What the fuck did you do?" Dodge growled, the threat of violence clear in his tone.

"I did …" he said between breaths, "what had … to be … done."

It wasn't a good enough answer for Trevor. He wasn't sure what he'd done to Sarah, but it was clear it had brought her an immense amount of pain.

Trevor pushed past Dodge in a flash, strode up to Benny, and punched him in the face. He roared in rage as Benny fell to the ground. "*What had to be done*? You nearly fucking killed her!"

Alric looked down at Benny, a mixture of shock and approval on his face.

Trevor expected Alric to jump in Benny's defense; instead, Alric shrugged. "I tried to tell you."

The others in the brotherhood, however, were ready in a flash. Steel was drawn, arrows were nocked, and voices were shouting. All was in chaos, all besides Warren, who still sat by a tree at a distance; Sarah, who lay unconscious behind him; and Benny, who was still recovering from whatever it was he had done to Sarah.

Before anything could go further, Benny jumped to his feet and lifted his hands into the air. "It's fine!" he shouted over the uproar, trying to restrain his comrades from attacking them. "Put them away. I said it's fine!"

Let them come.

Trevor reached to his hip when someone grabbed his wrist. He sneered to his right, his eyes set on Dodge, who shook his head.

Tom came up at Trevor's other side. "Hold fast, lad," he whispered to Trevor. "Last thing we need is to be crossing swords with this lot. Won't end well for us, or for her."

Dodge reassured Trevor of Tom's wisdom with the look in his eyes, pleading with Trevor to calm himself before doing something stupid, like starting a fight against seven strangers who could clearly kill them without breaking a sweat.

As Benny paced back and forth in front of the others, the two archers eventually lowered their bows, the man with the two axes relaxed his shoulders, and the uproar of the brotherhood began to quiet down.

Trevor tensed as Benny approached him, Alric standing behind him with his arms crossed.

"I am so sorry," Benny apologized. "That was not how it was supposed to go."

"It never is," Alric said from behind Benny.

Benny responded in turn with a roll of his eyes.

"What happened?" Trevor asked.

"If I'm being honest, I'm not quite sure myself." Benny wiped a small bit of blood from his nose. "But rest assured, Sarah is alive and well. She's a strong one, her. Very strong. But she has been through a lot. She'll need more rest."

Dodge took a deadly step toward Benny. "I know what you are," he growled. "I appreciated your help until now, but if you ever try that again—"

"He won't," Alric said flatly, staring hard at the both Benny and Dodge. "I'll make sure of it."

"And I'm supposed to believe that you'll make sure of it?" Tom spit to the side. "Because you were so keen on changing his mind before he decided to bewitch our lass here."

Bewitch? What does he mean by that?

Alric didn't seem offended with the slight. He shook his head. "I won't have to. We'll gladly let Trevor beat some sense into our old friend here."

Tom tilted his head to the side. "Yeah?"

Alric nodded. "You have my word."

Dodge spit toward Alric. "Word from the Wolf? Not worth shit. Not anymore. There may not be a lot of people left in the world to remember what you've done, but I still remember. I know what blood you have on your hands."

Alric's only response was an apathetic stare.

"If I may?" Evan pushed his way through the crowd. "There is the alternative."

Tom crossed his arms. "And what's that?"

Evan shrugged. "We kill you here and now so we can move on with our lives already."

"Shut up, Evan," Benny and Alric said in unison.

Evan raised his hands defensively. "Just trying to bring some light into the mood, is all. Don't need to get all testy. I was only kidding, of course."

Benny wiped the line of blood still dripping from his nose. A small smile crept across his face. "I admire your passion, Trevor. You hit hard."

"Well"—Alric cleared his throat and shifted on his feet—"did it work?"

Benny nodded. "Yes. Seems like we've a lot to discuss."

"Well, I'm all ears," Tom said as he walked forward. "Because there's a lot of shit going on around here that I don't understand. Why bandits attacked Robins-Port, how you just happened to be there, and then that witch-doctor bullshit of yours."

"It's not witchcraft," Benny replied, irritation clear in his tone.

"And we're no fucking bandits," snarled Merrick, his bow tight in his hands.

"Well," Garth said, looking to his brother, "not anymore, at least."

Merrick responded with a grunt, his eyes never leaving Tom's.

"And neither were the ones who attacked Robins-Port," Benny confirmed.

"That should be obvious to everyone by now," agreed Evan. "Bandits sack caravans, raid small villages under the empire's radar, and always they take something. They don't burn down the kingdom's heart of trade for fun and expect to get away with it. They were too ... too ..." He swirled his hand in the air, searching for the right word.

"Organized," Dodge finished for him, nodding in agreement.

"Right." Evan met Dodge's eyes as he snagged the word from the air. "I knew there was more to you than your looks."

Seroes scratched the side of his bald head. "Bandits tend to make a show of things, too. Gotta leave survivors in order to build a reputation, after all."

"Mercenaries, then?" suggested the hooded man, now tucking his twin hatchets at his beltline.

All silent eyes fell to Alric, who they found staring into the flames of the small fire away from the group. He stood quietly to himself, daydreaming into the flames as the rest of them awaited his verdict. Benny leaned in and nudged his shoulder.

He blinked quickly and looked at everyone, like he'd forgotten they were there. "Might be mercenaries. Might not be. It all depends."

"Depends on what?" Tom inquired.

"On what you saw," Alric said.

"You mean, besides people being dragged out into the street and butchered like fucking animals?" Tom quipped. "Not much else. I was in my forge with a late-night order when I heard the screams. Dunno if the bastards thought I was closed, or if they just hadn't gotten to me yet. Looked outside and saw a few men banging on a door, telling whoever was inside to get out or they'd burn it down. Poor folks didn't know what was coming … Soon as the door was open, one of them shoved the man with a blade in his gut, dragged the rest of them out by their necks, and put them to the sword right then and there, not even giving them a chance to speak."

Tom drifted off into the memory for a moment, watching the events unfold in his mind as he explained it. After a moment, he cleared his throat and continued. "Figured it was time to leave, so I relieved my axe from retirement and made my way to Dodge's place to make sure he was okay. Found a few of them there; figured I'd go out swinging. Killed them easily enough. Then we were attacked by another group of 'em."

Alric nodded to Garth and Baron. "And that's when you found them?"

"Heard the clashing before we saw them," the archer confirmed. "Probably what alerted the other group."

Again, Alric nodded and stared off into the fire. "What about you, Dodge?" he asked without looking up. "What'd you see?"

Dodge took a deep breath and glanced to Trevor. "Bastards kicked in my door, came rushing in with weapons drawn. We took care of them before setting out to find Sarah. Town was the way you describe."

Trevor remembered Sarah's parents lying in the street, facedown in a puddle of their own blood. He shuddered at the memory as Dodge continued.

"Looked to be worse at the other end of town, so we set back to make our escape. That's when we found Tom."

"Nothing else?" Alric eyed him suspiciously.

"Nothing else," Dodge answered.

"Yes, there was," Trevor said awkwardly, feeling like a child speaking amongst giants. "I remember something."

Alric said nothing, but inquired with a raised eyebrow.

"When we were making our way to Sarah's house, I saw a couple guys talking. They were … eh … talking to another guy."

Alric tilted his head curiously. "Talking?"

"Yeah, like they were … reporting to him? The guy looked like he was in charge, like he was giving them orders."

Alric looked at Trevor for a long while, feeling more uneasy as the time passed. There was something about the man's brown eyes, like a deep sadness hidden beneath a shell.

"Interesting." Alric nodded. "Very interesting. And what about you?" he called over his shoulder to Warren. Trevor had forgotten all about him, sitting quietly alone, away from the group. "Did you see anything?"

The question was lost on him. He said nothing before burying his face in his lap, his body shuddering repeatedly as he began to weep.

For a moment, Trevor took pity on him, not knowing what Warren had gone through during the attack. But then Trevor thought about his experience with Warren before the attack ever happened, which all but eliminated any trace of pity for the kid.

One nightmare of a night doesn't forgive him of a lifetime of tormenting me.

"You've been a great help," Evan shouted toward Warren. "Thanks, bud."

"Evan," Seroes said in a low tone.

Evan rolled his eyes. "Yeah, yeah. Sympathy. I get it."

"You said you saw someone, Evan?" Alric paced before them, a fist beneath his chin. "When you found the girl."

Evan shrugged. "Not much to go on. Man came running out of nowhere. Yelled to us that someone needed help. Tried to follow him, but we couldn't find his prints. It was like he'd vanished in the air." Evan nodded toward where Sarah lie unconscious. "We went in search of him when we heard her screams."

"And you didn't catch the man's face?" Alric asked.

"No," Seroes answered. "He wore a hood. Didn't look like he had weapons, either, just a walking stick and a small pack hanging over his shoulder."

Trevor's hope skyrocketed.

A hood, small bag, and even a walking stick? Could it have been ...?

"Well, so much for that," Alric grunted. "So, you are a blacksmith, then?" He looked at Tom.

"Aye?" Tom replied suspiciously. "Why you asking?"

Alric shrugged. "How skilled are you?"

Tom peered at Alric, irritation matching his suspicion, clearly offended with the notion of the question. "It's a family tradition. Started once I was a wee lad. Mother always told me I was born with a hammer in my hand."

"All the ones I've met say you can distinguish a good blacksmith from the rest when they can identify a piece of work just by looking it."

"Sounds like the blacksmiths you've been working with are a bunch of arrogant shits." Tom spit to the side, crossing his arms as he began sizing up Alric. "What are you getting at?"

Again, Alric shrugged, as if the matter was trivial. "Just wondering what category you fall into; that's all."

Tom shook his head, a grin spreading across his face. "You're something else, ain't ya? Go on," Tom encouraged. "Let's see it, then."

Alric pulled something from his belt and tossed it to Tom, who snatched it from the air. Tom held it close to his face and studied it in the dark. Trevor could tell it was an arrow.

"What can you tell me?" Alric pressed.

Tom studied the bloodied arrow for a moment longer, twisting and turning it. Then he scratched at the arrow point with his nail and flexed the shaft between his meaty hands. At one point, he even smelt the wooden shaft, quickly backing away with a curious look.

"Son of a bitch," Tom muttered more to himself.

"Yes?" Evan said suddenly. When everyone stared at him, he shrugged and looked away. "Sorry. Thought I was needed, is all."

Benny rolled his eyes again at Evan. Then he asked Tom. "You know something?"

"I know enough. Although, I hope I'm wrong. You." Tom nodded toward where the two archers stood. "Safe to assume you know your way from one arrow to the next?"

Both archers looked at each other before answering with a shrug.

"Suppose that's true," Garth said.

"Okay." Tom tossed the arrow toward them, and Garth caught it swiftly out of the air. "Tell me about the shaft."

Garth fumbled with the arrow, studying it much like the same way Tom had.

Evan laughed. "Are you really going to try to convince me that you can tell us who made that arrow just by the type of wood they used? You know, you blacksmiths aren't as arrogant as they say. You're worse."

"It's not wood," Garth said suddenly, handing the arrow to his brother next to him.

Seroes scrunched his face. "Not wood? What could it be, then?"

"It's stone," Tom confirmed. "Borderline metal, actually. It's called selphite. Harder than a bitch to mine and not cheap to harvest. You see, it's stone mixed with slivers of metal shards. Chipping it away is tough work, but you can smelt it easily, and it molds nice and light. Not much use for a sword or hammer, though. The force of it connecting with something else would shatter it in a single swing, but packs a hell of a punch for an arrow. Sharp, light, and flexible; could pierce through any armor known to man. And with the linear engineering, it holds enough support where the shaft won't snap on impact."

"Where's it found?" Benny asked, clearly impressed with Tom's diagnoses.

"Only one place in Navaleth where it's found," Tom said.

"Where's that?" Baron asked curiously, his face still hidden beneath his hood.

"Brackenheart," Tom answered.

Alric was taken aback with the information. "The Mountain city?"

Tom confirmed with a nod. "They've been carving their way through that mountain since they showed up. Where do you think the minerals go?"

"So, you are saying we provided these arrows." Alric folded his arms again, a puzzled look on his distant expression. "We know where the material comes from, but that leaves a lot of vendors, which leaves us with next to nothing."

"That's not necessarily true."

All eyes looked to Tom.

Alric shifted his interest and looked at Tom, too. "No?"

Tom shook his head. "Like I said, selphite is an amazing material, which means it ain't cheap. They don't just sell it in the market squares around the country. They save those arrows for a higher purpose. Military, specifically."

Alric looked to his two archers. "Garth? Merrick?"

Both archers pursed their lips, nodding to confirm Tom's analysis.

Tom gave a wry smile and looked at Evan. "How's that for arrogance, eh?"

"So"—Benny eyed Tom curiously—"you're suggesting that these arrows came from a blacksmith who has ties with the capital?"

"I'm not saying it; I know it."

Evan rolled his eyes. "It's a good thing there isn't an abundance of blacksmiths who work for the empire. Should be easy tracking them down."

"Won't be hard at all. selphite is easy to smith, but it still takes skill to handle. You'd need a blacksmith who's been doing their job for a while now. Maybe a smith that has been doing it for, well, let's say, since they were a wee lad?"

There was a moment of awkward silence that dragged on.

Trevor thought about what Tom had said, and just as it registered in his head, he saw Evan roll his eyes.

"Right," Evan said. "So, you're going to tell me that *you* made this arrow?"

Tom creased his brow, honest hurt in his eyes. "Would that be so unbelievable?"

"You're telling me"—Benny took a step toward Tom, gesturing toward the arrow they were debating over—"that you made *this* arrow?"

"I'm saying," Tom spoke slowly, "that once a year, I get a purchase order from Navaleth. They send me the supplies, I make however many arrows they want."

"Then, that would mean ..." Benny shook his head sadly. "Fuck. Alric, what do you make of all this?"

Alric took a deep breath. "Whoever these people are, they're no bandits. Possibly mercenaries, but definitely not bandits. They started from one end of your town and worked toward the other while burning and killing everyone they saw. They also placed a few scouting parties surrounding Robins-Port in case anyone managed to escape. A raid like that takes a lot of organization, control, and discipline.

"There's one thing that's obvious in all this, and it's that they wanted everyone dead. That's why they went house to house, cordoned off the town, and put everyone to the sword, burning the houses just in case someone was hiding.

They weren't taking any chances."

"Wanted everyone dead?" Dodge repeated. "You think they were looking for someone in particular?"

"Depends." Alric shrugged. "Any big shots in town? Any dukes? Business owners?"

"At Robins-Port near the end of harvest?" Tom asked sarcastically. "Not fuckin' likely."

"Right. So another thing that doesn't make any sense. I've known mercenaries to do almost anything for gold, but always there was an objective—capture this leader, or kill this group of bandits. But even the groups I know wouldn't just butcher a village simply to butcher a village. There had to be some sort of purpose."

"And what about what you did with her?" Dodge nodded toward Sarah. "Did she ... *remember* anything?"

Benny pressed his lips together. "She was attacked in her home. Her father came home and warned them, ordered them into the bedroom to hide. Her mother shoved her into a trapdoor under the house, but she didn't leave right away. She waited, heard the men above her break down the door into the room. They talked a bit before ... well, before ..."

Benny's words left a weight on Trevor's heart. He'd never gotten along with Sarah's father, Harold, but Sarah's mother had always been kind to him. Even so, both of them deserved a better fate than what they'd been dealt.

"Oh, Florance ..." Dodge said quietly to himself, "you deserved so much better."

"Florance?" Benny asked, head angled with curiosity.

"Sarah's mother. Her name is—name *was*—Florance." Dodge scratched his beard. "An old friend."

Benny peered around Dodge and stared at Sarah. "Interesting."

"Also," Alric continued, "I examined some of the bodies before picking that arrow off a child. Stab wounds were good, too good. Clean stab, straight to the heart. So, we have a large enough force to cordon and raid Robins-Port, with too much discipline for bandits, not enough motive for mercenaries, and with the equipment of Navalethian elite soldiers."

"Maybe some graverobbers," Evan spoke. "Could be there was a battle. Maybe some scavengers or survivors snagged some equipment from the fallen once the dust settled?"

"Last battle was quite some time ago," Dodge pointed out. "You'd think we'd have heard of one if it happened."

"You'd think," Evan said with a wink and a smile, the ambiguity of the statement making Trevor nervous.

"Either way," Benny said, "as unfortunate as it is, you may be the only survivors of this attack. Best thing for us to do is keep that to ourselves."

Trevor felt another surge of anger. "What? You don't want to tell anyone about what happened?"

"Trevor," Dodge whispered, "calm down."

"I won't calm down," Trevor snapped. "You're telling me that I'm supposed to keep this a secret while an entire fucking village was just slaughtered?"

If Benny was offended, he didn't show it. "Not exactly. We will tell someone, of course, but I'd rather tell the *right* someone instead of the *wrong* someone."

"And what the hell is that supposed to mean?" Trevor blurted, raising his arms in anger. "What are we even talking about here? And, why are you just standing there, listening to this?" Now facing Dodge, he said, "You've lived in Robins-Port your entire life. Everyone you knew is dead! We were just attacked. *I* was just attacked. I just … just …" Trevor's thoughts ran back to the skirmish outside his home, the bodies at his feet, the men swinging swords at his face … the man's lifeless eyes as he died by Trevor's hand. "I just killed someone."

Either nobody knew what to say or didn't care.

Now that the adrenaline had worn off, with nothing else to occupy his mind but these dark thoughts, the memory of the man's face slowly began to haunt him.

"It's Trevor, right?" It was Alric who spoke. "Look, your townspeople were just butchered like animals—"

"Please excuse his metaphor," Benny quietly added, now glaring a warning at his friend.

"You don't just murder an entire town unless you're also eliminating the risk of witnesses. And that's what you are—a witness. They wanted you dead, and you're still alive. That's a problem. Now, what do you think would happen if someone who organized the attack were to find out you were still alive?"

Pulled away from his dark thoughts, Trevor put the pieces together. "I'd be killed."

"Exactly," Alric confirmed. "Our only link to the attack is that arrow, which leads to the capital. We were headed there anyway, on business, so we can meet a contact once we get there. But, until we get there and can talk to someone we can trust, you've never even been to Robins-Port. None of us have. Understand?"

The silence spoke for them.

"Is there anyone you can trust in the capital?" Dodge asked.

Alric looked to Benny, who looked back at him. They both gave a lazy shrug.

"One? Maybe two?" Alric answered.

"It seems we've a heading, then." Tom stated. "When do we leave?"

"We move carefully. If we keep the fire small, we shouldn't give off too much smoke. Keep it going enough just to cook food, and that's it. If we travel hard at night, and I mean *hard*"—Alric met everyone's eyes—"we'll reach Servitol in a week. Unless someone else has a better plan?"

Trevor became suddenly aware of the tight pain in his legs and feet. For as long as he remember, he'd always wanted to leave Robins-Port, to go on his own adventure into the world he didn't know. But never did he think it'd be like this.

Now that he was leaving, he wanted nothing more than to just sit down and never move.

Trevor walked toward the tree where Sarah sat as everyone went about their business. Besides the dried blood that covered her entire body, she looked peaceful. She had a steady rise and fall in her chest and a soft look on her face as she slept.

It reminded him of the time when she'd been gone a month. When she came back, they did their usual routine—met at the wall, shared some chocolate, and told each other stories. He remembered how it felt when she leaned against his arm, the feeling of excitement rising in his chest. She'd fallen asleep, and no matter how badly his body had ached, he never risked moving.

Just like now. No matter how badly you hurt, you'll carry on. You'll do it for her. You owe her that.

A shadow cast over them and Trevor looked up to see Alric standing before him.

"A word, Trevor? If you don't mind."

It was just him. Dodge and Tom sat by the fire, seeming to be in a heated conversation. The rest of them looked to be searching through their bags or cooking food.

Trevor nodded, and Alric gestured to follow him away from Sarah.

"Your friends seem short with strangers," Alric said as Trevor met him a few paces from Sarah's reach. "Which I completely understand, so I figured I'd consult you. I've a couple questions."

"Sure." Trevor didn't know what kind of questions the man would have for someone such as himself.

"Your father, was he—"

"My father?" Trevor asked in confusion. "Oh, you mean Dodge. He's not my father."

"No?" Alric asked.

"He's my uncle." Trevor looked away shamefully. "I'm an orphan."

"Ah, there's that," Alric replied thoughtfully.

Trevor felt ashamed with the silence, half-expecting a judgmental comment, or even a look of disgust at the mention of Trevor's status. Instead, Alric shrugged, as if he didn't care.

"Look, here's the thing," Alric began, "your friend, Tom, I think? Well, he took a blow to his leg. Chances are it's going to get infected. You should tell him to clean it. Something tells me he won't take too kind to one of us telling him."

Trevor looked to where Tom stood with Dodge by the fire. "You're probably right on that."

"Right. Your uncle ... Dodge?"

Trevor nodded.

"Dodge. Was he a soldier?"

Trevor looked at his uncle. In all his years, he never talked about being in any battle, or ever being enlisted in the army. However, he did know more than his fair share with a sword.

"Maybe? If he has, he's never told me."

"Interesting. Well, here, I got this for you." Alric held out a crumpled note to Trevor. It was stained with dirt ... and blood. Written on the front of the sealed side was a name written in fancy swirls, *Sarah*. "Benny told me one of my guys found her holding it when she was ... attacked. We didn't open it. Not our business. Just thought you should make sure she gets it."

Trevor took the note and nodded his thanks.

"Also, I'll have one of my guys find some water." He now looked toward Sarah, who still slept peacefully in the shade under her tree. "You should wipe her down so she doesn't get sick." Alric looked back at Trevor with a look of concern. "What's her name again?"

155

"Sarah," Trevor answered.

"Sarah ..." Alric whispered.

"Sarah Michaelson."

"Right. Well, Trevor, that will do. Be sure to get some food in you and get some rest. That wasn't the easiest of hikes, and it's only going to get harder from here on out."

"Who do you think did this?" Trevor asked as Alric turned to leave.

It took a while for Alric to answer. "Not sure yet. But the important thing is that you're all safe. Just be sure to take care of each other."

Before Trevor could reply, Alric turned and made his way toward the others.

Trevor walked back over and sank next to Sarah, sitting beside her with his back against the same tree. His legs felt like lead, and his eyes held the weight of boulders.

Just as he felt himself drifting off to sleep, there was a gentle tap on his foot. He opened his eyes to see the one called Seroes crouching next to him, a bucket of water in his hand.

Without speaking, Trevor took the bucket and set it next to Sarah. He then took the small rag out of the cold water, squeezed, and then began to wipe the dry blood away from her peaceful face.

Part Two

Lessons of the Father

For the first time in a long time, possibly years, Francis's desk was clean of clutter. He leaned back in his wooden chair, one leg crossed over his lap, as he sat content in the shadow of his office. The sunlight carried a gentle breeze through the cracked window to his left, a swift smell of fresh grass and the coming of autumn.

It felt good to relax, to enjoy the heat of the sun, the chill of the wind. Most of all, it felt good knowing that all his hard work was about to pay off, to see the end of an old world and the beginning of a new.

Patience could be a man's downfall or his rise to power. Throughout the years of Francis pursuing the task bestowed upon him, he wouldn't be where he was now if it weren't for his patience.

"*Nothing good ever comes from being impatient,*" his father had always told him. "*A captain does not organize a raid within minutes, does he? No. He looks at every angle. He knows who to send, which direction to send them from, and what time of the day to send them. He accepts that they might die, that they will kill at their command. Patience, Francis. All good things come with patience.*"

Francis smiled with his reminiscence. *Oh, I've been patient, dear father, just not in a way you'd approve. I relish in the irony of what your teachings have brought me and the country you loved so much.*

Even though his father had been a knight in the Navalethian army, Sir Balorian, known to all Navalethians as Great-Hammer Balorian, Francis had never seen the point of bearing the weight of the Navalethian sun himself.

He never saw the logic of spending precious years of his life following orders from spiteful men until you were lucky enough to become the spiteful man in charge yourself, or die somewhere along the journey for people who never even knew your name.

Soldiers were expected to obey without hesitation, never to question. If a soldier was told to charge an enemy army on the frontlines, expecting certain death, they weren't only expected to make their ultimate sacrifice but also to thank their commander for the opportunity to die honorably. If they were ordered to burn a house filled with women and children to the ground, they were expected to smile as they lit the torch, cheering as the house rose up in flames.

"There are three things that get a soldier to fight," Sir Balorian had told Francis. *"Hate, fear, and love. Hate for their enemy, fear from death, and love for their family, country, and gods."*

Not my gods, Francis thought, wanting to spit somewhere, disgusted with the memory. *At least now I can disagree with you without fearing the back of your hand, Father.*

No, soldiering wasn't the life for Francis Balorian, which made growing up in the shadow of a legendary warrior absolutely dreadful.

There had been things expected of Francis, and no matter how hard he'd tried, he couldn't live up to his father's expectations. He just wasn't the warrior type, but that didn't mean the lessons of his father didn't stick close to heart.

Why fight and die for a cause you don't understand when you can help find a cause worth understanding? He wanted to serve his empire, but not strapped in chainmail, holding a sword. There was nothing glorious about war and battle, only bloody, mud, and the sound of dying men, something Sir Balorian had involuntarily mentioned during the nights he found himself enslaved to a bottle.

Francis did exactly what his father advised him to do. He was patient, just not in the way his father had intended. Instead of wearing armor, Francis donned a robe. Instead of strapping a sword to his back and marching into battle, he marched to the libraries in the School of Heralds with quill and paper. He lost himself in books, educating himself on the ways of his empire and its culture. It was there that he found his drive, his focus, his life.

My purpose.

Of course, his father had never approved. *"Why read about history when you can make it?"* he would argue. Francis's decision had put a wedge between the two of them, and it would remain there until the Great-Hammer drew his last breath, accompanied by years and years of that disappointed look that crushed Francis as much as his father's harsh lessons with his fists.

The following years after Francis's vow to the heralds were long over, half his life in fact, he always stuck with his father's wise words.

All good things come with patience.

Francis was changed beyond measure during those years of training. It was during those long hours of studying when he discovered the true idea of perspective, on how the idea of *good* and *evil* wasn't painted in black and white. Francis grew to not only question his monarchy but challenge it entirely. You could only read history so much until you realized that mankind's sole purpose in life was to wage war and take what you wanted from those who had it.

So long as we hold ourselves in charge of one another, war is inevitable, and war only results in death and grudges. Those of us who survive it never really leave the battlefield, and those who don't survive are forgotten.

Ever since then, Francis had direction. He found a solution to save everyone and everything. He studied endlessly in his tasks, performed his duties admirably and climbed the ranks in the herald hierarchy and was now second to the king. Well, with the guidance of the voice inside his head, of course.

Look at me now, Father. You may have been a great warrior, but I am head herald. You fought to bring order and glory; I will bring eternal stability. I suppose, in a sense, we will both change the course of history. Too bad you won't be here to witness it. Maybe then you'd feel a sense of pride in your disappointing prodigy?

"Father?"

Francis looked toward the door and was surprised to see General Destro and Vallis standing in the room. How long they'd been there, he didn't know.

"Oh," Francis mumbled, straightening in his seat and brushing the creases of his robe. *This is what happens when you get lazy, Francis.* "I apologize, gentlemen, I didn't hear you come in."

"We knocked on the door," Vallis said. "Several times, actually."

"Yes, of course." Francis cleared his throat in an attempt to recover his moment of negligence. "My mind was just elsewhere."

Destro crossed arms. "Something the matter?"

Francis gave a friendly smile. "Just thinking about how we ended up where we are. Have you ever thought back and wondered what life would be like if we made different choices?"

Destro bobbed his head slightly. "Someone once told me that, if we live in the past, we'll never be able to have a future. If we constantly question what *could* have been, we'll never know what *is*."

"Sounds like they were very wise." Francis leaned forward in his chair. "You don't think about it at all? Have you ever wondered where you would have ended up if you had never enlisted?"

Destro thought quietly to himself for a moment, his eyes searching the room.

Out of all the years that Francis had worked with Destro, something he had discovered was that Destro talked from the heart, giving no extra thought into what was going to be said but settled with what he simply felt. Watching him now, giving thought into what he was about to say, felt like progress to Francis.

"I'd be dead," Destro answered with a nod.

"Oh." Francis shifted in his seat uncomfortable.

So much for that.

Destro shrugged. "My village got raided by the natives when I was young. My family, friends, most of them dead. There was only three of us who made it out.

"Servitol was a few weeks away, but it seemed like our best shot at surviving. We lived in abandoned shacks and mud holes, living off rabbits and squirrels most of the time. We made it to Servitol, but only in time to starve. Apparently, you had to have money in order to eat in the city, something a young lad like me didn't fully understand.

"One day, just when we thought we couldn't go another day without food or drink, a man approached us. He was a soldier. He told us that the country was officially at war with the natives. He said that, if I enlisted, not only would we never starve again, but I could get revenge on those who had taken everything from me. I said yes right there and then."

"And what of the others?" Francis asked, deeply engrossed in the story. "The ones you escaped with?"

Destro shrugged. "Maisa fell in love with a drunk who beat her to death within the first year of her marriage. Erik lost his head our first battle. Well, we think. Never did find it, exactly. I suppose it could have been someone else."

Vallis stood off to the side, all but leaning away from Destro, his nose wrinkled as if Destro's grim life story literally soured the air. "For fuck's sake, man ..."

Francis softly shook his head. *Perhaps I never should have asked. This is why you keep your thoughts to yourself, Francis. What could you possibly say now?*

Thankfully, Destro spoke. "You see? Enlisting saved my life. Maybe not Erik's or Maisa's, but they made their choices, just like me. Life isn't always fair, and you have to deal with what you get."

Vallis laughed awkwardly, which got an unfriendly look from Destro. Vallis took a slow step away, his hands raised in defense.

"Well"—Francis coughed, hoping to clear the awkward tension in the room—"to business then. As of right now, everything is set in order. We're just waiting for the return of our ... acquaintances."

"That's actually why we're here," Vallis said, still eyeing Destro worriedly. "They've arrived."

"Really now?" Francis stood and pressed his robe to his body, excitement bubbling in his gut. "Then, who are we to keep them waiting?"

It seemed his father's advice had paid off yet again. *All good things come with patience.*

"I haven't met these men yet," Destro mumbled. "You trust them with our plan?"

Francis blew out a dramatic chuckle. "Absolutely not. They are hired men, and they believe what they are doing is a simple errand that pays more than its worth. Nothing more."

"Still." Destro bit his lower lip, shaking his head slowly. "I'm not one for loose ends."

"Neither am I. It will be taken care of. I assume you both know your duties?"

They both nodded in unison.

Francis looked to Destro, the brute of a man as solid as a statue. "How is our progress with General Gorman?"

Destro looked hesitant but held his posture straight. "He's grown suspicious that his riders haven't returned yet, but not enough to suspect something behind it."

"Perhaps not, but it's enough to start a search that could lead to possible suspicions. I cannot emphasis the importance of his cooperation any more than I already have. I *also* am not one for loose ends."

"Gorman is a resilient man, but he'll come around soon enough," Destro said. "He just needs to understand."

Francis nodded. "I hope you are right.

"Vallis? Is everything in order for tonight's final council meeting?"

"Ready," Vallis answered.

Francis met eyes with the two generals. Besides himself, Vallis seemed fueled with excitement, anticipation glossing over his eyes.

"Is this it?" he asked impatiently. "Does this mean we are ready?"

Francis took a deep breath then let it out slowly. He glanced toward his desk, toward the drawer that held the tablets that held the key to a perfect future.

"I believe it is," Francis said with a wry smile.

***

The midday sunlight burst through the stone windows of the palace, radiating warmth and giving color to the endless intricate decorations lining the marble halls of the castle. Vibrant drapes hung glowing from the windows and golden frames harnessing large tempuras of historical deeds burst from their hangings, guiding Francis through the maze of the castle from his personal quarters.

What a beautiful day.

He stole quick glances out of the passing windows, eyeing the luscious green hills and forests miles off in the distance. *How I long for a stroll through the forests again. Sometimes I feel my life is caged within these stone walls.* Francis knew, however, that the order of his life was soon to change.

The first thing he would do, once all of this was done, would be to pull one of his books off his personal shelf, find a trail in the Greenwood Forest to the north, and lie against a trunk, getting lost in the words.

And lost, I will get.

Destro and Vallis walked a few paces behind Francis, their footsteps echoing off the stone floors as Francis led them to the entrance hall. Nobles passed the three of them, giving small nods and whispering respectful greetings under their breaths.

"Father," one said with a bowed head, a man in a white robe whom Francis didn't recognize.

"Good day to you," Francis respond with a bright smile.

The people loved him, and he loved the people. People looked to him for comfort, guidance and hope, and it was because of that that Francis would do what was necessary.

No matter what I do, I do for you all. All the sacrifices that must be made, I will make for you.

"Good afternoon, Father Balorian," a woman's soothing voice called out, as elegant as her emerald dress.

"Sabrina, my dear, how fare's you and your family?" he asked while she passed.

Sabrina Evenson gave her usual, wicked smile. "The boys are in the east with their father for the next week. I never realized how lonely it could get here in the capital."

"I'll be sure to find you some entertainment, dear," Francis called over his shoulder as he continued to walk.

He glanced back one final time before rounding another corner to catch a glimpse of her shaking hips.

"I'm holding it to you, Father Balorian," she called over her shoulder, disappearing around a corner.

Another thing I may have to pursue once this is all over.

If Vallis or Destro had any concerns or thoughts on the engagement, they didn't show it. They walked tall and proud as they made their way through the castle.

One of the king's laws allowed certain areas of the castle open to the public, granting them access and a more personal relationship with their government. The entrance hall, where Francis now stood, was the most popular. The walls stretched to a vaulted ceiling, the architecture grand in every sense of the word.

The ceiling was painted in the Navalethian sun, depicting the gods all Navalethians worshiped—Elinroth, Mariella, Volron, and Arabella. The crowds swarmed around paintings lining the walls, engrossed in the history that Francis had grown to hate.

Francis looked to the ceiling, staring upon the faces of the gods. He might be the only person left alive who knew that another face should be among them.

And soon, my liege, the world will know your name again.

It didn't take long for Francis spot the two faces that he was looking for amongst the crowd of people. Two men on the far end were leaning against the wall with their arms crossed. It had been over a month since Francis had last seen them, but he would be able to make the two men out anywhere.

Both stood out like a new scroll in an old library. One had shoulder-length black hair and always wore a grimace on his face, like he'd smelled something sour. The shorter of the two kept a tight gray trim at the side of his head, long hair tied in a ponytail. Both of them wore dark gloves reaching halfway up their forearms, dark tunics with empty scabbards at their waist. Obviously, they wouldn't be allowed in the castle with weapons. Only soldiers in the king's army was allowed that privilege.

The shorter of the two seemed to be explaining something, waving his hand through the air like it helped prove a point that he was trying to make.

The taller one hardly seemed to be listening, only giving a soft nod every now and then as he watched the people, his eyes darting back and forth at each passerby.

Francis's heart raced when he saw the dirty sack on the ground next to their feet.

"Gentlemen," Francis said with a wide smile as he approached them, arms spread out in greeting. "On behalf of the kingdom, welcome back to the safety of our capital."

"It's always a pleasure, Father," Benjamin said with a welcoming smile. "We didn't expect to see you so soon."

"I made my way here as soon as I was given word of your arrival. How faired your travels? I must admit that I expected you much sooner. I hope everything went well?"

The two men looked at each other for the briefest of moments. Then Alric reached a leathered hand down and grabbed the dirty knapsack at his feet. "No problems." He held out the sack before Francis. "Took a bit longer to find this one, is all."

"Ah." Francis took the sack and handed it to Vallis, trying hard not to let his excitement show. "I should have known better than to doubt the capabilities of the infamous brotherhood."

"Well, ain't' this a surprise?"

Francis moved aside as Destro approached the two men.

"Alric Belinger and Benjamin Raylon, in the fucking flesh."

Francis watched as recognition slowly spread on Alric's and Benjamin's faces.

"Harvin Destro?"

It might have been the first time that Francis could ever recall seeing Alric smile. It was awkward, as the man was always such a brood.

He and Destro shook hands and grasped each other at the elbows.

"Wow. How long's it been?"

"The last time I saw you boys was …" Destro puffed his cheeks and dragged out a long breath.

"After Greengate," Benjamin finished for him.

"Right," Alric confirmed. "Right after Greengate."

The three men smiled to themselves, focusing on nothing in particular. Francis knew the look. It was the look that veterans had when thinking about their past, usually the memories of battle. He had seen it plenty of times on his father's face, especially the nights when a bottle was in his hand.

"How time flies," Benjamin said as he and Destro patted each other's backs. "It's always good to see an old friend."

"Always," Destro confirmed.

The three men begin to dive into conversation, the usual topics for old friends seeing each other for the first time in years: what they'd been up to, how life had treated them, where they'd been.

Great. More friends of Destro. More camaraderie, more passion, and more problems for me.

Vallis didn't look too pleased, either. He sat on the outskirts of the conversation with an irritated look, glaring at the three other men.

"My friends"—Francis held out a hand of subtle interruption—"may I introduce you to the commander of Servitol, General Vallis."

Alric burrowed his eyebrows. "General? What happened to Orlington? I thought he was in charge of the capital's garrison?"

"Oh, I do apologize. You have not heard. Of course you haven't." Francis cleared his throat. "Commander Orlington was struck with a fever. He passed not a week after your last departure."

Francis wasn't sure how the two men would react. They never met Orlington the last times they had done business with one another. To Francis's knowledge, they didn't know the man. Still, there was something about their reaction that worried Francis.

"Oh," Alric said, his face absent of emotion.

"A fever you say?" Benjamin asked, emotion overwhelming his face.

"A horrible one, yes," Francis answered. "The doctors said a sickness set in his stomach, had been growing there for a while, slowly breaking down his organs. As soon as the fever hit, the only thing we could do was help ease his pain."

Sorrow filled Benjamin's eyes. "Never thought something as simple as a fever would be the end of as hard a man as Orlington. He'll be missed."

Then it's a good thing poison doesn't care how hard of a man you are.

"Indeed, he will," Francis said. "The man was a military genius, courageous and just. Have no fear, large the boots may be left behind by Commander Orlington, but Vallis here is well qualified for the task at hand, and the capital trusts him fully to uphold his duties and obligations for the people of Servitol."

"I have no doubt," Benjamin agreed.

He looked to Vallis. "If you don't mind me asking, what battles have you commanded over?"

"Why?" Vallis rebuked heatedly.

"Uh …" Benjamin shrugged. "Pure curiosity? You just seem so young."

Vallis's lips curled. "I haven't had the pleasure yet."

"*Yet?*" Alric raised an eyebrow. "Have we gone to war sometime in the last two months?"

"Not a war," Francis interjected, attempting to defuse the situation. "But we are planning something against this bandit leader, Lazar. It's not exactly a campaign, but General Vallis will be overseeing the operation. It's about time we put an end to this bandit charade that's plaguing our farms."

"Right then." Alric faced Vallis. "Our general just seems a little eager to watch men die. What about fighting? What battles have you been in?"

Vallis flared with anger, all but snarling as he spoke. "I've trained with the highest and most renowned sword masters every day for the last decade. I've won countless fencing competitions, defeating many opponents that were unbeatable until they stepped in the ring with me. Not a man among my army has been able to best me to this very day. The king himself once referred to my skills as being *as swift as the wind*."

Alric didn't look the slightest bit impressed. "So … none?"

"What?" Vallis flinched, legitimate shock on his face. "Did you not just hear a word I said?"

Alric gave a nonchalant shrug. "Something about winning sword games and being referred to a phrase a cheap whore no doubt whispers into their client's ear."

Vallis's rage reddened his face to a tone Francis had yet to see. "I don't have to explain my deeds to the likes of simple mercenaries," he growled, spittle flying from his mouth. "To men who fight for nothing but gold and drink. Pardon that, to mercenaries that *don't* fight to begin with. Isn't that a rule of your *brotherhood?* A group of men who think that wearing armor with a sword strapped to their side makes them a warrior? News flash, *degenerates*: if you don't get paid to fight, it doesn't make you mercenaries. It makes you errand boys. Recognize your place, *errand boy*, and do not ever again question mine."

Alric wasn't fazed by Vallis's temper. "Well then, *Commander*, if not for gold, tell me what a person should fight for?"

"Honor and glory," Vallis answered without hesitation. "But I do not expect a lowly man such as your cowardly self to understand such a thing as that."

Alric chuckled to himself. "Honor and glory? I wasn't aware that put food on the table these days. Perhaps you should try explaining to those homeless citizens crowding your streets. Tell them everything is going to be fine as long as they have honor and glory."

Alric took a dangerous step toward Vallis, all humor draining from his face. "Seems a lot has changed in a couple months—Orlington, commanders, even how to make a living. Tell me then, General Vallis, *the maiden as swift as air,* if honor and glory are a legitimate currency in the capital, how have you managed to do so well for yourself, considering you lack both?"

Vallis took a step forward, reaching behind his back. "You worthless fucking—"

Destro put a firm hand on Vallis and stopped him from advancing. "I advise you to calm yourself," he said in a low rumble, his eyes searching to see if anyone was watching them. "You'll not raise your hand in the castle, especially toward men who've given half their lives to the crown. It was a jest. Control yourself."

Benjamin stepped between the two commanders. "I am deeply sorry if Alric has offended you, General Vallis. Just a little healthy prit-prat between two comrades, I assure you." Benny gave Alric a stern look. "He always does go a little too far."

Alric shrugged like nothing of his current situation mattered to him.

After a few heartbeats, the anger subsided and Vallis took a slow step back. "Of course," Vallis said as he brushed himself off. "Forgive my anger. I shouldn't let my emotions get the best of me, especially in such low company."

If Alric was upset by the jest, he didn't show it. "You calling the head herald low company?"

"What?" Vallis looked about worriedly. "No, that's not—"

"That's just rude," Alric mumbled, shaking his head.

"No! I was talking about—"

"My apologies, friends," Francis interrupted, fed up with the charade at hand, "but I must continue with my duties for the day. I do believe a reward is in order?"

Francis nodded toward Vallis, who hesitated for a moment before reaching into his tunic. Then Vallis tossed a bag to Benjamin without warning, the sound of coins clinking as the mercenary caught it.

"You will find what was promised upon delivery," Francis said. "As well as personal thanks from the crown for your hard work these last years."

Benny weighed the sack in his hand, bouncing it up and down before giving Alric a satisfied look. Then he glanced around the room to see if anyone was watching before tucking it behind his tunic and tying it at his waist. "All seems to be in order then?"

"As a matter of fact, I would also like to thank you for the services you've provided with a night of celebration. I can only guess you are wary and would like nothing more than to rest with a roof over your head atop a feathered bed. Rooms have been prepared for you in the castle at our expense. What you desire will be your reward."

Francis wasn't sure what he'd expected in return—a smile, a handshake, or even a thank you. Instead, both Benjamin and Alric looked at each other, and it was clear that they weren't thrilled about Francis's proposal.

"Actually," Benjamin said, "as comforting as that sounds, Father—"

"Please, call me Francis."

"We already have a room reserved for us in the city," Alric asserted.

Fuck. More complications.

"Not a problem at all, my friends," Francis said with a false smile. "There is still time to share our thanks. I understand there are three inns within the middle district; which one holds your reservations?"

"The Great-Hammer," Alric answered.

The Great-Hammer. It just had to be the Great-Hammer. Another sacrifice in the memory of you, Father.

Francis gave a wide smile. "I will send a messenger straight away. When you and your company are celebrating tonight, I'll be sure the owners know the expenses are on the crown." Francis gave a small bow toward the men. "If, in the future, you are in need of work, know that there is always room for the brotherhood in the capital. Take care and gods be with you."

Both men nodded their thanks.

Before Francis could walk away, Destro gave a heavy slap against Alric's arm. "Ale?" he asked them both, who looked to one another before showing their answer through a smile. "Good. I'll meet you at the inn in an hour. I know someone you'll be wanting to see."

"Yeah?" Benjamin asked.

"Oh yeah." Destro's face stretched to a mysterious smile. "Like you said, it's always good to see an old friend."

Benny seemed to approve. "Sounds good, Harvin. We've much to catch up on. We'll see you there."

With another nod, the two men were off, and Destro watched as Alric and Benjamin faded into the crowd of people.

Francis remembered his threat not a week ago, of what would happen if any harm came to General Gorman. *"If something happens to my friend, I'll fucking kill the both of you."* Francis had a gut-wrenching feeling that these two men had just been added to Destro's list of immunity.

"General Destro, as much as I'd hate to interrupt your reunion, please remember that we have our final council meeting tonight. It's important that you and Commander Gorman be fully prepared for it."

Destro's stare lingered a moment longer before turning to face Francis. "Aye, I remember." He nodded toward the sack Vallis held. "What'd they bring you?"

"That, my friend, is what we will discuss in the council chamber."

Destro grunted then turned and was lost in a crowd of people.

Francis watched as he left, knowing that something had to be done about the general. He knew the man would stay true to his word, at least until he fully understood what would take place on this night, and it was far too late to replace him like Francis had done with so many others.

No, I'll have to convince him. That, or I'll have to risk much more drastic measures. Desperate times.

Vallis didn't speak as Francis led them back to his office. At least, not directly. Every now and then, Francis would turn around and see the man grimacing, pouting, and swearing under his breath like a stubborn child.

Once they were in Francis's office, he slid the golden lock on the door then settled in his rickety chair. Francis pointed at the open chair on the opposite side of the desk, ordering for Vallis to sit.

Vallis handed Francis the cloth bag that the brotherhood had retrieved. It was the last piece.

Francis's heart raced with anticipation on reading the hidden scriptures carved in the stone.

For a moment, Vallis was completely forgotten, and the sound of the general clearing his throat nearly set Francis over the edge.

"I apologize—"

"Your impulsiveness is a great weakness, Vallis," Francis cut him off. "A weakness everyone can see. Especially our enemies. I will not stand for it, your men will not be expected to stand for it, and our king will surely not stand for it. Do you hear what I am saying?"

Vallis shamefully nodded. "Yes, Father."

As Francis watched the man shift uncomfortably, he couldn't help feeling himself swell with pity. It wasn't Vallis's fault, after all. He'd been sucked into a life-changing event at such a young age. He lacked discipline, wisdom, patience, self-control—all things that fell onto the teacher's shoulders. All things that Francis had failed to teach.

And he is not the only one. The world lacks wisdom, patience, control. It lacks ambition. After today, I will never fail another student.

"I am not speaking to you as a heretic," Francis said softly, keeping his own discipline in check, "but as a friend. I will expect much from you in our future endeavors, as will our master. So, do not be sorry, Vallis; be *better*."

Vallis nodded firmly and sat up straighter in the chair. "I will. I promise. I will not fail either of you."

"Good," Francis all but whispered, his focus again on the bag containing the last tablet. "Good."

"What should we do about them?" It wasn't anger Francis heard in Vallis's tone, but concern.

"Who?" Francis asked. "The brotherhood?"

Vallis nodded. "We can't rely on Destro and his men to do the job now, and my men will already be spread too thin."

Francis steepled his fingers beneath his chin. This was a complication, but nothing that couldn't be rectified. He thought long and hard, connecting what he could do and what would come of it; what his options were and what the consequences would be.

To kill them outright would raise awareness, and awareness could lead to questions, and questions need answers, and answers would need to be convincing. He couldn't just let them live, not after finding all the keys to the lock that Francis had found all those years ago.

Not to mention, there was still no word of General Gorman's riders yet, which meant they were either dead or they'd found the butchered bodies of Robins-Port's citizens. That would lead to more questions.

If only there was a way ... Ah! And there it is.

"For the most part, we stick to the plan," Francis said. "As for the brotherhood, you let me worry about them. Just be prepared for tonight's council. You know your task?"

Vallis gave a wry smile. "I do. You think he'll be on our side?"

Francis shook his head. "It matters little. I cannot work with someone if I do not know his intentions. Now, are you prepared to do what is necessary if it comes to that?"

Vallis nodded.

"Then I will see you this evening, General Vallis. Do enjoy yourself until then."

With nothing else to say, the general slid aside the lock and left Francis to his thoughts.

After getting up and barring his door once again, he turned about and gazed at the prize on his desk. Gently, he unlaced the sack and pulled out the stone tablet.

Finally.

Francis pulled out a thin piece of paper, dipped his quill, and began to write. When he finished, he melted his maroon wax and sealed the envelope with the royal sigil. Then he took the small key from underneath his robes and unlocked his drawer, adding the final tablet to his collection.

For too long you've been hidden from the world, your magic words silenced and forgotten.

After locking the contents in his desk, he made his way to the door with his sealed letter. It was time for action, and once this message was sent, there would be no going back.

Francis had waited a long time for this. Many sleepless nights of planning, all the years of serving as somebody he wasn't, all the lives sacrificed for his cause ... It was finally time to play it out.

Just as he stepped outside his door, he paused abruptly to a woman standing in front of him. Her blonde hair radiated with the sunlight, and her slim, emerald dress glistened as she rested a hand on her hip.

"Francis, I've walked these halls all day and still cannot find something to buy the time," she said.

Francis felt his face blush as he smiled. "Well, my dear, what sorts of entertainment are you longing for?"

Sabrina matched his smile, her pearly teeth adding to her radiance. "You're the one who knows everybody and everything. Do you have any recommendations?"

"I can show you a few things. However, I'm in the middle of running errands for the empire."

Sabrina bit her bottom lip and took a step closer to Francis. She looked up with her gorgeous hazel eyes as he felt a stiffen in his pants.

"But if you would like to come back in an hour's time, I'd be happy to find something that suits your needs?"

Her smile was wicked with seductive intent. "Are you sure you can wait that long?"

Francis couldn't help his chuckle while stepping even closer to Sabrina, their noses nearly touching. "Oh, darling, I am a very patient man."

All good things come with patience.

K.R. Gangi

The Traveler

Alric never understood why anyone would want to live in a city. Everything was so crowded; the buildings stacked within feet of another, wagons pulled up and down small cobblestoned streets, making it difficult for travel. Not to mention, the marketplace swelled with countless people bartering for goods, which made it nearly impossible to hear your own thoughts.

Even now, as he and Benny crossed the wooden bridge that connected the upper city and the castle, they had to squeeze between crowds of families, paying attention as to not let someone snatch their purse while in the process.

Alric felt that the city life was a distraction from the real world. If you got lost in the city life, you forgot what it was like outside its walls. If you lost touch with reality, you wouldn't know how to defend against it when it came knocking at your door.

Reality is a cruel bitch with a grudge. At least, in Alric's experience.

These people, the loyalists, beggars, merchants, barkeeps, shopkeepers, wouldn't last a day if Servitol were sacked.

Not that they had to worry. The capital had never once been attacked. The biggest threat nearly two decades ago. Even now, the city's defenses were more technologically advanced than before.

It just gives the guards more reason to grow lazy. Their safeguards will become their undoing.

Servitol curved along the coast of the Sun Sea. Its walls were massive— ten feet deep of solid stone with a ballista stationed every thirty or so feet. If that wasn't enough, trebuchets were at the ready in case the city's defenses needed even more fire power. The city was a fortress, the patrolling guards stationed on the walls merely a courtesy for what really waited for an attacking enemy.

Servitol had a geographical advantage, as well. The castle itself was nestled on an island with a mess of sharp rocks and shallow water protecting it from a naval invasion. Jagged stone reached from the rough waves, an inviting graveyard for any who would dare an attempt to invade Servitol from the sea.

The city itself was separated between two districts. The upper district, where most of the economy thrived with patrons and citizens of status, was connected to the castle by a wooden bridge that descended at the castle's will, therefore being in total control of who enters and who stays out. The bridge itself was over a hundred feet in length, yet that was only a spectacle compared to the enormity of the castle itself.

Beneath that bridge was a three-hundred foot plummet for any soul unfortunate enough to fall victim to the plunge.

However, Alric knew all too well that, even with the most advanced defending, the city had flaws. There was always a hole to slip through. He'd done it personally many times over.

No, these people would not survive. They relied on their protectors too much and had for far too long to remember how to defend themselves in a fight. If an attack came, Alric would prefer to be outside of the walls, not in.

Nowhere to retreat to if your back is against a wall.

Alric had bore witness on what happened in a sealed-off city, saw what people were willing to do to one another once they began to starve, when they lived in constant fear for their lives. Friends, family, all willing to gut one another over something as petty as a loaf of bread.

"You're brooding," Benny called from over his shoulder as they pushed through the line of people waiting to enter the castle.

"Not sure what you're talking about," Alric replied, picking up his pace.

"And you're in a mood," Benny replied, ignoring Alric's response. "What was that back there? Picking a fight over nothing?"

"I was fishing," Alric said firmly, though he and Benny knew it was more than that.

The truth was that Alric really was in one of his moods. He had been ever since they had left Robins-Port.

"And the man was a twit. Barely old enough to be a lieutenant."

"And yet, he is the commander of Servitol," Benny pointed out. "You thought what? To bait him into showing off his authority?"

"Like I said, I was fishing, dammit."

Benny raised an eyebrow at him, and Alric couldn't help but submit.

"And yes, I'm in a mood. Happy?"

"Far from it, actually." Benny's tone was now filled with worry. "Did anything feel … *off* back there?"

The brotherhood had been doing jobs for Father Balorian for years now, keeping them busy by searching for the old tomes, paying them handsomely for each one they found. The jobs were the same every time—they would find the tomes, hand it off to Father Balorian and Orlington, take their payment, and then set off to find the next one. Nothing more, nothing less.

"What are you thinking?" Benny asked, interrupting Alric's thoughts.

"Not sure," Alric admitted. "I don't think Vallis could have ran a raid like the one in Robins-Port. It was too clean, too precise. He's too hot-headed to think everything clearly."

"My thoughts, too." Benny tapped a finger against his bottom lip. "What about Harvin?"

Alric shook his head. "Doubt it. He always was a man for the people. Wouldn't sack a village for no reason."

"Maybe before … when we were young," Benny speculated. "Time can make even the most honest man a liar."

Alric was no stranger to how time could change someone's life. Something as simple as the concept of time could take a calm, honest life and twirl it into a living nightmare in the matter of minutes.

"Sure, but I still don't think he'd have it in him. He's come far from a simple grunt. You see his uniform? He's got some status on him now, and there's no way he'd send his men to do something like that, not if he knew what was being done."

They rounded a corner down a hill and descended toward the lower district. Even at this distance, Alric could see peasants in torn rags, holding out a begging hand for food, water, coin—anything that could feed them through the day.

Looks like the rumors were true.

Apparently, the loyalists, a large and overwhelming bandit group led by one named Lazar, was terrorizing farmers in the outer edges of each capital territory. They would burn the fields and kill the livestock but never once set a sword to a man.

If only it was Lazar and his gang who took your farm, Alric. Who knows how different your life would be if it was only your fields and home being burned away before your eyes?

"Could be the loyalists?" Benny suggested, as if reading Alric's thought.

"Might be. Might not be. Never heard of them butchering innocent folk, though."

"True," Benny agreed. "What about Father Balorian, then?" Benny asked, leading Alric toward the gates that separated the upper and lower district.

"What about him?"

"Don't tell me you didn't notice his persistence when it came to *tending to our needs*?"

"He's a herald, Benny, not a military genius. Besides, he takes orders directly from the king himself. Don't think it would please His Majesty if he found out his main trading village was slaughtered."

"And when's the last time you've heard anything from him, eh? It's been months since any public forums, speeches, or even a presence. Not since the queen's passing."

"Best keep that voice down," Alric warned Benny, searching the crowd for guards. "Someone might get the wrong impression."

"I'm just saying," Benny continued, lowering his voice. "If he knows already, he sure doesn't seem to care."

Alric spit. "Maybe the order came from him."

"I was going to suggest that maybe someone hasn't told him," Benny countered. "An entire village of his subjects *was* just wiped off his map. What purpose would our king have for that?"

A sour taste was beginning to build in Alric's mouth. "Even the worst of kings believe their twisted ways are for the better of their kingdom. Still don't think Father Balorian could manage something like that. At least, not without help and a sick sense of ambition. Don't see how it would benefit him the slightest."

"Wouldn't be so sure about that, considering his father and all."

"The Great-Hammer?" Alric asked, pretending to be interested. "You think they're connected?"

Benny raised an eyebrow. "Did you see that twinkle in his eye when we mentioned the inn? Flushed red at the sound of the name."

"So does everyone else who truly knew the Great-Hammer. He was as vicious with his family as he was with his enemies." Alric began chewing the inside of his cheek, a habit he'd fallen into when it came to being around crowds. He hated crowds. "Perhaps they are connected somehow. The timeline adds up, at least."

"Maybe little Balorian's choice of life wasn't the only rebellious plan he offered his father?"

Benny's suggestion put Alric more on edge.

"Perhaps, instead of living up to his late father's deeds, he'd much rather destroy the very thing he fought to build."

"Hm … Seems like a stretch," Alric thought aloud. "The man studies historic scrolls, tomes written in ancient languages found in caves around the country, not battle plans. He may be his father's son, but that's about as far as that goes. Don't really see a reason why he'd risk it. Being head herald isn't exactly a bad set up."

They reached the gate separating the lower and upper districts. It was surrounded by the homeless, begging to enter the castle so they could kneel before the king and beg for his help.

Benny kept a firm hand on his purse, being sure the payment for their last job didn't slip away unnoticed.

Wouldn't do to lose the coin from our final job, now would it?

They squeezed through the crowd, ignoring the crying pleas and gentle tugs at their tunics.

Alric began to sweat profusely. There were too many things going on at once, and it was near impossible to prepare yourself against a knife in the gut.

Guards stood around them, being gentle but firm enough not to let the homeless pass without invitation. Benny nodded to the guard, who then signaled to his fellow guards to make a path so they could pass.

Alric only felt at ease when he and Benny were farther down the street, away from the swelling throng.

"Well, we can always talk to Destro," Benny suggested once they could walk side by side. "If you believe he can be trusted."

Alric wiped the thick layer of sweat from his brow. "Let's hear him out first; get a feel on where he stands. This information might be as dangerous for him as it is for us. Better to not rush it."

"Fair point there. Best not to rush it," Benny agreed. "I knew there was still a part of you that could see things clearly."

"Just because I don't share your sense of optimism doesn't mean I don't see clearly," Alric teased.

"Stick with me, kid," Benny joked back with a wink. "You still got a ways to go."

Alric raised an eyebrow as his friend. "Kid? Really? You've got what

Bloodlines

…? Two years on me?"

Benny shrugged. "The older *are* amongst the wiser."

"Really?" Alric's tone was filled with doubt. "Wiser, huh?"

Benny's brisk walk now turned into a strut. "The young are always looking up to us for guidance. They accept us for who we are and live off our experiences."

"Very interesting" Alric said. "You know who would beg to differ?"

Benny's arrogant posture melted. He knew where Alric was guiding the conversation. "Don't even think about bringing up—"

"Matilda Hazwalt."

Benny sighed at the name. "Why is it that, every time we enter this city, you find pleasure in bringing up Matilda fucking Hazwalt?"

"Because I hate this city, and I'm not going to let you claim to be a wise man when you weren't even wise enough to—"

"Can't we just forget that whole ordeal?" Benny asked.

Benny scoffed. "She was a woman."

"A big woman," Benny corrected, his chin held high in defiance. "A *very* big woman."

"You started a fight with a *very big woman*."

"Please." Benny swatted away the notion with a flick of his wrist. "I'm sure I'm not the only one to land myself in a fight with a grown woman."

"And you lost," Alric stated.

"That's not fair, and you know it. I was still drunk." Benny shrugged in defense. "And the sun was in my eyes."

"You were inside," Alric corrected.

"I'm sure there was a window somewhere."

Alric shrugged. "You still went down in one blow."

"That's what happens when the blow is straight to your chops."

Alric chuckled to himself. He loved seeing Benny so uncomfortable. "Took you long enough to fight back, too."

"Her sisters were there!"

"A couple, strong-willed women shouldn't be a match for a former sun guard," Alric teased.

"There were six of them, dammit!" Benny explained. "You know that."

Alric couldn't prevent his laugh, enjoying the memory of it all, even more when he realized Benny wasn't.

"Yes, yes. Make fun of old, drunk Benjamin. You could have helped me with

179

that, by the way. I'm sure it was quite the show," Benny said bitterly.

"Lessons come more painful than others, I suppose. Bet that's the last time you tried to—"

"In my defense"—Benny held up his hands defensively—"she really seemed to be enjoying it."

"Still, man, you always ask permission; otherwise, it seems … *invasive*. There's a reason some women charge double for that sort of thing."

"It was just one finger," Benny argued.

"Just one finger too many, some would say," Alric retorted.

Benny sighed. "I was young. And *very* drunk."

"And brave, at that," Alric added to Benny's list of excuses. "Thinking you could pull a fast one like that on a woman of class like Matilda Hazwalt. Tsk-tsk."

"Yeah, well, my balls never really healed, if I'm being honest." Benny grimaced at the thought. "Even the memory turns my stomach."

"Nor your pride, apparently."

"Nor my pride," Benny agreed.

Weaving like ants through pebbles on a beach, Benny and Alric made their way through the maze of the city.

It was still afternoon, but Alric knew that the sun set fast this time of year. He dreaded the idea of sleeping in the Servitol, wishing he could set up camp somewhere else, somewhere he wasn't surrounded by thousands of people who valued profit more than people's lives.

Ironic, coming from one who calls himself a mercenary, Alric argued with himself, his mood beginning to shift again. *You've snuffed out more lives than you can remember, all for the lies of glory and duty. Like you've a right to judge these people after the things you've done.*

Lost in his thoughts, he turned a corner and bumped straight into a stranger. A basket tumbled and fell to the ground, apples and other fruit rolling about on the street.

"Oh no, no, no. That just won't do. Forgive me, good sir," an old man pleaded to Alric. "I meant no harm."

"No harm done," Alric said as he began helping the man gather the nearby scattered fruit. "Bound to happen to someone at some point in this damned city."

When the rest of the fruit was gathered, the old man set the basket in the back of a large cart that Alric hadn't noticed. The cart was loaded with different variations of foods: bread, apples, potatoes, bananas, tomatoes, carrots, and even squash.

"Best of luck to you," Alric mumbled as he turned to leave.

"Excuse me, good sir," the old man begged. "Would it be too much to lend a hand?"

In that moment, Alric took a good look at the stranger. He wore a ragged robe that dangled loosely off his shoulders. Wrinkles lined his face, arms, and hands as he leaned on a walking stick. He wore no boots, walking only on his bare, dirtied feet.

"It seems my cart decided to give out on me," the old man added.

"Uh ..." Alric grumbled. "What's the problem?"

The old man tapped his walking stick against the wheel of his cart. "Won't budge an inch. I think I may have gotten a rock wedged in there or something. I won't be able to move on unless it's removed, a thing some men can relate to, no?"

Alric looked at Benny for support, to see if the man's comment made him as uneasy as it did Alric, but Benny remained impassive.

Alric sighed to himself. "Head back to the others and let them know what's going on. I'll be there shortly."

Benny was confused as to why Alric would suggest such a thing, but he eventually shrugged. "Evan and I will run our errands. I'll meet you at The Great-Hammer." With that, Benny was lost in the crowd, leaving Alric with the strange little man, who was now smiling up at him like a pup to its new owner.

"Right then," Alric muttered to himself, his mood quickly taking a turn. "Let's see what the holdup is."

"Oh, you are too kind, sir," the old man praised. "I appreciate the help. Gods know there aren't many good men left in the world these days, but here I stand in the midst of one."

The compliment made Alric feel awkward, so he decided to ignore it.

Why is it that the elderly always believe everyone is a good person simply because they take pity on them?

Alric crouched on the ground and slid under the cart. It wasn't uncommon for a wheel to drag a rock into the gear; it had happened to Alric plenty of times on his farm. If he could just find it, he'd tug it out and this old man would be out of his hair in no time.

He lined his fingers down the crease of the wheel under the wagon's belly until he felt a prick. He pinched the rock between his fingers, pressed with his shoulder to roll the wagon back a bit, and then pulled the rock free.

"Got it," he said as he stood, tossing the previously wedged rock somewhere off to the side. "Shouldn't have any problems now. Although, I gotta say"—Alric turned to face the man who still stood there, staring at Alric with his sad eyes—"not too wise being alone with a food cart with a starving mob just around the corner."

"Around the corner, you say?" The old man perked up. "It seems I'm closer than I thought. Could you be so kind as to help me bring the cart over?"

Damn it all. This is why you shut your mouth.

"You plan on selling them food?" Alric asked, thinking that the old man could use some food himself.

"Not in the slightest bit," he replied, smiling.

Alric raised a brow. "Then why bring the cart at all?"

"Didn't you just say they were just around the corner?" The old man looked as confused as Alric felt.

Alric crossed his arms. "Plan on showing off a wagon filled with food and not selling it to them? Looks like you're right; not many good people left in this world."

"Oh, please." The old man waved away the comment. "You always suspect the worst in people, don't you?"

Alric eyed the stranger suspiciously, feeling that there was more meaning behind his words that what was said. "Well, can't say you're gonna get much from them if you don't plan to sell. Might piss them off a bit, though."

"On the contrary, I don't imagine they'll be upset at all when they find out I'm not there to sell them food."

"Oh yeah? Why is that?"

"Because I plan to *give* it to them, not *sell* it."

Alric was taken aback, his rebuttal stuck in his throat. He looked at the cart, at all the fresh food nearly overflowing the top, a fortune for a starving mob. "You're just giving it away?"

"Of course," the man said, shocked, as if Alric wouldn't do the same. "It's not like it was mine to begin with."

Finally, it hit Alric like a shield to the face. It all made sense now—the ragged clothes, lack of boots, dirt-covered body. "Right then. You're a thief."

The old man shook his head. "Wrong again, my friend. I am but a simple traveler."

"Then tell me, Mr. Traveler, how is it someone like you managed to get their hands on a cart filled with enough food for a banquet?"

"Why, I planted them, of course," Traveler said as if it were obvious.

"But you just told me it's not yours."

"They aren't. They're all of ours. It came from the ground, and who claims to own all the ground? It's nobody's, yet it's everyone's. Is a farmer a thief for giving away food that everyone owns?"

Alric's head began to hurt. "You know, you could have just said you were a farmer." It made sense, given Traveler's attire. "Although, I'm sure the king has a different idea about who's *ground* it is."

"Who said I was a farmer?" the man asked. "I'm not a farmer; I'm a traveler."

This is really beginning to annoy me.

"You know," Alric said before he could lose his temper, "why don't I just help you with this cart?"

Traveler literally leaped into the air with joy, much spryer than Alric could have imagined. "Splendid! I'll help lead the way. Do follow close by; we don't want to get robbed before we reach our destination, now do we?"

"Can't get robbed of something that isn't yours," Alric teased, a little more spite in his words than intended.

Traveler winked at Alric. "Now you're catching on. Even an old wolf learns new tricks."

Alric was gripping the handles on the cart when Traveler's words hit him. "What did you just say?"

But when he looked up for the old man, he was already halfway down the street, waving an impatient hand for Alric to hurry up.

I knew I'd regret this.

The cart was heavier than Alric expected for just hauling small foods. A lot heavier. It was also smaller, causing him to crouch low as he pulled it, making sure he didn't cause food to roll off the back.

Traveler waited for Alric to catch up, keeping a slow, solid pace next to him, leaning heavily on his walking stick with each step.

"You know," Alric said, his stomach cramping tight with each crouching step, "no offense, but you don't really seem like someone able to carry this very far, let alone from a farm. Where'd your help go?"

"You'd be surprised how old I am, young man, but you'd be more surprised at the level of my endurance, especially with a task at hand," he said vaguely, keeping his eyes focused down the street.

"I'm sure I would," Alric agreed, not risking another confusing conversation. "But you didn't answer my question."

The stranger looked directly at Alric, unexpected pain in his eyes. "The truth is that I have no one to help me. Not anymore. Not in a long time."

"Sorry to hear that and all, but if this is where you try to convince me that you've carried this all by yourself, don't waste your time."

"Such a strange phrase: *don't waste your time*," Traveler wondered aloud. "Life and time pass hand in hand, so who are you to tell me how to spend my life and choose for me how to spend my time?"

"Yeah." Alric nodded, already giving up the battle before it had begun. "That's just a road I'm not going down with you. How about we just don't talk at all, eh?"

Traveler ignored the comment. "And then there are those who think of time as an illusion."

"I guess not."

"Which is very interesting, indeed," Traveler continued. "Morning, afternoon, evening, all names delegated to certain times of the day so we can feel more in control of the world." Traveler now turned to face Alric. "If a man were to bid you good morning at sunset, would they be wrong?"

"Look, I don't want to play your stupid—"

"Oh, do indulge an old man, will you?"

Alric growled in irritation, but the old man smiled.

The weight of the cart was really putting a strain on Alric's back now.

"Fine," he said. "I would tell the man he's wrong."

"But why?" Traveler looked genuinely curious. "How could he possibly be wrong?"

"Because, when the sun sets, it's evening. It's night."

"So, what makes night ... *night*?"

"Besides the fact that the sun sets and the world goes dark?"

"When the sun hides behind a cloud and casts a shadow, does that mean it is nighttime, as well, then?"

"Well, no. It's just how we try to understand, I guess."

"Exactly!" the old man said. "And because of that, we've made time a linear entity. Last week, one month from now; we've developed a system that conveys time as a constant moving motion, but who is to say that's true?"

Alric honestly didn't know how to answer the question. Why did he ever agree to help this man? It was a mistake that he would never make again.

"I guess only the gods can answer that."

There was a sudden pause. He wasn't sure, but Alric thought he could hear the old man quietly laughing to himself.

"Strange," Traveler said finally. "Something tells me you aren't someone who believes in the gods."

Alric felt the ire building once more. "And what does a farmer know about the gods, exactly?"

"As I've said, I'm not a farmer. I am a traveler."

"Sure. You've said that." Alric kept his eyes focused on Traveler. "What exactly does a *traveler* do?"

"I search for purpose and serve it once it's found," the man responded without looking away.

"And it doesn't get any more vague than that," Alric declared. "Do you have a name, or should I just call you Traveler?"

The man tilted his head. "I suppose I've been called worse."

"Right then, Sir Traveler, any particular place you've wandered upon in order to get your hands on this?" Alric gestured to the cart of food. "Couldn't be too far."

"I've walked from one end of the country to the other and back again a dozen times over. Nothing is necessarily far."

Alric felt the heat rising in his face. "Anybody ever tell you you'd make a good politician? Where are you from, then?"

"A small village near Orange Fields," he answered vaguely with a wave of his hand.

Alric slowed his pace, letting Traveler drift farther down the street before coming to a stop. "Orange Fields, you say?"

The man turned about, not showing a sign of worry that Alric had stopped. "You've heard of it? I should have known. You do pass off as a man who's seen more than a few places, after all."

There was tickle in Alric's chest now. It was a feeling he hadn't felt in a long time—exposure, watched … threatened. "Where in Orange Fields?"

Traveler smiled ambiguously. "A small town named Rapport. Have you heard of it?"

K.R. Gangi

Suddenly, Alric felt very uncomfortable. He squeezed the handles of the cart tighter, picking up his pace as he passed the old man. "Never heard of it."

"You sure?" Traveler asked, now struggling to keep up with Alric's sudden pace. People passed by, pressing between them, but Alric was now a bull parting through the crowd.

"I'm sure," Alric answered assertively.

"Such a shame. It really is a beautiful place," Traveler declared. "I'm sure you would have loved it."

"I'm sure it is."

"Although, tragedy strikes even the most beautiful parts of the world, does it not?" Traveler proposed. "It's still a place worth visiting, though. Perhaps you should ... sometime."

"I'll pass." Alric began feeling more defensive by the minute, old memories ripping through his thoughts.

It hurts! Make it stop!

"Doesn't sound like my type of area," Alric stated flatly.

"Are you sure?" Traveler asked.

"Positive," Alric answered.

"Apologies. You just have the look of a farmer."

Alric said nothing. He could see the corner of the street now, only a few hundred yards to go.

"Well, who knows?" Traveler said, slowing his pace, leaning close to Alric to whisper in his ear, "Maybe you'll pass through during your travels. I'm sure you could *sniff* it out."

Alric dropped the cart abruptly and lunged at the man, one hand around his throat and another on his chest. He shoved Traveler against the wall of a shop, his arm pressing against the old man's throat.

"Who the fuck are you?" Alric growled, menace riding his voice like a wave of hate crashing against a bluff. "And think twice before lying to me."

Alric figured the old man would show some kind of worry, but his eyes sparkled and a wide smile crossed his face. "Such *fangs* on you, good sir."

The townspeople walked by, shooting shy glances toward the two of them then quickly looking away. They knew better than to get involved in a personal dispute in the lower district, unless they get involved with the guards themselves. The guards had a habit of treating the lower folk differently than the rest, whether you were at fault or not.

"You really think this is the time for jokes?" Alric let his anger drive his movement, pushing more weight into the man, expecting his throat to pop any second. Yet, Traveler seemed to hardly notice. "Now, answer me. Who are you?"

"I've already told you, Alric. I am but a traveler seeking purpose and serving purpose where it is found. I am not your enemy. I am, in fact, a friend."

"Can't say I've ever seen you before, *friend,* but something tells me you've seen me aplenty. Seem to know a few things about me." Alric peeled back his lips and growled through his teeth. "Things some people took to their grave. And that there lies the problem. Now, be straight with me or I'll—"

"You'll what, Alric?" Traveler's sparkling eyes turned more serious, the smile on his face sinking into a frown. "You'll gut me?" Traveler grabbed Alric's wrist calmly, prying his arm away with incredible strength. Alric fought back, but it was useless. Traveler was unpredictably strong. Too strong.

How the ...?

"Bash my head into the wall?" Traveler continued. "Strangle me, drag me into an ally and hit me until my face caves in? Not your style, Alric. Not anymore, and you know it."

Alric's anger began to sap away. He knew there was something off about the man from the beginning, but this was vastly beyond what he could have imagined. The old man looked withered and nearly broken, yet his strength was undeniable, inhuman.

Alric struggled to keep his face calm. "What do you want?"

Traveler shrugged. "What I want is for you to learn from this. A lesson, we'll say."

"And you think the best way to teach this lesson is through puns? Bring up my past? Make me carry your wagon?"

For that moment, Traveler looked more offended if anything. "Hey now, these are top class puns. And believe me; I didn't want to bring up your past. We've all made mistakes, Alric, and I don't mean to bring yours to light. I just had to make sure it was you. As for the wagon ... well, that's more of a metaphor."

"A metaphor?" Alric asked.

"For this lesson, yes."

Alric could feel the burn in his face returning. "You know, I'm just about fucking done with you."

"Oh, Alric"—the look on the old man's face sent a chill down Alric's spine—"we've only just begun."

"Fuck this." Alric turned to leave but was grabbed by Traveler, holding him tightly where he stood. The old man's grasp was unbelievably tight.

Before Alric had time to lash out, the man began to speak. "It's been too long, Aric. Years have passed since you *tucked tail*. The world has moved on without you, taking shape into something terrible. And if you don't defy this new world, all will be lost.

"What happened to you in Rapport was a tragedy, Alric. One I hate to talk about."

Alric felt a choke in his throat as he thought back to his life before—his home, his farm, his family.

"But," Traveler continued, "since then, you've been carrying this weight, a weight that's grown heavier with every passing year, yet you fail to notice because it's normal to you. It's heavy, weighs you down without notice, keeps you awake at night. It haunts your dreams.

"You think staying busy keeps the hurt at bay, and that's almost true. However, the longer you prolong to realize, the stronger it will be when you have to face it. Already it eats at you, in more ways you fail to acknowledge. You've no idea how close your mind is to break, and once that door breaks down, I fear that's it for you. There's no going back."

Alric wasn't sure how to respond. He wanted to lash out as soon as Traveler mentioned his farm. He wanted to punch him in the neck, to hear the spine crack with the blow. To reach down his throat and rip out his lungs. Then, at the moment he mentioned the nightmares, he felt more vulnerable than ever. Mostly because Traveler was right.

Alric wanted to channel his sadness into rage, to fuel his anger with his haunted past, but couldn't stomach the strength. Instead, he looked deeply into Traveler's eyes.

"Realize what?" Alric asked, more of a mumble than anything.

"Hm ...?" Traveler asked.

"You said, *before you realize*. What don't I realize?"

"Oh. Right." Traveler nodded past Alric's shoulder. "That's where the wagon comes in."

Alric nodded. "I get it."

"But, do you?" Traveler asked questionably.

"Yes. The wagon, the *weight* you so mentioned, I need to realize just how heavy this *weight* really is."

Traveler's posture slackened, conveying only disappointment. "No, Alric, that's not what I'm getting at. The metaphor isn't the *weight* of the wagon, but the *wagon* itself. The weight is something you've created, but the wagon never existed in the first place."

"What?"

"I said," Traveler repeated, resting a reassuring hand on Alric's shoulder, "there is no wagon."

The street was nearly the same as it had been when Alric came upon it—masses of people walked by, some people here and there, glancing at him quickly before shying away, the noise of chatter echoing the market. All was the same, besides the wagon.

The wagon he'd carried was gone.

He turned back and was startled. Instead of looking at Traveler, he was staring into the glass window of a pie shop, his own shocked reflection staring back.

Traveler was nowhere to be seen.

He looked about, glancing down both sides of the street to try to catch sight of him, to no avail. The man was gone, like he had never been there to begin with.

Instinctively, Alric ran down the street, back toward the way he'd come with Benny not long ago. He turned the corner to see the mob of beggars digging into a small food cart, much like the one Alric had carried for Traveler. Yet, it looked different. It was … bigger than it originally had been.

Alric stood in shock, knowing he should get moving but unsure of where to go. The encounter with the old man had happened. It *had* to have happened. But, if that were true, where was he now? How did the cart make its way to the beggars?

Alric didn't have an answer, so instead of searching for one, he began to make his way back to the inn, keeping his head low in an attempt to blend in with the crowd.

The Story of Legends

In the years of traveling with her family, Sarah had spent her nights in many places—local taverns, the houses of her father's patrons, even a royal guest at Duke Gunther's at one point, whose dukedom was only a week travel from Servitol. But, if she were lucky enough, her family would set camp in a field under a starry night.

A castle is vast and grand, but the stars were endless and beautiful, and the love for her family unfathomable.

It was nights like those that she would never forget. The smell of boiling stew cooking over a campfire, her father bringing bundles of sticks and twigs to fuel the fire, and the long nights of gazing upon the stars while her father told her stories of Navalethian fables.

She loved her father's stories. They were always filled with gallant knights slaying beasts that plagued towns and families, stories of small people doing great things and, of course, Asher the Conqueror. Out of them all, she idolized Asher the most.

Asher was a hero among Navaleth, a young boy born with the strength of ten men. Although he was only a fable, he remained a beacon of how all Navalethians should be—charming, strong, chivalrous, kind, brave. His stories gave all Navalethians the hope to become something greater than their normal self. Sarah's favorite stories all involved Asher, and she had no shame in that.

Being raised on a small farm, Asher was nothing more than a regular child helping his family make their way in the world. However, the world back then had been different. It'd been a world plagued with monsters— ghouls, giants, spiders as big as houses, dragons that breathed hellfire, cannibals that lived in caves, witches that abducted children and turned them into stew.

Asher's mother was the only one to take care of him. When his village was attacked by hellhounds, Asher fought them off with his bare hands, saving all the villagers.

Asher became a savior, and ever since that day, he dedicated his entire life traveling around Navaleth in search of other villages in need of his help. He defeated the mountain beast that raged bloody havoc on a town called Oakfurt. He defeated the Gellmar the Cruel, an ogre king, and singlehandedly saved the country from an invasion.

Out of all his triumphs, Asher's greatest achievement was when he defeated the necromancer king, who not only could resurrect and control the dead, but he also controlled a vast army of demons and monsters.

Asher and the necromancer fought a colossal battle for three days on the peak of a mountain. With the strength of the magical sword, T'vierith, the god slayer, Asher struck down the necromancer and rid the world of his evil doings.

Legend has it that Asher left the legendary sword stuck in the body of the necromancer, a beacon to all those who oppose the power of Navaleth, a warning against any more evil. However, three days following the epic battle, the mountain began to crumble and decay, turning Asher's warning into a tomb for the necromancer, burying his body, along with T'vierith, deep beneath the rubble. The legendary sword, along with the necromancers body, had forever disappeared.

Asher was crowned the first king of Navaleth with his victory against the necromancer king. He met a beautiful woman named Aeritis, who became the first official queen of Navaleth. Together, they lived happily, bearing three children, which started the royal bloodline of the Navalethian monarchy. The people loved them, and they loved the people.

Sarah knew that stories like Asher's were to teach children lessons and to distract them from the real horrors in the world, and there was a time when she strived to learn from the stories in order to become the Navalethian that Asher hoped everyone to be. However, given most recent events in her life, Sarah had changed. The only thing she wanted most in the world was another day by the fire with her family.

Nights by the fire was when Sarah felt like they were a real family. There were no tutors of her father's trade, no worries of politicians or kingdoms, and no worries of the future. It was just the Michaelsons lying in a field of tall grass as a regular family, doing regular family stuff. Nothing else mattered, nothing else existed. It was unbreakable memories like the fields that usually made Sarah feel invincible, as strong as the fabled Asher himself.

Never again would she feel that safe.

That was before, when the world was less evil, before the dying screams of her mother and father echoed in her head day and night, before the smell of burning flesh polluted the air miles away from a slaughtered village.

There would be no more meals cooked over the fire by her mother, no more stories whispered in the night by her father. Never again would she feel that absence of the world with her family, but only the absence of her family in the world.

Instead of lying in the fields with her family, Sarah sat in a dimly lit tavern in the lower district of Servitol with strangers. Evan sat next to her with his arms leaning on the table, his dark hair hiding his face as he looked down, as if he was deep in thought. At his right, Seroes sat quietly. Every now and then, Sarah would catch him staring at her before quickly averting her eyes. Across the large table sat Trevor, Dodge, Warren, and Baron. On more than one occasion, Sarah caught Dodge glancing at her awkwardly, yet he didn't shy away like Seroes. She could see the dark bags hanging heavily under his bloodshot eyes.

Warren sat quietly to himself, his head hanging low, not saying a word nor paying attention to anyone or anything. She hadn't said a word to him, nor even looked his way during their long march over the last week's trek through the endless woods. Nor did she to Trevor or Dodge. What would she say? What *could* she say?

The room around them was uplifted with conversations by other patrons. People clashed their mugs before taking a drink, slopped over bowls of porridge, and women flaunted their breasts and laughed obnoxiously for attention. None of it made sense to her—the drinking, the laughing, or even the eating. It was a vague memory she remembered cherishing but couldn't remember what it felt like in that moment. She remembered times when she'd laughed endlessly with Trevor on the broken wall in Robins-Port, but at that moment, she couldn't remember what that happiness felt like. The feeling was numb to her.

They sat at the Twin-Blade tavern, in the back, away from the other guests. None seemed to pay attention to them whatsoever. Sarah preferred that.

She thought back to the moment in the woods a week ago, when Benny held her hands, and suddenly she was thrown into her own memories, like she was watching a play acted out before her. Only, she was also the lead role, and her family and Trevor were secondaries to this tragic tale.

Ever since that moment, Sarah hadn't been able to sleep. In fact, she mostly avoided it, if she could. If she could stay awake for the rest of her life and function properly, she would. Anything was better than being thrown back into the nightmare that waited behind her closed eyelids. It didn't look like the others had slept much, either.

The nightmare was always the same. She would be crawling as fast as she could through that dirt tunnel, death whispering her name behind her. Whenever she would turn around, she would see the glowing eyes of a monster. And she had done the same thing in each dream—flee. But no matter how fast she crawled, the eyes would keep getting closer and closer. Then she would see a light near the end of the tunnel, an opened hatch just a few feet away with an arm reaching in for her. Just as she was fingertips away from that helping hand, the monster would grab her leg and drag her all the way back to where she had started.

No matter how many times she had the dream, it always felt so real. Each night, she would wake, kicking and screaming against the monster that hunted her.

Trevor was there every night. He would always have a cup of water for Sarah, reassuring her that it was just a nightmare and that she was safe. It was a cruel joke, because it wasn't just a nightmare, but also a memory. How did someone become safe from their own memories?

Sarah looked across the table to Trevor, and he looked right back at her. For a fleeting moment, she felt relaxed at knowing he was there with her.

She couldn't help wondering to herself, *Does he know what happened to me?*

Nobody had brought it up to her, and she never brought it up to any of them. It wasn't something she understood herself, so how could she possibly explain it someone else? The only way she could describe it was that it felt like something had been taken from her, something that she didn't know she'd had in the first place.

A shadow fell over the table, and Sarah looked up to see the bartender with his hands on his hips. He looked to everyone individually with a comprehensive stare. His hair was shortly cut, and he bore a scar across his cheek.

"Well, look who we've got here." His voice was as deep as the scar stretching across his cheek. "Been a while, I'd say. I see you've made some friends."

"Well, you know what they say," Evan said to the innkeeper. "When life hands you lemons, eh?"

"Something tells me yours were more sour than the rest of ours."

Dodge's lip curled beneath his rugged beard, and the innkeeper took notice.

"Meant no offense there," he said, holding up his open hands as a gesture of good faith. "A friend of the brotherhood is a friend of mine."

"No harm done, Twinny," Seroes said at the end of the table. "Just a long night, is all. What's on the gossip menu lately, anyway?"

Twinny tilted his head to the side. "Not much. Same problems, but only worse. More farmers come in each day, talking about their land being burnt by Lazar and his loyalists. One farmer told me Lazar himself made him watch as his cornstalk was burned away. Lazar told the man that it wasn't his fault, but the empire's." Twinny snorted. "Lazar apparently gave him a few pardoning coins, told him to use it only to reach the capital to spread his tale to the king. You believe that? A benevolent butcher."

"Hm." Evan shrugged. "Seems to me this *Lazar* is trying to start a rebellion of some sort. What's the king have to say about that?"

"That's just the thing. Nobody's heard from the king in months, and not even his herald's said a word on the matter. Either they're devising a plan or don't see it as a threat. Either way, that's about all the talk lately. Unless you have some news to share?"

The table fell silent, and Sarah prepared herself for what was surely going to happen next. They were, essentially, sticking to the plan on getting to Servitol and telling someone about the attack in Robins-Port. Twinny seemed like a trusted friend, so who better to trust that information?

"Well, as a matter of fact," Evan started, all eyes resting on him as he spoke, "we did have a sort of … close encounter of sorts. Didn't we, Baron?"

Baron's shoulders seemed to tense, and Sarah could see his lip curled beneath the shadow of his gray hood. "Don't know what you're talking about."

"Eh?" Twinny looked concerned for the moment. "You all right there, Flash?"

"Oh, he's fine," Evan continued. "Was nearly killed by an eight-legged friend of ours we found in a cave."

"For fuck's sake, Evan," Seroes said, fighting against a smile. "We talked about this—sensitivity."

Sarah's brief moment of hope was replaced with the familiar feeling of apathy. The plan had changed, she supposed. They were either planning on looking for a different contact in the city, or they actually didn't trust Twinny.

"Who's being insensitive here?" Evan asked, pleading innocence. "I'm just glad my good old' pal Baron here is still able to talk, given that scream."

"Not this again," Baron whispered quietly.

"In his defense," Evan said matter-of-factly, "it was a rather big spider. Squirmy little fellow. It didn't take long for me to catch it, let alone find a prime time to throw it at him."

"You *what*?" Baron pulled back his hood and looked hard at Evan. "You mean, you *put* that thing on me?"

Evan raised his arms at his sides. "Come now, Baron; what kind of friends would we be if we didn't try to help you face your fears?"

"What do you mean *we*?" Baron narrowed his eyes accusingly at Evan.

In response, Evan bit his lower lip as he scanned the faces around the room, finally settling on Seroes, who seemed to be doing his hardest to become invisible.

"You son of a—"

"You sniveling coward, Evan," Seroes said venomously. "You would drag me under with you."

Sarah didn't fully understand the story, but it seemed to get Twinny rolling with laughter.

"Every man's got a fear, friend," he said to Baron, who now looked away bashfully. "Can't say that'll get far for gossip these days, but a good story is always welcome. Where's the rest of your lot? How's Garth and Merrick? Benny and Al?"

The door was swung open, bright light warming the room, as Benny walked solely into the Twin-Blade Inn. He looked about the room, smiling broadly when he spotted Sarah and the rest of them at the table.

"Twinny!" Benny praised when he reached the table. "It's good to see you, friend."

"Aye, it's good to see ya," Twinny replied. "Where's the other half? Hardly ever see you two separated."

"Oh"—he waved his hand toward the door—"probably off brooding somewhere. He'll be about soon enough, I'm sure. How's business going?"

"Oh, you know. More people entering the city each day in need of a place to stay. Spend all day at the gates begging to see the king, but they usually come back near nightfall, using whatever coin they've left to fill their bellies and to find a soft bed to lay on. Which reminds me." Twinny pointed at Evan. "A merchant near the East-End seems to be bragging about a new stock he's got. Might be something you wanna look into?"

"Really?" Evan tapped a finger against his bottom lip, an intriguing smile spreading across his face. "Perhaps I'll pay a visit then."

"Sooner rather than later," Twinny said suspiciously. "Capital is filled with high-end merchants lately, always looking to fetch a good price for *product.*"

"In that case," Benny said, "we best be off to see this said merchant." Benny reached beneath his tunic and pulled out a small pouch. He untied the slipknot, revealed a few shiny coins, and handed them to Twinny. "If you'll please set up some food for our guests? Watch our gear in the back for a few hours?"

Twinny hardly looked at the coins before he slipped them into a pocket at his side. "You know I will. I'll get some fresh pork set up for you."

"Fantastic." Benny smiled widely. "Thank you, friend."

Twinny gave a nod toward the table then disappeared through a door that led to the back of the bar. The moment the barkeeper was gone, Benny turned to the rest of the table.

"Well then, how are our guests doing?" he asked, fidgeting with the fingertips of his gloves. "Is our good friend Thomas still with Garth and Merrick?"

"Well, they ain't' back yet," Dodge grumbled deeply.

"I see," Benny said with a nod. "Well, I had hoped they would be here for this, but … such is life."

"Where's your man?" Dodge asked suddenly.

"My man? Oh, Alric. He got tied up with something on the way. I'll be meeting with him shortly. Which brings me to my news. Things have become … *complicated.*"

"Not sure I like the sound of that," Baron said. "Annoying complicated or bad complicated?"

"Well, I wouldn't go as far to say *annoying* is the best choice of word, but it is perhaps a roadblock of a sort."

"So, annoyingly bad complicated," Evan confirmed.

"Where does that put us then?" Seroes asked.

"Al and I will be meeting an old friend at The Great-Hammer in a short while. We think he'll be able to help—"

"Why are we here?" Warren interrupted. He'd hardly said a word since their escape from Robins-Port, had always kept his distance, his arms cradled to his chest with a distant stare on his face. However, now his fury looked like it could melt steel.

"We're here," Evan replied, "to have a hot meal and cool drink."

Anger flared across Warren's face. "Fine, but why are we here in this flea hole? Why are we meeting with your *old friends* in the first place? It's the king we need to see. The sooner we tell the king what happened, the sooner my family can be avenged."

"Ah." Evan lifted a finger to Warren. "Then, by all means, pick up a sword and march your ass back—"

"Evan!" Seroes nudged Evan's arm. "What'd we talk about?"

Behind his mask of rage, there were tears building in Warren's eyes. Evan rolled his eyes, cleared his throat, and brushed himself off before leaning across the table toward Warren.

Evan rolled his eyes, cleared his throat, and brushed himself off before leaning across the table toward Warren. "Listen," he said in a hushed voice. "I know how you're feeling, okay? I get it. What happened to your family—to all your families—is unforgivable. Believe me; I'm all for a dish of blood pudding, but revenge is always dealt on your enemies and, right now, we don't know who the enemy is."

"But we do," Warren blurted impatiently.

Evan burrowed his brow in curiosity. "We do?"

"The *Mal'Fur*," Warren answered confidently.

The only thing Sarah knew about the Mal'Fur came from stories from her father, and none of them were good. From what she knew, they were a barbaric group of humans born with demon blood in their veins. During the War for Hope nearly two hundred years ago, the *Mal'Fur* were the main fighting force in Malicar's army, reaping across Navaleth and butchering anyone they deemed an enemy, which was just about everyone who wasn't Mal'Fur.

"It wasn't any Mal'Fur," Evan said with finality.

Warren curled his lip. "And how would you know?"

Evan raised an eyebrow in response. "Besides the fact that they never existed in the first place?" Evan laughed quietly to himself. "It wasn't them."

"Yes, it was!" Warren pleaded. "What they did …" Warren stared down at the table, tears pooling from his eyes, shaking his head. "What they did to the bodies? Only the Mal'Fur could do that."

According to Navalethian lore, the Mal'Fur were infamous for raiding small towns and murdering women and children. They used their victims as tribute to their demon god. These tributes were made from mass graves of dismembered bodies. It was said tribal chieftains would take a women and mate with them on top of the mangled corpses. They also believed that eating your offspring purified your soul and gave you strength, blessing you with the gift of never-ending youth. Over the generations of reincarnation, the power of the Mal'Fur's blood became more and more impure, with the natives being a direct descendent of that bloodline.

Before Sarah was born, Navaleth was at war with the natives. She never understood why, and her father had never given her a clear answer as to what the war was about. When Sarah would ask about the war, Florance, her mother, would also shut down and avoid the topic. All Sarah knew was that it was a bloody war, one that Navaleth almost lost.

With victory, the natives were pushed beyond Navaleth's borders. Years after the war, soldiers searched every corner of Navaleth, cutting down every native they found within the borders of the empire.

"People are evil enough," Baron said ominously. "Don't need to be a *Mal'Fur* to do something like that."

"But it was them!" Warren pleaded, slamming his fist on the table, his voice drawing attention from the other patrons.

"Listen, boy," Evan growled, real anger in his voice. Seroes reached across the table to try to calm his friend, but Evan shoved it away. "Fuck your *sensitivity*, Seroes. I'm not going to sit here and have this ungrateful shit spit on something he knows nothing about. It wasn't the fucking Mal'Fur. Your village wasn't butchered by mythical demons, nor was it killed by any natives, It was by regular people like you and me."

"Yeah?" Warren shifted in his seat. "How do you know the natives aren't hiding their true powers, taking all these years to plot their attack?"

It was Dodge who answered. "Because the Mal'Fur are nothing more than a nightmare story, and there are no more natives in Navaleth. It's been that way for fifteen years."

"We checked a body, as well," Seroes added, nodding toward Sarah who felt uncomfortable getting involved. "The one we pulled out of the hole. He wasn't native."

"And if nobody has seen a savage in fifteen years, how would you know what one looked like?" Warren pressed. "They could have used their devil magic to look like us, for all we know."

"I heard him speak." Sarah was just as surprised as the others to hear her own voice. "He didn't sound ... different."

Warren scoffed. "And I'm supposed to believe *you*? For all I know, you and that man were hiding away in that hole so you could fuck in privacy."

Dodge jumped from his chair. "What the fuck did you just say?" He towered over Warren. It might as well have been an ant standing next to a horse.

Warren refused to back down. "You heard me. For all I know, that whore could have been hidden away with one of her many lovers without a clue the village was under attack."

Some looked to Sarah, maybe looking for her to lash out at the ridiculous accusation, but Sarah sat there quietly. A week ago, she would respond with an insult of her own, maybe even go as far as to reach across the table and teach Warren some manners. But that was a week ago, and this was now. Sarah felt no emotion with what was said. Dodge, however, was feeling enough for the both of them.

"If I didn't know what you just went through," Dodge growled to Warren, "with your parents and the rest of my friends, I'd—"

"You wouldn't do a fucking thing." Warren stood now, trying to match Dodge's height. Trying and failing. "I know what blood runs through your veins, old man. I know you're as big a coward as your brother. We both know your family's curse."

"Let's all just calm down," Benny said, taking a step toward the table, keeping his voice hushed. "Last thing we need is to draw attention."

"I don't know," Evan said, leaning back in his chair comfortably. "This is the most that's come out of this lot since we set off. Could be a good show."

The tavern was quiet now, the nearby patrons all looking toward them, watching and waiting with insistent eyes, like animals waiting for their feed.

"What's that mean?" Trevor asked after a few moments of dangerous silence.

If Sarah thought the situation couldn't get any worse, a vicious smile creeping across Warren's face proved otherwise.

"Oh," he said quietly while peering around Dodge's massive arm. "He didn't tell you, then?"

Dodge tightened his fists. "Don't you fucking dare," he warned.

Sarah had never seen him so dangerous than in that moment.

"What'd he tell you? That your father died gloriously in battle?" Warren laughed quietly and shook his head, meeting Dodge's eyes again. "I suppose that's a better story than what really happened. About how his brother killed your mom."

It happened in a flash. Everyone was silent for a few moments, Warren's dark news polluting the air. Next, before Sarah knew what was happening, Dodge had his massive hands wrapped around Warren's throat, slamming his head repeatedly against the table.

Seroes and Baron leapt out of their chairs and went for Dodge's hands, peeling them away from Warren's throat. Evan leaned back in his chair, clapping softly at the show.

Bang! Bang! Bang! The sound of Warren's head hitting the table drew Sarah elsewhere.

Bang! Bang! Bang! She was no longer in the tavern, but in her parents' bedroom. She was facing her mother, who had her back against the door, which shook with each pound.

Bang! Bang! Bang! The door broke through, burying her mother underneath. A man stood in the doorway before her, a wicked smile on his face and a bloodied sword in his hand.

"*Here, little piggy.*" He stepped forward, raising his arm back, the sword point glinting in the air before sweeping down toward her face.

Sarah jumped out of her seat, her arms held out to shield her face from the incoming attack. Her body tremored, a screech of fear with each gasp as she slowly came to her senses. She searched around the inn for the man who was trying to kill her, even though she knew he didn't exist. Not anymore. His body was left back in the mess of Robins-Port. She stood there awkwardly as the rest of the tavern stared at her.

Something still felt off, like she was still in danger. She had to get away … and fast.

She turned to run when Benny stepped in close, his hands held up before her.

"Calm now, Sarah. There's no need to be afraid." He took a step toward her.

Instinctively, she backed away, looking for another route to freedom.

"Look at me, Sarah. I mean you no harm. Look at me."

The others at the table seemed to realize what was happening, their interests now all focused on her.

Trevor looked at her, his eyes full of worry that made Sarah want to break down and cry. He got up and walked toward her.

"It's okay, Sarah," he said, reaching out a hand toward her. "You're okay now."

"Just what the fuck is going on here?"

Sarah jumped at the sudden and loud voice from the barkeep Twinny. He stood at the table looking down at them all. He looked to Warren, who rubbed at the sides of his neck, and then back to Evan who faked an innocent smile. Twinny then turned to Benny with a look that made Sarah uncomfortable.

"I like your company, Benny—you know that—but my rules apply to everyone, one being that if you've a problem, you take it elsewhere." At that moment, he turned to the rest of the table, mostly focusing on Dodge and Warren. "Maybe you lot didn't know, so I'll clear it up for ya. They'll be no fighting in my fuckin' inn. Understand?"

When Dodge didn't respond, the barkeep raised his eyebrows. Dodge returned the look and gave a soft nod. "Understood. Apologies."

"You're forgiven. This time, at least. You get one. The next time, you're out. Benny?"

"Got it, Twinny. Won't happen again," Benny insisted.

Twinny turned and walked back to the kitchen.

Benny turned to face Sarah and Trevor. "Right, suppose we should make that errand, eh, Evan?"

"Suppose we should." Evan groaned as he climbed out of his seat. "Looks like the show is over."

"Sarah, Trevor, Dodge? Would you like to come?" Benny asked, his eyes never leaving Sarah's.

"Woah, now," Evan warned as he approached them. "That doesn't sound like the best idea."

"Neither does leaving them here after that … charade just now. Besides, Baron can stay here with Seroes."

"Since when am I the babysitter?" Baron complained.

"Well, someone has to stay here and wait for Garth and Merrick, and we can't exactly leave Warren alone."

"If the brat wants to leave, then, by all means, let him leave," Evan stated flatly.

"Evan?" Seroes called slowly.

Evan arched his back until Sarah could hear bones crack. "Yeah, yeah, sensitivity and all that shit. I'll be outside when you're ready."

Dodge answered by climbing out of his seat to join them. "Suppose I could use some air."

"And I some answers," Trevor said flatly, staring at Dodge.

His uncle looked away bashfully.

"Well then"—Benny straightened his tunic, took a slight bow, and then raised an arm toward the door—"shall we?"

The door opened to the clatter of conversation and the smell of the city. The sun shone bright, nearly blinding Sarah as she walked into the unfamiliar streets of Servitol, the capital of Navaleth.

A Stranger in a Strange Land

Trevor could sit and contemplate the grandeur of Servitol, imagining for days of what that massive city would look like, and still not even come close to its enormity. It was a gargantuan wonder, a city within a city, filled with people living whichever life they wanted without a care in the world. Every street was an endless line of shops and houses, a gentle wind blowing the faint aromas of both sweet and bitter smells, the sound of conversations whispering with the breeze.

There were people everywhere, crowding the large cobblestone streets and leaving hardly enough room for Trevor to squeeze by. Some stood at a stand, hollering at those passing by to take a gander upon the goods that they were selling. Children ran about, playing tag with their siblings or friends while their father tried on a coat from a tailor shop. A woman wearing an obnoxiously large hat laughed loudly as she nearly bumped into Trevor. The woman hardly noticed the encounter, deep in her gossip with a friend, not a worry in the world who might step into her path.

Regardless of the recent past events in Robins-Port, Trevor still felt a spark of excitement from being within the city, which was more than he could say about his companions. Benny and Evan seemed decent enough people, but Trevor couldn't help feeling they kept talking around him, saying certain things and having them mean something entirely different.

Much like what they were doing now.

What did that innkeeper say? Trevor thought to himself. *"Merchant with new product?" What does that even mean? For a group of people who were constantly talking about remaining in the shadows of Servitol, they sure seemed to know plenty of enough people to draw attention.*

Dodge, on the other hand, was quieter than ever. He didn't look like the conversationalist, but he usually could take even the dullest conversation and turn it into something worthwhile. Now he was as distant as a whisper on the wind, averting Trevor's eyes when he would try to meet his. Trevor couldn't help but feel it had to do with what Warren had said back at the tavern. Trevor hadn't believed him, of course, but Dodge's current attitude was making him think otherwise.

I've never seen him act so impulsive in my life. How could a man who preaches self-control burst so fast?

Trevor didn't want to think about it. He was in a new place, a new world, and the last thing he wanted was his experience to be once again ruined by a bully like Warren.

Unlike Dodge, Tom was as chatty as ever during their trip to the city. Though wounded, he walked about as if nothing bothered him, keeping a tight, blood-stained bandage wrapped at his side. More than a couple nights, he had heard Tom howling in laughter with some of the others, the two archers Garth and Merrick. Trevor didn't know what they had been talking about, he had kept most of his attention on Sarah.

She would keep quietly to herself, eyes mostly focused in the distance or toward the ground as she kept one foot in front of the other. When she was awake, at least she'd been mobile, but it was when she would sleep that Trevor grew more worried.

More than a few times, Trevor would wake from the sound of Sarah screaming, flailing around in her sleep and crying in pain as if she was being attacked. He would rush to her side every time, being sure to fetch a fresh cup of water. He never touched her, though. Something told him that it would just make things worse. So, he had to endure the horrific sight of Sarah struggling in her sleep until she finally woke herself up. When she did, Trevor did the only thing he could do in that situation—he handed her a cup of water and whispered that she was safe now, that whatever was happening to her was only a dream.

Trevor wanted to comfort her, to hold her tight and promise nothing bad was going to happen to her again. He wanted to show her that she was safe now, that he was there to protect her, but it was the same process when Sarah finally woke up. She would blink away tears, huddle her legs close to her chest, and silently stay awake for the rest of the night. All the while, Trevor would stay at a distance, also staying awake to make sure she was going to be all right.

Trevor had hoped that, when they finally managed to get to the capital, they would be welcomed by guards and ushered into the castle to speak directly with the king, to explain what had happened to them in Robins-Port.

However, things were not as grand as that fleeting thought. Instead, Trevor, Dodge, and Sarah followed three strangers through a city they knew nothing about, hoping they were trustworthy of their lives.

Trevor walked quietly behind them all, his mood shifting with his line of thoughts. He repeatedly told himself to ignore what had happened at the tavern, yet he couldn't get Warren's words out of his head.

Family curse? What does that mean? And why would Dodge be so upset about it?

Trevor was used to Warren vomiting nonsense to try to get under his skin, but this time was different. This time, he could tell Dodge was hurt by what had been said and pissed off enough to try to smash Warren's head through a solid oak table.

As he thought back to the scene, that little tickle in Trevor's stomach began to grow, spreading more fire throughout his body. Part of it was anger, but there was something else there, too. Something that Trevor didn't expect to feel.

Excitement?

Yes, that's what it was. He was angry but also excited. Part of him was curious as to why Warren would say such a thing, but another part of him really enjoyed watching his face smashed repeatedly on the table. It was nice seeing Warren hurt.

"What's this about a merchant, then?" asked Dodge, eyes focused up front at Benny and Evan.

"Servitol offers many possibilities to entrepreneurs," Benny said enthusiastically, only glancing over his shoulder toward Dodge as he kept the pace. "Traders come around the world to barter goods and services. Many of them you see on the streets, whereas some of them … well, aren't seen at all."

"I wasn't aware the brotherhood was connected to the black market." Dodge spit to his side. "What could they be selling that you're interested in?"

"Something that you'll not be telling another soul about, old man." Evan turned to Benny. "Are you sure this is a good idea?"

"What do you mean?" Benny replied, genuine concern on his face.

"What do you mean *what do you mean*? You saw what happened back at Twinny's."

Benny waved aside Evan's comment. "Trust me; they aren't like Warren. They'll be fine."

"And how exactly do you know that?" Evan asked angrily, refusing to drop the topic as quickly as Benny was attempting to.

Benny raised one of his gloved hands before Evan's face. "I know," he said.

Trevor wasn't sure of how it was an answer, but it seemed to do the trick with Evan.

"Fine," Evan said flatly.

More talking in circles about something that doesn't make sense.

"Still doesn't answer my question," Dodge said.

"What was that?" Benny replied from over his shoulder as he led the group around a turn down a cobblestone street. The street was flooded with people; some squeezing past others in a hurry, some pulling large wagons filled with barrels, and some groups just stood about in a circle, talking and laughing, while some playfully shoved another.

Dodge shook his head in frustration. "Fine. Keep your secrets."

"Seems to be a lot of that going on these days," Trevor said, just as surprised by saying it as much as Dodge was hearing it.

His uncle was hurt—it was easy for Trevor to see—but Trevor didn't care. It felt good to let go of his anger, and so he did.

Dodge looked back at Trevor bashfully. "Trevor, look, I—"

"Is it true?" Trevor asked impatiently, feeling angrier the sadder his uncle looked. He didn't care. His chest felt like it was on fire, and he let his anger fuel it. He spent so long keeping everything bottled up, always brushing his anger aside, because his uncle had taught him to, but not this time. It was good to let go, to let the anger take course.

"Tell me it's not true, Uncle," Trevor said, growling between his clenched teeth. "Tell me that filthy parasite was lying and that you haven't lied to me my entire life."

"It's hard to explain," Dodge said, stammering over his words, his eyes in search of an answer.

In that moment, Trevor saw his uncle at his worst. He looked weak, vulnerable, lost.

"No, it's not," Trevor replied, his patience wearing thin. "It's a simple fucking answer: yes or no." At some point, they all stopped walking, halting in the middle of the street, people giving awkward glances as they passed by. Trevor didn't care. There wasn't a day in his life that he hadn't received a dirty look from strangers. All because he was an orphan. All over something he had no control over.

"Come now, friends," Benny said as he tried to wedge his way between the two. "The last thing we need is to cause a scene."

Dodge kept quiet as he stared at Trevor, tears building up in his eyes. "Trevor …"

And there it is.

It was all Trevor needed. What Warren had said was true.

Trevor let his rage completely take over. In that moment, there was no Servitol, no strangers passing by, nobody named Benny or Evan or even Sarah. It was just him and his uncle.

"You've been lying to me my entire life," Trevor accused, his hands shaking with rage.

Dodge gave a soft shake of his head. "No, Trevor, I've protected you your entire life."

"Protected me!" Trevor couldn't help laughing at the nonsense. "Protected me? You lied to me! Every time I asked about my father, lies. When I wondered about my mother, more lies."

"I never lied to you about your mother," Dodge said quickly. However, Trevor was too lost in his fury to bother hearing it.

"Every passing day, I had to walk those streets. Every day, I was mocked, attacked, bullied, judged. I wondered why this was happening to me, why my life was so shitty simply because I had no parents to raise me. And through it all, the entire fucking village knew what happened when I was left in the dark."

Trevor turned to Sarah, who stood next to Benny, watching quietly with her ever-distant eyes. "Did you know, too?" Trevor asked her angrily.

She looked at him with that catatonic stare.

"Of course you did. How couldn't you? I suppose Warren was right about you, too, *pity* and all." Trevor stepped toward Dodge and Sarah. "Well, guess what? I don't want your pity. I don't want a fucking thing from you anymore!"

"Calm down, Trevor," Benny said quietly, looking around the street to see if anyone was watching, which just pissed Trevor off even more.

"Fuck off," Trevor told Benny. "You wanna keep your own secrets, so be it, but this doesn't concern you."

"Whoa now." Evan held up his hands and moved toward him. "Let's not forget who's helping who here."

Trevor stared angrily at Dodge, using his anger as armor. "I'm not confused on who has been helping who here." He watched his uncle's shoulders slump forward, exasperating a sigh of sorrow. "Not anymore. You didn't protect me; you betrayed me." Trevor looked back to Sarah. "You both did."

He couldn't believe the turn of events. His mind swirled with confusion from the sudden truth, and he couldn't grasp how he felt. Dodge was the closest thing he had to a father, but now he felt like nothing more than a stranger. Trevor had sworn to learn from his uncle, to live the ways he was being taught. He endured for him, suffered day-to-day life in Robins-Port for him. *I've killed for him!*

Before, when Trevor found himself close to seeing red, he would do his best to brush off the anger by using the exercises that Dodge had shown him. They consisted of breathing, steeling his mind, focusing his thoughts on something that distracted him from the problem.

Each time, he would think of Sarah and how lucky he was to have her. He would think about her golden hair blowing in the wind. Her wide smile as they laughed on the wall back in Robins-Port. The smell of the perfume she always brought back from her trips, along with the pieces of chocolate she would have.

None of that mattered anymore. Everything was different, and letting his anger out felt more right than all the times he had kept it in.

"So much for making it a quiet trip." Alric stepped out of an alleyway, his eyes darting back and forth between Trevor and Dodge. "All's well?"

"Not so much," Benny admitted. "Far from it, apparently. Yourself?"

Alric shrugged. "Same city, different day. Speaking of, what did you … uh"—Alric leaned closer to Benny, keeping his voice quiet—"what'd you see? Exactly?" Alric shifted uncomfortably, looking over his shoulder as if worried someone was following him.

"See?" Benny asked in confusion. "What do you mean?"

"Back there." Alric nodded in the direction he came from. "With that man. You notice anything strange? Did he look familiar to you at all?"

Benny crossed his arms and fully faced Alric. They spoke quietly to one another as the rest stood about. "Man? What man?"

A moment's hesitation passed from Alric before he nodded, brushing aside the quiet with a wave of his hand. "Yeah, yeah. I'm fine." He coughed awkwardly as if it would help in some way. "You plan on bringing this whole lot to The Great-Hammer?"

Benny eyed Alric suspiciously, waiting for an explanation that Alric didn't seem to want to give. "Of course not," he said finally. "Just our good friend Dodge. If I know Destro, he'll want to hear all sides of the story."

"Right. Then what's with the others?" Alric gestured to Sarah and Trevor.

"That's where I come in, apparently," Evan said with a sarcastic bow. "Got a tip from Twinny about some goods being sold on the other side of the lower district. Good ol' Benny boy here thought it'd be best to bring these two along."

"Oh yeah?" Alric said, his voice full of doubt.

Benny raised his gloved hands in defense. "I trust them. It's as simple as that."

Alric looked back and forth between Benny's hands. Then he gave a dramatic sigh and nodded. "It's as simple as that."

"Sorry to burst that ambiguous bubble of yours," Dodge said to the three men, "but I ain't going anywhere without these two."

Evan rolled his eyes and spun about. "Here we go."

"Look," Benny said defensively, "it's important that you come with us. The man we are meeting holds a certain prestige that could help us, and your side of the story is just as important as ours. More important, perhaps."

"I get it." Dodge nodded. "But it's like I said, I ain't going anywhere without these two. You want me to talk to your man, so be it. But they'll be coming, too."

"No," Trevor said with stern finality.

Trevor didn't know where he was, who he was with, or what they were doing. Everything was unfamiliar, a stranger to him. What he did know, however, was that he would rather be a stranger in a strange land than be anywhere near his uncle.

"No?" Alric asked.

"No," Trevor repeated.

"Trevor," Dodge said quietly, reaching a hand toward Trevor. "Don't—"

Trevor slapped Dodge's hand away. "Go with them. I don't want to go with you. I'll go with Evan." Trevor looked back at Sarah. "Take her, too. We've nothing to talk about anymore."

"Ouch." Evan squinted his face in a mimic of pain. "You might be the most savage little bastard I've ever encountered."

Trevor ignored the comment, eyes still fully focused on Sarah. "All the same."

For the first time since their journey to Servitol, Sarah looked at Trevor. Not the distant look he would get when trying to comfort her, but a real look, with feeling and focus.

"He'll be fine, Dodge," Benny assured. "I promise."

For a moment, Dodge said nothing. He looked down at Trevor, and Trevor returned with a glare.

To help settle the debate, Trevor walked toward Evan and stood at his side, arms crossed, still staring at his uncle.

Dodge nodded in defeat then stared angrily at Evan. "If any harm comes to him—"

"I'm sure you'll be a very grumpy, bitter old man," Evan replied. "I get it. As soon as we are done shopping, we'll head back to Twinny's to check up on your friend the blacksmith."

Dodge's only reply was a grunt.

"Right. Now that that's settled," Alric said impatiently as he started walking away.

"You've enough on you?" Benny asked Evan, in which the man replied with a nod. "Best not keep our company waiting then. Dodge, Sarah, if you will?"

Trevor looked one last time before turning his back on Sarah. He knew what he said was harsh, unfair even, but another part of himself was convinced that she deserved what was said. The idea of an apology made him sick to his stomach, so he just turned around and walked away with Evan at his side.

"Well," Evan sighed heavily, "this has got to be the worst case of babysitting I've ever done."

A Walk to the Forever Calm

There were no signs of the howlers the next day. Whether or not there were more, they'd yet to hear their cries, to fear their presence, as they marched through the forest toward their village. They were only days away, but with lack of water, food, and the utter exhaustion they all felt, Quiver and his pack—well, what was left of the pack—trekked on.

The adrenaline from the battle had gotten them through the first night and most of the next day. Yet, the longer they went, they slower they became.

They used their shirts as bedding for the litter they'd made, wrapping the thick fabric around two wide branches so they could carry Masco's unconscious body. Rasca managed to find some herbs to make a paste that would stop the bleeding and clean the wound, but Quiver feared that if they didn't manage to find fresh herbs to replace the old soon, which was unlikely, the youngling would suffer fatally.

He would like to say that he'd seen cuts just as deep during the war, that he'd seen warriors heal and walk away, but he would be lying. The youngling was in bad shape, and if they couldn't get him to a proper healer soon, all hope for Masco would be lost. But Quiver wouldn't give up that easily, not for the youngling who'd saved his life from one of the monstrosities. They would make it back to the camp. They would find him healing, and the youngling would make it. Quiver would make sure of it.

They managed to find a small creek the night after their fight with the howlers. As the sun set, they heard no howls in the darkness, so they decided to make camp and rest.

Oppo and Quiver set Masco next to the creek as Rasca ran off in search of more medicinal herbs and food. Oppo, who had been silent since the attack, simply stared at the water instead of indulging.

"Drink while you can, Oppo," Quiver told the youngling. "The village is still a bit farther. We'll need our strength."

The youngling made no sign that he heard Quiver.

After sitting silently for quite some time, staring at Masco's unconscious body, Oppo finally stood and walked to the creek to refresh himself.

Quiver peeled the cloth from Masco's back. The herbs were light green when he had first fingered them into the wounds, but now they were dark and brown. He noticed a smell, pungent and sour, a clear sign of a coming infection.

If we don't get him back soon, his muscles will decay and the sickness will take his life.

Quiver hadn't realized how bad the wound was until Rasca first filled it with the herb. The cuts were wide and deep, deep enough to scrape bones.

Quiver picked a leaf from a nearby bush and went to the creek. The water was chilling to the touch, and his mind screamed at him to take deep gulps from it, but he had other matters at hand.

He creased the leaf on its sides and folded a makeshift bowl to hold the water. Then he walked back to Masco and folded back his lip to slowly dribble the water into his mouth. Though unconscious, Masco took small swallows, which made Quiver feel a bit better.

"Keep fighting," he muttered.

Rasca emerged from the jungle, walking toward them, holding bright green leaves in both hands. "The water should help the salve last longer this time, but I didn't find much. How is he?"

Quiver looked down at Masco. "He's breathing,. Able to drink some water."

"That's a good sign," Rasca stated.

"It's a good sign," Quiver repeated, as if saying it again would truly make it so. "We've still some ways to go, though."

Rasca nodded, kneeling down next to Masco. "That we do. A couple days, at best."

Quiver sighed deeply. "My thoughts, too."

"What about Oppo?' Rasca asked, nodding toward the youngling who was now leaning against the trunk of a tree, eyes closed and fluttering. "He hasn't said much since the attack."

"The weight of Sparrow's death pollutes his mind." Quiver's heart sank with the memory of Sparrow. He'd been hard on the youngling ever since they'd left the village, and it made Quiver feel sick that he'd passed with that being among his final thoughts. "He's not the only one."

"Losing someone is never easy," Rasca said, a phrase Quiver knew all too well.

No, it's not.

"Here." Rasca tore off bits of the herb and held it out to Quiver, pulling his mind away from his dark thoughts. Rasca nodded to Quiver's wound. "For your side. We don't want that getting infected, too."

Quiver shook his head. "I'll manage. Masco will need as much as we can get our hands on."

Rasca didn't argue. He lifted back the rag on Masco's back. As soon as he saw the wound, he winced and wrinkled his nose. "Rot is starting to set in. Help me scrape this out?"

Quiver and Rasca dug their fingers up to their knuckles in the deep gash of Masco's wound, dragging down the cuts and scooping out the mush that was the old salve. Masco didn't move or make a sound. The more salve they removed, the stronger the smell of rot got. Quiver and Rasca only had to meet eyes to convey their concern.

When the new herbs were pressed into the cuts, Quiver nodded to Rasca. Then they huddled next to the creek, washed the blood from their hands, and took steady gulps of cool water.

Quiver felt the water chill his throat as he swallowed, feeling it settle in the pit of his stomach.

If only we had a few squirrels to go with it. I fear we have a long way to go before we get a decent meal, if ever at all.

***

They were farther away than expected. Much farther.

The next two days proved to be dreadful. The moisture of the hot forest pressed on Quiver's skin, his constant sweat mixed with dirt and grime pasted a thick coat around his body. The arches in his feet cramped with each step. His knees cracked and popped, tight and throbbing with the endless walking. It wasn't long after that before the rashes set in, spreading in the back of his knees, under his armpits, burning the sides of his thighs.

The cut at his side would open every day, burning constantly as the sweat caressed the wound. *But pain is good, sometimes. It means that you're still alive, that you've strength to carry on.*

Rasca managed to find a few squirrels that night. No longer worried about the howlers, they roasted them over a small fire, barely able to wait until fully cooked before they dug in. There were only two, so Quiver and Rasca let Oppo eat one while they split their own.

Oppo kept mostly to himself, staying quiet and distant behind them as Quiver and Rasca continued to carry Masco, who remained in a catatonic state. Quiver would frequently glance back, fearful that Oppo would no longer be following them.

His silence worried Quiver. He understood what it felt like to lose a brother, to lose a friend. Especially while so young.

We all deal with loss in our own ways. If this is his way, then so be it.

Quiver attempted to feed Masco, tearing the meat into bits in order to manage more easily, but the youngling wouldn't take. Water was scarce now since they had found the creek. Quiver saved what little he had left for Masco.

Rasca managed to find food, but failed to find any more herbs. Quiver hoped the water they used at the creek would help keep the wound moist until they reached the village.

"I'll take first watch," Quiver said once their bellies were as full as they would get tonight, which wasn't saying much. "We'll start at first light again."

Rasca didn't argue; he simply nodded then lay down, resting his head on a large root of a tree.

Quiver looked to Oppo, who didn't seem to have heard Quiver. "Oppo?"

The youngling looked at Quiver. His eyes were dazed, sad, empty. Then they creased, like it was the first time he'd noticed Quiver since they'd stopped. He then looked to Rasca, already lightly snoring in the grass and nodded. He stretched out on the ground near the small fire.

Quiver took out Nero's hatchet that they had found before their attack. Gripping it tightly, he sat against a tree underneath its heavy limbs to stay hidden in the shadow. He didn't expect anything to happen, but you couldn't go wrong with being prepared.

***

The next few days were a haze of sticky sweat and endless walking. Quiver wasn't sure how far they'd come since the creek, or how much farther they needed to go. He just kept one foot in front of the other and made sure his pack did the same.

Their walking began to falter. They stumbled over even the smallest of stones, ducking below branches and pushing past bushes, following the trail up and down hills, hoping that they were on a trail leading them the right way.

Quiver and Rasca took shifts carrying Masco. At first, Oppo had helped, but as Quiver watched, he saw the youngling's endurance fade faster with each day. He would let him walk alone for a few hours, keeping Oppo in front so he wouldn't fall behind, only to help for an hour before switching out with Quiver or Rasca. Eventually, they carried him the entire time, however many days that was. Quiver had no idea.

He kept his eyes focused front, watching Oppo sway back and forth, hoping he wouldn't topple over and add to the list of things to carry.

The water they had collected from the creek was completely gone, their rations from their packs eaten, and they didn't have the energy to find game to settle the endless cramp in their bellies. They did, however, stumble upon some berry bushes which, fortunately enough for them, weren't poisonous.

Each day drained them further and further beyond exhaustion, closer to their breaking point, and hopefully closer to their home.

It got to the point where Quiver wasn't even sure if they were going the right way, doubt creeping slowly in until it consumed his dazed mind.

We should be there by now. At least, I think we should be. Were we ever going the right way?

Regardless, they walked on. Either deeper in or farther out of the forest. He didn't think about it, couldn't think about it. The only thing he could focus on was Oppo swaying in front of him.

Quiver walked on, one in front of the other, hoping that Oppo didn't give up on him, so that Quiver wouldn't give up on Oppo.

***

Quiver sensed something in the distance. He wasn't sure how long it had been there— seconds, minutes, maybe even hours—but Quiver knew it was there. Maybe not to everyone else. Perhaps it was entirely in his own head, his mind playing tricks on him from lack of food and water and endless walking.

It wasn't a constant sound, one he occasionally heard past the throbbing in his head. It came in flashes, like spotting something in the corner of your eye, but it disappearing when you tried to find it.

Oh, how a deer would taste right about now.

It was the sound of people. When he first noticed, it was a cry. Or, was it laughter?

He looked back to Rasca to see if he'd noticed, but the man's eyes were shut tight, as if he was walking in his sleep, his tight hands on Masco's litter the only guide where to go.

In a way, his friend looked dead, and Quiver didn't expect he looked any better. They'd been walking for days with no water or sleep. Rasca's face looked pale, almost transparent. Dark circles surrounded his eyes, his lips blue like he was being suffocated. Rasca was a walking corpse.

And so are you, Quiver. All of you are already dead, wandering aimlessly in the afterlife. Walking to the Forever Calm.

"Shut up," he told himself, which caused Rasca to grumble behind him, but Quiver was too tired to even respond.

Oppo took a wide stumble on the trail and collapsed.

Quiver stopped abruptly, Masco's litter shoving into his lower back before Rasca realized they'd stopped. They set down the litter, and then Quiver went to Oppo.

The youngling's chest was rising and falling quickly, too fast for Quiver's clouded mind to keep up with. Using what strength Quiver wasn't aware he'd had left, he picked Oppo up and set him against a nearby tree. When he tried to stand back up, his vision spun and his face prickled with a cold heat. Before he realized what was happening, he was collapsing, as well.

He stared up toward the treetops, his head swirling as the green and yellow leaves blended together and swayed with a breeze. He wanted nothing more than to close his eyes, to lay in this spot until he withered away.

If this is what death feels like, I'll gladly embrace it. There are worse ways to go, Chief Quiver, and don't you know it.

Then he heard it again, the sound of someone yelling. It was distant, faint. Quiver knew he should get up, to tend to Oppo and Masco, but his body felt so heavy it might as well be sinking into the ground.

"Rasca," Quiver choked, hoping his friend was faring better than him. He shifted his head to the side, looking toward were Rasca should have been. Instead, Quiver only saw the bottom of Masco's feet lying in the litter, dirt stained and scabbed. "Rasca," he cried again.

Delusion clouded his mind. Time flashed in his mind, bringing him back to the days when he was younger, a time when he, his brother, and father would walk together in the forests.

He called out to his brother, only to remember that he'd been deemed exiled long ago. Then he called out to his father, the famous Nara'Seir who had brought all the clans together during the war, but then he remembered that dreadful day in the forest, the day his father had accepted a traditional duel and was rewarded with a hammer in the face from the southerner.

Then something else flashed before his eyes. A terrible memory that he'd hoped to bury long ago. In that moment, he wasn't in the forest. Well, not the same one, at least, but one hundreds of miles away from here. Hundreds of miles and nearly fifteen years ago.

He stood, his bow in hand and an arrow ready and drawn. Bodies lay about his feet, both bloodied with cuts, as well as peppered with the very arrows he'd set loose.

The sun was high, and he scanned the shadows of the trees, waiting for his target to come forth. He waited patiently until he saw the face of the monster before him. Yet, in this particular memory, it wasn't the man who he'd been hunting all these years, but a large wolf that revealed itself from the forest.

He stood with his bow drawn and arrow nocked, ready to fire at any moment, ready to take the life of his nemesis when, instead, he let the string go slack. He and the wolf stared at each other for a moment. Quiver spoke a few words, and then the beast gave a great howl before running back into the forest.

The memories slid by, reminding Quiver how he became the person he is today. Reminding him of the life he lived as it now leached from his body on the dirt ground in the middle of the forest.

He lay there, dark shadows of his vision closing in around him, death finally coming to sweep him away. That was when he saw a pair of feet approached him, followed by another, then another, and another.

Hands reached toward Quiver, but the faces that those hands belonged to were hazed in mist, blurred from his vision, as the world around him faded.

In his final moments, Quiver thought of Thread. As those hands reached out and began to take him to the afterlife, Quiver wished beyond everything that he could see Thread again, to tell her how much he cherished her ... one last time.

Yet, he was but a man, and this was the will of the spirits that he had betrayed. Who were they to take pity on a man who'd abandoned them so long ago?

Quiver's world turned to black.

The Language of a Whip

Trevor followed Evan through the eastern side of Servitol at a short distance, taking note at the sudden change in Servitol's scenery, all the while his guide spent his time muttering curses to himself rather than engaging in real conversation.

The streets were dirt rather than cobblestone, and the crowds of patrons and merchants that swelled the streets were all but gone, leaving the barren scene vacant of conversation and clutter. Houses were mere shacks, and if there was a home built from solid wood and materials, it was rotting and nearly crumbling to the ground.

Trevor didn't trust Evan. The only thing he knew about him was that he was quick to temper, never short of insults, unpredictable, and he didn't want Trevor with him for whatever it was they were doing. Even so, Trevor would prefer walking through a strange city with a man he didn't know, nor trust, rather than being anywhere near Dodge and Sarah. The thought of them alone boiled rage in Trevor's gut, sending more dark thoughts his way.

The eastern end of Servitol was about as opposite compared to what Trevor was used to seeing, coming from a warm, sunny town to a gray, melancholy slum. If there were people they passed, they looked more like farmers, mud staining their overalls and dirt covering their skin. Even the air smelled different here, more like spoiled food instead of the aroma of freshly baked goods.

How can two vastly different places exist in the same city? It's like a different world over here.

"Oh, for fuck's sake," Evan called from over his shoulder, looking back just long enough for Trevor to see him roll his eyes. "You're about the worst company I've ever had. Nothing but a brooding face and a quiet tongue. You know what they say about quiet people, right?"

Trevor was sure Evan would tell him whether or not he wanted to know, but he humored him anyway. "What's that?"

Evan laughed to himself. "They're boring."

They took a turn and began to descend down an empty street. Rugged houses lined close together on both sides. Windows were boarded up with planks of wood, front doors hung wide open, and the area was littered with garbage. A group of children hung about at the other side of the street, playing a game of sorts by kicking a rock back and forth between each other.

Evan slowed his pace and began to walk next to Trevor, eyeing the group of kids. "They may look innocent now, but they'll snatch your purse before you know it."

A boy, his face black with dirt stains, his clothes nothing more than simple rags, watched as Trevor and Evan passed.

Trevor wanted to run to the boy and help him, but he didn't know how. He had nothing to offer the child to make his life better. He only had the clothes on his back and a stranger for company.

In an attempt to not look rude, Trevor kept his focus on his feet as Evan led him farther down the street. Just as he was about to turn another corner, however, he looked back to see the boy watching him, his longing stare focused on Trevor as he disappeared around the corner.

"And here we are," Evan announced.

Before them stood a house, the largest Trevor had seen thus far. There was a large, steel gate separating the lush green grass from the deteriorating world surrounding it, a gold coin amongst a box of iron. At the entrance of the gate stood two men, both carrying a sword.

Evan faced Trevor for the first time since they had left the others. "You're quiet; that's good. Let's keep it that way. You follow my lead and do as I say when I say it. If things go south—"

"I can stay here, you know." The fact that Evan was treating Trevor like a child only annoyed him more.

Evan laughed. "And leave you alone in the heart of the East-End? Trust me; you're better off inside. People around here aren't exactly … hospitable, if you catch my drift. And if something were to happen to you, I'd have to answer to that brute of an uncle of yours, and I'm not exactly looking forward to that.

"Now, if things go wrong in there, just make it to the main district and don't stop running until you get there. Even if you're stopped by a guard, you keep running. You remember the way we came from, don't you?"

Trevor's look around, and when it was clear he had no clue as to which way led out of the city, Evan sighed.

"Well, let's just hope all goes well, then."

"What are—"

"Nope." Evan shut Trevor down with a raised hand. "No questions. No talking. No matter what you hear or what I say, you'll not fuck this up for me. Got it?"

Without giving Trevor time to respond, Evan turned around and made his way toward the two guards at the gate.

Trevor followed closely, keeping to Evan's shadow like he was told. *Always doing what the fuck I'm told.*

As they approached the two men guarding the gated entrance, both drew their swords and crossed them over the threshold, blocking the entrance with their blades.

"State your business," one of the men said in a deep voice. He wore a sleeveless vest of leather, which was littered with buckled pockets on the front and sides. Both of the men looked identical in attire, and both of their bare arms were decorated with scars.

"Just a farmer and his son here to do a bit of shopping," Evan replied, his voice more upbeat than usual.

"Go back the way you came or be run through," the second man said. "Ain't no conventional tools for a farmer here."

"Ah, but that's precisely why I'm here now," Evan responded, as if the guard had stated the obvious. "I was told I can find the best equipment a farmer could buy. *Unconventional* equipment."

The guard's scowl could curdle dairy, and the sight made Trevor weak in the knees.

He spoke with a deep voice, malice dripping from his tongue. "And who the fuck told you that?"

One of the guards smiled, his stare longing not at Trevor but past him. Trevor turned around quickly to see two more men. They were just as large and mean looking as the former two, standing only a few feet away from them with their swords drawn.

Trevor's heart quickened with fear. *They've got us surrounded.*

Trevor's first instinct was to run. He didn't have his sword, and he wasn't sure it would do much against these men even if he did.

However, if Evan was nervous, he didn't show it. "Oh, his name changes every year, it seems. Desiree, Ralfy, Corman. He did, however, give me this on our first meeting." Evan held up a large silver coin.

The guard's shoulders relaxed, his face slack and grimacing, as if Evan had robbed them of the opportunity to give someone a good stabbing. He looked to the other guard at his side and gave a soft nod before they sheathed their swords in unison.

Trevor glanced over his shoulder and saw the other two guards do the same and start walking away, back to whatever shadow they'd been hiding in.

"Three knocks, a pause, and then two knocks," one of the guards told them suddenly. "Marquis will answer."

"Very well. Thank you, gentlemen." Evan crossed the threshold of the gate and waved to Trevor to keep along. Then they climbed a flight of stone stairs that led up to the large house and gave the secret knock.

The situation was mysterious, setting Trevor on edge.

"Remember what I said," Evan whispered quietly to Trevor. "No matter what you see or hear."

Before Trevor could reply, the doors were swung open. A tall man, and very round man, stood with his arms on both sides of the door. His bald scalp shined through the thin hair combed over his head, a crooked smile matching his crooked nose. He was dressed in a decorated tunic, bright green and gold linings running in swirls. A thick gold chain dangled heavily around his neck, a large silver coin, which was near identical to the one Evan had shown the guards, hung from one of the links.

The man, who Trevor suspected to be Marquis, smiled widely. "I was beginning to wonder if you'd show up this year, my friend." He reached out and pulled Evan into a hug. When he pulled away, he noticed Trevor. "And with company, I see." He shifted his posture toward Trevor, cocking his head to the side as if judging the quality of a pig. "And who's this young man?"

"This is Marvin," Evan said as he put his hand on Trevor's shoulder. "My eldest son, here to learn the trade of a proper Navalethian farmer."

"Interesting. I don't recall you ever mentioning a family before?"

"There's a lot you don't know about me, *Marquis*," Evan said with a wicked smile. "It's one of the many perks of doing business with you. Speaking of ..."

Marquis laughed loudly. "Right you are. Fair is fair, I suppose." He stepped to the side and held an inviting arm toward the inside of the house. "Please, do come in."

The inside of the house was warm and brightly lit, the aroma of freshly cooked food wafting through the air. They stood in a large entrance hall, two sets of stairs winding around the sides of a fountain shaped like a sun, streams of rushing water spouting into a pool at its base. Red, lush carpet blanketed the floors, clean enough to be recently installed. On the walls hung large canvas paintings in golden portraits, all portraying faces that Trevor didn't recognize.

"I suppose wine is in order?" Marquis offered.

"Afraid not, old friend," answered Evan. "The hour is getting late, and I'm to be off bright and early."

Marquis gave a soft smile. "I suppose it'll be business over pleasure this time."

"Don't fret, Marquis." Evan bowed gracefully. "Business with you is always a pleasure."

Marquis returned the bow with one of his own. "I'm inclined to agree. Unfortunately, you'll have to forgive my hesitation with the company you bring."

"Marvin?" Evan waved dramatically in the air toward Trevor. "Nonsense. My father taught me the ways when I was young, so who am I to spoil tradition? Just teaching my son the way of the trade, sort of say."

"Well, it seems that you've been able to keep up with yourself." Marquis shook his head sadly. "Farmers are piling through the gates more recent now. I'm glad to hear that this Lazar bandit hasn't caused you harm?"

"Not yet, at least." Evan walked about the entrance hall, pretending to study the portraits with his hands behind his back. "Although, I've come to fear that possibility. I've worked too hard to lose everything my family has built to these loyalists. I'm hoping your goods can help me out with that, as well."

"I believe they will," Marquis assured, a sly smile spreading across his plump face. "Those poor souls outside suffered a great loss. Perhaps if they had seen the benefit of our ways, they wouldn't be here now. They made a mistake."

Trevor didn't know what the two men were talking about, but it didn't sit well in his stomach.

Evan replied with a nod. "A mistake I don't plan to make. I need some more protection as well as a few extra hands in the fields. Shopping with you gets me both of those things. Thought I might as well start training the lad in the ways of a true Navalethian."

Marquis's smile widened, his white teeth glistening with perfection. "Teach them while they're young. I like that. Fair enough, old friend. Do you have a particular interest this time?"

Evan shook his head. "Same as last year, and the year before that, my friend."

"You always were a man of high quality, Charles. Same amount as last year?"

"That all depends on your stock. I haven't the heaviest purse as of right now, but I know you're worth the investment."

Marquis chuckled to himself, his flabby chin shaking with the rest of his body. "You know I'm not one for flattery, but I must admit that I like your style. The thing is, I've a few other patrons who are interested, as well. I wouldn't look much like a gracious host if I were to take them away from what they've so willingly paid to see."

Evan tilted his head with a wry smile. "Dear Marquis, you wouldn't be trying to swindle me, would you? I thought we were closer than that."

The fat man gave a bashful bow. "What kind of merchant would I be without at least trying. If you'll wait right here?" Marquis walked across the large room and left through another set of large doors.

Trevor tried to catch a glimpse of the adjacent room before the doors shut, but only managed a brief look.

Silence hung in the air as Trevor looked about the room. Marquis seemed a decent enough man, so why was Evan so worried about bringing him along?

And why is he acting so ... different? And what did Marquis call him? Charles?

"What's—"

Evan cut Trevor off with a finger pressed against his lips. He shook his head and pointed around the room, and then toward his ear while mouthing, *"What did I say?"*

Trevor was beyond annoyed with being treated like a child. Clearly, there was nobody else in the room. Evan was being ridiculous with his paranoia.

He was about to tell him that when the sound of unlocking doors echoed in the entry room, followed by a sight that froze Trevor solid.

In that moment, the fog of understanding was clear as day—why they met with Marquis, the *tools* they spoke of, and why four, rough men needed to guard the entrance to a house in the middle of a burnt-out neighborhood.

K.R. Gangi

Three men walked in a single file line as they entered the room. They were taller than any man Trevor had ever seen. Their foreheads were wide, and their cheekbones angled out high on their face. Their complexion matched the darkening sky. Dark, long hair hung down past their shoulders, knotted with dirt and grime as if they hadn't bathed in weeks.

Natives.

Wrapped around their wrists were thick, iron shackles. Another set was around their ankles, a chain that connected each man together clanking loudly with each step they took. The only thing they wore was a brown, tattered cloth wrapped around their waists.

Despite their complexion, it wasn't hard to see the bruises on their faces. One's eye was swollen to the size of a fist, his nose angled awkwardly, obviously broken. Not only had they obviously been beaten, possibly tortured, but also starved. Their ribs pressed tightly at their sides, stretching their thin skin tighter with each breath they took.

Marquis stepped in front of the three chained men and spread his arms to his side, an evil smile stretching across his face. He looked back and forth between Trevor and Evan. "Behold, friends, the best tools a farmer could buy."

Trevor looked worriedly to Evan. There had obviously been a mistake. Obviously, they were in the wrong place.

They made eye contact for the briefest of moments before Evan matched Marquis's smile.

"May I just say ... *wow.*" Evan paced back and forth in front of the three natives, his arms crossed as he nodded approvingly. "You continue to impress me, good sir. Although ..."

"Although?" For the first time since they'd entered the house, Marquis showed a lack of confidence.

In that moment, Trevor felt afraid. The hairs on his arms stood up, a chill shivered down his spine, and his legs were getting weak. His hands shook at his sides, sweat nearly dripping from his fingertips.

Besides the inviting decor of the hall he stood in, he now knew that this was a dark place. He wanted nothing more than to be away from these men, away from this house, and away from this side of the city.

"Although," Evan repeated as he stood in front of the taller native, the one with the swollen eye, "my father did always tell me not to buy a broken

224

tool."

"Oh. You mean this?" Marquis asked, pointing a fat finger toward the native's face. "Put up a fight, is all. Hardest batch I've yet to get my hands on. Killed a few of my guards, in fact. Nothing but their bare hands. They're sedated at the moment, but I imagine that, when they come to, they'll realize their place. I'm sure you can understand the ... *repercussions* on such affairs? You are a businessman as much as a farmer."

"I understand entirely," Evan said ponderously with a finger pressed to his lips. "And if I've learned anything in recent transactions, I'm sure you're expecting some sort of compensation for the guards?"

Marquis shrugged with a bashful smile. "Business is business, after all."

"Business is business," Evan echoed. "Marvin, dear son, come here for me."

Trevor hesitated at first, wanting nothing more than to run out the front door. It took every instinct in his body not to.

Evan twisted back and smiled over his shoulder. "Come now. Don't be rude."

Trevor did as he was told, his legs like water as he stepped forward.

The natives looked much bigger up close, standing at least two feet higher than Trevor himself. Regardless of being starved, they were big, much broader than Trevor originally realized. Besides their physic, they didn't look much older than Trevor, which made him feel even more sick.

He tried to think back to everything he'd heard about natives: the demon blood that ran in their veins, the monstrous figures that ate human flesh, and worshipped death itself. But when he looked at the men before him, he saw nothing but slaves.

If there are any devils in the room, it's the man holding the key to these locks.

"Just like any tool we're interested in buying," Evan began saying, "they must first be inspected." Evan grabbed one of the taller native's hands, the one with the swollen eye. "The hands say a lot about someone—where they've been, what they've done, and what they're capable of doing. The first lesson of business, my ambitious son, is inspection.

"Although, we don't judge a plow by how sharp the blades are, do we? We check what it's made of, how wide it is, even the weight. All of this"—Evan dropped the slave's hands and gestured to all three of them—"is essential in our decision making.

"That's when our investment comes in. We don't invest in a trade because we know it will work; we invest because we know how *well* it's going to work." When

Evan finished, he turned toward Marquis, who stood by patiently with a fat smile, looking proud as Evan gave his lesson.

"Which leaves us at negotiations," Evan said plainly.

"It certainly does," Marquis agreed. "The price depends on which you prefer."

"I'd prefer them all."

Marquis's eyes widened, his jaw dropping slightly. "You want to purchase all three?"

Evan shook his head. "Correction; I *intend* to buy all three. That is, of course, if you're willing to throw in a few generous perks? A bulk discount, you could say."

Marquis nodded openly to the suggestion. "What'd you have in mind?"

"Well, if we come to a fair price, I'd expect something to help me on my travels—robes, a rope, maybe even a wagon?"

Marquis peered through the slits of his eyes, bouncing his sausage finger toward Evan. "Are you sure you've brought enough coin for such a deal?"

"I'm sure you know me better than to waste both of our time if I hadn't thought I'd enough for a fair price. Also, I expect some sort of discount on the … *condition* of my investment."

"As I've said before, dear friend, they are stronger than they currently look."

"Then let's strike a price," Evan declared.

"And that price is?" Marquis asked.

Evan bobbed his head. "Probably less than your original offer. And your counter offer?"

Marquis gave a wry smile, clearly enjoying their strange bartering system. "Probably more than your rebuttal. What'd you say to that?"

"I'd ask if that's the best package discount you could offer? And you'd say?"

"I'd say …"

Trevor watched as the two men played out their unusual negotiations. He'd witnessed bartering in Robins-Port many times, but never over one's life. It felt strange, arguing with someone over how much a life was worth.

As soon as he had a chance, he would tell Dodge what he'd witnessed so they could leave the brotherhood as soon as possible.

"I'm already putting my business at risk by letting you purchase all three," Marquis explained. "How am I supposed to keep my clients happy when I have no goods to sell them?"

Evan nodded sadly. "I suppose I can compensate for that."

"I'd say show me your best offer," Marquis crossed his arms defensively.

Evan reached into his tunic and pulled out the small pouch that Trevor had seen Benny hand him not an hour before. He heard the jingle of coins as Evan tossed it over to Marquis, who caught it before his face and weighed it in his hand. Moments later, he nodded and tucked it into a pocket at his side. "Robes and a rope, you say?"

"And a wagon, old friend," Evan confirmed. "You've haggled me enough as it is."

Marquis gave a satisfied smile. "A wagon, as well, then."

Trevor stared at the pouch as Marquis tucked it to his side, unable to comprehend how such a small thing had just bought three human beings into slavery.

When Marquis clapped his hands twice, the large doors were swung open and in walked six, mean-looking men. Their burly beards hung down to their chest, and their heads were shaved, thick scars stretching across their faces and arms.

"Unchain them and put them out back for our guests. Gather a rope and three robes," Marquis ordered the men. "Put them in a wagon and bring it with you."

The men obeyed without question, grabbing the leading native by the forearm and dragging him through the door.

All of this happened in one room. Makes you wonder what's happening in the others. The thought alone made Trevor queasy.

"Do they speak the common tongue?" Evan asked before Marquis could leave.

Trevor wanted to tremble with what the merchant said next.

Marquis smiled wild, baring his bright teeth once more. "The whip speaks every language."

K.R. Gangi

The Birth of a Legend

As Sarah stood in front of The Great-Hammer inn, she remembered a story her father had once told her. It was during one of her most memorable nights, when her family was caught between cities during their travels and they were hunkered down in their makeshift camp for the night. The only light being the glare of a small fire with the moon and stars above their heads.

Walking city streets while looking at tall buildings and pushing through crowds of strangers was one way to see the world, but sitting around a campfire in the woods with the people you love, sharing stories over a hot meal, was the way Sarah preferred to experience her world.

"What's the story for tonight, Dad?" Sarah asked.

Harold Michaelson tossed a couple of dry logs onto their fire as he teased, "Another story? I'll run out at this rate."

Florance's thin face peeked out from the edge of their nearby wagon. "I highly doubt that, dear," she hollered to her husband. Her face was gone as quickly as it came, and Sarah heard the sound of her mother rummaging through crates, gathering ingredients for the stew that would soon be boiling over their fire. Her mouth watered in anticipation.

Harold held up his hands defensively. "I'm just saying I'll have to pick up a few books on our next stop to get some more ideas."

"That sounds like a wonderful idea," Sarah said. "For now, I'll suffice for one of the top of that smooth noggin of yours."

"Hey now!" Harold instinctively reached up and rubbed the top of his balding head. "It really isn't that bad, is it?"

"Of course not," Florance cajoled as she approached the fire, a large cooking pot splashing around with fresh food. "Sarah, you know your father is overly sensitive about his lack of hair. No matter how much we wish he'd give up the fight and just shave it all off, we have to support his decisions. You know why?"

228

"Because we love him," Sarah answered with a small smile.

"Well ... yes." Florance nodded softly. "But more because second-hand embarrassment is a real thing, and he'd look even more ridiculous bald."

"Oh, come on." Harold shook his head bashfully.

Florance continued, "Our clients would get confused about who they're talking to because it'd be like talking to a mirror."

Harold sighed into the fire. "No man should have to endure this from his own family."

The night rang with laughter from the Michaelson family. It was a noise Sarah would never forget, nor ever wanted to end. No, this was the best part of her trips, where she could sit, eat, and laugh with her mother and father, not another care in the world.

By the time Sarah was uncomfortably full from her mother's stew, it was late in the evening and the moon was high in the sky. When the Michaelsons had cleared away their plates, brushed down their horses, and rolled out their sleeping packs, Harold cleared his throat.

"So, what kind of story are we up for tonight, then?" he asked Sarah from across the dim light of the fire. "Something maybe with a little ... romance? I know a great story about a knight saving a woman from a tower."

"Only if you want to see mom's dinner all over your lap." Sarah leaned forward, dramatically demonstrating her vomiting everywhere.

Harold and Florance laughed together.

"I figured as much." Harold smiled at her. "None of that, of course. Who would want to hear about damsels in distress being saved by chivalrous knights when you can hear about men fighting beasts like dragons, demons, or ghouls! About rugged men trekking through blood and mud, fighting off a hoard of Mal'Fur, spawned from Malicar himself!"

"Yes!" Sarah's eyes widened with joy, melting with the anticipation of her father's silver tongue.

"Another story of Asher, then?" Florance made sure not to hide her rolling eyes.

"No, you wicked women who stole my heart long ago. This story will not be about Asher the Great."

"It won't?" Sarah asked.

Harold shook his head. "This story will be about a man who fought on the frontlines in the War of the Natives."

"Oh." Florance put a hand to her chest and gasped with forced awe. "A heroic story of a Navalethian soldier?"

"Right you are!" Harold roared as if he were addressing a live theater. "This will be a story about a man so great that villains tremble at the mere mention of his name. A man so renowned that every soldier prays for his strength on the eve of combat. A knight so brave that he himself saved thousands of soldiers from the endless waves of enemy combatants by raining down iron and steel. A soldier who became the greatest warrior in our kingdom by single-handedly saving a lost platoon behind enemy lines."

"Oh ... Oh!" Sarah bounced with excitement. "Tell me."

Harold cleared his throat, something he always did right before he began one of his stories. "This is the story of ... "

"The Great-Hammer," Benny announced as he, Sarah, Dodge, and Alric stood outside the tavern's doors. "As great a structure as the man himself, don't you think?"

It took Sarah an awkward moment to realize that Benny was looking over his shoulder at her, waiting for an answer.

"Couldn't say," Alric answered. "Never met the man."

"Brood all you want, but you cannot deny the certain resemblance of the structure in relation to his stories."

"Funny thing about stories, there's always a different truth to them," Alric stated matter-of-factly.

"I cannot argue with that," Benny mumbled to himself.

They stood there for a moment, both of them looking about the crowd of people flowing around them.

Sarah studied the passing people. She'd only been to Servitol on one other occasion, and just this last year. She remembered being awestruck by the architecture that seemed to stretch into the sky. She remembered fantasizing about one day being able to dress in the puffy dresses that were popular and elegant. She once imagined herself as one of the sophisticated women who passed her now, walking with a strut that screamed wealth and prestige.

Now, everything and everyone seemed bland, as if Sarah was seeing the world for what it truly was. People's elegance was replaced with empty smiles and vague eyes. Those walking by paid them no mind, either too caught up in their own world or didn't give a care for anyone besides themselves.

"Where's your man?" Dodge asked suddenly. He'd been as quiet as the dead the entire walk to the tavern, probably sulking with how things were turning out with Trevor.

"Not here yet," Benny answered as he scanned the area.

Dodge replied with a grunt.

"I'm thinking we should sit at separate tables once inside," Benny suggested while taking in his surroundings. "Al and I will take a table near the front entrance while you and Sarah sit on the far wall across from the bar. Once our man shows up, we'll feel the situation and give you the signal to join us, and you can fill him in on what happened."

"*Feel* the situation?" Dodge tensed his shoulders. "I thought you said this man can be trusted."

"He can. Well, at least, he used to be trustworthy." Benny waved away his stumbling words. "We go back, the three of us, but a lot has changed in fifteen years. Better safe than sorry."

Dodge did little to hide his frustration. "Seems I might regret this, after all."

"Nonsense! You have my word, Mr. Dodge."

"Dodge will do just fine."

"As you say." Benny smiled graciously. "You have my word, Dodge. After tonight, you and your loved ones will be safe once more. Isn't that right, Al?"

Alric wasn't paying any attention to the discussion. Sarah could see that the man was tense. His shoulders straightened, his gloved hands squeezed tight at his sides, and his eyes focused on something across the street. Sarah could also see that the man was sweating profusely.

"Alric? Hey, are you all right?" Benny gently grabbed the man's forearm, which caused Alric to jump in fear, his opposite hand reaching behind his back for something. Sarah saw the glint of a blade tucked in the man's belt behind his back. Just as he was pulling it free from its hiding place, Benny gently caught the man's wrist.

"Easy, Al," Benny said softly in his ear. "Take it easy now."

Alric's flare of violence receded quickly and he let go the pommel of the hidden dagger. He returned his gaze toward the opposite end of the street. "The cart …" he mumbled, wiping the sweat from his brow. "How long has that cart been there?"

Sarah peered across the street, following Alric's stare.

Near the corner of two adjoining buildings, hidden in the shadow of their towering structure was a food cart. She didn't understand the significance. It looked like a regular food cart to her.

"I'm not sure …" Benny searched for words. "I don't understand. Al, are you sure you're up for this?"

It was another moment before Alric answered. "Right. I'm good."

"If you're not—"

"I said I'm fine, dammit," he snapped suddenly. "Plan sounds solid. Let's go."

Before any of them could protest, he made way to the tavern and opened the front doors, disappearing beyond the threshold. Benny gave a soft sigh and pinched the bridge of his nose. Then he looked at both Dodge and Sarah, gave them a reassuring smile, and made his way into the tavern.

Sarah felt a soft hand on her shoulder.

"Not sure about these two," Dodge said quietly to her, "but I don't see any other way. Let's just stick with their plan for now, but if I say go, you go. Do you understand?"

Sarah stared at Dodge a moment longer. She'd known him near her entire life, but in that moment, there was an unfamiliar aspect to him. In that moment, it felt like she didn't know him at all, like there was a side of him that she was never meant to see.

"Sarah, do you understand?" he asked once more. "If I say run, you run, with or without me. You find a guard, and you tell them what happened."

Sarah waited a moment, contemplating Dodge's sudden paranoia. "Okay," she answered.

Dodge looked at The Great-Hammer. "Well, that man did make a point. The Great-Hammer was always known for his …"

"Strength!" Harold exasperated. "The man could swing his hammer as quick as a feather. He could knock down trees with his mighty fists." Harold held his fists in front of him, striking the air in demonstration.

"Did I ever tell you he was the youngest anointed knight in Navaleth?"

Sarah replied with an awed shake of her head, unable to control the wondrous smile spreading across her face.

"Aye," Harold reassured. "It was a long time ago, years before the ending of the war. Years before the famous battle at Greengate, as a matter

of fact."

"The battle of Greengate?" Sarah asked, bewildered. "What's that, Father?"

"Oh, Greengate was the bloodiest fight of the war. We suffered the most casualties there. Nearly lost us the war. But that's a nightmare of a story to tell you."

"Or maybe in a couple years." Florance shifted uncomfortably. "The way my brother described it ... not sure if he was lucky to make it out alive or not."

Harold gave Florance's hand a gentle squeeze. "No matter what, I'll always count young Ben on the lucky side, and nobody respects the man more than I. I'm sure he's fine, love."

Florance replied with a sad smile, "Well, if you see him, give him my kindest regards, will you?"

Harold snorted, looking at his darling wife for a few seconds before turning back to Sarah.

"You see," he continued, "before being bestowed the title of Great-Hammer, our Navalethian hero was simply known as Charles Balorian, a low-level grunt who was good with a blade. The story is that Balorian was nothing more than a simple farmer who married the love of his life at a young age. He spent his last copper to give his wife her dream wedding, telling her that what he provided then was what she'd be getting for the rest of her life—everything she ever wanted. Yes, he married young, well before the age of mandatory recruitment.

"It wasn't long after the birth of their son, Francis, when Charles Balorian started hearing the rumors of the native front getting closer to the capital. Of course, no existing army in our past, present, or future could even dream of sacking Servitol, but that didn't mean there couldn't be casualties of war—villages pillaged; farms raised and burned; men, women, and children butchered and used as tributes to the necromancer king, the prince of hell himself, sole leader of the Mal'Fur. No. No army could scale the walls, but Charles wasn't one to let things up to chance.

"One night, Charles had a vision. A grand plan was bestowed upon him by the father god himself, Elinroth, and it changed the course of our history.

"Some say it was for the protection of his wife that he would rather die defending the love of his family than stand back and wait for possible disaster. Others will argue it's because Charles Balorian had a deep sense of love for his country. Either way, Charles Balorian enlisted as a foot soldier that following morning."

Florance handed Harold a cup of water, which he gladly took it with a generous drink.

Sarah, taking advantage of the opportunity, felt compelled to ask, "Why do you think he did it, Father?"

Harold's eyebrows raised with curiosity. "Why do I think he did what? Enlisted?"

Sarah nodded.

"Well, why don't you tell me, dear? Do you think it was love that compelled Charles to enlist early? Maybe a sense of duty? Or perhaps it was because of the vision that Elinroth sent his way, a vision showing him of the man he'd eventually become?"

"I think ..." Sarah started before she caught herself. Her father had always told her to think about her words before she spoke them. Even an unintentional lie could be seen as deceiving, especially in the business that their family was in. "I want to believe that he did it out of love, to protect his family, but why would he leave them when they could just move elsewhere?"

"Perhaps he did not have enough money?" Harold shrugged. "Moving across country isn't exactly cheap, especially for some who aren't as financially stable."

"So, maybe he did it for money? So he could provide for his family?"

Harold exhaled deeply, staring off into the fire as if searching for words. "If you ask me, I would like to believe he did it for love. Not for the love of country, as some soldiers will try and sell you, but deep, pure, passionate love for his people. I don't think a man like Charles Balorian could stand knowing that men died fighting to protect his family while he stood behind the safety of his walls."

"That's beautiful, Harold." Florance smiled, as lost in the story as Sarah.

"And I think," Harold continued, now smiling to himself, "that if Charles had known what would happen to him and his platoon, he would have second-guessed enlisting two years early into the Sun Army."

Sarah shifted curiously, recognizing the shifting atmosphere around the fire. "What do you mean?"

"I mean," her father continued, his voice now grim and full of sorrow, "that not every soldier sees combat. Hell, there are a lot who don't come near a battlefield. But we don't win wars by standing in a watch tower or guarding

the king's road. In every war, there is always a soldier somewhere, marching for two days with only a couple hours of sleep. Trekking through a swamp up to their knees, thirsty and starving, marching toward certain slaughter. I'm saying that nobody becomes a local hero such as the Great-Hammer without tasting the poisonous fruit war has to offer, and Charles was unfortunate enough to get a mouthful."

"Unfortunate for you, indeed," the heavy bearded barkeep said across the tall, mahogany polished counter. "But no worries; we've plenty to offer here at the Great-Hammer. Ain't nobody in Navaleth can tell you different. My wife's the best cook in the city, and she runs the kitchen, and I be the most skilled and resourceful brewer. Why don't you take a seat, and I'll send my son to help you out?"

"That sounds wonderful," Benny said with one of his smiles. He always seemed ready with a smile, and Sarah couldn't help wondering if it was genuine or not. She had her doubts with a lot of things lately.

Sarah stood by, looking about the interior of the tavern, scanning the patrons as they chewed their food, drank their mugs, and conversed between one another as if nothing was out of the ordinary. Her father had always hated taverns, so they had done their best to stay clear. Only on a few occasions the Michaelsons had had to spend a night in a tavern such as this. Most times, they'd been guests among a patron of the bank her father worked for.

My father ...

It was a flutter of a memory, but enough for Sarah to revisit the horrid recollection that she'd experienced at Robins-Port. She thought of her father's face, twisted in fear as he held himself firm against the battering door. The sound of her mother's scream. The tunneled walls scraping against her arms. The feeling of the rocks beneath her bare hands as she crawled on her hands and knees in the dark.

Here, little piggy!

"Sarah."

She could feel the man's weight on her body again, her hands locked above her head, held fast as her attacker pried her legs open with his knees. The aroma in the tavern made her nauseous, reminding her of the sour breath as the man had breathed into her face, grunting his words as spittle misted her face.

"Keep fighting me. I much like it when they put up a fight."

"Sarah." Dodge gently squeezed her elbow, prying her away from the horrific memory.

She was sitting in her seat, without a trace of remembrance of when she had entered the inn. She looked around, to the faces of the nearby patrons as they ate their food and drank from their cups. Though they paid her no mind, she still felt eyes on her from somewhere.

As Sarah sat in the wooden chair, her back against the wall, with Dodge at her side, she put her hands in her lap and studied the grain of the mahogany wood in front of her. She got lost in its pattern, tracing the lines and grooves across the table.

Her face shone back on the polished table, the deep red hue making her think of blood. Slowly, she slid her hand across the top of the table, feeling the sudden need to make sure it was clear of the stain. Her hand moved slowly, the polish feeling smooth and hard.

When she pulled her hand away, her heart nearly stopped in her chest. The blood in her veins began to chill, her lungs suddenly feeling tight in her chest. Dark blood dripped down her fingers, its sticky wetness flowing down her wrist, spreading its warmth on her arm like an unstoppable river. She knew Dodge was speaking, but she only heard mumbles, a distant buzz as she watched the blood flow.

She looked past her hand toward the table when her breath caught in her chest. Lifeless eyes stared at her. They belonged to her father. His severed head was before her, set neatly on the chest of his mangled body, which was sprawled on the table before her. Organs that Sarah couldn't even name crawled out of his open stomach and snaked over his lifeless arms, dangling off the table and into her lap.

"It's okay, dear," a calm voice echoed in her head. There was a familiarity to it, one that was impossible not to recognize.

Horrified, Sarah looked to her left. Dodge was no longer there, the chair empty, as was the rest of the tavern. It was just her, the mangled corpse of her father, and …

"We'll fetch him a bath and get him cleaned up," the voice said from directly behind her.

She slowly turned, trembling with fear as the haunting image stopped her cold.

Before her sat the living corpse of a woman. Her skin was pale as milk, purple lips spread wide, revealing blood-crusted teeth, her breath ranking like hot death. Below her chin was a large gap, deep enough for Sarah to see bone deep within.

Her lifeless eyes pierced Sarah from beyond the grave, the eyes that belonged to her mother. "We'll get him cleaned up, and then he can tell us a story. We know how much you love stories. Stories of fighting battles, of blood and death." Florance's smile stretched unnaturally, her rotted, yellow teeth lining her blackened gums. "How do you like living in one of those stories, Sarah? Is it everything you imagined?"

Florance stretched her hand toward Sarah, fresh blood oozing out of the gash in her forearm, dripping all over Sarah's knees.

Sarah tried to scream but found that she wasn't breathing. Instinctively, she jumped back, away from her mother's grasp, when she felt large hands reach around her back.

"It's okay," a voice whispered in her ear.

Sarah dug her nails into the hands gripping her, tearing at the flesh as she fought for freedom.

"Ouch!" The hands released her, and she stumbled forward, twisting in the air to face her attacker.

Dodge stood there, his hands up innocently, his eyes cringing with worry.

Sarah looked around her. She was back in the tavern. At least, the tavern she now remembered walking into. There was no body of her butchered father on the table, no sign of her mother's corpse. She looked toward the other end of the room, toward the table where Benny and Alric sat. Both of them had curious looks on their faces as they watched her worriedly.

"Sarah?" Dodge held out a hand to her, looking around the room. "Come sit with me, Sarah."

Sarah brushed Dodge's helping hand away, trying to get a grip on what was real. One minute, she had been sitting at the table with Dodge; next, she'd been living in one of her nightmares. She could avoid the nightmares by refusing to sleep, but what could she do when they haunted her when she was awake? Was there no escape for her?

She managed to climb back into her seat, her hands in her lap as she sat there quietly. It was a long moment before Dodge spoke, but when he did, Sarah tried focusing on his words.

"You know, there must be hundreds of knights this empire has had. Hundreds of different tales and hundreds of different accomplishments from hundreds of different people, but the Great-Hammer has always been my favorite above them all."

Sarah sat quietly, her mind intently focusing on Dodge's words, her body still shaking in horror of what she had just witnessed.

"Always been a fan of tales," Dodge continued. "As I know you are, too." Dodge nodded toward the bar across the room.

Sarah hadn't noticed when she'd walked in, but a large wooden hammer, a great hammer, was hanging from the wall above the entrance of the bar.

"You've got to respect a man who will put everything on the line for something, or someone, he loves. No matter how much pain it causes him, no matter if he thinks he'll live through it or not, but just does it because he knows it's the right thing to do."

Dodge was quiet then.

Out of the corner of her eye, Sarah saw his head hang low toward his chest. She couldn't be sure, but it seemed like Dodge was talking more to himself than he was to her.

"Did, uh …" Dodge took a deep breath, let it out slowly, and then looked at Sarah. "Did your father ever tell you how he became known as the Great-Hammer?"

Sarah's heart swelled with sadness at the thought of her father. She could feel her eyes bulging, tears near to come. She nodded with a sad smile. It broke her heart, knowing they were both talking about her father in past tense.

An unfamiliar smile crept across Dodge's face. It looked strange on the man, but Sarah couldn't help liking it. "I bet he did," Dodge said. "It's a great story. You mind if I tell it?"

Sarah nodded again, wiping a tear from her face.

Dodge straightened his back and cleared his throat, an image Sarah loved seeing her father do before he started a tale.

When Dodge began to speak, Sarah was brought back to that night with her mother and father.

"Charles left his family not even a year after his son's birth," Harold continued his story. "He knew there was a very good chance he'd never return, at least not for a couple of years. With a war on, soldiers didn't come back to their families until their enlistment was up, which could ultimately be

the latter half of a decade.

"But he knew deep down that he had to, that if he didn't, he'd regret it his whole life. Not only did he have a sense of duty to his family's protection, but to his country's protection, as well. Well, that's what people will tell you. We, as an audience, have the luxury to decide the meaning behind whichever decision our heroes made in their stories."

"I still want to believe he did it for his family," Sarah said without hesitation.

"Looks like we're having ourselves a love story, after all," Florance teased, pinching Sarah's leg playfully across the fire.

Sarah giggled and shoved her mom's hand away.

"Don't fret, sweet daughter." There was something about the sound of her father's voice that had a tendency of drawing her focus in quickly. "Love will always drive someone to do brave and dangerous things if they truly believed they were protecting the ones they loved. Love is always the culprit behind a hero's motive—Asher with the love of humanity, Elinroth with the love of creation. And whether it was love for his family or country that drove Charles to fight for his country, it still wasn't the reason we call him the Great-Hammer today."

Sarah frowned, confused how the story had turned. "So, you are saying it was love that made him great, but it wasn't love for his family or Navaleth?"

Harold squinted his face and shrugged. "I believe that, if you had the chance to ask Charles that today, he would say"—Sarah's father puffed out his chest, deepening his voice as to imitate the raw strength of the hero in the tale—" 'Yes, you young, beautiful, intelligent girl, what I did was for love of my family because, you see, my brothers-in-arms are just that—family.' "

Sarah laughed at her father's bravado. Then she and her mother clapped enthusiastically as Harold gave a theatrical bow of praise.

"So"—Sarah wiped her golden hair from her eyes—"what did he do? How did he get the name?"

Sarah watched as her father's faced sobered. She could literally feel the mood of the story shift, even before his next words were spoken.

"Strength, love, skill in combat"—Harold counted with his fingers—"these are important things that help bring our soldiers home. Whether you're patrolling the king's road or standing guard at a town, home is always on the mind of a soldier doing their duty. Unfortunately, some soldiers have a harder enlistment than others, and that could absolutely be said for Charles Balorian."

Sarah's eyes widened with anticipation. "What happened to him?"

Harold cleared his throat. "It was a foggy morning. Charles's unit had just received word of an enemy scout not a few days' ride from their location. If they pushed hard throughout the day, and also through the night, they could catch them unawares with a surprise attack. That was the plan, anyway.

"After marching the next day and night, they came to the edge of the Fang Forest to make camp. They were exhausted, hungry, and in dire need of water. They relied solely on raiding the enemy's camp to resupply, and it had been weeks since their last skirmish.

"It seems the natives knew this, too, for they were waiting within that forest for Charles's platoon. You see, the scout was mere bait to lure them into the forest. They hid in the trees, dug holes in the ground deep enough to fit three people standing and covered it with debris. Then, once they decided the Navalethian soldiers were at their most vulnerable, when most of their soldiers were sound asleep, with only a few guards at their post, they attacked."

Sarah couldn't help but gasp. Florance stared distantly into the fire, her focus more in the flames rather than the story.

Harold continued, "They went for the guards first, dropping them with an arrow or a quiet dagger in the back. Once they were dead, they surrounded Charles and his platoon, still asleep in their sacks, and started slitting their throats, one at a time.

"Thankfully, one of those sleeping soldiers had more than enough liquid courage before sleep and had to relieve himself. Once he woke and saw the figures of men crouching and sneaking around camp, he raised an alarm.

"Chaos boomed!" Harold slapped his hands together loudly, causing Sarah to jump at the sudden sound. "Steel was drawn, arrows took flight, bodies fell, one by one, on both sides, and blood misted in the wind. Within the first few minutes, over half the platoon was dead, the remaining troops either still fighting or dying on the ground. The Navalethians didn't know it then, but they were fighting just under two-hundred native warriors, and they were losing fast.

"Then, in the midst of the carnage of battle, a loud horn boomed, the sound shaking the trees around them all. The fighting stopped on both sides, which was a relief to our soon-to-be hero Charles. It was obvious that the Navalethians were defeated. To fight was to die a sure and gruesome death.

"A path opened between the native ranks. A man, large as a mountain,

the skin of a bear draped over his shoulders, red war-paint across his eyes, strutted through the battlefield like the reaper himself. He had a hatchet in one hand and a short sword in the other, blood dripping from the sharp iron.

"Walking at both of his sides were two boys. One had a sack of arrows strapped over his shoulder, a longbow in hand, an arrow nocked and ready to fly. The other was riddled with weapons; two hatches at his hips, twin daggers tucked at his ankles, several throwing knives strapped to his chest."

Sarah wasn't sure what the point of carrying so many weapons was. Then again, these were natives her father was talking about. They were brutes, raised only in warfare and slaughter.

"Who were they, Father?" she couldn't help asking.

Harold took a deep breath, sipped from his mug of water, and then continued his story. "The man with the bear skin was a native chief, a general who helped lead the war against our people. Beside him were his two sons. To this day, we still don't know their real names, but over the years, we've developed a fitting title for them both."

"You mean, they're still alive?" Sarah asked, her eyes wide with shock.

"Possibly," her father admitted. "It was a very long time ago, but there are no records of their bodies being recovered from a battle. They were merely children at the time this story took place, mind you, so it's quite possible they are alive even today.

"The one strapped head to toe with weapons was Quickdraw. He's known for his swiftness in skill with small weaponry. One minute you would be in a melee and, suddenly, instead of the axe he was fighting with, he'd be using a dagger, and then in the next, you'd be dead. Those throwing knives were also not just for show. One report said that he was seen throwing one fifty yards or more during a battle, only to find its mark in another man's eye.

"His other son, the one with the bow and arrow, believe it or not, was even more deadly than the former. It was said he could aim an arrow so true and fast that he could fire a second shot before the first one even met its target. Not only that, but it seemed that the warrior never ran short of arrows. He's remembered as Quiver."

"Quickdraw and Quiver," Sarah repeated to herself. "Was their father a king or something?"

Harold let loose a small laugh. "A native king? Nonsense. The native culture is complex, for sure, but even their sense of politics is primitive in nature. You see, *the native culture values the skills that someone can provide. Imagine different sections of a village. You have farmers, craftsmen, hunters, or even blacksmiths. Natives believe that political power should be elected by the people, not because of a bloodline. The skills you can provide is what natives value above all else*

"Nara'Seir, Quiver and Quickdraw's father, was the chief of combat. You see, it was said that, before the war, the native clans were adamant on fighting one another to prove which one was stronger. However, Swiftblade, this general, helped unite all the remaining native clans in Navaleth, to gather the largest force of enemies we've ever encountered. He gained the title of Nara'Seir once all clans pledged their loyalty, swearing to their gods never to take up swords against each other again.

"As barbaric as it sounds, fighting the natives was especially easy before the Nara'Seir. They were nothing more than an unorganized group of savages. However, once the Nara'Seir united the clans, he had them trained in the tactics of combat, strengthening them into becoming the greatest force we've ever fought."

"Nara'Seir," Sarah mumbled, the foreign words fumbling on her lips. "What does it mean?"

Harold smiled at Sarah. "Chief of Bak'am."

Sarah hugged her knees close to her chest. "What's Bak'am mean?"

The barkeep's son placed two large mugs of water on the table, accompanied by two bowls of bread and porridge. Dodge quickly tore off a smaller piece of the bread and dipped it viciously in the porridge before stuffing it into his mouth. It had been nearly a week since they'd had a meal besides dried jerky or deer. Sarah wasn't a fan of deer. Something about the meat always reminded her of a time when she had sucked on her finger after she'd accidentally cut herself with a kitchen knife.

She knew she was famished, her body running nearly on fumes alone, but she wasn't hungry. She just watched as steam rose out of the bowl, listening to the sound of Dodge loudly chewing his meal.

Dodge managed to swallow his bite and chase it down with a long gulp of water. After clearing his throat, he continued his story, not hesitating as he continued to eat his food.

"Bak'am is a strange word, one I might not even fully understand. But what I do understand is that it's some sort of spirit, or eh … something that the natives believe in. According to them, this spirit is present during every fight or battle. You don't see it, but *feel* it.

"I think the spirit represents some type of test for them—you being judged on how you manage a battle. If you run, you could be shunned by your clan. If you fight and die, and Bak'am found you worthy, you were allowed to join the rest of your tribesman in the afterlife.

"With that being said, you can only imagine the status the Nara'Seir held when named Chief of Bak'am. Out of all three generals during the war, Nara'Seir was the most respected, the one with the thickest voice of influence. He'd fought countless battles and survived every one of them, not one scar on him. We nearly lost the war because of him. A native he might have been, but nobody can deny that he was a military genius."

Sarah looked around the tavern. People seemed to be filing through the door, but there was still no sign of the man that Alric and Benny were supposed to meet. They sat five tables across from her, deep in conversation.

She didn't know what the other two were expecting from her, or why she was here in the first place. All she wanted to do was go home. Too bad her home was just a pile of dead bodies and burnt lumber.

"They didn't kill them all," Dodge said suddenly. "When Nara'Seir stepped through his ranks with his two boys, the Navalethian soldiers knew who he was. They dropped their weapons, got to their knees, and surrendered as hostages.

"Charles and his remaining twenty men were locked in cages. The natives kept them fed minimally, just enough to keep them alive, but not enough to regain their strength. They were there for three nights after the battle when Quickdraw, oldest son of the Nara'Seir, came at them in full rage.

"He'd been hollering at his father for days now, '*They're the enemy*!' he'd scream. '*Why do we waste our food on the enemy? If we kill enough of them, they'll stop sending them.*' "

Sarah's attention was interrupted as an older couple sat at the table next to them. Sarah felt a wave of fear surge through her.

The woman gave her a warm smile, but Sarah averted her eyes quickly. She scooted closer to Dodge, trying to hide the fear behind her silence. If he seemed to notice, Dodge didn't act on it.

"Maybe it was because the Nara'Seir found wisdom in his son's words, or perhaps he was running out of food to feed his own people, but he eventually ordered their execution.

"They tied up the prisoners and led them to the center of camp where a line of natives stood waiting, their hands fidgeting with their weapons. Thing about cultures is everyone views things differently, even executions. They planned to butcher them like lambs for the slaughter."

Sarah remembered this part of the story. It used to be her favorite. That was … until she knew firsthand what violence looked like.

As Dodge spoke, Sarah smiled softly to herself, nearly hearing the words of her father speaking instead.

"Charles bellowed at Nara'Seir and his clansmen while his fellow Navalethians knelt before the army in defeat. 'Coward! Is this how you've attained your status, Coward King of Demons? By strutting through the remains of a battlefield and taking the credit of your men?' "

Sarah gasped with shock, something that she couldn't help throughout the entirety of the story.

Her father laughed absurdly and pointed at her. "Yes!" he said loudly. "The exact reaction the natives had once Charles said the words!" Harold situated himself, brushed off his vest, and took another drink of water.

When Harold was ready, he continued the story, mimicking the voice of the Great-Hammer. " 'Aye, you heard me!' Charles roared at the Nara'Seir. 'I know you can understand me. I hereby challenge you, Nara'Seir, Chief of Bak'am, to a duel of ancients!' "

"A duel of … what?" Sarah asked.

"A duel of ancients is a tradition in the native culture. It's a melee between two opponents to prove themselves to their spirits, or gods, you could say. To deny the challenge would be a great insult, as it shows you don't think the spirits are worth fighting for. The duel is very simple, you see. Both sides of the parties surround the combatants, keeping them from running away, until one of those combatants were to surrender or die. Whoever won was granted one request, which everyone, by laws of their ancient spirits, must honor."

"Such a barbaric way to do things," Florance mumbled to herself.

"Maybe to us." Harold gave a soft pat on Florance's hand. "I'm sure they see our views as barbaric, too."

"What happened next?" Sarah asked impatiently.

"The first thing that happened was his son, Quiver, nocked a quick arrow and pointed it at Charles faster than the eye could see. Just before releasing it, however, Nara'Seir put up his hand, calling off the shot. Then, looking into his eyes, he accepted the challenge.

"The prisoners were cut free but stripped of their weapons as they circled the two warriors.

"Now, another thing about the duel of ancients is that, when you state a challenge, you do so willing to fight with any weapon. By tradition, if you are challenged by someone, you have the honor of choosing your opponent's weapon. Can you guess what Nara'Seir chose for our brave Charles?"

Sarah smiled wide with the answer. "A great-hammer."

Harold nodded his approval. "And a large one, at that. He meant is as a mock, you see, as Charles was starved and beyond weak. All Nara'Seir had to do was wait out his opponent, let him exhaust himself, and then go in for the killing blow. As we well know, that's not what happened.

"It was said the duel lasted days. Charles's hammer whooped through the air toward his target, but Nara'Seir was like a shadow. One minute, he was in the path of death; the next, he had the upper hand and was cutting at Balorian with a sword. Both sides of the crowd roared their encouragements.

"Charles knew he was wearing himself out. He knew that, in order to win, instead of relying on pure strength, he'd have to rely on his cunning instead. He knew if he kept up the way it was going, he'd soon find himself on the ground, bleeding out of a dozen wounds as Nara'Seir looked down at his dying body.

"So, Charles devised a plan. He roared like a bear as he swung down his hammer toward his enemy's face. Nara'Seir took a step back, just out of reach as the hammer's blow rocked the earth, embedding a crater in the ground. However, Charles had expected this, and just as Nara'Seir was feinting away, Charles moved with his momentum, letting go of his weapon as he charged his opponent.

"Nara'Seir didn't see the attack coming and was knocked onto his back. He tried rolling with his momentum, but Charles was too quick—he'd been fabricating his exhaustion for his enemy up to this point, saving what energy he had for this moment.

"Charles landed on top of the Nara'Seir, his knees pinning down the native's arms as he rained his fists on his enemy's face, his hands like boulders crumbling down a mountain." Harold demonstrated with his own fists punching through the air.

"The crowd was quiet with the sudden turn of events. The dull sound of Balorian's fists hammering against the native general's face was all that could be heard.

"After a dozen blows to his face, the chief native roared in defiance. He managed to roll Balorian off to his side and crawl away, retrieving his sword. Balorian, being much quicker than he'd been letting on, rushed to his own weapon, pulled it free of the crater, and faced his adversary again.

"For a moment, they stared at one another, both bloodied with battle, chest heaving with exhaustion. Then, in a uniform moment of decision, they charged.

"Nara'Seir, Chief of Bak'am, general of the natives, rushed with his sword coming down, cutting through the air like a thin sheet of paper. Then, Charles Balorian, a simple farmer, a man of love, only in his second year of enlistment, roared with rage as he charged with his hammer, swinging with all the strength he had left at the man before him.

"It's said the blow could be heard from miles off. Thunder boomed as bones shattered and a life was lost.

"Nara'Seir took the impact full force. The blow sent him flying back nearly ten feet and landing at the feet of his army. He was dead before he hit the ground."

"It was at that point where the man named Charles Balorian became the legend known as Charles the Great-Hammer," Dodge said, reaching the climax of the tale. "He fought with that hammer ever since. Upon victory, his one request was to release him and the prisoners to allow them safe passage back to Navaleth. Nara'Seir's sons weren't too happy, but then again, they were bound by their own ancient laws and had to grant the request.

"On his return, Charles was knighted by the king himself. Not only did he show courage for his fellow man, saving all their lives, but he managed, single-handedly, to rid the world of the leading general of our enemy. It's said that, if it weren't for him, we would have surely lost the war.

"He became a hero," Dodge finished.

The inside of the tavern was beginning to darken as the tale ended, and there was still no sign of the contact Alric and Benny was waiting for. Dodge had finished his plate of food long ago, and Sarah had yet to touch hers.

She enjoyed the story. It was told differently, which stories usually were when it came to differing narrators, yet she was happy that Dodge had retold it.

Not only did it remind her of the time she had sat with her family in that field, but also of the discussion following the story that she hadn't really understood until now.

"What'd you think, dear?" Florance asked Sarah.

"It was wonderful!" she exclaimed happily. "I always enjoy a good tale of good fighting evil."

"Well, I wouldn't necessarily say that," Harold said as he poked the dying fire with a stick.

"What do you mean?" Sarah asked her father.

"Well, who do you see as the villain in that story?"

Sarah was confused about the simplicity of the question. "Nara'Seir, of course. The natives."

Harold studied Sarah. "And why do you say that?"

Sarah was about to answer when she found herself at a loss for words. "Because ... Well ... I ..." She realized she had no real answer.

Harold smiled and nodded toward her. "I cannot explain how delighted I am to see how hard it is for you to answer that question. It shows that you are capable of understanding perspective, even though you don't realize it, and that's a luxury I hope we all can eventually understand.

"Charles is the hero of our story because I am the one telling it. However, do you think Charles is the hero of that same tale told by his sons Quickdraw or Quiver? No. Absolutely not. To them, the Great-Hammer is the enemy who killed their father right in front of them."

Sarah sat quietly at the lesson, a lesson she wouldn't fully understand until many years later.

"Always remember, Sarah, that just because people look different, act different, eat different, or even celebrate life and death different, it doesn't mean you are better than them. We are all still human beings on the same earth. The best you can do in life is make sure you understand both sides of a story, that you rely solely on yourself to determine what's good and bad, but not because somebody else simply claims it so.

"It was a tale of entertainment, for sure, but if I could teach you one thing from it, let it be this: a hero to us is always a villain to someone else."

"A hero to us is always a villain to someone else," Sarah mumbled quietly to herself, slow tears falling down her face with the memory of her father's lesson.

She felt a soft hand on her shoulder, a surprise, but not enough to be scared. It was comforting. She looked up into the eyes of Dodge, who was also on the verge of tears.

Dodge smiled sadly at Sarah, wiping a tear of his own from his face. "Wise words from a wise man."

To Old Friends

"Can't argue the quality of the place," Benny said, admiring the interior of The Great-Hammer Inn. He and Alric sat on the far side of the room, secluded from the rest of the patrons with a clean view of the front and back doors. Sarah and Dodge sat at the opposite side of the room.

The Great-Hammer was a proud establishment, decorated with intrigues of war and power. Different types of weapons hung on the walls like an armory, and paintings of famous battles fought by famous people.

Of course, nothing stood out well enough like the weapon hanging above the bar. It stood as a symbol of strength, courage, and duty. It was a weapon of history that would bring on stories for ages to come—a Great-Hammer.

"Do you think it could really be his?" Benny asked.

"Could what be his?" Alric replied, barely paying attention to the conversation.

When Benny gestured to the hammer hanging above the bar, Alric couldn't help rolling his eyes.

"We both know it's not," he said before focusing his attention back on the door, watching carefully to see who entered.

"I'm sure the barkeep would argue with you there," Benny continued. "I suppose it's not entirely impossible."

"It is, in fact, entirely impossible," Alric countered irritably. "Everyone knows his hammer is buried in the catacombs beneath the castle, rotting away with his corpse. It doesn't matter how good of a story the barkeep would make up. He'd still be a liar."

"Yeah, yeah." Benny sighed with defeat. "But maybe there's a good story behind it? It might not be the one he fought a duel with, but perhaps an original model from the blacksmith? One that—"

"You're doing it again." Alric had been around Benny most of his life, so he knew very well when his friend was trying to pry something out of him or keep his mind focused on something besides what was clouding Alric's head.

"And what is it that I'm doing?" Benny tried his best to look confused and innocent, but Alric knew better than that.

Alric didn't bother looking at Benny. "You're trying to bait me into a conversation that I don't want to have. I can honestly say I'm in no mood for your games right now."

"And what conversation do you think I'm trying to bait you into having?" Benny asked directly, the need for theatrics fading from his tone.

"Oh, just the usual. You think there's something wrong and that I'm going to tell you what that is."

"Except that I know for certain that there is something wrong and you should absolutely tell me what that is."

Alric readied his retort when the front door swung open. He swore under his breath when he noticed it wasn't Harvin and the mysterious guest he was bringing.

He felt uneasy with each passing minute he spent in the city. Everything seemed off. The meeting with the Herald, that twit of a commander, Vallis— *or whatever the fuck his name was*—not to mention Alric's run-in with this traveler who seemed to know everything about him.

Alric had been beginning to second-guess the encounter entirely. That was until he saw the same wagon outside of The Great-Hammer inn. In that moment, Alric felt nothing but a sense of panic. The air around him was crisp, his breathing steady, and his sense of smell keen and focused. All these attributes, he had grown accustomed with before blades started swinging and blood starting spilling. But in that very brief sense of danger, the wagon had disappeared again, and nobody else had seen it happen.

But it did happen, came a whisper in the back of his mind.

There was too much going on. He had witnessed the butchery at Robins-Port, the capital was flooding with farmers who were victimized by the bandit king, Lazar, and instead of putting an endless amount of miles between the brotherhood and Servitol, Alric sat in a dimly lit tavern with his closest friend who was, at that very moment, annoying the living shit out of him.

Alric didn't say all of this out loud, of course. Chances were Benny had the same thoughts on his mind, whether he shared his concerns or not. So, instead, Alric settled with, "We'll discuss it later."

However, Benny didn't seem eager to settle. "We've got some time. Humor me."

Alric knew he was lying before the words came out of his mouth. "We'll catch up about it later. Just not right now."

Again, Benny wouldn't budge. "I insist."

"I said"—Alric tried his best to channel his anger to the squeezing of his fists—"we'll talk about it later. It's not impor—"

"Oh, will you just shut the fuck up with that?"

The sudden burst of anger stopped Alric cold. Benny was the most restrained man he'd ever met, always calm and collected, even in the worst of situations. Composure was something he wore elegantly, like armor on a knight, and only on a few separate occasions, Alric had learned, his best friend's patience ended.

As he saw the clear anger in his eyes, he realized that this was one of those rare occasions, which also meant that he might as well sit comfortably while Benny gave him a nice, long lecture.

"Forgive me, Al, but I'm quite done having you tell me everything's all right, or that *we'll talk about it later.* That's horseshit, and the fact that you keep spoon-feeding me that line after so many years and expect it to taste any different is even worse." Although Benny was just above a whisper, the man might as well have been screaming in Alric's face. "So, let me make myself very clear. You're right; we *will* be talking about this later. We both know you are such a forgetful person with such occasions, so allow me to remind you of our current situation."

Well, this ought to be good.

"Just over a week ago," Benny continued, "Seroes had to drown you in a bottle of Nightshade, which, in case you forgot, is used as a *poison.* He did it because it was the only way we could get you to take care of yourself. Do you see the irony in that? Do you even see why that's completely fucked?"

"That—"

Benny held up a hand. "I said shut up. I've heard what you have to say; now you'll hear me." Benny let a moment pass, just to be sure Alric knew who was currently in charge of this conversation. When Benny was satisfied both parties were on the same page, he continued.

"Not three days later, a town gets completely butchered, something we haven't seen since the war, which clearly states someone wants us to believe it's someone who obviously didn't do it, which clearly means it's a coverup from somebody who holds enough power to kill hundreds of innocents and keep it hush." Benny gave Alric a rough poke in the chest. "And I'll not let you forget that we saw it happen before we even arrived in Robins-Port. Did we not?"

Alric thought back to the dream that Benny had made him remember on the night they spent on the cliffside. He wasn't wrong. There were very distinctive moments where parts of his dream was seen on that night in Robins-Port, specifically the boy with the arrow sticking out of his chest, that arrow that was now tied to the side of his hip.

"So," Benny continued his rant, the anger still lingering in his tone but still quiet enough so only he and Alric could hear, "now we have a conspiracy theory. We planned to find a contact in the city so we can explore that option, as well as provide safety to the only survivors of that attack, and you decide to pick a fight with one of the most influential commanders in the entire fucking city?"

"Vallis is a—"

Benny slammed his fist on the table. "Vallis is a *commander*, dammit! And not only do you attack the man, but you attack his pride? That's beyond foolish, even for you. Oh, but it doesn't stop there. Not only do you attack the pride of a man who could simply whisper to the wind and have it sweep us away without a trace, but you nearly draw your dagger on me in the middle of the street?"

There was a pause, but Alric knew better than to say something. If he said anything, it was likely Benny would shut him down with a punch in the face. So, he waited, and as he did, he could see the tension release in his friend's shoulders.

Benny sighed and shook his head. "And then I, the man you know you can trust with anything, the one you know would do absolutely anything to help you, try to see if you're okay, and you tell me to *fuck off.*"

The barkeep made his way toward their table, took one look at the atmosphere of the conversation, and turned back, making his way into the kitchen.

If only you knew how much I envy you in this moment, Mr. Barkeep.

Alric knew Benny wasn't exaggerating. Benny would do absolutely anything to help him if the need called for it.

Alric sunk as the weight of guilt dragged him down with enough pull to sink a ship to the depths of the deepest ocean.

"There was a man in the market today," Alric started, not knowing exactly where he was going with his story. "I ran into him. You saw it. Or, well, you *should* have seen it." Alric picked at his nails as Benny watched him intently, a somber look on his friend's face.

"He knew things about me," Alric said finally. "Not just about all of us, but about … me." *Such fangs on you … Years have passed since you tucked tail.* "He knows about my time during the war, and the time after. Benny, I think he knows …" Alric felt a choke just at the mere thought of her name.

It'd been years since Alric had said her name aloud. Years since the cruel world he lived in was gifted with the memory of her. It felt strange hearing it out loud, and not just a word floating around in his Alric's head. "I think he knows about Meyra."

Alric watched Benny intently as he processed the words. *He's thinking about what to say, about how he should say it. He's scared of how I'll react. By the gods, I'm even scared how I'll react.*

When Benny did eventually speak, it was in a flat voice, and his eyes never left Alric. "You think he knows about the fire?" he asked.

Alric nodded.

Benny sighed, leaning forward on the table. "About the murders?"

Alric shifted uncomfortably, the memory of the life he once had shaking him to his core. "Possibly. He asked about the Orange Fields. Rapport, specifically."

"Shit," Benny swore quietly. He leaned forward on the table and shook his head. "Did you at least hide his body well enough?"

It took a moment for Alric to realize that Benny wasn't kidding. "No."

Concern lit up Benny's eyes.

"No—I mean, I didn't kill him. I wanted to, but … well …" Alric remembered Traveler's strength, so easily overpowering. "Well, I didn't."

Benny frowned and nodded in bewilderment. "Guy's lucky to be alive. Did you get a name from him at least?"

"No. He, uh, got away."

"Got away from *you*?" Benny looked genuinely surprised when Alric nodded. "Looks like miracles do still happen. I see why you're suddenly on edge. If this man is following you, then we'll have to be extra careful. We'll leave the city tonight and make our way to the Crooked Tooth." Benny took a sip from his mug. "Suppose Evan might be right. Perhaps it's time to go home."

"And what if he follows us there?" Alric asked hopelessly. "What if he follows us back, Benny? What if I lead him there?"

There was no emotion with Benny's reply. "Then we'll kill him."

It was moments like these that Alric was reminded on just how far Benny was willing to go for him. It only made him love the man even more, but there was still a lingering fear in his gut.

"And if he brings men? If they see what the Crooked Tooth really is, they'll send soldiers as soon as they can. Everyone would be killed, or worse."

Benny shrugged. "Then we'll just have to kill them all, now won't we? But, for now, let's hope it doesn't get to that. We'll leave Dodge and his group here tonight after we speak with Harvin, and then we'll make our way back. We'll cover our trail, circle about and look for scouts. When the coast is clear, we'll go on. We'll go home."

"Home," Alric mumbled to himself, a sadness overwhelming him with the memory of the true home he'd once had. Of the home he built with the woman of his dreams, and then the fire that had taken it all away from him. Alric could rest anywhere with anyone in the world for the rest of his life, but he would never truly feel at home ever again.

The door to the tavern was opened again, and Alric immediately recognized the two faces that strode in. Even out of his armor, Harvin apparently liked to don the color of his stature. His richly maroon attire was simple enough not to draw too much attention, but enough to display status if the moment called for it. He wore a mahogany vest over his red undershirt with black embroidered stitching.

It wasn't Harvin Destro that caught his attention, but the man who followed at his heels. Like Harvin, the man dressed in a similar fashion, but instead of a rich red, he wore an emerald green tunic with gold stitching. It was only suitable for one who prided himself on status, and Alric couldn't blame the man. Out of the very few men left alive that Alric could call a friend, he knew this one had been through enough to earn the right to present himself as such.

They sat down at the table with Benny and Alric.

"Well, look who crawled out of his grave only to plague the world once again." Marcus Gorman looked the same as Alric had always remembered him—clean shave, a short, cropped haircut, and a mouth that could fend off a castle under siege. "Looks as if you win this time, Harvin. You'll be drinking under my tab tonight."

Marcus stretched out his hand with a wide smile, and Alric gladly took it.

"Kid didn't believe me when I told him who I saw in the castle earlier,"

Harvin explained. "Had to bribe him with a night of drinking in order for him to come see for himself."

"I see he's still calling you kid." Benny laughed as he shook hands with Marcus.

"Ah, and the reaper himself." Marcus motioned for the barkeep for a round of drinks. "Alric still can't get rid of you, eh? How the hell are you, Benjamin?"

"You know how it is for us, old friend." Benny gestured to Marcus's attire. "Yet, I can't say much for you. Did you finally marry that rich and elegant woman you always said you would find?"

"The world's too unfair to let that dream come true," Marcus replied vaguely.

The barkeep rushed over and set four large mugs of ale down on the table before them. "Is there anything else I could get for you, m'lords?"

Marcus waved a nonchalant hand at the barkeep. "There'll be none of that. We're off duty as of an hour ago, and we've got some time to kill. Think of us as a couple of old veterans ready to knock back a few pints and share a few stories with some very old friends."

The barkeep nodded and smiled. "Very well. I'll set on some food for you guys and keep the drinks coming. Nothing better than slinging back some Great-Hammer ale with a belly full of food, eh? On the house, of course."

"That's well appreciated, friend." Marcus slapped three silver bits onto the table. "I'm always looking for thriving businesses in the city, so consider this my first investment. Just keep the drinks coming, the food hot, and the fire burning."

The barkeep nearly toppled over at the sight of silver. He looked back and forth between the four men at the table, hesitating, before slowly reaching out for the coins as if a snake waiting to snap at his hand. He quickly pocketed it at his side and nodded graciously then made his way back into the kitchen without another word.

Even Alric and Benny were shocked. It wasn't often you saw silver bits being thrown around in the likes of a tavern, even if it were in Servitol.

Marcus gave a sly smile when he noticed his friends looking at him. "What?" He shrugged in defense. "Ain't much use being on a commander's salary if you aren't willing to spread the wealth, right?"

"Oh, curses," Benny scoffed. "So, you've married yourself to your country, as well. Is that it?"

"I did always say she'd be beautiful and rich, didn't I?" Marcus picked up his mug and raised it in toast.

"All three commanders of the Navalethian army on the same day?" Alric grabbed his mug of ale and joined his friends in the toast. "I should consider myself lucky."

"Ain't no one drinking to lady-luck tonight." Harvin lifted his mug before them. "But I will drink to old friends."

"To old friends," they echoed.

They took a deep pull of their ale, all besides Alric.

When the others had finally finished their own drinks, Harvin wiped his scraggly beard and belched quietly. He studied his mug and nodded slowly, smacking his lips with satisfaction. "That was very, *very* good."

"I'm way ahead of you, brother," Marcus said as he signaled for another round.

When the barkeep had returned with a new set of drinks, he looked on the verge of a heart attack after realizing that Alric hadn't touched his own drink. "Was there something wrong with the drink, sir? I can bring you something a little sweeter if you'd like? I have the finest wine—"

"No, thank you," Alric said, suddenly feeling embarrassed. It had been years since Alric had a drink, and as much as he craved the warmth a bottle promised, he wasn't about to break his vow. "I'll settle for some water?"

"Ah, yes. Of course, sir. Right away, sir." The barkeep hurried off toward the kitchen again.

The room was beginning to heat up with conversation. Alric glanced over to where Dodge and Sarah sat patiently, eyeing the company that he and Benny were keeping. They didn't look worried, but he did know that, soon, they would have to explain their purpose in the city.

The barkeep came back quickly, and Alric was soon holding a mug of cold water toward his friends. He half-expected a couple of judgmental looks, but then he remembered who they were and all fear of judgment disappeared.

Harvin cleared his throat and raised his mug once again. "Well, looks like Al's volunteered to babysit us while we try our best to make a fool of ourselves, eh?"

"Looks like it," Alric agreed with a smile.

"Hang on tight, boys," Marcus said, undoing the buttons on his tunic. "There's nowhere I've got to be in the next few hours, so I'll be sure to make this is one bumpy fucking ride."

Alric suddenly had the unfamiliar feeling of warmth spreading across his chest, and though it was a stranger to him, he knew it was happiness. Here he was, sitting in a tavern with his oldest and closest friends, with the bravest men he'd ever known, sharing drinks and food like they were simple grunts in the Navalethian army once again. In that moment, Alric had forgotten what it meant to feel worry. In that moment, however brief it was, he was content.

It was a shame that his world would soon take a harsh turn, and his life would be made into a living hell.

The Three Shapers

The moment they left Marquis's house, Evan changed completely. Trevor just couldn't tell if it was for better or worse. He seemed back to his normal self—quick to anger and muttering curses quietly to himself as he marched the three natives, who were now tied with a rope and dressed in robes to stay hidden, toward the farthest end of the lower district.

Slaves, Trevor thought dreadfully. *They're slaves, and I helped it happen.*

A crop of thick brush lined parallel to the, what was most likely, outer wall surrounding Servitol. The wall itself was five times the height of Trevor. If there were guards patrolling up top, he couldn't see them.

" *'The whip speaks every language'*," Evan mocked as he brushed aside the thick brush, revealing a large hole in the wall that led outside the city. "So does a dagger, you fat fuck." Evan stepped through and disappeared, tugging roughly on the rope.

It was a minor miracle that the natives managed to squeeze through the gap in the wall. There was a moment when one of them, the one with much broader shoulders, was nearly stuck. That was until Evan managed to yank on the rope hard enough to pull him the rest of the way.

When Evan and the slaves were through the gap, Trevor thought about the opportunity he was now in. If he planned to escape Evan and find a guard, now would be the best time. By the time Evan would know, Trevor would already be reporting his story to a guard. All he had to do was turn and run.

Trevor shifted his feet in the dirt, readying himself to flee, when he heard Evan's muffled voice through the gap in the wall.

"Don't bother,. I suspect you'd make it down a few streets only to find some bullyboy's waiting for you. You'll learn that their swords are much sharper than my tongue. Might as well put on your big boy face and follow me."

Trevor wanted to yell back, suddenly feeling very brave with the wall between the two of them, but he also knew it was pointless. Evan was right; he had to go with him, regardless of how much he hated the living shit out of him at that moment.

He took a moment to gather himself before Trevor squeezed through the hole to join the others.

"Good boy," Evan said as Trevor pushed his way through. "Now, if you're done being an idiot, would you be so kind as to follow me? We've gotta make good ground if we want to make it back before dark."

"Then you should probably untie them." Trevor nodded toward the three natives, their faces hidden in the shadow of their hoods. Trevor tried his best to keep his composure, but it was hard to hide the anger when he spoke. "It's kind of hard to walk with your hands and feet bound together."

"Don't worry about them." Evan clearly noticed the anger in Trevor's tone, but it only seemed to fuel his malicious intent. "Drugs probably still have them woozy enough. Now, start walking."

Before Trevor could protest, Evan had walked past the prisoners and made his way toward an open valley of rolling hills that stood between Servitol and the rest of Navaleth. The sun was beginning to set, the orange horizon shedding light upon the endless hills that rolled to what might as well have been the edge of the world.

They traveled for what seemed like hours, Trevor mostly keeping to himself as Evan continued to mumble to himself. Every now and then, the natives would slow their pace, and Evan would encourage them to keep moving with a quick tug on the rope that bound them.

Trevor looked back over his shoulder. The massive walls guarding the capital looked small in the distance. "Won't the guards see us?"

"Guards are being switched out," Evan said flatly. "That or off getting drunk. Nobody expects an attack on the capital any time soon, so why not piss away your coin rather than stare off into nothing all night?"

"Then, where are we going?" Trevor pressed. "And why are we taking … *them* with us?"

"You know, you ask a lot of fucking questions. Aren't you the one who wanted to come with me? Guess this is what you get for throwing a temper tantrum like some little shit-mouthed kid. Can't you just settle with the fact that you don't know anything?"

"I know enough," Trevor replied, irritation building up once again. He was getting really sick of being left in the dark, as well as being called a kid. "I know it's illegal to own slaves."

"Ah, there's the brooding bugger that claims to know it all. Best be careful now. Might give me the impression you plan to run off to a guard once we get back."

"Maybe I will." Trevor suddenly felt power with his threat. "Maybe I'll go find one and lead them to that friend of yours. Save whoever else they have chained up in there."

"And you would no doubt become the hero you were born to be," Evan said, doing nothing to hide his sarcasm. "Wouldn't that be something? Sorry to rain on your parade, but that would be a mistake. A big mistake."

"What?" Trevor asked, a challenge in his voice. "You going to kill me?"

Evan scoffed. "Wouldn't need to. The guard would take care of that."

Trevor was about to object when Evan beat him to it.

"Thing about being a city guard is that it's dreadfully boring and the pay is total shit. Any guard would turn a blind eye to a robbery if they were cut in on the score, and what's a bigger score than selling a few slaves? No. The guard would probably have you lead them to me just to slit your throat and get me to pay him some sort of "toll of passage" for each slave. They'd make a fortune then kill us all after handing off the money. Wouldn't be the first, and sure as hell wouldn't be the last time that would happen.

"Didn't you notice a certain lack of guards in the East-End?" Before Trevor could answer, Evan continued, "No, not one guard, and that's because there's no profit in the East-End. No merchants to rob. No food to steal. It's poor, and it'll stay poor, because that's how the city wants it."

"I don't believe that," Trevor replied plainly.

Evan laughed to himself. "Like I said, *you don't know shit.* You think I'm some monster, but you clearly haven't looked in a mirror lately."

"What's that supposed to mean?"

"Baron told me what happened back at your little village. How you split a man's neck, watched him choke to death while he still hung off your blade. Nasty way to go, if I may say so myself."

"That was different," Trevor defended, thinking back to the dying man at the end of his sword. "That was self-defense."

Evan laughed again. Trevor was beginning to hate the sound of it.

"That's true, sure. Doesn't matter, though. Whether you're fighting your way out of a mess or making the mess yourself, a killer is a killer. And you, kid, are a killer."

"Shut up." Each word Evan said helped ignite a fire in Trevor's stomach. "Just … shut up."

"Oh, don't get so heated now." Evan was clearly feeding off Trevor's anger, which only pissed him off more. "We all fall to the sword, eventually. It *is* one of the three shapers. And don't get me wrong, kid, it's always better to kill than be killed. Number one rule in a fight is to gut the other man before he can gut you. Just don't go convincing yourself your means are justified. I'm sure that poor bastard you drove through thought he was justified to put your village to the torch. That's the problem with perspective—everyone believes they're doing the right thing. Still doesn't change anything."

"So, you think owning slaves is the right thing?" Trevor accused angrily.

"Oh, these guys?" Evan tugged on the rope again, the three natives nearly falling over in the process. "Don't worry; they won't be with us much longer. Still a bit woozy with the drugs, so we'll walk a bit more first." Evan spat to the side. "So, what was that show all about back there? Upset that your poor, old uncle kept a secret about your daddy?"

"You don't know what you're talking about," Trevor said bitterly, picking up his pace toward Evan. He wasn't sure what he would do once he was close, but he did know what he *wanted* to do.

Evan tugged on the rope to stop the three men and quickly faced Trevor. "*I know enough*," he mocked back. Then he stood straighter with a sly smile on his face when he realized Trevor was making his way toward him. "Well, look at that. You've a look of murder in your eyes, kid. You'd like to run me through, too, wouldn't ya? You know what they say about killing; once you start—"

"Shut your—"

"No, you fucking listen." Evan, no longer smiling, lip curled in anger, stepped toward Trevor. "Let me see if I've got you sized up. You're an orphan. You've never met your parents. You've gone around your entire life with people giving you the stink eye. That kid back at the tavern? Probably some entitled fuck that bullied you, right? And the girl? Someone special. Anything I'm missing?"

Trevor was about to say something, but Evan cut him off. "Didn't think so! Now, let me see if I'm right about this, too. That man—your uncle?—raised you, fed you, taught you right from wrong, and even taught you how to fight, right? And you *still* care a shit who your poor old daddy was? The man takes you in, raises you from birth, and you still wanna tell him to fuck off because he wouldn't tell you a secret? Now, I've done some real low shit, kid, but even I know that's cold."

"Stop calling me kid!" Trevor tried his best to sound angry, but the lump in his throat was getting in the way.

"Take my word for it; fathers are overrated." Evan stepped to the side and gestured to the captive natives who kept their hooded heads tilted toward the ground. "Look at them, Trevor. Where do you think their fathers are? How about those kids you saw before? You think they have parents they can go home to?"

"That's different," Trevor said, feeling stupid as the words left his mouth.

"Let me tell you a story." Evan took a step closer to Trevor, only a few feet of distance between the two of them. "Growing up, I had this friend, Jacob. Real solid kid. Wasn't afraid of anything. Well, except for one thing. You see, Jacob's father was a war hero. That being said, nobody ever questioned the relationship Jacob had with his dad, no matter how many bruises he had, no matter how many times he walked the town with a swollen eye or a broken arm.

"You see, Jacob's father was a drunk. A real piece of filth. He kept saying he saw the faces of the people he'd killed when he tried to sleep, that only the drink helped keep them at bay. But then he started seeing them during the day, walking around, standing off at a distance, peeking behind the doors in his own house. So, Jacob's daddy tried to drink them away, too. It wasn't long after that when things got worse.

"Before it was too late, Jacob's dad believed that the ghosts of his victims possessed some of the people in the town. He said he could see them in their eyes, floating around, laughing at him while they screamed curses in his name, blaming him for sending them to the afterlife. And the worse his dad got, the worse Jacob's beatings became.

"I begged Jacob, '*Let's run away. Let's go somewhere he'll never find us.*' But Jacob was a great kid, you see, his heart pure as gold. He kept saying he couldn't leave his dad when he needed him most." Evan paused for a moment and smiled to himself. "I always respected him for that." The smile didn't last long, and Trevor slowly watched it fade to a grimace.

"In the end, I convinced him. We were going to run away to a cousin of his that lived in the next village. The following morning, as I waited at a nearby creek where we agreed to meet, Jacob never came. I waited all morning, for hours, before I decided to find him myself ..."

Evan's face softened, tears building behind his eyes, his bottom lip trembling. There was a long pause before Evan straightened his back, cleared his throat, and crossed his arms. "I went to his house, never even bothered knocking on the door. That's when I saw Jacob. Well, what was left of him, at least. You see, Jacob's dad thought that the only way to be rid of the ghosts for sure was to *cut them out* of their new hosts. Purging, he called it."

Evan stared off distantly. The rope he held in his hand was loose, the natives behind him shifting uncomfortably. Trevor felt uncomfortable himself, not really knowing whether he should say sorry or say anything at all.

Evan tightened his grip on the rope. "The way I see it, *you* have a choice to pick *your* family. I'm sure there are plenty others out there wishing they could. You've no idea how good you have it."

Trevor felt awkward, and the only thing he could think to say was, "I'm sorry about your friend."

"Yeah," Evan mumbled, nodding to himself, deep in thought. "Me, too. Point is"—Evan turned about and nodded to the three native slaves—"you're an orphan. Don't hate the world for it, don't blame your uncle or that girl for it, and especially don't hate yourself for something you can't control. *Do* something about it. *Prove* to the world you're better than what they see every time they look at you.

"The world isn't fair, kid, and it sure as shit doesn't owe you anything. Good men die in the mud while bad men hide behind a uniform. People like pig-faced, fat fuck *Marquis* sit in high places while men like these poor bastards are beaten and starved. It isn't fair, but we work with what we got."

Trevor took in consideration of what Evan was saying. When he spoke, it wasn't angry. "For being so familiar with your friend back there, you've quite the opinion of him."

"That tub of shit is far from my friend," Evan said bitterly as he walked along. "In fact, I intend to kill him the first chance I get. Can't decide how I'd prefer to do it, though ..."

"Then why do you *buy* from him?" Trevor asked.

"Because if I don't, someone else will."

"But, why slaves? And why does he think you're a farmer?"

"Believe it or not, some farmers still use slave work to help them in the fields.

They make enough money from production to pay off the local guards in order to turn a blind eye and still pull a profit before taxes. It's fucking sick."

Trevor shook his head. "Says the guy who just bought three slaves."

"Like I said, better me than someone else."

They walked in silence for a while. They'd gone so far from the city that Trevor could only recognize the large walls as a black shadow on the horizon, the evening sun casting a beautiful landscape.

Last week was just another day in Robins-Port. Today, I'm walking the countryside by the capital of Navaleth with a stranger holding a rope that binds three native slaves. Who knows where I'll be once the snow falls?

"What are the three shapers?" Trevor asked as they descended a hill, another long distance of silence between them.

"What's that?" Evan tugged on the rope, halting the natives in the saddle of two adjoining hills. All was quiet and still, as if they were the only ones alive in the valley. "You don't know what the three shapers are?" Evan dropped the rope as he walked behind the three men, who, in response, kept their hooded heads facing the ground. He put a hand on the back of one of their necks and forced him to his knees, causing the others to be dragged down with him.

Trevor was beginning to feel uncomfortable as he watched Evan stand above the kneeling slaves. "Can't say I've heard of it."

"Interesting." One by one, Evan pulled the hoods off the heads of his captives. "There are three things that shape the world. Three things that guarantee the course of history. The first one is bloodline. Somewhere in our time, we decided someone was *purer* than the rest of us, that *they* should lead while others follow.

"Some say it started with Asher the Conqueror, but I've never been one for fairy tales. Either way, if a monarch decides to expand his territory, he expands his territory. If a king decides it's illegal to own slaves, it's illegal to own slaves. Royalty decides how our world works, just as their heir will, and just how their heir will, as well. All because of their bloodline. All because we believe they are better than us."

Evan pulled a hidden dagger out of his boot, spinning it around in the air as he spoke. "The second one is a blade. A man with a blade holds the power of life and death. Once you kill a man, he's gone forever, only their name to be remembered by, and even that doesn't last very long. Well, unless you've managed to kill yourself enough men, then you become a hero. Strange, isn't it? We chant and praise these heroic names as if they were the greatest people who ever lived, when, in reality, they were just better killers than the rest of us."

Trevor hadn't known that Evan had a blade and seeing it now worried him. Not for himself, but for the three slaves kneeling before them.

Being careful not to show his worry, he asked, "And the third?"

A panic surged through Trevor as Evan turned and stepped toward the natives. He looked down at them as he picked under his fingernail with the dagger. "This world is doomed, kid. We've been so corrupted with the first two shapers that we've forgotten the most important one."

Evan knelt down before one of the slaves. Their eyes locked on one another as Evan's blade hovered inches away from the native's nose.

I've got to do something. I can't just let him kill them.

Trevor wasn't sure if he should charge Evan straight on or try to sneak up behind him, but before he could make a decision, something unexpected happened.

Evan began severing the knot binding the native's hands.

"The last one," Evan continued without looking away, "is choice. We can choose whether or not to follow our chosen monarch, choose to kill, or choose to try to change the world in our own way. We've been so caught up with the bloodshed and the hate that they tell us to have that we forget one thing." The rope snapped and the captives were now free. "We're all people of the same world."

Once all the bonds were cut, the three natives stood tall before them, all rubbing their wrists where the rope had been.

Evan flipped the dagger in his hand, handle pointed out to the native with the swollen eye. "You understand me, yes?"

Trevor was shocked to see the tall man nod in response.

They understood us this entire time? Even in Marquis's house?

"Good." Trevor saw Evan smile in that moment. "There's a place for you. It's called the Crooked Tooth. You've heard of it?"

"Yes," the native with the swollen eye said in a deep voice. "We know of it."

Evan nodded. "Head up the mountain until you find a cave."

"Wrong. Crooked Tooth impossible to climb."

Evan put a reassuring hand on the native's shoulder. "I promise you, it's not. There will be a path for you. Follow it up and around the mountain until you find a cave, then follow the cave through. You'll be in good hands."

The native looked to the others at his sides, who only exchanged words with their eyes. After nodding toward one another, the one Evan had been talking to took the knife by the handle. "Will go. We thank you."

"Don't thank me yet. Best be on your way, and I recommend you travel by night."

The native nodded his thanks then turned and fled without hesitation.

Trevor watched Evan closely as he stared off in the distance after the natives. "You freed them?" he asked dumbfoundedly.

"I freed them," Evan answered.

"I don't understand." Trevor gave up on trying to figure out what type of person Evan truly was. "What exactly is going on?"

"It's like I said." Evan turned to face Trevor. "We can choose to try to change the world in our own way. This was my choice." Evan pushed his way past Trevor and began walking back toward Servitol. "You really do ask a lot of fucking questions."

The False Idol's Promise

"I cannot express the importance of your mission tonight." Francis watched as the man shuffled through the shelves around the kitchen, rummaging behind jars of liquids and powders in search for a specific ingredient. Once he found his mark, a large bottle filled to the rim of dark powder, he added it to the pile of dozen others on the table.

"I understand that it will be a difficult task." Francis picked up one of the jars and studied the contents. He never was one for cooking, but that didn't mean he failed to understand just how difficult it could be, especially under the pressure of an empire. "But the king and I have the utmost faith in the cooking staff, especially his lead chef."

"And your faith is well put, Father Balorian," the chef said, still rummaging through the cabinets for a specific ingredient while Francis stood by as witness. "I'll be sure to make the finest feast for our guests."

"Please, do call me Francis. And tonight's feast isn't necessarily about quality as it is quantity."

The chef paused from reaching into another cupboard. He looked as if Francis had slapped him in the face. "Not of quality, you say? I don't understand, Father—er … Francis. If I'm to cook for the king and his royal guests, should I not aim for the finest meal?"

Francis shook his head. "I understand your worry, good chef, but tonight isn't of tradition. We are simply aiming for enough food to fill enough bellies."

The chef looked confused. "And how much am I to make?"

"Well, you'll actually know better than I. Tell me, have you happened to get outside of the castle walls today?"

The chef nodded, his hand still reaching toward a cabinet. "Aye. The wife and I took our daughter to the market. Why do you ask?"

"And when you came back to the castle, did you happen to see a few stragglers trying to make their way into the castle? The homeless farmers, I mean."

"It's sort of hard to miss them."

"Indeed," Francis agreed.

"Not sure what this has to do with anything," the chef admitted.

The fact that the man was failing to see the significance of the conversation was beginning to bore Francis. "How many homeless people do you suppose are crowding our gates at this very moment?"

The chef thought to himself for a moment. "By now, I'd say ... a few hundred?"

Francis shrugged. "Then I suppose you'll have to cook enough food to fill a few hundred mouths."

Finally, the chef's hand dropped from the cabinet as he realized his current situation. "Oh."

"*Oh*, indeed," Francis confirmed.

The chef took a deep breath, another thing that Francis found annoying. "Are you sure the king will want to use his own supply of food to feed a bunch of pests like that?"

"Pests?" Francis dropped his arms to his sides. "Do you mean the citizens who are victims of banditry? The men and women who have sacrificed their lives in order to keep your kitchen filled? Surely, you can't mean the farmers who need our help?"

The chef put his arms behind his back, clearly embarrassed and regretting his poor choice of words. "I, uh—"

"Those *pests*"—Francis pointed toward the ceiling—"were left with nothing after a group of cowardly bandits decided to destroy everything they had. They've labored endlessly every day for their kingdom to make sure our countrymen were fed, spending their whole lives enslaved to the fields. Who would we be to abandon them in a time of need such as this? We owe those *pests* whatever it is we can offer them, even if it is a basic meal and a warm bed. Or do you disagree?"

The chef shifted nervously, doing his best to avoid Francis's glare. He picked at his thumbnail, which irritated Francis even more, and studied the contents of the floor. "No, Father, I only meant—"

"Shall we let them starve on our very doorstep? Is that what you would prefer?"

"Absolutely not, Father." The chef kept his focus on the ground. "I meant no offense, of course. A slip of the tongue."

Francis perspired with irritation. It was down to the final stretch of his plan. All he needed to do was make sure this pompous, overqualified chef could follow through with a simple meal.

"And I'll let that one slide for good measure. I understand you are overwhelmed with your task tonight, but let me make it as simple as can be."

The chef quickly nodded. "Aye, Father. Whatever our king commands."

Francis ignored the comment. "There are just under five-hundred seats, not including the royal table, in our hall. I expect you to provide enough food for each man, woman, or child occupying that seat in just a few short hours."

The chef looked utterly terrified. "But you ask the impossible, Father. Perhaps with a few extra hands I could cook porridge, but to do that on my own would be too much."

As I expected.

"Then I shall provide a few extra hands to help suit your needs. As I've said, tonight is about quantity, not quality. There will be a lot of mouths to feed, good chef, and as I've said before, the king and I have the utmost faith in you."

Francis watched as the task dawned on the man before him. After a few moments of looking around the kitchen and taking two deep consecutive breaths, he looked at Francis with determination in his eye. "Aye. I'll not fail you, nor the king."

Francis smiled warmly, yet not entirely genuine. "Good. I'm glad to hear it. I will be back in just a couple of hours to see the progress of your work." Francis turned to go, the sound of clattering jars echoing behind his back as he left the chef to his work.

Just before Francis left the kitchen, he turned back and looked at the chef. "People will remember tonight's feast, my friend. It will never be forgotten, nor will people forget the chef who graciously and valiantly fed the country in its greatest time of need."

A wide smile spread across the chef's face and, for a moment, Francis actually felt sorry for the man.

In recent years, Francis had grown to know the chef more personally. He was a man who was passionate about his cooking, not because he was good at it, but simply because he loved to provide. He had a beautiful wife and a wonderful daughter who liked to visit his father in the kitchen from time to time. He was a good man, and an even better cook. If anyone could complete such a task with such short notice, it would be him.

In just a few short hours, the man would stress beyond belief, but he will also

{

do exactly what Francis needed to be done.

And then he will be dead.

***

Although just a few hundred yards away, across the sturdy bridge that connected the two islands of the castle and main district of Navaleth, he could hear the shouts and pleas of beggars swarming the gates. Still, he kept his head held high, his back straight, and his mind focused.

He gave one of his most friendly smiles as he approached the crowd, spreading his arms in rejoice as he looked upon the faces of his next victims.

The shouting muffled down into near whispers, the hush of his name passing throughout the crowd.

"Look, it's the head herald!" a man screamed, his son held tightly against his chest.

"He's come to save us!" Francis heard a woman holler hopefully.

They praised him as he approached. A savior in their eyes, yet a liberator within his own.

Of course playing his part was easy in the eyes of the crowd. They didn't see Francis, not the true Francis, at least. They saw a herald in his robe, a man who dedicated his entire life to the laws of faith in order to aid the crown. His image and status alone had won him over just about every obstacle he'd encountered on his path.

Why is it that people grow so weak at the sight of a man of faith?

"Citizens!" Francis bellowed to the silent crowd.

The few remaining guards took a moment to relax. They had been guarding the entrance to the castle all day, no doubt fatigued with the constant task of holding the beggars at bay.

"Fathers, mothers," Francis spoke, each time looking into the eyes of another person before him, "sons, daughters, brothers, sisters … all who have suffered at the hands of this barbaric horde of bandits. All who have fallen victim by those who have burned your homes and butchered your cattle, your livestock, and your life.

"You have waited patiently here at our gates, and for that, I and your beloved king greatly appreciate your boundless patience. Now, you shall be rewarded. You shall be saved!

"You have spent your lives providing for your kingdom, for your country and all its citizens. Now I say, it is time that we provide for you! Tonight, you will dine in the halls of the castle, feast on the food provided by the country you love so greatly! For the country you've sacrificed your very lives and homes for."

A cheer went up in the crowd. Francis could see tears of joy coming from faces of men and women both.

You've got them in your grasp. Now give them their well-deserved false hope.

"Fear not, friends; this is only the beginning. As of right now, your fields are being tended to by other farmers, your homes are being rebuilt by our finest architects, your new livestock is being herded by our most trusted shepherds. You will not only be able to return home soon, but the first three years of your new lives will also be without tax!"

Another cheer went up, louder than the first.

Francis continued over the roar of the crowd, his voice a whisper through a storm. "Your king will never fail you, just as you have never failed him!"

He turned his back on the beggars to see the line of guards making their way across the bridge toward them. "These"—he motioned to the approaching guards—"will be your escorts to the dining hall, where you will be provided with bread and water. Then, in a few hours, your bellies will be full with a hot meal and your hearts warm with your king's love. Do not fret, nor stray, anymore, my friends, for you have been saved."

Francis motioned for the guards to let crowd through.

When they stepped aside, the swarm flowed like a river, engulfing just about every inch of space the bridge could manage as they made their way across. They walked by, praising their love to Francis. Francis, all the while, smiled and played his part perfectly.

As the crowd cleared, and Francis was left relishing in his achievement, one man remained. He stood across the street, away from the entrance to the bridge, a dirty cowl over his face as he leaned on a cane. His skin was dark and grimy, and Francis realized he wasn't wearing shoes.

Francis studied the man, overwhelmed with curiosity and the inability to look away.

The old man stared for a long moment back, and in that moment, Francis felt a swell of sadness in his chest that he couldn't explain. He remembered the feeling as a child when he'd failed, on multiple occasions, to gain his father's approval.

In that moment of sadness, the stranger shook his head dismissively, turned, and walked away.

***

Francis was back in his room, contemplating tonight's festivities, when there was a light knock at the door. He unlocked the golden deadbolt and creaked open the door. When he recognized the face behind it, he widened the door and invited them in. Once the door was closed, the golden lock shut, he returned to his desk.

"Everything set up?" Francis asked his guest.

"Everything's set up," Vallis answered with a smile.

"Good. How many men did you get?"

"Thirty," Vallis answered with a quickness that said he was waiting for the question. "Thirty men total. More than enough to do the job."

"And their families?" Francis took a sip of the liquor he'd used only on celebratory occasions.

And this is absolutely such an occasion.

"No families, no loved ones, no ties, and nobody will recognize them. Perfect for the job."

"Good." Francis took another sip, letting the burning contents reach his stomach before speaking again. "Timing is everything. Once I leave the dining hall, you'll lead them into the city. There can be no mistakes now."

Vallis nodded in confidence. "Understood, Francis. You can trust me."

"Yes, I can. Which is exactly why you'll be leading them. As soon as I leave the dining hall, you are to begin. Start off quietly, and only kill enough people to send a message. What do you do after?"

"After the city is attacked, I'll send them to the location where they'll be ambushed by our guards."

"Where they'll be ambushed and *killed* by our guards," Francis corrected. "There can be no survivors."

"I understand," Vallis confirmed. "Once I hear the bell toll, they'll rally there, and I'll meet you and the others in the council chamber."

"And you understand your task there?" Francis looked at his accomplice long and hard. "There can be no hesitation in this matter. I wish it were otherwise, but we have to work with what we've got."

"I won't hesitate. The man may be arrogant, but even I'd be a fool to doubt the potential he has as an ally, or even recognize what he's sacrificed to get where he's at. He's a hero, but I promise you, I will not hesitate."

"Good." Francis swirled the liquor around in his glass. "Unfortunate it had to be this way, but sacrifices must be made."

Vallis nodded his thanks.

He might be a hot-headed fool, but Francis still saw potential in the man. He just needed some guidance, and soon, the entire world would be guided well enough.

"So, it begins. Tonight is the end of the world as we know it, and tomorrow is the start of a new one." Francis took a long swallow, finishing off his liquor. The burn in his throat spread warmth through his belly. He placed the glass down on his desk, wiped his mouth, and smiled at Vallis. "Let's begin."

A Ghost in a Shell

"Who was that arrogant fellow?" Benny snapped his fingers repeatedly, as if the name would magically appear out of thin air. "You know, the one who always ranted about marrying a princess once he got out?"

They had been at it for over an hour now. What else were you to do when this was the first time you'd seen your closest friends just shy of fifteen years, and it just happened to take place in a bar? You had a few drinks, you told old stories, and you tried to forget the outside world.

Alric didn't participate in the drinking, though, and he was grateful that the others didn't question why. He hadn't had a drink in quite some time now, back when he preferred living his life in a drunken blur. Back when he found all his solutions at the bottom of a bottle.

"You're talking about Pretty-Boy Williams." Harvin took another sip from his mug, which Alric had to question just which number that particular cup was. The man could down ale quicker than a man dying of thirst yet showed no signs of inebriation. "Or, in other words, The-One-Who-Never-Shut-Up."

"Yes!" Benny slammed his hand against the table, causing the foam of his third ale to spew over its rim. He, along with Marcus, had no shame in conveying just how many drinks they'd had. "Pretty-Boy Williams. Such a theatrical man. He always did like bolstering a crowd, didn't he?"

Harvin grumbled, "I remember seriously considering sewing his mouth shut just to have some peace and quiet. I never understood how the man could have such energy after a full day's march."

"He always did try to make our days something of a fairy tale." Marcus, compared to Harvin, had just about as much to drink as any of the rest. However, he was always the one to let loose when he had the chance. The man had no shame as he leaned drunkenly over the table, the aroma of stale beer wafting before them all. "Do you guys remember the speech he gave the morning of his first march? Kid probably practiced it in the mirror for years, waiting for that very moment to recite it before his first mission."

Alric sipped his water. "I remember holding up in a small town east of Rylath when he had his first ale."

"Oh gods, please no." Marcus chuckled like a giddy child. "Not this story."

"Was that the night Orlington actually *let* us take the night off to have some drinks?" Benny asked.

"Yup." Harvin leaned back in his chair and crossed his arms. "And drink Pretty-Boy Williams did."

"It was nearing midnight when he came sprinting down the stairs with two mugs in his hands," Alric continued. "Shit, never seen the boy move faster than that, not even when his tent caught fire one night."

"Yes!" The memory came back to Benny. "Is this where—"

"Guys, please don't." Marcus struggled with holding his drink while he was too busy cradling his stomach. His face was purple with laughter as the story brought him to the brink of hysteria. "Seriously, I'll fucking die."

" '*Guys, I've found her! I've found my princess!*' " Benny said in a mocking voice.

Harvin grinned with the memory, a rare sight to witness for most men. " '*Tonight, we'll make love like none has ever made love before, for tomorrow morning that love must be put on hold until I can once again return and take her hand in marriage.*' "

Benny struggled to catch his breath from laughter. "Seriously, where did he come up with that shit?" When Alric shot Benny a raised eyebrow, his friend shrugged and took another drink. "I'm not *that* bad."

Harvin took another drink from his mug. "And there I thought the theatrics were bad enough when he was sober. Give the man three pints, and he turns into a fucking bard."

"I think all theatrics died the next morning when he saw his *princess*," Alric added.

"Hold on now." Benny raised a defensive hand. "She wasn't terrible."

"Guys, seriously," Marcus pleaded, his face as red as a fresh picked tomato. "I can't take it."

"By all means, no." Harvin shrugged his broad shoulders, ignoring Marcus's plea. "Especially if your idea of a princess is an elderly lady who also happens to be a dwarf."

Marcus exploded in a long, singular laugh, his face turning near purple as tears of merriment rolled down his cheeks. "What—" His words gasped out between breaths as he clenched his stomach tightly. "What was it … she said … to him?"

Harvin joined in the laughter that echoed around the table. " '*My grandchildren will be so happy to see their nanny riding the wagon again.*' "

The table erupted in laughter. Some of them couldn't help pounding the table a few times, not a care in the world for their spilling mugs, nor the questionable looks they were now undoubtedly getting from the nearby patrons.

Marcus was the worst. He was the type of man who, when he laughed, it made others laugh. The fact he could still laugh so easily after everything he'd been through gave Alric a sense of pride in simply knowing the man personally.

"Fucking hell," Marcus said as he wiped the tears from his face. "I'll never understand why you all hated on him. He always was a good laugh when you needed it."

Harvin smiled to himself, staring off distantly with the memory as he nodded. "I can agree with that."

Benny took a deep gulp from his mug. "What ever happened to that guy?"

And just like that, that heavy blanket of warm happiness was sucked away and replaced with the true and bitter face of the world. Once again, the ugly face of reality invaded their conversation, that comforting warmth of happy memories only a fleeting thought.

"Green-Gate," Alric answered bitterly.

Alric watched as Marcus's smile melted from his face. "Right. Green-Gate."

Harvin sighed, that rare sight of happiness melting into his usual grimace. "Fucking Green-Gate."

Silence hung over the table as the four men pushed about their mugs.

You can always count on the memory of dead friends to butcher a mood swifter than a leaf blowing in the wind.

They all sat in silence for a moment, thinking of the countless names of everyone they knew that had fallen that terrible day. Names that matched the endless line of bloodied faces belonging to those who were now buried months away in a shallow grave, far from their home, forgotten in the sands of time.

"Well," Benny said after the quiet dragged on. He grabbed his mug, now with nearly half its contents spewed about the table, and raised it before them. "To Pretty-Boy Williams."

The rest followed suit, lifting their own in salute. "To Pretty-Boy Williams," they echoed.

Alric half-expected for Marcus to order another round, yet he waved away the approaching barkeep and pushed his empty mug to the center of the table. He'd apparently lost his appetite. "You know, I looked for you guys after the war."

"You did?" Benny asked after draining the last of his ale.

"I did." Marcus set his arms on the table, tucked his chin to his chest, and belched quietly to himself. "Don't get me wrong, I was ecstatic when we got home. Everything seemed so … bright, you know? Like everything was new and welcoming."

Alric did know. The thing he remembered most when he first came home from the war was how everything was so *quiet.* No more orders being barked as soon as you opened your eyes. No more echoes of stories being told around fires, or sleeping in the same tent with three other companions. No more clinking of metal on metal caused by thousands of marching men. Everything was blissfully silent.

"But that dulled out faster than a rusted blade." Marcus picked at his fingernails, a tick that Alric recognized immediately. His friend had a tendency to do that whenever he felt vulnerable. "You guys remember Old-Fist Payne?"

They nodded. Old-Fist Payne had been the oldest man in their unit. He'd been enlisted since he was able to swing a sword and committed his entire life in Navaleth's army. Alric had learned a lot of things from Old-Fist Payne, mostly on how to be a soldier in the Navalethian army. Despite being a great teacher, Old-Fist Payne was also known for his dark side.

"He used to admit to beating his wife," Marcus ranted on. "I remember, one night he told me how he let the drink go too far once, that he nearly killed her in a drunken rage."

Alric had also been witness to hearing such stories.

"From there on, I always thought the man evil. I swore to myself that no matter what happens, I'll never end up like that old bastard.

"I always knew there was something wrong with him, but I just brushed it off. *He's earned his grief, Marcus Gorman,* I told myself. *It's your job to learn from him, not judge him.*"

Alric remembered the word traveling around his company about Old-Fist Payne. Thing about being so close with dozens of people, word traveled fast, and sooner rather than later, Old-Fist Payne became the talk of the company.

"Then there was that one night when he got drunk on patrol," Marcus continued, Alric knowing full well where it was about to lead. "I told our team leader, and he just brushed it off. He said that, if I didn't get back in line, he'd have me flogged and cleaning latrines for the next month." Marcus bit his lower lip angrily. "*That arrogant prick!*"

Marcus had mentioned the story a few times before, and each time he struggled to tell it the same. The man had seared that memory to himself, a brand of regret burning his heart. "Sure enough, Old-Fist Payne was drunk enough to mistake a poor private coming back from a piss as the enemy. Killed him right there and then."

Harvin nodded sadly, staring off at nothing in particular. "He was a new guy. Pretty sure he wasn't even a year in his enlistment."

"And I fucking *told* command about him." Marcus hit his fist on the table. "I warned them, and they brushed it off simply because it was Old-Fist Payne, because who should trust a word of a simple grunt over the word of an admired officer. I'll never forget that arrogant bastard Lieutenant Milson. If he would have just fucking listened to me, if he would have just taken a short look at Old-Fist, he could have saved someone's life. And because of that negligence, a mother lost a son. A sister lost a brother. For all we know, a child lost a father, and a wife lost a husband. Not to our enemy, but to the very people who swore to fucking protect him!"

The ire burned in Marcus's eyes. It boiled there, a rage of regret that had obviously been haunting him all these years.

Alric and the others let him sit quietly for a moment as he gathered himself, not letting the anger settle, but simply putting it back in the box where it stayed hidden with the rest of the bad memories old men like them possessed.

"Anyway," Marcus said when he calmed down, "I was back home, not even for a few months when I started doing everything I swore not to. I drank a lot, I fucked even more, and I started more fights than I could count. To be fair, I couldn't go to a bar without being recognized, which only helped the crowd feed me drinks all night. They praised me like I was Asher himself! I couldn't even go to local market without some poor fool patting my back, thanking me for everything we did in the war.

"Can you believe that?" Marcus asked, grimacing at the vile memory. "They *thanked* us for what we did, for killing all those people. I didn't even feel like … like *me* anymore. I was like a ghost in the shell of who I was."

Benny nodded solemnly. "Fame always does come with a bitter price."

"It does, and it really did." Marcus wiped his nose, his eyes on the brink of tears. "One night, I woke up in a tavern—with absolutely no recollection of how I got there—three towns over from my home. I got up and looked in the mirror. And I mean *really* looked in the mirror, and I swear, Old-Fist Payne was staring back at me.

"That morning, I walked back to my house, packed my things, and I was off. I started walking endlessly, hunting game for food, sleeping next to fires at night, nothing but what I could carry with me hanging in a knapsack over my shoulder. I did that for about a month before I started asking around for you guys. Wasn't hard back then, given who we were."

"Huh," Harvin grunted.

"Anyway"—Marcus cleared his throat—"thing was, I heard you were all doing pretty well. Benny, I heard you were looking for your family."

"Aye," Benny agreed. "Heard my sister had a husband and child, but they spent a lot of time traveling for work. He worked for the banks or something—can't recall. Anyway, never did catch up with them."

"I'm sorry to hear that."

Marcus looked at Alric. "Took a while to catch some solid news about you, Al. Last thing I heard was that you owned a farm somewhere east. Had a wife of your own, actually."

Alric felt a heavy pain in his gut at the mention of his wife, the memory of his farm coming back to him. Him working the fields as his beautiful Meyra pranced around in her sundress. The way she looked as she rocked in her chair next to the fire with a book in her hands. It had been years since he had heard her voice, since the day she was taken from him, and every day since felt like the first day without her.

"Had," Alric said, trying his hardest to channel his sorrow into anger, a feeling that was easier to live with. He suddenly had that old familiar feeling of a need to drink.

"That made me happy," Marcus said. "And I am so sorry."

Marcus looked at Harvin. "Then, one day, here in Servitol, nonetheless, I ran into an old friend wearing a captain's uniform. I had heard rumors of the 'Merciless Harvin' taking command of his own company, and I just couldn't resist the urge to see it for myself."

"Always thought you'd get out," Benny said to Harvin.

Harvin nodded softly. "I was on my way to do so when I ran into our old commander. He said there was a lieutenant spot with my name on it if I wanted it. Got captain a few years after that."

"And now you're the commander of Brackenheart," Alric said to Harvin, who just grunted with a slight nod in reply.

"After that, I decided to search for my own purpose," Marcus continued. "I was not even a few miles away from my home, a few years after the war, when I came upon a bandit gang trying to rob a married couple."

"That must have ended badly for them," Benny said.

"I didn't kill them," Marcus said suddenly.

"You didn't?" Alric was actually stunned with the news.

Marcus shook his head. "No, because I recognized them. They were in our unit during the war. That poor private that Old-Fist Payne had killed? They were his friends. They helped me bury him. " Marcus let the turn of events settle for a bit before continuing. "That's when I realized what I wanted to do, what I wanted to spend the rest of my life doing."

"And what was that?" Benny asked patiently.

Marcus leaned over the table. "I wanted to make sure that Old-Fist Payne never existed again." There was no mistaking the seriousness in Marcus's eyes. "That officers like Lieutenant Milson were more involved with their troops.

"I enlisted as an officer not a week later and worked hard to climb the ranks. I made sure that every one of my men were heard, that all their concerns were taken seriously, and that the army was taking care of their soldiers the way it should have been when we were simple grunts."

They all sat quietly for a while, taking in the story of their friend's journey after the war. It filled Alric with pride looking at his old friend in that moment, and if there was anything the story told, it was that they could trust this man with the terrible news that they had yet to deliver.

How could he have doubted them in the first place? These were the people he'd gone through hell and back with. They'd marched across the entire country together, sometimes marching day and night, only to spend the rest of the day fighting face to face with an enemy. How could he have doubted the integrity of his friends so easily just because he hadn't seen them in a while?

Alric looked to Benny, and he could see they were of the same mind. If they were looking for someone in the city to break the news to, to share a possible conspiracy theory that cost hundreds of innocent lives in Robins-Port, these were the men to speak with. Not only were they great friends, but they commanded two-thirds of the entire Navalethian army. They were their best option.

Alric looked to the other side of the room where Dodge and Sarah sat quietly at their own table. Dodge watched them curiously, his eyes squinting as if to size up the situation. Sarah, as usual, sat with her hands in her lap and a blank stare on her face.

If there ever was a time to do this, it's now.

Alric looked at Benny and nodded.

Benny cleared his throat and leaned across the table, his voice barely above a whisper. "We, uh … need to tell you something. And it's going to come as a bit of a shock … I'm hoping, at least."

Marcus eyed Benny curiously. "Takes enough to shock men like us, wouldn't you say?"

"This is serious," Alric said.

"Very serious," Benny confirmed.

Both Harvin and Marcus looked inquiringly at their friends, and when it was clear Benny was waiting for them to move closer so they could keep their conversation private, they scooted their chairs a bit and waited for Benny to speak.

"Robins-Port was attacked," Benny whispered.

The two men eyed quizzically gazes at Benny, as if he'd just said something in a foreign language. They replied with blank stares, no doubt waiting for the punchline to the joke they were just told. When it was clear that it was, in fact, not a joke at all, and Alric could see realization mask their faces, Benny continued.

"We were passing through to come here when we saw the flames."

"What do you mean *attacked*?" Marcus said, sobriety kicking in. "Attacked by whom?"

"We don't know," Benny admitted. "We didn't recognize their type."

"Bandits?" Harvin asked aloud, scanning the room for any unwelcome listeners. "There is this bandit king, Lazar, pillaging farms and sending the residents here to the castle. Didn't think them so bold as to attack a trading city, especially such as Robins-Port."

"We couldn't tell," Alric said. "We showed up near the end of it."

"Wait, wait, wait," Marcus said impatiently. "When did this happen?"

"About a week back," Alric answered.

Marcus shook his head. "No, that can't be right. That's impossible. We would have heard of it by now."

Marcus could never understand just how uneasy the comment made Alric feel. Not only did it confirm that word hadn't reached the city about Robins-Port being ransacked, but not even the highest ranking officers in the Navalethian army had even caught wind of it.

"I assure you, it is quite possible," Benny said. "We were there. We saw it."

"That doesn't make any sense," Marcus continued to deny. "I sent riders to Robins-Port last week. They would have reported back already if they saw it was attacked."

Alric could see the cold moment of realization hit his friend like an arrow from a bowman. He realized that if his men hadn't reported back by now, then it was most likely because they were dead.

"Well, fuck," Marcus cursed quietly to himself. Marcus didn't just lose two men, but also two friends. "Fuck, fuck, fuck."

"Wait." Harvin, who had been quiet nearly the entire time, looked to Benny. "Why wouldn't the guards send a messenger?"

There was no easy way to say it, so Benny said it plainly. "Because everyone there is dead."

"Bloody hell," Marcus said under his breath, pain clear in his eyes. "Everyone, you say? Why in the hells would someone attack Robins-Port and not use it as leverage?"

"Are you sure everyone was killed?" Harvin asked abruptly.

Alric looked to Benny once more, and he met his eyes.

Well, it's already out there. It's all or nothing.

"No, not everyone," Alric said, looking past his friend toward Sarah and Dodge.

"What do you mean?" Marcus asked, hope now giving him more life. "What does that mean?"

Benny shifted in his seat. "He means, not *everyone* is dead. We saved a few. They're here with us now."

"You mean *here*, in the city?" Harvin asked.

"I mean here, in this tavern." Benny gestured behind the two men, toward the table where Dodge and Sarah sat quietly. "Right there, actually."

Harvin Destro and Marcus Gorman turned around and stared at Dodge and Sarah, who now straightened in their seats, knowing that their secret had just been shared. Alric and Benny had done what they'd promised. They had found someone in the city they could trust, which meant they could be on their way soon, putting miles and miles of open country between Servitol and the brotherhood.

Marcus turned back around and let out a deep sigh. He pinched the bridge of his nose and shook his head. "Well, bring them over then. I'm sure they a wicked story to tell."

The Heart of Navaleth

The dining hall was one of the largest rooms in the entire castle. The walls vaulted high toward the skies, and balconies upon balconies reached up the sides an additional three levels, each section fitted with velveted chairs and a large marble table. Were the royal party, such as dukes and ambassadors to the king, bankers and trading companies, they would be assigned their own balcony with a personal kitchen staff member to provide them with every need they desired.

Everyone knew that it was a great privilege to eat in the dining hall of the castle, which was exactly why Francis took it upon himself to give access to the homeless citizens who were pounding at the castle gates not hours ago. It was a small favor that made people feel more valued by their government. A small aspect of value they craved in order to feel equal with their leaders.

Little did they know their petty and charitable moment would soon be their undoing.

"Mom, look," a child hollered to his mother, pointing toward a large painting on the eastern wall. "It's Asher, Mom! Just like from your stories!"

The painting depicted the fabled story of Asher the Conqueror, protecting a town from a pack of hellhounds with only his bare hands. It showed a man of massive strength holding two hounds at bay by their throats, acting as a human shield to protect the family behind him.

Francis smiled wickedly as he stood on a raised lectern in the front of the dining hall, looking down over the crowd as they flooded into the vaulted room.

Perhaps one day they'll do a painting of you, he thought to himself. *At least it would be better than the lies that has polluted this castle for centuries.*

Behind Francis sat a massive, golden table fit only for the king and his family. Although the king's wife had died years ago, long before the king himself had been taken ill and was left rotting in his bed, one chair would always remain vacant in the loving memory of the past queen of Navaleth.

There were other chairs, as well, reserved only for the king's offspring, a princess or prince to his ancestral bloodline. Unfortunately, the queen had died too soon to produce an heir to the throne. Currently, there was no heir to take the king's place if something were to happen to him.

Well, not a rightful heir, at least. But we'll take that secret to the grave, my king. At least, you will, and very soon.

Long tables lined parallel down the long room that stretched to the front of the dining hall. Guards were escorting families of the former farmers to their table and seats, shaking dirty hands with one another with hopeful smiles on their faces.

Vallis stood at the back of the hall near the main doors. He was looking around at the hundreds of people who were now about to dine in one of the most privileged rooms in the castle, a sour grimace on his face. When he met Francis stare, he gave a small nod. Francis nodded back.

And just like that, everything began.

Vallis walked out the front doors and signaled to the guards behind him to close the doors. When the echo of the shut doors boomed through the hall, the conversations that floated across the room shrank to mere whispers, which ultimately ended as hundreds of faces now stared up at Francis.

"Mothers," Francis's voice echoed off the stone walls, his arms raised at his sides, welcoming people with open arms, "fathers, brothers, sisters, children, and friends. You sit here today for two reasons and two reasons alone. The first is because you are a citizen of Navaleth. You have spent your livelihood honoring that by ploughing the fields, milking the cows, and harvesting the grain. You have honored that by providing your fellow countrymen and women by putting food on their plates, by feeding our troops when they are in the field. It is because of the sweat of your brow, the aches in your backs, and calluses on your hands that we were able to create such a great and wonderful kingdom!

"Even so, because of reasons I could never begin to fathom, there are others who do not take pride in what we have built. Where you choose to work tirelessly every day to provide food for those in need, others would rather hide in the shadows and strike out with a knife and torch. They would rather see your creations burn to the ground and all your hard work crumble before us all. This is one reason why you sit here! Because you are a working Navalethian, and this bandit king chose to try to destroy everything we stand for!"

Francis took a moment to look at the faces in the room. He saw the power of his voice resonating in their eyes. He saw the sorrow of his truth weighing heavily on those before him. These were the faces of those who had been broken down, and now it was time to build them back up.

"But you do not give up," Francis roared over the heads of the people sitting before him. "You do not give in! You do not tremble and cower away from the ones who seek to destroy our creation. No, you do not fret, for that is the second reason why are you are here!

"Because you belong to the greatest kingdom in the world! Because, where others will struggle to watch you fall, we take pride in holding each other up! Because, in this kingdom, in this beloved kingdom that you, by your own hands, have built from the ground up, *we will never let our brothers and sisters fall to such evil!*

"You sit here, in this great hall, because you are Navalethians, the greatest people the world will ever know!"

Cheers thundered from the tables, from families of farmers and guards alike. He let the roar take flight, letting the chants boom off the walls as the entire dining hall erupted in praise. Francis could see tears of joy in the mothers, he could see pride and determination in the fathers, and he could see hope and love within the children's eyes.

"When those in the shadows kick us down," Francis continued, "we get back up, we brush the dirt off our clothes, and we *ask for more!* Because that's who we are, because that's what Navaleth stands for!"

More cheers followed, claps, and whistles continuing to echo around the room.

"So, please"—Francis struggled to get his voice above the roar of the crowd—"feast tonight, enjoy this humble and the first of many gifts from your king to help us get back on our feet. Fill your bellies with warm joy, and never forget who you are. Never forget that you are the heart of Navaleth!"

***

"Quite the speech, Father," the chef said as he peppered three large cauldrons of bubbly stew. "Made the hairs on my arms stand up. It reminded me of why I love this country so damned much."

"I'm glad you thought so," Francis thanked, fiddling with the small pocket of fabric in his pocket. "It's important to remind those in need that we will never fail them."

"Aye." The chef nodded. "Indeed, it is."

"I see that you've done well on your task." Francis gestured to the bubbling cauldrons.

After his speech in the dining hall, he had made his way to the kitchen where he'd found the chef hovering over the task that Francis had given him a few hours ago. "Was the staff I provided efficient enough to suit your needs?"

"They were, aye." The chef took a step back, put his arms on his hips, and gave a deep breath. "It's all done, just as I promised. I told you I wouldn't fail ya."

"And I never had a doubt in my mind of your capabilities. Thank you."

"What we got here"—the chef held his hands out toward all the food—"is rabbit stew, mixed with carrots, potatoes, and a creamy broth. Spiced to all hell, but the flavor will melt away their sorrows in just one bite." He looked upon his meal as if it were a prized creation. "It'll be the best damn stew they've ever had."

"May I?" Francis asked. "The king will be having a bowl himself. Not that I don't trust you, of course, but policies are in place for a reason."

"No need to explain to me." The chef waved to the stew invitingly. "Be my guest, Father." The chef handed Francis a wooden spoon.

He tasted each cauldron and was rewarded with an unbelievable taste each time. It was, as the man had so easily put it, the best damned stew he'd ever had.

When Francis gave the man his verdict, the chef clapped his hands loudly. "You see! Perfect in every sense of the word."

"So it is," Francis agreed with a friendly smile. Then he went to the door and cracked it open. In the hallway stood two guards awaiting his command. "Get the staff ready to host their guests. The chef and I will take our leave here soon, but make sure every bowl is filled to the brim and that nobody starves tonight. Understood?"

"Understood." The guards marched off up the stairs. Once they were out of sight, distant enough to risk being heard, Francis closed the door.

The chef was again rummaging through the cabinets on the far wall, now putting back the ingredients he had searched so hard to find earlier.

With the man's back to him, Francis pulled out the small pebbles he'd been fiddling with in his pocket. With a quick flick of his wrist, he dropped a pebble into each cauldron of stew.

"I'll take a bowl to his majesty now," Francis announced. "Do you have any ceremonial bowls about I could use?"

"Yes, yes, of course." The chef hurried across the room to the far corner where he opened a door to a large closet. Before him stood shelves lined with cutlery, bowls, and plates. Francis knew that the golden bowls, which were used only for the king, were in the very back shelf of that closet.

The chef walked deeper into the closet, and Francis was right behind him, as quiet as a mouse but as deadly as a viper. Francis felt his heart beat through his entire body, his blood boiling hot as he rolled up his sleeves and revealed the hidden dagger tied to his arm.

"They'll be telling the story of tonight for years to come, Francis," the chef was saying, oblivious to the danger he was currently in. "Your speech will be in it and everything. One day, when I'm too old to cook myself, perhaps my daughter would—"

Francis wrapped his hand around the chef's mouth and plunged the dagger underneath the man's armpit. He ripped it free and drove the blade into the chef's ribs. Again. And again and again. All the while, the man reached for Francis, trying to pry away his clamping hand.

Warm blood washed over Francis's arm as the chef began to choke on his own blood.

Francis's adrenaline vibrated through his entire body. The rush was euphoric, and it grew more intense with the sound of the chef's gurgles choking in his throat.

After a few more plunges, Francis felt the chef's body go limp in his grasp as his life floated away into nothing, leaving behind an empty bag of bones and meat.

The body crumbled to the floor at Francis's feet. He spent the next minute looking upon his work, the blood spreading across the stone floors better than any fresca in the castle. He let the adrenaline subside, rolled down the sleeves of his robe and tossed the dagger onto the lifeless body of the chef.

Francis then took a bowl from the top shelf and closed the door to the closet, leaving the corpse of the chef in the shadows. It would be a few hours before it was found, just like Francis had planned. He grabbed a nearby towel and wiped the dark blood from his hands before filling his bowl to the rim with the stew.

And now it's time to end a bloodline.

The Curse

"You're brooding again," Evan quipped.

They had made it back to the outer wall, and Evan was just beginning to crawl through the hidden gap that led inside the city.

Trevor kept silent as he crawled through the hole. Once he was on the other side and, once again, in the slums of Servitol, Evan eyed him suspiciously.

"What? Finally run out of insults? Not pissed off anymore?"

"I'm definitely pissed off," Trevor reacted. "I'm just … thinking."

"Huh." Evan sniffled and wiped his nose on his dirty sleeve. Then he shrugged as he began leading Trevor through the dirt streets. "Thinking of …?"

At first, Trevor wasn't going to answer, and he wasn't sure why he did. Maybe it was the way Evan had spoken to him before. Sure, it was ugly, but an ugly truth, nonetheless.

"Look," he began awkwardly, "you were right about how I acted before. It was hard to hear, but maybe I needed to hear it."

Evan didn't fully turn around, but the shake of his head was enough for Trevor to know he'd said something wrong. "Fuck, kid, you really are cold, aren't you?"

Trevor was taken aback, nearly stopping in his tracks with the comment. "What are you talking about?"

"I'm just saying," Evan said defensively, an obvious act for his own pleasure, "not a week back, your entire village was murdered. Every house was burned to the ground, along with every resident butchered like animals. Yet, here you are, in a strange city with strange company, and you act as if you don't care whatsoever of what happened to your home."

It was true. He never really did think back to the innocent people in Robins-Port who had lost their lives. Truth be told, he'd never cared for them in the first place. Nobody had put him to thought when they had been alive, so why should Trevor put them to thought just because they're dead? Maybe he should feel bad about that. But the truth was that he didn't.

As much as Trevor would like to, there was no forgetting what had happened in Robins-Port.

Goosepimples crawled up his arms, spreading around his neck and making the hair stand up on his arms as he thought about the man he killed. He thought of the sound his sword made as it slid through skin and scraped its way past bone. He thought of the way the blood looked as it flowed down the steel of his blade and caressed his hands with a warm touch.

Trevor also dreamed of his victim every night since the attack. Each time, it was the same. The man would come at him in full strength, swinging a long sword at Trevor's face. Each time, Trevor knew what he had to do, what he had already done before, but in his dream, he couldn't bring himself to do it. Instead of blocking the attack, Trevor would guard his face with his hands, and just before he would thrust his giant blade through his guard, Trevor would jump awake.

He didn't regret killing the man, though. Not because of what the bandits had done to Robins-Port, but because, out of everything that happened, he, Dodge, Sarah, and Tom were safe. Trevor hated Robins-Port, and he felt nothing for its former occupants.

"Why should I mourn those who wouldn't mourn me?" Trevor said to Evan as he led him around a corner, the entrance to the middle city a few hundred yards away. "It's like you said, the ones who made it out are my family, and we're safe now."

"Well, nobody is ever safe," Evan retorted ominously. "I can respect that, though. A word of advice?"

Trevor rolled his eyes. "Something tells me you'll give it anyway."

Evan laughed again, more genuinely. "See? Now you're learning. But before you get back with the others, just think on this quick. Sure, you and *your* family made it out, but that pretty little blonde and the other kid? They just watched *their* family murdered before their eyes. Your uncle and his friend? They'd seen the faces and heard the voices of those people every day for most of their lives, and now they're gone, snuffed out like a candle. You may not miss them, but they sure as hell will."

Trevor thought long and hard about what Evan was saying, and as the moments of the lesson past, he felt a weight of guilt on his shoulders.

How many friends did Dodge have in Robins-Port? And Sarah? She just lost her family and was violated, yet I'm sinking in self-pity.

"Fair point," Trevor acknowledged. He half-expected a retort from Evan, but the man just grunted and kept leading Trevor through the empty streets.

They walked in silence until they passed through the gate that separated the slums from the main city. Men and women walked about with large bags from their shopping, children skipped joyously while holding hands with their mothers. Trevor watched as a kid jumped excitedly, pointing to a small stand on the corner of the street.

The boy cheered loudly. "Chocolate! Mommy, I want chocolate."

A man stood behind a table of chocolates, a monocle in one eye and not a strand of hair atop his head. His thick mustache curved around his upper lip and lined the side of his cheeks all the way to his chin. He was busy organizing bags neatly into rows on two separate tables.

"Wait," Trevor said abruptly and, to his surprise, Evan actually stopped and faced him.

Evan raised a brow. "For?"

Trevor hesitated. He had never asked for anything, not expecting anything from Evan, but this was important to him. "Could I ... get some money?"

"Excuse me?" Evan stood motionless as if he was offended by the question.

"I want to buy some chocolate," Trevor told him.

Evan looked at the crowds passing him by until his eyes found the chocolate stand. He looked at Trevor as if he were crazy. "So?"

"So, you're the only one with money here, and I just helped you buy *farm equipment*, in case you've forgotten. Help me out?"

Evan wrinkled his face in disgust. "No."

"Please," Trevor pleaded.

To Trevor's surprise, Evan slowly reached into his pocket and revealed a handful of coins. He looked from his hand filled with coins then back to Trevor.

Trevor didn't hesitate. He took the money quickly and made his way to the chocolate stand. "Thank you."

The clerk gave him a grand welcome, but Trevor ignored it.

Sarah had brought them chocolate every time she'd returned home; it was high time Trevor returned the favor with an apology he knew he owed.

"Questions, my lad?" the merchant asked as Trevor mulled over his options. "This one has a caramel glaze mixed with salt. It really gives you that bitter-sweet flavor. Oh, that one? My favorite. A rich cocoa with a hint of—"

Trevor pointed to a dark bar wrapped in a clear wrapper. "That one."

"Whoa, now. First, let's see if you have enough." Trevor opened his palm to the clerk, who in return studied the bits of coins. "Well, you're in luck. You've just enough for it, my friend."

Trevor dumped the coins into the man's hand and took the chocolate bar with no questions asked. "Thank you," he said before running back to Evan.

Evan held out his hand toward Trevor. "Well then, I think it's fair to say I've contributed enough for a piece?"

"Oh." Trevor showed his chocolate bar to Evan. "You only gave me enough for one."

Evan tilted an ear toward Trevor. "I'm sorry?"

Trevor fidgeted with the bag of chocolate. "I didn't have enough."

Evan's jaw dropped. "You're telling me you spent all that on *one* chocolate bar? I gave you seven coppers!"

"Was that too much?" Trevor asked genuinely.

"*Was it too much*, he asks!" Evan began pacing about, ignoring the looks from passing people as he threw his temper tantrum. "Out of all the evil doers out there, why do you continue to punish me, gods? Why me? I know I've done some shady shit, and I mean some *real* questionable things, but why have you cursed me with this boy?"

"Evan?"

Tom and Merrick stood on the side of the street, watching as Evan paced about in circles, throwing his tantrum.

When Evan looked up and saw Merrick standing there, he took two long strides and threw his arms around his shoulders.

"What the …?" Merrick tried leaning away, but Evan refused to let go.

"Merrick!" Evan praised. "Merrick, my friend, thank you. Please, save me from this walking plague." He gestured toward Trevor, who stood awkwardly in the center of the cobblestoned road. "I can't bear it any longer."

Merrick looked at Trevor. "I see you've gotten him in one of his moods."

Trevor replied with a shrug.

"The kid has a knack for it." Tom limped his way toward Trevor and gave him a slap on the shoulder. There was a large bandage wrapped around his leg, a dark stain Trevor could only conclude was blood.

"How's your leg?" Trevor asked, beyond happy to see a familiar face.

"Oh, this?" Tom wiggled his leg wildly. "Nothing but a scratch. Nothing to worry about but a limp for the next few days, then it'll be all the better."

"We talked about this." Garth emerged from the alleyway behind Evan and Merrick. "That ointment wasn't exactly cheap. Don't go opening that wound again."

Tom barked a laugh. "Yeah, yeah, I heard ya. Can't take all your money, aye? Not when you're about to owe me more."

Garth smiled. "Still up for that bet, eh?"

"Unless you feel like backing down?" Tom laughed heartily. "I'll give you one last chance."

Merrick grinned. "I've never been one to pass on free drinks."

"The only one drinking for free tonight will be me," Tom declared "And you bet your ass I plan on burning a hole in that deep pocket of yours."

"Deal?" Trevor asked, confused by the conversation and sudden change in demeanor amongst Tom and the others.

They seem a lot friendlier than before.

Tom nodded toward Merrick. "Man's been bragging all day about being the best archer in the country."

"Well, that's debatable," Evan added. "I'm sure Alric could tell you a story or two about a certain archer he'd rather spend the rest of his life never seeing again."

Tom rolled his shoulders and stretched his back. "Said that he can split an arrow one hundred yards out, but I bet he couldn't. Whoever loses buys the rounds for tonight."

"I just hope your words are as big as your purse, old man," Garth jested. "I've worked up quite the thirst dealing with you and your lot."

"Ha!" Tom barked another laugh. "You see the balls on this guy?"

A week ago, Tom was ready to throttle anyone in the brotherhood if the situation called for it. Now it was as if they were old friends.

Strange how much your life can change within a week. A week might as well have been a lifetime. Things had changed and people were dead.

"The others still back at the inn?" Tom asked Evan.

"Ah"—Evan pressed a determined finger to his lips—"about that. Last time I saw your brute of a friend, they were heading their way with Al and Benny to The Great-Hammer inn. They're meeting some people there that might be able to help you out."

All playful humor drained from Tom's face. "Are these people friends of yours?"

"Not necessarily." Evan bobbed his head back and forth. "No, actually, never met them before. But it's a bit of a walk, so we best be off. Plus"—he winked at Trevor—"I think you two have some catching up to do."

Merrick, Garth, and Evan quickly dove into a quiet conversation as they began walking away. Evan was no doubt filling his friends in on recent events regarding Trevor and Dodge.

Trevor looked at Tom, who stared at him curiously, and then followed after Evan and others.

"Something I should know?" Tom asked as he limped slowly next to Trevor.

It occurred to Trevor in that moment that, if Warren was telling the truth about his father, which Dodge didn't exactly defend himself against, it was highly likely that Tom had known, as well. If that were the case, Tom was also lying to Trevor. Well, not lying, just hiding the truth from him.

But, is that really any better? It seems like people know more about my life than I do.

Trevor tried his best to remain calm, but he was already feeling the heat rise to his cheeks. "Warren said that my father didn't die in the war, that he killed himself after murdering my mother."

For a few moments, Tom didn't speak at all, but when he did, it was just enough to confirm Trevor's suspicions. "Did he now?"

"Yup," Trevor said bitterly. "He did."

Tom sighed. "How's Dodge doing?"

"So, that's it?" Trevor snapped at Tom. "This entire time, everyone knew the real reason why I'm an orphan, while I got to grow up thinking my dad was some kind of hero?"

"Your father was a good man," Tom said, a hint of his own anger in his voice. "Just because he wasn't a hero to others doesn't mean he wasn't to some. He was one of the best people I've known."

"How can you even say that?" Trevor pleaded. "Explain to me how a man can murder my mother and still be seen as a good man!"

In all the years, Trevor had never seen Tom so uncomfortable, at such a loss of words. Trevor would probably feel bad if he wasn't boiling with anger at the moment. But he was, so he didn't give a shit.

"That's not my story to tell, lad," Tom answered. "I'm sorry."

"Yeah, that sounds about right." Trevor spit to the side. "Seems like nobody feels like sharing it with me. Why bother? Who cares whether or not

I know what happened to my own parents? They're dead. Just like everyone else in that fucking town."

"Hold on now," Tom said with a warning hand hovering before him. "I know how some of them treated you, but that doesn't mean they deserve what they got."

Trevor wasn't about to be swayed otherwise. His was anger near to taking complete control of himself. "*Some?* That whole fucking town hated me, spit on me, cursed me, bullied me, shunned me, and for what? All because I was born into the wrong family? Because of something I had zero fucking control over? No, fuck that, and fuck them."

"Watch it!" Tom grabbed Trevor by the wrist and pulled him closer, and Trevor knew he had gone too far. He remembered what Evan had said to him earlier, "*You may not miss them, but they sure as hell will.*"

Tom took a brief moment to gather himself, letting go of Trevor's wrist. "It's not my story to tell. It's Dodge's, and he will, I promise. So don't ask me to tell that story. That's not fair to Dodge, to you, nor is it fair to the memory of your parents."

"The memory of my parents …" Trevor shook his head, laughing at the nonsense of the phrase. "The memory of my parents is already stained with blood. How much worse could it be?"

Tom was quiet then, searching Trevor's eyes for an answer that wouldn't come. "Just trust me on this. Wait for Dodge to tell you. Please?"

Trevor was about to spit back an angry retort when he thought better of himself. Again, he found himself sulking in his own world when Tom's had ended a week ago in the attack. It wasn't fair that Trevor should make him feel worse, especially since Tom had always been there for Trevor, regardless of his image as Robins-Port's orphan.

"You're right," Trevor said as he and Tom began walking again. "It's just … I want to know about them, you know?"

Tom was quiet for a moment as they walked, but when he did speak, Trevor could tell he was struggling to keep the sorrow out of his voice. "Regardless of how he was in the end, your pa was one of the second greatest men I'd ever known. We used to play with sticks back when we were kids. Me, Dodge, and your father. We would pretend they were swords, that we were saving the country from hordes of demons, or stopping a pack of centaurs from kidnapping a princess. You know, stuff like that."

Trevor listened, the imagery of Tom's story unfolding in his mind like a page

K.R. Gangi

being turned in a book.

"One day, we came by a pack of wolves that had trapped a family of black bears in a little grove. The momma bear must have taken a few of them down herself, but we could tell she was on her last leg as she stood with her cubs behind her.

"Now, you've got to understand that we were kids, much younger than you even. But your pa? He never saw himself so little. Not once.

"Before we knew what was going on, your dad jumped down there in the grove, standing between a huge black bear protecting her cubs and a pack of starving wolves, nothing but a broken stick in his hand.

"Hell, Trevor, that was the first day I realized I could always count on your dad. '*Come on!*' he screamed at us. '*Get in here and put those swords to use!*' " Tom laughed to himself, lost in the memory.

"What'd you do?" Trevor asked.

"Well, it's not like we were left with much choice! Dodge and I jumped down in there, our backs to this bear and her cubs as we faced off a pack of wolves with sticks. Thankfully, there was really only like … three of them. So, since they saw themselves outmatched, they scurried off quick.

"But *that's* who your dad was, Trevor. At least, that's how I choose to remember him. It didn't matter where he was or who was involved, it always came down to what was the right thing to do. And no matter what story you hear when you ask your uncle about him, I want you to remember that story. I want you to remember your dad as the kid who faced down a pack of wolves, of the man who was always there for someone."

Tom wiped a tear from his eye. It was the very first story that Trevor had ever heard about his father. Every time he'd ask Dodge about him, his uncle would shut down. Tom had helped Trevor in more ways that he could express.

"Who was the first?" Trevor asked.

Tom tilted his head. "The first?"

"You said my dad was the second best man you've ever met. Who was the first?"

Another warm smile passed Tom's face. "Dodge."

"I see." Trevor replayed the story over and over again in his head, trying to imagine what his dad would have looked like based on the way Dodge explained. "Thank you."

"You're welcome, lad. I know you're angry. By the gods, I'd be angry, too. But just do me another favor, will you?"

"What's that?" Trevor asked. He could see tears building in Tom's eyes again.

"I know you want answers, and you no doubt deserve them, but just consider Dodge for a moment. Yes, this is your parents we are talking about, but it's also his *brother*. It's not something he can easily talk about. So, when he tells you—and he will tell you—let him tell you in his own way, at his own time, will you? Just do that for me."

Trevor wanted to shrink to the ground with guilt at the realization of what he was truly asking. Where Trevor wanted to know about his parents, two people he'd never met in his life, what he was really asking was for his uncle to describe the worst thing he's ever witnessed.

It seems I owe two people an apology today.

Trevor nodded solemnly. "I will."

"As for the boy Warren"—Tom looked sideways at Trevor, managing to worm his way through the oncoming crowd of people—"he's grieving in his own way. Best to let him just ride it through."

An endless supply of retorts passed through Trevor regarding Warren, most of them involving how Trevor wished he'd have died with his parents, or someone suffered a worse fate than that. Surely, the world would be better off without Warren Robinson. However, Trevor didn't say any of those things. Instead, as Trevor thought back about Warren's outburst in the Twin-Blade inn, there was another question on his mind.

"Warren said something about a curse. That I'm cursed because of my parents. What does that mean?"

Tom thought momentarily to himself. "Just a bunch of superstitious hogwash from the church."

"Sure," Trevor pressed the issue further. "But what did he mean?"

"Well ..." Tom cleared his throat as they turned a corner past a bakery shop, another stampede of men and women flooding the street, and Trevor could glance the Twin-Blade inn near the end. "In the beginning, the gods created man, right?"

Trevor nodded.

"Well, the church will tell you that the gods were the first beings to live, and that they had the power of life and death itself. So, when they created mankind, who can also create life of their own, they technically gave us the gift of life."

"All right," Trevor said, shrugging. "What does that have to do with a curse?"

Tom shifted, and Trevor could tell he was becoming uncomfortable. "Now, keep in mind this really is just superstition. Hell, the church runs solely on superstition, curses, myths, or anything that would help control the masses. So, really, don't overthink this."

"All right then."

"Well, when we ..." Tom gave a rough scratch at the side of his beard. "Well, the gods gave us the gift of life, and we have the freedom of enjoying it and spreading it to others. But when we kill ourselves, we betray that gift. We took that gift and rejected it, perverted it, the church would argue. Because of that, the gods take that gift away."

Trevor tried to keep up with what Warren could have meant. "So, if my father killed himself, how could they take that gift away from him? He's already dead."

"They don't take the gift away from him; they take it from his bloodline." Tom watched until recognition set within Trevor. "It's the gift of *life*, Trevor."

"Ah," Trevor said as he began to understand what Tom was getting at. "I see then."

Tom nodded sadly, keeping a worried eye on Trevor's reaction. "Right. That would mean that his next of kin no longer possesses the gift of life."

"That's ..." Trevor searched for the right word. "Dark."

"It's fucked, is what you mean," Tom grunted. "Can't run a country of people who kill themselves, right? Better to give them a reason to stay alive and plow the fields."

Trevor raised his brow to Tom. "That's even more fucked, if you ask me."

"Ha!" Tom barked a laugh. "You might be right there."

"So, that would mean I'm not able to have kids?" Trevor added. "That my bloodline can no longer go on?"

Tom shook his head, waving away Trevor's question. "Only if you believe that superstitious bullshit. Just because the church says it's true, doesn't mean that it is."

They made it to the Twin-Blade inn. Merrick, Garth, and Evan turned toward them to make sure they were ready to go in with them when Trevor spotted something that sent a jolt through his entire body.

Across the street, as people kept walking by, he spotted a man standing next to a wagon near an alley. For a split-second, Trevor could see him clearly before he disappeared as a large crowd of people passed before them.

Trevor couldn't be sure, but he could have sworn the man wore the same dirty cowl around his head and shoulders as he leaned on that same old wooden stick. And then, in a flash, the man was gone.

Or was he even really there?

"Trevor?"

Trevor only then realized that Tom was looking at him, a worried expression on his face.

"You good, lad?"

"Sure," Trevor answered. "Just thought I saw someone … familiar."

"Hm." Tom perched his lips, looking about the crowd passing by. "That's the thing about big cities, all the faces start to look the same. Listen, I wanted to tell you one last thing."

Tom stepped in front of Trevor, turning his back toward the alley where Trevor thought he had seen Eli. "Listen, I know that Warren and you have a past. A not too friendly one, at that. But"—Tom set a gentle hand on Trevor's shoulder—"you have to remember that there's nothing left for us. Everything we had? Everyone we knew? It's all gone. We are literally the last that remains of what Robins-Port was. Regardless of what happened before, we have to be there for each other now, because we are all we have."

Trevor creased his brow at what Tom was asking of him. "You want me to forgive him?"

Tom shook his head sadly. "No, never that. But I want you to promise you'll try to move on from it."

It was a lot to ask, especially given what growing up in Robins-Port had been like for Trevor, but Tom was right. There was nowhere to call home anymore, for any of them. And like it or not, they really were all they had left.

Trevor was about to give his answer when he caught another look just over Tom's shoulder. He stepped to the side to get a full view when he noticed the group of men emerging from the alleyway across the street.

What troubled him most was that they were wearing masks that concealed their faces, and the fact they were holding swords and other weapons that spoke more of danger rather than fashion.

At first, he thought maybe they were guards, but all that went to shit when one of the hooded men grabbed a nearby woman by the back of her hair to expose her throat. Trevor tried to scream a warning, but it was too late.

Tom managed to follow Trevor's gaze just in time to see the woman's throat cut wide open, her red blood spraying in the wind.

A Matter of Conspiracy

The man who introduced himself as Marcus Gorman pinched the bridge of his nose. It was a thing he had done frequently during the conversation. "So, you're saying you saw a couple of those guys reporting to a single man?"

"It looked to me he was in charge," Dodge confirmed. He'd been more open with the two commanders than Sarah had expected.

"Well, someone had to be, the way you explain it," Marcus said. "It seems a little too organized to be chalked up as mere bandits."

"That doesn't mean it's a matter of conspiracy," the other one, Harvin Destro, added. He'd been quiet most of the time, eyeing Dodge and Sarah as they went over the series of events multiple times. "The loyalists are running about the country, pillaging farms every other week. Some of the pilgrims that show up to these gates report hundreds of them all together. There's a small army of them. Could have easily been them."

"Doesn't really add up, though," Marcus retorted. "The pilgrims are here to tell the story because the bandit king wanted them to. In fact, each and every report from them is the same—the loyalists burn down homes, butcher livestock, and then send the people on their merry way here to complain to our king. They didn't hack them to pieces and throw their mangled corpses into piles, or hang them from trees for someone to eventually find."

The look on Dodge's face could break a rock.

"No offense," Marcus said apologetically.

"Still, we have nothing else to go on besides speculation." Harvin was persistent, and it made Sarah uncomfortable. He was probably just being thorough, but it was as if the commander was trying very hard to hide the fact that it could have been the Navalethian army. Harvin then looked at Benny and Alric. "You should have come straight here. We need evidence if we suspect treason."

"And if we had evidence?" Benny asked vaguely. "Say we do have that type of evidence. Into whose hands would that turn up in, exactly?"

"If you did have some sort of evidence that linked our own army leveling a city," Marcus speculated, "it would go straight to the king himself."

"And if it was the king who gave the order?" Alric asked. "He'd cut your throat and toss your body out the window, and nobody would dare ask him why."

"Fair point," Marcus agreed. "Then it would be a matter up for discussion, *if* you had such evidence."

Benny looked toward Alric and gave him a soft nod.

Alric reached to his belt and tugged free the arrow that was tied there. He set it on the table before them.

"What's this?" Harvin asked, eying the arrow.

Alric pushed the arrow across the table. "We have a very reliable source who's confirmed that these arrows were made for Navalethian troops."

"Eh?" Marcus took the arrow in his hands and studied it, rubbing his fingers up and down it's shaft, picking away at the crust of blood that covered the wood. "And who is this source of yours? What makes him so reliable?"

"He goes by Tom," Alric answered. "He's the blacksmith who made it."

Marcus chewed at the side of his lip. "Whose corpse did you pull this from?"

"It came from a little boy," Alric answered. "Not even old enough to shoot one."

Marcus closed his eyes and slowly shook his head. "Such a shame. That's not fair. That's not fair one bit."

"Wait," Harvin said suddenly. "You're saying there's more than just you?" he asked, gesturing to Sarah and Dodge.

They let the question hang in the air for a few moments before Benny answered, "There's two other lads and the blacksmith. They're at the Twin-Blade right now."

"Why aren't they here with you?" Harvin asked.

"There's been, uh ... some complications between our traveling companions," Benny replied.

Sarah looked at Dodge, who stared off into nothing.

"We decided to split up for a little bit, is all."

"No doubt to see if we were still legit, is what you mean," Marcus accused, letting the uncomfortable silence drag on before innocently holding up his hands. "Don't worry; I understand, especially if this checks out."

"So, this blacksmith." Harvin leaned forward, the smell of ale fresh on his breath. "How can he be sure that he actually made this arrow for our garrisons?"

Benny nodded toward the arrow that Marcus held before him. "That's selphite. Comes from your mountain, doesn't it?"

Harvin inspected the arrow then confirmed Benny's claim with a soft nod. "Sure is. Stuffs tough as steel, but as light as a feather. There's no doubt this came from Brackenheart. But even if it is selphite, that doesn't mean our own troops did this."

"You two command your own garrisons," Alric pointed out. "Any news of a shipment disappearing or being attacked recently?"

"Not in the east," Marcus answered.

"Nor in the north," Harvin responded. "But I'll admit, it does stink as an inside job."

Benny cleared his throat, a look of caution as he asked his next question. "What about the new commander in the city? This Vallis. Could he be responsible?"

Both Harvin and Marcus chuckled to themselves, but it was Harvin who answered. "The man's full of pride, but he lacks the strategy this needed. The boy's all about the fame and glory. He'd most likely charge head-on alone against the entire bandit army rather than destroy one of his own cities."

"Harvin's right," Marcus joined. "Vallis is a prick, but he's a witless one at that. No way he could manage to pull something like this off."

"No, we're looking for someone less green," Harvin explained. For during the conversation, he was actually considering the possibility of a conspiracy. "Someone who's been in command before. If this is an attack from our own troops, the one behind it has to have some prestige. He's got to have status to get his men to do something like that."

"Which means"—Marcus put the arrow back on the table—"we've got a rogue officer."

"Unless this particular officer has deep pockets"—Harvin pushed his mug around the table—"then I think we need to explore bigger options."

Marcus leaned back in his chair. "Meaning?"

"What I mean," Harvin continued, "is that there's a lot of money involved in something like that. Not only do you have to arm your troops, but you've got to buy their silence, as well. Keeping something like this quiet? That's a whole lot of money."

"Money *and* power," Alric said, following Harvin's train of thought.

Benny sunk in his chair, despair all but radiating off of him. "You don't mean …"

"If that's the case," Marcus said, studying the contents of their table in thought, "then we have a rebellion on our hands."

Silence befell the table. Both commanders, Alric, and Benny thought quietly to themselves.

Dodge shifted nervously in his seat. "Somebody want to speak clearly for once?"

It was Alric who answered. "We think it might be one of the dukes."

"A duke?" Dodge shook his head in bewilderment. "Why would a duke do such a thing?"

"Because all four of them are power-hungry madmen," Harvin explained, real bitterness driving his words. "If it weren't for the king keeping them in line, they would have tried usurping the throne long ago."

"Why try now, then?" Benny asked. "And which one would go for it? Scyllis?"

Harvin scratched the side of his head. "He has a motive, I suppose. Lazar and his loyalists have been sacking his dukedom. He's been requesting help from the king but hasn't gotten any."

"Last time I checked, Scyllis isn't a military strategist," Harvin speculated. "He couldn't have organized something like this."

Harvin shrugged. "Doesn't mean he didn't buy someone who is."

"What about Duke Vaerin?" Benny asked. "He has a military background."

Harvin chuckled. "He was a scribe during the war. He's never seen a battle in his life, let alone organized one." Harvin took a drink from his mug, emptying the contents before slamming the cup back on the table. "Where Scyllis organizes the agriculture in the country, Vaerin is in charge of the trading routes. Wouldn't make sense to ransack his biggest trading city."

"Which leaves Gundell and Roland," Alric said. "And out of those two, we know who's the likely suspect."

"Roland," Benny confirmed, eyeing Alric worriedly.

They all sat quietly at the table. Alric had his hands on the table, staring off distantly as the others glanced at him. Sarah didn't understand why, but she had a feeling that there was a history between Duke Roland and Alric. A history that put them on edge.

"I suppose Roland would have a better motive than all," Marcus said, breaking the uncomfortable silence. "We all remember his cousin, Captain Marlot, during the war. Ruthless bastard. He didn't make too many friends. I guess his entire family was butchered one night. His entire estate was put to the sword, and they never found the people who did it. They killed them all—men, women, and children, too. Hell, they even killed the help. There wasn't a single soul who survived the attack, and Roland has been teetering on good terms with the crown since."

Alric shifted in his seat, scanning around the room from person to person, his nerves suddenly on edge. If Sarah didn't know any better, she would almost believe that Alric was on the verge of tears.

"Well," Benny said, coughing into his hand heavily, "in any case, we find ourselves with more dangerous news that we originally anticipated. I'm sorry we brought you into this."

"No." Harvin shook his head with finality. "I take back what I said. You did right to come to us and take caution." He looked to Dodge and Sarah. "I'm sorry for what happened to you and your family, but you're here now, in the city. You're safe with us."

Sarah looked at the man and wanted to believe him. She *really* wanted to believe him, but she couldn't help feeling a sudden chill down her spine as she looked at him. There was something behind his words, like he was hiding something from them.

Sarah looked to Marcus, and her heart nearly stopped in her chest. Where his eyes should be, two black orbs sat, a vast abyss of cold darkness. She nearly jumped back in her seat, but as he nodded to her, his eyes switched back into their original blue. The whole ordeal happened in a flash. Or maybe it didn't happen at all?

You're right not to trust him, a voice whispered in her mind, a whisper that sounded much like her mother's voice. *Don't trust any of them.*

"What now, then?" Dodge asked as the silence dragged on.

"Now," Marcus answered, "we've got to go to the herald about what we've discussed."

"Can he be trusted?" Alric asked, worry clear in his tone.

Marcus began chewing at the side of his lip again. He thought long for a moment, looking at each of them in turn, and then nodded. "I trust him."

"Me, too," Harvin added. "The man's dedicated his entire life for our people.

Not to mention he's essentially second, next to the king."

There was a moment of silence at the table. Sarah could tell from the lack of light in the windows that evening was only a few hours away, and the thought of the dark that followed made her pulse quicken a bit. It made her feel trapped, covered. Trapped in a cave and covered with dirt.

Here, little piggy ... don't struggle now ...

"Right then," Marcus said as he stood. He grabbed the arrow off the table and tied it to a small knot at his belt. "We should take this to Father Balorian right away. I'll send an escort to retrieve you here soon. Men I can absolutely trust, that is," he added when he saw the look of worry on their faces.

"I'll return with them," Harvin said. "Any way you can find these other survivors and bring them here? I'm sure the herald will want to hear their reports, as well."

"They'll be here when you get back," Benny answered.

"Right then." Harvin stood and joined Marcus. "We'll be back soon. I wish things could end on better circumstances, but regardless"—he reached out, and Benny took his hand in a rough shake—"it was a pleasure seeing you boys again." He took Alric's next. "A real pleasure."

"You, too, my old friend," Benny said quietly.

They shook hands with Marcus then turned to leave.

Just as Marcus and Harvin were about the exit the inn, Marcus looked over his shoulder, back to Sarah. He gave her a soft nod as he smiled sadly at her. However, his kindness only shook Sarah to her very core, for what she saw wasn't the man named Marcus at all, but a wraith in the flesh. His eyes were bold and black, the face pale like the moon. Then he turned to leave.

Maybe it was the voice in her head, the voice that sounded like her mother, but Sarah knew that the next time she saw Marcus Gorman, it wouldn't truly be him. It would be something else, something as old as time itself.

Shadowroot

"Yes, Your Majesty, I'm here now." The king's hand was limp, his clammy cold fingers trembling as Francis held them gently.

The king of Navaleth raised his head, leaving a dark stain of sweat on his golden velvet pillow as he seated himself up in his luxurious bed. "Oh my." The king rubbed the sleep from his eyes. "Oh, Francis, I was having a terrible dream. Is there water?"

"There always is, Your Majesty." Francis handed his king the golden chalice that sat on his nightstand.

"Enough of that, Francis. We're quite secluded here. No need for formalities." The monarch drank deeply from the goblet. He gave a satisfied sigh before returning the goblet to the table.

"Of course," Francis replied. "How do you feel, Victor?"

"You know how it is." Victor waved a hand in the air. "Mornings are always better. The rest helps. But it's the latter half of the day that drags on. This sickness will be my undoing, I tell you."

Yes, it will.

"Nonsense," Francis assured. "We employ the best doctors in the world, and they all say the fever will break; that it's just a matter of time."

"Doctors?" Victor scoffed. "Did the doctors help my wife? Forgive me, but I find it hard to trust the word of those who have contributed to my greatest failure."

"Failure?" Francis asked, treading carefully with his words.

Victor nodded. "Keeping her alive, Francis. Throughout my entire life, failing to keep my wife alive is my greatest regret."

Francis nodded sadly. "That was some time ago. We've made some new discoveries to medicine since then, my old friend."

Victor laughed to himself. "Do tell me, how long has this illness strapped me to this bed?"

"A few months," Francis answered.

"And do I look any better than I did a few months ago?"

Francis remembered a time when his king gleamed like a sword in sunlight. A few months ago, he strutted the streets of his kingdom, his head held high as he radiated strength and love. Now, however, his skin was pale and his body frail, looking nothing like the man he was before. It was as if his body had aged ten years in the matter of a few months.

"To be fair, you didn't look the best then, either," Francis replied with a smirk. "You always did prefer drink and food over physical activity."

Victor laughed softly. "Always one to take advantage of our times alone to practice treason, aren't you?"

Oh, you have no idea, Your Grace.

"The sickness will run its course, I assure you," Francis encouraged.

Victor looked out of the opened window, toward the setting sun. The king's bedchamber was in the tallest tower of the castle that overlooked the western ocean. The orange glow of the sun glimmered off the ocean water.

As he stared out the window, he sighed. "Three months stuck in this damned room. To this damned bed. Doing nothing but sleep and fight a fever as my country, my beautiful home, carries on without me."

"The only reason why our country thrives in a time like this is because you've made it so," Francis stated. "Never forget what you have done for your people, for they never will. It has been able to carry on without you *because* of you."

"Huh." Victor pursed his lips. "Good answer."

"Did you expect anything less?"

Another small laugh from Victor. "By the gods, your ego is relentless."

"I am only an image of my teachers, of course, and I've always been told I was your best student."

Victor laughed again, and that laugh honestly hurt Francis.

There was a time when Francis admired the man, when he craved approval from the king more than he did his own father. He knew that none of this was Victor's fault, that sacrifices had to be made, but that didn't mean he didn't still love the man.

"The worst part isn't the fever," Victor said, all playfulness draining from his face. "It isn't the vomiting, sweating, or even the constant shitting that's the worst of it. It's the *dreams*."

Francis eyed the bowl of porridge on the nightstand next to the goblet. "Tell me about them?"

For a moment, Victor didn't speak, just stared out the window that overlooked the ocean. "I hardly understand them," he admitted. "Some of them are from the war, while others are just me here in the castle. One moment, I'm leading the charge into battle, men roaring their battle cries with mine; then, in a flash, I'm sitting by the fire while Val reads a book beside me."

Val, or Valleria, was the previous queen of Navaleth. She had died some years ago. Francis had known her very well. She'd been an inspiration to him at one point, just like Victor had been. She had been a young, beautiful woman, full of love and joy, hope and strength. She was loved by everyone in the kingdom, and so missed deeply by everyone after she passed.

"I miss her so much," Victor said, tears building in his eyes. "She was the best a man could ask for, a gift given by the gods themselves. She was taken too soon. You know how they say time heals all wounds? Well, sometimes it still feels as if yesterday I heard her laughs echoing in the halls of the castle."

Francis, too, missed those laughs. "Maybe these dreams aren't so bad, then?"

Victor smiled softly to himself, no longer a king, but a humble widower reminiscing about his former wife. "If I could stay in those dreams for the rest of my life, I would die a happy man."

Something shifted in Victor, the sadness of his smile forming into worry. "No, it's not those dreams I worry about. It's the ones where I'm standing on a mountain overlooking my kingdom. Each and every time, I watch as a dark mist swarms over it, spreading from city to city, leaving nothing behind but graveyards and fire.

"Other times I'm in a meeting in the council chamber. You're there with me, but there's another. He's always sitting at the end of the table, dressed in a dark cloak and a hood covering his face. Always, he's watching me. And every time I notice him, the room always grows so cold, like death itself is trying to take me."

"It's just a nightmare, Victor." Francis put a reassuring hand on the king's arm. "Nothing more."

But the king didn't seem convinced. "Of course, but it just feels so damned *real*."

For a long moment, Francis watched as the king stared out the window, a crease on his brow, no doubt contemplating the dreams haunting him. After a few minutes, he shook his head and looked around the room.

"Is there any food, Francis? I'm famished."

"Of course." Francis grabbed the bowl from the end table, trying hard to control his shaking as he handed it to his king. "Fresh from the kitchens."

"Ah." Victor took the bowl and placed it in his lap. "Thank you. Send my thanks to the chef, as always."

That'll be a difficult task, my king, as his body is currently rotting in your kitchen.

"I will be sure to," Francis stated.

He watched as the king swirled the contents in his bowl, steam rising from the thick broth, the aroma sweetening the air. He lifted the spoon to his mouth and blew. For a split moment, Francis wanted to reach out and save him, but he knew that, deep down, it had to be done.

Victor slurped his first bite, only to groan in satisfaction and continue eating.

And just like that, I've ended an ancient bloodline.

"Mm ..." the king moaned. "That is absolutely delicious."

Francis watched as the king took a few more mouthfuls of the stew. It was only a matter of time before he would be raising the alarm, and considering they were, in fact, old friends, the least Francis could do was give him an explanation.

"Do you know what shadowroot is, Victor?" Francis asked.

"Hm ..." Victor slurped loudly at his food. "Haven't heard of it."

"I don't blame you," Francis replied. "Not many people have. In fact, there are probably only a handful of people left in the world who have actually single-handedly held its contents, give-or-take. One in the city itself."

"Oh?" Victor looked intrigued. "Is it rare?"

"Yes. It's very rare. It's a strong hallucinogenic that can be grounded into powder. Needless to say, the effects are very strong. It's said that, once ingested, the powder mixes in with your bloodstream, leaving it impossible to trace."

Victor wiped a bead of sweat from his pale face. "What are the effects?"

"Well, that's the thing. I only found a single book in our archives that briefly mentions it, along with arguments against the author that his claims are, in fact, false. That he's mistaking this shadowroot for something more biological.

"What I found interesting, however, was how it works. If, unfortunately enough, you happen to come in contact with the shadowroot, which apparently grows as a very deep purple plant found only in the Haunted Forest, it takes absolutely no effects to you whatsoever. But, if you were to ground up this plant and heat it to a certain temperature, being sure not to burn the contents in the process, it becomes reactive."

"I never was one for botany." Victor took another slurp of his stew. "But you definitely have my interest."

"The effects are very vague, however," Francis continued. "The author claims that it takes high dosages of the flower to react, and it also has to be periodically ingested. If you take it once, it would be ineffective. Overtime, however, after frequent exposures of the shadowroot, one would start to experience the effects."

Victor cleared his throat with a cough before taking another portion of his bowl. "Sounds like this is a very complicated substance. You take up studying herbology recently?"

"Just this last year, actually," Francis answered with a smile. "The beginning effects are minor. It starts out as a simple cold, developing into something more serious, like coughing and vomiting. Eventually, one would fall to a fever.

"But those aren't the only recorded effects. Apparently, since the root flows in your blood, it affects your brain, as well, leaving the victim with very lucid and vivid dreams." Francis let the information sit in the air for a moment. "Mostly nightmares."

Victor glistened in perspiration. Beads of sweat ran down the sides of his pale skin, dripping from his chin onto his lap. He looked toward his bowl of stew for a moment then returned his gaze to Francis, hurt shining brightly in his bloodshot eyes.

"That's about it, though," Francis finished. "And the cure is to simply stop taking it. The poison will run its course before disappearing entirely.

"But …" Francis grabbed the bowl from his king and set it on the end table next to the golden chalice. "And here's the fascinating thing about the poison. If you were to grind up the pedals into a powder, boil it in water, then strain it, it dries to another form of poison. As the shadowroot dries, it begins to crystalize into small shards.

"Unlike the former essence of the poison, this form is absolutely traceable. Now, if someone were to ingest the crystalized shadowroot, it would be an entirely different experience."

Victor's lips began to purple. Dark veins stretched across his face as the poison began to take a toll. His eyes were a deep red now, a drop of dark blood dripping from his nose.

"All the recordings of the crystalized shadowroot conclude in the same way."

Francis stood above the monarch. "A quick, yet agonizing, death."

Francis watched as the poison took its full course. Black veins closed around Victor's face, thick blood fountaining from his nose, traces of a white liquid dripping out of his ears. All the while, the king reached for his throat that was no doubt beginning to swell. With his other hand, he reached toward the bedroom door where, not just a few feet away, guards stood watch in order to protect the king who was now dying.

A tear fell down Francis's cheek. "I did not want this, old friend. I wish it could have been different, but there was no other way. I will always remember you as the man you once were. The brave, passionate leader that everyone loved. I will never forget that."

A putrid smell wafted the air. The poison was now beginning to attack the intestines, causing the king to extricate all over the bedding. Blood mixed with shit and piss soaked the sheets where the man had spent the last three months of his life trying to defeat a sickness that his most trusted friend had given him. A sickness that Francis himself had fed him in the goblet of water each and every morning.

In the final stretch of his life, Victor Craul, King of Navaleth, the last living member of his royal bloodline, died in his bed, choking on his own blood and vomit.

Francis watched as the life paled over his green eyes as they stared into nothing.

"Goodbye, my friend." Francis wiped the tears from his face. "You'll be missed, but your death was necessary."

Francis, Head Herald of Navaleth, Prophet of the Church, walked calmly to the door and rested his head against it, gripping the golden handle. "Let's get on with it, then."

He ripped open the door and screamed, tears now steaming from his eyes. "Seal off the city! The king has been poisoned!"

Accepting Who We Are

It happened in phases, the first being confusion.

The masked murderer kicked away the woman whose throat he had just slit. Her body crashed to the ground, a pool of blood spreading around the cobblestones in a flood. People slowed as they walked by, coming to a halt as they stared at the woman's body at their feet. Meanwhile, as the bystanders stared dumbfounded at the first victim, the masked murderer wiped his bloodied blade on his trousers.

Then came the next phase: shock.

All was quiet, even Trevor, as everyone took a moment to process what had just happened. Like a flock of crows eyeing a spoiled rabbit on the side of the road, everyone stood by and waited for something to happen, for something to snap them out of this sudden dream that couldn't possibly be real.

Then it did.

Unfortunately for the shocked bystanders, the third phase was absolute chaos.

The knifeman launched himself over the woman's corpse, toward a man wearing a tall hat.

For a moment, Trevor didn't understand why someone would wear such a hat, but after realizing that man had a dagger buried in his eye, the thought didn't matter anymore.

"Get inside!"

Screams snapped people out of their trances as they began to scurry about like a plague of rats. Those who were in the back of the surrounding crowd had the advantage to get away, but the closer victims weren't so lucky.

Four more men poured from the alley, all with their faces hidden behind a mask. They swung their weapons wildly at anyone in their immediate vicinity, not looking for a particular victim, just anyone with blood to spill.

Trevor felt a pull on his arm but ignored it. He watched as the bloodbath unfolded before him.

One of the attackers swept the legs from under an old man in a fancy suit. The man landed on his back and tried crawling away, bringing his hands up and pleading for his life. The attacker simply laughed at the pathetic sight, holding a terrifying mace high above his head. He brought it down with a fury on his victim's face. The killer lifted it up high and chopped down again. Then again. And again. The old man's body spasmed with each blow, twitching as blood squirted in the air, the sound of his crunching skull sickening Trevor to his very core.

Another one of the attackers had a woman backed against a wall. Tears flowed in streams down her face as she pleaded for her life, begging the murderer to let her go. The person in the mask held his sword level with her nose. She closed her eyes and began sinking against the wall, but the masked bandit wouldn't stand for that. He grabbed her by the throat and dragged her to her feet, pressing her hard against the brick. He brought back his arm and plunged the sword into her gut. The woman tried to scream, but no sound escaped her.

The murderer stepped away, holding his sword firmly in place, an artist observing his greatest masterpiece. The woman's hands traced the steel blade now protruding from her stomach, confused as to why this was happening to her. then she shrieked in pain as the masked bandit ripped away the blade.

As she fell, the bandit grabbed the back of her head and forced her to the ground, bashing her head roughly against the ground. Trevor could hear laughter behind the mask as they began hacking away at the woman's body like an axe man against a tree.

"Run for your lives!" people screamed, running about like mice trapped in a maze of horror. "Quick, get inside and bar the doors!"

A woman held her child under her arm as she fled away from the scene, crying for help from anybody willing to lend a hand. Trevor knew he should run to her and offer help, but he just stared at the horror that followed.

A man materialized from a nearby alley, springing from the shadows at the lady and her child. Using his momentum as force, he shouldered her and the child to the ground.

"Go!" The mother pushed her child away, pointing down the street. "Run! Find your father!"

The man from the alley leapt on the woman, and before she could register what was happening, there was a dagger in her chest. Once, twice, three times the man jabbed at her, each time sending lines of blood through the air.

"Trevor!" Tom turned Trevor about, their faces inches from one another.

"I said get inside!"

Before he knew it, Trevor was being pushed through the doorway of the Twin-Blade inn, the sounds of chaos outside muffled with the closing door. Patrons still sat at tables, drinks in their hands, some still even chewing their food as they looked at them all.

"Twinny!" Evan shouted. "Twinny, get the fuck out here."

The barkeep from earlier that day rushed from the door leading into the kitchen. "What're you shouting about, eh?" Twinny cocked his head to the side, eyes on the door that led outside. "Is that fighting I hear?"

"Not a fight. Murder," Evan answered. "We need our bags right now."

Without hesitation, Twinny disappeared through a door leading into the kitchen.

Baron, Seroes, and Warren rushed toward them.

"What's going on?" Seroes asked.

"People outside are being attacked," Garth answered. "We need to get out there."

"No, we need to help them," Evan corrected. "Twinny, where the fuck are those bags?"

Not a moment later, Twinny was back, carrying two large bags. He set them on a table and undid the straps.

Evan pulled out two long sticks, one ending with a large curved blade. He began screwing them together, locking them in place to reveal his halberd.

"How many?" Baron asked as he began slipping numerous daggers into the hidden pockets beneath his coat.

"Four, I think," Evan answered. "Not sure. Couldn't see much once the mess started happening."

Garth and Merrick, the twins, tied a quiver of arrows to their hips while strapping another one over their shoulders. They pulled out their bows, both lined with a thick string and built with a dark polished wood.

The rest of the patrons continued their meals and drinks, either too drunk or completely naïve of what was happening just outside where they sat. Meanwhile, the brotherhood continued their discussion as if they were the only ones in the room.

"I counted five," Merrick replied. "Couple with swords, others with maces and daggers. Looked like bandits, to me."

"Small bandit group attacking the capital? Not likely," Baron suggested as he pulled his dual swords out of the bag and held them at his sides.

"Six," Trevor said, remembering the one who attacked the mother and child. "Another one came out of an alley farther down the street. That makes six."

"He's right," Garth confirmed, testing the strength of his bow string. "Six total."

"Good eyes, kid," Evan said, a crooked smile on his face.

"Coincidence?" Garth asked.

"What? To Robins-Port?" Evan weighed his options as he rolled up the sleeves of his tunic. "Could be, I suppose."

"If that's true," Seroes joined, handing an axe to Baron, "then this is bigger than we thought. *Much* bigger."

"Where's my axe?" Tom grumbled, pushing through the arming crowd. "If these bastards have anything to do with Robins-Port, then there's a lot of swinging that needs to be done."

Seroes tugged free a large axe from one of the bags. Tom's axe. "You're wounded."

Tom scowled at the bald man. "Don't try to talk me out of this."

"Never would, just don't let them see it." Seroes handed Tom his large battle axe. "They'll take advantage of it."

Tom smiled wickedly. "They can try."

"What? We're supposed to just go out there and fight?" Warren's voice cracked with fear, though he tried hard to hide it. "That's insane. You don't even know how many are out there."

"Didn't we already cover that?" Evan asked rhetorically. "Seems you might as well stay here, then."

"Wait!" Warren stepped away slowly, real fear in his eyes. "You can't leave me here."

"Suit yourself, kid. Stay here and hide, or go out there and die. In any case"—Evan tightened the straps on his belt—"you're officially no longer my problem."

"Evan ..." Seroes bumped Evan's arm.

"We don't have time for your empathy, Seroes," Evan snapped. "People are dying. Now, are we fucking ready?"

"Ready," Baron stated.

The twins tugged on their bow strings. "Ready."

"Aye," Tom answered as he gripped his axe. "Best stay clear once I start swinging."

"Noted." Seroes rolled his shoulders. "Let's get on with it then."

Before Trevor knew what he was doing, he reached inside the bag and pulled out the sword that Dodge had given him back in Robins-Port. It was still in the sheath, tethered to the side of the leather belt.

"What the hell do you think you're doing?" Tom asked as Trevor strapped the belt around his waist.

"I'm going with you," Trevor answered, as if the answer was obvious.

"Like hell you—"

"Dodge and Sarah are on the other side of the city, and we've pretty much agreed there's more of these guys. They could be in trouble." With the belt tight at his waist, Trevor pulled the blade free of its scabbard. "And I'm bringing this for when the fighting starts."

"Trevor—"

"You can't change my mind in this, Tom," Trevor stated firmly. "I'm going."

Tom looked as if he was about to protest but held his tongue. Trevor knew Tom was worried. He'd known Trevor hadn't been the same ever since he killed that man back in Robins-Port. Trevor knew that, too. He had ended a man's life, and that still made him feel sick to his stomach. But, if he would have to kill again in order to save his uncle and Sarah, then he'd fight any amount of enemies that stood in his way.

Tom saw the determination on Trevor's face, an understanding in the briefest of moments, before slightly nodding.

"You remember what we talked about?" Evan asked Trevor suddenly, and Trevor realized the man wasn't mocking him. It was genuine consideration, referring to their recent conversation.

A killer is a killer.

In that moment, Trevor was willing to accept what he was becoming.

He nodded to Evan.

"Okay, then." Evan walked toward the door, the others following behind him. "Garth and Merrick, pepper anybody wearing a mask. Seroes and I will rush them and make sure none get away. Baron, just pretend they're spiders with a death wish; I'm sure you'll work it out. Twinny?" Evan looked over his shoulder. Twinny was still standing where he'd been moments ago. "Put it on our tab, will you?" Before the barkeep could reply, Evan lifted his leg. "Let's go kill some bad

K.R. Gangi

guys."
    The door was kicked open with a crash.

The Face of Death

The door to The Great-Hammer inn exploded, shards of wood shattering across the entrance of the room as men in masks began rushing in. Three, four, five, Sarah counted, all swinging their weapons toward the patrons at their tables. One man spun about in his chair, a fountain of red gushing from an open wound in his throat.

Patrons, half-drunk and dazed, were rushed by the masked men. They were pulled from their chairs, dragged to the ground where they were stabbed repeatedly. Others were murdered where they sat, a dagger lodged in the side of their necks, or their heads taken completely off by the swing of a sword.

The tavern erupted in pandemonium, the muffled conversations replaced by cries of pain and agony. The smiles of friends and family was replaced by the bloody face of death. Sarah, frozen with fear as the slaughter unfolded before her, was glued to her seat.

Her attention was drawn toward the door where two more men filed in, both armed with crossbows. One of the crossbowman locked eyes with her from across the room. Seeing an easy target, as Sarah just stared in awe, he put the stock of the crossbow to his shoulder and took aim. There was a loud *twang* that cracked the air as the bowman released his shot.

The table flipped over in a flash while Dodge pulled on Sarah's arm, dragging her to the ground as the bolt of the arrow splintered through the wood that now shielded Sarah from certain death.

"Keep your head down," Dodge yelled above the sounds of people dying. "Don't make yourself seen!"

"What the fuck is going on?" Alric shouted. He and Benny hunched behind the table, peering over the edge as the events of death unfolded twenty feet away from them.

"I don't know," Benny answered. "This is not good."

"Oh, you think?" Alric shook his head. "This isn't random. We're being fucking hunted. I told you this was a bad idea."

"We don't know that they're after us," Benny stated.

Alric rolled his eyes. "Right. We just happen to be escorting the survivors of a secret massacre, and as soon we tell someone, we get these bastards."

Benny shook his head. "It doesn't make sense."

"It makes perfect sense," Alric countered. "We were betrayed, plain and simple."

"But—"

"Think about it. They asked where we were, and we told them here. They betrayed us, Benny."

Benny's face was a mixture of confusion and sorrow with the realization that there might actually be a connection between the sudden attack and their presence in the city, that he might have been betrayed by the ones he called friends.

Screams of pain ripped through the clatter. Broken bottles scattered across the ground, chairs and tables snapped apart as the men in masks began tearing through whoever and whatever came into their path.

"Looks like seven of them," Alric counted. "We need to take the initiative before they run out of distractions."

By distractions, Sarah knew what he really meant was out of other people to kill.

"We have to get out of here," Benny declared. "Back door?"

Alric glanced above the table quickly before settling back behind its protection. "Occupied."

"Fuck," Benny cursed. He peeked over the table, his eyes darting from place to place, weighing his options. After a quick study, he shrugged. "Then it looks like we've got to go through them."

"He's loading another crossbow," Alric stated, his eyes just above the edge of the table.

Sarah didn't need to see what was happening to know what it looked like, the sounds of people screaming and dying were enough to paint the image in her mind.

"What do we do?" Dodge asked Benny, a hand firmly set on Sarah's. "We have to get her out of here."

When Benny looked at Dodge, for the first time since Sarah had encountered him, Benny looked afraid. "We need to get up and do something before these guys can focus entirely on us. Now, Al and I are going to distract those bowman—"

"We are?"

"—and they're going to fire at us. When they start reloading, that's our chance. We rush them and gain the initiative. Now"—Benny pulled a dagger from behind his back and held out the hilt to Dodge—"can we count on you?"

Dodge looked from the dagger to Benny a quick moment before taking the blade. "On your mark." He nodded in answer.

The sound of violence drowned the room. Sarah could hear people begging for their lives, their dying screams being cut off with a grotesque ripping sound. The only thing separating her from joining the dying was an oak table and the three men beside her.

She felt trapped behind that table, free to move but only in the direction she knew would end in her torment. Just like Robins-Port. Just like that tunnel.

Here, little piggy.

"Sarah!"

It took a moment to realize that Dodge was kneeling before her, his hands on both of her shoulders.

"Did you hear what I said? You need to stay here. Don't come out until I tell you to. Got it?"

"We need to go now," Alric stated.

"Dodge, are you ready?" Benny asked.

Dodge didn't wait for Sarah's reply. "Ready."

"Right, then." Alric stood and walked around the table, spreading his arms in invitation. "Hey, fucker!"

Waking the Demon

I know I'm going to regret this.

Alric spread his arms at his sides and stepped away from the table, locking eyes with the bowman who rested the stock of his crossbow against his shoulder. "That just for show?"

The first bowman nudged the other one at his side, in which they both put the stocks of their crossbows to their shoulders and took aim.

Alric felt the sudden urge to turn and flee, a feeling any man within the sights of two crossbows would indefinitely feel. However, he shoved those feelings aside and focused. Timing was everything in this, and even the slightest distraction could lead—

Twang!

Alric dodged to his lower right, feeling the thick bolt ripple through the air past his ear. As soon as the arrow had past, he rolled with his momentum further.

Twang!

The second bolt cracked the floorboards where he stood moments ago. It seemed these guys had experience, using the first bolt as a decoy and the secondary to follow up with the kill shot. Whoever these guys were, they had some sort of military training.

But so had Alric. He'd been trained how to fight since he was a boy. His father had made it clear that only fighting men get ahead in a world full of violence, so he'd taught him everything he'd known, just like his father had done for him.

The more Alric had trained, the more he had become aware that he was different than others.

One night, his father had sat him down next to a fire and told him that he was special, that what seemed normal to him was indifference to others. It was a secret kept in their family forever, and it was vital to never tell a living soul about it.

Alric could size a soldier up simply from their demeanor during a fight, so he recognized that these men were dangerous. But none of that mattered. Regardless of how much training these guys had, or how confident they were in their skills, they would still be lying on the floor dead in just a few short moments.

The adrenaline surged through Alric. He welcomed the bloodlust like an old friend. His hearing was crisp, his hands steady.

"And now"—he gripped the dagger tightly, a deadly smile on his face—"it's your turn."

He rushed toward his attackers. At the same time, Dodge and Benny leapt over the table to join him, both of their battle cries catching the attention of the masked murderers. They were three men with simple weaponry, charging against a squad of professional killers, but Alric could see the fear in his soon-to-be victim's eyes.

The bowmen hesitated, just as Alric knew they would. They had Alric outnumbered two to one, only now to be facing three men rushing their ways with blades drawn. They tried to reload their crossbows, but as soon as they went to reach for another bolt, Alric and the others were already upon them.

The first bowman was hunched over, fitting a bolt on the railing of the crossbow, when he was personally greeted with Alric's boot. The kick sent him stumbling back to the floor.

Alric didn't relent. He leapt in the air, a wolf pouncing on its prey, and drove his dagger into the side of the masked man's neck. He roared as he ripped the blade away, opening a large gash where the man's throat had once been.

Blood splattered across Alric's face, the taste of death dripping from his lips. In just a few short seconds, Alric had sent another soul to the eternal journey of the beyond. He smiled, relishing in the bloodshed.

Benny had just finished gutting the second bowman when Alric finally took in the rest of the scene. Four attackers remained, and a few of them didn't even know that their friends were dead on the floor. They stuck with the easy prey, killing innocent people rather than picking an actual fight.

The bandit closest to Alric was standing over someone, a boot firmly pressed to his chest, pinned defenselessly to the ground. Alric kicked him in the back, sending him flying forward, crashing through a wooden table. He rolled quickly back onto his feet, his sword held out before him in a guard. He locked eyes with Alric.

He was sure he could end the masked killer in mere seconds, but what would be the fun in that? It had been so long since he had felt the intoxicating euphoria of a fight. He had spent so much time running and hiding from it, and for what? If death wanted to dance, then Alric would take the lead. Killing was second nature to him, after all.

If bloodshed was an art, then Alric was the best artist in the entire fucking country.

Alric let the man stand. "Come on, then," he antagonized, his teeth shining bright white behind his blood-speckled face.

The bandit rose to his feet, looking back and forth between his own sword and Alric's dagger.

"Odds aren't in your favor, friend," the bandit assured, his deep voice near quaking with fear.

Alric flipped the dagger in his hand, his smile more deadly than the blade. "Just how I like it."

The bandit made his move. "You should have taken your chance while you had it." He came at Alric fast and hard, putting all his strength in his swings.

In Alric's experience, most men fought in two different ways. The first were those who put everything into their offensive. If you could put enough pressure on your enemy's defense, you could cause them to make a mistake, which would give you the chance to coordinate your next attack to their flaw and, hopefully, end them with a quick blow.

The second were those who used their enemy's strength against themselves, which was the way Alric liked to fight. Regardless of how experienced you were, swinging a sword was exhausting work, and if you couldn't find a blow to end your opponent before tiring yourself out, you were doomed.

The first blow was a downward arc toward Alric's face, which he easily dodged with a scoop to the right. Knowing what his opponent would do next, he then jumped back out of the way, the wide swing clearing his chest by inches. The bandit was fast, but Alric was faster.

The bandit continued his assault, his voice a rage as he pressed the attack on Alric. Alric simply stepped out of the way, the blade cutting nothing but air. He was deflecting it off the small blade of his dagger.

As time went on and Alric made a façade of the duel, the bandit began to tire. His attacks slowed, his breathing more haggard and deeper. Alric ducked under a lazy swing, laughing at how pathetic his opponent had become.

"Seriously?" Alric laughed out right as he stepped out of reach from another attack. "This is all you've got? Are things not going the way you hoped?"

Rage boiled in the bandit's eyes as he jabbed the point of his blade toward Alric. As soon as his arms fully extended, Alric was already rolling under the attack, coming up behind the bandit. He gave the bandit a steely kiss behind his heel, sending him to his knees as the tendons severed. Instinctively, the bandit dropped his sword and reached toward his ankle. It was the last mistake he would make.

Alric stepped behind the bandit, pulled his head back, and then wrapped his arm around his neck. He dragged the blade across the skin and ripped away, a spray of blood gushing across the tavern floorboards. Alric sent the body to the floor with a hard kick, adding him to the mess of butchered bodies that littered the floors.

He looked around the tavern, at the massacre he stood in, and suddenly the rush of battle began to leave him, replacing his frenzy with a cold memory.

He looked down at himself, soaked head to toe in blood. It had been a long time since he had been in a fight such as this. It was always easy for him to get lost in the killing, but now that he looked upon the mess of the tavern, he remembered why he had tried his best to avoid it in the first place.

"*You're not that person anymore.*" He could hear Meyra's voice in his head, giving him one of the many lessons she'd never failed to give. "*I know who you were during the war, and I know what your father told you when you were young but, Al, you don't have to be that person anymore. Not with me.*"

Someone crashed into Alric's side. The blast knocked the dagger out of his hands, causing him to skitter across the floor through a couple of chairs. He lay on his stomach as he felt the air leave his lungs. Pain numbed his back and shoulders.

Pain was a good sign in a fight. It meant you were still alive. But numbness? Not so much.

Someone gripped the side of his arm and flipped him onto his back. Alric saw the point of the blade coming down toward his face, but he caught his attacker by the wrist before the blow could connect.

A bandit sat on top of Alric's chest, using their weight to drive the blade into Alric's eye. Alric felt a pop in his chest that was followed by a sharp pain stretching across his shoulders and arms.

Alric relented a bit, and it was enough for his opponent to realize they had the upper hand. Any moment now, Alric's arms would give, and he would be dead.

Alric looked around the room. Benny was grappling with one of the other bandits, weaving left and right as the attacker swung wildly with his sword. He wouldn't be much help.

To Alric's fleeting surprise, Dodge was managing to fend off against the remaining two bandits, each coming at him like a storm with their blades. The attacks came swift and hard, yet Dodge managed to duck out of their reach just in time to strike his own blow. Although it was two against one, Dodge was clearly in control of the fight. Either way, Alric wasn't going to get much help from them.

Sweat beaded down the sides of his face as the blade inched closer and closer, the weight above him getting heavier by the second.

"You're done," the man behind the mask said. "Just let it happen. Don't struggle."

Alric felt hot. He could struggle all he wanted against the man, but he was right. With his dislocated shoulder and his strength sapping with each breath, he was done for. It was only a matter of seconds. The spark of battle frenzy was fading, quickly being replaced with the overwhelming fear of death.

Would it really be that bad? Why is it that you continue to struggle?

A shadow fell across them. Alric could see someone standing beside the bandit, and his heart sank when he saw the tip of a very sharp blade next to them. He struggled to wiggle free, hoping against all odds he could just gain an inch in his favor, but he couldn't.

"There you go." The bandit's dagger was now at the bridge of Alric's nose. "Just let it happen. It'll all be—*Ugh!*"

Dark blood wrapped around the bandit's neck like a gripping hand. His weight lessened, and his eyes rolled in the back of his head, blood dripping onto Alric's face.

Another blur, and Alric saw the line of a sword coming down toward the bandit's neck. His head hung limp above Alric, more blood gushing from the wound and washing onto his.

Taking advantage of the change in struggle, Alric rolled his hips and swung the bandit off to the side. Alric readied himself for an attack when he saw the large gash in the back of the bandit's neck, revealing meat and bone. He was already dead.

Alric turned and looked upon his savior. She was still holding the sword as blood dripped from it. She must have picked it up from one of the fallen bandits. Either way, Alric was grateful.

Sarah just stood there, looking at the body at her feet, her eyes wild as she looked between Alric and the dead bandit.

"I killed him," she said quietly.

Alric reached out toward Sarah when he heard a familiar *click* that no unprepared fighter wanted to hear.

He turned and saw a man standing in the doorway of the tavern, the stock of his crossbow firm against his shoulder, aiming down his sights toward Sarah.

"You little bitch!" the man roared at her then set the bolt free.

Twang!

Alric didn't hesitate; his reflexes didn't let him. He honestly couldn't tell you why he did it. Maybe it was because the girl had just saved his life, literally, and he felt he owed her, at least a little. Or maybe it was because he felt, deep down, that it was just the right thing to do, that sacrificing himself to save someone else was the only decent death he would get in a world such as his.

Whatever the reason, his choice left him standing in front of Sarah, the long bolt of a crossbow protruding out of his chest.

At first, there was no pain at all, just a numbness spreading warmly across his back. Then he felt the throbbing of his heartbeat vibrating throughout his body. He tried to breathe but couldn't. It was as if a wall blocked his throat and closed off his lungs.

Sarah was looking up at him, blood speckling her face. Fresh blood. Alric's blood.

He followed her eyes down to the broadhead sticking out of his chest, his lifeblood dripping from the tip. His vision began to blur, a hot prickle on his face. He collapsed to his knees, the sounds of fighting only a distant thing.

As his vision continued to blur before him, the sound of his heartbeat was all he could hear as everything began to grow black.

Butterfly Wings

Sarah wasn't sure what had compelled her to do it. She'd hid behind the collapsed table just as Dodge had told her to do, knees tucked to her chest as the sounds of death echoed around her—screaming, cries of pain, the sound of clashing steel. Then there had been a crash at the table that she hid behind, followed by the sounds of scuffling.

She peered around the side of the table, seeing Alric on his back with another man, one of the ones wearing a mask, leaning over him, straddling his chest while trying to bury a knife into his face. Sarah watched as that knife drew closer and closer.

'*It needs to be you,*' a voice said to her, the one that sounded so much like her mother.

Something glinted out of the corner of her eye, catching her immediate attention. A sword lay on the ground, a bloodied hand still gripping the blade. She didn't need the voice to tell her what to do next, she could *feel* it.

She crawled from behind the table, keeping low to the ground as she made her way toward the sword.

It had belonged to one of those wearing a mask. Sarah could tell by the pale glaze over their distant eyes that they were dead.

She pried his stiff fingers off the hilt of the sword and stood. Then she walked up behind the bandit straddling Alric, the blade hanging heavy and limp in her grip, and that's when she could hear the man in the mask speaking.

"There you go," he said. "Just let it happen." The words echoed in her mind, much like the ones that had been haunting her since Robins-Port, the voice she' heard every time she closed her eyes.

In that moment, Sarah didn't see the man in a mask, but the dark monster that haunted her dreams. *Here, little piggy. Don't struggle now. Nobody can hear you scream.*

She raised the sword above her head then brought it down with all her strength.

There was something familiar about the sound, like trying to chop down a tree with a dull axe. It reminded her of a snapping branch. Instead of dried flakes of wood, though, the warm spray of blood misted the air. Rivers of black gushed from the man's wound, wrapping around his neck and dripping onto Alric's face.

But it wasn't enough. The man still fought on, so Sarah decided to give him another *whack!*

The wound peeled out, reminding Sarah of the way a butterfly would spread its wings. She could see chips of the man's spine, tendons and muscles flexing as the blood pooled even more. The body went limp, and Alric rolled it over to his side.

He managed to climb to his feet, nursing his arm as he stared at Sarah still holding the sword.

"I killed him," she mumbled to herself.

Alric stared at her in disbelief. He was covered in gore, the dripping remnants of those he had recently killed painting his body. He began reaching toward her, either in thanks or scared she might attack him next.

"You little bitch," Sarah heard someone shout, and as she looked to her left, she saw a man pointing a very large crossbow at her.

Twang!

Warmth sprayed Sarah's face as a man stood before her. She watched Alric's face as he studied the thick wooden shaft sticking out of his chest, just beneath his collar bone. He probed the bolt with a gloved hand then collapsed to his knees.

"No!" Benny ducked under a swinging blade and brought his own dagger under his attacker's chin. Not wasting time, he shoved the man away with his other hand then charged toward the bowman, who was currently stretching back the string on his machine and lining another bolt onto its frame.

Benny kicked the crossbow out of the man's hand, grabbed the back of his head, and began smashing the hilt of the dagger into their face. *Crunch! Crunch! Crunch!*

The body went limp in Benny's grasp, yet Benny didn't relent. He plunged his dagger once, twice, three times into the man's abdomen, roaring with each strike.

Leaving the blade buried, he ripped away to the side of the man's stomach, intestines spilling out of the wound. A roar of pain shrieked through the tavern, the man in the mask doing his best to catch his falling organs as he sank to his knees. The sight alone made Sarah sick.

Dodge had just finished leaving a deep gash in one of his attacker's thighs. The bandit twisted around, his blade level at Dodge's head. Dodge ducked beneath the attack and brought a heavy fist into his attacker's throat, sending him to the floor as the second bandit pressed in for his attack.

If the second bandit thought Dodge wasn't ready for the attack, he was dead wrong.

Dodge jumped out of reach as a blade came at his chest. The bandit pulled back for another attack, but Dodge was already leaping into the man's guard, releasing a fury of pain on the bandit with his meaty fists, as graceful as the wind but as strong as a mountain.

Dodge plunged his dagger into the man's ribs, followed through with his heavy fists, then pulled his dagger free before burying it into the side of the man's neck. In just a few short moments, the bandit was dead at his feet.

Wasting no time, he shoved away his victim's body and walked over to the first masked man who, unfortunately for him, was still choking from his previous blow. He lifted a hand as he saw the mountain of Dodge towering over him, either hoping Dodge would take pity and spare his life or confident his hand was strong enough to shield the attack that was sure to come. Dodge replied with a quick jab, leaving the blade of his dagger sticking out of the man's skull.

Benny was at Alric's side now, kneeling next to him, cautiously inspecting the bolt that was lodged in his body. "Might be wedged against some bone but missed all vital organs."

Dodge joined them, standing tall behind Benny and Alric, looking down at them, a face full of rage. "Your man betrayed us." The dagger was still in his hand, fresh blood dripping from the steel. He was a look from a nightmare, an enormous brute drenched in blood, murder bright in his eyes.

"We don't know that," Benny defended. "Even if so, we need to get out of here."

Any moment now, Sarah expected Dodge to bury the dagger into Benny's back. Instead, he tucked the blade at his belt, knelt down, and wrapped an arm around Alric's waist, helping him to his feet.

"Anywhere we can go?"

"There's a guard post just down the street that should have some healing equipment. It missed all his vital organs, but he's losing a lot of blood."

The tavern was eerily quiet. One minute, patrons had been sipping their mugs, laughing at jokes with their companions, and hollering for refills. Now, those patrons lay about the ground, their lifeblood pouring from open wounds, their glassy eyes distantly staring into nothing. That was the worst part for Sarah as she looked about the slaughter—the eyes.

Her own eyes settled on the corpse of the man she'd killed. The man was just like any other person in the world. Like everyone else, he'd had a childhood, a mother and father, maybe a couple of siblings. They had gone through their own struggles, had dealt with their own fears. None of that mattered because, in the end, it would ultimately be Sarah who had sent them to the afterlife. The thought mind-boggled her. It took so long to grow a life, but only a few swings to end one.

"Sarah." Dodge brought her attention back. He was situating Alric, who now looked to be on the verge of passing out, by wrapping his unwounded arm around his shoulders and grabbing the other side of his belt. "It's time to go, sweetie. You need to stay right behind us, okay?"

Sarah didn't say anything, only a small nod was her reply.

Limping with the weight of his passenger, Dodge moved toward the door. Benny, however, walked over to the bar top and pulled down the large hammer from the wall.

"Know how to use one of those?" Dodge asked.

"I know enough in case we need to use it," he replied.

"Benny ..." Alric grumbled.

With worry in his eyes, Benny rushed to his friends' side and leaned in close. "I'm here, Al. What is it? We'll be at the guard post in a short bit, then we'll get that arrow out of you. I promise."

"I ... told you ..." Alric spit blood onto the floor, a line of thick drool dripping down his chin. " ... that thing isn't real."

Benny stared at Alric in bewilderment. "Excuse me?" He held the large hammer out in front of him. "Are you seriously ...? Even on the brink of death, you're still going to argue with me?"

"Don't be ... so dramatic," Alric said between breaths. He looked up toward Dodge. "He's always so damn ... dramatic ... isn't he? I'm not ... dying yet. Just tired."

Benny stared at his friend in disbelief. Then he shook his head and made his way toward the door leading outside. "For fuck's sake, Al. We are going to have a serious talk about your priorities when we get out of this."

The strangest part for Sarah wasn't the argument, but the sound of Alric's laughter as they left the tavern.

A Game of Deceit

The doorframe shattered with an audible *crack*, shards of splintered wood flying in the air as Trevor rushed through the door, staying close to Evan's heels. He expected to see evidence of an attack when he had agreed to join the fight, but he still wasn't prepared for the brutality he now rushed toward.

Even in the small amount of time that Trevor and the others had spent preparing inside the tavern, the bandits were able to turn the peaceful street into a bloody graveyard. Bodies lay sprawled, bent at awkward angles, with open wounds and slit throats. The bandits' thirst for carnage was insatiable, and Trevor knew they had no bounds to their violence as he spotted the small bodies of children amongst the battlefield.

The street was pandemonium. Bandits broke windows to shops and threw lit torches inside while others continued to stab victims attempting to crawl away from the attack. They stood on the opposite end of the street like a gang of thugs, relishing in the remnants of their ambush, living gods amongst the graveyard they had created.

The sound of Evan kicking the door drew the attention of six masked men. Together, they turned to face them, a sight from a nightmare, sending an eerie chill down Trevor's spine. They flexed the weapons in their hands—swords, large clubs with a spiked ball attached to a chain, and some with crossbows. The group of men screamed of violence, and their eyes showed a thirst for more.

Evan led the charge toward the masked men. "Bowmen!"

Trevor felt a rush of adrenaline as he followed, sprinting full force toward the bandits who were now rolling their shoulders and twirling their wicked blades in welcome. Two men holding the crossbows put the stocks to their shoulders, taking aim directly at Evan and Trevor.

Fear hit Trevor like a wall.

Something whistled through the air past Trevor's head, and then the two bowmen sank to their knees, arrow shafts sticking out from their chest.

Trevor glanced back over his shoulder and saw Merrick and Garth nocking another arrow and taking aim. Like a single entity, they drew their strings back as one, took aim as one, and drilled the two masked bowmen in their faces with their arrows as one.

"Focus," Tom roared at Trevor's side. "Stick to what you've been taught."

Time slowed as the men drew closer.

During Trevor's sparring lessons with Dodge, his uncle had told him that time felt different in a real fight. Every move could either be your victory or your death, and the mind tended to focus differently when you knew that.

They were close enough to see the whites of the bandit's eyes, all of them wrinkling in rage. They held their weapons out before them, the sharp ends pointing straight toward Trevor.

Trevor felt the urge to stop his pursuit, to turn about and flee from the certain death that he rushed toward. That was until he remembered why he was doing it in the first place.

I have to get to Dodge and Sarah. If that's through these guys—he tightened his grip on his sword—*then so be it.*

As he rushed toward certain death, either for him or his opponent, Trevor thought back to a lesson he had been taught long ago. A lesson he never thought he would put to the real test.

"Rushing an enemy has two effects." Dodge reached out and pulled Trevor from the ground. They'd been at it for hours, nearing the end of their morning lessons. "It either puts fear into your enemy, or it doesn't. So, if you're going to charge, you better hope it does the former."

Trevor dusted dirt from his arms then picked up the practice sword from the ground. "Noted."

Dodge took up his stance again as Trevor watched. "Every man being charged will hope the same thing—that they can use their enemy's momentum against them, that they need to simply hold out their blade while the rushing army skewers themselves. That's why, when the lines of an army are being charged, pikemen are at the front. They use the reach of their weapons as an advantage to help their line of defense from breaking.

"Like this." Dodge held out his wooden sword before him. He took his right heel and brought it back, bending at an arch to give himself more stability. His elbows were slightly bent, a buffer for the hypothetical force

coming his way, the blade straight out before him, locked in two hands.

"Why would someone charge against that?" Trevor asked.

"Because, regardless of how confident that pikeman is, there will always be a fraction of fear in the back of his mind. I've got plenty of stability from my arms and legs to fend off my attacker's weight. However"—Dodge waved the sword left and right—"my wrists now lack any stability, leaving vulnerability in my defense. That, and I'm watching an entire army running at me."

"So"—Trevor observed his uncle's stance—"how do I continue to charge but take advantage of their weakness?"

Dodge gave a wicked smile. "Timing."

Trevor focused on one of the bandits with a sword, and as he drew close enough, he swung his sword against his defending blade, knocking it to the side as he kept running. He used the force of his momentum and shouldered the masked man in the chest, sending him back but not knocking him over. Trevor took advantage of his press and swung toward the bandit's chest, but the man leaned out of the way and jabbed quickly at Trevor with the end of his sword.

Fear jolted Trevor into action, reflex and muscle memory from his practices driving his movement. He didn't need to think where the blade was going to go; he simply knew.

He leaned back, just far enough to let the incoming attack slice through the air before his face.

Trevor jumped away from his opponent and held his sword out defensively, but the bandit didn't press an attack. Instead, they locked eyes, slowly walking in a circle as the sounds of battle rang around them.

Trevor knew the others were in their own fight but tried to ignore it. He had his own fight to focus on, and if Dodge had taught him anything in his past, it was that a duel needed his full attention.

"When it comes to a duel like this"—Dodge pointed back between himself and Trevor as they stood a few feet apart—"it's a game of offense and defense. We already know that both sides have their benefits, that they can be as effective as the other. Do you remember?"

"I remember," Trevor answered, leaning over his sword, trying to catch his breath. The sun was high in the sky, but Dodge insisted they keep training.

"Tell me, then," Dodge invited.

Trevor stood up straight. "When you're on the offense, you're pressing your enemy, wearing down their stamina and pressuring them into panicking, which could lead to a mistake."

Dodge nodded. "But?"

"But," Trevor continued, "if you aren't used to it, you'll tire yourself out and leave yourself open, which is the benefit of defense. You can parry and dodge and tire your enemy out, waiting for an opening."

"So, which is better in a fight: offense or defense?"

"I ..." Trevor didn't know how to answer the question. "I think they both have their benefits and faults. Can we really say one is better than the other?"

Dodge gave an approving smile. "Very good." He began twirling the blade in the air, a clear sign to Trevor that their training wasn't yet finished. "The best any fighter can do is master both sides. For example, if I'm pressing an attack, I'm hoping my opponent can't keep up, so they leave an opening. On the other hand, if I'm parrying and on the defensive, I'm waiting for my opponent to tire themselves out, hoping I still have enough strength in me to use that to my advantage.

"So, the thing is, you want to trick your enemy. You want to control the fight but have your enemy believe they're the ones in control. Press your attack for a bit, then leave yourself open in their eyes. Once they believe they have the advantage, that's when you've already won. When you're on the defense, leave a slight opening for your enemy to see, and when they press for it, turn it against them.

"Always remember"—Dodge locked eyes on him—"a duel is a game of deceit."

Trevor stared quizzically. "Then why doesn't everyone fight that way?"

Dodge spread his arms wide. "Who's to say they don't?"

Trevor nodded at the lesson.

Dodge continued, "Always expect your opponent to be a step ahead of you so you can remain three steps ahead of them. And just remember, this skill is also your weakness. If your enemy notices what you're doing, he'll use it against you."

"So, how do you pull it off?" Trevor asked.

"Simple." Dodge squared off against Trevor, his sword held before him. "You just have to be the better liar."

Trevor leapt at his opponent, chopping down with his sword. The masked man saw the attack coming and blocked it easily, but Trevor didn't relent. He followed up on the offense, pushing the bandit back as he rained down blow after blow.

Trevor was gaining ground, his opponent nearly with his back against the wall of a building, but it wasn't enough.

The masked man wasn't a mere bandit, but someone with more than enough experience with a blade. Each blow Trevor delivered, the bandit rejected, sending it flying wide or easily dodging out of the way.

Trevor swung wide toward the bandit's waist, but they twisted their body and easily blocked the blow. Trevor changed his tactics and went for his opponent's head, but the bandit ducked below that attack.

Trevor let his attacks drag on, always pressing forward to drive his opponent away. Their swords clashed in song, the art of their duel singing loudly in the street. The more Trevor fought, the more comfortable he became in his abilities. However, Dodge had always told him never to let his pride and confidence be his undoing, and so Trevor continued to play his part.

His arms grew heavy, and Trevor began to slow his attacks. His blade came down from the top, and the masked man stepped to the side, leaving Trevor's ribs open and vulnerable. The bandit saw his opportunity and lunged out with his blade, but Trevor feinted right and let the blade pass by while bringing his own in a wide slash toward the bandit's face. For a brief moment, Trevor thought the fight would be over but, surprisingly, the bandit ducked low and leapt back out of Trevor's reach.

The fighting continued out of his peripherals. Tom swung his axe wildly while Evan and the others were locked in a melee with the other bandits, tempting to distract Trevor from his own duel.

Dodge had taught him the lesson many times. *"You can train all you want, but the moment a warrior loses focus is the moment they lose their head."*

The bandit breathed rapidly, dark stains of sweat spotting their mask. Trevor picked up his pace of breathing to match his opponents. He had to play the part, after all.

At first, before the battle, a surge of fear had stiffened Trevor's limbs. He knew that the smallest mistake wouldn't just be a crack in the ribs like his practice sessions with Dodge. Instead, it would end in a painful death. Now, as the battle raged on, Trevor became more confident. His enemy was skilled, but Trevor knew he was better.

"*Let him study you,*" Dodge's lesson echoed in the back of Trevor's mind, "*and just when he thinks he has you, finish it.*"

Trevor lunged forward, slower in his speed but precise with his attack. He chopped down toward the bandit's face again, just like before. And, just like before, the bandit stepped to the side and prepared for another attack toward Trevor's open ribs. Trevor, again, twisted out of the way, much slower than the first time, and swung a counterattack toward the bandit's knees. The bandit leaned away from the attack, only to spring toward Trevor with a rain of his own blows.

Time to play the defensive.

Trevor backed away, giving his enemy ground as he deflected blow after blow, sparks flying with each clash of steel.

The bandit lunged toward Trevor's gut, a deadly blow that could have easily skewered and disemboweled him. Just as the point of the sword was inches away from his gut, however, Trevor twisted sideways and let the blade pass inches from his waist.

The two of them clashed, the ring of steel on steel adding to the echo of battle in the street. Trevor's breathing was heavier now, loud enough for his assailant to notice. He kept pace with his blocks and dodges, but his movements became more sluggish as his opponent became more aggressive.

Each attack was followed by another, which led to another opening on Trevor's part. This was absolutely a skilled fighter, one who stayed a step ahead of his opponent.

But Trevor was three steps ahead.

The bandit pressed his attack, driving Trevor across the street, treading carefully not to trip over one of the corpses that littered the ground. Trevor could see victory glistening in his attacker's eyes, could feel the wide smile hidden behind the mask.

Knowing Trevor was weak and tired, his movement would be slower, the bandit resorted to the technique that had nearly gutted Trevor from before. He followed through with a wide swing that came toward Trevor's side. Trevor made sure to dodge the same way he had before, just a bit slower to make sure his opponent followed through with a counterattack, the same as before.

Trevor exposed his gut once again, convincing the man that he'd found his way to victory.

The bandit lunged out with his sword as if it were a stick, driving the point of the blade toward Trevor's abdomen. Instead of twisting like before, though, and letting the blade pass, Trevor stepped to the side, the blade hovering at waist level before him. With all the might and speed he could muster, Trevor then brought his blade in an upward swing toward the bandit's exposed wrist.

"Very good." Dodge wiped the sweat from his brow as Trevor picked himself off the ground.

"Easy for you to say," Trevor said bitterly, wiping mud and sweat off his arms. "Can't see how that was good in any way."

"That's because you're focusing on the win and not the fight. Yes, you lost, but I could tell you were trying to balance your tactics, drawing me out to make a mistake with deceit. That is what's good."

Trevor scoffed. "It's not like it mattered."

"But it did." Dodge walked to Trevor and placed a reassuring hand on his shoulder. "Once you become a master of these three tings—offense, defense, and deceit—you can win any fight. But there is one more lesson I'll teach you today, and it's the most important one of all.

Trevor listened intently. "What's that?"

Dodge looked at him for a moment, that familiar look that said there was nothing more serious than what was about to be said. "Fighting me, in this yard, will be much different from fighting a true enemy. You have to be fully invested, fully focused to walk away from a real fight. Not only that, but you can never hesitate and never relent.

"If by a cruel hand played by the gods you find yourself fighting for your life, Trevor, never give your opponent remorse. No matter how much pain you cause that person. Just remember, they were your enemy before, so they are your enemy now. Show no mercy."

The bandit shrieked in pain as his severed hand spun through the air, still gripping the sword he was so sure would end Trevor's life.

Trevor wasted no time. Before the severed hand could reach the floor, his sword was already plunging into the man's open mouth, silencing his screams instantaneously as his blade split through the man's skull, a few inches of steel sticking out from the back of his head.

Trevor ripped his blade away, the body turning rigid as the blade ripped free, a wet, sucking sound noticeable as his assailant crumbled to the floor.

Trevor looked about the carnage. Tom's axe was currently wedged into a man's chest, whereas Baron and Evan were still locked in their own melees.

Baron was a blur, his twin swords hacking wildly at a man defending himself with a mace. He began to falter, but Baron didn't let up. His feet were just as quick as his swings, hopping back and forth around his opponent, causing the man to stumble over himself rather than getting his weapon up for defense. The masked man began to stumble, and Baron hopped back, only to make room for a heavy kick to the man's chest.

As he began to fall, Baron was already in the air, leaping onto his falling target with his blades angled down. As they crashed to the ground, Baron was straddling the man, both blades in each of the bandit's eyes.

Seroes fought like a brute, using a sword to draw a defense out of his opponent. Just as the bandit parried a blow, Seroes struck out with an unsuspecting fist. The bandit rushed toward Seroes, anger driving his attack as he held his blade high. Gracefully, Seroes lowered his body to the side, holding out his sword lightly, and let the man rush past him.

The bandit drunkenly sank to his knees, eyes creasing in confusion as his sword dropped to the cobblestones. He looked down to witness the open gash in his abdomen, dark blood rushing out. He reached down, his lifeblood flowing through his open fingers, and then sunk forward, face-first onto the street. He didn't move after that.

Evan fought with a halberd—a large stick with a deadly arched blade attached to the end of it. Trevor had asked many times about the benefits of this weapon, and each time, Dodge had insisted that it made for a better offense by keeping an enemy away from you.

Evan swung the halberd in wide circles, causing the last standing bandit to jump back out of reach. He readied himself for a counterattack, only to see the blade suddenly coming from another angle, which caused him to duck low this time, and then to jump away from the next. It was a sad sight, like a cat batting a mouse back and forth between its paws, deciding on its own terms when to devour its prey.

And in a split-second, the bandit made the deadly mistake of trying to duck when Trevor knew he should have jumped back. The blade of the halberd passed by in a flash, leaving behind an open gash in the masked man's throat.

The bandit dropped his blade and reached for his neck, gurgling as he began to drown in his own blood. Like his comrades before him, he sank to the ground, his body still as a pool of blood spread across the cobblestones.

The entirety of the scuffle had lasted only minutes, but in a way, it had felt much longer to Trevor. Sweat dripped from his face, his chest tight as he fought to catch his breath.

Trevor looked around the massacre before him, and now that the adrenaline of the fight was fading, his stomach began to turn at the sight.

"Well, that's over." Evan wiped the gore from his blade on the tunic of one of the dead masked men. "Everyone good? Seroes?"

"Good," Seroes called out. He, too, was cleaning his sword, but only with a small cloth he had pulled from his coat. "Haven't we talked about respecting the dead?"

Evan patted the corpse a couple times before rising to his feet. "I only have respect for the ones deserving." He waved his hands at the bodies before them. Besides the men in masks, there were at least double that of men, women, and even children. "These bastards deserve nothing but the cold ground, so I'll reserve that empathy for those who aren't complete degenerates."

Seroes stuck out his bottom lip, surveying the carnage while nodding. "Fair enough."

"Baron?" Evan stood then walked toward Trevor and Tom. "Garth, Merrick?"

"We're good," the twins said in unison, an arrow nocked and ready to be drawn at the slightest notion of a threat.

"Good here." Baron sheathed his twin swords across his back, his hood up, hiding his face in a shadow.

"What about you?" It took a moment for Trevor to realize that Evan was talking to him. "You did well, I see." He nodded toward the man that Trevor had killed not a few minutes ago. "You all right, kid?"

It was just a general question, but Trevor felt that Evan was implying more than whether he was injured; he wanted to know if he was okay with the decision he had made when he'd chosen to fight.

Trevor looked down at his victim and said, "All good here."

Evan stepped past Trevor, but before he broke his line of sight, Trevor saw a small smile of approval on the man's face.

"How about you, old man?" Evan gave a rough slap on Tom's shoulder. "Pull a muscle? Break a hip?"

"Son, I've worked in the forge my entire life." Tom stood tall with his battle axe hanging at his side. "Believe me when I say it'll take more than a simple bandit to be the end of me."

"They weren't just bandits," Seroes declared. "Bandits want something from their victims, something valuable. That's why they're bandits. But this"—he gestured to the bodies scattering the street—"this was just a *massacre*."

"Shit."

All eyes turned to Baron. Though his face was hidden in the shadow of his hood, Trevor could tell he was looking past them all.

Trevor followed his stare and understood why.

They all turned their heads, gazing upon the dreadful sight, and what Trevor saw shook him to his core. In the sky, hovering in multiple places above the tall buildings that crowded the streets, were black pillars of smoke.

Servitol was on fire.

The Alpha and His Pack

Scattered fires engulfed buildings, red hands of scorching flames reaching high toward the sky. Food wagons were ablaze, the crackle of the fire popping loudly as the dry wood was entirely consumed.

Her arms and face tickled with prickly heat as they stepped through the door; Dodge at the front with Alric hanging from his shoulder, and Benny at Sarah's side, with a ridiculously large hammer in his hands.

Smears of red splattered building walls, evident trails leading to the fallen victims of the massacre. Across the street, a shop with a large window, the impaled body of a man hung over the shards of broken glass. A woman was lying in the street, her face a mess of gore of red meat and broken bone. One of her hands reached out, her fingers near touching the body of another fallen victim, one of a man with a thick mustache and a slashed throat.

Despite surviving her own personal hell, Sarah had never witnessed the carnage that took place in Robins-Port. She'd been too busy wishing she were dead and had never gotten a first glance of what death looked like. This, she supposed, was the closest comparison.

People swarmed the street in a hasty rush to freedom, like a school of fish funneling through a trench, caring for nothing but their own safety as they shoved others aside and left them behind. Some managed to keep their balance; others weren't so lucky. The unlucky few found themselves sucked under the current of stampeding residents, still reaching out for help as they were trampled to death. The current flooded down the street, away from the bridge that connected the castle and upper city.

"This looks much bigger," Benny said, his composed voice muffled by pure pandemonium. He stretched his neck to get a view above the fleeing crowd of pedestrians. "I can see some guards up there. They're fighting off a mob of those masked men. Looks like there's a lot of them."

"Then we should be off in the other direction." Dodge fixed Alric's weight at his side. "Make to escape the city. Those men inside, they were sent there for us."

"We don't know that," Benny replied, his heavy hammer at the ready. "There's no telling why this is happening, but if it's as big as it's starting to look, we might just be caught in the crossfire. And if that's the case, you can forget about the exit."

"Benny."

Dodge shifted Alric's weight again. "And why's that?"

"Because those guys"—he nodded toward the end of the street—"are fighting off the city guards, which means someone's reported back to the castle, which means the first thing they'll send is an order to close off the city, trapping us inside until they can figure out what's going on."

"Benny."

"Then we should find a place to hold up," Dodge suggested. "Meet with the others and plan an escape."

"No time for that. Besides, if they find us hiding away in a house, they'll most likely think we are part of it all. We need to get out of the city *now*."

Dodge shook his head impatiently. "I thought you just said—"

"There's a place," Benny said suddenly, "in the lower district. A place nobody knows about that we can slip through. We'll have to go now."

"No," Dodge said sternly. "I'll not leave without Trevor."

"Trevor is with Evan and the others. Most likely—"

"Most likely isn't good enough," Dodge interrupted. "Either we can move together, or I drop your man here and now and make my own way. I'm not leaving without Trevor."

"Benny!"

When Alric finally managed to gain Benny's attention, he nodded down the street toward the crowd had nearly entirely disappeared, leaving only a few scattered individuals left.

A few scattered individuals who were currently being attacked by men in masks.

"Shit," Benny muttered.

Dodge followed his gaze. "How many?"

"Looks like five more." Benny flexed his hands on the hammer. "Doesn't seem like they've spotted us yet, though."

One of the bandits, this one wearing a red mask instead of black, had just finished hacking down a man trying to scurry to safety with a tiny dog in his hands. He looked about the scene as his brethren continued to prey upon the fleeing people then tilted his head toward Sarah.

"Oh, bloody hell," Benny cursed to himself.

The man in the red mask whistled, catching the attention of his comrades like a pack of wild dogs. Clearly, he was the one in charge.

Leaving their most recent prey behind, they strutted forward, the man in the red at the front with the others at his sides. He pointed his blade toward them, and despite the distance currently between them, Sarah saw droplets of gore dripping from it.

In a flash, the men in black leapt at a command, racing off like rabid wolves, hungry eyes set on their next meal.

"Stay behind me, Sarah!" Dodge dropped Alric. An instant later, a dagger was in his hand.

Sarah's heart hammered in her chest, soon to burst, as she watched the four men sprinting her way. Her vision narrowed, her breath became short and shaky.

The masked attackers howled in delight, pointing their blades at her, promising to join her with the corpses around them.

Benny stepped in front of Alric and took a defensive stand next to Dodge. "Can you fight with two?" He pulled a dagger from his beltline and tossed it in the air toward Dodge.

Dodge snatched the blade from the air, twirling it between his fingers before giving it a tight grip. "You just worry about that hammer," he told Benny, readying himself for the bandits who were no more than ten feet away.

The first one to reach them leapt into the air, his bloodied blade angled down at his intended victim. However, as the man leapt, Benny was already winding back his hammer. In the matter of split-seconds, just as the man in the mask was inches away from driving his blade home, Benny's hammer connected, smashing the bandit in his chest and sending him flying back. The bandit slid across the ground, his body limp like a ragdoll as he rolled.

As soon as the blow landed, another one came from the next bandit. Benny leaned away as a sword passed inches from his face then struck out with the butt of his hammer, but his new opponent was too quick.

The bandit struck out with his sword again, leaving a bright cut across Benny's ribs. Benny roared in agony, a hand pressed tightly over the wound.

The bandit followed through with a final attack, and Sarah's heart skipped a beat as she was about to witness Benny's death. However, despite the pain, Benny managed to block the blow with the hilt of his hammer.

Dodge was vicious, a bear defending its cubs from a pack of starving lions. With a dagger in each hand, he managed to fend off his two attackers with a series of jabs. However, as one of the men was directly engaged with Dodge, the other slipped behind his back.

Sarah's eyes widened, her mouth opening, ready to scream out in warning, but not a moment later, without as much as turning his head, Dodge grabbed hold of his attacker and spun about, using him as a human shield. In a flash, with no time left to second-guess the attack, the blade from the second bandit was buried deep in the back of the bandit that Dodge had replaced himself with.

Dodge kicked heavily at the body, sending both bandits flying back. The one who had managed to sneak behind Dodge landed in a thud, the lifeless body of his heavy companion on top of him.

Dodge rushed in for the final attack, but the bandit managed to squeeze out from underneath the corpse and wiggle free. Just as Dodge's blade came crashing down, the bandit rolled to freedom.

Benny swung his hammer about, using the reach of the weapon to keep his enemy at bay, but his opponent was quick. The bandit ducked low and saw a clear opening in Benny's guard. They rushed in and shouldered Benny in the chest, making him stagger back a few steps, but he managed to stay on his feet. However, with his wound, his movement was sloppy and slow.

The bandit rushed in, his blade point leveled out and directed toward Benny's torso. Just as the man was inches from him, Benny spun around, the hammer leveled with the ground as he twirled in a full circle and swept the legs out from under his attacker. As the bandit hovered defenselessly in the air, Benny used the momentum of his swing and brought his hammer down on the bandit's chest.

There was a sound of splitting gravel as Benny pinned his opponent between his hammer and the ground, the weight of a mountain crashing on a tiny nail.

He wiggled the hammer, pulling it free from the wide hole that was now the bandit's chest.

Benny lifted the hammer before him and studied it. The wood of the polished hilt had split, severing the hammer portion, leaving nothing but a heavy stick for a weapon.

Dodge ducked beneath a blow from his opponent. He twisted his body to the side, letting his attacker reach past. Before the bandit could pull back their arm, Dodge brought his dagger up, leaving a steel kiss on the man's forearm.

The bandit cried out in pain and dropped his blade, but Dodge didn't relent. He kicked at his assailant's knee, and there was a large *pop* as the leg buckled inward. Then, as the bandit fell forward, Dodge swung up toward their chin, burying the tip of his dagger deep into their brain. He let it sit there for a moment before shoving the body away.

The bandit in the red mask was just approaching his flock as his last pigeon was plucked from the sky. From their build, Sarah could tell it was a man. Before his feet, a mess of his gang, nothing but bloody heaps of meat left to rot.

He studied Dodge and Benny, who were now hunching down at the ready; Dodge with both daggers in his hands, and Benny with nothing but a fancy stick in his.

Sarah watched as the bandit looked past them, toward Alric lying on the ground. Although his face obscured, it looked as if he were scowling.

"Come on, then," Dodge growled, his body tense with his next fight.

The bandit was just lifting his sword, revealing a dark swirl of a tattoo on his wrist, when a bell tolled, its loud banging echoing over the city.

The bandit hesitated, looking from one opponent to the other, then down to Sarah. Their green eyes pierced Sarah like a snake set on a rat. For a moment, she thought he would try leaping through Dodge and Benny to get her, but he just took a few steps back, turned around, and ran away.

Dodge took off in pursuit when Benny grabbed his arm. "We have to get out of here."

"He's clearly their leader," Dodge protested, trying to pull his arm away from Benny's grip.

Benny shook his head, refusing to let go. "They'll seal off the city. We need to get out of here."

There was a commotion from behind them, and all eyes turned to see a group of men in shiny armor walking in formation. The three at the front had long spears with sharp blades at the end of them. Others beside them carried large swords and shields. Their armor shined bright silver, and Sarah could make out a picture of an orange sun on their breastplates.

"The city guard," Benny declared, picking Alric off the ground and fixing him around his shoulders. "We make for the lower city."

"I fucking told you," Dodge growled, his voice near a shout, "I'm not leaving without—"

"And I'm telling you," Benny interrupted, "if Trevor is still in the city with Evan and the others, their making for the same spot. We have a rendezvous set outside the city where they'll go. It's what we all agreed on. Now, you won't get far with those daggers, especially on the wrong side of the city guards. Help me, and I'll help you. That's a promise."

Dodge looked down at his weapons, red staining his hands and up his arms. Then he looked to Sarah, worry clear in his eyes. After a moment's pause, he nodded in defeat. "Fine. But if we make it to your hidden path and they aren't there, we part ways."

"Suit yourself." Benny began walking forward, Alric hanging at his side, when he heard his friend grumble. "What's that, Al?"

Alric replied with a nod toward Benny's free hand, the one that still gripped the handle of the broken great-hammer.

Benny rolled his eyes. "Alric, if you say, *I told you so*, I swear, by every god in this world that I'll hit you in the face and leave you here to die."

Despite the arrow still lodged inside Alric's shoulder, the man managed a small smile, and as she, Dodge, and Benny made their way down the street, away from the mess of bodies they'd just made, Sarah could hear him laughing.

The Right Thing to Do

"This is more than just a bandit attack," Garth said, tightening the strap on his shoulder.

Merrick nodded in agreement, rolling his neck from side to side. "It's an invasion"

The smoke was far off, but Trevor was convinced that it was close enough to where he had parted ways with Dodge and Sarah earlier. "We have to find Dodge and Sarah."

"We can't risk it," Seroes said. "If this is as large of an attack as it's turning out to be, the first thing the guards will do is seal off the city, which means, if we rush to the gates *now*, we might actually make it."

"What about your men?" Tom asked, wiping the blood from the large blade of his axe. "The brotherhood may leave behind their friends, but we don't."

"As soon as Benny and Alric realize what's happening, they'll do the same thing. In fact, they're most likely on their way to the gates now."

"There's a lot of hope riding in those words"—Tom flexed his axe in his hands—"and when it comes to between hoping my friends are all right and being able to help them, I'll always swing with the latter."

"You don't know where you're going," Baron said, his face still hidden beneath his hood.

"And neither do they," Tom added.

Seroes shifted on his feet uncomfortably. "I understand you're worried, but we have to be smart about this."

Tom shrugged his large shoulders. "Who says I'm worried? It's the right thing to do. If they're in trouble, I'm going to help. It's as simple as that."

"Yes, but—"

"I'll go with them." Trevor was surprised to see Evan stepping in to help. In fact, just about everyone stared in disbelief as Evan volunteered. "What? Why is that so surprising?" Seroes was about to reply, but Evan cut him off. "There's no way in hell these two are going to just run off with us and leave their friends behind. It's only a few blocks away—"

"Ten blocks away," Baron corrected.

Evan rolled his eyes. "Thank you. It's only *ten* blocks away. We'll rush to the inn, check to see if they had any trouble, and then we'll make our way to the lower city wall."

The same wall we smuggled the natives through.

The sound of a bell toll resonated through the city from the direction of the castle. Trevor hoped that it was a good sign.

"That's a bad sign," Garth said. "They're sealing off the city. If we don't move now, we'll never make it."

Seroes rubbed his chin, his bald head glistened with sweat as he thought to himself. "I don't like it. You'll have to be quick, and I mean *very* quick."

"And if there are more of them, which it looks like there are"—Evan looked down to Trevor—"we'll be quick *and* deadly."

"I'm going with you," a voice called out, and then Warren shimmied out from a crack between the wall of a building and a cluster of barrels.

Trevor felt pity for him as he slunk awkwardly across the street toward them, terror on his face as he stepped around the corpses. He looked like a child sneaking through the kitchen at night to steal from the cookie jar.

"Just stay close," Tom said as he patted Warren's shoulder. "It'll be all right."

Evan looked from Warren to Trevor. There was a message in his look, and he didn't have to say it out loud for Trevor to understand.

"He's not the enemy right now," the look said.

"Best be off, then." Evan looked to Seroes. "Meet at the rendezvous?"

Seroes nodded. "We'll give you a week before we start looking for you. Don't lollygag."

"Me?" Evan took on the image of an innocent child. "Why, Seroes, would I ever?"

Seroes rolled his eyes and turned away, but Evan wasn't finished.

"Best of luck, my dear friends. Garth, Merrick, don't go shooting your eyes out now. And Baron? I absolutely did *not* put a spider nest in your bag last night, so don't go thinking I did. And Seroes—"

"Will you just get a fucking move on?" Merrick called from over his shoulder, leading the others down the street at a jog.

It was an uncomfortable feeling. Not even an hour before, you had to weave between small gaps between people in order to cross the street. There was always the sound of conversations, even though you couldn't find who it was from. The street had been loud with life.

Now you had to weave between corpses, making sure you didn't step on someone's head as you moved about. Instead of the joyous sound of life, you were left with the eerie silence of nothing.

Evan looked at Trevor, Tom, and Warren, his posture more serious. "Let's get going," he said as he began jogging down the street.

Trevor followed close behind him, mentally preparing himself for what he was about to see.

It didn't take long for them to hear the screams.

A Message of Fear

The halls of the castle boomed with disorder. Fearful citizens grouped near corners of the rooms, huddled together, hugging each other, making promises to one another that everything was going to be okay. Castle guards marched in formation, patrolling from room to room, searching every nook and cranny of the castle for the "assassin."

The crowd parted for Francis as if he possessed an invisible barrier that surrounded him. He walked with a purpose, a large crate held tightly to his chest as he followed the booming echoes of orders being shouted.

"And you've searched the second floor?" Gorman asked two officers who stood at attention before him.

Francis kept a few steps away, observing Gorman.

"Yes, sir," one soldier answered. "We searched every room and found nothing. We have a checkpoint at every entrance to the stairs with orders not to let anyone pass."

"Good." Gorman rubbed his chin. "Keep a watch out for the cook. He's a—"

"We've an update on the cook, sir." The officer shifted uncomfortably with the interruption.

Gorman crossed his arms. "Good news, I hope."

"We found him stowed away in the back of a closet in the kitchens," the second soldier answered. "He's dead. We think he walked in on the assassin poisoning the food. Killed him before he could raise an alarm."

Gorman nodded and sighed. "Shame. When all this is over, find out if he had a family. The least we can do is put their mind at ease and let them know he died a hero."

The guards gave a stiff salute. "Yes, sir."

"Now send your squads to the third floor and check *everything*. Vases that could fit a man could also fit an assassin. Pull the curtains from windows, check behind statues. Remember, gentlemen, that there is still an assassin on the loose."

Oh, how right you are, General. He stands just ten feet from you.

"Right away, sir," the soldier said.

"Dismissed."

The guards snapped a quick salute, turned around, and then ran off to their duties.

Before they turned the corner down the next hall, Gorman shouted, "And be safe, for gods' sake! I'm talking no less than three-man teams, got it? Get a headcount and keep track of your men."

The soldiers nodded then disappeared around the corner.

Gorman pinched the bridge of his nose and groaned. When he lifted his head, he spotted Francis off to the side. "Father Balorian. It's not safe for you to be about. There's still the possibility of a threat in the castle."

"I understand your worry, General." Francis looked around the room. Off to their side was a man with a bloodied rag held over his arm, a doctor hovering over the wound, inspecting it. Next to him, a mother held her children in her arms, whispering quietly as tears fell down her face. "But I'll not leave my countrymen to suffer while I hide away in a locked room. We're all in this together."

Gorman nodded his approval. "You have my respect, Father."

"And you have mine, General. Now, how does the castle stand?"

Gorman cleared his throat. "The ground and second floor have been searched, but nothing was found. We suspected someone had paid off the cook to poison the food, but it turns out he ended up dead himself, along with …" Gorman looked past Francis, eyeing the double doors that closed off the entrance to the dining hall, a room now filled with over two hundred corpses. "Well, we can add him to the list of victims. I sent a platoon to search the third floor now. They're looking everywhere for the assassin, but it's taking too long. They most likely fled the castle as soon as the poison was added."

Or they could be standing within stabbing distance from you. But who's to say?

"Regardless," Francis replied, "it's good to be thorough. Have we heard from General Destro yet?"

"Aye," a voice boomed. "I'm here."

They both turned and saw Destro materialize from a gap between the swelling crowd, a brute of a man surrounded by flocks of sheep. "I sent a messenger to my men outside. They're ordered to cordon off the entrance and set a perimeter around the city."

"Do we have enough men for that, General?" Francis asked, fabricated worry in his tone.

"They'll be stretched thin," Destro admitted, "but it'll be better than nothing. With the exits secure, nobody gets in or out of the city."

There was a commotion coming from the entrance of the castle. A woman screamed as she was shoved aside by an approaching figure.

"Out of my way!" the man roared. "I'm on an urgent mission for the king. Move, damn you, move!"

It seems our city general is in a mood, Francis thought, *which is not an entirely good sign.*

"General Vallis," Francis announced as the man approached, trying hard to keep the venom from his voice. "Where does the city stand?"

Vallis donned a look of disgust as he analyzed the room. His lip curled as he surveyed the citizens huddled in corners, fearing for their lives. "What are all these peasants doing here? What point is it to have hospitals in the city if our people refuse to use them when needed?"

Gorman's lip curled in rage. He looked like he wanted to reach out and strangle Vallis right there. "The hospitals are all burning."

Vallis sneered, shaking his head with irritation. "Well, have some guards set up a base outside. This place is way too crowded. Any one of these peasants could be the killer we are looking for."

Gorman, with clear restraint on striking out at Vallis, leaned closer to his fellow general. "Let's remember that these are the people that truly run the city. The ones that you swore to protect. They look up to you in times like this, so how about you lead by example and show a little fucking compassion in their time of need?"

Francis expected that, at any moment now, Vallis would do one of two things. Either he would make some snide comment about Gorman, which would in turn infuriate the man enough to throttle Vallis right there in the entrance hall. Or, he would simply try his very best to get a few swings in before Destro separated the two of them.

Francis was deeply surprised to see that Vallis did none of these.

"I'm sorry," Vallis apologized, looking timidly toward the ground. "You're absolutely right. These people are looking to us for answers. For help. My apologies. I lost myself there."

Destro's eyebrows could have lifted stone as they climbed his forehead, a look that Francis himself no doubt mirrored.

Gorman seemed satisfied with the apology. He gave Vallis's shoulder a tight squeeze. "It's a strange time, and a stressful one, at that. You're doing fine. Just keep focused, calm, and collected."

Vallis scratched the side of his head. His sleeve was unbuttoned, falling away to reveal a tattoo of a swirling sun on his wrist. "Father," he said to Francis, "I have the city guard patrolling the streets in search of these mysterious masked men. Attacks have been reported across the entire city."

"Reports of shops and inns being put to the torch and pedestrians being attacked on sight," Destro added.

Francis made sure to look worried. "By the gods, what do these bandits want?"

"That's the thing, Father; they don't seem to want anything. They just want to kill. To burn everything down."

"That's preposterous," Francis complained. "That makes no sense. There has to be a meaning to all this, why they're doing this. Why else would they?"

Vallis made a move to shrug. "Fear? We've yet to have a list of demands from anyone. It's as if they've up and vanished."

"And with the advantage of being masked in the first place," Destro added, "it'll be easy for them to get lost in the crowd."

"Of course," Vallis concluded.

"These can't just be bandits," Gorman added. "They've targeted the hospitals and taverns. They picked the most crowded places in the city. It may look like a random attack, but there's deep planning behind this. There's something we don't know yet."

How very observant of you, General. If only we could have been on the same side. What a wonder we could have accomplished together.

"You said that some inns were put to the torch?" Francis asked. "Do we know which ones?"

"So far, only two," Vallis answered. " The Twin-Blade, which is in midtown. That, and"—Vallis looked to Francis, sadness in his eyes and tone—"The Great-Hammer."

Silence fell upon the group. It was no secret that Francis was the son of the famous Great-Hammer Balorian, but it was a secret that his relationship with his father was nothing short from a few drinks and more than his fair share of drunken nights, which usually resulted in a beating. Francis was glad the inn had burned to the ground.

Any remnants of that man can perish along with it, memories included.

"What about survivors?" Gorman asked. "Do we know if anyone was inside The Great-Hammer?"

Vallis shook his head solemnly. "I just know it's burning as we speak. That's about it, unfortunately."

Francis looked away, trying his hardest to catch a tear in his eyes. "All of this for fear?"

Destro scoffed. "Poisoning over two hundred people and starting a coordinated attack in the heart of the city will do that."

"Those weren't the only ones who suffered poisoning this night," Francis said quietly.

Gorman burrowed his eyebrows. "What do you mean?"

Francis shifted the weight of the chest that he carried, the contents shifting about inside. He leaned in closer to the three of them, being very aware of how quietly he spoke, "The poison reached the king. I was there when it happened. Thankfully, we were able to catch the doctor in time, and he's being tended to right now."

Gorman's shoulders sank. "Oh fuck," he sighed.

"Have faith, General," Francis reassured. "The gods are watching over us. Now, I realize that you are all very busy, but it's imperative we speak. I'm rescheduling our meeting. Delegate what needs to be done then meet me in the council chamber tomorrow. We have a very important matter to discuss that cannot wait."

"You got it, Father." Destro nodded to Vallis and Gorman before walking away, calling another soldier to him from across the hall.

Gorman nodded gently before slapping Vallis on the arm as he passed. "You got this, General Vallis." And just like that, he was off to his duties.

Crazy how utter chaos binds friendships in those who were sworn enemies the day before.

"Do you need help with that, Father?" Vallis nodded toward the chest that Francis carried.

Francis shook his head. "Nonsense. We all have a job to do. Do you remember yours?"

Vallis nodded. "Yes."

"Then go about your duties and meet me in the council chamber. Remember not to be late."

Francis turned away from the doors then made his way down the hallway. He passed guards stationed along the hall, each of whom nodded to him as he passed. It was like that as he made his way to the council chamber.

When he was out of sight from the guards, Francis donned a wide smile. Not because he was happy to see the city working together in a crisis, not because he was putting on an image to help comfort those in dire need, but because he could feel the power vibrating throughout his body, and he was genuinely excited with what he was going to do with it.

Grains of Sand

The brisk air nipped at Sarah's arms like a starved animal as she followed Benny's lead through Servitol. They hunkered in the shadows, hid themselves behind crates of food or around alley corners, anything that would hide their presence from the men in masks.

The sun was setting fast, the sound of chaos fading away with the daylight. Servitol was a ghost of its former self. Before, a radiant garden full of life and color; now, nothing better than a vacant farm of rotten crops. There wasn't a soul in sight, a whisper to be heard. It was as if all the citizens had upped and vanished. The city was an empty shell, and Sarah was a mere grain of sand trapped inside.

Or they're all dead, and you're walking through a graveyard; your tombstone waiting for you just around the corner.

It wasn't a far walk to the lower city, but with current events, and Alric slowing Dodge down, it took longer than Sarah would have liked.

The farther they got from the inn, the more paranoid she became. Every time they crossed a street, took a corner, or hide themselves out of sight, Sarah expected the bandits to spot them.

She quaked with anxiety, treading the city streets like shark-infested waters. Every shadow was a man in a mask, every sound was an alarm of where they were. However, they were either very sneaky or very lucky because, between the time of their encounter with the man in the red mask and actually arriving to the lower city, their experience was as eventful as a stroll through an empty museum.

Sarah heard of slums before, low-income districts within the borders of a city, but to say that the lower district was a slum would be an understatement. The village itself appeared to be on the brink of collapse. Houses leaned at awkward angles, nothing but rotting wood standing between its life and utter collapse. Dirt and gravel replaced the grass. Creaking, rotting wood replaced the polished stone. The windows were glassless, some doors hung open on its hinges.

The only building that looked fully intact was one they had passed near the center of town, but even that looked to be vacant. It was a three-story building, only its gray environment fabricating an image of impressive architecture. A large green door stood center of two large stone pillars. The entirety of the house was surrounded by a gate.

"Where is everyone?" Dodge asked, pulling the very question from Sarah's mind.

Benny kept his pace, actively looking from house to house, from street to street as he led them through the maze of Servitol. "Not much happens in the lower-city. The king made it specifically for low-income housing, but it eventually just turned into a place for the homeless and an office for crime lords. The homeless usually keep to themselves, whereas the slum lords pay off the guard to turn the cheek while they conduct business."

Dodge growled, "You sound like you have experience here."

Benny sighed. "I do hope there is a day in your future where you can trust us. It's not as if we helped you in Robins-Port, helped you get here, gave you a warm fire and fed you hot food, and are, again, helping you escape a terrible situation with your lives. Is this how you always repay those who show you kindness?"

It wasn't spoken in anger, but the message was plain to hear. Benny was right. The brotherhood had done nothing but help them since that horrific day in Robins-Port, yet Dodge repaid them in nothing but anger and distrust.

If it hadn't been for the brotherhood, Sarah most likely would had been buried in an unmarked grave, dirt filling up her mouth as her corpse rotted in a tunnel below a bloodstained city where nobody would find her.

She shivered at the thought of that image, whispers of that night coming back to her like always.

Don't struggle now. '
here you go.
Here, little piggy.

"Thank you." Sarah looked away from her feet toward Benny, who now stopped and turned around to look at her. They were now standing near a giant wall, large bushes planted like a garden next to house with a slanted roof.

Benny scratched the side of his head with a gloved hand. "You're very welcome, my dear." He came over to her and, for a split-second, a surge of fear jolted through Sarah's body as he reached behind his back. "Here. I'd like to give you something."

Sarah wasn't sure what to expect, yet the image of a dagger did cross her mind. However, what Benny held before her was something Sarah didn't expect at all—a pair of gloves.

"I want you to have these." Benny handed them out to her, which she slowly took, treading carefully as if the gloves themselves would come alive and lunge at her like a pair of snakes. "They belonged to my sister. They are the last thing I actually have of her. Go ahead; try them on."

Sarah pulled on one of the gloves, her hand slipping into a soft interior while the dark blue shone like polished leather. It was a slim fit, reaching halfway up her forearm. She wiggled her fingers. A perfect fit to her small hands. It reminded her of something her mother might wear, and the thought spread a smile across her face.

Benny leaned closer to her, keeping his next words between the two of them. "They help with the touch." He pulled off his own glove and held out his bare hand to Sarah.

She stared at it in worry as she inched her own gloved hand toward his.

"Don't worry," he reassured her. "Trust me."

She reached out and roughly grabbed his hand, but nothing happened. She sank in relief, and Benny smiled warmly at her. She remembered what happened the last time she had touched him, of the memories shifting like vague clouds in her mind, a bystander to her own memories. But to Sarah's relief, that didn't happen.

"A trick of the trade, my dear." Benny winked at her and stood back up. "And there are many more."

"How much farther?" Sarah could hear the concern in Dodge's voice as she slipped on the other glove, flexing her fingers with satisfaction.

Benny waved an arm toward the wall before them. "We're here. There's a gap in the wall behind the bushes. From there, we'll—"

"No!" Dodge set Alric down against the wall of the house, being conscious of the arrow still sticking out of his body. His fist curled with rage. "You said they would be here." He took a dangerous step toward Benny. "We had a deal."

"And nothing has changed," Benny retorted, irritation clear in his voice. "I said that, if they were still in the city, they would have come this way. If they did, they wouldn't waste time sticking around. There's a cottage outside of the city about ten miles off, hidden in the woods that nobody knows about. That's our rally point."

Dodge clearly wasn't happy with the answer; the bulging veins in his neck and forehead were proof enough. He looked around where they stood, shaking his head as his face purpled with anger. They had come to Servitol in the trust of the brotherhood to find justice for what had happened in Robins-Port, but the only thing they'd found was a spitting image of what they'd escaped from.

It's as if we're being followed by death, like he's close at our heels, stalking us like the shadow of death he is.

After a minute of raging silence, Dodge turned back toward Benny. "You swear that's where they're going?"

Benny didn't blink as he gave a solitary nod. "I give you my word."

Dodge looked to Sarah and, for a moment, they just stared at one another. She could tell he didn't want to make this decision alone, not sure what he should feel about their companions, but Sara couldn't help feeling it was the right decision.

She nodded at Dodge.

"All right," Dodge said, looking at Benny with pleading eyes. "I'm trusting you. Please"—Dodge's voice began to shake—"don't let me down. I *need* to find Trevor."

Benny matched his stare. "The house is the only spot they'd go if they escaped. If they aren't there, I promise you, I'll help you find him."

Dodge exasperated a deep sigh, his shoulders hunched in defeat. He nodded without saying another word.

Benny looked down to Alric, who was surprisingly still conscious. The bleeding seemed to have stopped, crusting his dark tunic with a crimson red. "There's one more thing we have to do," he said, not taking his eyes away from Alric. "And I'll need your help."

"What's that?" Dodge asked.

Benny nodded toward the thicket of bushes lining the wall. "It's a thin opening, so it'll be a tight fit. We'll have to squeeze through."

"Oh?" Realization dawned on Dodge's face as he looked at Alric. "Oh."

"We can't pull it through, or we risk tearing more muscles." Benny went over and knelt next to Alric, whose face was pale, eyes fluttering to stay open. "We'll have to snap it off."

For an odd reason that Sarah didn't understand, Alric smiled, blood glistening on his pearly teeth. "*You'll* have to snap it off."

Dodge positioned himself behind Alric and inspected the bolt. "Cross bolts aren't easy to break."

"And we don't have our supplies here," Benny added, never taking his eyes from Alric. "We'll have to make do with something else to staunch the bleeding."

"Here." Dodge tugged on his shirt, tearing the sleeve off in a mighty pull. "It's dirty, but it should do until we can get our hands on some supplies."

Benny smirked at Alric. "Better than nothing, eh?"

"Better than nothing," Alric mumbled. Then, with what little strength he could muster, Alric twisted his body to face Benny, leaning forward with a wince of pain. "Let's get this over with."

With a nod from Dodge, Benny grabbed the front of the shaft, dark blood squeezing through his grip. Alric groaned to himself.

Benny took a couple of deep breaths. "Try not to pass out."

"Please," Alric replied with a smirk. "Doesn't even hurt. You won't even get a scream out—"

Snap!

Alric did scream … and then he passed out.

The Loss of Innocence

Trevor wiped his brow, the brisk air failing to prevent his perspiration from soaking his clothes, sticking against his arms and thighs as he, Evan, Tom, and Warren continued to sprint down the vacant streets.

At first, Trevor let his adrenaline fuel him, his running a simple jog as he watched out for more of the men in masks. However, as they made their way farther and farther into the city, sneaking down alleys and through empty shops, sticking to the shadows like a cat on the prowl, they didn't come upon any more of the men in masks. It was as if they were gone as fast as they had appeared, leaving nothing but devastation behind in their brief existence.

Trevor and the others had only witnessed a minimal amount of the real damage that was dealt to Servitol. They were right; what had happened back at the Twin-Blade was only a minimal amount of damage the city had taken. The deeper they got into the city, the worse things appeared.

Wagons glowed like beacons in the night as they were consumed by flames, blood pooling the ground reflecting in the firelight, the streets nothing more than a recent graveyard as bodies were scattered about. The worst part, however, was the silence. It was as if the entire city was dead.

His worries grew when they turned down the street where The Great-Hammer inn was, and his heart sank when Evan told him it was the large building in the center, the one that was currently on fire. They could see signs of a battle near the entrance, but the flames were too hot for them to get any closer to check.

"If they made it out," Evan said, turning around and backtracking down the street, "they would have gone to the wall. Let's hurry before—"

"You!"

Trevor looked to his left, down the street where he came from, and saw four people running toward them. By the way the firelight shone off their bodies, Trevor could tell they were wearing armor. "Don't move! Stay where you are!"

"Guards," Evan cursed. "Best hurry now. Go!"

"Why?" Warren scrunched his face, confused as to what they were doing. "If they're guards, they can help us. Why would we run?"

Trevor looked back toward the guards. They were close enough where he could hear the clinking of their armor, but what raised the hairs on his arms was the fact that it seemed they were more running *at* them rather than *to* them.

"That doesn't look good," Tom declared, all of them but Warren fully understanding what was happening.

"We're nothing but bandits to them," Evan said. "They aren't looking for survivors; they're looking for the culprits."

Warren began to shift uncomfortably, his eyes remaining focused on the guards rushing them. "But—"

"But nothing! You want to live? Then that means you saddle the fuck up and follow me. If you want to die, then, well, just keep standing there, making that face." And without another word, Evan was off.

Trevor didn't wait to see if the others followed, but he felt better when he glanced over his shoulder to see them close behind. Well, he was happy to see Tom. Trevor secretly wished Warren would either fall behind or stay and wait for the guards. They would either help him or not. Either way, he didn't care.

It wasn't hard to lose the guards, and Trevor figured it made sense considering it was a lot harder to run in a full set of armor. That, and Evan seemed to know every nook and cranny of the city, leading them down short alleys, only to cut across the street.

They leapt over a set of barrels and into another alley. Trevor felt like a cat on the run.

They turned a corner down the next street, quickly dipped into a small alley, and pushed through an open door. They found themselves in a shop. But, like the city itself, nobody was around.

Just as Evan was about to leave through the front door, he suddenly stopped.

Trevor was about to ask what the matter was when Evan held up his hand for silence. Then Trevor heard it—a muffled whimper coming from behind a closed door to their right. Then there was the sound of scuffles followed by a loud thud.

Evan slowly crept toward the door and placed his ear against the wood.

Trevor watched as the observant look on Evan's face turned into a look of pure, malicious rage. He took a step away, brought his leg up, and kicked at the door, shattering it off its hinges.

"What the—"

A man flew through the doorway, sliding another couple feet across the floorboards of the shop in front of Trevor, Tom, and Warren. He was wearing armor; a bright, golden sun emblazoned on the center of his chest. He was sweating profusely, stammering over his heavy breathing as he desperately tried to situate his dropped trousers back around his waist.

Sounds of scuffling came from the open doorway where Evan had rushed into.

The guard, who managed to fix himself, was beginning to crawl to his feet, confusion replaced with a scowl of rage. He reached for a dagger that was lodged in his boot as he stood, but Tom rushed forward and punched the guard in the face, sending him back to the ground.

Warren cowered against the wall behind a bookshelf, peeping around the corner at what was happening. Trevor, shaking himself from a daze, walked toward the open doorway as Tom sat himself on top of the fallen guard, sending a hammer fist into his face one last time, knocking him unconscious.

Just as Trevor was peering around the edge of the doorframe, another body took flight through the air, landing not far from where the first guard had fallen. Only, this time, this guard was bleeding from what seemed to be a dozen different wounds.

The guard ignored Trevor, crawling on his back away from Evan, who now stood mightily in the doorway, his fist clenched and a bloody dagger in his hand.

Behind Evan, Trevor could now see a woman huddling in the corner of the adjacent room, her arms wrapped around a bundle of rags. Her dress hung torn from one shoulder strap, and her arms and face had dark, purple bruises. She rocked back and forth, shushing the faint whimpers of the infant wrapped in the clothes that she cradled. She stared at Trevor, wide-eyed with terror.

"We weren't doin' nothin," the second guard was saying as he managed to back himself into a wall.

Evan replied with a grimace as he slowly walked toward the guard, the curl at his lips promising certain pain.

"Honest, we were helping her—"

"By raping her?" Evan said, tilting his head to the side. "Strange way to help a woman, especially coming from the city patrol who've sworn their lives to protect people such as her."

The guard, who saw no chance in reasoning with Evan, converted his tactic to threats. "If you're smart, you'd turn the other way. You don't want to get on the wrong side of the sun guard. An act against us is an act against the king him—"

Evan threw the knife without warning, burying the blade up to the hilt into the guard's forehead, which bounced back against the wooden wall of the shop then hung limply as his body sagged.

Evan's heavy boots boomed on the floorboards as he walked to the guard's body and ripped the blade free. Then he wiped the blood off on the guard's pants and tucked the blade away into a pocket behind his waist.

Evan entered the adjacent room where the woman was still huddled in the corner, her baby now openly crying in her arms. Without warning, he took a knee in front of her and reached for her hand, but she pulled away in fright.

"You don't have to fear me," Evan told her plainly. He nodded over his shoulder toward the two guards; one dead, the other unconscious. "They're the enemy, not us. What's your name?"

The woman looked worriedly from Evan to Trevor then toward the two guards. "Merrian," she answered. "This is little Jezel. We found the guards when the fighting started, and they said they would protect us, but when we got in here, they closed the door and started for us. They told us things … things they wanted to do to us, things they were *going* to do to us." Merrian began to weep, shaking her head back and forth.

Evan reached out and put a comforting hand on her shoulder. "I know. Merrian, do you live nearby?"

After a moment, she nodded.

"Good. Now, when we leave, we're going to shut that door, and you're not going to open it until tomorrow." Evan reached into a pocket and pulled out a handful of coins. He reached once more for Merrian's hand, and when she let him take it, he dropped the coins into her palm. "Wait out the night, and when morning comes, rush home until everything calms down. Don't go to anyone unless you're within a group. Do you understand?"

Merrian looked at Evan, tears falling from her eyes as she nodded.

Evan left Merrian where she sat, closing the door behind him as he left without a farewell.

"What do we do with this one?" Tom asked, still sitting astride the unconscious guard.

Evan looked puzzled. "Is he still alive?"

"Yeah," Tom answered.

"Why?" Evan asked plainly.

Tom shook his head. "I try not to murder unconscious soldiers of the empire."

"Even when they're rapists and murderers themselves?"

Tom didn't seem offended, nor did he seem worried when he gave Evan a shrug.

"Fine," Evan said. "Looks like this task needs someone with a little less heart. Take the others, and I'll meet you outside."

Tom considered for a moment, then ultimately decided it wasn't his problem. He left the unconscious guard sprawled on the floor as he made for the exit, waving to Warren and Trevor to follow. Evan, however, stood over the guard.

Just as Trevor was moving past Evan, he asked, "What will you do?"

Evan gave a look that surprised Trevor. It almost seemed as if he was ashamed of his answer. "As much as it sickens me, I'm going to turn these degenerates into heroes. I'm going to make it look like they died protecting the woman and her baby." Evan nodded over his shoulder toward the closed door where Merrian waited. "For her sake. Now go wait outside." Evan grabbed the sleeping soldier by the collar, pulling him up to a sitting position. "This won't be pretty."

***

Another ten minutes of fast running and hard breathing, Trevor was back in the East-End, back to where he and Evan had smuggled the native slaves.

As they paced through the streets, Trevor kept a lookout to see if he could spot any of the children who had been there before. Like the other districts, it was a ghost town. He was, however, relieved to discover that the violence didn't seem to have reached this part of Servitol.

A scream roared through the night, distant enough to echo but close enough to be of concern.

Evan crouched low, Trevor and Tom following his lead. Keeping at a slow pace, they continued down the street, keeping an eye out for any threats of the men in masks.

They passed the large house on their right where they had met Marquis earlier. No guard stood by the front door. It was as empty as everything else.

Another scream pierced the night, louder and more pain-filled.

As Evan led them around the final turn before they made it to the wall, Trevor saw three men hovering over a third that laid sprawled across the ground. To his relief, he also saw a slender blonde girl standing close by.

Trevor sprinted their way once he recognized who they were, disregarding the protests of his aching muscles.

"Sarah!" Trevor stopped before her, concerned about what he was seeing.

She'd, no doubt, seen her fair share of trouble. Her face was sprayed with droplets of blood, and dark stains splattered her shirt. She rubbed at the sides of her arms, her hands now covered in a pair of dark gloves.

He wanted to ask if she was all right, but given her current appearance, it seemed stupid to ask. He also wanted to go to her, to try to comfort her somehow, to show her that he cared, but he couldn't bring himself to do so.

He'd spent the last hour racing to find her, but now that he had, he wasn't sure what to do with himself. He was just glad she was okay.

"He fainted," Benny announced.

When Trevor looked away from Sarah's distant eyes, he watched as Dodge and Benny struggled to position Alric's unconscious body to a sitting position. Blood covered Alric's chest, leaking from a wide hole just below his shoulder.

"Hold him there. Now grab that and stuff it in the wound; we need to staunch the bleeding quickly. Evan, get ready to—"

"On it." Evan twisted the shaft of his halberd, disconnecting the two pieces before tying off both ends at the sides of his hips. Then he leaned down and grabbed Alric's shoulders from the front, his head rolling to the side, pale as the moonlight that cast over them.

When he was situated, Evan ripped Alric's tunic open, revealing pale skin and a dark wound where blood continued to flow. The sight made Trevor queasy.

All three men worked quietly together, shifting Alric's body back and forth, leaning him forward then back as they began working on his wound. None of them spoke, but they coordinated their positions and worked together.

"Crossbow?" Evan asked, followed by a sigh when Benny nodded.

Benny continued to stuff a dirty rag into the open wound with the tip of his finger. "That'll have to do," he declared, leaning back with his hands on his knees. "I'll get his feet. Think you can manage his upper body?"

"I can manage just fine," Dodge replied.

Dodge looked to Trevor. His face was masked in the shadows of the night, but Trevor could see a gleam of worry in his eyes. They didn't speak; just stared silently at one another. Then Dodge nodded his way, a gesture that meant more than words, and Trevor replied with a nod of his own.

"We should leave him."

All faces turned toward Warren, who stood with his arms across his chest, either cold or shaking with fear. Trevor assumed the latter.

Evan stood up straight and faced Warren, a challenge in his posture that screamed danger. "And why would we do that?"

Warren's face twisted, as if what Evan had asked was complete nonsense. "Because he'll hold us back from escaping. Look"—he gestured toward Alric, sprawled out in Dodge's arms—"he's probably dead already."

As if nature itself wanted to spit in Warren's face, Alric twisted his head slowly, groaning as his eyes began to flutter open.

Warren curled his lips. "We'd still have to carry him, and that'll take too long."

"Oh yeah?" Evan took a deadly step forward.

Warren, suddenly aware of the possible danger he was in, took an involuntary step away.

"Why don't I just kick your knee in? Then we'll see if it's a good idea to carry you, too."

Tom positioned himself between Warren and Evan. "There's no time for that."

"I can agree there." Evan made an effort to peer around Tom's large shoulders, sure to make eye contact with Warren. "There certainly is no time for *that*."

Dodge set Alric aside and stood. Trevor shifted uncomfortably as he spotted the two daggers in Dodge's fists.

If it came to a fight right there, how would he react? If he sided with Evan, he would be betraying the very people who had risked their own lives to save his. On the other hand, if he sided with Dodge and Tom, he would be defending the very person in the entire world who had spent every free moment of his life making sure Trevor's was in absolute ruin. He would be defending the only person in the world that he could honestly say he truly hated.

His thoughts went back to that night in Robins-Port when he and Sarah were ambushed by Warren and his goon-squad at the broken wall. *"You're the sheep, I'm the fucking wolf."*

Not much more than a sheep now, Trevor thought, deciding in that moment that, if it came down to it, he would not interfere at all. He would much rather that Tom and Dodge let Evan gut Warren there and now, rid the world of another plague.

"You see?" Warren, still cowering behind Tom's back, leaned around and yelled to Evan. "Everyone thinks—"

Given the size of the man, Trevor couldn't believe how fast Tom was as he whipped around and snapped at Warren, "Will you just shut the fuck up before I let this man throttle you? For your own good, keep that trap shut!"

With confidence fleeting like a quick breeze, Warren stepped back even farther, his arms crossed and cowering, reminding Trevor more of a lost pup than a wolf.

"We're not leaving anyone behind," Tom said, looking at Evan, who smiled back at him. "Right?"

Evan held up his hands in defense. "Right you are, old man."

As the tension faded, Dodge crouched down and hooked his hands under Alric's arms. "No point in waiting around," he said as he lifted Alric to his feet. "Let's get going."

The Casualties of Betrayal

Alric's head swam, a hot prickle on his face as the world swirled before him in waves of color. If being raised during a war promised you anything, it was a fair share of wounds and more than a few scars to tell a story. But, out of all the wounds he shared—well, besides the ones he kept hidden beneath his gloves—he absolutely fucking hated being shot.

First, you felt the impact, which wasn't short from being punched very, *very* hard. Following that, the warm spread of numbness crawling away from the wound, inching out slowly and spreading its warmth to your body. Lastly came the fatigue, the slow and aching feeling of your muscles as you began to tire. So, in a sense, being shot wasn't necessarily painful.

It was surviving how you fix it.

The method used to remove an arrow all depended on the state of the wound. If you were unlucky enough, which Alric had seen once or twice during the war, the arrow would remain lodged in your body. Not fully pushed through, but buried in your muscle and bone. This, Alric came to the conclusion long ago, was the worst state to be in when shot.

To pull back the arrow would be more devastating than leaving it in there. The angles of the broadhead would grip the meat, tearing the muscle as you pulled, causing much more damage than the original wound itself. If it happened to be stuck in a muscle, you would most likely do permanent nerve damage. If you happened to take an arrow in the stomach region, you would most likely tear your inner organs, catch an infection, suffer internal bleeding, and die a very, very slow, agonizing death.

However, you couldn't just snap the shaft and leave the arrow lodged in, so the only options were to either dig and cut away small amounts of tissue as you tried to pull the arrow free, or you had to push it all the way through and make an exit wound. This way, you could snap the arrow and remove both ends with, well, relative ease.

Fortunately for Alric, given his current circumstances, the arrow had pushed through his shoulder entirely, the tip of the bolt sticking out front, and the fletching out of his back.

Walking had been hard, given his fatigue, but the arrow didn't necessarily hurt as long as it was left alone. However, life couldn't just continue on with an arrow lodged in your shoulder, no matter how hard Alric wanted to just pretend it wasn't there.

He knew it would be rough. You needed a strong pair of hands to snap a cross bolt in half, given how thick and durable the wood typically was, but Dodge's hands were the size of mountains, more than capable for the task. The last thing he remembered was the feeling of sharp needles prickling in his shoulder, then he heard the snap of the bolt. It was soon after that he passed out.

When he came to, he was staring up at the stars while two dark silhouettes looked down on him. There was no numbness in his body, no warm spread through his shoulder; only the hot burning pain racking his body.

He reached out to steady himself, catching someone's arm from behind him. When he realized it was Dodge, he nodded his thanks and began to step away. He struggled against the urge to vomit, but with a few more steps, he was able to catch his balance.

Trevor was there, along with Sarah, Evan, Tom, and Warren. Alric didn't have to ask to know there was tension in the air. Evan was squared off against Tom, his hands slightly hovering close by the pommels of his halberd that hung at his sides.

"Can you walk?" Benny asked Alric, worry creeping into his voice. "Maybe we should—"

"Nah." Alric worked his way to the bushes where the gap in the wall lay hidden. "I think we've warmed out our welcome."

He pushed past the brush, nearly tripping on a rogue twig and falling to the ground, but he managed to make it to the gap. Without looking back, he then twisted his body, wincing at the pain and fighting against the cloud that now began to fog his mind, and squeezed through. He made sure to move slowly, careful not to let his hasty bandages tear against the concrete, as he stepped beyond the city walls.

A chill, refreshing breeze greeted Alric outside the city. He looked upon the open country before him, gazing at the vast miles of open land as the others crawled through the hole behind him.

The first to emerge was Benny, who came to stand next to Alric as Dodge followed in his stead. Next was Evan, followed by Trevor and Sarah, her golden hair all but glowing in the moonlight. Then was Tom, followed lastly by Warren.

With everyone outside of the city, they began to leave Servitol behind them, when a voice hollered out, "Halt!"

They turned to see four figures running toward them, the sound of armor clanking in the night, the steel of their metal catching the light of the moon.

"Don't move," one said as they surrounded them, drawing their blades.

There's nothing that gets the nerves going quite like the sound of steel being drawn.

"Hands up," the one who seemed to be in charge ordered.

The only protest came from Evan, who cursed quietly under his breath.

They raised their hands and did as they were commanded.

"Gunther, run back and give a message to L.T.; tell them we have some stragglers on the eastern wall."

One of the guards, Gunther, gave a tight salute. "Aye, sir," he said before taking off at a sprint.

"Look, guys." Benny pushed his way to the front of the crowd, his hands still out to show he meant no harm. "We're just trying to escape the mess in there. We've been attacked, too. We just want to be off and on our way."

The guard kept his eyes focused on Benny as he pleaded their innocence. He was a tall figure, with broad shoulders and an intimidating aura radiating from his body.

"Is he gone?" he asked, and it took a moment for Alric to realize he was talking to the other guards.

One of the guards peered over his shoulder. "He's out of sight. He's a slow lad, but the lieutenant ain't."

"What do we do, sir?" the third guard asked.

"Strip them of their weapons," the man ordered immediately.

Evan stepped out of the crowd. "And why would we do that?" he asked, a slight challenge in his voice.

"Evan." There was a warning in Benny's tone. "Now is not the best time to pick a fight. We can talk this through, isn't that right, Sergeant?"

Something's off, Alric thought. *Standard procedure during an attack is to rescue civilians, not treat possible innocents as hostile.*

The only time a soldier was ordered to proceed upon suspects as hostile was during a siege, and this was no siege. The city should—*would* have ordered the guards to search for survivors and guide them to safety.

"Can't you see it, Benny?" Evan was slowly moving his hands toward his hips, both handles of his halberd mere inches away. "You don't want to help us, do you, *Sergeant*?"

The soldier said nothing, but his smile sent a chill down Alric's spine, a chill that usually walked hand-in-hand with violence.

"What do we do, sir?" the third guard asked again.

The leader looked them over, sizing them up like cattle for the slaughter. After a moment, he fixed Alric with a vile grin, menace glistening in his eyes. "Can't you see, Private? These men are attacking us."

Alric's heart sank.

"Besides"—the guard tensed his shoulders, and by that time, Alric knew it was too late—"we're to leave no survivors."

Fighting in the dark is never an easy task, especially with a hole the size of a small branch punctured through your body that throbbed with each movement. There were, however, advantages. For one, it was difficult for your opponent to spot weaknesses in your form.

In a normal duel, a wrong twist in your body could lead to a poor follow-up, leaving your attack easily parried, which would leave your vitals open. However, petty mistakes that could cost you your life were more forgiving in the dark since they were harder to identify.

There was, though, the state of the obvious when fighting in the dark—it was hard to see. It was just as difficult to spot a weakness in your opponent's form. Also, it was harder to track their eyes. The most efficient tactic of a swordsman when dueling was to read your opponent without letting it show in your eyes. In the past, Alric had been able to walk away from most of his battles due to the fact that his adversary had a nasty habit of paying more attention to where he wanted to put his blade rather than where Alric was about to put his. It was a nasty habit that usually left most with a nasty wound.

Fighting in the dark was definitely tricky business. For most people, at least. For Alric, fighting in the dark had never been a problem. It was one of the many secrets that only a few people knew about him, and one of the few fitting reasons behind his title when he'd been in the army. Because, when the blanket of night arrived and hid the world from most, Alric could still strut through a forest and leave without as much as a scratch on his arms.

Alric could see the blade coming from the first soldier. He didn't have anything to defend himself, nor could he manage to lift his arms much higher even if he tried, so Alric began to duck out of the way, but he knew he wasn't fast enough.

Just before the blow was connected, sparks crackled in the night as somebody stepped in front of Alric, two daggers crisscrossed with the incoming blade stuck between them.

Dodge grunted at the weight of the blow. "Get in the back," he ordered Alric as he shoved the guard away.

Alric was stepping away when he could hear the whirl of Evan's halberd whipping through the air, the low tone of its momentum building as he spun it about and shot forward against the second guard who was leaping toward Benny.

The wicked blade missed by inches, burying into the dirt with a heavy *thunk*. Benny leaped into the soldier's guard, reached out, and grabbed ahold of his wrist, pinning his sword arm in the air as he began pushing forward, driving his assailant back and away. It was a tough struggle, given the wound that still bled at his side, but Benny managed to wrap his leg behind the soldier as he pushed. As the guard tripped and fell backward, he managed a firm grip and dragged Benny with him.

Dodge was locked in a melee with the leader, his daggers jabbing quickly from every direction. Despite the armor sapping his strength, the captain managed to slip by Dodge's attacks with ease, ducking low and to the side as Dodge's blades sliced nothing but air.

Tom was currently swinging back his battle-axe toward the third and final guard, a death roar bellowing from his deep lungs. The guard sidestepped from the incoming blow as the axe buried itself in the dirt. Then the guard reached out with a metal fist and struck Tom in the face. Alric could hear the connection of the blow and was more than sure it resulted in a few shattered teeth and a broken nose.

Tom staggered away, being sure to drag his axe with him while the guard pressed the advantage, pulling his arms back and beginning a heavy, wide swing toward Tom's gut.

Trevor was there in a flash, swinging his sword up and knocking the blade wide as Tom gathered himself.

The guard rocked back on his feet as Trevor rushed, using his shoulder to add to the guard's weight and throwing him onto his back. Trevor then hacked down quickly, but the guard managed to roll away just in time.

Springing to his feet, the soldier fixed his stance and squared off against

Trevor. For a moment, they simply looked at one another, bathing in the calm before the inevitable storm.

Then the soldier rushed. His sword point jabbed toward Trevor's chest, but Trevor managed to get his blade up in time to deflect and counter the attack. Trevor fought with ferocity, and his form was near perfect. He'd clearly had some type of training before.

But he fights against a Navalethian soldier, and one who has seen his fair share of battles.

Sparks shattered in the night, the sound of clashing steel a solemn melody for any warrior.

Trevor was on the defensive now, stepping back cautiously as the soldier pressed his attack, but Trevor held strong.

The soldier swung low, but Trevor managed to pivot the point of his sword down, forbidding the blade to take off his ankle. With Trevor's flank open, the guard saw his opportunity and took it, and for a moment, Alric was sure the boy was done for. However, the guard swung, only to be rejected once more as Trevor managed to twist his body, putting his full stance into his guard, sending the attacking blade bouncing back toward its owner as he followed up with another counter.

Alric couldn't help admiring Trevor's skill. His moves were as graceful as the calm waves of an ocean, constant with persistence, but patiently devastating. Not only had he managed to draw in his opponent's attack, exhausting himself in the effort, but now Trevor was on the offense.

Tom, who had finally managed to gather himself, fixed his axe in his hands and flanked the soldiers locked in a melee with Trevor. Without looking about, the soldier began leading Trevor on, pulling in his attacks as he began circling around, keeping Tom and Trevor near shoulder to shoulder.

Some would say it was certain death to fight off two attackers, but, like everything else in the world of combat, there were as many advantages with the defendant as there were with the attacker. Sure, keeping track of two people fighting against you was manic, but only if one was kept out of your line of sight. When fighting against two opponents, the best thing you could do was keep them close together. That way, they had to worry about hitting each other just as much as hitting their target. It was hard to swing a sword when you were cramped up next to your buddy. The soldier, being as skilled as he was, managed just that.

Trevor and Tom might have been a force to be reckoned with, but it wasn't easy swinging a blade, let alone a huge battle axe, at a dodging man while making sure you didn't butcher your comrade in the process. Their attacks slowed, focusing more on precision than strength, and the Navalethian soldier took advantage of that.

Just as Trevor swung wide toward the soldier's waist, Tom managed to poke out with the tip of his axe, hoping his assailant would try to parry Trevor's blow and leave himself open. What the soldier did, however, was twirl to his left and sweep around to Trevor's flank. Using his momentum, he rushed in and struck out at Trevor, the pommel of the blade smashing into his right knee.

Trevor went down with a yell.

The soldier kicked him back as he began to fall. Being so close together, Trevor crashed into Tom's side, and they both tumbled to the ground. The soldier then followed through with his final attack, but Trevor managed to get his up in a weak guard and deflected the blow. The soldier leapt back as Trevor waved his sword wildly, slowly crawling to his feet, favoring his right knee that now throbbed with pain.

Seeing the advantage, the soldier was about to leap in when he halted, turning his head to the side, his eyes fixating on a very, *very* close and frightened boy.

Warren might as well have been staring up at a dragon of legend, a wraith from hell itself. He began muttering to himself silently, and Alric could hear, even above the clatter of the battle—because his sense of hearing was yet another reason why he'd survived so long in his bloody life—that Warren was praying.

The guard looked from Warren to Trevor, measuring the distance between each other. Then the guard fixed his eyes back on Warren, and Alric felt his gut sink. Whether afraid of an attack or just taking advantage of the opportunity to spill blood, the soldier stepped toward Warren.

Alric began making his way across the small field of chaos. A sharp pain racked his body with each step as he wobbled slowly toward the guard, spittle flying with each wince and groan of agonizing pain.

The guard kicked out with a heavy boot, sending a defenseless Warren flying onto his back. In just a few moments, he would be no better than a skewered rabbit roasting over a fire.

There was movement from the side of Alric's vision, a giant blur of a man rushing forward.

"Roll, boy!" Tom roared as he rushed in. "Roll!"

Solid advice, but Warren was frozen with fear, a look that most men suffered when the promise of their certain death dawned on them.

Alric picked up his pace. Dodge and the leader of the guards were locked in a brutish melee, the white blur of steel whistling through the air as they ducked, parried, and countered each other's attacks. Benny was on the ground, wrestling with his attacker as Evan circled about, looking for an opening to poke the guard with the deadly end of his halberd.

To Alric's surprise, Warren tucked his knees toward his chest as the blade came at him, which was absolutely better than nothing, but his movement wasn't fast enough. A shriek of pain pierced the night as the blade passed through his calf.

"No!" Tom was only a few feet away now as the guard pulled his blade out to follow up with the final blow.

Trevor was still on the ground, nursing his knee with both hands as the chaos continued around him.

He scanned the battlefield and rested his eyes on Sarah, who stood by on the outskirts with her hands clasped in front of her chest, that familiar blank stare on her face.

Tom leapt forward just as the guard's blade was coming down toward Warren's face. The sword bounced off the metal, sending it wide from its mark.

Tom placed himself between Warren and the guard, but Alric could tell he was favoring his leg, dark blood spotting the bandage from the blacksmith's previous wound. And in that moment, Alric could tell the guard had noticed, too.

The guard swung to his left, his blade like a shooting star as it came down toward Tom's weak side. Tom planted his foot back to guard against the blow, but his leg began to buckle under the pressure. The guard swung again and again. From left to right, left to right. It was a simple method—drive your opponent to exhaust themselves by twisting their body back and forth—and Alric knew of numerous ways to counter it. But, with each passing blow, Tom's wounded leg buckled just a little bit more. It was only a matter of seconds before it gave completely, giving the swordsman the advantage.

Tom seemed to notice this as he leaned back suddenly, letting the blade's edge swing by. At the same time, he brought his axe swinging over his head. The amount of speed Tom had managed was impressive, and in any case, it was a fine killing blow. With his wound, though, he just wasn't fast enough.

The blade of his axe swooped down, the weight of a mountain crashing down with it. Alric felt the impact as the blade buried itself in the dirt. The guard, however, sidestepped the blow with ease, now at Tom's flank. He kicked out with his boot against the handle of the axe, and the wood splintered and cracked with a loud *snap*, leaving Tom with nothing but a broken stick as a weapon.

Trevor seemed to recognize the danger his friend was in and began to move forward, but he was twenty feet away, not nearly close enough to rush to Tom's defense in time.

"Dodge!" Tom roared, hopelessness clear in his voice as the guard continued to rain down blow after blow. Tom tried fending off the attacks with the pommel of his broken axe, but it was useless. "Stay strong for the little ones. They'll need your help. All of them."

The soldier stepped closer to Tom, his acidic smile filled with venom.

"No matter what happens," Tom continued, "you need to forgive yourself. I forgave you long ago, and so would she. You're the greatest man I've ever—"

The guard struck Tom in the face with a gauntlet fist, and that was when his wounded leg gave way, the blow sending Tom to his knees. Then the soldier jabbed forward with his sword, burying nearly half the blade in the gap between Tom's neck and shoulder.

Tom's body shuddered for a brief moment, blood pouring from his open mouth as he gurgled blood. Then the guard pulled free his blade, the wet sound of tearing flesh clear in the night, and Tom's body crumbled to the floor.

K.R. Gangi

No Mercy

Tom's body crumbled beneath itself as the soldier pulled his sword from his corpse. It almost didn't look real.

Trevor had witnessed death more in the last few weeks than in his entire life yet, when he started to realize that Tom, who Trevor had shared a laugh with not a few hours ago, wasn't going to get up from the ground, the cold grasp of despair gripped his heart, clenching in a wretched fist and sucking the air from his lungs.

Tom had always been kind to Trevor, had always been there in his time of need. In fact, some could say that Tom had raised Trevor just as much as Dodge. When Warren and his pack of goons had jumped him in an alley one night, it'd been Tom who had found him nearly beaten to a pulp. Others had just walked by, turning a blind eye as the orphan of Robins-Port rotted in the gutter. Not Tom, though. The instant he saw Trevor lying there, inches away from death, he had scooped him up in his burly arms and raced him off to a doctor.

Not a week from that day, Tom had visited Trevor in the hospice, a basket full of bread and a bowl full of porridge. He had talked as Trevor ate, telling him about what it meant to be a man.

"I had a friend growing up," Tom said. "You see, his mother had a nasty habit of drinking when she was pregnant. So Arnie, my young friend, was born with nerve damage and half his face was paralyzed. He may have looked different, but I saw past that awful monster that others claimed he was. Arnie was a sweet and gentle soul; wouldn't hurt a fly.

"One day, some folks were passing through town when they saw Arnie throwing rocks down at the pond. They called him names like cyclops, or sag face. You know, anything that would get under Arnie's skin. But Arnie never flinched, never raised a hand against these strangers who had intended him harm.

380

"The kids didn't like that, you see, and they decided that a beating would show Arnie who were his betters, and beat that boy to a pulp they did. They broke his nose, a few ribs, and bruised his face so badly it was swollen for what seemed like months.

"All was fine until a few months later when those very same folks rolled back into town. Arnie had spotted them from his window, and right there and then, something in the boy's mind just snapped.

"That night, Arnie grabbed a cutting knife from his kitchen. He waited in an alley for hours until those boys walked by. He killed them all.

"Thing is, Arnie had grown up being called a monster his entire life, but it wasn't until that night when he proved everyone right.

"Vengeance, Trevor, makes a monster out of us all. So, you sit here and heal, think on that, and remember it well. Let your wounds heal, but don't grow to be the very thing people fear you are. A man proves to those who doubt him that he's the very thing they believe he could never be."

Not a few days after he was released from the hospice, Trevor had begun his training with Dodge. Not to take vengeance on Warren, but to be the very thing the town could never expect him to be; a person with the power to become the monster they claimed he was, but deciding to be everything they claimed he wasn't—a decent person.

There were small moments with Tom that Trevor would never forget, like the time Dodge had too much liquor for his own good. He'd passed out on the kitchen table in his own drool, and Tom had come to help Trevor carry his uncle to his bedroom. Other times, Tom would just stop over the house when Dodge was running errands in town. He would sit with Trevor at the table and talk about anything and everything. Many times, though, Trevor would talk about Sarah, and Tom would, in return, console him through everything going on.

Tom had played a huge part in Trevor's life growing up as an orphan. He, along with Dodge and Sarah, had been a river that shaped him into the person he was today. Tom was a pillar that stood tall and mighty, a symbol of what Trevor strived to become. Now, as Trevor looked at Tom's corpse, that pillar was nothing more than broken rubble on the cold ground.

"Tom," Sarah whispered from behind Trevor, tears building in her eyes.

Warren managed to crawl away from the attack, coming right up to Trevor's feet. He looked up toward Trevor, his eyes wild with fear, rivers flowing from his eyes, spittle lining his lips.

Trevor tightened the grip on his sword. It would be so easy to end him right there and then.

Why shouldn't I? It's his fault Tom's dead. Gods know he deserves much worse.

Trevor tightened the grip on his sword, the point angled toward Warren's weeping face. Slowly, he raised the blade, moments from swiping it across Warren's neck, when the sound of laughter stopped him cold.

"You're a pathetic lot." The guard laughed, wiping the red from his blade onto his leggings while walking toward them. "Look at you, cowering like a lost pup. It's a shame these folks are about to die protecting—*Urgh*!"

An arm appeared from behind the soldier, wrapping around his neck while pulling him back. Trevor could see Alric from behind the man, arching his back and leaving the soldier's chest wide open.

Trevor pushed past Warren and rushed forward, but as he began moving, the soldier struck out at Alric's thigh with the pommel of his sword.

Alric grunted as the soldier shrugged him off.

Alric began staggering away, but the soldier was quick. In a flash, he turned and grabbed hold of Alric by his wounded shoulder. With a mighty roar, he lifted his sword and brought the bottom of his pommel down on Alric's face with a sickening *crunch*. Alric dropped to his knees, his arms sagging to his sides as a line of blood flowed steadily down his forehead.

The guard was pulling back his blade, a mighty swing with clear intention of separating his victim's head from his shoulders. Just as his charge reached its full length, however, Trevor brought his blade in the small gap in the soldier's armpit. The blade was precise, passing through the man's ribs and piercing his heart.

The guard dropped his sword and fell to the floor.

Alric was on his knees, his eyes rolling as blood began pouring down his pale face. He began to wobble, and Trevor reached with a steadying hand as Alric fell onto his side. He lay sprawled awkwardly on the ground, still and silent.

Dodge rolled underneath the passing blade of the captain, placing himself at his side, and lashed out with a quick jab to the man's ribs. If it weren't for the armor, the soldier would have been done there and then, but the blow simply bounced off as the soldier leapt back out of Dodge's reach.

Dodge was facing Trevor now, and as he squared his shoulders for another attack, his eyes quickly wandered over to wear Trevor stood, toward the large body of Tom not a few feet away.

Dodge's eyes creased in pain with the realization that his friend, quite possibly the only friend he had left, was now dead. Then, just as quickly as that despair materialized, it was replaced with pure rage, a fierce snarl on Dodge's lips as he roared at his opponent.

Dodge leapt forward, one of his blades jutting out from the side toward the captain's shoulder. It was easily deflected and parried with a counterattack, one that left a clear line of red across Dodge's left shoulder. If the soldier anticipated Dodge to waver, however, he was dead wrong. Ignoring the wound, Dodge pressed another attack.

The unexpected captain was oblivious to just how much rage fueled his adversary's strength It was only a brief moment of uncertainty, but it was enough for Dodge to throw off his opponent.

The captain tried to backstep away, to put distance between him and the bloodthirsty barbarian in front of him. Dodge was too fast.

He swung out with his left dagger, piercing through the metal armor and puncturing soldier's ribcage. Then Dodge swung with his right, also passing through the armor and jamming the blade into the soldier's chest plate.

With a ferocity Trevor had never seen, Dodge yanked down, using his punctured daggers as leverage as he drove his opponent to his knees. Dodge then brought up his knee into the man's face, tugging free both his daggers as blood flowed heavily from the wounds. The soldier dropped his sword and cried out in agony, but it wasn't enough for Dodge to relent. He kept to his own lesson—show no mercy.

Dodge brought a blade up high, twirling the grip between his fingers before swinging down and driving it into the side of the captain's neck. He struck out with the second dagger. burying it up to the hilt in the man's temple.

Dodge roared with a rage that shook the very earth as he pulled both daggers free and kicked the body to the ground with a heavy foot, a spray of blood and gore following in its wake.

A Sad Farewell

Once they had been found by the city guards, there had been a small, tiny spark of hope in the pit of Sarah's gut. They wouldn't have to run anymore, wouldn't have to hide in the shadows and escape the city. The guards had only simply asked for their hand, and they would whisk them away to safety, faster than a bird taking flight in a windstorm.

But then one of the guards had been sent away, and that small flame of security and hope in Sarah's gut had begun to wither and fade.

Knights in shining armor were always referred to as knights of chivalry and code in all the stories. They were supposed to save those in need and fight off the monsters and bad men. Although, it seemed there was hardly a difference between monsters and bad men these days, considering the turn of Sarah's recent events.

That flame, the one shining a dim light in Sarah's heart, the one hidden beneath the numbness of what her life had become, had been snuffed out when she'd seen the first guard attack, casting that familiar shadow of despair that Sarah was beginning to become so familiar with.

She stood by as the battle unfolded before her, a bird perched on a tree watching as a world she didn't understand passed her by. Blades were flying, their rings echoing in the night, but it was difficult to see who they were.

She watched as the shadows of men jumped back and forth, dodged left and right, swung high and low, all while she stood silently on the precipice of the battle.

And just like that, it was over. Only a few brief moments of chaos, then four men were suddenly dead. Three were strangers who had lives of their own, and one who wasn't a strange at all, but a friend. It felt alien, looking at Tom's body. Even as she watched the blood pool out from beneath his still body, she kept anticipating him to get up, brush of his trousers, and give that hearty laugh that he was so fond of giving.

But he didn't.

His body was still.

He was quiet.

He was dead.

"No." Dodge dropped both daggers and rushed to Tom's side. He searched with his hands as he collapsed to his knees, patting Tom's corpse with his shaky hands. "Oh, please, Tom. No, no, no, no, no. Not like this."

All was quiet. All but the whimpers of pain from Warren, who was cradling the deep cut in his calf. He, too, was looking at Tom's body, confusion and sadness taking control of him.

"He saved me," he whispered to himself. "He saved me."

Dodge tilted his gaze toward Warren, tears flowing down his blood-splattered face and a grimace that could make even a god second-guess their decision. He rose slowly, his hands balled into fists. Sarah could practically feel the violence emanating from him. He took a heavy step toward Warren when Benny cried out.

"Al?" Benny knelt next to Alric's body. He wiped the blood trail lining Alric's forehead, smearing it across Alric's milky face. "Shit. Someone get over here and help me."

An instant later, Evan was at his side. He leaned in and put his head against Alric's chest. "It's faint, but he's still alive. We need to get him to the others *fast*."

"It'll be three days at best," Benny said, a hint of doubt in his tone.

"Not if we run. Me and the big guy—*Hey!*" Evan realized Dodge was marching toward Warren, his fists tightly fixed on his daggers that screamed murder. "There's no time for this. We need to be going before that soldier grabs reinforcements."

Trevor was at Dodge's side, his sword tight in his hand as he, too, stared directly at Warren. When it was clear to Warren that he was yet free of danger, he began dragging himself away, putting distance between Dodge's and Trevor's insidious glare.

Dodge tried pushing Evan aside, but regardless of the man's mass, Evan refused to budge.

"Look," he said, stepping back in front of Dodge's trail, "I'm sorry about your man—really, I am—but if we don't get out of here now, we're all dead, and he would have died for nothing."

Dodge wasn't listening.

Evan began to plead with Trevor instead. "Look at me, kid." Evan grabbed Trevor by the shoulder. "Look at me! You need to talk some sense into your uncle.

We can't carry Alric alone, and if we don't make like a bird now, we'll be eating dirt before you know it. Please, kid, find some sense!"

Like his uncle next to him, Trevor refused to budge.

That was when Sarah stepped in. She walked slowly over to Trevor, took his hand, and gave it a hard squeeze. "Please, Trevor," she said, a small tear rolling down her face. "Don't do it."

She had no reason to defend Warren. Sarah could list off an endless amount of reasons why Warren deserved more than he was inches away from receiving, but in that moment, she wasn't thinking for Warren.

Trevor stopped and faced Sarah, a mixture of confusion and shock clear in his eyes. "You're defending him?" he asked, his face mixed with betrayal.

Sarah shook her head. "I'm defending Tom. He died saving Warren, and if you kill him now, then you murder his dying wish. Don't betray that memory of him."

Dodge had slowed his pace, as well, eventually coming to a halt. He looked down at Sarah.

Behind the gore that stained his body, Sarah could see the old and familiar Dodge who she'd grown up with.

He looked from her to Trevor then back to Warren. Without a word, he turned about, walked straight passed Evan, and knelt next to Benny.

Trevor kept his malicious stare at Warren, who remained curled into a ball, sobbing to himself. Then, whether or not Sarah managed to convince him, Trevor shook his head and walked away.

Sarah looked to Warren, and for the briefest moment, their eyes met. Though he wouldn't say it, Warren looked grateful.

"It's not far from here," Benny reassured Dodge. "It's a small cottage in the middle of the woods to the northeast, about a few days walk from here. If we hurry, we can hopefully save him."

"What then?" Dodge asked, his distant eyes focused on Tom's corpse.

Benny must have been expecting a protest, because once Dodge vaguely agreed to help, Benny's shoulders sagged with relief. "Then we make our way to the Crooked Tooth. There's a safe haven there. It's our home."

Dodge knelt down and placed a hand on Tom's chest. He closed his eyes, saying nothing for a few moments. When he was done giving his respects, he grabbed the blade of Tom's axe from the ground and tied it to his hip. "Until we meet again, old friend."

Without another word, Dodge scooped Alric from the ground and cradled him in his brutish arms. "Lead the way, then."

"Well, all right then," Evan mumbled to himself as he scooped Warren up in his own arms.

"You know," Evan said to Warren as he began following in Dodge's footsteps, "you're a little shit, and a heavy one at that."

Warren's only response was a painful wince as he bounced around in Evan's arms.

"And I strongly suggest you keep your mouth shut for a while. It's a long walk, and there are plenty of rocks to trip over."

Benny was close behind Evan, which left Sarah and Trevor alone for the moment. They looked at each other quietly.

A million things swarmed in Sarah's mind that she wanted to say, but it was the way Trevor had looked at her that stifled her tongue, a look between hurt, rage, and disgust. She had a deep sense to apologize, but before she could manage to clear her throat, he gave her a cold shoulder and followed the others.

Sarah looked behind her at the city of Servitol, a charitable memory she once associated with happiness and family, only to be replaced with the endless void of despair.

She turned her back to it and walked into the dark night.

A History Built on Lies

The panic was clear in the muffled voice that came from behind the large oak doors leading into the council chamber. Francis smiled to himself, relishing in his success, basking in the power that pulsed through his veins.

The stone statues lining parallel on both sides of the hallway looked down on him, casting their eternal grandeur on all those beneath them. Francis sneered at each of them.

You are nothing more than a fabricated memory built of stone, but I am flesh, and I will be great. Soon, very soon, your memory will crumble, and I will strut through the rubble and grind you to dust beneath the heel of my boot.

With the heavy box in his arms, Francis shoved the doors open with his shoulder.

Destro and Gorman were in a heated debate, probably having to do with the attack on the city . Both of them still wore their armor but, respecting the traditions of their empire, none of them carried any weapons.

"That's impossible." Gorman shook his head. "You heard the reports yourself—attacks *all around* the city. There's no way they could have all slipped away that quickly before being spotted by our patrols."

"The size of that hole, it's obviously been there a while, which means these guys have been planning it for some time now," Destro rebutted, clearly irritated by the discussion, as if they had been over the topic more than once already. "They could have been planning it for weeks, for all we know. Months maybe."

Francis smiled to himself. *Years, actually.*

Gorman didn't seem convinced. "So, you're telling me at least twenty men managed to chisel their way through the thickest wall surrounding the capital of the kingdom, under the very nose of the most powerful army the world has known, sneak in, plan a coordinated attack miles away from each other around the city, and then sneak off through that same hole without being caught?"

Destro grunted in response. "You forget. They *did* get caught. They killed my men during their escape."

"Even so, that's thin." Gorman crossed his arms, obviously unsatisfied with Destro's response. "That's very fucking thin, and if you choose to believe that, then you're either growing naïve with your age or your willingness to accept such a stretch of an excuse proves you've just grown lazy."

If Francis knew any better, Destro was seconds away from throttling Gorman. However, he kept his composure and stared at his fellow general. "And if that's the case, then you've grown too paranoid to see reason."

Francis dropped the chest onto the council table, the clatter booming off the stone walls. Destro and Gorman looked at him, noticing Francis for the first time since he entered the room.

"As we speak, we have men hauling out hundreds of bodies from our dining hall. Bodies of men, women, and children who choked on their own bile and blood. Men, women, and children whose lives were taken by *cowards*.

"Not to mention, your king, *my friend!* among them. All of this is happening. Meanwhile, when you two should be exploring solutions to our current predicament, you sit and bicker like children."

Both men were quiet for a while, the tension in the room clearing out like daylight with a setting sun.

"Apologies," Gorman said, a slight bow of his head in sign of respect.

Destro nodded, as if that was an apology enough.

Francis sighed as he pinched the bridge of his nose. The electricity that surged through his veins begged for release. It was a strange feeling. It was as if the power had been there all along, but only needed to be awakened with the scripture of the tablets that he'd spent the last years studying. Nobody had felt such power in centuries.

And in a very short time, the world will see it used once again.

"No, I am the one who should be sorry," Francis said. "We have all lost someone tonight." Francis tapped a finger on the chest before him, anxious to reveal the contents inside. "Let's hear your reports, Generals."

Destro cleared his throat before speaking. "There were reports of nine attacks, all about a mile away from each other in the city. Same reports all over—men in masks attacking citizens, burning down what they could, and killing those unfortunate enough to get in their way."

389

"And the damage?" Francis asked.

"Still being assessed. We should know more by the end of the day."

Francis nodded, turning his gaze to Gorman. "What's this about a wall?"

Gorman wasted no time, as if he'd been waiting to be asked. "There's a gap hidden in our walls in the lower district. Looks like it's been there for a while now. We think that the bandits"—he gave Destro a sideways glance—"or at least *some* of them, managed to escape there."

Francis looked to Destro. "And your men were attacked?"

Destro nodded. "Lost three good men. My report said he was heading back to command for support, but when they got there, they'd already managed to escape. Said he saw at least six people. A few kids were with them."

Francis eyed Destro suspiciously. "And when did this happen?"

Destro crossed his arms. "It was dark. Not long after sunset."

Francis scratched the side of his chin. Unless Vallis had made changes to his plan, which Francis doubted, his men would have been on the other side of the city by then. It couldn't have been the men who Vallis enlisted for the job.

The bandits weren't meant to escape. Then, who were these people?

"I see," Francis said.

Gorman shifted uncomfortably, and Francis could tell the man had more to say.

"Is there something else, General?"

The door was opened and Vallis appeared. Dirt and sweat stained his face and hands. If it wasn't for the velvet, well-cleaned, intricate robe, one might have thought he had spent the evening in a mud pit.

"Sorry I'm late, gentleman." Vallis shut the door behind him and walked to an open chair at the table. He sat down, threw his feet on the table, and crossed his arms.

"Report," Francis said, a hint of impatience in his words. He had expected Vallis to be there when Francis had originally showed up to the meeting.

Vallis didn't show any sign of worry. "I just got a report from one of my captains. They found an abandoned house near the western end of the upper city. They found masks, weapons, and clothing inside."

Gorman's shoulders tensed. "Which means they're still in the city."

"Well, in a sense." Vallis's smile was smug as he reached into his robe and pulled out a small knife, accompanied with an apple.

This time, Gorman didn't challenge the man about bringing a weapon into the council chamber. He simply waited in silence for Vallis to continue.

Vallis, clearly relishing in the fact that he knew something the other men didn't, took his time. "They're in the city, yes."

"Then let's round up our men and get them," Destro stated.

Vallis shook his head as he cut a small piece of his apple and tossed it into his open mouth. "No need. They've currently taken up residence in body bags. Soon, their heads will be put on pikes around the walls for all to see our victory."

"Your men managed to track and kill them?" The doubt was clear in Destro's voice.

"Is that so hard to believe?" Vallis looked offended, whether or not he truly was.

Destro stammered, at a genuine loss for words, shaking his head back and forth as his eyebrows danced on his forehead. It was a comical image seeing the brute of a man struggling with something as simple as praise. "Just ... surprised, is all."

"Huh." Vallis tossed another slice of his apple into his mouth. "Stick around. You'll soon see I'm full of surprises."

"Good work, General Vallis," Francis praised. "But I'm not sure displaying our success at apprehending our attackers in such a ... *colorful* manner would be the best option for the city right now. In the matter of a single day, countless families have lost loved ones and a kingdom has lost its king. It's best we find out where these men have come from so we—"

"Wait." Gorman shook his sunken face. "Lost a king?"

Francis took a deep breath, shaking his head to add to his theatrics. "Our doctors said the poison made its way to his heart. We were too late. He's gone."

Gorman put both hands on the table, leaned forward, and breathed deeply. "Fuck."

"This is a very difficult time," Francis said. "It's best if we focus on where these men came from and if they're still a threat."

"We have a lead," Gorman said, leaning away from the table.

Francis raised his eyebrows in question, curious as to where this was going. "A lead already?"

Gorman looked from Destro to Vallis then took a step forward, fully committed to his decision. "I met with a contact yesterday just before the attack. They passed through Robins-Port a week back and said that it had also been attacked by bandits."

"What?" Francis inhaled a sharp breath, stepping back a few steps, playing his part perfectly. "What do you mean *attacked*? Why is this the first I've heard of it?"

"He told us that—"

"Us?" Francis tilted his head. "Who is *us*?"

Gorman nodded toward Destro, who returned Francis's stare with a look of his own. A look that Francis struggled to understand.

Francis flexed his fists at his sides, keeping his mixture of irritation and raw power at bay the best he could.

"General Destro and I met with them at The Great-Hammer inn before the attack. They said the town had been put to the sword. All the residents butchered in the streets, the houses and shops burned to the ground."

"Why wasn't this reported?" Francis asked. "Why didn't they come straight to the king?"

It was Destro who answered. "It gets a bit more complicated."

Does it now? We all know how much I love complications.

"Explain," Francis ordered, his reserve of pleasantries depleted.

"Well ..." Gorman looked at them all. Francis, who had masked a look of concern; Destro, who was as difficult to read as a sleepwalker; and Vallis, who now chewed obnoxiously at his food. "They managed to save a couple of people."

Francis was worried the others would be able to hear the pounding of his heart. All demeanor washed away, all charade of the great herald who stood as a symbol of Navalethian Faith, of one who walked the path of the god Elinroth himself was gone. All that was left was the true Francis Balorian. The ambitious student of the world, thirsty to make it a better place through the awakened power of the ancients he so recently discovered.

"Survivors?" Francis asked plainly, giving Vallis a sharp look of malice.

The man put his feet down from the table and stood to join the others. All three men now stood across from Francis, nothing between them but a large chest sitting atop the large council table.

"Any children, General Gorman?"

"Fortunately enough, yes. A couple, supposedly." He thought for a moment. "Three, in fact."

Three children with the survivors, and three children reported escaping outside the eastern wall. Coincidence?

"But there's more," Gorman continued, placing something on the table before them—an arrow. "Our contact pulled this from a child's chest that night before escaping with five others. One of those escapees is the blacksmith of Robins-Port. He recognized this arrow. It's selphite, a—"

"A metal that's used for our troops' arrows," Francis finished. "I'm familiar with it." Silence fell over the room. He didn't say the words, but Gorman's intent was clear as day. "You're suggesting our own troops attacked Robins-Port?"

Gorman sighed deeply before he spoke. "I'm saying that maybe this is all connected. There's no way the attack last night wasn't just by mere bandits. Think about it. The attacks were spread out far enough where they had our forces split too thinly, with no chance of resistance, and in small enough groups where they could lose our men easily during the escape. This reeks of treason. Someone in power is behind this. Perhaps even one of the dukes."

"What about your contacts?" Francis asked, realization settling in. "You said that you met them at The Great-Hammer, but it was put to the torch during the attack."

"They ..." A look of worry passed briefly over Gorman's face. "We've cleared some of the rubble, but there are a lot of bodies—most of them with stab wounds—but we've yet to find one that matches their description. It's possible they're hiding out in the city, waiting for things to die down."

Francis looked Gorman in the eyes. "Or perhaps Alric and Benjamin managed to escape with the survivors you mentioned?"

Silence fell on the room. Gorman was a mix of confusion and worry, no doubt piecing the threads Francis had tied in place so long ago. Francis could see the moment Gorman began to realize just how deep his conspiracy theory went.

Francis pressed the question further, his body throbbing, pulsing with the heavy beat of his heart. "You obviously speak of the brotherhood, do you not?"

All was revealed now. The long years of planning. The years spent manipulating Vallis and Destro to his aid, plotting the attack on the country in order to vanquish an ancient bloodline, only to resurrect another. All of Francis's hard work, the sleepless nights, the constant anxiety of playing his part while keeping others in the dark even as they did his bidding by finding the true heir, eliminating those who opposed him, hiring the brotherhood to retrieve the tablets.

All of these dark secrets had been set in motion long ago and were now completely brought to light.

All was ready for the final act.

"I'd like to tell you a story, General Gorman," Francis said. "So, please pay attention." Francis walked to the table and opened up the chest. It creaked as he slowly lifted the lid, revealing the seven tablets resting inside, their golden words all but glowing in the shadow of the chest. One by one, Francis took out each individual table and set it on the table, his hands tingling as he handled the ancient stone.

"As you well know, this land was in disorder once. It was plagued with witches, cannibalistic demons, giants, trolls—everything you can imagine from a nightmare. Mankind was a dying species, the lowest predator on the food chain. Our species was on the brink of extinction, but then our gods came along and changed everything.

"And so, the gods ruled this land. Not just this land, mind you, but *all* lands. Navaleth isn't the only kingdom on this continent. Did you know that deep in the Haunted Forest hides a castle even bigger than this? And below the very ground we stand on are ancient underground cities?

"But one kingdom stands older than all else, for it was the first signs of civilization. Mind you, all its occupants have long deserted the place, thousands of years ago, actually. Once before, it thrived with life; whereas now, it only collects dust and long-forgotten memories.

"It's a wonder how nobody remembers this. There are books *littering* the grand library on our history, all mentioning the *Great Kingdom.* It seems our arrogant species has yet again limited their imagination by simply settling with a kingdom built on the fabricated truth of our forefathers."

Gorman took a cautious step away from the table, his eyes creased with worry, but Francis took a step closer, refusing to give the man any more room to hide from the truth.

"However, in that castle is a throne room, much like the one above our heads. In that throne room was a seat for each god. These gods"—Francis tapped the council table, waving a hand over the godlings depicted in grandeur on the top—"you already know.

"Elinroth"—Francis tapped to each individual god as he spoke—"the All-Father, creator of life and the world around you. His wife, Mariella, creator of our love, our passion, our livelihood. Together, they bore two children; a daughter, Arabella, and a son, Volran. The daughter of wisdom and passion, and the son of strength and bravery.

"You know these names as well as any other Navalethian in the country. We speak the name Volran when we pray before a battle, and pray to Arabella for our loved ones who fall ill.

"We use their names when we simply cannot fathom an alternative explanation to the unknown, specifically death. Yes, we know these names well, for they are engraved on our hearts as soon as we are able to use our ears, because our freedom of thinking has been poisoned by those who came before.

"But a name you do not know, General Gorman, is *Malicar*." Francis let the word ring in the air. Just saying the name aloud, after so many years of it being kept secret, after only a mumble on his lips during his late-night teachings, was a physical relief.

The name had power. *And soon, I will release it.*

"Malicar ..." Francis repeated, a wicked smile promising wicked intentions. "No, this is not a name you know. Is it, General Gorman?"

Gorman stood quietly to himself, his lips curling with worry and his brows creased with confusion. After a long pause of silence, he shook his head softly.

Destro stood quietly to himself at Gorman's side, his arms crossed as the story unraveled before him. Vallis chewed slowly on his apple, placing himself behind Gorman, not a care in the world. He, unlike the others, had already heard this tale.

"Of course you haven't, General," Francis continued, "for that name has been hidden from the world long before this castle was even a thought. You see, in the *Great Kingdom*, hidden deep in the Haunted Forest, there are *five* thrones for each god. You see, Malicar was Elinroth and Mariella's third and youngest child, and he possessed the power of death. You see, where Elinroth is the bringer of life, Malicar is our bringer of death."

Gorman, still possessing the same demeanor as a stubborn child, took a slow step away from the table, away from Francis and his ancient tablets and his ancient secrets. "I'm not sure what this has to do with anything, Father."

"*Do not call me that!*" Francis snapped, his body now boiling with the power surging through him. "I have lived my entire life in that lie, flaunting your perversion of truth among you flock of sheep. You are all so willfully blind, basking in your bliss of ignorance, thinking of nothing of the future beyond the bridge of your nose." Francis took deep breaths, gathering himself before continuing. "As for the meaning of this lesson, I promise you, you'll soon understand. I promise you, General, that you will become *enlightened.*"

Gorman shifted his hands to his waist, only to remember that he'd suffered the penalties of his own ancient traditions. He was beginning to recognize the danger he was currently in.

"This is where the history has been lost in the fog of generations, but the conclusion is the same. At some point, Elinroth fell madly in love with his creations, becoming sick with lust. Volran questioned his father, claiming he loved human life more than the life of his own family. At some point, in their heated debate, Elinroth struck down Volran, killing him with a single blow.

"Malicar flew into a rage and immediately searched the realm of death, his very domain, for the lost soul of his brother. After years and years of searching—for the realm of death is an endless plane of despair—he could not find his brother Volran. What he did find out, however, was the secret of his godly blood.

"The blood of a god is powerful beyond measure and comprehension. Malicar, using the power of his blood, decided to manipulate our genes and create an army for himself. With the power of death mixed with the gift of life, Malicar created a legion so powerful that the very name echoes through even today's age. Although, the meaning has become perverted, much like the rest of our history. The name of his army was the Mal'fur."

Francis relished in the sight of Gorman's eyes widening at the name. Of course, everyone in Navaleth knew the Mal'fur as a demon army, but that was only half true.

"You see, the Mal'fur aren't a demon horde, led by manifested evil wraiths that we were told. That's what our history wants us to believe, because we have been lied to, made to believe that, because Malicar challenged his father for slaying his own bloodline, we are to believe he is nothing more than a devil waging war on mankind. That is not the case. In fact, they were no different than an army you see today—warriors who have sworn their lives for the cause of their king.

"The Mal'fur was led by two generals: Belicar and Dekarta. With the blood of their god in their veins, they became a force of reckoning! Their senses heightened, their skills in combat superior to all. They could see clearly in the dark, hear a whisper and catch a scent a mile off. Their reflexes were so heightened that it was said they could pluck a flying arrow in mid-flight. They were a supreme force above all else as they waged war against, not mankind, but Elinroth himself.

"For nearly a century, the Mal'fur fought against the armies of Elinroth and, in the end, the All-Father was inevitably the victor. You see, where Malicar manipulated mankind to his own, so had Elinroth. The war was fought by two sides of a superhuman race, whose blood had been perverted to serve one purpose. War.

"Over the years, the bloodlines descended, creating a family tree of both gods and humans. During the final battle of the war, the descendants of both bloodlines dueled for days on a mountain top; Dekarta fighting for his liege lord, and Asher the Great fighting for his."

Gorman shook his head, finally finding the strength to speak as the wave of information began to drown him. "That's impossible. Asher is a myth." Gorman looked to the two men at his sides. "This man is mad!"

"Oh"—Francis laughed softly to himself—"I know how this may all sound, but I assure you that I am far from mad. You are not at fault for your blind ignorance. It is mine for not showing you the way sooner. But it's never too late, General. Allow me to *enlighten you.*"

Vallis struck out with the small knife that he'd been carving his apple with. The blade passed in a flash, leaving a red line at the side of Gorman's neck.

Destro, realizing what was happening, flew into a rage and made for Vallis, but was too slow. Vallis had anticipated the outburst and dropped low to the ground, jabbing his knife into Destro's knee.

Destro roared in pain as he sunk to the ground. "You bastard!" he yelled to Francis, eyes watering with tears. "What did I tell you? I said if anything happened to him—"

"That you would kill me. Yes, I remember your threats very well. But before any more blood is shed, allow me to finish my story." Francis looked at Gorman. "He at least deserves to know what cause he's dying for."

"Fuck you!" Destro roared. "Don't you fucking—"

Destro's rage was silenced with a heavy boot from Vallis.

Gorman crashed on the table, his hand pressed to his neck as blood flowed between his fingers. Blood was also beginning to dribble on his lip, a line of drool sinking onto the table. Regardless, he glared at Francis through pain and rage.

As Gorman bled out before him, his dark lifeblood spreading in a pool across the table, Francis continued.

"As you know, it is said that Asher the Great was the first king of Navaleth, and that our monarchy is a direct descendent of his great bloodline. That, however, is a single truth amongst the graveyard of lies we've been told."

Francis tapped the tablets on the table. "These tablets speak of a prophecy. It says that once the bloodline of the '*traitorous blood*'—Elinroth's blood—has been eviscerated from the '*traitor's creation*'—our world—then the world can finally live in peace, without fear of death and famine, without starvation and greed. The world will be led by a new creator, and they, with the power of the ancients, will bring peace amongst everything.

"It wasn't long ago when I sat with our king, drinking too much wine and having too many debates about how the world should work, when he let slip an affair he'd had with a woman during his campaign in the Great War. Can you believe that? For someone who displayed so much passion for his beloved wife, he'd had a mistress the entire time."

Francis lost himself in nostalgia for a moment, reminiscing about the earlier days when he had decided to commit his life fully to his cause. "She was ... a beautiful woman—the queen. Remarkable. I admit that I would have grown and died a happy man watching their children grow." Francis met Gorman's glossy eyes. "But the bloodline needed to end, and unfortunately, she was with child at the time."

Gorman clenched a bloody fist, the promise of vengeance burning in his eye but lacking the strength to do so.

"Oh, don't look at me like that. It's the same look General Orlington had when he also learned the truth, as he died right where you stand. Don't look at me as if I'm a monster. A monster is someone who hides the truth from us, like Elinroth did with Malicar. A monster is a father who strikes down his child in a rage, putting an end to their very existence because of political disagreements. A monster is a hero who slaves himself to the bottle, blaming his only child for the death of his mother, who dishes out his lessons with a fist and the back of his hand!"

Francis breathed deeply, lost in his childhood memories, struggling to calm himself and refocus on the task at hand.

The power surged through him now, on the very brink of breaking loose. He knew it was time.

"The bloodline needed to end in order to bring peace, and sacrifices had to be made. The power of death can't be harnessed without death itself. It's a fickle thing, magic. Everything has to be precise. Everything has to be exact. When the body dies, the soul naturally fades toward the realm of the dead.

But there are moments when they are at pause, when they search for the door to the realm. In those moments, anyone with the proper technique and skill can harness those souls and channel them into power. This was the true power of Malicar.

"The power of the soul is … *insatiable*. It's like giving a man dying of thirst only a sip of water—he'll crave more and think of nothing else. Now, to harness hundreds of souls, you have to have those souls in transcendence simultaneously." Francis pointed above him with a stoic finger. "Much like our dinner guests last night. Their passing was necessary for what is needed to be done. Shadowroot is a complicated poison, but its timing is remarkable."

"You bastard!" Destro tried standing, but Vallis punched him in the face, sending him back to the ground.

"Perfect timing, General Destro, for that was the important factor of this charade. You see, as I've said, our loving king had a mistress, and rumor was she had birthed a child. Now, even if I respect her not bringing that child forth and demanding a crown out of it, it was, however, *very* difficult to track her down. You see, she lived a life of travel, but I was able to narrow down her location to a small yet very productive trading town … Robins-Port.

"The details on this particular woman was hard to decipher. I didn't know who she was, nor whether I was searching for a male or female heir to the throne. But I did know that the bastard lived in Robins-Port. Naturally, just to be safe, I had the town put to the torch. Sacrifices must be made to achieve the greater good."

Gorman was a pale ghost, and Francis could feel the power of the man's soul struggling to stay within the magical boundaries of his physical body.

"One thing I've learned over these years, General, is that a body is nothing more than a vessel. You see, bodies, though different in shape, are the same—empty. It's the soul that's alive, the soul that is the conscious entity, which fuels our physical body. Which brings me to the final part the prophecy."

Francis waved his hands over the tablets on the table, channeling out that feeling of energy through his fingertips, the words glowing with a gold light. "Harnessing souls gives you power, for it takes an unspeakable amount of energy to summon the souls of the dead, and much more to transfer that soul into another vessel. Fun fact about the transfer of souls is that those who are summoned are forever enslaved at the hands of those who did the summoning."

Francis's mouth widened, displaying his white teeth with a vicious smile. "So, die you will, but die knowing that you had the privilege of offering your body for a resurrected god." Francis held out his arm, his open hand flexed as thin trails of black smoke began to wrap around it in swirls of gray.

Gorman's eyes rolled to the back of his head. He collapsed onto the table and began to violently convulse, white foam spewing from his mouth as the magic began to take a toll.

Francis couldn't remember a better feeling than in that moment. The power had been building up, expanding and put close to the breaking point within his body. As he let it loose, as he called forth the name of his king beyond the realm of the dead, all that steam power was set loose, channeling with a single purpose.

Gorman's soul began to separate from his body. It hovered between worlds, searching for the door to the afterlife. Francis didn't see it, but *felt* it.

Francis concentrated and, in that moment of limbo, Gorman's soul began to writhe in agony, stretching thinner and thinner as it was consumed by Francis.

Now, with all the souls he needed for the ritual, Francis focused on Gorman's corpse.

With his hand stretched out, the power on his fingertips, he forced the pressure of his power fully toward the body sprawled on the table.

Releasing the hundreds of souls that Francis had consumed was pure ecstasy. The world around him brightened with power, and once the last soul left his body, his world lit up in a flash of bright white.

Instead of the council chamber in Navaleth, Francis stood atop a rock cliff, overlooking an endless site of barren mountains and rocky plains. Beneath a purple sky, flashing with streaks of lightning, were ranks upon ranks of neatly lined soldiers. An army awaiting their command.

"You have done well," a voice said.

Francis turned around and was standing before a man. No, not a man. A wraith. It stood tall before him, a dark cowl hiding his face in black, his massive figure drowning Francis in shadow.

Francis wrinkled his nose as a hot wind blew against him, wafting with the sour aroma of death.

"Now," the figure said, reaching out and pressing a cold hand on Francis's chest, "serve your purpose."

In a white flash of pain, Francis screamed. He screamed as loud as he

could, but nothing escaped his lips. In one moment, he was floating before the
figure, his back arching in the air as pain racked his body.

He was back in the council chamber, hunched over the large table, the ancient tablets scattered beneath him. By the look of Gorman's rotting body, Francis had to have been unconscious for quite some time.

Gorman's skin was as white as a cloud, his lips purple with death, and a large pool of blood had spread wide across the table.

Vallis still stood over Destro, his foot on the side of his neck, keeping the man firmly pinned to the ground.

Vallis met Francis's eyes. "What happened?" he asked as Francis managed to stand back on his feet, wobbling awkwardly as he caught his balance. "You passed out for a while. You were mumbling in your sleep."

"I ..." Francis shook the dizziness from his head. The feeling of power was still there. Dormant and quiet, but still there, deep down in the consciousness of his own soul. He thought about his dream, about the desolate plain of endless rock and shadow. About the figure that stood before him. "I'm not sure what happened," he admitted.

Destro spat on the ground, his face heavy with sweat. "You lied to me," he accused, eyes piercing Francis. "You said that the king was dying, that we needed to explore other options of government. We agreed we would leave things up to the people, to end the monarchy in all!"

"Our king was dying," Francis confessed, "and we had to explore other options, correct. But leave the choice of how a country is run up to the *people*?" Francis scoffed at the absurdity. "Mankind has been poisoning the world since it began to walk. We are limited to our sense of what is wanted rather than what is needed, and you want to leave the fate of the world in the hands of *that*?" Francis looked at Gorman's body, feeling a sense of disappointment. "No, General, I have other plans. But, as it seems, even those I have—"

Francis's words were caught in his throat as the body of Gorman began to move. It started small. A twitch of his head. The fluttering of his eyelids. Then his arms began to bend at awkward angles, his bones cracking and popping loudly in the process. Then, as if his limbs were unnaturally controlled by invisible strings, he slowly began to stand up, blood dripping from his neck wound and falling away to the floor beneath him.

He stood there quietly for a moment, his eyes closed as a tinge of color began to glow in his skin, showing a gray tone rather than a deathly white. Then he opened his eyes, revealing two black orbs staring directly at Francis.

"Are you well, my liege?" the thing that used to be Marcus Gorman asked.

Francis's heart fluttered with his joy as he looked upon his creation. "All is well, Lord Malicar. Welcome back to the world of the living."

The figure didn't move, just stood there and accepted Francis's greetings.

"What have you done?" Fear quaked in Destro's voice as he looked upon his old friend. "This is black magic. Necromancy! What have you done, Francis?"

Francis walked over and stood above Destro. Vallis shifted his heavy foot against his neck. "I had such high hopes for you, Harvin Destro, but you've made your intentions very clear. There's no place for you in the new world."

Malicar took his place, standing next to Francis, his black eyes staring down at Destro.

Vallis handed Francis the knife.

"There's no place for you amongst the new gods."

Part Three

An Unwelcome Reunion

The world hurt as he lay on his back, even worse when he tried to open his eyes. Piercing pain ached through the joints of his body as he tried to sit, making it only a few inches before collapsing.

His spine throbbed, the stiff pain in the soles of his feet. Everything ached.

He tried to shift his body once again, and once again he succumbed to the sudden pain.

"Give it a moment," a familiar voice told him, and suddenly the pain didn't matter. He knew he was back in the village. He knew who was tending to him. And so, beyond the pain that racked his body, Quiver's heart fluttered with ease.

Quiver felt a gentle hand on his chest. The woman's voice gave him a sense of security because, if it really belonged to the person he thought he was hearing, that would mean he'd somehow made it back to the village.

"Let your body wake a bit before moving," Thread told him.

"Thre—"

A sharp pain tore at Quiver. He began to cough, knives cutting at his throat as he gasped for air.

"Drink this before talking," she said, pressing a wooden cup to his lips.

After Quiver gathered himself, he let the water flow down his throat. The water was warm to his lips, but Quiver might as well have been swallowing shards of ice.

"Small sips now. There you go."

Quiver coughed again once he'd drained the cup. He gasped with a deep breath of cool air. "Thank you, Thread."

"You are welcome," Thread replied warmly.

Quiver could just make out Thread's face as his vision began to clear. She looked much the same before he had left with his pack; her dark brown eyes matching her long hair, the small bend in her nose accompanied with her strong cheeks, her thin chin that ended at a sharp point.

Thread smiled at him. "Glad to see a friendly face?"

"I'd prefer waking up to yours compared to the one I expected to see."

Thread bit her lip. "If you're referring to Elder Roku, you missed your chance. He came to visit you when you first arrived but has been quite busy with himself since."

"When I first arrived?" Quiver grimaced as he struggled to sit, pushing through the throbbing pain as he swung his legs over the side of the cot. "How long have I been out?"

"A little over a week," Thread answered quietly. "We sent out another pack in search of you when you didn't return. Elder Roku argued that it was a lost cause, that your personal struggle with the spirits had caused you to abandon us all."

Quiver grunted. If his body hadn't felt like it was made of stone, he would have left the tent immediately to find Elder Roku and confront him.

Thread gave a satisfied smile. "I can't explain how good it felt to see that others disobey him, and even how better it felt to see Elder Roku's face when they came back with you."

Quiver looked to Thread, the question hanging in the air that he didn't need to ask.

Thread frowned, a sight Quiver never liked seeing. "They found you just a mile away from the village. You, Rasca, Masco, and Oppo. They said they looked but couldn't find Sparrow." Quiver could hear the sadness in Thread's voice. "What happened out there?"

Quiver wanted to tell her everything right there and then. He wanted to tell her how they followed Nero's trail to a clearing where they were ambushed by monsters that he'd never seen before, monsters as big as bears but could climb trees as quiet as squirrels. Monsters with red eyes that they fought and won against, but at the cost of one of their youngling's lives. He wanted to tell her all of this, but it was too soon. There were other things he had to do before he talked about his experience in the woods.

"The others?" Quiver asked. "Rasca, Masco, and Oppo?" He grew worried, realizing that it was only the two of them in the tent. "Where are they?"

Thread met his eyes with a smile. "Do you ever worry about yourself?"

"You know me better than that."

"More than most." Thread nodded. "Rasca is fine. He woke up only a couple days after they brought you back. He was just here this morning to see you, actually." She smiled at Quiver. "He'll be excited to see that you're awake. I don't think you've got a closer friend than him."

"Oppo?" Quiver began another coughing fit as Thread handed him more water. Once he downed the cup quickly, he pressed the question. "What about Oppo?"

"He shows no bruises on the outside, but I fear that he is hurt here." Thread pointed at her head. "In his—"

"Mind," Quiver finished for her. Thread had always struggled with southern words and ideas.

"Yes." She looked bashfully away. "We bring him food and check if he's okay, but he refuses to speak to us. Mostly just keeps to himself, never even touching his food. His mother says that he doesn't sleep much anymore, but when he does, he talks. She said he keeps mumbling the same thing over and over again."

Quiver's heart sank with the news. "What does he say?"

Thread looked at Quiver sadly. "That it's all his fault, and that he's sorry."

He blames himself for Sparrow. Quiver knew the guilt of loss was heavy. He'd seen it become the undoing of even the strongest warriors, including himself. *No youngling should have to face that guilt, especially not alone.*

"He's been through a lot," Quiver said. "Give him some time to heal; he'll work it out.

"And what about Masco?" Quiver feared to ask, dreading what answer Thread might give him, but he needed to know.

At the mention of Masco's name, Quiver saw sadness glisten in Thread's eyes. "Not good. He's had a fever ever since he was found. Poppy says the fate of the youngling's life rests in the hands of the spirits now."

As somber as the news was, Masco was still alive, and that was better than the alternative.

Quiver made to stand, pushing through the pain burning in every joint of his body. Thread helped guide him by taking his arm, steadying him as he climbed to his feet. He stood there a moment as the vertigo washed away and the world began to focus clearly.

Quiver hadn't felt this vulnerable in years, and it was moments like this where he valued Thread more than ever. They'd known each other since they were kids, and she'd been there for just about every moment when Quiver was at his weakest. Even when Quiver and his brother were dragged off to war on his father's campaign, he had always imagined coming back to Thread. It was a bond he could only explain verbally through a southern word.

"Thank you," Quiver said to her, studying her face as if he was seeing it for the first time.

"There's no need for those sad eyes," Thread told him with a small smile. "I knew you'd be coming back."

Quiver looked into her face, not a trace of doubt in his voice. "I didn't."

Her smile faded, replaced only by sadness in her oval eyes. "Bad news, then?"

Quiver stepped forward and took her by the shoulders. He nodded softly. "Bad news." He pulled her closer to him and kissed her firmly on the lips. The boldness in his grip caught her by surprised, but as the shock of the moment passed by, Thread gladly returned his embrace.

"Wow," Thread said, smiling as she pulled away. "That was … unexpected. Not that I'm complaining."

"You always did say that I should stop being so predictable." Quiver smiled lightly. Then he looked toward the flap of the tent. "I should check on the others."

"I know better than to try to hold you back, especially when you've a mind to check on old friends. But I'd stay away from the elder for now. He's glad to have you back—at least, that's what he's saying—but I think he has other plans for you and your pack."

"Sounds like he's as predictable as me," Quiver jested when, in fact, he was dreading the reunion he would have to have with the elder.

Quiver's quest had been an utter failure at finding Nero, but that didn't mean he didn't have important news. However, Elder Roku was no longer the type of leader to accept news that threatened his power.

"Can't wait to see what he has in mind."

"Come back after?" Thread asked.

Quiver smiled at her. "Of course."

She returned his smile, watching him move toward the exit of the tent. "I suggest you keep out of trouble, too. I don't think you can handle much worse."

"You know me," Quiver said as he made to exit the tent.

"Exactly my point," he heard Thread say as the flap closed behind him. "I know you."

The sun was beginning its descent, casting a warm glow across the place that Quiver called home. It didn't look like much; simply tents sprouting from branches

407

of wood, wrapped in numerous pelts, fitting only a few as two or three occupants comfortably. When it came to Quiver's people, they didn't see the point of wasting material given to them from the world on building grand or enormous houses or buildings. They were a humble people, using only the bare essentials provided to them by the spirits to manage their lives.

A southerner, Quiver discovered in his younger days, would argue the opposite. They would argue that their gods had given them the resources to build something grand in honor of their existence. They owed it to their creators to build something in tribute. Where Quiver's people only used what they absolutely needed, southerners would exploit just about every resource available to them, or make more available to them, in order to satisfy their own personal ambitions, and then hide behind their claim of it being a tribute for their gods.

And they call us savages.

To some people in the world, they would look at Quiver's village and use words like *uncultured* or *uncivilized*, but, to Quiver, it was a beautiful sight, regardless of the recent transgressions on his faith. He might not share the same ideals as his ancestors, but that didn't mean he didn't respect and love his people.

Quiver wasn't naïve enough to see fault in his own people, either. He knew that both sides of the country had their flaws. Native people might dedicate their lives to the tradition of the old world, but that also meant that they dedicated their lives toward old world problems, as well. Disease being one of them.

What his people saw when it came to disease was merely a test by the spirits. They believed that, if a person were to be stricken with sickness, it was because they had offended one of the spirits, and that it was their own responsibility to prove themselves back to health. If a child were to get a simple cold—a word used by southerners to describe a minor illness—it meant that he probably did something that most younglings do, which is cause mischief and make mistakes. It was their responsibility to prove themselves to that spirit in order to get healed.

The severity of the illness represented the seriousness of the offense. If a villager, even in some cases younglings, got the shakes or a cold sweat while suffering a high fever, it meant that they had greatly offended a spirit, and that the recompense would be great in order to heal. If they proved themselves, they would get better in the end. But if the spirit deemed that the villagers had not proven themselves enough, that person would only get worse and, in some cases, die.

Quiver had seen it many times over. It was one of the very few reasons he envied the southern lifestyle. The southerners weren't held down by their beliefs like his people were. They didn't sit back and *hope* a deity would forgive that person and heal them. They took matters into their own hand and expanded the capability of medicine that Quiver could hardly understand. They weren't tied down by their pasts, but seeking for better alternatives, something Quiver wished his people would do.

He had seen southern medicine used a few times before, only during the war fifteen years ago. He'd seen a man stricken with fever, moments away from the field of the Forever Calm, only to be walking not three days after a southern healer slipped a few drops of dark liquid into his drink every few hours. Quiver's people had called it blasphemy, that cheating the decisions of the spirits would cause them even greater rage.

Quiver knew better than that. He had always been skeptical when it came to the spirits. But, just because you don't understand something doesn't mean it's blasphemy. Although he followed the ancient beliefs that his ancestors taught him, he couldn't help but feel that the teachings became more of a means to control than a means to live and thrive.

In this case, villagers didn't see a need to hide from another with a sickness, which was why the healer's hut was built near the housing huts at the western end. It was, after all, a sickness of the individual given from the spirits. And if the illness was given by a god, sent upon an individual, then there was no worry of contamination, right?

Quiver was lost in his thoughts as he made his way toward the healer's hut.

Some villagers, most of which Quiver knew very well, greeted him with a respectful nod or smile. Meista, who Quiver remembered taking on a hunt when she was just a youngling, passed by and patted her closed hand against her chest twice. "Home, Chief Quiver."

Quiver mimicked the same to her with a polite smile. "Home, Meista"

Other villagers, however, did not share the same excitement as they passed Quiver. Still, they gave their respectful nods. Quiver could tell it was out of custom to who he was rather than actual gratification on his return. Some of these villagers Quiver knew quite well. Some were people he had trained in hunting, or even in fighting. Others he knew to be very close with Elder Roku, who did not have a very good opinion of Quiver.

At some point in his life, Elder Roku had seen Quiver more as a rival than a chief. His paranoia had drawn him to believe that Quiver had actually sought out to claim elder himself, to claim authority over the village and cast Roku out as a traitor. He'd no idea when or how this paranoia began, and the last thing Quiver wanted was to become elder. He'd learned long ago the cost of leading a great many people. It was a lifestyle he would never ask for again.

Something is off. There should be more people about at this time of hour. Where is everyone?

Usually, when the sun began to set, the villagers would gather just enough supplies for a feast with the entire village. They would meet at their ritualistic firepit and praise the spirits, thanking them for the day's harvest. However, there were hardly any at all.

He hooked around a large tent, and Quiver's tension began to ease when he saw a familiar face leaning against Poppy's hut. Their face was at ease, their posture relaxed, and if it wasn't for the bandage wrapped around one of his hands, hiding the missing fingers, Quiver would never have guessed Rasca had been a part of their fight against the howlers.

"It's good to see you up," Rasca said as Quiver approached. "I wish it were sooner. I've been trying to stall the elder for days now, and I'm starting to think he's had just about enough of me."

"Stall him of what?" Quiver looked around, acknowledging the absence of other villagers. "Where is everyone?"

"It seems"—Rasca stood straighter and met Quiver's eyes—"that the elder is gathering the villagers for a ... I forget the word. You always were better with those southern words." Rasca scratched at his scruffy beard. "Where they ask you a bunch of questions in front of everyone, and then everyone decides what to do with you? I forget the word ..."

Quiver felt a deep sense of worry. "A trial?"

Rasca snapped his fingers. "That's the one. A *trial*. We are to trial before the entire village."

"You mean we are to be put *on* trial before the village," Quiver corrected.

Rasca leaned back, his face a frown of confusion. "Wait—they're going to put us on a trial?"

"No, no, no." Quiver shook his head, pinching the bridge of his nose.

"Not put *on* a trial, but put on trial."

Rasca shrugged. "Same difference."

Quiver shook his head impatiently. "Actually, no, it's not." Quiver waved his hand in the air. "Forget it. A trial for what?"

"Not sure," Rasca admitted. "Elder Roku has been interviewing people in his tent all week. The only people allowed in are those being questioned and his personal guard."

Since when does an elder need a personal guard in his own village? It seems Roku has grown even more paranoid that I was found alive.

"Maybe he just wants to know what happened out there?" Rasca suggested.

It was a nice thought, but Quiver guessed otherwise.

"Then why not just ask us? Why the formality?"

"Formality?" Rasca asked slowly, the word sour in his mouth.

Quiver rolled his eyes at Rasca. "How is it you've campaigned the same war with me and never picked up on a few simple words from our enemies?"

"The southerners thought of us as barbarians. That's the only word I needed to know."

Quiver briefly thought back to the haunting memories of the war. *It wasn't as if we didn't give them cause.*

"Well, the village needs to know what happened to Nero and his pack, and to us, as well," Quiver said. He studied Rasca's face as he spoke his next words, hoping that his friend had the same mind. "We need to get them out of here. It's only a matter of time before the howlers find our trail again and follow us back here. They could be a few days out by now."

Rasca looked around the huts surrounding them, and then back to Quiver. "Don't think everyone will agree with you there. In fact, I'm sure that's what the elder has been warning everyone else about."

Quiver creased his brow. "About the howlers?"

Rasca answered the question with a shake of his head. "About you trying to lead them away from him. He's worried you want control."

Quiver spat on the ground, an old habit he picked up from his older brother. "I don't want control of the village. I want to save it."

"I know you do, but he's not going to see it that way. Best wait to make that suggestion before the trial, make sure they hear our story first."

"That's time we don't have." Quiver was good and irritated now. He'd come back hoping to warn the village and hopefully save those who saw sense. Instead, he was going to be put on some sort of trial—probably the first in his people's history—to defend himself instead of explain?

Sensing his frustration, Rasca put a reassuring hand on Quiver's shoulder. "Regardless of what happens, I'll back you up. I was there. I saw what happened, and nobody can stop us from telling them what's coming. Not Roku, not the howlers, not even the spirits."

Rasca had always been a good friend to Quiver, but over the years, with the absence of Quiver's older brother, Rasca had been the closest thing to family. In some ways, Quiver felt that Rasca might be the only other villager to understand, if not, empathize for how Quiver saw the world. Nothing was black and white, but mostly shades of gray, and the fact that Rasca understood that was enough for Quiver to trust the man more than anyone else.

"Thank you," Quiver said.

Rasca nodded silently in response.

When the moment passed, Quiver was reminded of why he'd sought out the healer's hut in the first place. He nodded toward the entrance of the tent. "How is he?"

Rasca waited a moment before answering, and Quiver prepared himself for the bad news he was sure to get. "He's better, actually."

Quiver was shocked with the sudden change of news. "Better?"

"Better," Rasca confirmed. "But that's only because, as of yesterday, we were sure his heart had stopped beating. But today, he's breathing again, better than before. He still stinks of infection, but the ointments are helping. I think he's going to be all right."

"That's good news." Quiver felt a weight lift from his shoulders. He'd grown to like Masco. It would have been a shame to lose him like this.

"For Masco, yes." The sudden change in Rasca's voice caught Quiver's attention. "But Oppo is a different sort."

Quiver nodded. "Thread said he's been keeping to himself. Have you seen him?"

Rasca scratched at his beard again. "I have. He won't speak. Only to himself. He blames himself for Sparrow, and it's driving him sick. I've seen it before, Quiver, and so have you."

It was true. Oppo was showing all the signs of a man with a guilty conscience, a man struggling to deal with himself. And if there was anything Quiver had learned from it, it was that you could be the strongest warrior in the village and still be beaten by guilt.

"I should speak with him."

"You'll have to wait," Rasca said flatly.

"Why is that?"

"Because he's with the elder right now, in his hut."

Quiver rolled his eyes and Rasca nodded his agreement.

Younglings on their deathbed, monsters from the dark on their way to destroy everything and everyone, and you're trying to manipulate a child in your favor for a trial that goes against everything you stand for? Just what are you trying to do, Roku?

"Well, you're fine enough, at least," Quiver said. "I might as well see how the other one is doing."

Quiver never liked being inside of a healer's hut. It was something about the smell; the sour pungent odor of the sick or dying, or maybe even the spices of their healing powders or musky scent of sweaty or, in his experience, bloody clothes.

All these things Quiver expected when he walked into the hut, along with Poppy hovering over a dying Masco, probably reassuring him that he'll soon be with his loved ones.

Quiver always did find that strange. His people always referred to dying as a passage to the next life where your family, loved ones, and ancestors waited for you. That you should be happy, not to grieve. The way Quiver saw it, the ones you left behind were your family and loved ones, the spirits on the other side were merely strangers. He would choose this life over the next any day.

He never spoke of these things, of course. It would be against the norms of his people. It was something they wouldn't understand and something Quiver couldn't make them understand.

He thought of this as he entered the hut, bracing himself against those unbearable aromas of death—just walking into the hut sent a piercing pain into his temples—when what he saw left him frozen in the doorway.

The hut was long and narrow. Four cots lined both sides of the walls, leaving just enough space in the center for the healer to walk from patient to patient. At the end of the hut was a wall of shelves littered with vials of oils, powders, and anything a healer might need to cure a wound or ease the pain of the dying.

Poppy was where he expected her, tending to Masco's wounds. However, where the young boy should be lying unconscious with a fever, he was sitting upright and taking large gulps from a wooden mug of water.

"Take it slow, young one," Poppy encouraged Masco, her voice soothing and gentle. "Let the medicine work its way into the body. Slow sips now."

"Shouldn't he be resting?" Quiver asked Poppy as he took a seat on the cot next to Masco.

Masco drained the last contents of the mug with a satisfied sigh.

"Well, look at that." Rasca joined Quiver at Masco's side. He looked between Poppy and the boy, trying to understand what was happening. "This morning, you were as pale as the moon, hardly an ounce of strength in your body." He looked to Poppy. "What did you give him?"

"Nothing you weren't there to see," Poppy answered. "One minute, he was tossing in his sleep with a fever, mumbling about things, very ... *odd* things." She stared at Masco, whose eyes were now closed as he breathed deeply. "I went to grab some water, and when I turned back, he was trying to stand up. The fever broke after that."

"Impossible," Rasca exclaimed. When Quiver looked at his old friend, he saw genuine confusion in his eyes. "I just saw him this morning. He was better, but not *this* better."

"Nothing is impossible to the spirits," Poppy assured, still eyeing the youngling. "What they deem fit to live, they let live. It is simple."

If it's as simple as the spirits deciding who lives and dies, then the spirits are as twisted as our worst enemies.

"Can I see it?" Rasca asked Poppy, who was now refilling Masco's cup from a large pitcher.

When she handed Masco the medicine, she beckoned him toward her. He didn't even so much as grimace as Rasca slowly peeled away the bandage that Poppy had fastened across the boy's back.

Quiver thought back to how the wound had looked in the forest. Rasca was right; it was impossible that it was fully healed and now a scar.

The howler attack had left the boy with three large scars across his back where he'd been hit, stretching from between his shoulders and down to his lower back. But that's all they were now—scars. Where deep gashes of torn flesh should be, raised, pink skin was all that remained. Not a week ago the wound had been infected, swelling with pus and bleeding from the open wound, but now it remained only a story to tell.

"Impossible," Rasca repeated, regardless of Poppy's previous lesson with the power of the spirits.

"She was protecting her cubs, no?" Poppy asked suddenly.

Quiver responded with a tilt of his head, confusion clear on his face.

"The bear. She must have had cubs nearby."

"It wasn't a bear," Quiver said.

"I've seen many wounds before," Poppy observed, her gaze going back to Masco. "Many of them animal wounds. This was from a bear."

"When's the last time you've seen a bear with three claws?" Rasca challenged.

Poppy shrugged. "Nights ago, I helped a man with only three fingers," she replied, nodding toward Rasca's bandaged hand. "First time for everything, I guess."

"We saw them," Quiver said before Rasca could retort. His mind went back to that night in the woods. He thought about the ambush he had set with his pack, about the way the beasts had moved as silent as the night, how weightless they were as they scaled the trees. How their red eyes glowed in the dark.

That haunting howl.

"They weren't bears," Quiver concluded, more to himself than to Poppy.

Quiver looked long at Masco. He was still sitting up, but his eyes were closed. He was taking deep breaths, sweat beading down his forehead.

"You said he was mumbling in his sleep?" Rasca asked Poppy.

She nodded in answer.

"What was he saying?"

Poppy struggled as she tried to put her thoughts into words. "It does not make sense to me. Something about … a tooth?"

There was a long pause as Rasca raised a brow. "A tooth?"

"A tooth," Poppy confirmed.

Rasca was losing his patience waiting for Poppy to further explain. "Anything else about this—"

"Chief."

It was only then that Quiver noticed Masco looking right at him. His eyes sank heavily, swelling with exhaustion. His mouth hung open, breathing deeply between his words.

"I … heard her … Chief," Masco said. "I heard … her tell me …" He grimaced, clearly in pain as he tried to speak.

"Easy." Quiver gestured to Poppy with a nod.

She replied by handing Masco another cup of water.

415

"Drink, then talk. Easy now."

When he'd finished drinking, he looked at Quiver in earnest. "She showed me. I saw you."

"Who showed you?" Quiver leaned forward so he could hear better. "Saw me where?"

Masco gently shook his head. "I didn't see her, but she was talking to me. She showed me things. Things about you. Things about the world."

Quiver reached out to the boy, trying to calm him, but Masco shook his head more vigorously.

"I saw two men fighting. They were standing in a ring of villagers. Warriors, I think. The man fighting looked like you, only I *knew* he wasn't. He was much older."

Quiver listened intently as Masco painted the melancholy memory in his mind.

"He fought against a man with a giant hammer. The man looked ... strange. White skin and long hair. He killed the man who looked like you, and then was ... set free?"

Quiver's heart sank with the memory. He was about to speak when Masco continued.

"Then she spoke to me. She said, 'This is where his path began.' "

Where my path ... began? Quiver thought back to that day when he had been a youngling himself. A youngling dragged into a war he didn't understand. A youngling dragged to a dueling ring to watch his father die.

"Then I saw you the way you are now," Masco continued. "Younger, though. In the woods, standing there with your bow in hand. You were surrounded by death." In that moment, Masco looked horrified. "So much death. I couldn't see it. I could only ... sense it. I felt it. It felt ... cold ..." His words trailed off.

"It was just a dream," Quiver assured, even though he knew he was lying. "Listen to the healer now. You need to rest."

For a moment, Masco just stared off in thought. Then he set his eyes on Quiver, his jaw tight and his voice clear enough to make you second-guess he'd been wounded at all. "You were just standing there when a wolf came out of the woods. A massive wolf. One with green eyes. You spoke to it. You said, 'This war has made us all monsters, but nobody will be more a beast than yourself.' "

Quiver sat frozen with the memory of those words. They echoed in his mind, bringing him back to that day of blood, to the last day he'd seen the Wolf.

It's been nearly fifteen years since that day. A few years before the youngling was even born. How could he possibly know this?

Masco continued his story, on the verge of losing consciousness again. "When I looked back, the wolf was gone, but a man was standing there. A man covered in blood. He was holding swords, one in each hand." Masco squinted in thought. "I think there were two more at his waist."

The Wolf and his fangs. How could I ever forget those?

Quiver looked at Rasca, who looked just as concerned as Quiver felt. Poppy, however, just shook her head.

"Like I said," Poppy explained, "he makes no sense."

"Did she say anything else?" Rasca asked, ignoring the healer entirely.

Masco remained focused on Quiver. "She said it was the moment you gave up on our way of life. The moment you let go of your hatred. She told me, 'All paths will cross at the Crooked Tooth,' and that I should follow you there when you leave."

Quiver squinted, his chest tight with anxiety and worry. "When I … leave?"

Masco responded with a simple nod.

The entrance to the tent was opened, and two men stepped inside. They looked between Quiver and Rasca. When Poppy got up to fetch Masco another pitcher of water, one of the men spoke.

"The elder wishes for you to rest easy, Chief Quiver and Chief Rasca. Rest now, for three days from now, you are to report to the elder hall and report your quest in front of the entire village."

The men were about to leave, clearly told to simply deliver their message and do nothing more, but Quiver wasn't about to play these games. There was simply no time for that.

"Where is the elder now?" Quiver asked impatiently. He half-expected the men to ignore the question and leave. To his relief, they turned to face him.

"He remains in the elder hall to bless the food for tonight's feast," one of them said.

Quiver looked to Rasca. His friend stared back at him for a moment before nodding, answering the question that Quiver didn't need to ask.

Again, it was moments like these when Quiver couldn't express how thankful he was for such a loyal friend.

"Tell Elder Roku we'll be at the hall soon," Quiver said, stretching the stiff sores from his body. "Then we'll give our report, and he can have his trial."

The Trial of the Heretic

"It seems the elder believes we are at war," Rasca said, speaking the very words on Quiver's mind as they approached the elder hall.

Wartime tradition was second nature to Quiver. He had been raised during one of the bloodiest wars his people had ever experienced. Throughout the Days of Old, when his people consisted of scattered clans that would war against one another in order to attain power, it had been a grueling, dark time. However, his people had never experienced devastation the way they had when they fought against the south, and they would have been all but massacred if it weren't for Quiver's father.

There were two sides of the man Quiver knew as the Nara'Seir: the general and the father. The general had trained Quiver how to become the greatest fighter. Quiver remembered times when Quiver had been running drills with his bow for nearly a month every day, shooting from places like high in a tree or tucked low underneath a bush. How to draw and nock an arrow in the blink of an eye. How to hit split an arrow from a hundred yards out. He was being trained to be the perfect killer.

Then there was the father that Quiver remembered. The father who would steal away Quiver and his brother whenever there was a chance. They would disappear for a few nights just to set up camp away from the clan and spend time with each other. He would tell them stories about life, about how to be a man *for* the world rather than a man *of* the world. They would stay up late at night, looking up at the stars for hours without a word passing between any of them.

He had loved nights with his father more than anything, mostly because they could all be themselves rather than warriors preparing for a war. Yet, as time went on and the war began to drag on longer than Quiver's father had expected, those special nights with his father and brother had become more brief. In the end, Quiver had known his father more as the Nara'Seir than father.

Quiver let out a long, deep breath. "It seems that way."

He had spent the day tending to Masco, who had fallen into another deep sleep soon after the visit from the elder's guards. Poppy had assured him that it was nothing more than sleep, and Quiver had no reason to doubt Poppy's capabilities, so he had decided to leave Masco to rest.

Quiver and Rasca would have gone in search of Oppo soon after that, but the boy was being questioned by Elder Roku.

The boy needs some rest, not an interrogation.

"But why?" Rasca waved to the two guards before them. "What is the point of it all?"

Quiver knew exactly why the elder had posted guards outside the hall. It was the same reason he had two of his guards fetch him and Rasca earlier that day. The same reason they were having a trial in the first place.

"He wants to prove his power to his enemies."

"Enemies?" Rasca looked to Quiver, a raised eyebrow and a slight shake of his head. "What enemies?"

Quiver made for the tent. "Me."

Never in his history had Quiver heard of a trial being held by his people. It was a southern tradition, one that his culture was exposed to during the Great War. Quiver knew that there would be a great gathering of people, in a grand building that represented some sort of political power, to question someone. That individual or, in some cases, individuals were given the opportunity to shed light on a situation that everyone felt needed explaining.

Thing was that the people who were put on trial were usually being accused of something, typically something that would ultimately lead to a guilty sentencing, in which they would receive some type of punishment. All of this Quiver had learned from his father.

As time went on during the war, his father had continued to teach the way the southern people lived their lives, their traditions, what they valued, their political structure. One day, during a fit, Quiver's brother had asked why he was teaching them how the southerners lived. Quiver would never forget his father's response. *"In order to defeat your enemy, you must understand your enemy."*

The more Quiver grew to understand the southerners, the more he began to see less differences between them and his own people. He questioned how there was conflict between them in the first place. Maybe, in the grand scheme of things, that was exactly what his father had wanted his two sons to understand all along.

The inside of the tent was packed. It seemed that just about every villager had shown up for the trial, all standing near the sides of the large house, all faces of who Quiver had grown to know and love over the years. They all looked at him.

As he scanned about, Quiver could see Thread near the back corner of the room, her arms crossed and her hood up. Even with the attempt at hiding her face, he could still see worry in her eyes.

The uproar of the crowd began to fade as he and Rasca entered, and as the silence drew on, those villagers he knew so well began to part toward opposite ends of the room, revealing Elder Roku sitting in his large wooden chair against the far wall. The two guards who had fetched Quiver and Rasca earlier stood at his sides, long spears in their hands, as still as a stone but as cautious as leopards. Between Elder Roku and Quiver was a large bonfire pit that burned with a low flame, a haze of smoke thickening the air.

All was silent in the room now.

A smile crept across Elder Roku's face as he looked at Quiver across the fire, a smile that, despite the warmth of the room, sent a dreadful shiver down Quiver's aching spine.

"No matter what happens," Quiver mumbled quietly to Rasca beside him, "do not get involved. These people will need you in order to survive. Swear to me, by them, you'll do what's right, regardless of how this turns out."

Rasca growled to himself. "We are both chiefs. You can't ask that of me."

"I'm not asking you as a chief," Quiver replied. "I'm asking you as a friend. Please, swear to me."

Rasca turned sideways toward Quiver, not a trace of humor on his face. "I swear to you that I'll do what is right."

With that, Quiver matched Elder Roku's stare and stepped forward, leaving Rasca where he stood, placing himself in the center of the elder hall before his sworn leader and before the entire village.

"Chief Quiver," Elder Roku's voice boomed throughout the hall, "you stand before your people because I wish to give you the opportunity to explain your experience regarding the task I assigned to you. I understand that you have had dire tidings regarding your search for Chief Nero, and it would not be right of me, elder of these people, to deny you the chance to share the story of your experience. I can only imagine you have much to say."

Quiver looked around the room, to the faces he'd sworn to protect. "Yes."

Elder Roku leaned forward in his chair, the old wood creaking with his weight. "You may proceed then, Chief Quiver."

Quiver looked to the faces around him as he told his story. He began by stating what his duties were from Elder Roku, about how he had set out with Rasca and the three younglings in search of Nero. He talked about how they caught sight of their tracks, which led to the clearing where they found evidence of an ambush. He mentioned finding Nero's hatchet, now wondering where that was, and about the tracks they'd discovered on the trees.

"And you truly believe Nero and his pack were attacked by this unseen force?" Elder Roku asked Quiver.

"I do," Quiver answered.

"And did you find any bodies?"

Quiver could see where this was going, and he could already feel the heat rise in his cheeks. "No, but—"

"No bodies of Nero and his pack, nor of an enemy tribe?"

"There were no signs of bodies, nor any blood trails leading to one." Quiver curled his lips and glared across the fire to Elder Roku. "And there hasn't been an *enemy tribe* since the Days of Old."

Elder Roku spread his arms to his sides, looking back and forth between the crowd of faces that stood by. "You claim there was evidence of a fight, yet you show no evidence."

"As I've said, we—"

"Could it be possible you simply lost his trail?" Before Quiver could answer, Elder Roku was already smiling wide to the crowd, cutting off any chance for Quiver's response. "The jungle is a big place. Perhaps your eyes are not what they once were, Chief Quiver."

Half the crowd rumbled with laughter while the other half stood by quietly.

He's trying to use the crowd against you, Quiver thought to himself. *He wants to make a fool of you, to make you out as a failure in front of the village.*

"My eyes see more clearly than before I left, Elder Roku." Quiver struggled to keep the ire out of his voice. Tried and failed. "I did not claim that Nero was attacked by another tribe, nor anything … human, at all."

Gasps erupted around the elder hall, echoing from person to person, and the villagers around Quiver began to shift uncomfortably. Elder Roku, however, only raised an eyebrow in question.

"Nothing *human*, you claim?"

"Can you not hear me atop your throne?" Quiver rolled his shoulders back, puffing out his chest in defiance. "Perhaps your ears are not what they once were, Elder Roku."

Laughter among the crowd faded to silence, all but the quiet chuckle coming from Rasca.

For a moment, the room was deadly still. Villagers looked from Quiver to their elder, their jaws dropped and eyes white and wide.

Quiver saw a flash of anger pass over his elder's face, his lips curling behind the flames of the fire. "Explain," he sneered.

Quiver told his story about the howlers, about their relentless pursuit through the jungle. When he got to the part of their journey when they discovered it wasn't the eyesight the beasts were using to track them, but their smell, he mentioned how he and his pack had agreed to set an ambush for the beasts.

He heard gasps in the crowd as he described the howlers; their guile tactics as they entered the ambush site, their glowing red eyes, and the enormity of their bodies. Then he mentioned Sparrow's fall and inevitable death. For the sake of the youngling's parents who were undoubtedly somewhere amongst the faces in the crowd, he left out the bit where he'd been mauled to death by the beats, how the youngling had died one of the worst possible ways Quiver could imagine.

He then explained their journey home, about their lack of food and water. They talked about the medicine they had found for Masco's wounds, how they fought the infection while doing their best to carry on. When Quiver finally arrived at the part when they collapsed in the woods and were eventually found by their clan, all was silent in the elder hall.

Elder Roku looked at Quiver from his chair, replaying the series of events in his head. Quiver just stood quietly to himself, relieved that he was able to warn the villagers of the howlers before it was too late.

"It seems," Elder Roku said from across the room, "that you have had dire experiences, indeed, and that we should be lucky for you to be alive."

Quiver nodded, genuinely shocked at the sudden praise from Elder Roku. Perhaps he was too hasty with his anger, and that his elder genuinely did want to understand what had happened in the forest.

"However," Elder Roku continued, and in that moment, Quiver knew that things were not going to go the way he had hoped, "that's if all of this is true."

Quiver balled his fists at his sides, trying hard to keep them tucked toward his back so no one could see. "I assure you," he said patiently, "it is true."

"Maybe parts of it, yes." Elder Roku stood now, pacing before the crowd. "I do believe you tracked Chief Nero to a clearing, but I also believe that it was there you failed to pick up his trail. I believe you did not want to look weak in front of the younglings, nor Chief Rasca, so you conjured a plan that would allow you to keep your reputation.

"I also believe that you were, in fact, pursued by beasts, but not of these monsters you describe. I myself have visited young Masco in Poppy's hut, and I think we can all conclude that his wound was caused by nothing more than a bear. It wouldn't be the first time they've been spotted in the forest, and I'm sure it won't be the last."

Quiver was about to protest, but the elder shut him down with a rise of his hand. "And what I most definitely believe, Chief Quiver, is that in order for you to keep your status as chief, and to save face amongst your peers and fellow villagers, you've conjured up this entire story because of the one thing you and I can firmly agree on—you failed to protect your younglings. In the end, one of them is dead, and the other one scarred for life."

Oppo materialized from behind one of the guards.

"If it wasn't for this brave youngling here"—Elder Roku waved a hand toward Oppo, who in response kept his eyes glued to the floor and his hands in front of himself—"we might never have known the truth of you."

"And what truth is that?" Quiver challenged.

Elder Roku paced in front of the crowd, looking from face to face of his people, a shepherd amongst his cattle. "You all know what I speak of. It is in plain sight before you today and has been for years now. There is no denying that this man has become corrupted for some time, banishing his faith in our spirits to adopt the heretical faith of our sworn enemies.

"For years now he's tried spreading his poison among you, teaching you in the ways of the south; having you speak their words, learn their ways, practice their traditions and, although it brings me great fear to say, worship their gods!"

Some in the crowd began nodding their heads, their eyes wide as they fed into Elder Roku's manipulation. Others held passive stares, neither accepting nor denying Roku's accusations.

Quiver feared that Roku would somehow spin this into an opportunity to alienate him, and it seemed that was exactly what he was trying to do.

"On countless occasions, you have seen Chief Quiver go against my wishes. Before I set him out in search of Nero, I begged him to take a group of younglings. I pleaded with him that it'd be a great opportunity for our young to learn our ways, to see how we choose to live life in the eyes of the spirits and how to make those spirits proud of us. But, of course, he openly denied me until I reminded him of his duties as chief."

Elder Roku's head sank to his chest, his voice becoming very quiet. "And perhaps I should have listened to him, for if I had, young Sparrow would still be alive today. That is my burden to bear, not Chief Quiver's, for the very life of my clan is my sole purpose."

"Your sole purpose in life?" Rasca, who had until that moment done what Quiver had hoped him to do, took his place beside Quiver. "Years ago, you took your oath to lead these people, to watch over them and grow them as a clan, sacrificing your own needs to put theirs above your own. That is what you swore to do, Elder Roku. But what you swore to do years ago and what you have done since then are two very different things."

"What in the hells are you doing, Rasca?" Quiver growled at his friend, not knowing whether he should hug the man or punch him in his face.

Rasca never took his eyes from Elder Roku. "I'm doing what is right."

"See before you the truth of what I speak!" Roku waved his hand toward Rasca and Quiver. "See how his poison spreads, how he openly defies the spirits and his very own elder.

"Let me tell you what happened to Nero." Elder Roku now looked upon his flock. "We have had reports of attacks from other clans. I know I should have told you all, but I did not want to spread worry amongst you. You see, like Chief Quiver here, our fellow clansman have been corrupted by the south, living their lives in the eyes of the false gods while our spirits are pushed aside.

"I believe Nero and his pack were attacked, yes, but not from these monsters you describe, but by the monsters of these heretics. I thought this could be something that would pass, that we could save them but, as you can see, their poison has spread to our village. It is my duty, by you and the spirits watching over us, as chief amongst us all, to find a solution."

Quiver mumbled to himself, shaking his head in frustration.

"What was that?" Elder Roku took his place in front of his chair, beyond the fire, beyond Quiver's reach. "There is no point in hiding your intentions now. You have finally been brought to light. If you wish to plead your sanctity, do so where we and the spirits can hear."

"I said"—Quiver looked up, his fists balled at his waist, his lips curling in rage—"you are no elder of mine. You are a savage."

Gasps and pandemonium exploded in the elder hall. Chaos boomed as Quiver's clan burst into fits of anger, shock, and fear. The guards at Roku's sides tensed, their spears dipping low to the ground, ready to fend off an attack, or spring their own.

In that moment, Quiver knew Elder Roku had won.

"I see," Roku said, sitting back down in his seat. "Then my greatest fear has come true. It seems you are truly lost. I had truly hoped that you'd have overcome your internal struggles, but it seems that the south has corrupted your soul beyond redemption. Yes, I can see it—"

"You've already told us what you've seen, Roku!" Quiver all but roared. "Now let me tell you what I have seen." To address an elder solely by their name was beyond disrespectful, some might even call it heresy, but Quiver saw no reason to hold back anymore.

"Before," Quiver began, "there stood five separate clans of our people, each clan led by those who craved power and glory. For centuries, we waged war against each other, fighting for things like land, or currency, even slaves. We did all this to prove ourselves to the spirits we worship. We lived a life dedicated to the bloodlust of our gods.

"And then came the Great War, led by the southerners who, for some reason, we still fear today. They studied us in the shadows, watched as we fought against our own, watched as we butchered one another so we could boast the reputation of our own clan. They saw us for what we truly were." Quiver searched the faces of those standing before him. "Who here remembers what they called us?"

Quiver let the silence drag, waiting for an answer. When it came, it was from Rasca beside him.

"Savage," he answered.

"Savage!" Quiver shouted the word. "They called us savages, and that's what we were! We'd rather kill our own people than work together. And because of that, we were easy targets for the south. We had no line of defense, no organized army. Not until the Nara'Seir."

Whispers echoed the crowd. People looked to one another, a nod of acknowledgement with mention of Quiver's father, the one man in the entire tribe who had managed to band together all clans.

Even Elder Roku nodded with acknowledgment. "We have not forgotten what your father has accomplished, of how he saved us all from peril, Quiver. However, it is not he who is on trial."

"No, he is not," Quiver spat back. He took a step around the firepit, and Roku's two guards tensed as Quiver stepped toward them. "It is *you* who is on trial, Elder Roku."

"How dare you!" Roku signaled with a flick of his hand.

One of his guards struck out with his spear, intent on skewering Quiver where he stood. Quiver, however, stepped to the side, grabbed the spear, and pulled the weapon toward him, grasping the guard's wrist and dragging him forward, as well. He tripped the guard with a well-placed foot, who then instinctively let go of the spear as he fell. In the end of the brief encounter, Quiver stood above the guard, the spear firmly in his hand.

Roku leaned away in his chair, scared of the blow Quiver was surely going to strike. Instead, Quiver broke the spear over his knee and threw both parts behind his back.

"Since my father united the clans, we defended our own lands against the southern invaders. We may have lost the war, but what we gained was victory enough. We gained a united people, living together and *for* one another. Something nobody had managed to do since the beginning of our history.

"Now *you!*" Quiver's finger was inches away from Roku's face. The elder was now cowering in fear, trying hard to slink through the cracks in his chair and out of Quiver's reach. "*You* have become the very thing we escaped from all those years ago. You crave power and blood, using our spirits as a shield to hide behind as you seek to separate our people, to bring them more pain and suffering at the expense of our united survival.

"For years, you've become corrupt with your position. You plan to expand your territory, to make an enemy of our own people, and to enslave the very people who you promised to lead. You worry more about your throne than the people who gave it to you. You, Elder Roku, have become a *savage!*"

More roars erupted from the crowd, but Quiver didn't let it stop him. He looked to the faces of his people as he walked to the other side of the fire.

The guard he had tripped was just managing to get off the floor. As he stood to rise, Quiver offered him a helping hand, taking hold of his arm and dragging him to his feet. He nodded to the guard, and although there was clear anger in his eyes, the guard nodded back.

Quiver turned back toward Elder Roku, who had suddenly found enough courage to sit straight in his chair now that Quiver was out of arm's reach, a menacing look on his face that screamed murder.

Yet Quiver didn't falter.

"I came here today for one reason, and one reason only. I came to warn my clan, *my people*, about the threat in the woods. They are still my people even though you have poisoned them against me."

"You openly defy me in the face of our gods, and then expect these people to heed your warning?" Elder Roku laughed. "You are a fool."

Despite the turn of events, of how dire things had suddenly become, Quiver matched Roku's laughter. For the first time in years, Quiver truly laughed. Not a chuckle, not a giggle, but a deep, genuine laugh.

"You have the audacity to mock me?" Roku's voice boomed in the hall. "To mock the spirits?"

"The spirits?" Quiver looked around the room. He saw Thread watching with calm composure, but even Quiver could see how tense she was. Rasca, the oldest friend he had, the only person who he could truly trust with anything, stood by him, nodding in approval, as if he'd already agreed with the realization Quiver had come to.

"The spirits have either abandoned us, or they're dead," Quiver said, no remorse in his voice.

Loud gasps and cries passed through the crowd.

"If they are dead, it is because we drove them to kill themselves. And if they have abandoned us"—Quiver looked directly at Roku—"then fuck them."

Quiver let the cries ring through the crowd, pandemonium shaking the very foundation of the elder hall. Roku's guards tensed, deciding whether or not they should attack Quiver there and then.

Then Quiver spoke again, his voice loud as he roared over the crowd. "The spirits do nothing but crave blood from the very people who worship them, and I refuse to spill another drop in their name. But even still, I hold faith in my heart. Not of the spirits, no! I hold faith for *you*—the people, my clan, my friends and family. I did not come here to answer to Roku; I came here to warn my people. And I pray to whatever bloodthirsty wraith that claims to be a god that you heed my warning."

"Out!" Roku sprang to his feet. "Out now! You are banished. Go into exile like your brother. Live with the very people who took your own father's life. Go live and worship those false gods. You have brought shame to your ancestors and to these people. Be gone tomorrow, or I swear I will send you to the spirits you claim absent."

Quiver was already moving toward the door, turning his back on the people he'd sworn to serve and protect, no matter what the cost. One moment, he had been chief among the greatest clan he'd managed to live with, and the next he was nothing but an exile, a traitor in the eyes of the people he had so recently called a family.

The crowd was in an uproar, shouting vulgarities and insults as he passed them. Some of them even went as far as spitting on the ground next to him. And even amongst all of that, even as Roku continued his threats, how his own father was disowning him in the afterlife, Quiver wasn't mad.

In fact, he felt a great sadness in his gut. Not because he was exiled. Not because he had managed to become a traitor among his people. But because he knew that once the real monsters came to this village, almost all the faces he had just seen, the ones he has grown to know and love, would be amongst the dead.

Fit For a Fairy Tale

They'd been walking for two days now, trekking across the endless plain with little sleep or rest. The sun was setting, the tall green trees only a blur on the horizon.

"Just beyond those trees now," Benny said, sweating profusely with the struggle of Alric's unconscious body wrapped around his shoulders. "Not much farther."

"But far enough," Evan replied, taking his place at Benny's side. "Let me carry him."

"No," Benny said sternly, not bothering to meet Evan's eyes as he answered. "I'll be fine. You're a better fighter, and we'll need you if the guards track us."

It had been like this since they had managed to escape Servitol. The first night, they had walked for hours, finding an island of trees a few miles away from the walls of the capital where they rested the remainder of the night. Benny had addressed Alric's wound, wrapping the torn-off sleeve of his tunic around his head to help control the bleeding. Warren, with his wounded leg, had actually been lucky enough—the blade was a clean cut, through and through. He wouldn't suffer any permanent damage, but he still struggled to walk.

Benny refused to sleep. He spent the entirety of his time focusing on Alric's well-being through day and night, refusing the extra help that others, especially Evan, had offered. Even when the cut at Benny's side had reopened on more than a few occasions, though he had settled with a hasty bandage from his torn shirt. It was like this every night, and before the sun fully rose in the morning, they were off again.

Evan looked over his shoulder, past Sarah, Trevor, Warren, and Dodge, scanning the open terrain. The night was young, for they had marched all day. Besides the starlight guiding their way, nothing could be seen through the darkness. If they were being followed, they would never know.

"They'll never get us before we reach the tree line, but they will if you pass out and we have to carry you, as well. Here." Evan tried taking Alric from Benny, but Benny shoved him away with his free hand.

"I said no," Benny snapped, and beyond the sweat dripping from his face, Trevor could see tears in the man's eyes. "I'll carry him to the tree line, and then you'll help me make a litter. Until then, just keep your mouth shut and your eyes open."

Besides the occasional grunt and heavy breathing from Benny, everyone mostly kept to themselves. Evan didn't intervene or try to help Benny anymore. Instead, he kept his notorious comments to himself and scanned the surrounding area just as Benny had told him to.

Trevor couldn't pry his mind away from the image of Tom dead on the ground. There was a part of him that expected to still see the man when he would return to Robins-Port. But he knew that would never happen, since Robins-Port was burned to the ground and Tom was lying facedown in the dirt.

I wonder what they'll do with his body, he thought. *Would they bury him outside the city? Find a place in the crypts beneath the city streets?*

It was unlikely. Where he and the others knew that Tom was only trying to protect himself and the rest of them, the city would only see him as an enemy. Trevor doubted they would treat his body with care for the burial, if there was a burial at all.

After about another hour of sulking in silence, they finally made it to the forest. Large oak trees stretched high toward the sky, blocking out the light of the stars above them.

They'd walked about a hundred feet into the tree line when Benny set Alric down against a tree.

"We need … some sticks …" Benny said between deep breaths.

"What you need is some fucking rest," Evan replied, his concerned tone borderline irritation.

Trevor's legs were tight, but the pain didn't bother him. It was something that existed beyond the numb of Tom's recent death. He set himself down next to a tree, leaning his head back against the rough bark. He saw Dodge and Sarah doing the same across from him, their eyes downcast and bleary with exhaustion.

"What we need …" Benny said, casting his eyes up at Evan who stood above him, "is some gods damned sticks … to make a gods damned litter."

Evan knelt down next to Benny and spoke quietly to him, beyond the reach of Trevor's ears. They were nodding back and forth, whispering to each other, all the while nodding slightly toward Alric, whose head was hunched over his chest.

A twig snapped, and Trevor jolted with worry. He was just beginning to rush to his feet, reaching toward his waist for the hilt of his sword, when he saw that the sound had come from Warren.

Warren had been quiet for the entirety of the trip. He had kept his distance between himself and the rest of the group, limping along in silence. His leg was wrapped in a tight cloth, stained with dark red, yet he seemed to manage just fine, which only pissed Trevor off even more. Tom was dead, and Warren was able to walk away with his life just fine.

Warren searched around the clearing for somewhere to sit then settled for a tree not too far from Trevor's left. Close proximity of Warren alone was enough to boil Trevor with anger.

"Fine ..." Trevor heard Benny say, defeat in his voice as he looked at Trevor and the rest of them. "We'll rest, but only for a bit. We're not too far now."

"That's what you said hours ago," Warren replied, his legs tucked to his chest and his arms wrapped around them. "You said we'd be there soon, yet we're still in the middle of nowhere."

Benny's eyes were tight with anger. The man had always seemed so upbeat and positive, so to see the anger flaring in his eyes sent a small chill down Trevor's spine.

"Precisely," Benny said plainly.

Warren's face twisted in disgust. "You mean to tell me that you've been leading us to the middle of nowhere *on purpose*."

"That's enough," Dodge said, leaving Sarah sitting against a tree and taking his place kneeling at Alric's side.

"No, I'm not going—"

"I said *that's enough*." Dodge didn't shout, but the threat of violence in his voice was loud and clear. He looked over Alric, parting his hair and tilting his unconscious head back and forth. "His skull is cracked. Probably a concussion." He pulled aside Alric's jacket. "Not to mention the amount of blood he's lost from that arrow. We can't afford to rest. We need to get him to a doctor quick."

Dodge wrapped Alric's arm around his neck and dragged him to his feet, shifting the weight where he could carry the man around his shoulders. Benny rushed to his feet and began walking toward his friend when Dodge lifted out a hand for him to stop.

"I get it," Dodge said, "but we can't risk carrying you, too. How much farther is it?"

Trevor thought Benny was sure to protest, but he just hunched his shoulders and blew out a deep breath. "Just over an hour if we keep the pace. There's a cabin hidden in the brush. If the others aren't there now, they will be soon. Seroes can fix him up."

"Just over an hour," Dodge repeated to himself, nodding. He looked to Trevor, real worry in his eyes. "Well, we better set off, then. Lead the way."

Trevor was about to follow when he noticed Sarah still hadn't moved from her spot. Slowly, he walked over to her when he heard the faint and quiet sound of snoring. He knelt down next to her, a sad smile on his lips as he watched her sleep peacefully. Her hands were in her lap, her head tucked to her chest, the rise and fall of her chest matching the rhythm of her quiet snoring. He wished he could leave her to rest, but they had to keep moving.

He reached out and gently took her hand in his. The snoring stopped suddenly, and Sarah slowly raised her chin and looked at Trevor. She then looked down to their interlocking hands before meeting Trevor's eyes again. They were quiet for a moment, and then Sarah pulled her hand away from his, twisting Trevor's guts in his stomach.

Feeling foolish, he cleared his throat and stood. "We're moving out again. They said it would be about another hour."

Before waiting for a response, Trevor left Sarah where she sat.

***

Realizing everyone else had moved on, Sarah jumped to her feet and began following after Trevor. She couldn't remember the moment of falling asleep. Honestly, she couldn't even remember sitting down. One moment, she was entering the forest, keeping close to Dodge, and then the next, she was lying against a tree, waking up with Trevor holding her hand.

She didn't know why she had pulled away from him, but she had, and she instantly regretted her decision the moment she saw the hurt on his face. As Trevor turned his back, Sarah had wanted to reach out and drag him to the ground with her, to wrap her arms around his neck and squeeze tightly.

She kept an eye on his swinging hand as she walked behind him, tempted to

433

run up and take it in her own. But she didn't. Instead, she walked in silence, keeping her eyes glued to the ground, watching her feet as they took repeated steps.

Blame it on her exhaustion, but it took her a minute to realize that Warren was walking at her side. She heard his voice but couldn't make out what he had said.

"What?" she asked him, sleep dragging her words.

Warren didn't meet her eyes. He kept his focus on the ground, his hands clasped before his stomach as he limped on. For a moment, Sarah wasn't sure that he had spoken at all, that maybe it had been just something she had imagined. But then Warren said it again.

"I didn't …" Warren struggled with his words. "What happened, I didn't want that. I didn't want … him to die."

A moment passed before Sarah realized he was referring to Tom, and then a rush of sadness washed over her. She had known Tom her whole life, and now he was gone. Gone because he tried to protect a person who, in Sarah's opinion, was the least deserving person of protection from anything.

"I know," Sarah said.

Warren raised his head and looked at Sarah, tears dripping from his cheeks as he sniffled.

"But he did."

Warren wiped his nose on his sleeve, patting the tears away from his eyes. They walked in silence for a while longer until he spoke again.

"I saw it, you know," he said.

Sarah kept her eyes forward, her gaze still drifting toward Trevor's hand. "Saw what?"

"Back home. The attack." Warren's voice began to shake, quaking with fear. He took a deep shuddering breath then breathed out slowly. "I was sitting in my room when they came in. I rushed out to see what was wrong when I saw them beating her. They just kept … beating her face for no reason. I yelled at them to stop, but they didn't listen. My pa came stumbling out of his room, half-drunk, wobbling over to them with a cutting knife in his hand. They didn't even hesitate. One moment he was mumbling at them to leave my mom alone; next, his throat was slashed open, and the men were laughing.

"I can still hear the sound, you know?" He looked at Sarah, hoping she would understand. And she did. "The sound it made as the man kept pounding my mom's face. Whenever it gets quiet, I can hear it. Whenever I lay down to sleep, I hear it. I can't …" Warren hugged himself, his shoulders shaking at the memory. "I just can't stand the *silence*."

He was quiet after that, no doubt reliving the memory over again as they walked along. Sarah could relate. Every time she tried to sleep, she was back in that tunnel, crawling through the dirt as the man called out to her in the dark.

Here, little piggy!

"Anyway"—Warren sniffled and wiped his face—"all I'm saying is I didn't want Tom to die, too. I'm sorry."

"Sorry?" Sarah all but laughed to herself, knowing full well that there was nothing the least bit funny. "It doesn't matter that you're sorry, Warren. He's still *dead*. He died keeping *you* alive. What matters now is what you do with that second chance."

Sarah expected a retort, a vile rebuttal to make himself feel better, but to her surprise, Warren kept quiet, his face no longer belonging to the childhood bully she knew, but a victim of tragedy, just like her.

"I know," Warren said. "I want to do better." He nodded, wiping the final tear from his face. He looked at Sarah with determination. "I'm *going* to be better."

Sarah shook her head. She didn't believe a thing Warren was saying, no matter how much she wanted to. "Try harder."

They kept a quiet pace for a while longer, the crunching of fallen leaves and the heavy breathing from Dodge near the front of the line the only sounds within the woods.

Sarah kept her eyes on Trevor's back, wondering what was going through his head at that moment. On more than a few occasions, she nearly picked up her pace, leaving Warren alone behind her as she met with Trevor at his side. She wanted to take his hand in hers, tell him she's sorry about how distant she's become. Explain to him that it wasn't his fault, that it was the man's she kept seeing in her dreams. She would confess what happened to her parents, about what happened to her in the tunnel. She'd let him wrap his arms around her as she wept in his arms with the memory of her dead family.

But every time she made to move, her body froze, her chest clenching with anxiety, and her muscles went numb with content. So, instead of seeking help from the one person who was dying to offer it, she settled for her childhood bully in absolute silence.

***

There was a certain beauty to the woods that Benny led them through. It was something beyond the idea of quiet. It was the absence of the world existing outside the threshold of the trees.

The woods are a world of its own, still and quiet, peaceful and harmless. It's everything the world beyond the tree line lacks.

Regardless of the circumstances, Trevor couldn't deny the beauty of the world he walked through in that moment. The way the moon gleamed through the spaces of the trees, the shadows of branches stretching out above his head, the occasional howl from an owl, the feeling of the gentle breeze, and the scent of leaves on the wind.

Of course, Trevor never had a chance to see much of the world outside of Robins-Port before, so anything beyond the dirt roads and the wooden confines of his walls was all new to him. There was, however, the best part of Trevor's past that remained, and it was only twenty feet behind him.

Yet, it seems so much farther.

"It's just through here," Benny said, swatting a thicket of bushes aside. After a few moments of searching with his hand, he pulled against the brush, parting it away to reveal a hidden trail leading farther in.

Trevor was right behind Dodge, who wasted no time proceeding down the hidden path. The path led around thick trees, underneath a fallen log, and past another thicket of bushes. It seemed to be leading to nowhere when, suddenly, Trevor was standing before a cabin that stood on a small hill. A wide patio was lit with torches, the glow of the torchlight spreading its gloom across an open yard.

The cabin was next to a pond, a small dock stretching into its center. Wisps of dragonflies soared above the surface of the water, fish splashing as they jumped from the water to catch their dinner.

The yard blinked with fireflies that buzzed everywhere. The trees surrounding it circled, stretched toward the sky, the thick branches leaving a small opening where the moon beamed down on the lake. It was a scene fit for a fairy tale.

Benny, however, was not fazed by the scenery. He stumbled past Dodge, hobbling his way toward the cabin lights. "Torches are lit," he breathed deeply. It was a wonder how the man was still standing. Not only had he been wounded in the skirmish outside of Servitol days before, but he'd carried Alric's unconscious body nearly the entire way there. "Seroes, we need you out here *now*! Bring your kit!"

Warren and Sarah stood by Trevor, no doubt lost in the beauty of the scenery before them. Meanwhile, Evan rushed past, taking Alric from Dodge's grasp and dragging him toward the cabin. Benny continued to yell, and just as Trevor began to doubt the others had made it there before them, the door opened and Seroes came running out, carrying a large bag in his hand. Garth and Merrick were right behind him, their bows nocked and ready to fire. Baron pushed his way between the two archers, a hood covering his face and a hatchet in both of his hands.

"What's happened?" Seroes ducked, shouldering Alric's other arm, assisting Benny by walking him to the entrance of the cottage.

"Hit in the head," Benny replied between short breaths. "Been unconscious since. Shot with arrow in his left shoulder."

Trevor and the others stood by and watched the events unfold as Garth and Merrick all but leapt down the wooden stairs, rushing to help Seroes and Benny. Evan rushed past them into the cabin without a word, and Trevor could hear the sound of clatter from inside just before Evan reappeared.

"Table's cleared off," he announced. "I've got a blade on the fire to cauterize his shoulder. What else?"

Seroes nodded toward the lake. "Some water. Lots of it. Baron—"

At the mention of his name, Baron tucked his twin hatchets behind his back.

"—grab the gauze out of my bag.

"Garth, in my pack should be a bottle of yellow herbs. Looks like powder and smells rancid. I'll need it to fight the infection.

"Merrick, you see to Benny and the others. Looks like they've taken a hit, as well."

Benny was about to protest when Seroes shot him a quick look. "I'll not hear any of it. I need my space to work, and you'll do nothing but worry and distract."

"I'll need to—"

Seroes nodded to Evan as they reached the door. Evan nodded back and began to relieve Benny of Alric's weight, pulling him away from the door as Seroes carried Alric inside.

Garth walked past Seroes, mumbled something under his breath and stepped off to the side just as Seroes began closing the door.

"I've got this," Seroes said to Benny just before the door shut.

Amidst the prior chaos, all was silent around the cottage. Everyone stood for a moment, letting the life around them chirp and sing, a melody by none other than pure nature. Then everyone began moving again.

Evan, keeping quietly to himself, walked down the steps of the cottage and passed Dodge toward the lake. Dodge, who had been standing by as the others had rushed to Alric's aid, took his spot next to Trevor, Sarah, and Warren. In that moment, there was a line—the survivors of Robins-Port and the brotherhood.

There was a splash, followed by a praising holler. "*Damn*! Now that'll make a fine meal, indeed." The wet sound of boots squished in the dark as Evan strutted back into the glow of the lamp light, his chin held high and just about the biggest fish that Trevor had ever seen flapping on the end of a pointed stick. "Don't know about you all," Evan said with a bright smile, "but I'm famished. Who's ready for a snack?"

Revealing Memories

Sarah had always hated fish. There was something about the smell that lodged in the back of your throat, that soured your nostrils, the pungent smell lingering longer than anyone had bargained for. The smell always brought her back to a time when her mother and father had stopped by a small village near the coast.

Sarah fell into trance with the memory as she watched Evan rotate the fish over the fire.

Small huts lined a bay at the edge of the village, all dedicated to a certain job contributing to their harvest. Where a couple huts were tasked with emptying nets filled with fish, others were tasked with separation of species, while others were tasked for flaying and packaging.

Sarah grimaced as she watched a dark man drag a large net out of the water, the contents of his catch flapping and jumping around vigorously. "Why don't they trade something else?"

"What's that, dear?" her father replied, scanning the manifest his assistant had given him.

"Fish." Her nose crinkled, the word itself bringing that vile smell. "Why would the bank want to invest in a community catching fish? Can't anyone do that?"

"We are here to determine whether or not it's in the bank's best interest to invest in this community based on whether or not their contribution can strengthen our economy."

Sarah looked across the vast body of water before her, the sight making her feel like a tiny ant among the enormous world she knew. The glow of blue stretched endlessly before her, only small dots she knew as fishing boats a few miles off the coast.

"But people sell fish everywhere," she pointed out, hugging her arms as a cold mist blew from the beach.

"They sure do." Harold Michaelson folded up the manifest then tucked it into

his pocket. "But if these numbers are correct, there's been a steady increase of demand for their product since they've begun their trade. According to our data, they can't meet their demand with their current production. We need to not only determine whether or not this can benefit our economy, but if we can even provide a service that helps them with their harvest."

"And how does money help that?"

Harold laughed at her question, a sound Sarah loved to hear. "My dear, banks do not just loan out money. They invest in communities, provide goods to better them so we may better ourselves. Tell me; with a village like this, what do you think the bank could provide to help meet their demand?"

Sarah looked around her. The huts were simple, made of sticks, ropes, and canvas. The people were far from starved, the muscles on both men and women large and swollen from their daily tasks, so food didn't seem like the right answer, either.

"You're not looking in the right direction," her father pointed out, nodding his chin toward the open water.

Sarah took in the sight, smiling as the answer came to her. "Boats."

Harold nodded with an approving smile. "If the bank invests in the building of ships, we not only provide more jobs for the builders, but we invest in trade of wood and materials, as well as increase this community's production of goods. We increase more production here, we produce more trade, we build more ships, and the circle continues on and on. Who knows, dear, this could be the very beginning of a new city in our country, simply by providing nothing more than a few boats and a road for trade, which will also provide more jobs to our citizens."

"But, if it's that easy, why don't we just go for it? What does the bank have to lose?"

"Well, it's not just the bank's money we are investing; it's our citizens'. The bank owes an ethical obligation to be sure our investments will turn for the better. Our kingdom is still young with developing communities we don't even know about yet, and the bank can't provide for them all. To put it simply, we have to make sure our investment is worthwhile."

"And how do we do that?"

"For something like this? It's simple." Harold held out his arm with an inviting smile. "We make sure that the goods will be worth the purchase."

Evan set a fillet onto a ceramic plate, passing it to Garth on his left, who then began passing it around the circle. They sat around the fire, Dodge to Sarah's left and Trevor to her right, as Evan boasted continuously about the quality of their dinner.

"Best you'll ever have," Evan praised, sprinkling some salt onto a fillet as he passed it to the next person. "Won't be able to say otherwise."

Sarah's stomach managed to growl as the plate reached her, regardless of how much she loathed cooked fish. Maybe it was because she was half-starved, or maybe Evan was as good a cook as he claimed to be, but the food before her was ever so inviting. Her mouth salivated as the heat and smell wafted before her face, and without the dignity to use the fork that Dodge had passed her way, she grabbed the fillet with her hand and took a large bite.

Her mouth exploded with flavor, hot grease spreading inside her mouth, the flow of seasonings winning her taste buds over within just a few short seconds. She was familiar with the texture of the meal, but besides that, she'd never tasted anything so good, and some had claimed she'd eaten the best fish in the entire world.

"And what makes this the best fish in the world?" Harold asked the village leader.

The fisherman smiled as if he had been waiting for the question. "It's the only fish you'll have that keeps the integrity any way it's cooked. In my experience, the more you season fish, the drier it gets. You have to cook it as to not get sick, but even the smallest mistake in its preparation will also dry it out.

"But this"—he waved a hand over the table before him, neatly cut and displayed portions of the fish spread out nicely—"you can cook this just the same, but the consistency of the meat won't crumble or break away. It's thin enough to smoke, bold enough to roast over a fire. The meat is so tender, your seasoning won't drip away with the grease, but hold within the body, giving you a much richer and lasting flavor."

Harold perched his lip, weighing his options as he studied the neatly displayed bites of the fish. "May I?"

The fisherman took a step back, opening his arms in invitation. "By all means, please. Help yourself. You and the young one, I mean."

Sarah tried her best not to be rude, but she failed to control the wrinkle of her nose with her first bite of the fish. She wasn't deceived—heavy juices flowed in her mouth—but nothing about the experience was appealing to Sarah. The meat was slimy, the taste was sour, and it lingered in her mouth long after she'd swallowed the contents.

"Mm ..." her father praised, a satisfied look on his face with his third bite. "That is tasty. Very tasty." When he looked down to Sarah, who was fighting back the urge to vomit, Harold laughed. "You'll have to excuse my daughter; her pallet is just as fussy as her mother's."

Sarah half-expected the fisherman to take offense but, to her surprise, he rushed up to the table and gestured to another section of his product. "Too bitter? Try this one. It's smothered in lemon and salt. The sweet and salty helps hide that natural flavor."

"I wouldn't bother with that," Harold teased playfully. "She hates fish. If you can convince her otherwise, then you'd have managed to achieve something I couldn't within her fifteen years."

The fisherman laughed to himself. "My daughter's the same way. Once she's got her mind set on something ..."

"There's no changing it," her father finished, smiling down at Sarah as he took another bite of his food. "I'd catch myself dead the day I see her enjoying a fish fillet."

Sarah's plate was empty within minutes. She had scarfed down the remaining bits of her meal, licking her greasy plate with satisfaction.

As the plate dipped below her eyes, she realized they were all staring at her. Some looked impressed, others shocked, but Evan looked bewildered.

"See?" Evan nodded to Sarah's empty plate. "I told you. I don't know why you people ever doubt me."

Now that her belly was full and warm, sleep was beginning to dawn on her. Her eyes were getting heavy, and a few times, she caught herself drifting off into the glow of the fire, only to catch her head bobbing as she began falling asleep. Now that she was finally settled in and not walking endlessly or running for her life from men in masks, her exhaustion was taking its toll.

She wasn't ready for sleep, though. Not yet, at least. It wasn't that she didn't feel safe, which seemed to become all too familiar as of late, but there had been a question on her mind ever since Servitol.

She looked passed the fire toward the cabin where Benny rocked by himself in a chair on the porch. Seeing as good an opportunity as she was probably going to get, she left the others at the fire and joined him.

It took a moment for Benny to realize Sarah was standing nearby, no doubt trapped within the worries of his friend's condition. When he did see her standing there, however, he gave her a half-smile and gestured to the open seat beside him.

Without saying a word, Sarah sat herself down in the chair.

"Evan always was the best of us when it came to cooking," Benny said eventually. "He always did say that, when we finally decided to retire, we should open up a restaurant up north. He'd be the cook, Garth and Merrick would usher people to their seats, and I'd keep track of the books." Benny laughed to himself sadly. "Evan used to say that Seroes would be a waiter, that all his talk of sympathy would provide the best customer service anyone could offer. And Baron? He'd be the best butcher in the country, just as long as we didn't have any spider nests nearby."

"What about him?" Sarah nodded toward the cabin door.

A tear fell from Benny's face. He quickly wiped it away with his sleeve. "Evan said we'd have the restaurant on a farm, and that Alric would be the one running it.

"It wasn't always like this, you know. There was a time where Al laughed and smiled more often than any of us. He had a farm once … before all this. He and his wife—" Benny stopped suddenly, as if he'd already said too much. Then he shook his head softly, looking away from Sarah, hiding his grief.

"He has a wife?" Sarah asked, knowing she was pressing her luck.

For a moment, she didn't think Benny would answer. He shook his head silently, and just as Sarah was about to ask the question she'd originally come over for, he spoke.

"Alric and I know each other from the war. We'd enlisted at the same booth, was sent to the same training camp, and stationed in the same battalion. We fought the same battles with one another, fought endlessly in the worst parts of the war, only to complete our time of service, retire, and separate.

"You see, I ran away from home to enlist, and I thought about my family every day on the job. About my mother and my sister. There was the three of us, and that's all we had. Well, that was until I ran away to fight for my country. So, when I got out, I told myself I was going to go home, use the money I had to build a better life for my sister and mom."

Benny was silent again, and Sarah knew that talking was helping him keep his mind off the current situation. If she had the opportunity to distract the man from his grief, then that's what she would do.

If only I had something to distract myself from mine.

"And did you go home?" Sarah asked quietly.

Benny nodded. "I did ... for a little bit. Took me all of a month to get there. It seems that no matter how hard you fight during a war, you still only get a small horse and a few coins to get you on your way after being separated, along with a piece of paper you have to bring to the bank to retrieve your payment of service."

"A memo-exchange," Sarah said, managing to get a small smile out of Benny.

She couldn't explain why, but she felt that it was an achievement.

"Seems you've quite the head on your shoulders." He nodded approvingly before looking back toward the others at the fire. "I deposited the money into a bank when I got back home, and then searched out for my mom and sister." Sarah watched as Benny's smile slowly faded. "It wasn't hard to find out what had happened. Everyone in town knew who I was and thought it was their duty to explain it to me.

"My mom had fallen ill with a fever that took her life, and my sister had moved away with her childhood sweetheart. I can't blame her, though. He was a good, smart man. Always talked about money flow, banks, and how the economy should work. All of it went over my head, you see. I was a man of fighting, while he was a man of numbers. The only numbers I cared about was how many were standing next to me on a battlefield, and how many friends I'd lost."

It was a small joke, but not even Benny laughed.

"It was an odd feeling. I spent ten years away from home, but when I got back, it felt like I'd never left. And then, when I found out that my mother had passed and my sister had moved on with her life, I felt like a complete stranger within the very place I grew up.

"I visited my mom at her grave, said my peace, and left a week later. At first, I left in search of my sister, but I couldn't help feeling she was better off with the life she had now.

"I was passing through a small town east of here that was having a parade. Apparently, they'd just hit a contract with the banking system that would help them establish themselves as a major trading city. When I was talking to the locals, they described a man working with his wife, a woman who I found closely detailed to my sister. I don't know what it was, but something told me that it was her, and I nearly wept with happiness when they told me she was with child."

Benny smiled widely to himself, and the image actually got a small smile out of Sarah herself. They sat there for a short time, enjoying the quiet happiness that hung over their heads, enjoying it while it lasted.

"I didn't search for her after that," Benny said a few moments later. "She found her place in the world, and I decided that it was time for me to find mine. I started moving from town to town, traveling the country that I had just spent the last decade fighting for, when I found Alric."

Sarah could feel the mood change, that quiet happiness dissipating like a thin fog in the morning sunlight. He was quiet for a while, chewing his bottom lip as he studied the wooden floor beneath him.

"He'd had it bad during the war. Much was expected out of him, and he was good at it. But the skills of a foot soldier don't always carry over to the skills society needs when a soldier retires. He did, however, buy himself a nice pocket of land in the Orange Fields, found himself a wife, and settled down nicely. I'm sure he was the happiest version of himself during those times."

"What do you mean?" Sarah tugged nervously at the tips of her gloves. "You mean you never saw him there?"

"No, not exactly. When I saw him, he … he was …" Benny sighed to himself and shook his head. "I'm sorry, dear, but that story is not for me to tell." He shifted in his seat. "But something tells me you didn't leave the company of your friends to hear an old man ramble about his past. If I know any better, it seems to me you've asked just about every question besides the one you came over here for."

Sarah shifted uncomfortably, feeling suddenly vulnerable. She looked to the fire, to Trevor, Dodge, and Warren, who still picked at their food, and then back down to her gloved hands. "I wanted to ask you about this." She held out her hands before him. "I don't … understand it. But I think you might."

Benny nodded. "I understand only a little bit, I'm afraid. What I can say, though, is that, throughout all my years, there was only one other person I've met who has this"—Benny lifted his own hand, his leather gloves flexing as he bent his fingers—"ability."

"Who was it?" Sarah asked.

"My sister." Benny smiled to himself again. "Flo."

"Flo?" Sarah was taken aback from the name.

Benny nodded. "Just a name I used to call her when growing up. We were playing one day in our mother's garden. We liked to lock our hands together and swing in a circle for as long as we could before we fell over. Then, one day when we touched, something happened. Images flashed within our heads. I saw images of her playing alone, picking flowers by herself, while she saw images of me playing with a stick, pretending that a tree was a monster as I fought it off with a sword.

"We asked our mother about it, but she brushed it off and told us to stop making up stories. Eventually, we began to realize that they were memories.

"Do you remember what you saw when we touched hands before Servitol?"

Sarah nodded. She remembered the flashes of images; first starting as memories of the attack on Robins-Port, of her mother and father being killed. Then she began seeing things she didn't recognize—a trench full of soldiers, an army horde rushing down a vast, green hill toward them, chanting a war cry with their weapons held out before them.

"I remember … something," Sarah confessed, still unsure of how to explain what she saw.

Benny explained instead, "When Flo and I began to understand how it worked, we realized that we couldn't just see memories, but we could *search* for them. That's what I was trying to do with you. I wanted to search your mind to see if there was a detail that would help us understand who attacked Robins-Port."

Sarah nodded her understanding. "Which is why I was reliving those memories. It felt like I was there all over again, standing on the side while the memory played out."

"Exactly," Benny said. "The best way I can describe it is like watching a play as it unfolds before us, but only in our mind's eye."

"Our mind's eye," Sarah repeated to herself, nodding in understanding. "It was your memories that I was seeing, then?"

"Yeah," Benny admitted, a bit of shame in his voice that confused Sarah. "What you saw was my first battle during the war."

"And the man in the hood?" The hair on Sarah's arms stood on their ends. "The one I saw. What was that?"

Benny looked as worried as she did. "That was …" He searched for his words, shaking his head in defeat. "I honestly can't say. That was no memory of mine, and I doubt a memory of yours. That was something … different. Something beyond my understanding."

Sarah was quiet for a while, building the confidence to ask her final question, afraid of the answer she might receive.

She looked at Benny, who looked right back at her. A look in his eye told her that he had been waiting for this particular question, as if it was something he also considered in his life.

"Can we … change it?" she asked finally, her body jolting with anticipation as the question left her mouth. "The memories, I mean. We are reliving them, after all. Can we change it at all?"

The look on Benny's face answered it for her, and she felt all the hope that she had built up fade away with a shake of his head. "We relive the memories, yes, but that's all they are in the end—memories."

Sarah blew out a deep breath. She had expected the answer, but the fairytale girl inside her had truly believed that there was a way to use this newfound ability to change her past. It had felt so *real.*

Watching Benny's memory unfold in her mind wasn't just like watching a play; she had been there. She had felt the wind on her face, felt the ground shake with the approaching horde, had smelt the sweat and dirt from the soldiers in the trench.

If it felt that real, surely there was a sense of reality within it? And if there was a sense of reality within in, then surely she could relive her memory again, but instead, this time, she would plead with her mother and father to warn someone of the incoming attack. She would save everyone, and her mother and father would still be alive.

Deep down, she wanted to believe she could do it, regardless of the information Benny had just fed her. Deep down, she still wanted to try. But another part of her knew that it was impossible. There was nothing Sarah could do to save her parents from their cruel fate.

"I'm sorry," Benny said quietly. "Truly, I am sorry."

Sarah nodded in defeat. "Will you teach me?" She wiped a tear from her cheek. "How to control it? How to use it?"

And then Benny did something that made her heart weep. He shifted so his body faced her, took her gloved hand in his, and looked her straight in the eye. "Absolutely."

She looked at her gloved hand resting in Benny's as he gave a gentle squeeze.

A week ago, she would have shunned away the kind gesture out of fear, but she knew there was nothing left to fear from Benny, especially with her new discovery of the man.

The door opened, and before Seroes could fully step out, Benny was out of his seat and rushing to meet him. Seroes put a hand up before Benny as he closed the door behind him, cutting Benny off from entering the cabin.

"I've done what I can, but he still needs to rest." He placed both hands on Benny's shoulders. "It's not good, friend. He's lost a lot of blood, and he's in a deep sleep. One that I've only seen a few come out of."

"What does that mean?" Anger was clear in Benny's voice. Not at Seroes, exactly, but at feeling utterly useless. "There has to be something we can do to help wake him up."

Seroes shook his head, and Sarah could see Benny's shoulders shake in sadness, could see the tears forming in his eyes. "I've stopped the bleeding and treated his wounds, but the only thing that is going to wake Al up is Al. It's up to him whether or not he wants to come back to us."

Benny scoffed at the diagnosis. "You're telling me that it's all up to whether or not Alric wants to keep living?"

"Have *faith*, my friend," Seroes consoled, tilting his head lower to meet Benny's eyes. "Have faith in him and us."

Benny shrugged to release himself from the giant's grasp, taking a step away and setting himself back into the rocking chair. "Have faith in his will to live?" Benny chuckled to himself. Not a genuine one, but one of misery. "You forget who we're talking about."

It was a strange sight to see Benny, who was mostly upbeat and witty, now sulking quietly to himself, looking more defeated than ever.

There was nothing Sarah could say to console him the way he had for her. She decided her best choice was to leave him to his thoughts.

She walked toward the fire. Trevor was still there, watching her intently, saying nothing as Sarah gazed into the glowing embers and reached into her pocket. She pulled out the crumpled envelope that her mother had given to her on that night in Robins-Port. Holding in her hands the last words she would ever get from her mother, the idea brought a tear to her eye. With a shaky hand, she tore it open, unfolded a thick parchment of paper, and immediately recognized her mother's writing as she scanned the letter.

She stared at the words in disbelief, even minutes after she had finished reading it. Her mouth hung slack and open; her breaths had seized in her chest.

After the initial shock of the letter passed, she crumpled it up, rolling it into a tight ball, and tossed it into the fire. She watched as the paper began to take flame, bursting into a small ball of fire as its secrets burned away. Then she turned away from the fire and slowly made her way toward the tree where her packs sat, leaving Trevor staring in confusion on what had just happened.

"So, we are going to invest in the village?" Sarah asked as her dad led her across the beach toward their travel wagon, the sour taste of fish still potent in her mouth.

"Not exactly," her father answered, scanning the beach and its contents as if in search of something. "We are going to develop a proposal for the bank, urging them to take an interest in the village, hoping they see the opportunity it holds the way I see it.

"Now, where is ...?" He smiled widely as he found what he had been looking for. "There she is, chatting away with the locals as usual. Hey, Flo!" He waved wildly to Sarah's mother, like a child trying to catch the attention of their parents in a crowd.

Florence saw Sarah and Harold walking back toward their wagon, nodded her thanks to a pair of women dressed in fishing clothes, before rushing back to her family.

"Such an interesting story of how this place was found," she said as Harold opened the door to the carriage, ushering his beautiful wife and daughter inside.

Florence took her seat on the cushioned bench next to Sarah. "Did you know that this was just a mere beach before? That the founders were actually lost on the water when they discovered this place? How lucky is that, to come across an opportunity such as this? It could almost be described as fate."

Harold shut the door before taking his seat opposite of Sarah and Florence. Then he pounded on the roof to signal the driver to set off. "Fate that, weeks before its discovery, they were fighting off starvation? If that's fate, then I'd much rather stay out of its path."

"Oh, please." Florence waved the comment away, setting her eyes on her daughter. "Your father never did believe that we serve a much higher purpose than our day-to-day lives."

"I'm just saying," her father said defensively, "that I would rather put my faith in what I can provide for my family rather than leaving it up to something as

vague as a word such as fate."

"And you don't think it's fate that has provided you this family?"

Harold shrugged. "I'd much rather believe it was my charm that got me this family."

Sarah rolled her eyes. "Oh gods, please don't do this."

"Charm, eh?" Florence crossed her arms. "Are you saying it was charm you had on our first date?"

"Can we please not do this?" Sarah pleaded again.

"You'll never let that down, will you?" Harold's face blushed with embarrassment.

Florence turned to Sarah. "Your father cooked a meal for us on our first date. Did you know that? We were about your age at the time, and he thought he could impress me by kicking his parents out of the house and setting up a private dinner."

"Please don't tell her this." Harold looked bashfully away, staring out the carriage window. "She'll never look at me the same."

"Problem was," Florence continued, ignoring her husband's plea, "he wasn't a very good cook, and he put way too much pepper into his ingredients. Oh, the setup was well enough. He pulled out my chair for me, pushed me closer to the table, set a napkin on my lap. You should have seen him, all dressed up handsomely in an oversized suit."

"I hit my growth spurt late," Harold interrupted. "You know that."

"Oh!" Florence hugged herself with a huge smile. "He was so cute, trying so hard to impress me."

"Seriously!" Sarah laughed. "You need to stop."

"Yes, please, dear," Harold added. "Don't do this, for your daughter's sake."

Florence ignored her family's pleas once again. "And he did impress me ... until he had his first bite of the chicken. He started sneezing rapidly, spit flying all over our dinner."

Sarah laughed at her father, who was currently trying to hide his face behind the window curtain.

"Oh, that's not all, though," Florence continued.

"Please stop," Harold begged.

"After the tenth sneeze, I rushed to his side and handed him some water ... when he let go the biggest fart that shook the very walls."

Harold's face was as red as a tomato as he tried to hide behind the curtain.

Sarah laughed until she was fighting for air, gripping the velvet seat of her carriage.

"And that," Florence said as she smiled across the carriage to Sarah's father, "is the charm your father speaks of."

Though clearly embarrassed, Harold laughed to himself, shaking his head toward his wife. "I hate you."

Florence smiled at him. "You love me."

Harold smiled back at her. "I love you."

They both looked at each other in silence as Sarah sat there with a raised eyebrow. "Seriously, if this is how the ride back is going to be, I'm going to vomit all over you both."

Sarah Michaelson fell asleep within minutes, in the middle of nowhere, in the company of a band of strangers, her childhood bully, a mentor of sorts, and the boy who she had once fallen in love with.

Her world had changed months ago when her home had been destroyed, but it had changed even more within the last hour of her life. For the first time in her existence, Sarah felt she truly did not know who she was. She fell asleep not a hundred feet away from the uncle who she had only heard of in passing moments from her mother, an uncle who didn't know he had a niece. It was a secret she would keep to herself for now, but that was only one of the secrets that Sarah fell asleep with.

The Phantom of an Unknown Father

His plate was empty, his belly full, and the fire in his heart all but died out as an unfamiliar silence fell upon the cabin, leaving nothing but the sounds of nature echoing in the night. An owl hooted nearby, the beat of its wings thumping in the darkness, flapping away to the song of crickets chirping and coyotes crying to the white moon that brightened the sky.

The cabin had felt safe since their arrival, the secluded land hidden by a natural fence of brush and debris, providing a shell of protection from outside, from the world full of blood and destruction.

Trevor reflected on the past three weeks of his life. Given the sudden change of events he had suffered, life had seemed so simple in Robins-Port. Sure, he was an orphan, a shunned, parentless boy who people had freely scolded on a daily basis, but his biggest worries had been running into Warren and his squad of goons, or helping Dodge and Tom with their errands, along with waiting for Sarah's return.

It had seemed so hard then, but nothing compared to how things were now. Sure, he'd heard curses as he would walk by other townsfolk, but at least those people weren't trying to stick a sword through his gut. Yes, he would go out of his way during errands to avoid running into Warren, but at least he wasn't skittering down foreign allies like a lost cat, expecting a knifeman to leap from the shadows and stab him bloody. No, life had been easy then; it had just taken going through hell to realize how much worse it could get.

I was a boy back then. Now? A killer.

The residents of the night's fire had cleared out once they were all finished with Evan's meal. Evan wasn't lying. That just might have been the best meal Trevor had ever had. But Trevor wouldn't admit it. The last thing he needed was to boost Evan's ego.

That was another thing that had recently changed. He'd been skeptical about the brotherhood at first, given the fair share of secrets they obviously kept. But, in the end, when it came to trusting them with his life, Trevor hadn't been disappointed. They had fought together, killed together, and survived together. Two weeks ago, they'd been strangers. Now, he felt a close bond with them all.

Trevor liked them.

He looked over his shoulder to where Sarah was lying against a tree, her head sunk to her chest. Trevor thought back to weeks ago when they'd been sitting on the wall in Robins-Port, talking about her last trip and where she had been, what she had seen, and what she had brought back.

When Trevor looked at her now, he didn't see the same woman who he had fallen in love with. She didn't speak much anymore, and when she did, it was quiet mumbles that usually implied she wanted nothing to do with him.

For some reason, Trevor couldn't help feeling it was his fault. It was a frustrating feeling, considering he was trying to be there for Sarah ever since they escaped Robins-Port. But every time he would try to comfort her, she would pull away from him.

She was different. They were all different, for their lives had taken a hard turn from a day of sunshine to a month of thunderstorms.

Trevor had killed a man. Multiple men, actually. He had taken their lives, and he would spend the rest of his life dealing with that.

The thought of being a killer wasn't the worst part; it was the thought of having to do it again, which seemed like a possibility with how life had been lately.

Above all of that, the worst part wasn't all the blood Trevor had helped spill. It wasn't the amount of bodies he'd had to carve through in order to get where he was now. No, the worst part was the fact that Sarah had made it perfectly clear that she wanted nothing to do with him.

Perhaps she's afraid of you because of what you've done. Maybe when she looks at you, instead of seeing the boy she grew up with, she sees a monster.

Trevor sat staring at the fire as the large figure of a man approached. Even through the dark, Trevor could see the pain on his uncle's face, and that made Trevor feel guilty, which, in turn, made Trevor angry.

Why should I feel guilty? He's the one who lied to me this entire time. If anything, he should feel ashamed, not me.

But when Dodge sat down next to him, and Trevor could tell that he'd been crying, that anger disappeared, for he knew that Dodge was also hurting.

He just lost his best friend, and here I am, sulking in my own self-pity.

Trevor wondered what Evan would say about that. He figured it would be a very colorful and rude remark, which would no doubt set Trevor in his place.

Dodge leaned his head back and took a deep swig from a bottle. After a couple, large gulps, he let out a deep breath, the aroma of spiced rum wafting in the air. Without looking his way, he held the bottle out for Trevor to take. Trevor accepted and lifted the bottle in the air.

"To Tom," Trevor said before taking a drink. He felt the liquid burn through his chest and settle in his stomach, the warmth of the liquor spreading with ease.

He handed it back to Dodge who, with a weak smile, returned the salute. "To Tom."

They sat with each other in silence for a while, the orange glow of the burning wood warming the night.

Trevor searched the camp again and took account of the others. Benny, after Seroes had explained that Alric was in some sort of deep sleep, found himself inside the cabin for the rest of the night, along with the twins Garth and Merrick. Evan had found a spot away from the cabin near the entrance to the clearing. Baron, who Trevor hadn't seen since earlier, walked off toward the cabin and disappeared into the shadows.

Trevor felt the hint of anger rise in his chest when he spotted Warren on the porch, wrapped in a small blanket in one of the chairs, either still crying to himself or asleep.

The silence dragged on, the only sound being the crackle of fire and the liquor swishing about as Dodge knocked back the bottle. He and Trevor hadn't spoken since Servitol, which had been a few days ago. It was the longest Trevor had ever gone without saying a word to his uncle.

"Will you tell me about him?" Trevor asked quietly, even though the question seemed loud in the night.

Dodge took another pull from the bottle then handed it back to Trevor, nodding without meeting Trevor's eyes. "What would you like to know?"

Trevor shrugged. "Anything," he answered before he took a sip from the bottle.

Trevor handed the bottle back to Dodge, who lifted it to his mouth. Before he took another drink, however, he let the bottle hover near his lips. After staring off for a moment, he put the bottle in his lap. "My brother was … a great man. Best man I ever met. Much better than me."

"How can you say that after what you told me?" Trevor scoffed. "After he killed my mother."

Dodge wasn't mad at the question. He spoke plainly, more or less mumbling into the fire rather than talking directly to Trevor. "He was brave since the day he learned how to walk. Always finding a challenge and overcoming it. He always had my back, no matter what. Either during the war or at home, he never let me down."

"And my mother?" Trevor asked. "What was she like?"

Dodge, smiling unexpectedly, stared distantly into the fire. "Your mother was everything my brother deserved. She was a beautiful woman, a fun and loving friend, as well as the strongest woman I've ever known. She had a mouth on her like a sailor, mind you, and wasn't afraid of setting someone in their place."

Trevor smiled at her description, trying hard to picture the woman within his mind. Trying and failing.

"What was her name?"

Dodge's smile spread wider. "Marielle, after the goddess. And the name suited her well."

The goddess of beauty and hope.

"She loved my brother," Dodge continued, taking another pull of his drink, "and my brother loved her."

"Then, why did he kill her?" Trevor couldn't help but feel betrayed with the mention of his father possessing any love for a woman who he murdered. "If he loved her so much, then why did he do it?"

"I can't sit here and tell you what brings someone to do such a thing, Trevor, but I also won't betray the true man my brother was. The only thing I can do is explain what I know. It's up to you to determine what to make of it."

Trevor rolled his eyes. "This isn't another lesson—"

"You're right; it's not." Dodge looked at Trevor, his eyes blood red and weary with intoxication. "I'll tell you about him, but only if you sit there and listen. Got it?"

Trevor took a deep breath, pushing aside the retort he wanted to spit at Dodge. Instead, he bit his tongue and accepted with a nod.

When Dodge was satisfied with Trevor's answer, he continued, "My brother and I enlisted together. Like everyone else, we grew up with the notion that the greatest thing we could do was fight for our country. To get on the frontlines and fight those who opposed us.

"To celebrate our enlistment, we decided to have more than our fair share of drinks at the tavern in town a week before we shipped out. That's where we met Marielle."

Dodge shook his head, a wide smile on his face. "From the moment they started talking, they fell for one another. Before I knew it, she was at our house near every day before we left.

"It's not as if they locked themselves in the bedroom. It was more than that. She would leave at night then come back the next day to see how we were doing. We would stay up all night, talking about our lives, mostly of what we wanted and what we planned to do with the money we earned.

"But, like all good things, our time was up, and on the final morning before our departure, my brother promised Marielle that, once we returned, he'd ask for her hand in marriage. She wept there and then with his promise. Then she hugged us tightly, gave us a kiss on the cheek, and watched us set off."

Dodge went to take another pull from the bottle when he realized it was empty. He tossed the bottle over his shoulder into the darkness behind him where it fell silently into the soft grass.

Dodge's tone seemed to change suddenly, going from the enjoyments of reminiscing to the dreadful experience of explaining a nightmare. "We thought the first battle would be the worse. At least, that's what they told us. Our leadership has always said that, if you made it through your first fight, the rest were easier. But as time went on, the bloodshed grew more frequent, the number of graves stacked up. But, no matter what we went through, my brother and I made it through together, for better or worse.

"One day we were walking a patrol south of the Haunted Forest, about a month's walk from here. We were cresting a ridge when we were ambushed. The first arrow took a friend of mine in the throat. I thought he'd just lost his footing and tumbled down the hill. I remember laughing at the sight, only to choke on that laughter as an arrow ripped through the air not an inch from my own face.

"I rushed to take cover behind a fallen tree when I slipped. I was just pulling out my sword when I began tumbling down the hill, toward where the enemy fire was coming from. I remember hearing the sound of rushing men when I hit the bottom, saw them baring their teeth as they rushed toward me; four native warriors with very sharp spears pointed my way.

"I tried to stand and defend myself when I realized I sliced my leg on my own sword when I'd fallen. I managed to raise my sword when the first man reached me, but I knew it'd be too late. I watched the look in my murderer's

456

eyes as he struck out with his spear toward me.

"Then, in a flash, his weapon flew from his grasp, and not a split-second later he was folded over the tip of my brother's sword.

"I watched as the other three men closed in on my brother. They attacked like a pack of wolves, biting and nipping at him, but my brother was the best warrior in our company.

"The odds didn't matter to him. Whether he was going against three men or ten, if it came down to saving one of his friend's lives or, in this instance, his brother's, no amount of force would stop him. He cut through those men like a butcher, and within a minute of our ambush, four of our enemies lay dead at his feet.

"Then we started getting peppered with arrows again. One of those particular arrows found a nice home in my brother's shoulder. But, like I said, nothing would stop him. Instead of taking cover, he picked me up and carried me all the way up the hill to safety. I was hunched over his shoulder, watching arrows land inches away from us in the ground, yet my brother never slowed his pace."

Trevor couldn't hold back the admonishment in his voice. "He saved your life."

Dodge nodded. "He saved my life. That wasn't the first time, but it was the last.

"You see, a shoulder wound is easy, but a leg wound? If a soldier couldn't walk to the battlefield, there was no chance of him fighting in it. So, being as wounded as I was at the time, I was sent home with a few coins and a medical discharge. They told me to come back once my leg was healed. I came home, and my brother stayed."

Dodge leaned on his side and dug around in a pocket at the side of his pants. When he pulled his hand out, he revealed a second bottle of liquor; this one much smaller in size, but the contents just as dark as the first. He popped the cork, tossed it into the fire, and then took a small swig before continuing his story.

"Couldn't tell you how she knew, but Marielle was waiting for me at the house when I rode in on my horse. We talked all night about the war, about what was happening. I reassured her that my brother was safe, and never once did she seem concerned about him. It was like she'd already known he was coming home.

"It wasn't until a year later that he did, riding upon his horse in an officer's uniform and a pouch full of gold coins. He told us that the war was over, that Navaleth had won it at the battle of Green-Gate.

"Being a man who kept to his word, the next morning, he got down on one knee and proposed to your mother."

Dodge took another pull of his bottle, nearly emptying the entire contents and struggling not to fall over. He was good and drunk now, a sight Trevor had only seen on a few occasions.

It helps him talk about it.

With the last drop gone, Dodge tossed his second bottle behind him and just stared into the fire.

After a few moments, Trevor spoke. "Then what happened?"

Dodge answered without turning away from the fire. "War, Trevor. War happened."

"I thought the war was over?"

Dodge shook his head solemnly. "The first few months back were great. When two people plan to get married, everything seems perfect. It's all laughter and butterflies with a promise of a happy ending.

"I'll never forget the look on my brother's face when Marielle told him he was going to be a father …" Dodge sniffled and wiped a tear from his eye. "I knew, in that moment, my brother was the happiest he could ever be."

Tears fell from Dodge's face as he shook his head, doing his hardest to still his trembling lip. "War, Trevor. We may leave the battlefield, but the battlefield never leaves us. It was the worst for my brother. The war I left my brother in grew worse than what we'd seen together. The year I missed was the bloodiest year of the war, and my brother had been in the thick of it. He had to do some terrible things in order to make it home, and eventually, those things came back to haunt him.

"A lot happened behind the curtain of their relationship. A few fights here, a few fights there. Something that I found admirable about them was how they were able to keep it to themselves. They didn't let anyone get involved or risk having it become someone else's problem. But then it began to grow more public, and eventually, they were the talk of the town.

"My brother began drinking more and more, spending more money on drink than providing for the family he was soon to have. Tom and I did what we could to sober him up, but the more time went on, the more paranoid and violent he became.

"During the worst of his drunken fits, he kept calling himself a monster, telling us that he was evil and that he deserved misery. When Marielle would try to comfort him the best she could, he would shun her, push her away, call her a traitor. He would accuse her of adultery, declaring that her baby wasn't his."

Dodge's shoulder heaved with sobs. His voice broke as the tears crashed to the ground around him. "I thought he would get better. Tom and I both did. He wasn't my brother anymore, and I wanted him back, wanted him to be the same man I grew up with. I wanted the big brother who would protect me against anything, not the man who came back that day on that horse."

Trevor wiped a tear of his own, an unexpected pressure building in his throat. Not once had he seen his uncle so vulnerable, so open, so sad. It made his heart break, and he began to understand why Dodge had never told him the story of his father. He placed a hand on his uncle's shoulder, and Dodge met it with his own.

Dodge shuddered with a deep breath and wiped the tears from his face. "It was a week before the ceremony when Tom and I went to surprise them. It'd been a few days since we'd seen them. We knew they were having some trouble, but we wanted to remind them of the reason why they fell in love in the first place.

"But, what we found ..." Dodge struggled with his words, finding it difficult to finish the story between his deep sobs. "She was just ... lying there. Gods, there was so much blood. And Marielle ... she looked ... she looked so sad."

"I know." Trevor scooted closer to Dodge, wrapping an arm around his large shoulders as his uncle wept into him. "You don't have to explain. I know."

For a while, he let Dodge cry, let him weep with no shame as they sat at the fire. Eventually, though, his uncle gathered himself, leaned away from Trevor, and wiped his face on his sleeve. He took out a handkerchief and blew his nose before tossing the cloth into the fire where it was consumed and burned away.

"Don't blame him," Dodge pleaded to Trevor, his voice quaking. "Don't blame my brother for what he did. It's not his fault. I know that sounds strange, and even wrong, but it's not."

"I ..." Trevor wasn't sure what to say. He had asked for the story about his parents, and he'd gotten it. It wasn't a happy story, he had known it wouldn't be, and now it was hard to decide whether or not it was worth knowing in the first place.

Does it even really matter?

"I don't," Trevor said, unclear of how he felt. "I don't blame anyone. I just ... wanted to know. I'm sorry."

"Don't be sorry." Dodge wiped the last tear from his face. "Don't you ever be sorry."

After a short while of thinking over the story, Trevor knew exactly what he wanted to say. "I wish things could have been different."

Dodge looked at him and gave him a sad smile. "A part of me does, too, Trevor."

They sat quietly with each other for a while after that, both of them staring into the fire.

The night was growing late, and Trevor was beginning to feel the strain of his exhaustion tugging at him. His eyelids were getting heavy, his legs aching with stiff pain. He knew he needed rest, but he didn't want to leave Dodge alone. Not yet, at least.

Trevor shifted, his butt going numb in the cold dirt. "Seems like we can add one more title to my name."

Dodge burrowed his bushy eyebrows as he looked at Trevor. "What's that?"

Trevor gave a playful smile. "Looks like I'm a bastard as much as an orphan."

Dodge just stared at him for a moment, his face unreadable. Then a small smile hooked the side of his mouth before he turned back to the fire. "I guess, technically, that's true."

"Can you imagine the look on Warren's face once he figures that out?" Trevor giggled to himself. "Who knows what sort of insults he'll have in store for me?"

Dodge shook his head. "Not sure it matters anymore."

"No," Trevor agreed, "I don't think it does."

They sat quietly together again, watching as the glow of the fire all but dimmed, and the chill was beginning to soak into Trevor's bones.

He stood, stretched his legs, and looked about the cabin.

"Go find a spot," Dodge said suddenly, still staring off into the fire. "You could use some rest. I think I'll stay up a while longer."

Trevor stood, but before leaving Dodge to his solitude, he turned back. "Thank you," Trevor said.

Dodge looked toward him, a small smile on his lips.

"I'll see you tomorrow, Uncle."

Dodge gave one small nod. "Until tomorrow."

Trevor left Dodge at the fire and walked to his pack. It wasn't far from where Sarah slept. He opened it and searched the contents until he found what he was looking for. He looked toward the cabin to the open chair next to where Warren slept. Then, before making his way to his bed, he looked one last time at Sarah and smiled, wishing that things could be different between them.

He wanted to convince himself that he wouldn't give up on her, but the truth was that it was too late. They were completely different people now. They had both gone through too much in order to go back to what things were. Trevor knew the best option was to give up.

No. It wouldn't be giving up; it would be letting her go. And if that's something that would make her better, then it's something that I will gladly do.

He unfolded the blanket that he had grabbed from his pack then gently laid it over Sarah.

Smiling to himself, he took a seat in the empty chair on the porch and closed his eyes for the rest of the night.

A Shadow of What Was

It was a simple pack; a canvas bag threaded with a line of horsehair stitching. A small rope lined the top hole, two snaked ends on each side that tightened when you pulled them away from another. It was dirty beyond its years, yet it remained one of the most reliable belongings among the very little that Quiver possessed. The canvas was old, stained brown with dirt and sweat. The horsehair bit at your hands as you tugged the bag closed. Yet, through all the years that Quiver had slung that very bag over his shoulder, even during the war, that bag had never torn.

Like the bag, Quiver had become dirty and stained over his years, stretching thinner and thinner at the threads of his existence with the weight he carried. However, unlike the bag's integrity, Quiver had been pushed beyond his limits, tearing and breaking apart as he had lost control of himself during the trial in front of his village.

Roku hadn't been lying. Quiver had become more distant with his faith and the traditions of his people for many years now. He imagined a world where his new ideals could exist with his old, never having cause to clash; that life could be lived more than one way. People should have been able to explore all the ways of living rather than clinging to the way they are simply comfortable with. His people were a superstitious culture, always fearful about changing their way of life, shunning things like modern medicines and ideals simply because it was unknown.

It's not that Quiver wanted to pull his people away from their beliefs. He just wanted them to explore other ways of making their lives easier. He wanted his people to start thinking more openly. But it was people like Roku who would rather live in the shadow of what was instead of thriving in the light of what could be. It was because of Roku why Quiver was now stuffing the little amount of belongings into his pack, packing up what he saw fit to carry before he left his village, his people, and their way of life … forever.

Quiver was fearful of what would come next, but he couldn't deny the sense of relief that washed over him as he left the elder hall, and that was how he knew he'd made the right choice.

He realized that he had been a shadow of his old self, trapped in a world that refused to let him grow. For years now, he had been a cloud of gray, living in a world of black and white.

Despite the fact that Roku had exiled him, Quiver felt that he was leaving on his own terms, and because of that, he felt relieved.

A shadow fell over the room as Quiver reached for a pouch of dried beef. He looked to his tent flap and saw Rasca leaning against the entryway.

"That didn't go as planned," Rasca said.

Quiver turned and continued his packing. "And yet, I can't help feeling this was something planned all along."

Rasca stepped toward Quiver, looking around the interior of the tent then down at Quiver's dirty bag. "Not sure it'll all fit in there."

Quiver lifted the bag before his face, weighing the contents within—a few loaves of bread, dried beef, a sack of water, and a few dried biscuits. "It'll fit enough."

"Where will you go?" Rasca asked. "Where will Chief Quiver, war hero and sole remaining heir of the great and powerful Nara'Seir, go?"

Quiver grumbled, "Didn't you hear? I'm an exile. I'm no chief. My name holds no meaning anymore, and I've no claim to any bloodline. I'm nobody's hero."

Rasca's stance was more serious, his tone deep with conviction. "You're a hero to me, Quiver. No villager would stand up to Roku like that, no matter how much power they had."

"Right." Quiver chuckled to himself, tossing his bag to the side of his tent as he stared at Rasca. "No villager with a lick of sense, that is. Which makes you a fool."

Rasca crossed his arms. "Then a fool I'll be."

Quiver shook his head in disbelief. "Why, Rasca? Why did you do that back there? You promised me you'd stay out of it."

"No, I promised you I would do the right thing. And I did. If you expected me to just stand by while that parasite made you out to be some type of heathen, then you're the fool, Quiver. Not me."

Quiver stared at his old friend. Rasca had known the struggles Quiver had gone through, not only dealing with his experiences in war, but how he began to deal with his perspective on life. He'd known that Quiver wasn't as attached to tradition the way the others were, and all the while, he had still remained at Quiver's side, never once forsaking him.

"Well"—a smirk angled on Quiver's face—"looks like we're both fools, then."

Rasca matched his smile. "Lucky us." He scratched the side of his face with his mutilated hand. "Where will you go?"

Quiver let out a deep breath. "Don't know, actually," he answered. "I'll head south for now, then probably head east to try to find another clan."

Rasca shook his head. "We both know you don't belong in another clan. There's no place for you among our people, Quiver, and even you know that."

Quiver nodded solemnly in response. It was true; it didn't matter which clan he would become a part of; he would still feel like a stranger in a strange world. "Guess I'll just have to find my own way."

"Can I make a suggestion?" Rasca walked past Quiver, sitting down on the cot that had served many nights as a comfortable bed.

"You have a suggestion on where I should spend my life as a deserter?"

Rasca nodded. "I know a place where all ideals and ways of life are accepted. Where you can live your life to the ways of your own choosing, and not someone else's. It doesn't matter if your southern, or like us. All people are accepted."

Quiver breathed a sad laugh, shaking his head in disappointment. "No place like that exists."

"Yes," Rasca said seriously, "it does."

Quiver burrowed his eyebrows. "Then, why is this the first time I'm hearing about this? Why haven't you told me before?"

"I've kept in contact with their leader for some time now. The village doesn't know about it; would probably shun me if they found out. He sends a runner every now and then, mostly asking how things are here, letting me know there's a place for us among his people."

"What do you mean a place for *us*?" Quiver dropped his bag and faced Rasca. "What are you talking about?"

His friend stood, suddenly very tall and unfamiliar. "I'm talking about a place where we can be accepted, a place where *all* are accepted."

"And if you've known of this place the entire time, why haven't you told me of it? You've known all along the collapse of my faith, how I've felt a stranger amongst my own people, and *now* you tell me about this?"

Rasca replied with a single nod.

"Why?" Quiver asked, his hands shaking in irritation. "Why keep that from me?"

"Because I know you would have wanted to leave, and you couldn't do that until you've made peace with yourself."

Quiver stared at Rasca, surprised by the sudden confession. It drew more questions than it answered. "He's an elder, then?"

"He's a leader, yes"—Rasca crossed his arms—"but he's not an elder. He built the community, but he doesn't decide the fate of the people living in it."

"A leader appointed by his people. Doesn't seem much different from here."

"It is," Rasca reassured. "*He* is. He understands what it's like living tied to tradition, and the only thing he wants is to coexist. Not just with tribesmen, but *all* people."

There were only a few people left in the world who Rasca would risk being exiled over, and Quiver knew them all.

"You didn't answer my question," Quiver said, bracing himself for the answer that he already knew. "Why does this elder have an interest in me?"

Rasca stared at Quiver for a moment, the silence and worry from his friend all but confirming Quiver's suspicion.

"Because he's your brother."

"My brother," Quiver said, his body shaking with emotion. It had been a long time since Quiver had even heard a whisper of his brother's fate.

He shook his head, fighting back the tears that burned his eyes. "My brother is not the man you describe."

Rasca nodded, well aware of Quiver's feelings toward the only family he had left in the world. "Your brother is not the same man as you remember."

Quiver's mind raced back to the last memory he had of his brother. It'd been so long that he couldn't even remember what he looked like, but the details of that last night stuck with him, nonetheless. The stink of drink on his breath, the smell of death staining his clothes. The blood washing over his body.

Quiver shook his head at the idea that his brother was who Rasca described. "My brother—"

"Has sent a runner to meet with me every week outside of the village, each time asking about how you have been."

"And this entire time, you have kept it a secret from me?"

Rasca bobbed his head up and down. "You were not ready to hear it. Like I said, you had to come to terms with yourself, but now I think it's time we can move on."

"*We?*" Quiver shook his head. "There is no *we*, Rasca. You are still chief amongst the village. They need you here."

Rasca stared at the entrance to the tent, his eyes distant with thought. After a moment, he slowly shook his head. "They do not need me here." He looked at Quiver, determination in his hard stare. "I swore to you *both*, remember, that I would stand with you no matter what. These people do not need me. They do not want me, for I have become something they fear. *We* have become something they fear."

Quiver struggled to grasp the sudden turn of events, at the secrets Rasca had confessed. "Do not forsake these people because of my misdoings, friend."

"Sadly"—Rasca put a reassuring hand on Quiver's shoulder—"we both know that they have forsaken themselves."

"There is still hope for them," Quiver added.

Rasca looked away for a moment, staring at the confines of the hut as he chewed his lip. After a short moment, he looked back at Quiver. "No, there's not."

Someone entered the tent, and when Quiver and Rasca saw who was standing in front of them, a bag over their shoulder and a dagger at their hilt, Quiver closed the gap between them and took a knee.

"Masco, what are you doing here?" Quiver looked the boy all over and was shocked to see how well he had recovered in such a short time. "You should be resting."

"She said I have to go with you." Quiver noticed the small bag thrown over the youngling's shoulder, bulging with supplies.

Quiver eyed the youngling. "The voice from your dreams?"

Masco nodded. "She said to follow you through the trail of the mountain, to where the bloodlines meet and where the final war begins."

Rasca came to stand beside Quiver. "What are you talking about, young one?"

If Masco heard the question, he chose to ignore it. Instead, he stared at Quiver, his eyes never leaving his.

Quiver stood, crossing his arms and taking a deep breath. He wasn't about to let Masco throw away his future because of him. Quiver might be lost in the world, but that didn't mean Masco had to be.

"You—"

"Will follow you," Masco finished, anticipating Quiver's objection, "whether you accept it or not."

Quiver was taken aback by the outburst, but before he could react, another person had decided to enter his tent. She stood tall, and the moment Quiver and her eyes locked, he felt a sense of sadness deep in his gut. Saying goodbye to her was going to be the hardest part about leaving, and it was something Quiver had been dreading with each passing second. By the look on her face, Quiver could tell she felt the same.

"I told you we'd see each other again," she said with a sad smile.

"Thread," Quiver breathed, fighting back the cramp in his throat. "It's good to see you."

Rasca cleared his throat. "Well, best be off, lad." He took Masco by the shoulder, ushering him out of the tent. "We better let these two be for a bit."

They exited the tent, leaving Thread and Quiver standing in silence, the only words being passed in that moment through their bleary eyes.

After a quiet moment, Thread said, "So, this is it, huh?"

Quiver wanted to apologize to her, explain to her what he had been feeling for so long, but it would only be stating the obvious. Thread knew him better than anyone, so it was already likely she knew everything.

"I ... I don't know what to say," Quiver admitted.

Thread gave another sad smile, walked past Quiver, and sat on his cot. "How about we talk like it's the last chance we have."

Quiver matched her smile and took a seat next to her. "Suppose it is," Quiver said, feeling stupid as the words left his mouth.

Thread kept her eyes on Quiver. "Where will you go?"

Quiver sighed. "I don't know. Thought I'd try to go east, find a clan. But"— his mind was brought back to Rasca's story—"Rasca says he knows a place."

"With your brother?"

"How did—" Emotions flurried through Quiver, leaving him conflicted on how to feel toward Thread. "You knew, too? How could you keep that from me, Thread?"

Thread didn't turn away. "Rasca told me a while back. We didn't want to tell you. Not yet, at least. We had to wait until you were ready."

467

"I suppose I didn't have a say when that could have been?"

Thread shook her head.

"Wow." Quiver sighed. Not out of anger, but of honest exhaustion from the sudden news. "I just ... don't understand how you could keep that a secret."

"If we had told you, you'd have run off looking for him. You'd have abandoned everyone here and later hated yourself, because you'd still question where you belong."

"And how does that matter now?" Quiver searched Thread's face for an answer. "Whether I left then or now, I'm still leaving. What difference does it make?"

Thread reached for Quiver's hand. "Because now you can leave and accept who you are. You didn't abandon these people, Quiver' they abandoned you."

Quiver hunched over his knees. "It doesn't feel that way."

Thread put a hand on Quiver's back, the simple gesture causing his heart to skip a beat. "You are the last image of what your father did all those years ago," she said. "Without your father, we would have never grown. Now that he's gone, we've resorted to the old ways. That's our fault, not yours."

"I just ..." Quiver shook his head. "I just wish it were different. I don't know."

Thread giggled, a sound Quiver never wanted to forget. "I suppose it will be now."

Thread and Rasca were right. If he had heard the news of his brother asking for him, he would have left long ago in search for him. And, if he had done that, he would have felt like a failure to his people.

They seem to know you better than yourself.

They sat there together for a while, not speaking, not needing to. Just to be around Thread brought Quiver peace, easing his endless questioning mind. He thought of all the things he wanted to tell her. He wanted to beg her to come with, to leave the village before the risk of the howlers finding the village. As he began thinking about his time in the forest, his mind came back to the dream he remembered having.

"I dreamt of you, you know," he said to Thread, breaking the comfortable silence.

Thread raised an eyebrow, a smirk on her lips. "Oh?"

"Not that kind of dream," Quiver said, nudging Thread's elbow with his own. They laughed together for a short while before Quiver continued, "It was a couple of days after we left. I dreamt I was standing on a cliff, looking down over an endless forest. There was a bridge leading over a canyon, and on the other side, pacing in front of the trees, was a wolf."

"Hm ..." Thread searched Quiver's eyes. "What kind of wolf?"

Quiver took a deep breath. "It was just an ordinary wolf, but I couldn't help feeling it meant something. I couldn't help thinking back to that soldier from the war. The Wolf, or Red Fang." Quiver shook his head in thought.

"What was his name?" Thread asked.

Quiver thought to himself a moment, digging into the memories he would rather forget. After a couple minutes of reminiscence, it came back to him. "Alric," he answered. "They called him Alric."

Thread nodded. "And, do you think this wolf was Alric?"

"I don't know," Quiver admitted.

Quiver was quiet for a while, lost in thought, until Thread scooted closer to him. "This doesn't sound like a dream about me, you know."

"Right." Quiver shook away his dark thoughts. "I heard your voice. It said, '*You have to help show him the way.*' What do you think that means?"

Thread tilted her head and shrugged. "I'm not sure. It's all very ... I can't think of the word."

"Peculiar?" Quiver suggested.

"Weird," Thread said with a smile. "It's very weird."

"Oh," Quiver said, laughing to himself.

"But I do think it means something. Maybe you are meant to cross that bridge and see what's on the other side. Perhaps that moment is now?"

Quiver chewed the inside of his lip. "Perhaps," he said. "I suppose you might be right."

"I usually am," Thread said, wiping a tear from her smiling face. "Who's going to teach me all the southern words when you're gone?"

Quiver hugged her close, tears now burning in his eyes. "I can teach you one more."

Thread wiped her nose on her sleeve. "Please do."

Quiver took a deep, shuddering breath. "There's a word they use to describe a feeling. Now, not everyone feels this. It's something only a few get a chance of experiencing."

"What does it feel like?" Thread asked.

"It sort of …" Quiver waved his hand in the air, then gestured to his stomach, "tickles around here."

"So, it's tickles?" Thread asked, a smile forming beyond her tears.

"No, not exactly. It just feels that way. But it also hurts. Usually, here." Quiver tapped his chest.

"It hurts, too?" Thread scoffed.

"It hurts, yet you miss the feeling once it's gone. It settles in your stomach and spreads, driving you close to madness."

"Sounds complicated," Thread observed. "Why do southerners have to complicate a simple thing such as a name for something?"

"It's the most complicated word in their language," Quiver declared. "It's something I don't fully understand myself, but I think I've been feeling it for a long time. I feel it every time I think of something."

Thread wiped a tear from her eye. "Can it happen when you think of *someone*?"

"Yes," Quiver answered, placing his hand on top of Thread's. "It can."

Thread nodded. "I think I have this feeling, too. What's it called?"

Quiver kissed the top of Thread's head. Before pulling away, he took a deep breath of her hair, searing in the memory of her smell so he might never forget. "Love," he answered.

Thread leaned her head on his shoulder and, for that moment, nothing else existed outside the walls of his tent. She smiled deeply, resting her eyes as she took comfort in Quiver's embrace.

"Tell me one last thing," Thread said after a few minutes of silence.

Quiver squeezed her tightly. "What's that?"

It took a moment for Thread to answer, for her sobbing cries cut off her words. When she did answer, however, she looked at Quiver, her radiant eyes glistening with tears. "Tell me you'll be all right."

***

Quiver exited to the tent, acknowledging that it would be for the last time. He held his travel bag in one hand and Thread's hand in the other.

Outside the tent stood Rasca and Masco, both of them sitting on a log nearby. They jumped to their feet when they saw Quiver.

He looked about his village for the last time. He had spent most of his life in this village, providing for it daily while teaching others how to live according to his people's rules. It was strange to think that he would never come back, that when he left, it would become nothing more than a past life and a distant memory.

He turned to Thread and gave her a tight hug, taking in every second of that moment and forever branding it into his memory—the smell of her hair, the feel of her body, the way she tucked her face into the crease of his neck. All of these things, he cherished for what seemed like hours, but only seconds later, she pulled away, giving his hand a tight squeeze as she walked past him, disappearing around the corner of his tent. Disappearing from his life forever.

He wanted to beg her to come with, to leave this place and spend the rest of their lives together, but that wouldn't be fair. Like Thread had done for him, it was time to find her own path.

He fought the tears in his eyes as he walked past Rasca and Masco.

"Where to?" Rasca asked as he matched Quiver's pace. Masco, too, placed himself on the opposite side of Quiver.

"Don't know," Quiver answered, keeping his eyes clear and focused ahead of the trail that led south out of the village. "You're the one who knows the way." He didn't have to look to see the smile on Rasca's face.

Quiver looked to Masco at his left, eyeing the youngling suspiciously.

"Yes, I'm sure about this," Masco said to Quiver suddenly.

"Because of what the woman said in your dreams?" Quiver asked.

Masco shook his head, "Not just because of that. But for Sparrow. For Oppo. None of the others believed what happened, and if it weren't for you, we'd have all died. You may not be chief among them, but you are to me, and my promise still stands. I'll follow you through it all."

Quiver felt a sense of pride in the boy, and he couldn't help ruffling the top of his head playfully, which Masco appreciated with a smile.

They walked in silence and eventually made it to where the path began to descend down the cliffside in which their village had taken residence on.

Quiver was lost in his thoughts as the familiar trees passed him for the last time. He didn't know what to say. His mind raced with the events of the past month of his life. He had fought monsters, watched younglings die, held the woman he loved in his arms, and had been exiled. Now he walked beside a youngling, who'd spent nearly a week in a coma, and the closest friend he could ask for toward a brother who Quiver thought he would never see again.

"So," Quiver started as he began to descend the beaten path, "just where has my brother been all these years?"

Rasca trailed behind Quiver. "We head east for a couple of days, then cut north toward the mountains. A hidden trail will lead between a small valley, then we make our way toward—"

"The Crooked Tooth," Quiver finished.

Rasca confirmed with a nod. "The Crooked Tooth."

Quiver stopped in the middle of the path. They had been walking for over an hour now, the village still seeming to be just around the bend of the hill. His stomach sank with the sense of loss. Not for the village itself, nor most of the residents it held, but for one resident in particular. He could still smell her hair on his clothes, a scent he hoped never washed away.

"You'll see her again, you know."

Quiver looked down to Masco, who followed Quiver's eyes up the path they had descended.

"I will?" Quiver asked.

Masco answered with a nod.

"When?"

"When the old blood comes," Masco answered ominously.

The look the youngling gave him sent chills down Quiver's spine, and in that moment, he didn't see the boy, Masco, but something else.

"Another thing the woman's voice said?" Rasca asked the youngling.

Masco never took his eyes away from Quiver, nodding in answer. "You'll see her again when the old blood comes and the village falls to its shadow."

The Void of Sorrow

Alric stuffed the apple into the bottom of his sack. Meyra wasn't too fond of the green ones, but that didn't mean he wasn't allowed to spoil himself from time to time. She was, after all, getting an entire bag of reds all to herself.

The market was heavily packed today, which put Alric's nerves on edge. His heart beat heavily in his chest, his pulse throbbing his temples as sweat dripped down the sides of his face.

There was something about crowds that uneased him. Even after getting home from the war years ago, he still half-expected to see the glint of a small dagger jabbing out of the crowd. It had been a while since his last panic attack, and it wasn't something he wanted to revisit in the middle of the market, a mile away from his farm. Rumors would spread and eventually lead back to Meyra, who would make it her sworn duty to spend the next week asking if he was all right. Arguing with her was more taxing than plowing the fields.

So, to avoid another lecture from Meyra, Alric did what he usually did in his given situation; he handed the trader a few coins for the apples, kept his head tilted down, pushed through the cracks of the crowd, and headed home.

He was mere feet from escape when three large men, dressed in velvet robes, stepped into his path.

Alric managed to trip over the foot of a nearby patron, losing his balance as his bag of apples was lost from his grip. He tried to catch himself, but the man he fell toward stepped aside as Alric fell to the gravel.

"Watch it, peasant," the man yelled at Alric. "This robe is worth more than your life."

Saving what dignity he had, Alric climbed to his feet, picked up his bag, and faced the men before him. "Apologies. Lost my footing there. Meant no offense."

He turned to leave when the man shot out a hand and caught Alric's wrist. "I know you," he said. "My father said you lived nearby, but I refused to believe him. You're Alric the Wolf, aren't you? The Red Fang?"

Alric shifted uncomfortably, scanning the crowd, noticing several pairs of

473

eyes set on him. "It's just Alric now."

"Well, fuck me sideways." The man scanned Alric up and down, none too impressed with what he was seeing. "You're nothing what I imagined. Figured you'd be taller."

The two men behind the stranger laughed, an image that reassured just why Alric hated noblemen.

"Aye, I get that a lot," Alric said, trying to defuse the situation quickly enough to take his leave.

"My father said you were the bloodiest of his lot. Said you stacked more bodies than the amount of men in his company. Said he's seen you plow through a horde of savages, taking no wound as you left a trail of dead and dying in your wake, hacking down those animals like a living devil. He said you could track a pack of savages in the dark using nothing but your nose and ears."

Alric nodded bashfully when he realized just who he was talking to. "I take it you're Captain Marlot's eldest, then? He was a great man," Alric lied, knowing that Marlot was an incompetent prick who had gotten more men killed protecting his honor rather than doing his job. "One of the best leaders I've ever followed. Send him my regards, if you will. And my respect."

Alric turned to leave, but the boy snatched at Alric's other wrist, his smile replaced by a sneer. "He also said you gave him a fair amount of trouble. Said you called him a coward in front of his men, tried to spring a mutiny on him."

Alric could feel his heart quicken, the blood pounding in his ears. He clutched the bag of apples tighter in his free hand, making sure not to provoke the boy in any way.

"Soldiering is a stressful life," Alric said. "Your father had the hardest job of us all, and I'm sure he'll—"

"Don't mock me," the boy growled as he tightened his grip.

Noticing the sudden change in the conversation, the two people behind him straightened their posture, flaunting their chest to convey strength.

"You're a long way from a battlefield, Wolf, and you hold no authority here. My father took a great grievance from you, and I'm sure he'll be more than happy to hear I've rectified the situation. You've poisoned his name and brought shame to our family, and I'll be sure to make you suffer for it."

Alric nodded, taking in his surroundings with a quick scan before taking a step toward the boy. "You're right," he said quietly, leaning in so that nobody but the boy could hear. "Your house name is poisoned, but only because your father cared more about his title than the men who fought and died to give him it. The truth is that he was a coward, ready to shield himself with his comrades rather than with his own sword.

"But I won't call him a liar. He's right. I've plowed through more people than I care to count. Death praised me, for nobody in this world has sent him more souls than I. Sure, I'm a ways away from any battlefield, but if you don't release your hand, I'll be sure to make this market the only battlefield you'll ever see. I'll stain the fucking walls with your blood and decorate the stables with your limbs. Let go and be on your way, or you'll learn why they call me Red Fang."

Alric held his gaze until he felt the pressure on his wrist fade as the boy released his grasp. When he was free, he took a step back then turned to leave when he heard a mumble from the others, followed close by with a few laughs.

In normal circumstances, he would let it pass—he was never one to let his pride be his downfall—but what he heard sent a boiling rage through his muscles as his vision began to close in with red.

He turned around and dropped his sack of apples on the ground. "What was that?"

The three of them were just turning to leave when the son of Captain Marlot made a grave mistake. "I said, my father told me you found yourself a pretty wife. Perhaps she'd like a visit from her betters. I'm interested to see what kind of woman it takes to tame a wolf."

Alric took a step forward, and then everything went black. When he came to, he was standing in a circle formed by the crowd. People were cheering, while others stood with their hands covering their mouths, terror in their eyes.

Alric, his fists still clenched and covered in blood, stood over the bodies of the three men. Two of them were unconscious, possibly dead, but Marlot's boy was trying to crawl away from Alric, his face a bloody mess.

"You'll pay for this!" he screamed through his swollen mouth, his jaw undoubtedly broken as it bounced loosely. "My father will—"

Alric brought his heel down on the boy's face, careful enough not to crack his skull but with enough force to knock him unconscious. He regretted it as soon as it happened, knowing that he should have just taken the boy's insult and turned away. But threatening him was one thing and threatening Meyra was another.

He picked up his bag of apples and pushed his way through the crowd, making his way out of the market and heading back home to his wife.

All this happened before Alric, for he stood among the crowd and watched the memory unfold before him. He didn't understand what was happening, why he was reliving the memory like this, but he begged whatever god made him witness a past he longed to forget to show him mercy, to spare him the pain of what came next.

But the gods never did deem Alric worthy of mercy, and even Alric knew, deep down, he didn't deserve it.

The memory flashed forward. Instead of the market, Alric was standing in the kitchen of his home. Meyra was currently handing him a bag, accompanied with her infamous scowl that said a thousand words to him, and not one of them friendly.

"No fighting," Meyra said, her voice set with contempt.

"How many times are you going to remind me?" Alric accepted the bag while he fit his remaining arm through the sleeve of his jacket.

"How many times are you planning to disappoint me? I'm serious, Al. No fighting. The last thing we need is someone knocking on our door, looking to put the local hero to shame."

"You know I hate it when you call me that."

"And you know I hate scrubbing blood from your clothes. Looks like we'll just have to settle for what we've got."

Alric abruptly turned away from her. "Then maybe you should stop sending me there. You know I hate it. I don't understand why you insist on making me do this."

"You're doing it because *you hate it, that's why. Al, you can't even be around more than five people without sweating through your clothes. It isn't healthy."*

"What isn't healthy is a woman torturing her husband with petty errands in order to get him over his fears." Alric paused at the door, keeping his back to Meyra. "You keep saying it'll help me, but I haven't felt any better."

Meyra didn't respond right away. Instead, she slowly walked toward Alric and wrapped her arms around his waist, leaning her head against his back. That was the thing with Meyra, and something Alric loved deeply about her—she was passionate about what she cared for.

"I know it seems like that, but you just have to trust me. It will get easier, Al."

Alric let the moment linger before turning around and taking Meyra's hands in his. "It would be easier if you came with me."

Meyra smiled then, a sight that could send Alric to the moon. "You know I can't, dear." She dragged Alric's hand and set it on her swollen belly. "It's too far a walk for us. She'll throw a fit all night."

Alric felt a jolt in his stomach. "He is going to throw a fit no matter what."

Meyra chuckled, the sound sending a wave of warmth through Alric. "Right, because that's what we need. A little lad running about, taking his father's lead and picking fights with strangers."

Alric kissed his wife's cheek. "Then we'll just give him a sister. No doubt she'll have her mother's attitude to keep him in line."

"Very funny," Meyra said without laughing. She wrapped her arms around Alric's shoulders and hugged him tightly. "Just promise me you'll be careful. Please."

"I promise," Alric whispered as he embraced his wife.

Alric watched the moment pass from the entryway of his kitchen. He screamed at her, begged her to go with, begged to change her mind and leave the house, but no sound left his lips. His words fell into empty air, into a void of sorrow as the image flashed before him.

It was night, a cloudless sky with the full moon lighting his path as he journeyed home. Meyra would be proud of him. Not only had he successfully fulfilled her grocery list without a problem, but he managed to find someone in town willing to give him a helping hand around the farm.

He was overcoming the crest of the hill that overlooked his farm when he saw the glow of flames. He froze, his heart pausing in his chest, unsure of what he was actually seeing.

The flames were spreading fast. It had been a dry summer, and his home was more than fit for kindling.

He dropped the bag of apples where he stood and took off at a sprint.

Alric wasted no time. Ignoring the heat, he kicked at his front door and shattered it off the hinges. Rushing in, he called to his wife, "Meyra! Where are you?"

The roar of flames was deafening, and the violence of the fire was already spreading to the ceiling.

He rushed to the bedroom to find it nearly engulfed in flames, but beyond the burning glow, he could tell nobody occupied the bed.

That's when he heard the screams.

"Help me!" The sound of Meyra's screams were distant, beyond the scorching flames. "I can't get out! Please, someone help!"

Alric held out his hands to the flames, trying desperately to fend off the heat long enough to find Meyra. He left the bedroom and passed through the living room. A haze of smoke polluted the air, but beyond the blur, Alric could see the door leading to the kitchen. He went for the door handle, but it bit at him with an intense heat.

He used his shoulder to break open the door. It took a few tries, but the door eventually broke from its hinges to reveal Meyra in the kitchen, sitting in a chair with her back to him. Alric rushed forward when something heavy crashed against his back, dragging him to the floor and nearly knocking him out.

Trying his hardest to push through the pain, he rolled onto his back and saw that the ceiling was completely consumed in flame, charred wooden beams raining down on top of him.

He rolled onto his belly just in time to dodge an incoming plank. The house was breaking apart.

"Alric, please! Help me!" Meyra screamed, looking over her shoulder, watching a slow flame spread across the floor, eating all that fell into its path as it snaked its way toward Meyra.

Crawling on his knees, Alric rushed to his wife's side. He got there before the flames, only to find that the knot binding Meyra's hands were not only thick and twisted but doused in a slick liquid.

Oil.

Doing all that he could, Alric clawed at the knot, but it was too slick to get a grip.

"I'll get you out! Just hang on!" Alric quickly traced the path of the rope. Her feet were also locked together and tangled in a mess of knots constricting her to the legs of the chair. "Just hold on!"

"Please, Alric! I'm scared. I'm so scared."

"I know, honey. I promise I'll get you out." Alric continued to try to undo the knot, but it was no use.

"The baby, Al. Oh gods, the baby!"

"Just hang on, Meyra. I'll—"

Alric's assurance was cut off by Meyra's piercing screams.

478

It was too late. The flames had made it to her chair and were now snaking up her bare legs.

She convulsed violently, desperately trying to flee but remaining tied to the chair.

"It hurts!" she shrieked, her cries deafening the sound of the fire. "Please make it stop!"

Within a flash, the flame exploded in a blast of heat, igniting the oil and completely consuming Meyra.

Wet with the oil from the rope, Alric's hands went up in flames. He fought against the panic in his chest and kept trying to untie the knot that bound Meyra, but the pain was excruciating.

The smell of burning flesh poisoned the air, and the sound of Meyra's bubbling skin was all Alric could hear as he got to his feet.

Ignoring the burning of his own arms and the flames that had consumed his wife, he grabbed the bottom of the chair and began dragging it from the kitchen.

He wasn't sure exactly how, but he managed to get Meyra clear of the house ... much too late.

Her screams might have silenced, but because Meyra was nothing but a bulk of black meat crumbled into a ball next to Alric.

Alric lay on his back, his charred hand reaching out to his dead wife. His vision began to blur, his lungs tight in his chest as he cried out his wife's name.

Everything went black.

Alric's eyes shot open as he bolted upright on the table. His vision swam before him, the swelling in his head nearly sending him back down into unconsciousness, back to the nightmare that awaited him. He steadied himself, though, leaning forward on the table to catch his breath and balance.

He lifted his hands before him and saw that his gloves were elsewhere, revealing scars that spread up his forearms for all to see, naked and vulnerable. He flexed his hands. Even though it had been a dream, he could still feel the lingering pain of the burns, prickling at his deformed hands.

The room was dimly lit, and it took him a minute to realize that he was at the cabin.

How much time has passed?

He thought back to his last memory. He remembered running through Servitol as it was attacked, sneaking through the crack in the lower district where they had

K.R. Gangi

been met by a squad of Navalethian soldiers. Other than that, he had no recollection of making his way to the cabin, which was a bad sign.

A fire burned in the hearth, the only source of warmth and light. Close to the fire was a body, and from the large shoulders and the glare of the fire reflecting off his clean shaven head, he knew it was Seroes. Beside him, lounging with his feet stretched out on a second chair, was Benny, his chin tucked to his chest and his light snore faint in the air.

Alric swung his legs over the table and sat for a moment. His head was a mess, a sharp pain digging into his skull with even the bear movement of his eyes. With a couple fingers, he searched his head and nearly jumped from the table when he came across a quick burn near his forehead. When he looked at his hands, his fingers were smeared with blood. No doubt the culprit behind his amnesia.

As quietly as he could, he slid from the table. He waited a few moments before he caught his balance then made his way outside of the cabin.

The woods around him was alive with life as the moon beamed down on him. At both his sides were two others, the boy named Trevor and the other Warren, both sound asleep in rocking chairs.

He walked around the camp, gathering his surroundings and trying to piece his memories together. The fire had burnt out some time ago, and as he approached a figure hunched against a nearby tree, he twisted his ankle on an empty bottle.

He cursed to himself as he made his way to the edge of the opening where he found the girl Sarah incapacitated underneath a thick woolen blanket, the man named Dodge snoring loudly a few feet away from her.

Alric found the twins sleeping side by side, a packed blanket under their heads and their bows within arm's reach. Baron snored lightly next to them, a thin blanket covering the lower half of his body, no doubt his hands still gripping his hatchets, and his hood covering his face to ward off the bugs.

Alric didn't see Evan near the crowd, so he made off in search for him when a sound caught his attention, the sound of splashing water, much too big to be caused by a fish.

Alric focused on the dock, at the figure sitting at its end with their feet dangling in the water. His vision was superb, even at night, so he knew it wasn't Evan, but someone else. Someone that didn't belong.

"You can join me if you'd like." It was a voice of a man. He didn't turn around as he spoke, just kept his focus on the water before him. "The night is warm, and I would like the company. I know it's a full moon and all, so please refrain from howling."

Alric's heart jumped a beat with recognition. It wasn't possible for the man to be here, and it sure as hell wasn't just a coincidence that he'd managed to find one of the most secluded and well-hidden areas Alric knew about. So, how could he be there?

And who is he?

"We'll talk about that later," the man said, as if reading Alric's mind.

Alric walked the rest of the way down the dock and took a seat at the stranger's side.

"I hope you'll excuse that last pun," Traveler said. "I just couldn't help myself. I know you lack a sense of humor."

Alric hung his legs off the dock, the water tickling the bottom of his bare feet. "My sense of humor is just fine. You're just not that funny."

"Ah." Traveler marveled with a smile. "I stand corrected. Still, I shall try to hold my tongue."

Traveler looked much the same than when Alric had last seen him in Servitol. His baggy shirt was dirtied and riddled with rips and tears, his feet were stained with mud and dirt, and his walking stick lay on the dock next to him.

"I'm sorry for self-inviting," Traveler said. "But I found our next conversation to take precedence over formalities. And what are formalities, anyway, between strangers?"

"I'm sure the king would disagree with you there," Alric retorted. "Formalities usually take precedence over mutual respect in this country. Plenty have died over lack of formalities."

Traveler shook his head. "I doubt the king would disagree with much anymore, considering he's dead."

"Dead?" Alric looked quizzically into Traveler's eyes.

Gods, how long was I asleep?

"Only a few days," Traveler answered Alric's thought. "And yes, dead. Murdered, in fact."

Alric was hesitant with his next question, unsure of how this man was able to hear his thoughts. He eyed Traveler, searching his eyes as he asked, "Murdered by whom?"

Alric tried to think back to the attack in Servitol, about the men wearing masks who were attacking anyone they could and burning down whatever they wanted.

Traveler swung his legs back and forth, his bare feet just grazing the surface of the water. "Who killed our monarch is less important as to why."

"There are plenty of reasons why men want the death of kings," Alric replied. "Is there ever really only one?"

"In this case, there is only one reason, and a reason you'll soon understand," Traveler said ominously.

"Well," Alric scoffed, "doesn't get any more vague than that."

Traveler sighed to himself. "I'm sorry."

"You're just full of apologies tonight, aren't you?"

"Yeah," Traveler agreed. "I sincerely mean it."

"And I sincerely don't care." Alric was getting good and angry. "It doesn't matter which king dies. There will be another one soon enough. There might not be an heir, but there will always be someone with a thirst for power."

"And if I told you there is an heir?" Traveler eyed Alric. "Would you care enough then?"

Alric didn't give the idea any thought. "No doubt there is. I'm sure women are flooding the castle, pleading that their child is the true son or daughter of our dead monarch. It's prime time to be a bastard in Navaleth."

Traveler didn't try to hide the disappointment on his face. "I say, are you always so cynical?"

"You seemed to know a lot about me the last time we spoke," Alric addressed. "How about you tell me?"

Traveler nodded to himself solemnly. "I admit, I was a bit harsh with my ambush there, but it was something that needed to be done."

"And what's done is done," Alric said with stern finality. "Including the king. I spent over ten years fighting for my king, and never once did I meet the man. I owe him nothing, not even the sympathy of his death. I don't care who he was, I don't care about his legacy, and I don't care about any heir. Right now, there's only one thing I care about."

"And that is …?"

Alric turned his head and looked Traveler right in the eye. "Who the fuck you are."

There was a quiet between them. Then, with a wry smile, a faint chuckle came from Traveler.

"There's that fire we need. I'll answer your question to the best of my abilities. But, for now, I'll ask you the same."

"Ask me the same what?"

"Ask you the same question. Who are *you*?"

Alric laughed to himself, shaking his head at Traveler. "You're the only one in this conversation who knows the other's name. I think it's time for you to start answering some questions before I give you any information you probably already know."

Traveler raised an eyebrow, his lip perched with deep thought. "I'll admit that I know a lot. More than most. But what I don't know, Alric, is who you are anymore. And who you are may decide the fate of many lives in not only the country you've grown to hate, but the entirety of the world."

"I think you're taking the death of our king a little too seriously," Alric observed.

"And you aren't taking it seriously enough!" Traveler snapped back, irritation clear as day. "You may think your life choices are inconsequential, but the truth of the matter is that the fate of our world rests on the shoulders of a bitter old man whose hate has burned him to his very core. A man who walks a fine line between realism and insanity. A man who believes the only way of saving the world is by letting it kill itself and start over."

Alric bobbed his head back and forth. "Seems like you know me well enough."

Traveler's eyes burned with fury. "In that case, congratulations, Alric. You're broken. You've let the world defeat you. You've given up on the world and everyone in it, and now you have the chance to sit back and watch it destroy itself."

"I guess that means this conversation is over, then?" Alric made to stand when Traveler put his hand on his. Making the move, Alric expected him to use the inhuman strength he'd shown at Servitol, yet the touch was gentle, not malicious.

"Just wait," Traveler begged. "Please, just … just stay a little longer. I'm sorry."

Alric froze for a moment, stuck between sitting and standing, debating whether he should stay with Traveler or not. After a few seconds of thought, and for reasons he couldn't comprehend, he decided to stay.

"Thank you," Traveler said. "I just … need you to understand this."

"Nothing you have said has made any sense," Alric stated. "How am I supposed to understand any of this?"

"It's not easy to explain. Here, think of this." Traveler turned his body to face Alric and held up both of his hands. "This"—he waved his left hand—"is a bee. Now, it's the bee's job to bring pollen back to his hive. However, this particular bee is smart and knows that it's collecting too much pollen for the flowers around his hive. If it keeps it at this rate, the pollen will run out and the hive will have to move. So, instead, he searches out into another garden and finds another flower"—Traveler waved his right hand—"and decided to collect from there.

"So, this bee reports to the queen and says that it found another garden not too far from the hive. And so the queen orders all the bees to harvest from the garden, and the hive grows three times in size within the next month."

Traveler paused then, and Alric wondered whether he was done with the story or not.

"I'm not sure what this story has to do with—how'd you put it?—*saving the world.*"

Traveler smiled at the question, as if Alric had asked the right one. "A month later, in a town nearby, little Timmy is being bullied. Three boys chase Timmy out of town and to that very tree the hive hangs from. Trapped between the tree and Timmy's three foes, he tries to rush through them, but it doesn't work. One of the boys shoves Timmy against the tree with enough force that the hive shakes from the branch and crashes at their feet, sending a swarm attacking all four kids.

"Billy, one of the bullies, is deathly allergic and gets stung. He rushes back home but doesn't make it. He dies not a hundred feet from his house, where his mother sits at the kitchen table, getting lunch ready for Billy's little sister.

"Years pass on, and Anita, Billy's mom, develops a drinking habit. It's the only thing that helps her forget the face of her young boy who had died from a simple bee sting. It's late after a night in the tavern when she's walking home. She's crossing the street when a man grabs her from behind. He drags her into an alley and butchers her against the side of her neighbor's house.

"Claire, Anita's daughter, sister to Billy, is now motherless and has to resort to other ways of survival. She starts with stealing from shops in the market. Then, as time goes on, she becomes better at thievery. She moves on to bigger jobs. She's just going on twelve years when she's caught by the guards. She's thrown into a dark cell, chained to a wall, where she is beaten, raped, and starved. That cell becomes Claire's grave."

Alric sat quietly as Traveler finished his story. It was dark and twisted, something he didn't expect from the old man.

The clearing around the cabin was silent, and Alric only then recognized the sounds of crying coming from Traveler.

"That's a sad story," Alric finally said, feeling uncomfortable as Traveler wiped tears from his eyes. "And here I thought I was the cynical one. Did anyone ever tell you that you've got a taste for the drama? Hell, you and Benny should have a conversation some time. Wouldn't that be something?"

"There's no reason to be rude, Alric."

Alric responded with a nonchalant shrug. "Just being honest. If that's rude, maybe you should pick better stories."

Traveler sniffled. "Oh, Alric, if only I could say it was just a story. You were only fifteen when Claire died in that cell. She died a stranger to the world, without anyone but the guards, who buried her in a shallow grave, knowing she ever existed."

He could tell Traveler was deeply upset, so he decided not to say anything. Instead, he looked across the lake, watched as the flies glided across the water, as the fish jumped out to snatch their meal.

After a few minutes passed, after the tears had stopped and Traveler had pulled himself together, he spoke. "The point of the story is quite simple, Alric. And I want you to consider it before I ask my final question."

Alric shrugged. "Okay, then."

"Imagine what would have happened if that little bee didn't find another garden."

"You said that the hive would have had to move," Alric replied.

"Correct." Traveler continued to swing his feet off the dog. "And if the hive had moved, would Claire be alive today?"

"I …" Alric thought hard about the question. If the hive had moved, then Billy wouldn't have been stung by a bee. If he wasn't stung, he wouldn't have died, which would mean Anita wouldn't have become a drunk and wouldn't have been murdered. "I … suppose?"

"Exactly," Traveler said. "We don't know for sure, do we?"

Alric shook his head. "Not for sure, no."

"But"—Traveler held up a finger—"we can decide that she wouldn't have died in that cell at the age of twelve, right?"

"Probably not," Alric admitted. "At least not in that way."

Traveler nodded, his eyes looking down toward his bare feet. "Now, I want you to think deeply on this question. I don't want an answer; I just want you to think it over. Got it?"

Alric sighed and shrugged, looking toward the stars above them. "Sure."

"Look at me, Alric."

Alric did, waiting quietly for the question.

It was a few seconds before Traveler spoke, but when he did, he asked, "A single action can determine a catastrophic consequence. Now, what if I told you there was an heir?"

Alric mulled the question over in his head, trying to place the significance of the question. When he realized just what Traveler was implying, he looked over his shoulder to the others who were sleeping soundly amongst the trees.

Alric looked back to Traveler. "And if we get this heir back to the capital?"

Traveler pursed his lips. "Then you'll all be murdered before you knew what happened."

"Then what am I supposed to do? What's the point of all your talk about saving the world if it's not to get the heir on the throne?"

"Because our heir will not sit on the throne. They're much more important than that. It's your job to protect them. To fight for them. You must *fight*, Alric. That is your destiny."

"My destiny?" Alric scoffed. "Destiny is a warm blanket for those afraid of the unknown." Alric spit into the pond. "Fuck destiny, and fuck the idea of a grand plan determined by fabled deities. If the gods are real, then that means it was destiny that my wife and child burned away. That it was all in their *grand plan* that they were taken from me. And if that's the case, then fuck the gods, too."

Traveler was quiet then, letting Alric soak in his anger.

His head was more than throbbing now, his body tingling with rage. He brought his hands before him, studying the scars that covered them, eternally reminded of the worst day of his life.

"Is it so hard to believe that we were born with a purpose?" Traveler asked.

Alric spit again. "I refuse to believe that my wife's purpose in life was to be burned alive."

Traveler nodded. "And how many people have you sent to their grave, Alric? How many lives have you snuffed out? Tell me; what did you do after the fire? What'd you do to those men who took Meyra from you?"

Alric grimaced at the memory, too far gone in his anger to wonder how Traveler could know such a thing, of how he could know about that night filled with blood and screams.

"I hunted them down."

Traveler raised his brow. "And what'd you do once they were found, Wolf?"

"I murdered them," Alric said, his memory racing back to that bloodlust night, the night he snuck into Captain Marlot's private estate and butchered his son, along with the rest of his family. Hell, he even killed the staff working that night. He found those responsible and tore them apart, bit by bit, as he scattered their limbs and memory to the wind. "I murdered them all."

"You murdered them all," Traveler confirmed. "Nobody ever said destiny was rainbows and sunshine."

"So, you're telling me that life's grand plan is death and destruction?" Alric rubbed at his scarred hands, tracing the lines of raised flesh that will forever remind him of his past.

He expected an angry retort, a snide remark from Traveler; instead, the man used his cane to help push him to his feet and said, "Fate is not a grand plan for everyone, my friend, but only a chosen few. It is not a web of interconnected lives. It may look like that, but fate is a maze; there are many paths, but only one destination."

Traveler looked toward the stars. "There are many versions of our lives in different versions of our world, Alric, and only minor differences between ourselves ultimately lead us to a very different conclusion. However, with those of us cursed with destiny, we are but walking within a maze, an estate with many hallways, but with one destination in mind."

"And you're telling me that I'm making my way through my maze?" Alric asked.

"No." Traveler looked down at Alric. "I'm saying that you're *lost* in your maze."

Alric wiped his face as he chuckled to himself. "Whatever the fuck that means."

"It means," Traveler stood as he spoke, "that you have a choice."

"Destiny leaves me with a choice? A little contradictory, isn't it?"

"Not at all. As I've said, we are different versions of ourselves within our different versions of life. However, in this life, in this world, you still have one more choice to make."

"Mmhmm," Alric grumbled. "And what's that?"

Traveler again gazed at the stars above them. "Whether you are the bee or poor Claire."

"And you're the queen bee who gets to decide who does what. The grand architecture of this shit-show of a world." Alric stared at his open hands, studying the scars that danced up his arms. "I don't know how to be any of those things now, but what I do know is that I don't want anything to do with your grand plan."

Traveler nodded , fetching his cane from the ground. "I hope you figure it out. Our time is up now, Al."

"Hold on." Alric stood and faced Traveler. "You said that there are different ... *versions* of myself. Different worlds?"

"That involves a very complicated explanation, along with specifics you couldn't possibly fathom. But, to put it simply"—Traveler shrugged—"sorta."

Alric rubbed his hands. "How many?"

"Well"—Traveler gave a sad smile—"how many choices have you made in your life?"

Alric laughed softly, mind-boggled with the possibilities, but there was one reason why he was curious, and if Traveler was as all-seeing as he claimed to be, he already knew what Alric was going to ask.

"Does she live through any of them?" Alric asked quietly, rubbing his thumb deep into the palm of his hand. "Meyra. Do we ... have a family?"

Traveler nodded to Alric with a sad smile. "You do. In a lot of them."

A tear fell down Alric's cheek, crashing to the wooden dock beneath his feet. "Tell me about it?"

If it weren't for Alric's ability to see clearly through the dark, he never would have seen the tears building in Traveler's eyes. "You named her Kaira."

"Kaira," Alric whispered the name, tears streaming down his smile. "So, a daughter. I wonder what Meyra would have said to that."

"That she was right," Traveler said. "That she's always right."

"That sounds about right." Still smiling, Alric wiped the tears from his face. "What happens?"

The smile ran away from Traveler's face. "It's always the same, Alric. You are in a maze with one destination. Your path is always different, but your destination remains the same."

"Right. And, uh, out of all these *versions* you speak of, do I make it to the end?"

Traveler leaned heavily on his cane and sighed deeply. "Most times, yes."

"And ...?" Alric pressed.

Traveler sighed. "This is ... the only version that I can't see an end to. Most times, you make it to the end, while in others, you lose your way. What I have found out, however, is that my specific guidance does not benefit whatsoever. Quite the opposite, actually."

Alric shook his head, dissatisfaction clear to the man, or thing, before him. "Anybody ever tell you that you'd make a good politician?"

Traveler laughed to himself, the first genuine laugh Alric had heard. "You've asked me this before. Not here, of course. Well"—he waved with a wide hand in the open air—"here, but not *here*. Are you sure you want to know?"

Alric nodded, arguing with himself as to why he was buying into this fictitious charade.

"The end has always been the same for you," Traveler told him. "You die."

"I ... die?"

Traveler nodded solemnly. "But it's why you die that matters."

If what he says is true, and all the versions of myself end the same, that would mean ...

Traveler nodded in reply to Alric's realization. "Like I said, it's not always rainbows and sunshine. I truly am sorry."

"Yeah, well"—Alric wiped the remaining tears from his face—"if destiny is real, she sure is a nasty bitch."

Traveler smirked. "She can be." Traveler then turned his back on Alric and began leaving the dock.

"I suppose you'll drop in unannounced again?" Alric asked aloud.

Traveler paused before turning toward Alric. "That all depends on you." He leaned heavily on his cane, his face long and sad. "I wasn't lying, Alric. You're broken. Trust in your friends, for they are the only things that will help you distinguish realism from insanity.

"Also, if you could"—Traveler looked toward the cabin, a small smile on his face—"keep an eye on Trevor, would you? He's a good lad, and he has his part to play, as well. As for the other, I believe her protection will come naturally. You are a good man, even if you have buried it deep down." Traveler turned and began walking away.

Question beyond question raced through Alric's mind. He had to shake his head to steady himself. "No, you can't do that." He walked toward Traveler, the man ten feet from him. "We're not done ... here ..."

Traveler wasn't walking away, but toward Alric. To Alric's sudden surprise, however, it wasn't Traveler at all, but Evan who stood before him with a confused look on his face.

"Who are you talking to?" Evan asked suspiciously.

"Erm ..." Alric struggled with the situation. One minute, Traveler had been there, and the next, he wasn't. "Nobody," Alric lied. "I was ... sleepwalking."

Maybe my head is a little more cracked than I thought.

Evan didn't seem to bite, but he eventually just shrugged. "Surprised you're walking at all, after that. I knew you'd come out of it. It'll take more than a fucking guard to bring you down. Hungry?"

"Yeah," Alric answered, dazed with the turn of recent events. He rubbed his stomach, which agreed with a loud growl. "I could eat, I suppose."

"Right. I'll put a fire on," Evan said as he walked away.

Alric looked about the cabin yard for a sign of Traveler, but found none. He stood there for a while longer, shaking the fuzz from his mind. Then he made to move when he noticed someone blocking his path. Alric was frozen to his core, fear locking his body in place.

From head to toe, she was covered in one giant scar, one that matched the same pattern on Alric's arms. Her eyes were dark rings, crisp blue eyes shining hungrily from the darkness. Blood dripped from her deformed face, the craters of her burns glistening with a yellow goop. It was a literal image from his worst nightmare.

"Hello, dear," the phantom of Meyra said to him, a cruel smile stretching her demonic face. "I thought you promised no more fighting?"

Epilogue

"How long has he been like this?" It was a gruesome sight, seeing the youngling sway from side to side, his shadow casting a horrid sight as the dry rope creaked with a tear.

The guard looked away in dejection. "We found him an hour ago, but his mother said he's been missing for days." The guard wrinkled his nose. "From the smell of him, I'd say it's been longer than that."

Elder Roku covered his mouth as he studied the youngling's body. His face was flushed purple, his swollen eyes bulging from their sockets, his neck stretched unnaturally with the weight of his body. Flies swarmed the corpse, buzzing in delight as they took refuge in the rotting cave that was once the youngling's mouth.

"I think you are right," Roku agreed. "What of his father?"

The guard cleared his throat. "Walking the fields of the Forever Calm."

Roku nodded. "Have you told the mother yet?"

The guard shook his head. "I came to you first."

"Good," Roku answered, taking a large step away from the hanging corpse. "I remember this one. He was there, at Quiver's trial. He was part of their pack."

Again, the guard nodded, his eyes sinking with sadness as he looked at the corpse that swung back and forth from the rope. "His name is Oppo."

"No." Roku turned to face his guard. "His name *was* Oppo, but he forfeit his life in front of the spirits, forsaking the ultimate gift they bestowed upon us. He will never walk in the Forever Calm. He will never pass into the afterlife. He will forever wander in the realm between life and death. That is the choice we make when we take our own lives."

"I understand."

Roku looked back to the body. "You were right to come to me first. We will tell the mother nothing of this. She believes he has run away?"

The guard nodded in silence.

"Good, then that is what we will tell her. These are trying times, and a mother should never have to see the corpse of her child."

"As you say, Elder." The guard pulled a dagger from his belt and severed the rope that hung Oppo's body from the peak of the tent. The body crumbled in itself as it hit the ground.

"This is not entirely our fault," Roku assured the guard. "He was betrayed by his mentor, Quiver, when they went in search of Nero. His mind was confused, lost with the lies he was fed. This just proves my greatest fear. Even in Quiver's absence, our people suffer his blasphemy."

The guard nodded. "It is as you say, Elder."

Roku sighed at the youngling's corpse. "I will find the mother and assure her that we will send a party in search of her son. Once she's—"

The flap of the tent opened, the fresh air cleansing the thick scent of death as a woman stood in the entrance. She looked from Roku to the guard, and then settled her eyes on the Oppo's body. "What are you doing?" she screamed at Roku.

"Hush your voice," Roku said in a loud whisper, moving closer to the woman. She was one of the healers of his clan, the one that Roku knew had been close with Quiver. Her name was Thread.

Thread's eyes were wide with terror. She rushed into the tent and sank at the youngling's body. "What happened?" she asked, her eyes full of hurt.

Although there was a clear fire building in his chest with knowing that Thread had grown close with Quiver over the last few years, Roku took a knee and met the healer's eyes. "He took his own life. I fear that he grew confused with his former chief's perverted faith, that it poisoned his mind and brought him past the point of redemption."

Thread's lips curled in rage. She stood up, her fist clenched at her sides as she stared down at Roku. "Quiver has been gone for weeks now, yet you still seek to poison his name even after you've driven him away from his people."

Roku all but leapt to his feet. "Quiver drove himself away when he abandoned the spirits. He has nobody else to blame for his transgressions but himself."

Thread pointed to Oppo's corpse. "As do you for what lies at your feet!"

"You dare put blame on *me* for this?" Roku gestured to the corpse on the ground. "You direct blame to your *elder*?"

Thread took a threatening step toward Roku. "I put the blame on the man who wears my people's faith as a mask for his own vile intentions."

The guard, who had all but stood by and watched the conflict unfold, placed himself between Thread and Roku. "Take a step back from the elder, Thread," he said with a soft yet firm hand on her shoulder.

The fire still blazed in Thread's eyes, but she backed down.

Roku felt a great sense of accomplishment at her submission. Although she was weak, another person who Quiver had poisoned over the years, it seemed that his power was still effective.

"Now," Roku said quietly to the both of them, "the sun sets, and once night fully comes, we will take the body a few miles into the forest where he can be buried."

"Bury him?" Thread shook her head. "You would put him in the cold ground instead of sending his ashes to the spirits?"

"He did not earn that right," Roku countered. "He has taken his own life. To send him to the spirits would give them great offense. No, Thread, we cannot save his soul, but we can still save his memory. I will tell his mother that we will send out a party in search of him. Once we find nothing, we will tell her that he has run away due to the shame he must feel."

Thread scowled at her elder. "You'd rather let his mother live day after day, waiting for her son's return?"

"I would rather tell any lie that will save her from the truth of her son's suicide," Roku countered with finality.

"It's a lie," Thread spat back. "She deserves to know."

Roku shook his head. "That is not a decision you get to make."

"And what makes it yours?" Thread asked.

"I do," Roku answered. "I am elder. I am *your* elder, and this is *my* decision."

Thread shook with rage, and at any moment, Roku thought she would strike out at him. He hoped that she would so that he could resolve the matter of this blasphemous healer in a quick manner. To his disappointment, though, Thread simply shook her head and left the tent, leaving Roku and his guard to tend to the current situation.

Roku straightened and faced his guard. "Wait here. The sun is still setting, but once it's fully dark, I will send another to help you dispose of the body. Take him to the woods and bury him a couple miles out. Do you understand?"

The guard nodded silently.

"Good," Roku answered. He then left the tent in a hurry, making his way toward the center of the village.

He thought of Thread, acknowledging the danger she posed to his position. She had grown close with Quiver, and that was a problem. It had taken years to alienate Quiver and his family, and he wasn't about to let it all be for nothing over a pretentious, low-born villager.

At least there was one thing Roku and Quiver could agree upon, and that was that his people had changed over the years. They had grown weaker, settling contently with the day-to-day life without even a fleeting crave of ambition in their blood.

It was true. They had lost the war to the south, but that didn't mean they should forever lick their wounds and hide from the world simply because a man wearing a golden ring atop his head had declared it so. No, instead of sulking in the shadows that their blasphemous neighbors cast on them, they should be rallying their tribes and striking back.

Unfortunately for him, Roku seemed to be the only person who saw the opportunity at hand. Years ago, Roku had received word from one of his spies that the southern king's wife had fallen ill, taking her life, leaving the king with no heir. Roku understood southern politics, and a king with no heir was problematic. What was more problematic, however, was the recent news of the king's death.

Roku's heart raced in excitement with word of the southern king's death. No doubt the entire country was in uproar. Soon, the dukes would be pushing for power, and eventually, the country would be at war with itself. It was the perfect moment for Roku and his people to exact revenge on their southern neighbors for the eternal pain they had caused them over the years.

Once upon a time, Roku's people ruled all the land. They had farmed to their own purpose, fought to their own purpose, and served for their own purpose. Then came the southerners, who had raged war against the clans, driving them deeper and deeper into the forests.

Now, after the bloodiest war that his people had faced, they were forced into hiding, living in constant fear of slavery, savagery, and murder from those who wronged them.

For no longer. We will face our enemy once again, and under my rule, we will win.

With the southern king dead, and no heir to the throne, it was time to unite the clans, to amass an army, and march south. They would burn down homes, kill every last soldier that stood and faced them, march on the great castle, and raze it to the ground.

And I will become the next Nara'Seir.

All these things, Roku thought about as he made his way toward his tent, passing by the very people who put their full trust in him leading their way to glory. However, there were still minor obstacles to overcome, Thread being one of them. If she had the same mind as Quiver, which it seemed that was the case, she was standing in the way of Roku's ultimate goal.

She will have to be dealt with, and quickly.

It took Roku years to rid the tribes of the former Nara'Seir's bloodline, and those were the years that he didn't have. Roku had to resort to more aggressive tactics to take care of his problem. It wouldn't be the first time he'd sent one of his men to assassinate a clansman. Nero, even though he was a distant connection to the Nara'Seir bloodline, had also been a risk that Roku couldn't chance against.

No, he would send one of his guards tonight to find Thread, murder her in her sleep, and take her body to the woods, like Roku had ordered on many other occasions. His guards were fully committed to him, fully believing that whatever he did was for the sake of preserving the clan. He wished it didn't have to be this way, but if he was to bring his people out from their enemy's shadow, it was something that must be done.

Roku saw his tent off in the distance, the two lit torches on both sides of the entrance. He smiled to himself, taking pride in his work, relishing in his sense of excitement for what was yet to come.

It was fully night now, and as soon as he had the privacy of his own tent, he would write a simple letter, hand it to one of the guards outside and, just like that, his Thread problem would be resolved as he slept through the night.

He was nodding to one of the guards when he heard a sound to his right. It was the sound of snapping twigs. Then the sight of large brushes shaking in the windless night set him on edge. Whatever it was, it was big.

Something emerged from the brush. Roku thought it a massive shadow, but as a deep growl rumbled through the night, he finally understood just how massive the beast was.

It tilted its head back and gave a deep roar.

Roku watched as hot breath fogged the air, steaming through a mouth full of very large, sharp fangs. It stared at Roku with one large red eye that glowed amongst the blackness of the night.

It stomped a paw on the ground, scraping loose dirt with intention to pounce.

It was as big as a bear, but also shaped like a wolf. It was a beast from a nightmare.

Roku pissed himself when it dawned on him that he was looking at the very thing Quiver had warned the village about. Then he began to tremble with regret for not listening.

The beast leaned back on its hind legs, muzzle pointing toward the stars as it shrieked with a frightening howl. After a moment of silence that followed, in the distance that didn't sound too far from where Roku stood now, came the echo from more beasts, all howling in answer to the one that bared its teeth before him.